# About the Author

Theo is a half-Dutch Kiwi currently living in Amsterdam with his wife, Maddie. Inspired by the stories and adventures hidden in the past, coupled with a love of writing, Theo was inspired to share his love of history and write his debut novel, *Saga: A Clash of Jarls*.

# Saga: A Clash of Jarls

# Theo de Monchy

# Saga: A Clash of Jarls

Olympia Publishers
*London*

**www.olympiapublishers.com**
OLYMPIA PAPERBACK EDITION

A CIP catalogue record for this title is
available from the British Library.

ISBN: 978-1-80439-228-7

This is a work of fiction.
Names, characters, places and incidents originate from the writer's imagination.
Any resemblance to actual persons, living or dead, is purely coincidental.

First Published in 2024

Olympia Publishers
Tallis House
2 Tallis Street
London
EC4Y 0AB

Printed in Great Britain

# Dedication

To the family and friends who have indulged my love of history over the years and have listened patiently to an endless stream of unsolicited facts and stories. Here is one you can read in your own time.

# Acknowledgements

Thank you to everyone who has helped and supported me on this journey. Writing this book was an incredible experience, and I couldn't have done it alone.

A special thanks to my mother, Mandy, for her endless encouragement and confidence that I would one day write a book of my own. To my father, Alex; my brother, Oliver, and my good friend Dej, who all read through my first draft and provided valuable feedback on the story.

To my wonderful wife, Maddie, for her tireless patience and support throughout this journey and for being the final pair of eyes to review the manuscript. Your feedback can only be described as invaluable.

Finally, to my grandmother, Bobby, for her wonderful imagination, her love of English and the incredible games she created for us as children. I'm sure that the adventures we shared together all those years ago were the spark that ignited my imagination.

# Dear Reader

Writing a book of my own has been a lifetime ambition of mine, and I've stopped and started numerous stories over the years, as I'm sure most authors do.

I wanted to take a moment to thank you for buying a copy of *Saga: A Clash of Jarls*, and for supporting me on this journey. I truly hope that you enjoy the adventures within these pages, and that you are as entertained reading the story as I was writing it.

Thank you.

    —   Theo

# Foreword

This work of fiction is the result of over a year spent researching and writing, and a lifetime passion and love for history, historical fiction and the stories hidden amongst the annals of time.

As much as possible, I have tried to be historically accurate, and to use the original Nordic words to bring the story to life. You will find a glossary of the different words that I have used, and their meanings, at the back of the book. I have made a few exceptions to this accuracy, such as using minutes as a measure of time to make the overarching story more enjoyable. I hope that such liberties won't detract from the overall experience.

To the best of my knowledge, none of the characters or places in this book, apart from England and Norway, are real, and were instead created from my own imagination.

# List of Characters

### Shorewitchshire

**Arleigh** – Bjørn's mother, Torr's wife and Erik's bed-thrall.
**Torr** – Arleigh's husband in England, killed by Yngvar.
**Old-Manton** – A fyrd man of Shorewitchshire, Torr's father.

### Vágar

**Arleigh** – Bjørn's mother, Erik's bed-thrall. See also Shorewitchshire.
**Erik** – Known as the Golden Hand, Bjørn's father and Arleigh's captor.
**Sven** – Erik's prow man, one of his húskarlar. Torsten's brother.
**Yngvar** – Erik's closest friend, Bjørn's mentor, captain of *Sleipnir*.
**Olaf** – Bjørn's half-brother, the oldest of Erik's sons.
**Sigurd** – Bjørn's half-brother, Erik's second son.
**Toke** – Bjørn's half-brother, Erik's third son.
**Bjørn** – The half-English, half-Norse fourth son of Erik Golden Hand.
**Fen** – Yngvar's dog.
**Sanu** – Once Yngvar's thrall; a Moorish blacksmith and trader from Spain.
**Hoelun** – An eastern thrall of Erik's.
**Gørm** – Erik's goði.
**Green Alf** – The old prow man of *Fjord Uxi* who died while shaving.
**Uffe** – Jarl Erik's lead ranger.
**Halfdan** – Captain of *Fjord Uxi*.
**Turid** – Erik's wife, mother to Olaf, Sigurd, and Toke.
**Leif Geirsson** – Garrison commander of Vágar.
**Bjarni** – One of the crewmen on *Sleipnir*, Bjørn's friend, Bersi's brother.
**Red Orm** – One of the crewmen of *Sleipnir* and Bjørn's friend.
**Guttorm** – Bjørn's friend, one of the younger men from *Sleipnir*.
**Knud** – One of *Sleipnir's* prow lookouts.
**Arne** – One of the young bóndi in Erik's fleet, sails on *Sleipnir*.
**Sweyn** – One of the young bóndi in Erik's fleet, sails on *Sleipnir*.
**Knut Troelsson** – One of the younger men in Erik's fleet, sails on *Sleipnir*.

**Troel** – Knut's father, dead.

**Uffi** – A ranger from *Sleipnir*.

**Galti** – A ranger from *Sleipnir*.

**Sindri** – A ranger from *Sleipnir*.

**Bo** – A retired warrior of Vágar.

**Bersi** – A Warrior on *Fjord Uxi*, Bjarni's brother.

**Orm** – A warrior on *Fjord Uxi*.

**Bergathor** – A ranger on *Fjord Uxi*.

**Odd** – A ranger on *Fjord Uxi*.

**Tolstan** – A ship's boy on *Fjord Uxi*.

**Frode** – A warrior on *Fjord Uxi*.

**Váli** – An independent land owner, loyal to Erik.

**Astrid** – Váli's wife.

**Ragnar** – Váli's son.

**Signy** – Váli's daughter.

**Torsten** – Váli's prow man, one of his hirð, Sven's brother.

**Ulf** – The blacksmith of Vágar, father to Fafnir.

**Revna** – Wife to Ulf, blacksmith of Vágar, mother to Fafnir.

**Fafnir** – Son to Revna and Ulf.

**Hrolf** – Leader of the three úlfheðnar warriors who fight for Erik.

**Finnir** – A warrior from *Fjord Uxi*.

**Fótrfjord**

**Jarl Ake** – Jarl of Fótrfjord.

**Rolf** – One of Jarl Ake's scouts.

**Dag** – One of Jarl Ake's scouts.

**Siv** – One of Jarl Ake's scouts.

**Carr** – One of Jarl Ake's scouts.

**Canute** – Jarl Ake's first warrior and prow man.

**Steinar** – Jarl Ake's only son.

**Audun** – One of Jarl Ake's scouts.

**Ottar Svensson** – One of Jarl Ake's men.

**Aven** – One of Ake's men and a close friend and confidant of Steinar.

**Jungulf** – One of Jarl Ake's men, serves Steinar.

**Rune** – One of Jarl Ake's men, serves Steinar.

**Trygva** – One of Jarl Ake's Húskarlar.

**Skarde** – One of Ake's bóndi warriors.

Saga:
A Clash of Jarls

*The smoke-dulled sky was broken by whispers of ash rising from dry thatch roofs as it burned orange and red against the sky. Two ravens circled above the ancient oak in the village centre, croaking death and gloom into the world before coming to rest on the lowest branch, watching hungrily as the mayhem unfolded below them. Everywhere, the sounds of screaming echoed through the burning village, the cries promising a feast, come sundown. Death was walking amongst the living.*

# Prologue

Arleigh woke with a jolt, the smoky blackness of her home shrouded in silence but for the sound of wood gently striking wood as her husband lifted his father's battered shield from where it hung on the wall. His smiths-hammer was tucked through the leather belt around his waist with his hunting knife sheathed at the small of his back. The brass-decorated bone handle caught the light and glinted dully in the dark room.

Outside, Arleigh could hear the distant alarm horns warning the villagers of danger, and she knew what had woken them. Torr was no warrior, at least not by profession, but his height and build, moulded by years of beating metal into submission at the anvil, had seen him recognised by their *thegn* as a man of strength and muscle. When the horns called, Torr was expected to stand in the front of the *fyrd's* shield wall and defend his home. Some called it an honour. He had been called up before, his movements almost routine, but something told Arleigh that this time was different. It would be the last time. As she watched him heft his ash spear and remove the leather sheath protecting the leaf-shaped blade, her mind filled with visions of him walking towards his death, never to return. The thought stilled her breath for a moment, and she imagined she felt the flutter of new life – their new life – kick from deep within her belly. But the fyrd had been called up, and no sentimental begging from the blacksmith's wife would change the fact. The dragons from the North had come. Bending to kiss his wife, Torr smiled his tired, soot-stained smile, filling her nostrils with the metallic smells of the forge as his toughened leather jerkin scratched roughly against her cheek. As the blacksmith, Torr had managed to scrimp and save enough iron to craft himself a simple helmet and a single iron-backed glove to protect his spear hand. Beyond this, he wore nothing but toughened leather and a thick quilted jerkin for protection.

'*At least he has a spear,*' Arleigh thought to herself as she looked into her husband's forest-green eyes for the last time. As a wall-breaker, Torr was fortunate enough to carry the length of ash-and-iron to accompany his shield, a gift from the thegn for those he asked to stand in his front ranks. Anyone

21

behind the second line carried what they could find. Some were fortunate enough to carry spears, but others went with whatever was close to hand. Mae's husband carried nothing but a three-pronged pitchfork, and her own brother had only a scythe.

'Goodbye, my love,' he whispered in her ear, a gentle smile playing in his eyes.

'Don't go, Torr, not this time,' she whispered suddenly. 'Take your bow and hide in the woods. We can tell the thegn you were hunting when the horns blew. If you answer the call this time, you won't return to me; to us,' she said, taking his large hand and placing it gently on her belly, her eyes on his. 'I know it as surely as the Lord is my witness.' Even as the words left her mouth she regretted them, feeling as if she had sealed his fate by giving voice to her fears.

'I have to, Arleigh. As a man and as a *warrior*. I have to go.'

The emphasis on warrior wasn't lost on Arleigh as he took her hand and gently closed it around something hard and metallic.

She could only watch as he stood and hefted his war gear. To her, he looked like Mars, the ancient Roman god of war. To the men from the North, he would be little more than a farmer with a spear. The wolves came with swords and axes, wearing shirts of iron and watched by their heathen gods, silver-sick and hungry for blood. Torr would be nothing but a lamb for slaughter in their eyes.

Arleigh knew this, just as she knew that this was the last time she would see her husband or wake up in their small home in Shorewitchshire. She didn't know how she knew – perhaps it was a premonition from the Lord – but somehow she was sure, beyond a shadow of a doubt. Just as she knew that nothing she could say would change Torr's mind.

'Get a stew going, my love,' Torr said, breaking her train of worry. 'The hares from yesterday will need cooking. I'll be home for the evening meal. I promise.'

And then he was gone, closing the door quietly behind him on its leather hinges. Only then did she open her hand, finding Torr's small silver cross resting in her palm. It was the only shred of silver they owned, earned as part of a payment from the thegn for his son's sword. With a sigh, she slipped her head through the cord and let the warm metal rest against her heart.

Preparing for the inevitable, she wiped her tears away and dressed quickly, donning a simple dress with a stained and patched apron over the top before going outside to retrieve the hares. She quickly skinned and gutted them before chopping the meat and adding it to the pot over the central fire, adding onions, carrots, chopped cabbage and some wild rosemary, as well as ale and water from the well. The stew would slowly cook through the day for a husband who would never return to eat it. Only additions of water would be needed to keep it from getting too thick. When she had finished with the stew, she began preparing for the reality of Torr's death.

Walking outside, she took a deep breath as she made her way towards the smithy. Torr kept a pony there in a small stall that he'd taken in payment a few years prior from a farmer who couldn't pay for a scythe blade he'd ordered. The piebald was small and strong, with healthy yellow teeth and a pattern that reminded her of flowers in a meadow. She quickly set about loading the mare with blankets and food, a small wood axe, a flint, and her needles and thread. Last, she threw two waterskins over the saddle and secured Torr's hunting bow and quiver before ducking back into the inky blackness of her home to retrieve her own belt and the eating knife she carried on her side. If the Norsemen came to Shorewitchshire – when they came – they wouldn't find her on a bed of straw waiting for them with her legs open and her breasts bared.

At eighteen, she was still youthful and beautiful, and stood out amongst the older women of the village. She knew that men lusted after her long brown hair and green eyes, and her smooth skin that was untarnished by age or disease. More than once Torr or her brother had had to step in when men from the village drank too much and forgot themselves. She knew that to the heathen-Norse she would be a prize worth taking, and there would be no hesitation if they sought to satisfy their desire when they found her, especially after their time at sea. She would run, and her son would survive to grow tall and free.

Fighting back tears, she tied their meagre purse of coins to her belt as she watched the rest of the village women and old men go about their daily lives. Shorewitchshire had fought off the Norsemen once before, and everyone appeared confident that they would do it again. The thegn was a skilled tactician, and all the men who fought for him – both his household warriors and the fyrd – had experienced battle under his leadership. When the war horns blew, he could muster an army of sixty-three men; twenty from his own household with the rest coming from the village and surrounding farms. Given enough time, that figure could grow to eighty-five as the men from the outlying farms joined the ranks. They had every reason to be confident.

But still, Arleigh wanted to be prepared. In her heart of hearts, she knew that this was the end of Shorewitchshire. So, pony loaded, and knife sharp, she stirred her stew and watched the horizon, waiting for the inevitable.

*** 

The sun was passing noon when they finally came. All around the village, wheat and barley swayed slowly in the afternoon breeze, the wind carrying with it an ominous iron tang. Blood. Like a goshawk preparing to strike, Arleigh's vigil was at an end. Now was the time to flee. She dropped the basket of wood she had been carrying and ran for the pony, leaping onto the mare's back and kicking in her heels. She could hear the screams of fear amongst the homes closest to the coast, and looking back she watched as the few greybeards left in the village scrambled to form a shield wall on the road to repel the invaders.

Too old to fight with the fyrd, the elders of Shorewitchshire still had teeth, and they would bare them now. With ancient spears and rusted blades, they formed their shield wall. She watched as old-Manton hefted a wood-and-wicker window cover in place of the thick planks of wood he had carried in his youth. Standing in a line, the last men of Shorewitchshire stood against the men of iron who came to steal and thieve, to rape and pillage.

The Northmen barely slowed as they approached the line of shields. A volley of javelins thrown on the run downed three of the greybeards in a single volley, with more staggering as shields and limbs were pierced. Fresh tears flowed down Arleigh's face when she saw old-Manton fall with a spear through his chest, pinning his shield to his body. He would have been a magnificent grandfather, she thought, crying as she watched him fall. Within seconds the wolves were amongst the sheep, swords and axes rising and falling with ruthless abandon as they slaughtered Shorewitchshire's final defenders. Only one of the sword-Norse was laid low in the fight, his throat ripped out by a rust-kissed spear.

Watching from her small hill to the east of the village, Arleigh had seen enough. Shorewitchshire was finished. She had to look to the future. Crying freely, she rode for the forest praying that the men of the North would never venture so far from their fearsome dragon ships, not with a village to plunder and undefended women to enjoy. Feeling the pony stir beneath her, she kicked in her heels, savouring the drum of the hooves as they struck the earth beneath her. She pushed her mount as hard as she could, leaving the village in her wake.

She looked back just once and saw the smoke beginning to rise from a fired thatch roof.

'Goodbye, Torr,' she whispered, tears coursing down her face as she galloped from her past.

As the forest grew ever closer, she began to feel hope welling in her chest. She was going to make it; she could almost taste her escape. Once she reached the safety of the forest, she could begin making her way up the coast. Her oldest brother worked in Ipswich as a boat maker with his family. She would be safe there if she could just reach them.

Confident in her decision, she was just beginning to allow a glimmer of hope to bloom when she saw it, a flash of movement between the trees and the glint of iron before her pony screamed in pain. She could see the arrow's fletching as the brave mare carried her a few final steps, the iron tip clean through its heaving heart. Arleigh screamed in anger and pain as the horse crashed to the earth, broken, throwing her from its back to tumble in a mess of limbs.

In the time it took for her to find her feet and stand, five men were moving towards her from the woods. One carried a bow, three carried axes, and the largest carried a sword. All of them began to grin hungrily when she stood, her ripped dress parting to expose her left leg from ankle to hip. Without thinking she pulled the bow from where it was tied on the quickly dying pony, silently thanking God it had survived the fall as she nocked her first shaft. She drew the string back to her cheek with a smooth, practiced motion before releasing.

By the time the archer's choking cough reached her she already had a second arrows on the string, her eyes searching out her next target. She would sell her life dearly for what these men had stolen from her, she decided. There was little more she could do.

Her second shaft took one of the axemen in the right shoulder, making him drop his axe and cry out in pain and surprise as blood blossomed from the wound. The remaining warriors came on more carefully now, grouping together to form a small shield wall as they continued their advance.

She took careful aim, focusing her attention on the eye-slit in the swordsman's helmet and praying silently to God to guide her arrow. Exhaling slowly to steady herself, she released, following the arrow's curve as it shot towards the target. For a moment she thought she'd struck true, until he dropped his face behind his shield at the last minute and the arrow dinged harmlessly off the rounded iron of his helmet to land in the dust behind them. Snarling in frustration, she threw the bow on the ground and took up the wood axe before turning to run, her arrows spent. She screamed in shock as she collided with another raider, this one covered in blood. His thick arms quickly grabbed her wrists and twisted them, forcing the axe from her hand. Holding tight, he turned her around so her back was against him, grasping both of her small wrists in his one giant hand.

'Where go you, girl?' he asked in broken English, his right hand slowly creeping up the back of her exposed leg to grip her behind.

'Wherever you're not, heathen pig,' she spat, slamming her head back into his nose, breaking it.

Gasping in pain, he released her to hold his ruined nose, a look of shock surprise crossing his face. Arleigh drew and slashed in one clumsy motion, running her knife across his exposed throat. She wasn't prepared for the spray of blood that exploded from the wound, the iron warmth painting her face and briefly blinding her. Without thinking, she turned and ran for the woods, the choking sounds from the dying warrior following her as he coughed his final, gargled breaths. Even as she ran, she knew it was over. The remaining three men from the forest gained on her quickly and surrounded her. She slashed wildly with her knife, but she could barely chip the paint decorating their shields.

But just as Arleigh couldn't reach the men behind the shields, they too weren't sure how to capture the raging, spinning wildcat they'd caged. She drew strength from that, and from the feeling of Torr's cross bumping against her chest as she spun and slashed in her wild fury. She was going to die, she realised.

Gritting her teeth, she steeled herself for death and threw herself against their shields with ruthless abandon, determined to die undefiled by a heathen prick. 'I will see you soon, Torr,' she whispered, closing her eyes for a second before throwing herself at a red-and-white painted shield, wildly slashing her knife over the rim as she tried to pierce the owner's eyes. Before the blade could connect, another man grabbed her hand and twisted violently, making her scream out in pain and surprise.

The sudden agony forced the knife from her hands, and she watched absently as it came to rest bloodily in the grass at her feet, out of reach. Unarmed, the surrounding men's confidence grew quickly, and she could feel their hungry eyes wander over her exposed leg and hip as the fabric fell aside.

'Forgive me, Torr,' she whispered as she sought out the swordsman, closing her eyes before throwing herself towards his blade, hoping to skewer herself on the sharpened length of iron.

'Halt! Stans alle sammen!' A voice boomed from behind her. Arleigh stopped in her tracks at the bellowed command, her plans for death forgotten as the warriors surrounding parted like the Red Sea for Moses to reveal an iron-clad Norseman, the likes of which she had never seen before. He towered over the men surrounding her, with a gilded sword at his hip and a silver-decorated helmet with a swooping raven to guard his nose and eyes tucked under his arm. Around his neck sat a finger-thick torc of twisted silver-and-gold, and his beard was plaited with rune-covered rings. There was even one in gold. She knew without a doubt that where this man led, others followed.

'Hun er min,' he said, his voice carrying in the early afternoon breeze.

Unable to understand a word he said, Arleigh could only watch hopefully as her would-be captors grunted in frustration and began to move away from her, heading back towards her ruined home. It was only now that she noticed the crying and the screams coming from the village, the sound unlocking a fresh stream of silent tears.

'You are mine,' the warrior said calmly as he turned back to her, his accent giving his English a rough edge.

'Yours? I'd rather die,' she cursed, spitting in his face.

He didn't move or blink. He just wiped the spit away and stared at her, his pale blue eyes freezing her in place. 'You can come with us, and live like a wolf, or die here like a sheep. The choice is yours, but it would be a shame to see such spirit wasted. There is Freyja in you, girl, both beauty and war. So, I give you this one chance; live or die. I won't ask again.' He finished.

'And what would I do, were I to come with you?' she snarled, baring her teeth. 'You've taken everything from me, everything!' she screamed. 'Why would I come? What could you possibly offer me!' Bursting into tears, her shoulders began to heave as the gravity of what had happened to her began to sink in. Torr was gone. The village was gone. Everything she had known, was gone. Beside her, the giant Norseman watched silently as she spent herself, patiently waiting to speak again. Oblivious to his presence, Arleigh cried until there was nothing left. Only then, when her tears had dried up and receded to quiet sobs, did he speak.

'Life,' he said simply. 'Our fates are woven by the *Nornir* from the day we take our first squalling breath. But, through it all, we are given rare

27

opportunities to change the weave and take control of our futures and change our destiny, such as you face now. Come with me, and live, or stay here and die. Decide.' Iron entered his voice on the final word, stilling the raging fire that fired her blood.

Now that the other men had left, and she was unarmed, she knew in her heart that she didn't want to die. She wanted to live. Not for herself; her life ended the moment Torr died. She would live for the child growing inside her. For the memory of Torr.

'I will live,' she whispered, ignoring the tears as they streamed down her face.

'Good.' He nodded, satisfied. 'I am called Erik, I am jarl to these men. From this day on, you are mine, and you will be safe.' With that he turned his back and began to walk back to the village. 'Sven!' he called, gaining the attention of a giant warrior carrying a two-handed axe, clad entirely in iron rings under a wolf-fur cloak. 'Tie her up in the large hall for me,' he called, motioning back towards Arleigh. 'She's coming with us.'

Arleigh had never seen such a large man before in her life, and she felt her stomach clench in fear as his eyes passed over her briefly at Erik's command. The giant axeman nodded briefly to the jarl before walking towards her and taking her arm with surprising gentleness and quietly leading her back towards the burning ruins of Shorewitchshire.

Tied to the thegn's chair in the dark of his abandoned hall, Arleigh strained against the ropes that held her as she listened to the Norsemen pillaging her home. Her ears filled with the screams of women she had known all her life and the hysteric crying of newly-orphaned children, the miserable orchestra punctuated by the crackle of flames as her world burned around her. She listened as the *vikingr* gave into their basest desires, the basest of sins. Arleigh listed the names of women she knew quietly to herself, praying for them even as she listened to their horrific fate, the sounds inescapable in the dark emptiness of the hall.

'Abigale, Thea, Agnes, Trea, Hild, Nelda…' The list seemed endless, and all the while, she cried. She cried for the life she had known, the man she had loved, and the future she had lost.

No man came for her in the cold dark. No man except the jarl. It was full dark when he finally came, his breath heavy with ale and mead. It was clear what he wanted, and having heard her world burn around her, she had decided to twist her own fate and survive. She would survive and endure, and protect the child growing inside her. She had to. She didn't fight or struggle as the jarl untied the ropes holding her and lifted her onto the table. Instead, she met him with open legs and breasts bared, and while he spent himself inside her she cried and thought of Torr, and the life they had created together.

***

The next morning, Arleigh woke to someone lifting her to her feet and guiding her outside into the new day. She was given water, bread, cheese and smoked pork by the giant named Sven. They'd found the winter stores. All around her the remains of Shorewitchshire smouldered, the flames long since spent.

The homes, the church, Torr's smithy. Everything was gone, survived only by splinters and charred beams. Only the homes that the men had used for the night, and the thegn's hall, remained untouched, but not for long. Erik's warriors were already moving amongst the remaining structures and setting them to the torch.

Arleigh was led to where the final survivors of the village stood, their eyes dull with grief and their bodies showing signs of hard use. She counted only thirty-two in total, all women and children who would likely be sold in foreign slave markets, their futures uncertain. She knew she would never see any of them again beyond the coming journey. Erik had confirmed as much the night before.

At spearpoint, they were marched through the burned husk of their home, pushed towards the coast and the waiting ships. It wasn't long before they passed the remains of their menfolk. They knew they were close long before they could see them, the cries of circling carrion birds giving away the position.

Arleigh stopped when she saw him, the shock hitting her like a physical blow. Lying to the right of the thegn's shield wall was Torr. Two dead Norsemen lay in front of him – one of them barely into his first beard. She could see the vivid wound that had killed him in his chest, the red blood turned brown overnight. '*At least he died quickly...*' Arleigh thought, her eyes welling with fresh grief.

She grasped the cross hidden at her neck and whispered a prayer for Torr to wait for her, and to forgive her her survival, and how she had found it. The rest of the villagers were picking out their husbands, fathers and sons, fresh

29

tears running through their soot-stained faces as they caught sight of their loved ones. Several of the Norsemen left the column to collect their dead, and to strip the English of the valuable weapons and armour that had sat there overnight. Arleigh shed fresh tears as she watched one bend and pick up Torr's weapons and helmet, his prized knife amongst them. The Norsemen moved quickly, and it wasn't long before the column began moving again, burdened down by their dead comrades and looted equipment. The English were left where they had fallen as a feast for the ravens. Arleigh couldn't help but notice that the number of dead warriors they collected was pitifully low compared to the deaths of everyone she'd ever known or loved.

As the survivors were pushed towards the three ships waiting on the shore, Arleigh turned back just once towards the ruins of her home. She could see the smoke rising from the village, blackening the early-morning sky. They'd be long gone before anyone arrived and found the ruins; before anyone found Torr. She watched as two ravens flew over the group towards the sea, leaving death and ruin in their wake. All around her, she could hear the laughter and conversation of the Norse, and their rough, heathen voices as they made the ships ready for the journey home, stowing their plunder and slaves, while others built funeral pyres for their dead. All around her the crying continued as the survivors realised the finality of their situation. Their lives in Essex were over; their lives amongst the Norse had begun.

# Chapter 1

Bjørn wiped the blood from his eyes and exhaled slowly, adjusting his grip on the heavy wooden spear and linden wood shield he carried. Across the rough-marked square from him stood his opponent, patiently waiting behind his painted shield wearing a gleaming iron helmet. The flying raven on the nose guard taunted Bjørn, as did the golden fist that decorated the brow. Both men wore *brynja*, the heavy iron rings offering them greater protection than most men could hope to find in the shield lines of the *skjaldborg*. Unlike his foe however, Bjørn's helmet was a simple iron construction, with unadorned eye holes, decorated with only a small, polished brass fist on the brow to match his opponents. Checking the grip on his spear, Bjørn moved quickly, feinting to the right before smashing his shield against his opponent's, trying to throw him off-balance. It didn't work, and the man before him remained as immovable as an ancient oak, rooted fast. Before he could regain his balance, his enemy counterattacked with his own spear, mercilessly striking the left side of his neck and causing his vision to explode with light. Before he knew it, he was falling backwards, helped onto his arse by a spear shaft between his legs, tangling them.

'Yield?' he heard his father say through the ringing in his head.

'Yield,' Bjørn gnarled, gingerly rubbing his neck. It was the fourth time that morning that Erik Golden Hand, Jarl of Vágar, had generously deposited him in the mire of mud and snow. The irony wasn't lost on Bjørn. His father had earned his by-name – Golden Hand – through the generosity he showed to his warriors.

'Fall on your arse again and you'll spend another season here with the women and old folk, Bjørn. This is your last chance,' his father said, his voice gravelly from the exertion.

Bjørn regained his feet, the mud sloughing from his hands and arms as he moved. He spat, blood and saliva mingling together in the mud and snow beneath his feet. Looking around him, Bjørn briefly registered those who had come to watch the fight. There were his three half-brothers, jeering good-naturedly at his efforts and betting amongst themselves on the outcome. As the youngest of the brood, and half-English to boot, Bjørn was the last of Erik's sons to face him in combat. The trial was similar to a *holmgang*, with two combatants fighting in a dedicated space, although they weren't on an abandoned island as tradition dictated. Instead, they fought for all to see in an open space near the walls of Vágar, not far from Erik's hall. Unless Bjørn could defeat his father in single combat, he would spend another summer at home while his father and brothers sailed for distant lands to raid for wealth and glory. Jarl's son or not, Erik's boys had to earn the right to sail the whale road. Birth alone didn't guarantee them an oar, and generous as he was, Erik Golden Hand wasn't one to suffer the weak or the incompetent on his ships.

'What are you waiting for, boy? Your mother can't help you now, nor can your brothers – it's just you and me. Prove you have what it takes to stand in my skjaldborg and ride the dragons, to write your own saga. Prove to me that your English blood hasn't made you weak!' Erik snarled.

Bjørn knew that his father was goading him, trying to make him angry and lunge without thinking, to give himself to Óðinn and go *beserk*. But he knew his biggest strength: patience. Erik was a true man of the North. He thought quickly and acted quicker, never looking back. Bjørn, on the other hand, had learned patience, and cunning. While his father revered Óðinn – as all good Norsemen must – Bjørn sought only the Allfather's wisdom. Óðinn is a jarl's god, Erik's god, and to best his father, Bjørn's prayers were better given to one known for his guile and trickery: Loki. If Bjørn ever wanted to claim his place in his father's shield wall, he would need cunning and trickery. For years he had listened to stories of the sword storm and the skjaldborg, had been forced to wait while others raided and sailed to distant shores. This summer, he would at last take his place in the wall of iron and wood, earning fame and fortune for himself and his father. Come next winter, it would be his sagas that the skalds told around the fires at night while the world outside was painted white with snow and glittering ice. But to achieve all that, he had to first put his father in the mud.

Breathing slowly, he dropped his shield and spear to the ground and began moving slowly around the roped-off arena to turn his father towards the sun, blinding him with Freyr's golden rays. As he moved, he drew the weighted and blunted sword and axe from his belt, nodding at his father. He could feel the dried blood and mud cracking on his face as his lips parted to form a small smile, his teeth flashing white.

'No man in my *skjaldborg* drops his shield, lad,' Erik growled dangerously.

'This is no skjaldborg, Father. This is *holmgang*,' Bjørn replied.

'Careful, Bjørn. I've put more men in the ground than you've got hairs in your *beard…*' Erik gnarred.

Erik struck before Bjørn could reply, his spear lunging forward with a speed that belied his massive bulk. Sweeping his shield across his body to block Bjørn's sword, Erik's spear lunged straight for his son's unprotected belly with enough power to threaten the iron rings, blunted blade or not. Bjørn had seen his father's subtle shift in footing while they swapped taunts, his right foot sliding backwards in preparation of the lunge. As soon as Erik moved, Bjørn dropped to the ground and rolled to his left, hooking the beard of his axe over his father's spear and yanking downwards for all he was worth. Erik's momentum did the rest for him as the spearhead was buried deep in the mud's gluttonous embrace. Screaming Loki's name, Bjørn drove his sword between his father's legs and twisted, forcing him to lose his balance on the unstable ground. Time seemed to slow as Erik fell, his feet moving awkwardly as he fought to right himself before landing squarely in the mud alongside his buried spear. Bjørn was on him before he could blink, the blunted edge of his axe nestled tight against his father's neck. Blood slowly ran down his face and dripped from his nose, painting the polished and patterned iron of his father's raven helmet.

'Yield?' he asked, feeling the battle frenzy leave his body as he allowed a smile to reach his fjord-green eyes. Outside the ring, his brothers had fallen silent, as had the rest of the onlookers. They'd all beaten Erik in their turn, but they'd never dared to claim the victory so brazenly.

'Yield,' Erik grunted, smiling despite himself. 'That'll do it, Bjørn. You'll have your oar.'

Bjørn smiled and held out a hand to help his father rise, both of them grinning as clumps of mud rained from the iron rings of Erik's brynja. Overwhelmed with emotion, Bjorn briefly retained his grip on his father's forearm and squeezed. 'Thank you, Father. I won't let you down. I swear it, as Óðinn is my witness.'

Sensing the severity of his son's mood, Erik met Bjørn's eyes as he returned the grip, ignoring the twinge that always came when he thought of his son's English blood. 'I know, Bjørn,' he said seriously. Squeezing once, Erik nodded, satisfied, before dropping the grip.

As his father moved away, Bjørn began comprehending the enormity of what had just happened. With one lunge of his sword, he had rewritten his future. Erik had three ships that he took on the whale road each season, and at long last, he would sail in one of them. Erik's flagship, *Fjord Ulf*, was a great sixty-oared *drakkar* that carried a crew of sixty-six men, and was joined by two smaller, sleeker forty-oared *snekkja*. Named after the Allfather's eight-legged steed, *Sleipnir* carried a crew of forty-two, while the slightly smaller *Fjord Uxi* carried forty. There were less auspiciously named ships carrying crews of Northmen to fame and fortune, and, in a few short months, Bjørn would finally join them. At last, his own saga could begin.

He soon became aware of the silence around him. His brothers were staring open-mouthed at their mud-covered father, while the older warriors – Sven and Yngvar among them – were trying to hold back their smiles. No one had seen Erik take such a beating from any of his older son's when their time in the square had come.

It was Yngvar who finally broke the strange *seiðr* that had settled over the watchers. Slight of build and rarely armoured with more than hardened leather, Yngvar was often mistaken for a *nithing*, a weakling, by his enemies. Looking at him now, it wasn't hard to see why. He wore no beard and his head was shaved on the sides, with a long braid down his back. Standing next to Erik, or his massive prow man Sven, Yngvar looked more like one of the *dvergr* dwarves of *Svartalfheim* than a man. But all those who thought him weak were dead, while Yngvar remained very much above ground. Yngvar was a born killer and one of Erik's closest and oldest friends and, with Sven, was his most loyal follower. Bjørn, just like his father, trusted Yngvar with his life, and would happily give his own for him.

Snorting like *Hildisvíni*, Freyja's battle boar, Yngvar spat into the mud as he walked across the square towards Bjørn, taking his hand in the warrior's grip. 'Well done, lad, well done! Inspired by Loki and guided by Tyr; a dangerous combination, wouldn't you agree, Erik?' he said, turning to his friend.

'Yes, and dirty,' his father grunted through his own smile, pointlessly rubbing his mud-covered hands on his already soiled breeches.

'It seems your sons are all destined for skalds songs in the years to come.'

'Aye, Yngvar, that they are.' Erik smiled again, watching with pride as Bjørn returned his helmet and brynja to his brother, Sigurd. They could hear them all talking, discussing and complimenting their brother on the manoeuvre. It wasn't long before they began trying it themselves, and the two friends watched in companionable silence as Sigurd and Olaf recreated the fight together while Toke and Bjørn watched with grins on their faces. At sixteen, Bjørn stood as tall as his brothers, with skin painted brown from years learning to sail and fight and shoot from Erik and his warriors, Yngvar and Uffe among them. Erik had never coddled his sons, and they'd grown tough through hard lessons. Only Bjørn's piercing green eyes and brown hair marked his English blood, standing in stark contrast to his brothers' – and father's – light blue eyes and rich blond manes, except for Sigurd, whose hair shone as red as Thor's.

'Their mothers will kill me,' Erik whispered with a wink. 'Taking all four boys vikingr in one season. I'll never hear the end of it!'

Yngvar smiled, but said nothing as he watched Olaf send Sigurd spinning into the mud, the ground erupting in a spray of brown and white slush.

'Bjørn will sail with you, just as he trained with you,' Erik said softly as he watched his sons. 'The boy fought well today, but I still worry that his blood will out, in the end,' he added, oblivious to the frown that flashed across his friend's face. 'He's a credit to you, my friend, and I'll honour my promise.'

Yngvar remained silent, nodding at his friend's words. Inside he was seething, and his heart broke for the boy he had trained and loved as if he was his own.

Although Arleigh remained Erik's thrall, he had accepted the boy as his own, and treated him as equal to the rest of his brood, while his mother had embraced her life amongst them, raising Bjørn as a true man of the North. Her only exception had been to raise the boy bilingual, teaching him her native English. To Yngvar's mind, Bjørn couldn't be more Norse if he tried. '*What does blood have to do with anything anyway?*' Yngvar mused, spitting again. None of this showed on his face as he turned his attention to his friend and nodded.

'It will be as you say, Jarl Erik,' Yngvar said, patting his friend on the back before crossing the square towards the boys.

'Congratulations again, Bjørn. It seems you will sail with me come the thaw. I will be proud to have you as part of my crew.'

Bjørn beamed at the words, his conversation with Toke forgotten. 'I won't let you down, Yngvar. I promise,' he said, dipping his head.

'Come and visit me this evening. I have something for you.'

'I will,' Bjørn nodded as he tried to control the smile on his face.

Smiling, Yngvar turned and walked towards the open gates and the fjord beyond.

As Bjørn turned to leave, he saw his mother watching him, a slight frown furrowing her brow. '*I suppose the risk of Valhöll is real now?*' he mused with a shrug, smiling at her. The thought hardly bothered him. His fate would flow as the Nornir had woven it. *Wyrd.*

Overhead, the sky was beginning to turn grey, and the first drops of rain were starting to fall gently into the mud and snow. Erik and Bjørn's brothers were all making their way back to the longhouse, but Bjørn wanted time to himself to process the reality of the situation. He had dreams to dream, and a bit of water wasn't going to stop him.

As the rain began to intensify, Bjørn donned a seal skin cloak and made his way along the shore to Yngvar's solitary home. Set back from the shore, Yngvar farmed a small plot of land a few *rôst* from Vágar's walls. With a small forge and enough land to raise a few animals and grow vegetables, Yngvar kept himself to himself as often as he was seen in the town, tinkering away at his anvil and forge. On a clear day, the sound of his hammer striking iron could be heard from a rôst away. Although not a blacksmith by trade, Yngvar loved to create and experiment, and as Bjørn drew closer to the house he began to make out the gentle *ting ting ting* of his hammer at work as he walked along the muddy path. Off to his right he could see a mist creeping down the fjord towards the homestead, blanketing the world around it.

'Yngvar!' Bjørn called into the wind, his words whipping away as he spoke. 'Hold the dog, I'm coming in.'

'He's ...side, lad. You ca. ...en the ga...' the wind called back, carrying only fragments to his ears.

*'Here goes,'* Bjørn thought to himself, opening the gate.

Yngvar's dog, Fen, was an exceptionally large elkhound that held keenly to its wolfish heritage, and had been named after the Fenrir wolf. He was the last thing Bjørn wanted to come across on a dark night like this. Despite the hours he had spent with his master, it always paid to be cautious where Fen was concerned.

Walking along the roughhewn planks, Bjørn was able to avoid the worst of the mud as he crossed the final few steps towards the buildings. He made a beeline for the comforting glow and warmth of the forge, the constant *ting ting ting* growing louder with every step. Through the rain he could see Yngvar hammering away, the red glow of the iron spitting sparks with every strike. Fen was curled up against the heated stones of the forge, enjoying the heat radiating from the glowing coals.

'Yngvar,' he said, nodding as he stepped into the warmth.

'There you are. I wasn't sure you'd come in this weather,' Yngvar said with a smile as he returned the length of iron to the coals. 'Get that cloak off you, boy. You can hang it there by the forge. No not there, I don't want water falling in the coals. Hang it there, behind the bellows. That's it.'

Bjørn sighed. When it came to the forge, obsessive was the word that sprang most readily to mind. *'What would a few drops of water matter in a furnace of that heat?'* he mused.

Steam was already rising off the oiled skin, mixing with the smoke from the coals before escaping through the hole in the thatch roof. 'So, Yngvar, what was it you wanted to speak to me about?' he asked, moving to sit by the flame and warm his frozen bones.

'It's not so much something to speak about, as to give you. Ale?'

'Aye, an ale would go down well,' Bjørn sighed, welcoming the warmth as Yngvar pushed the drinking horn into his hands, the lightly heated brew warming his frozen fingers, not that he'd ever admit as much. 'So, what is it that you want to give to me, then?'

'This,' Yngvar said, retrieving a package from a chest by the wall and handing it over. 'I've wanted to give it to you for some time, but I decided to wait until you had proven yourself ready for it, like you did today. I was proud of you, Bjørn,' he said quietly, his blue eyes reflecting the fire's light. It might have been his imagination, but Bjørn thought he could see tears welling in the corners of the grizzled warrior's eyes. *'Probably the smoke,'* he thought.

'Thank you,' Bjørn said seriously as he took the package and began unwrapping it. Stripping away the final layer of fabric, he found a knife with a bone-and-brass handle in an elk leather sheath decorated with an embossed raven. Glancing up at Yngvar he saw a smile dance across his face as he watched him. Drawing the knife, he found a wicked sharp, slightly curved blade that was a little shorter than his forearm. The blade itself bore the same raven design as the sheath, the bird appearing ready to take flight as it sat poised in the metal.

'I took this dagger the day we captured your mother,' Yngvar said into the silence. 'We took her from some scrappy little nowhere in Essex; I forget the name.'

'Shorewitchshire,' Bjørn said unconsciously, his attention focused on the blade in his hands. As it turned in the light of the forge, he imagined he could see the Raven moving.

'Yes, that's the one,' Yngvar continued. 'Anyway, the owner of the blade put up one hell of a fight; a giant of a man who sent two of ours to the corpse hall before I got to him. I remember it as if it was yesterday. He'd lost his spear in one of our lads and was swinging a blacksmith's hammer like a man possessed. But by then the fighting had taken its toll on him and it wasn't long before my sword ended him. He wasn't a warrior-born like us, but he could fight, I won't deny him that, and I'd be glad to share an ale with him when the *Valkyries* come for me, if his God denied him. Anyway, I worked my way to him, looking to put an end to his fury and spare more of our men. I made sure he died quickly and cleanly, honouring his bravery. I even took his hammer, rather than see it rot in the field. It's over there on the wall, see it?' he said, pointing to his tools. 'It's the one with a lighter shaft. A man who fought so bravely with such a mundane tool deserved remembering. Aside from the hammer, I also took his knife, and now I want you to have it. It would honour me to see the blade at your side in the voyages to come, to know it had found its way to a worthy owner. One with English blood,' he added with a grin, making Bjørn chuckle.

'I don't know what to say, Yngvar. It's beautiful, and the sheath… thank you. I'll carry it with me for as long as I sail the whale road.'

Yngvar grinned as he watched Bjørn slide the sheath onto his belt, replacing the aged seax he usually carried.

'I have one more thing for you,' he grinned, moving to open another chest at the rear of the forge. 'A jarl's son shouldn't sail without a *proper* blade.' As he spoke, he pulled a rigid length of cloth from the chest. He began unwrapping the package as he walked, seemingly oblivious to Bjørn's excitement.

For his part, Bjørn could feel his blood pumping in hopeful anticipation. Only his father's *húskarlar* – his hearth warriors – and some of the hirð carried anything that could be called a sword. Most made do with axes, spears, or, if they were lucky, long seaxes. Olaf and Sigurd were included in that number, earning captured swords from Erik during previous raids. Toke had been less lucky, and they spoke often of their desire to capture swords of their own in the future. Being gifted one before even leaving was something he never would have dared hope for.

Ignoring Bjørn's rushing emotions, Yngvar continued his story. 'A few years ago, when we were raiding the lands of the Franks, I came across a man with skin the colour of soot. He told me he was a blacksmith turned merchant, and that he had learned our language from his thralls. I can tell you now, when I heard he'd kept Norsemen as slaves my blade was half out of its sheath. "I freed them," he told me quickly, his eyes glued to my sword. When I asked him why, he told me that "it pleased him to do so", before telling me about how his thralls had saved his life when men tried to rob him in the street. Apparently, his unarmed Norsemen killed them all without hesitation. In exchange for saving him, he offered them jobs as his guards, and paid them to protect him whenever he left his home in a city called Toledo. Apparently, travelling through the lands there could be dangerous because of religious disagreements between the White Christ and some God from the East. His plan, he told me, had been to sell weapons to the Franks and passing Northmen, but in the event, his guards abandoned him and escaped on a passing longship. Abandoned and alone, he soon became a slave himself.'

Yngvar stopped to take a sip from his mead horn, grinning as he travelled the roads of his youth. 'Remember that, Bjørn: a sheep does not ask a wolf to keep it safe and protect it, because a wolf will always be a wolf, and will always seek the freedom of the forest. But I've gotten distracted,' Yngvar said, putting down the horn to remove the final scrap of cloth. Bjørn could barely contain himself when the fabric fell away to reveal a sword in a matching elk skin sheath with an embossed raven in the leather, this one flying in the opposite direction to one on the knife.

'This is Huginn,' Yngvar said, drawing the sword to reveal the raven on the blade. Grinning, Bjørn half drew the knife to reveal the raven Yngvar had carved into the iron.

'Huginn and Muninn; thought and memory,' he said, nodding at the knife. 'A good warrior will act fast and move on, but a great warrior will think and remember; he will learn and grow, constantly working to better himself. Do this, and Óðinn will surely watch over you for as long as his ravens fly in your hands.'

Sliding the knife home, Bjørn reverently took the sword from Yngvar, admiring its craftsmanship and balance. The patterns in the iron reminded him of water as it danced in the forges flickering light. He was mesmerised.

'As I was saying, the trader. I brought him home as a thrall – you would have been about five at the time? Do you remember him? Never mind – I brought him back to Vágar and had him working in my forge and teaching me his secrets. His name was Sanu, and he taught me to make a blade like that, so the iron looks like ripples in a fjord. He told me that his home in Toledo, and another city far in the East – Damascus – were both renowned for their swords, and he had travelled there in his youth to learn the Eastern craft and then combine the two methods. He called the Eastern technique Damascus or damascene, something like that, after the city. It makes the sword stronger and helps it hold an edge for longer. Personally, I prefer to call it a *fjord blade* because of the patterns that appear in the iron. It's made by layering the metal on top of itself during the forging process, layering it over and over to give it increased strength with every fold. Hold the blade up tomorrow in the sunlight, after this gale blows out, and you'll see what I mean. Anyway, Sanu stayed with me for four years, teaching me to create and work iron like this, and helping in the forge. In return, I gave him food, ale, a little silver, and the first knife I made in his style before putting him on a passing Dane ship, telling him to head south-west towards his home. As he had freed his own Northmen, it pleased me to free him.

'Over the years I've experimented and played with the technique, working hard to perfect it. After all these years, this is the first sword that I've made that I'm happy with, and I want you to have it. You can show your father when he asks, and tell him I have another in the forge for him now, to celebrate twenty years of his arse on the high seat. But this one is for you,' he said, smiling.

Bjørn didn't speak for several moments, mesmerised by the priceless gift and the waving patterns. Yngvar smiled as he watched, pleased to see the blade so well received. After a while, he reached over to refill his drinking horn, the sound of sloshing liquid breaking Bjørn out of his reverie.

'Yngvar,' he finally said, 'I don't know what to say. I don't deserve this…'

'Yes, you do,' Yngvar said quickly, cutting him off. 'I have no son of my own, and while you're Erik's boy, I was given the *dubious* honour of teaching and training you, and I've grown fond to you, in my way. This is a gift I *can* give you, to recognise how hard you have worked and how diligently you've trained. And also, to prepare you for how hard you will have to fight. The whale road is anything but safe, and the places it will take you can be even more dangerous. Take the sword, Bjørn. Huginn is yours now, and come the spring, he will fly.'

Bjørn reached his arm forward and looked his mentor in the eyes, his gaze serious. 'Thank you, Yngvar. For everything,' he said, gripping the older man's arm tight. 'I'll never forget what you've given me.'

'You're welcome, lad,' Yngvar grunted, embarrassed.

Smiling, Yngvar's thoughts flew to his own son, long dead on an English shore – killed by the very man whose knife now rested on Bjørn's belt. *'There's some Loki devilry at play here,'* he thought to himself as he refilled his horn. He imagined he could hear bones clicking in the wind, he shivered despite the warmth from the forge. 'Come on, lad,' he said, breaking the moment and putting his arm around Bjørn. 'Let's have some food. I've half a pig on the spit in the house that the thralls should've finished cooking by now, and plenty of warmed ale to keep our tongues wet from now until *Ragnarök*. We've a summer of a-viking to plan, and you've much to learn between now and then if you want to make it home again.'

Bjørn nodded absently, his gaze wandering back to the sword – his sword – as he followed Yngvar into his home.

***

'He has another for you, Father, he is forging it even as we speak,' Bjørn said excitedly.

He was sitting at his father's high table with his brothers, showing them all Yngvar's gifts. Around them, the carved wooden walls were decorated with trophies, battle standards and painted shields from Erik's past adventures and raids. The hall was big enough to house Erik's entire hirð for feasts, with two tables running parallel along the two longest walls, flanking the giant central hearth that ran the length of the building, warming it from stem to stern. At the far end was Erik's high table, which sat across the length of the hall. Outside, fresh snow was falling, but it was much lighter than it had been in the previous weeks, hardly settling on the chilled earth before turning to an icy slush. The spring was rising, warming the world, and heating the blood in people's veins.

'The blade is a fine gift, and well earned. You bested me, Bjørn, fair and square. You've earned your sea chest and your oar. But from me, you will also have your shield. You've proved that you have what it takes to stand in a skjaldborg and think on your feet.' So saying, Erik turned and boomed into the depths of the hall towards the passage that led to the store rooms. Behind them were the disconnected kitchens which sat off the hall to reduce the risk of fires. 'Hoelun! You can bring it out now.' The silence following Erik's battlefield bellow was broken only by the flames as they ate away at the wood in the hearth. They were soon joined by a low shuffling sound as someone approached. While they waited, Bjørn's gaze was torn between Hoelun, his father's beautiful, almond-eyed Eastern thrall as she came into the light, and

41

his sword as it made its way back around the table, each of his brothers taking their time with the blade before passing it on.

'It's beautifully balanced,' Sigurd said, holding the hilt towards Bjørn. 'I just hope all those waves in the iron won't weaken it when you need it.'

'Yngvar assures me that they make the blade stronger, but we won't know until we're in the sword storm,' Bjørn said, a smile dancing in his eyes.

'We'll see,' Sigurd said, lifting his drinking horn to his lips.

'Don't you doubt Yngvar's word, boy,' Erik rumbled. 'He's made plenty of blades over the years, and not once have I seen one break. He knows what he's doing.'

'I don't doubt him, Father,' Sigurd said quickly. 'I've just never seen iron worked like this before…'

'Regardless, the gift is beautiful, and well deserved, brother,' Toke said, jumping in to break the tension and save Sigurd – and all of them – an unwanted lecture.

'I agree!' boomed Olaf, standing and rising his horn. 'To Bjørn!'

'To Bjørn,' they all cheered.

'To my father and brothers,' Bjørn replied, smiling at them all before downing his own drink.

Hoelun arrived at that moment with her arms spread wide, carrying her burden. In her arms was a giant, circular parcel, wrapped in scraps of linen and leather and tied off with a thin cord. As always, Bjørn was taken by the girl's beauty and grace, even under the heavy weight she carried. Petite and elegant, Hoelun's darker-skin and raven-black hair instantly marked her as an outsider, but it was her yellow, almond-shaped eyes that always took Bjørn's breath away. Wolf eyes.

'Any son of mine who wants to stand in the skjaldborg,' Erik said with a smile, 'will need a good shield.'

'Father, I already have a shield…' Bjørn began.

'…I'm not talking about some rough-around-the-edges circle of old keel planks! I'm talking about a shield, boy; a man's shield. Something for the skalds to sing of that will match that fine blade of yours. Hoelun, give the gift to Bjørn, then fetch us more ale!'

Hefting the awkward package in her arms, Hoelun lifted the parcel onto the table in front of Bjørn, while Erik and his brothers watched in curious silence. Taking the package from her, he began removing the linen coverings, letting them fall to the ground beside him. Underneath was everything he

42

could have wished for in a shield. Made from banded layers of linden wood, the iron shield boss sat proudly in the centre, bearing the same wave-like patterns as Huginn.

'It matches my sword?' he asked questioningly, turning to Erik.

'Of course, I knew about the sword.' Erik chuckled. 'Yngvar asked my permission well before you turned sixteen, knowing you would challenge me. A sword-gift is a father's right, but Yngvar is fond of you and has dedicated time and knowledge training you. It seemed fitting that he should forge and gift the blade you will write your saga with. However, I had no idea that he was making a second for me. It will be a strange thing to hang Geri on the wall,' he said, reaching up to pat the sword that hung on his chair's back. With a polished bronze pommel in the shape of a fist, the sword was as much a part of his saga as Erik himself. All of his sons coveted the legendary blade, although they knew they would never carry it. Erik had long ago decided that when his time came, he would be buried with Geri, ending his saga and leaving his sons to write their own.

Nodding, Bjørn turned his attention back to the shield. The rim was surrounded with beaten iron carrying the same waving patterns as his sword, while the face had been painstakingly divided into six equally sized triangles, painted red and white in an endlessly alternating order. In the centre of each white section sat a yellow fist, Erik's sigil, while black painted runes dominated the red segments. One for Loki, one for Tyr, and one for Óðinn. The workmanship was beautiful. '…And the runes, Father?' Bjørn asked, tearing his gaze away from the shield.

'To protect you, Bjørn, and to keep you safe on your voyages. You carry Loki, to acknowledge and remind you of your cunning and guile in earning your seat and oar. Tyr, the lord of battle, to keep you safe and fierce in war, and to guide your sword. And Óðinn, for his wisdom and war-fervour, and to remind you that you are a jarl's son. Three runes; three gods, each with a role to play in your life. As with your brother's shields, I have watched you grow over the years, and thought long and hard about which gods seem most interested in the man you have become. After our duel yesterday my decision was made, and I painted the runes myself. Live by them, son,' Erik smiled, raising his silver-embossed mead horn high.

'I will. Thank you,' Bjørn said seriously, smiling.

'To Bjørn!' Sigurd and Olaf said at the same time, raising their horns again.

'To Bjørn!' Toke and Erik echoed.

'To the sagas we will carve for ourselves!' Bjørn shouted as he raised his own horn, spilling ale over the table in his excitement.

'There is one last thing, Bjørn,' Erik smiled, interrupting them before the drink flowed too freely.

'Father?'

'Here,' Erik said, reaching under his high seat and tossing a final package to his son. 'I want you to have this, too.'

Bjørn dropped his horn in his haste to catch the parcel, spilling the rest of the contents across the table to splash into the fire with a hiss of steam.

'Your brothers all have helmets of their own. This one is yours,' he said with a smile.

Looking at the bundle in his hand, Bjørn untied the cordage and let the covering fall to the ground, revealing a polished iron and brass helmet, the same style as the one he had so recently borrowed from Sigurd.

'That mop on your head won't do much to keep your brains in place if you take a hard hit!' Erik chuckled, enjoying his son's evident happiness at the gifts. 'Hopefully this will help a little.'

'Thank you, Father,' Bjørn said, lifting the helmet to his head. It fitted perfectly.

'To my sons!' Erik boomed, lifting his drinking horn again and taking a deep swig. 'I am proud of you all! Olaf, Sigurd, Toke, Bjørn. I am proud of the men you have become. But now, heed my words. Olaf, Sigurd, Toke, you have sailed with me before, and you know the dangers that await us on foreign shores. Watch out for your brother and remember the excitement you first felt when you sailed with the fleet. And Bjørn, listen to your brothers, honour their experience, and protect them. When life is boiled down to the bones, family and fame are all that matter. One you earn, and will give you immortality. The other is a gift that can be taken away at any moment. Remember this, my sons, now and forever. But for now, raise your horns!' he boomed again. 'To the sons and sire of the hall of the Golden Hand! Let them hear our oars in the waves and see our standard fly! Let them know the Golden Hand has come!' Erik's voice boomed through his hall, his words met by the fierce cheers as his sons added their voices to his and raised their horns high in celebration.

Arleigh watched as the men celebrated, drinking horn after horn of ale and mead. She watched her son – Torr's son – cheer with them, raising drink-after-drink to his *father* and *brothers*, as they boasted of the feats they would perform come the summer. She shuddered to see what her son had become compared to the life she had once imagined for him. Yet she knew she couldn't tell him the truth. Erik was ruthlessly protective of his brood and bloodline. If he thought for a moment that Bjørn wasn't his, there was a chance he would cast them out without a moment's hesitation.

*'And why should I tell him? What did England ever do for me? We were little better than slaves there. Yes, I had Torr — my darling Torr — but that was it. No power, no wealth, no real security. Nothing. Here at least I have a shred of power, some respect. Yes, I'm a thrall — a bed thrall — kept pretty and proper for the jarl. But that promises real food in my belly, and a roof over my head. And Erik isn't a bad man; he just isn't Torr... But Torr is gone, and with him my old life. What should I care if England and everyone in it burns? Why should I tell Bjørn anything other than what he knows? Here, I am Norse, Bjørn is Norse. He is happy here, and safe — as safe as he can be — and already higher in society at sixteen than he ever would have risen if he'd been born Torr's son. At best he would have followed in his footsteps and become the village smith... And what's wrong with that? It's honest work, and good work... But here Bjørn is a jarl's son. He has power and prestige and opportunity beyond anything he would have had in Shorewitchshire. And he's safe. Torr died to keep him safe ...'*

Arleigh had had the same argument with herself a thousand times over the years in every conceivable variation, and as she watched Bjørn and his brothers through conflicted eyes, the same concerns ran through her head again. It was impossible not to let memories of her past and hopes for her future swim across her mind as she focused on the present before her.

*'Bjørn can be told if ever there is a need for him to know. At least he is already better equipped than many of the men who will sail with Erik. My son will be safe... as safe as he can be. At least I have that...'*

# Chapter 2

As the snow began to melt and life returned to the cold north, Erik's dragons emerged from their winter lairs.

Erik kept two older thirty-oared Snekkja's – *Fjord Elg* and *Jörmungandr* – tied at the wharf year round, ready to slip their moorings and protect his land at a moment's notice. But his prized raiding ships – *Fjord Ulf*, *Fjord Uxi*, and *Sleipnir* – were kept ashore through the winter months in specially built boat houses beyond the town walls. Standing off the ground on raised platforms, the three ships were painstakingly cared for until their time to sail came again. With the first hint of spring, the work shifted from maintenance to preparation as the promise of open seas and adventure spread through Vágar like a plague. Decks and hulls were scoured and re-tarred, sails were stitched, bilges cleaned, while rotten or worn planks were replaced, and the prow beasts repainted. Erik loved raiding almost more than anything else and was eager to leave as soon as possible and shed the jarl's cloak of responsibility and simply be one raider among many. Like his father, spring had always been Bjørn's favourite time of year. Long before the brothers had begun to grow their first beards, they would always be found in the boat sheds, either watching from the rafters or helping the men prepare the ships, learning everything they could for when their time came. Their days had been filled with dreams of their own adventures and the glory they would carve for themselves. Age had done nothing to temper their excitement, and they spent the days filling holes with horsehair-and-tar bungs, helping to sew sails, painting the prows, or plaiting rope. Jarl's sons or not, they worked just as hard as any man. Stripped to the waist, they worked until steam rose from their sweat-covered bodies, constantly competing amongst themselves to work the hardest and prove their worth. Come evening, it wasn't uncommon for one or more of them to fall asleep at their father's table during *nátmál* – the evening meal – completely spent. Bjørn was working even harder than usual, striving to strengthen his muscles through the labour.

'So, here you are at last, little brother,' Sigurd smiled, puffing a little as he pushed and pulled a coarse stone along the decks of *Fjord Ulf* to make the new planks smooth. 'Do you think you'll be able to keep up with us, carrying *such a heavy sword*? Or would it be best you leave the fighting to us and stand at the back with your bow?'

'I could ask you the same question. I still have the energy and vitality of youth, while even now you huff and puff like an old man from simply pushing a little stone along a deck! Are you sure you're fit enough for the trails to come?'

'It means he has rhythm, Bjørn,' Toke cut in before Sigurd could reply, pausing from his painting. 'Listen to his breathing, timed with the motion of the rock. You should try it. The sounds of your scraping and huffing down there makes you sound like an ox with a punctured lung!'

'This from the man who nurses a splinter!' Bjørn bit back, subtly adjusting his breathing to match Sigurd.

'A little more than a splinter – don't you think?' Toke replied, unconsciously looking at his bandaged hand. Blood had soaked through the white fabric again.

Toke had fallen from *Fjord Uxi* the week before and a piece of wood had gone straight through his left palm. He assured everyone he would be healed by the time they sailed, but Erik had confined him to light duties to be sure.

'Anyway, it's not like you three are anything to compare myself against,' Bjørn continued. 'I'm younger, faster, and blessed by Loki and Tyr both. I'll keep up just fine; I just worry that you'll all fall behind!'

He smiled to hear his brothers chuckling with him.

For all the mad energy in town, their own mood was calm as they worked, enjoying each other's company and the time together. Despite their differences in blood, the four brothers were close and had already shared many adventures together in the wilds around their home, from hunting deer and climbing the fjords to sailing the waves and camping on abandoned islands. The prospect of new adventures on distant shores was infecting them all, and the closer the time came to sail the more time they spent together. Preparing the ships, training their weapon craft, and meeting the men as they arrived in Vágar from their outlying farms to answer Erik's call was only increasing the excitement.

'We're going to need more, you know,' Bjørn said, taking a drink of water.

'More what?' Olaf asked, looking up from his own stone. 'I swear, brother, Óðinn himself couldn't decipher your thoughts, sometimes.'

'I hope you're talking about time with the bed thralls,' Sigurd butted in before anyone could speak, a mischievous grin across his face. 'I tell you now, weeks at sea with only men for company can do things to a man.'

'No! Well, actually, yes. But I was talking about meat. We should go

47

tomorrow. Who knows when we'll get the chance to hunt together again once we sail? If we take a few horses and ponies, we could bring back a few deer and maybe a fat boar – rare as they are. *Sleipnir* and *Fjord Uxi* could still do with more meat for the journey. Only *Fjord Ulf* is fully provisioned so far, and any extra would mean more food here for the men left behind to guard the town.'

'That's true,' Olaf said, furrowing his brow. 'There are more than enough men to finish work on the ships, now that the men have started coming in from the outer farms. We'll need to spin it for Father, though; otherwise, he'll think we're shirking work to go hunting. If we leave early enough tomorrow, we could get to the top of King's Leap by early afternoon.'

'Uffe said he and his men saw tracks up that way just last week,' Bjørn added. 'It would be as good a place as any to begin.'

Olaf turned conspiratorially to face Toke, his gaze matched by Bjørn and Sigurd. 'You're up, Toke,' he said.

'Gnn,' Toke grunted, eyeing his brothers slowly before returning his horse-hair brush to the paint pot. 'Fine, but I'll be sure to tell him it was your idea, Bjørn,' he grunted as he tied off his belt and left the byre.

'Better him than us,' Bjørn smiled. Since the accident, Erik had been much more lenient towards Toke. It wouldn't guarantee them anything, but Toke had the best chance out of any of them of succeeding, even over Olaf.

A happy silence settled over the remaining three brothers as they resumed their work on the planks, broken only by their breathing and the rhythmic sounds of their stones as they scraped along the wood. It didn't last long, however. No sooner had they each sunk into their individual thoughts and rhythms than the silence was broken by the coarse, crackling voice of Gørm.

'Bjørn! Where are you, boy?'

Standing from his work, Bjørn stretched his back before fixing his fjord-green eyes on his father's *goði*. The man had an uncanny ability to arrive unheard. Bjørn shivered involuntarily.

Dressed all in furs, stained black with dried blood and soot, Gørm carried a staff like a shepherd's crook, ghoulishly decorated with small animal bones that rattled as he walked. His long black hair was pulled back and braided, hanging down his spine with yet more bones and small animal skulls tied through it in place of the iron and silver rings more commonly seen. At his belt he carried a bone-handled knife that was more often than not red with the blood from his most recent *blót* sacrifice. The old man hadn't always been a priest; years before he had been a prominent chieftain in Iceland, a goði. But a rival had driven him from his lands in a feud. Only by finding passage on a trading ship was he able to escape, eventually finding his way to Erik's hall where he pledged his life in service of the gods.

'You haven't been to see me yet, boy. Your father claims you will be protected by the gods... bah! What would he know? Only I can tell you the truth of the gods' protection, and I tell you now: if you sail without hearing what I have to say, you will die without the gods declaring your fate. Without them, Rán's daughters will claim you five days out from Vágar, long before you ever see a foreign shore. That will be your whole saga, boy. A body entombed in the deep; eyes and tongue claimed by crabs and fish... this... this I... have seen! Come with me, boy! And hear what the gods have for you!'

Without waiting for a response, Gørm turned and left, presumably to return to the hide-covered shack he called a home.

'You better go, Bjørn,' Sigurd whispered, the days light-hearted mood shattered by the intrusion. 'We all went to see him before our first raids, to hear our fate. He's a creepy bastard, but like it or not, he can speak with the gods. He told me things I'd never told another living soul,' he said, shivering unconsciously.

'Aye,' Olaf said, nodding. 'Remember Green Alf, the old prow man from *Fjord Uxi*? He refused to see the goði when he was summoned, saying that Gørm's words were nothing more than stories to scare children. The day they sailed, Gørm warned Alf that he would die by his own hands twenty days into their journey, but still Alf ignored him.'

'I thought Alf died in a storm?'

'Nay, Green Alf cut his own throat while trimming his beard. A rogue wave came out of nowhere and hit *Uxi* amidships, causing his arm to jolt and sending the blade straight through his throat. Exactly twenty days out from Vágar. When I spoke to Gørm when we retuned, he told me that all he had to do to avoid a straw death was to always shave on dry land. Go and see him, Bjørn. Gørm is mad, but then so would anyone be who spends their days speaking with gods.'

'Gørm makes my skin crawl,' Bjørn grunted, handing the stone to Olaf. Looking at the figure walking along the shore, he huffed and leapt over the side of *Fjord Ulf*. 'I'll see you later,' he said, bending to pick up his sword and return it to his belt.

Making his way along the windswept shore, Bjørn followed Gørm's crouched silhouette back into the walls of Vágar, arriving at his home in time to watch him disappear into the hide-covered hovel. Preferring the company of gods to men, Gørm lived on the edge of the main settlement, having built his home in a corner of the wall where it lay in permanent shade year-round.

Bjørn had only ever been there once before, and he didn't remember the day. It was when he was born and Erik brought him before the goði to confirm his name. It wasn't the sort of place one went to share a horn of ale. As he drew closer, he noticed a horse's head skewered onto a pole in the ground by the door. Uncleaned, the head was slowly being devoured by ravens and the elements, surrounding itself with the sickly smell of putrefaction. '*If nothing else, Gørm loves blood,*' he thought to himself before taking a final deep breath of fresh air and entering the sultry darkness. A feeling of claustrophobia began to kick in immediately, and Bjørn stopped to take stock of his surroundings before moving deeper into the hovel, his breathing shallow. He could see a small fire burning in the centre of the structure, with an assortment of vials and gourds laid around it. Above the flames hung small vermin and birds. Of Gørm, there was no sign, but that wasn't a surprise given the inky blackness and the thick smoke.

'Welcome, Bjørn Eriksson,' came the gravelly voice from the shadows.

'Where are you?' Bjørn replied, focusing on the fire as he moved into the room.

'I'm here, Bjørn, so named for the Ironside. Take this, and drink,' Gørm grunted, holding out a roughly hewn wooden bowl which he thrust over the flames into his hands.

'What is it?'

'*What is it?*' Gørm mimicked, his voice cruel. 'Don't ask, boy. Do! The Gods aren't patient, and have vastly more important concerns than you. I can hold them here for a few moments, but not for long. Drink!' he barked impatiently.

Bjørn sighed and looked again at the bowl in his hands. He could just make out a reddish tinge to the brew, and a few suspicious clumps floating around giving texture to the liquid.

Steeling himself, he swallowed his indecision and lifted the bowl to his lips. He immediately tasted the iron-tinge of blood, followed by the kick of ale and an earthy flavour that reminded him of mushrooms.

'Now what, *goði?*' Bjørn gasped, wiping his mouth on the back of his hand. The drink was disgusting, there was no two ways about it.

'Now we wait. It won't be long now,' the voice crooned, softening.

Bjørn sat quietly and concentrated on his breathing, striving to fill his lungs in the space's cloying atmosphere. His body was already craving fresh air. Lifting his hand to scratch an unidentifiable itch on his thigh, he was surprised to see his arm leave a trail behind it. At first, he thought it was the dim light, but the same thing happened when he turned his head back towards the fire. The world was beginning to slow around him, and seemed to vibrate subtly, like a beaten drum in firelight. When he turned his head to ask Gørm what was happening, the rest of the room moved independently from his eyes, beginning to spin slowly around him. Shaking his head, he put his hand out to stabilise himself, but he felt nothing but emptiness. The last thing he saw before he hit the ground was Gørm's arms emerging from his cloak, feeding the fire with herbs from the pouch at his waist, causing more smoke to fill the small space. Through the blur, he watched the goði open a small cage by the fire and pull out a pure white raven. His head began to fill with murmurings in a language he didn't recognise, his head swimming as the goði drew the blót knife from his belt and slit the bird's throat. The raven died in silence, and he watched Gørm pluck three wing feathers from the twitching bird before placing it on the fire, adding the smell of burning flesh and feathers to the acrid smoke surrounding them. Then there was nothing.

Nothing.

Nothing.

Then a voice.

Though it came from Gørm's mouth, it belonged to another. Someone not of *Miðgarðr*, of Middle Earth. Gone was the gravelly croak and cackle of his father's goði, replaced by a deep and rich sound that could have come from Asgard itself. Pervading the creeping deep of the hovel, Bjørn could do nothing more than listen as it began to speak, the words resonating within his head, sinking into his consciousness.

*'So, you're to sail, to leave the lands of your youth and visit distant shores. To write a saga to endure the ages that will bring you fame and renown wherever you go. One that will immortalise the name Bjørn Eriksson amongst sword Norse and Christ worshipper alike.*

*This you will do, and more, Bjørn Eriksson. Tales of you will survive the ages and live for eternity. However, whether your saga is one of honour or infamy can only be decided by you, and you alone. That particular thread you must weave yourself.*

*As you embark on your adventure, and write the first true verses of your life, remember this: your word is iron, Bjørn Eriksson. Never break it, not with friend, never with foe. Never forget the importance of family, and the bonds that bind you. Blood is thicker than water; history is stronger than both. Finally, do not think to find weakness in the liquid that courses through your veins; your deeds will speak volumes where your blood only whispers.*

*Go now, Bjørn Eriksson. Seek your glory, write your saga, and remember the words we have shared with you. Beware the twists of fate woven in the Nornir weave, for somewhere amongst those threads lies one you will sew yourself.*

Nothing.

Nothing.

Bjørn was awoken by the gentle spray of rain hitting his face, the fresh air slowing his spinning senses after the smoke in Gørm's hovel. Sitting up slowly, his vision began to clear and he began to collect his bearings. He could see the town walls and their crown of guards as they walked their rounds, while beside him the waves gently pushed and pulled the pebbles lying on the shore.

He could still taste the iron tang of blood on his tongue from the thick brew he had drunk, the aftertaste coating the inside of his mouth no matter how many times he spat the cloying liquid onto the pebbles. Sighing, he climbed to his feet and began to strip his clothes, desperate to clear his body from the stench that clung to him. Tugging his tunic over his head, he felt the fabric catch on a piece of driftwood in his hair. *'Must have got caught while I was lying here,'* he thought, reaching up to untangle the flotsam. Finding the offending scrap, his fingers closed on the soft hair of raven feathers. Tied in his hair were three white feathers from the raven Gørm had sacrificed, each marked in black with the runes for Óðinn, Loki and Tyr.

*'Gørm must have taken them before I arrived,'* he mused, stroking the feathers. *'I saw the bird burn...'* he thought, shivering involuntarily.

Feeling foolish, he shook his head before quickly stripping off the rest of his clothes and diving beneath the fjord's frigid waters, cleaning the filth from his body, unaware of the feathers as they broke free and drifted away into the silent fjord. He luxuriated in the cold water, feeling it cleanse his body of the foul odours that had seemingly soaked into his skin before rolling onto his back and floating, gently rising and falling as the gentle waves moved under him.

*'Was it a prophecy? Or a warning?'* he mused, thinking about the words he had heard. *'Whatever it was, I am the master of my own fate,'* he decided, spitting a

fountain of water into the air before tucking tail and diving for the seafloor, failing as always, to come close to the bottom.

***

'I hope you know what you're doing, Erik. All four of our boys! Woe betide if you lose any of them!' Turid hissed.

'You heard, then?' Erik replied, looking calmly at his wife. Three strong sons she'd given him, and he loved her dearly. But she could be vicious as a *vaalkyrie* when she wanted to be. Tall and strong, with piercing, glacier blue eyes and golden-yellow hair with just a few grey strands breaking through, she was the most beautiful woman he had ever seen, and the most ruthless he'd ever met.

'Of course we heard! Erik Golden Hand and his brood, *Scourge of Britain*. Arleigh agrees with me: at least send them to different places, so some are likely to return!'

'And diminish my strength! Would you have your husband weaker, his men more vulnerable, for the sake of his sons? No! My ships will stay together, with me!' Erik growled, allowing some of his anger to show as his voice rang out like a struck bell in the empty hall. They'd been arguing the same point for over an hour, and his temper had finally broken free.

'And if something should happen?' Turid replied, unbending in the face of Erik's rage. 'What if the English destroy your force, a storm swamps your ships, disease hits your camp? What then? How will you protect them then? At least leave Toke behind; he's injured already, and a risk because of it.'

'He can stay, or he can come, that is his decision. But neither his father, nor his mother will force his hand in this! His fate is his own, and if the Nornir have decided to cut his thread in the coming raids, then so be it! But I will not stop him from coming, and nor will you!' he thundered with finality, the words echoing around the hall and crushing his wife's pleas.

'And Bjørn?' Arleigh asked from her seat, entering the conversation for the first time. Unlike Turid, Arleigh remained quiet and detached when she argued with Erik. She knew her place, and that her way of talking to him had always unnerved him.

'What of Bjørn?' he asked in exasperation. 'He's earned his seat and oar as much as the others. I won't deny him his right to join us for the sake of his mother's worry. He has the right to sail with the fleet.'

'He's only sixteen, Erik. Make him wait another year, just one more. You already have Sigurd and Olaf, and Toke if he is able. Bjørn is still so young...'

'No! They are men now, all of them, and they will make these choices of their own accord. I will not forbid them this, and nor will you!'

'And if they die, or if you die, what then?'

'Then they will sit at the Allfather's table and prepare for *Ragnarök*. My boys will sail with me if they so choose. If it will allay your fears, I will put them on different ships, with different crews,' he said after a while. 'I will take Sigurd and Olaf in *Fjord Ulf*. Toke will sail with Halfdan in *Fjord Uxi*, and Bjørn with Yngvar, in *Sleipnir*.

'I will tell both to protect and guard my sons. Olaf and Sigurd are older, and have the experience to protect themselves, but I will tell good men to watch them all the same. This is the only concession I will make. This conversation is over,' he said with finality as he turned and walked towards his high chair, calling for Hoelun to bring ale and meat as he went.

'Will they be safe, Turid?' Arleigh asked, watching Erik as he walked through the hall.

'He rages and shouts, and raises the roof, but he loves those boys fiercely, Arleigh. He will protect and watch them. Trust me. He will bring them back alive, if he knows what's good for him. He has women back home who will punish him for the loss of their sons, and he knows it.'

'I want to believe you, but you've seen your sons sail away and come back again. I've never watched it before, not my own blood.'

'Erik will keep them safe, Arleigh. And Bjørn is no fool. I saw the fight the other day, same as you. He's ready; we just have to hope that his weave will bring him back to us again. Now, I'm going to get a drink. Go and find what's taking Hoelun so long, will you?' Turid said, turning to follow her husband.

'I pray to Christ that you're right,' Arleigh murmured as Turid left. 'Erik or no, I pray that Christ watches over my son and forgives him his sins. Oh Lord, my son, born in sin, knows not what he does following these pagan gods. Keep him safe and bring him home to me again. Oh, Torr. What has become of my life, my love...' she whispered.

'Arleigh! Tell that useless woman to hurry up with the ale! And then come join us!' Erik's voice boomed from the end of the hall.

'Yes, Erik,' she called back, moving quickly towards the kitchen.

'Hoelun? Hoelun, hurry with that ale, girl! Erik is thirsty!' she shouted as she left the main hall for the steam and smoke of the kitchen.

'Yes, miss. Sorry, miss,' replied a flustered Hoelun, coming out of one of the store rooms, her hair dishevelled as she rearranged her clothes.

'What have you been doing back here? Erik called for ale an age ago!'

'Sorry, madam, I was… I was just looking for it, miss.'

'It's right here,' Arleigh replied, picking up a fresh pitcher. 'What were you doing? Hurry up, speak!'

'Nothing, miss, honestly.'

'Honestly… You take this ale out to Erik, then you come straight back, you hear?'

'Yes, miss,' she stammered, lifting the pitcher and running towards the hall.

Once she was gone, Arleigh moved quickly to the store room door and pulled it open.

'Mother!' Bjørn started, rushing to cover himself with his shirt.

'Aha! So, you're the *nothing*, are you? Bjørn!' Arleigh said, bemused, switching to her native tongue.

'What?' he mumbled, switching languages easily despite the sheepish look on his face, his cheeks matching the burning coals in the brazier behind him.

'Oh… nothing.' Arleigh smiled, her mind flashing back to her first furtive tryst with Torr in her father's hay shed. He'd had the same embarrassed expression on his face when her mother had walked in and caught them. 'I suggest you make your way to the table and talk to your father. I'll be there presently.'

'Fine,' he shrugged, pulling on his shirt and cloak. 'But perhaps knock next time, mother?' he said, standing up to buckle up his belt.

'Hmm' she muttered, raising an eyebrow as he made her way past her and made his way towards the hall. 'Oh, and Bjørn, perhaps make your way around by way of the back door. It'll give you some time to *cool off*.' She laughed. 'It wouldn't do for your father to think you'd prefer to stay here playing with thralls all summer.'

Stopping mid-stride, Bjørn stopped and turned around. 'True,' he said, a sheepish smile playing on his lips. It was the same one he'd worn eight years earlier when she'd caught him stealing honeyed mead from Erik's personal store with his brothers.

'*Clearly his tastes are changing,*' she thought to herself, watching as he moved for the door. '*All men are the same,*' she thought, rolling her eyes as she made her way back towards the hall.

# Chapter 3

'Wake up! The sun's already rising.'

Bjørn felt as if he was underwater, with Sigurd calling from a distant shore. He might as well have drowned after the amount of ale he drunk the night before.

The kick in the ribs was less gentle.

'Hunting. Your idea… Remember? Now get up! The sun is already high, and Olaf and Toke are ready with the horses!'

'I'm up, I'm up,' Bjørn groaned, pushing his brother's prodding foot away. 'Where's the waterskin?' he asked, rubbing his eyes to try and bring the sharpness back to his vision.

'Here,' he heard, followed by the thump of something hitting the wall by his head before tumbling down to land beside him, the sloshing liquid loud in his ears.

'Thanks,' he grunted sluggishly. He hadn't planned to drink so much.

'I'll be outside. We've got everything else organised, just bring your bow and whatever else you think you'll need. Bring your sword, as well. Toke said one of the rangers found tracks up there last week.'

'Probably just some hunter who got himself lost in the snow.'

'He didn't think so. There were too many prints for a hunting party. Father has extra men on the walls as a precaution. It should be fine, but there's no harm in being safe.'

'Very well. Give me a few minutes and I'll be ready. Shall I bring my shield as well?'

'We've all got ours, and our helmets.'

'Fine. I'll see you outside.'

'Hurry up,' called the receding voice.

Rubbing his eyes, he sat up and looked around the room, his head throbbing from the evening before. *'If I were boots, where would I be?'* Bjørn mused, taking a deep draught of water from the skin before pushing the hair back from his face and tying it with a strip of rawhide.

*'I'd be under the cot, wouldn't I? Gotcha!'* he smiled, sitting up to pull on the

rouge footwear and gasping as the movement set his head thumping. When he finally opened his eyes again, they drifted absently to the sword and shield that now hung proudly above his bed. *'Now to earn you properly,'* he grinned, pulling the long blade down and belting it around his waist before sliding his hand axe into the loop on his right hip.

Taking another deep draught of the water, he focused on trying to clear his head of the incessant throbbing behind his eyes, slowly bringing the rest of the world back into focus. Outside, the sounds of people going about their day came flooding through the open window cover. Somewhere a child was crying, the sound punctuated by the repetitive *ting, ting, ting* of the blacksmith as he beat stubborn metal into submission. He could feel his excitement growing as the winter loosened its grip on the world, giving way to shorter nights and longer days as people threw off the dark months with an almost festive fervour.

'Come on, Bjørn! Hurry up!' his brothers chorused, their voices breaking through his thoughts.

'I'm coming, I'm coming,' he grunted.

Rolling up a sheep-skin sleeping sack, he tucked it under his arm before shouldering his shield, the weight unfamiliar. Finally, he picked up his bow and quiver of arrows, and threw on a fur coat against the cold.

'Good morning, beautiful,' Sigurd called with a grin as his youngest brother emerged at last, gaining only a gnarled mumble for his efforts as Bjørn covered his eyes against the sun. 'I remember when I had my first beer,' he continued, enjoying the rapidly growing smiles spreading over Toke and Olaf's faces. 'I was younger than you, I think, perhaps fourteen. The next morning, I was up with the dawn and climbed to the top of the fjord, proud of my youth and strength. Clearly a difference between us. I've heard the English struggle to hold their ale,' he added, chuckling good naturedly.

Bjørn didn't respond, he just walked towards his brother and smiled up at his bearded face as he sat comfortably on his horse.

'Not even a word in response! Perhaps we should just leave him here with the women to sew and weave while we find some meat for the voyage? What do you say to that?' He chuckled, looking at Olaf and Toke.

Bjørn struck as soon as his brother turned away to face the others, whipping Muninn from the sheath at his back and drawing it across the belly strap of Sigurd's pony, severing the leather and causing his brother and everything he was carrying to lean heavily to the left before falling into the mud with a splash. Everything seemed to happen in slow motion before returning to a normal speed when Toke and Olaf's booming laughter broke the shocked silence, ringing out loud in the morning air. More than a few passing townsfolk stopped and laughed at the sight as Sigurd struggled, roaring to his feet with mud running off him.

'Careful, brother,' Olaf said through his laughs. 'A hand that moves that fast and slices so cleanly after a night in the ale should be kept calm. Don't you agree?'

Sigurd stopped his raging as Olaf's words broke through the roaring in his ears. The brothers fought with fists almost as much as they trained with their blades, but lately their scuffles had led to more painful bruises than any would care to admit. Swallowing his pride with a sigh, Sigurd showed his teeth through his muddied beard.

Bjørn, in the meantime, had calmly walked to his own pony and pulled himself up into the saddle, watching with a bemused smile on his face as Sigurd swallowed his anger and calmed himself.

'Ready, brother?' he said, a teasing tone to enter his voice.

'Give me a minute,' Sigurd grunted back, spitting mud as he picked up the ruined saddle and walked to the stables for another, calling to one of their father's thralls to take the ruined one away and repair it. It was a testament to Erik's wealth and status that he was able to have a stable of horses and ponies, with thralls to care for them. It was a wealth that more than one jarl jealously watched from their own halls, although none yet had shown themselves to be fool enough to challenge Erik.

'Couldn't you have just tipped him off?' Olaf asked, still laughing. 'You know how long it takes for Sigurd to saddle a horse!'

Behind him, Toke was struggling to control his laughter and was at risk of falling off his own horse as the tears ran down his face.

'This was easier,' Bjørn grunted, closing his eyes. 'Anyway, I thought he could do with a bath.' He listened to the amused chortling and conversation of his brothers as he dozed in the saddle, letting his mind wonder and dream of the future while they waited for Sigurd. When he finally returned, the four brothers formed a line and followed Olaf as they made their way through the streets of Vágar towards the walls and the hills beyond.

A few hours after leaving the streets of their home they were easing their mounts single file through the narrowest section of the trail, with a sheer drop falling away into nothingness on one side, and rising cliffs that touched the sky on the other. Holding their breath as they made their way along the precipice high above their home, they finally emerged into the clearing known as King's Leap.

A small stream babbled alongside the clearing before disappearing over the edge, where the water was carried away by the winds to form a veil of mist. At that height, parts of the stream that had yet to feel the sun's rays still showed shelves of ice that had been eaten away by the water flowing beneath them. Looking down on their home, Vágar looked like some sort of child's toy as people moved around the fortified town. It was easy to believe in the gods when you looked down on the world from such a height, and the insignificance of man was laid bare.

'A stupid name for a cliff,' Toke mumbled, breaking the silence as he spat over the edge. 'What sort of a king would leap from such a height?'

'One manipulated by the trickster god,' Olaf grunted without taking his eyes from the view. A few moments later he became aware of his brothers watching him with expectant eyes. 'If you want to hear the story, let's at least rest our arses and water the horses,' he said, climbing down from his saddle. 'Bjørn, Sigurd, go find some firewood while we get some kindling going and start a fire.'

Once they had the blaze lit, and a small stock of wood ready for the flames, Olaf began his story, taking a deep draught from his aleskin before beginning.

'Years ago, in an age long past, an ancient king ruled these lands, whose deepest desire was to have a name that would echo through eternity, and to be remembered as the greatest king the north had ever known. He often travelled up to this cliff, looking down on the world and whispering his desires to the wind, hoping for a sign or a spark that would point him in the right direction. It was through the wind that Loki heard the king's desires, his prayers inspiring a moment of entertainment for the trickster god that would break the tedium of his timeless existence.

His plans laid, Loki surprised the king one day as he prayed to the wind, startling him as he appeared from the woods disguised as an aged wanderer, his face hidden by a hooded cowl, leaning heavily on a knobbed staff.

"I can give you what you seek," he croaked, his hidden face broken by a cunning smile.

"Who are you to make offers to a king, thrall?" the king asked imperiously, his eyes narrowing as his hand grasped the leather-bound hilt of his sword.

"Do you not know me, Great King? Nor the stories of the Æsir wandering the world in disguise? I can give you what you seek," the hooded man repeated. "Or I can leave you to your *prayers, oh Great King,*' he grumbled before turning and making to walk back into the forest.

The king watched in confusion as the mysterious figure turned and moved slowly, returning the way he had come as he headed for the forest path that would quickly see him lost to sight. "Wait," he called at last, his decision made, fearing suddenly that the Allfather, Óðinn, had heard his prayers, for it was often said that the wise one often walked the world of men cloaked and bent, wearing a crooked hat and carrying a knotted staff.

"Yes?" Loki said, hiding the smile of delight that crossed his face as he turned.

"Tell me, then. How can you give me what I seek? How can my name, my saga, be remembered for all time?"

"Jump," Loki answered simply, shuffling back to where the king stood at the edge of the cliff. "Jump, Great King, for you shall not fall, but fly, and behind you shall be a legacy that survives the ages."

"Jump?" he asked sceptically, watching the old man in surprise before turning his attention back to the cliff, and the fall beyond. "That is a death sentence."

"Not for you. For you, it is the key to immortality, and a name that will last forever."

"How do I even know you to be one of the Æsir or Vanir, to be a lord of Asgard?"

"You doubt me?" Loki replied, his voice growing cruel. "But then why shouldn't you, a great king being met by a beggar on a hill, a man who by rights of his age should never be able to make such a climb. But still, I see the doubt in your eyes? Well then, Great King, observe," he said, clicking his fingers and holding the knotted staff high. Instantly, its head burst into flames that glowed bright in the early morning light, the colours changing through the different hues of a rainbow before disappearing, wood once more.

The king's face stood frozen from the spectacle; his eyes transfixed on the ancient figure before him.

"What say you, Great King? Will you jump, and find your immortality? Or will you die, unknown and forgotten by the passage of time?" Loki gnarled.

His grating voice snapped the king from his stupor, shaking the life back into him before, without a word, he turned and ran towards the edge, spreading his arms wide as he leapt into the abyss, his eyes filled with images of fame and immortality.

Laughing, the duplicitous Loki transformed himself into a seagull and followed the king down to the bottom, asking him what he thought of his ability to fly. Before the hapless king could think of an answer, the gull-formed-Loki shrieked once and flew away, his cawing laughter filling the sky as he watched the doomed sovereign plunge to his death.

His name has long since been forgo'ten,' Olaf said, finishing his story, 'but he was immortalised through the story of King's Leap, just as Loki promised.'

For a while, they sat in silence as they mused over the story, each lost in their own thoughts as they gazed into the fire.

'Well he got what he wanted,' Toke said quietly, breaking the silence as he poked the fire with a stick and sent a shower of sparks into the sky. 'He was a fool to trust a god without knowing who he faced,' Bjørn muttered, eyeing the cliff once more.

'He thought he spoke with the Allfather,' Olaf said quietly, turning to his brother.

'Gnn,' Bjørn grunted. 'Still, I wouldn't be so quick to believe, nor think that fame is something to be so easily given or earned.'

It was Olaf's turn to grunt as he considered his brother's words, seeing the truth in them.

'Some people are consumed by their greed,' Sigurd said, his eyes lost in the flames. 'I can understand his desire to believe, although I agree with you. He was a fool to trust so readily.'

'This place gives me the creeps,' Toke muttered.

'Why? Because Loki was here? Or because you're another king about to fly to the bottom?' Bjørn joked, turning to face his older brother.

'I just don't like it.'

'Do you think it's true?' Sigurd asked suddenly, spitting into the fire.

'Who knows? But I like the idea that the trickster was here.'

'Perhaps,' Olaf said. 'And perhaps not. We'll never know, but no matter what, it is beautiful here. You can see forever.'

'Agreed,' Bjørn and Sigurd said together, looking once more at the view beyond the cliff.

The silence stretched amongst them, each lost in his own thoughts.

After a while, Olaf stood with a sigh and began to kick dirt onto the dying flames. 'Let's get moving. It will be dark before we know it and the cabin is still a fair distance from here.'

Moving quickly, the brothers checked their kit before mounting and riding into the forest, guiding their mounts onto the path that wove gently between the trees.

As they left, a larger-than-normal seagull swooped down unseen and stared at the retreating figures before cawing once and plunging down the cliff face towards the waiting ocean, its screeching cry breaking the still silence of the fjords.

Before long, the brothers were surrounded by dense forest, the trees packed together so tightly that little sunlight could penetrate the thick canopy.

'The cabin is a few rôst from here. We can set up camp there and organise ourselves for tomorrow,' Olaf said, as he led them along the narrow trail. 'Bjørn, you're best with a bow. Once we're a little further into the forest, why don't you cut through the woods and see if you can catch something for dinner. I saw a few rabbit tracks in the snow behind us,' he added.

'Would we say best?' Toke butted in. 'Or luckiest…?'

'Regardless of what you'd say, I'd prefer to eat something other than dried meat and bread tonight if we can. Bjørn goes,' Olaf said.

'Yes, Toke, *you* see to the horses,' Bjørn purred, smiling at his brother. 'I'll sort dinner. Wouldn't want you getting lost in the woods now, would we?'

'That was one time,' Toke groaned before lapsing into silence.

Chuckling, the others let the matter drop as they focused on the path under their horses hooves.

The deeper they moved into the forest, the less sound carried until they couldn't hear anything of the gulls and wind they'd left behind at King's Leap. Occasionally they would hear birds singing in the trees, and once Sigurd called out when he spotted a deer disappearing into the undergrowth, stirring up leaf litter and snow as it fled. After an hour or so of riding, they began to hear running water coming from between the trees.

'Here's a good spot,' Olaf whispered, pulling on his horse's reins so he was facing his brothers. 'Leave your horse with us, Bjørn, and go ahead on foot. One of the rangers mentioned that deer and wild goats come into the clearing by the cabin to feed and drink from the creek. They'd make a far better eating than a few rabbits.'

'A good opportunity to show us if you really are the best with that bow of yours, eh Bjørn?' Toke grinned.

'You could go yourself, Toke,' Bjørn replied, climbing down from the saddle and pulling his bow from the quiver and stringing it. 'Or you could come with me,' he continued as he lifted his quiver down and fastened it around his waist.

'I wouldn't want to be there when you miss, little brother.'

'Bjørn, keep the sun on your left until you hit the water,' Olaf said, ignoring them as he pointed off the path. 'When you reach the creek, follow it to the right. The trees will begin to thin out before you reach the clearing. Good luck,' he said, throwing him a small pouch of dried meat. 'For the walk,' he added.

'Right, I'll see you at sundown.' He nodded, tying his sword to the saddle horn, and slotting his axe through his belt, next to Muninn.

'Be careful, Bjørn,' Sigurd said as he made to follow Olaf and Toke. 'Remember what Uffe said about finding tracks up here. It's probably nothing but keep your wits about you.'

'See you this evening,' he nodded, before disappearing into the woods.

'He is the best, Toke. You do know that, don't you?' Olaf said, turning to his brother.

'Of course.' Toke chuckled. 'But it wouldn't do for it to go to his head so soon after beating Father now, would it?'

Before anyone could reply, an arrow flew from the woods and pierced Toke's grey woollen cap, carrying it off his head before coming to a quivering stop in the elm tree next to him.

'It might be a little late for that,' Sigurd chortled, struggling to control his laughter as he pointed at the stilling arrow.

'You're as bad as Bjørn,' Toke grunted as he liberated his hat and the arrow from the tree with a heave, inspecting the unwanted alterations.

'I heard that,' came a voice from the woods.

'I rather liked this hat,' Toke grumbled, ignoring Bjørn as he poked his index finger through the newly punched holes.

'You still have it. It's just been... *decorated*,' Sigurd said, masking his smile with concern. 'Here.' He chuckled, slicing off a small pine bough from an overhanging branch and leaning over to slot it through one of the holes. 'Good as new.'

Toke just grunted in response; his attention fixed on his damaged headpiece.

Bjørn smiled to himself as he drew another arrow from his quiver. It was a
risky shot to take, and a cruel prank, but he knew that the story would spread
through the town when they returned. It wasn't much, but it could be the
beginning of his own saga. Or it could bring down Erik's fury. Either way a
story would spread. Plus, Toke was always good prey. They were closest in age,
and they shared a special bond, having stood together on the shore year after
year as their father and brothers sailed away.

Moving slowly, he began to make his way through the undergrowth in the
direction Olaf had indicated, keeping the sun on his left as he went. As he
walked, he drew his knife and sliced off a generous helping of the dried meat,
munching contentedly as he made his way through the undergrowth. It wasn't
long before the trees began to thin out a little and he came onto the creek. He
could see signs of life everywhere along the bank, with deer, goat, and rabbit
tracks staining the mud every few steps. He could see tiny fish darting to-and-
fro with quick, erratic movements just below the surface.

Turning to his right, Bjørn moved back into the woods a little way and
kept walking along the bank. As he moved, he began to sink into himself,
focusing fully on his surroundings as he locked his finger over the shaft to
keep it from banging against the bow stave. The forest was full of signs that it
was coming back to life after the cold, dark winter. Like at King's Leap, the ice
left on the edges of the creek was beginning to recede as the weather warmed,
and small saplings were beginning to bloom with their first new leaves.

'*I could never live anywhere else,*' he mused, luxuriating in the fresh air as it
filled his lungs.

After covering a little over a rôst, he became aware that something was
missing, out of place. He couldn't put his finger on it, but something was
causing the hairs on the back of his neck stand up. Opening his mouth slightly
to sharpen his hearing, Bjørn stood still in a small clearing and listened to his
surroundings. He stood there for five minutes, listening. Then five minutes
more.

Still nothing.

'*Must be in my head,*' he thought, beginning to move again. Keeping his arrow
on the string, he followed the bank, but at a much slower pace than before.

The further he went, the more unnerved he became, but he still couldn't figure out what it was that was worrying him.

'Birds!' he thought suddenly. 'There are no bird sounds. There should be birds everywhere this time of day... And I can smell smoke.' His brain went into overdrive. 'What did Sigurd say? The rangers found tracks up here. Shit. The others won't pick it up, and if they do, they'll just think the smoke is me, and there's no way they'll notice anything out of place until it's too late. How far have I come? One röst? Two?' He ran, following the water as quietly as he could towards the smoke. 'Whoever it is, they won't be expecting anyone to come from the creek.'

He could feel the blood beginning to course through his veins as his body tensed in preparation, unsure of what he was running towards. After ten minutes of running, the smell of smoke grew stronger, and he could hear the sound of someone cutting wood. 'They wouldn't be doing that if the others were there already; I'm getting close.' Slowing his pace, Bjørn stretched his bow string a few times as he walked to loosen his shoulders. The creek was flowing faster here, babbling over rocks and fallen branches. A hundred paces ahead he could see the trees beginning to thin out onto the clearing. 'At least they won't hear me coming,' he thought as he followed the water's shimmering silver path.

'I bet you Bjørn comes back empty-handed' Toke said, examining his damaged headwear once again. 'Anything you want, name your price.'

They were moving slowly along the beaten path, the ancient pines bending above them as the wind flew through their needles, singing the final songs of winter.

'I wouldn't be so sure,' Olaf responded. 'He's surprised us before in the past. I wouldn't take him lightly. Chances are he'll come back with a bear.'

Toke chortled, the sound coming loud in the close stillness of the surrounding trees.

'I'll take your bet,' Sigurd chimed in from the back of their small convoy.

'Oh, aye?' Toke asked, turning.

'Aye. I'll bet you your axe that Bjørn comes back with something dead; and more than that, I bet you he beats us to the cabin.'

Toke fell silent for a moment at that, mulling over the wager. It wasn't a small challenge. His hand axe was beautiful, inlaid with gold and long coveted by Sigurd, and many of the warriors in Vágar. He'd taken it as a prize on his first and only season raiding, capturing it from a young Frankish lord. It was the crowning story in his fledgling saga, and he carried the axe with pride.

'And if I win?' he said at length, his eyes boring into Sigurd, silently willing him to change the bet.

'Name it.'

'Your brynja,' Toke said suddenly, his eyes lighting up at the idea. Now it was Sigurd's turn to be silent. Only he and Olaf owned the coveted iron ring shirts amongst Erik's sons, both taken as prizes in past raids. For Toke and Bjørn, they would have to find theirs the same way, and so far, Toke had been unlucky in his quest.

'You'd bet your prized possessions on Bjørn's ability to kill a rabbit?' Olaf asked incredulously, turning around in his saddle to face his brothers.

'I would,' Sigurd said finally, holding out his hand to bait his brother.

Olaf shook his head in exasperation as Toke clapped his hand into Sigurd's, sealing the deal.

'Children,' huffed Olaf, kicking in his heels.

'May the best man win.' Sigurd chuckled, punching his brother on the shoulder.

'Aye,' Toke grunted, already reconsidering the wager.

Coming up from the creek, Bjørn knelt among the moss-covered rocks and long grass by the bank and scouted the clearing, noting the footprints in the mud next to him as he settled himself. Leaning against the cabin walls were spears and shields, all within easy reach of the men who were spread around the cabin. One, a giant of a man, was chopping wood with a large axe while two others lay by the fire eating and drinking. A fourth was sleeping on the grass.

'Five shields... there must be another one somewhere...' Bjørn mused as his eyes continued wandering across the scene. The men weren't from Vágar, he knew that much. Not one among them was familiar, and he doubted he would find men from their nearest neighbour – Váli – this close to Vágar without them announcing themselves. His men would hunt closer to his own lands. Even if they were, he thought he would recognise Váli's men, having visited his home several times.

Sliding back up to take another look, he winced as his knee rolled over a dead branch, breaking it. The result was instant, and he watched with dismay as the men in the clearing reacted to the sound with the confidence of seasoned warriors. As one, the men resting by the fire rushed for their shields and spears while the giant axeman began to immediately advance on Bjørn's position, the giant weapon looking all too comfortable in his enormous fists. Behind him, the remaining men had formed a small skjaldborg. While the axeman advanced, the rest remained still, searching the woods for danger over their shield rims.

'*They have no idea what's out there,*' he realised.

Unbidden, Yngvar's words came to him, his deep voice resonating in his head. '*A good warrior will act fast and move on, but a great warrior will think and remember; he will learn and grow constantly working to better himself.*' 'Act fast and move on, think, and remember. Go.'

Climbing to his feet, Bjørn drew the bowstring to his cheek in one smooth motion, aiming and releasing in a single breath to take the advancing axeman through the throat. He ignored the choking gurgles as the giant warrior fell to the ground, his fingers clawing at the shaft through his neck, more aware than ever that every moment counted. As calmly as he could he drew and aimed his second arrow, focusing on the advancing wall of shields. None of them had helmets on their heads which helped. Exhaling slowly, he waited for the moment when his lungs were completely empty and he felt the need to inhale again. At the moment of stillness, he released, sending the arrow spinning across the rapidly diminishing space between him and the advancing warriors. He watched in sick fascination as the shaft drove straight through the right-most warriors eye before exploding out the back of his head. He was dead before he hit the ground, the feathers coming to rest in the destroyed eye socket like some kind of grotesque mask.

The remaining two spearmen were closing fast, and Bjørn could read the fury in their eyes after seeing their companions cut down so easily. In quick succession he loosed two more arrows, aiming for heads and legs, but they had learned their lessons and made themselves as small as they could as they advanced. Gritting his teeth in frustration, he realised that his position in the woods with his back to the creek would give them an unfair advantage with the greater reach of their spears. Loosing a final arrow, he dropped his bow and drew the axe from his belt, taking comfort from the familiar feel of the wood in his hand as he freed Muninn from its sheath. By luck more than design, his final arrow had pierced one of the men's shoulders, forcing him to drop his shield and advance with his spear held awkwardly in one hand. He took comfort from the man's groans as blood flowered from the wound. Grunting, the warrior stopped briefly behind the cover of his friend's shield to snap the shaft, releasing a fresh groan of pain.

Exhaling slowly to calm himself, he stepped forward into the clearing and moved to his left, giving himself space for the fight to come.

\*\*\*

'Did you hear that?' Olaf said, snapping around to face his brothers.

'It came from where the cabin should be…?' Toke whispered back; his eyebrows knotted.

'Do you think it's Bjørn?' asked Sigurd, shrugging his shield from his back.

'It could be. Or it could be whoever left the tracks Uffe's men found,' Olaf said, surveying the forest ahead as he placed his helmet on his head. 'Toke, follow us with the mounts. Sigurd, you're with me.'

'Olaf, I can fi…' Toke began, eyeing his brother.

'I know you can, brother, but your hand is injured and we need someone to watch the horses. Meet us at the clearing as soon as you can. Sigurd, let's go! Heeyaa!' he shouted, kicking his heels in.

'Don't be too far behind us, brother,' Sigurd said seriously before whipping his own reins.

Toke watched sullenly as his brothers disappeared into the forest ahead. With a sigh, he drew his own shield from his back and held it firm in his left hand, ignoring the pain as he gripped the handle. 'Chuh,' he clicked, kicking his heels in to set his own horse after his brothers, Bjørn's mount and the packhorses following obediently behind.

'How much farther is it, Olaf?' Sigurd asked, his eyes constantly moving to the left and right as he searched for threats.

'Not far now, slow up. We don't want to ride into a trap. When we round the next bend, we should leave the horses and go on foot. Toke can pick them up on his way in. It's only a few hundred paces from there.'

'Where is your shield?'

'Shit! It's on Bjørn's horse. The strap was rubbing my shoulder.'

'Stay behind me. At least you have your helmet…'

'Gnnn,' Olaf grunted, pulling back on the reins as they rounded a bend in the road. Ahead, the two brothers could see the light breaking through a gap in the trees, revealing the clearing ahead.

Jumping from the saddle, the brothers drew their swords, leaving the scabbards tied to the saddles. No one wanted to risk a straw death because their sheath got tangled between their legs.

'Put this on,' Sigurd whispered, passing his brother a thick bearskin cloak. 'It won't be much protection, but it's better than nothing.'

Olaf nodded and wrapped himself in the heavy fur, his face fierce under his helmet.

Moving towards the light, Sigurd held his shield high, resting his sword on the rim as he felt Olaf place his left hand on his right shoulder to follow him. The two had fought side-by-side many times before and no instructions were necessary. They knew what was needed as they crossed the final few paces towards the clearing, and Bjørn.

Bjørn didn't give the men a chance to recover from his barrage of arrows, or the injury he had inflicted on one of them. Moving onto the offensive, he took two sharp steps forward and brought his axe down in a sudden chopping motion, forcing his uninjured opponent to raise his shield to protect himself. As the shield came up and obstructed his vision, Bjørn was moving again, rolling under the clumsy spear thrust to bring himself into range of the injured man as he fumbled awkwardly with his own weapon. Bjørn instinctively brought his knife up under the man's ribs, burying it to the hilt before ripping it free with a vicious tug, sawing it across his belly as he did so. As the blade came free, his victim released an ear-splitting scream before falling to the ground where he writhed in agony, his spear forgotten as he struggled to hold his innards in place.

Bjørn was already moving, dancing out of range as the first man's spear skewered the air he had occupied seconds earlier before coming to rest a few steps away, waiting for the next attack.

Rolf watched uneasily as the man before him stood quietly and calmly with all the self-assurance of youth. It was a shock when he realised that his own confidence had been knocked by the sudden violence, despite the countless times he had found himself in the sword storm. In just a few minutes he had gone from eating and joking with his companions by the fire to watching two die and a third roll screaming on the ground as he struggled to hold his body together. He noticed absently that Dag's breathing was becoming more strained. Regardless of the outcome, his time in Miðgarðr was over.

The silence stretched as the pair watched one another, each waiting for the other to move. As he waited, Rolf had to remind himself that the boy before him was flesh and blood and would die like any other man. '*Hopefully*

*Siv and Carr will have the sense to stay away if they're watching...*' he thought absently.

'Fuck it,' he muttered quietly, drawing back his arm to lunge forward with his spear, aiming for the boy's unprotected chest. An axe and knife could do little against six *alnir* of wood and iron.

'*Fuck it.*' The two words penetrated Bjørn's unconscious mind even as his body waited for the spear to thrust forward, warning him of the attack. He watched as if from above his body as the man pulled his arm back slightly in preparation, waiting until the last second to throw his body out of the way. While his body was fighting the man before him, his mind was focused on Erik, and their duel just days before. Absently, he noted the soft earth beneath his feet, and without conscious thought he swayed to the right as the spear came for him, hooking his axe over the shaft before dragging it down into the earth, just as he had done with his father. He was moving before the spearman could react.

Rolf watched in horror as his spear buried itself in the earth, sticking fast and exposing his unprotected flank. Everything else happened in slow motion as he watched the boy dance around behind him, ready to strike. He felt more than saw the length of iron that slipped between his unprotected ribs to puncture his lungs. Some part of him was screaming, telling him to draw his own axe and fight, to put the youth down and send him to the corpse hall. But even as he formed the thought, he felt a dull impact on the side of his neck forcing his body to tip over before he was surrounded by nothingness. Just infinite blackness and the faint beating distant wings overhead.

\*\*\*

Sigurd and Olaf burst into the clearing with a roar, the two moving quickly towards the cabin to protect their unshielded flank against an attack. It was with a mixture of disappointment and relief that they watched Bjørn bury his axe in the neck of his adversary.

'Bjørn! Clear?' Olaf called, looking around for more potential threats.

'No,' Bjørn called back, sheathing his knife before picking up one of the discarded shields. 'Olaf, shield,' he called, pointing his blooded axe towards the pile by the cabin.

'Form up with Sigurd!' Olaf called as he crossed the ground towards the cabin.

Bjørn crossed the ground quickly to join Sigurd by the cabin while Olaf ducked inside to clear it. It wasn't large and he came out seconds later shaking his head.

'Empty,' he said as he took up a shield of his own and stood with his back against the cabin, alongside his brothers.

'How many more are there?' Sigurd asked, his eyes searching for new threats.

'I counted five shields, including these two,' Bjørn replied, gently banging his axe shaft against the steel rim.

'And four dead,' replied Olaf, counting the bodies.

'Where's Toke?' Bjørn whispered, looking towards the trail.

'Following behind with the horses. Do you think we should go to him?'

'It could be a good way to draw out the fifth if he thinks we've left the area,' Sigurd muttered under his breath. 'And we can't stay here all day...'

'Agreed. We move on three,' Olaf whispered.

Beside him, Bjørn wiped blood from his eyes where it had sprayed, painting a grim war mask over his face.

'One,' whispered Olaf.

'Two,' followed Sigurd.

'Three,' grunted Bjørn, pushing off from the wall.

'Krab,' Olaf grunted, swinging his back against his two brothers.

The four brothers had come up with the crab manoeuvre when playing with practice swords and spears against the other boys in town. Whenever they'd found themselves outnumbered, they'd go back-to-back and create a circular skjaldborg like a crab's shell, with swords and spears slashing and stabbing like pincers. They could protect one another's backs and flanks while still doing wicked damage against a larger foe.

'Now, move,' Olaf ordered, stepping forward. He began to beat a rhythm on his shield, marking the pace for them so that the crab never fell apart, moving inexorably forwards towards the forest path, and Toke.

\*\*\*

'Stupid hand,' Toke muttered, spitting in frustration. Alone, he could admit to the pain. Every step his horse took sent a flame of agony up his arm as the rough leather grip of his shield rubbed the linen bandage. Already he could feel blood soaking the wrapping. He was surrounded by trees on all sides, noting the ash and elm amongst the denser stands of fir and spruce. He was alone but for the horses, with nothing but the wind for company, and the gentle *clop, clop, clop* of their hooves as they struck the earth beneath.

He held the reins lightly in his injured left hand with his shield, while he unconsciously flexed the fingers of his right as they gripped his axe shaft.

'Come on,' he said, clicking his tongue to urge the horses into a gentle trot. 'Let's see what all the fuss is about.'

As he leaned forward to pat his pony's neck, an arrow shot past his head, missing the back of his neck by a hair's breadth. It passed so close that he felt the passage of the feathers fletching before it buried itself in the tree next to him.

'Bjørn?' he called, facing back towards the forest where the arrow had come from. 'Bjørn, this isn't funny...'

All around him the woods stood silent, seeming to steal the oxygen from the world. Even the horses had fallen still, sensing something was wrong. Beneath him, his own mount nickered, shifting uncomfortably. Without taking his eyes from the woods, he gently patted the animal's neck, calming it.

He was about to shout again when he caught sight of movement in the woods. He just had time to see the archer as he drew his bow back to full draw before he threw himself from the saddle with a roar, covering himself with his horse's body. He moved just in time, feeling his head shoot back as the arrow pinged harmlessly off the crown of his helmet before disappearing into the surrounding woods.

'Show yourself, nithing,' he snarled as he lifted his shield, gasping as he tightened his grip. 'Fucking splinter,' he cursed as another wave of pain shot up his arm.

'Who's there?' came a voice from the woods.

'Hel!' Toke snarled. 'Show yourself and perhaps I'll kill you quickly. But I warn you, I am not a patient man. I'm going to count ten breaths,' he continued angrily, 'and if I don't see a bow thrown onto the path by then, you'll see Óðinn's mead hall before the day is out.'

'I don't think you're in a position to negotiate, friend. I hold the bow while you cower behind a horse. If anything, you should be the one dropping your weapons.'

As the man spoke, Toke slowly counted in his head, slowly edging closer to the woods. 'One... two... three...'

'...Drop them, lad. No one needs to die here today.' The voice came as another arrow flew from the woods, burying itself in the dirt at Toke's feet.

'... *Six... seven... nine...*'

'Make the right choice.' Another arrow came whirring out of the forest to bury itself in the ground. Toke didn't flinch.

'... *Ten.*'

Like a bull, Toke threw himself around the side of his horse and charged, having placed roughly where the archer would be. '*Óðinnnn,*' he bellowed, his shield held high to cover his body as he rushed into the undergrowth.

Another arrow struck, the heavy iron head piercing through the wood to expose itself inches from Toke's eye, quickly followed by another a few inches lower. He ignored them, charging on until he caught sight of the man a few paces in front of him, hastily drawing another shaft.

He heard the man groan as he fumbled the arrow, dropping it amongst the needles at his feet.

Toke almost laughed as the man dropped his bow and turned to flee, his courage disappearing in the face of Toke's fury.

'Hold!' he yelled, his deep voice following the retreating figure, but shout as he might, the archer kept running. Quickly slipping his wrist from the loop around the axe handle, Toke turned the blade towards himself, took aim, and threw with all his might. He watched as his prized axe disappeared into the gloom, following the retreating figure before striking true in the back of the man's neck with a satisfying thump. 'Haa!' he yelled in triumph as the archer tripped and fell, rolling through the dirt before coming to rest, still. Drawing his seax, Toke dog-trotted towards the body to retrieve his axe, his eyes constantly roving the darkening gloom in search of more enemies.

'Disabled my arse,' he grunted as he stood above the prone figure, grinning to himself.

# Chapter 4

'I think you'd better stay home this year, Toke,' Bjørn joked, rubbing his hands over his face and releasing a shower of dried blood. He watched as they fell to the ground in a grisly stream of bloody red flakes.

'He won't have an axe to carry, anyway,' Sigurd added with a smile. 'Bjørn had three dead by the time we reached the camp, well above the quota we set. Wouldn't you say, Olaf?'

'Gnnn,' Olaf replied, ignoring them as he watched the woods for new threats.

'The hell I won't!' Toke growled. 'Animals, Sigurd. Dead animals! This is why we call you the slow one.'

Beside him, Sigurd's smile grew even larger in the face of Toke's frustration.

'Why would he lose the axe?' Bjørn asked, confused.

'Some idiotic bet about you killing something before we got here,' Olaf said distractedly.

'Sigurd, even if he keeps it, it's not like he can use it right anyway...' Bjørn said with mock seriousness, his voice trailing away as he bent over in laughter.

They had come across Toke as he emerged from the forest with his unconscious quarry thrown over his shoulder. The jokes had started almost as soon as he finished telling his story.

'Enough!' Olaf shouted suddenly, his voice bringing his younger brothers back to reality. 'We've got bigger problems than Toke's axe-throwing abilities. Sigurd, get that body up onto ahorse, and tie his hands together. Make sure he can't escape if he wakes up. Bjørn, you and Toke ride ahead and check the camp and make sure there aren't any more of them waiting for us. Get their weapons and equipment in the cabin and keep your wits about you.'

'And grab your helmet, Bjørn,' Sigurd added, bending down to tie the prisoner's hands together.

All around them the forest was silent, broken only occasionally by a branch falling from a tree, or birds chirping in the green darkness.

'And Toke...?' Olaf added, watching as his brother drew the axe from his belt.

'Hmnnn,' he mumbled, turning.

'Sharp end first…' Olaf said innocently, setting Sigurd and Bjørn laughing again.

'*Fifls*,' Toke muttered, kicking his heels in. 'I'm surrounded by fools.'

Grinning, Bjørn spurred his horse after his brother's, leaving Sigurd and Olaf alone with the prisoner.

'Come on, Sigurd, get him up,' Olaf said once they'd gone, pulling his attention back to his younger brother, and the captive he'd managed to drop. He watched as Sigurd brought himself back under control before bending to take up the limp body, grunting under the weight.

'You could get down off your high horse and help, you know.' He sighed, heaving the archer onto his shoulders.

'I have much more important things to worry about,' Olaf said innocently, picking his teeth as he eyed the surrounding forest.

Nothing had changed. The birds had fallen silent again after the sudden bout of laughter, or from Sigurd's heaving and gasping as he hefted the unconscious body into place. Olaf spat idly onto the ground beneath his horse's hooves, patting its neck as he did so. He was rewarded with a contented nickering in response.

'Done.' Sigurd sighed behind him, climbing into his own saddle, the pack horse's reins loose in his hand.

'Good, let's go.'

A quiet grunt was all the response he got as he threw his eyes over the silent trees one more time before clicking to get his horse moving.

Neither one could shake the feeling of unseen eyes watching their progress through the brush as they followed the path behind their brothers.

\*\*\*

Bjørn and Toke remained silent as they rode, constantly listening for the tell-tale signs of an ambush; the gentle swish of cloth on cloth, birds suddenly taking flight, or the exhalation of breath that pre-empted an arrow. It was only when they came within sight of the clearing – and the cabin – that Bjørn broke the silence, confirming that nothing had changed. The bodies were still lying where they'd fallen while the fire, left unattended, had burned through the wood to leave only charred logs and embers growing in the rough firepit. Toke grunted in response; his more experienced eyes not willing to relax until they'd broken the treeline proper.

'It all looks clear. I'm going to find my bow,' Bjørn whispered, sliding down from his saddle. 'Can you take the horse?'

'Be quick, Bjørn. We don't know if there were more of them out hunting.'

'I will.'

Nodding slightly, Toke took the reins from his brother as he disappeared into the undergrowth, moving towards the sound of running water.

Behind him, Bjørn could hear the gentle steps of the horses as Toke moved towards the cabin, the sound seeming loud and ominous against the silence of the surrounding trees. He loosened his Muninn in its sheath, readying the blade in case he needed it again.

Moving towards the creek, he quickly retraced his steps back to where he had launched his arrows and bent to retrieve his bow from where it had fallen among the grass. The silence was total in the clearing, and as he made his way back to Toke past the bodies of the men he'd killed, the imposing weight of the forest began to weigh on him.

'*I killed them,*' he thought, looking down into the now glassy eyes of the last man he'd fought. His face was white as snow, devoid of blood and life.

'Bjørn? Are you okay?' Toke asked quietly, moving to stand alongside his brother.

'I killed him,' Bjørn said, realising he had been standing there for a while. 'It was almost exactly like the fight with Father, but real.'

Toke was silent for a while, staring down at the body with his brother before he responded, understanding the reaction.

'It's never easy,' he said. 'Not the first time, nor the second, nor the third. It gets easier, but never easy. Nor should it.'

'But it was easy,' Bjørn said, turning. 'As easy as pulling my shirt on in the morning, or saddling my horse…'

'Aye, but I'm not talking about the action, brother, but the act. The ability to live with yourself after knowing that his thread was cut so yours could keep weaving. You killed this man,' he said, nudging the body with his foot. 'But it's not something to feel guilty about. It was you or him, and the Nornir wove his fate the day he came screaming into the world. This was his wyrd – his fate. He was supposed to die here, under your blade,' Toke finished, reaching up to clasp his brother's shoulder, squeezing once before walking away, pulling arrows from the dead men as he went.

Left alone, Bjørn stared at the body a while longer, processing his brother's words and taking comfort from them. He realised that all the time he had spent learning to fight, and dreaming of the sword storm, he'd never fully appreciated the weight that ending another man's life would bring.

In a family of brothers, teasing was as common as ale. Toke could have made a mockery of the moment of weakness, made light of the fight, or simply ignored it. Instead, he'd recognised feelings he himself had once experienced. There was comfort in that; in knowing he wasn't alone in feeling this way. Not for the first time, he thanked the fates for the family he had been born into.

'Bjørn. Let's start moving them out of the clearing. Their bodies will begin to foul, and we don't want visits from Óðinn's beasts keeping us awake all night.'

Bjørn nodded absently, his mind still working as he bent down to take up the dead man, grunting at the weight. As the body moved, the shirt came open to reveal a simple Mjölnir pendant on a string around the man's pale neck. Without thinking he reached down and freed it and put it over his own head. '*Something to remember today by,*' he thought as he took up the limp limbs again and heaved the dead weight onto his back.

The light was turning gold by the time Sigurd and Olaf rode back into the clearing, their hostage awake and cursing them tirelessly from the back of the horse. He only stopped when he saw the bodies of his friends, positioned along the path as a warning for anyone else looking to come into Jarl Erik's lands uninvited. The sight of his dead companions shocked him into a stunned silence that was replaced by the crackling of a fire when they finally reached the small cabin. Hidden by the flames, Bjørn and Toke sat facing the path with their backs to the hut as they slowly turned two rabbits over the fire, watching hungrily as the fat fell sizzling into the blaze.

'HA! Two rabbits! What do you say now, Toke?' Sigurd said, climbing down from his horse and tying it off against a pole set in the dirt. 'I believe that that axe is well and truly mine, wouldn't you say?'

'I think, under the circumstances, that perhaps he should keep the axe, wouldn't you say, Sigurd?' Olaf said as he climbed down from his own saddle and eyed the rabbits hungrily.

'What?' Sigurd grunted in frustration. 'Bjørn has killed two rabbits, and the men. Hand it over, Toke.'

'The axe isn't yours, Sigurd,' Bjørn said, watching his older brother with a bemused look. 'Toke killed them. By the time we finished dragging the bodies down the path, and gathering wood for a fire, I didn't have the energy to hunt anything, so Toke took my bow and off he went.'

'Toke shot them?' Sigurd asked incredulously. 'He couldn't hit the side of Father's hall if he stood two steps away from it!'

'Honestly, Sigurd,' Bjørn sighed, sitting back down by the fire. 'Take it or leave it.'

'I think, we can consider the bet void,' Olaf interrupted. 'Yes, Bjørn killed something before we arrived, but I don't think armed warriors was what either of you had in mind.'

'I'll accept it if Sigurd will,' Toke grunted.

Sigurd looked from brother to brother in disbelief. He didn't honestly care about the axe, but the idea that Toke had shot two rabbits with a maimed hand beggared belief. Toke was by far the poorest shot amongst them.

'Aye, I can accept it,' he said finally with a sigh. 'I suppose congratulations should be offered. Not only was Bjørn blooded, but Toke has finally learned to feed himself!' he said as he sat by the fire and pulled a leg from the nearest rabbit. 'Let's see if you've learned to cook as well!' He chuckled.

Their excitement grew when Olaf produced a skin of ale and a few loaves of bread from one of his packs to wash down the meal.

Between the rabbits and Olaf's bread and ale, they ate well on their first night in the woods, speaking long into the night about the events of the day and the adventures still to come. Beyond tying their prisoner to a tree and throwing him a crust of bread and a waterskin, they ignored him. As far as they were concerned – now that they knew they were safe – he was their father's problem.

Around them the forest had fallen asleep, the chirping of birds and whispering of wind replaced by the more sinister nighttime sounds. Owls hooted in the dark and once they heard some unseen beast rooting around the edge of their camp from the direction of the bodies. None of them got up to explore, well aware that the night was home to more than just beasts.

'So, you fought him like you did Father?' Olaf asked, slicing another strip of meat from one of the rabbits.

'Aye, almost exactly,' Bjørn said, staring in the flames, making himself night blind.

'You did well to survive it,' Sigurd said seriously, lowering the aleskin. 'One against four is rough odds, even for someone like Father or Sven.'

'It wasn't really one against four,' Bjørn admitted. 'Two were dead before they knew fully what was happening, and the third was so wounded he could hardly hold his spear. It wasn't as rough as it sounds.'

'Nay, but that's not what people will say when they hear the story,' Toke grinned.

'He's right,' said Olaf. 'By the time you sit down for your first meal back home, people will be asking how you managed to single-handedly fight off eight men, each iron clad and armed with good swords while you carried little more than your eating knife.'

Bjørn chuckled at the image, picking a piece of meat from between his teeth. 'Just dumb luck, I suppose? Anyway, all I know for sure is that I need to sleep. I'm exhausted.'

Before anyone could respond, Bjørn rolled out his sleeping sack and climbed into it, his sword lying ready by his side.

'Aye, we should, too. Sigurd, let's do a final check to make sure no one is waiting for us to fall asleep. Toke, you have the first watch; wake me up in three hours, Sigurd, you're after me, then Bjørn. Nothing tires a man out quite like a fight, and Bjørn's had more than his fair share today.'

'All right,' Toke nodded, watching the two figures disappear into the gloom.

'Thank you, Bjørn,' he whispered once the others were out of earshot. 'I really couldn't hit the side of Father's hall,' he admitted quietly.

'It's what brothers do,' Bjørn yawned lazily.

Bjørn was up before the sun, standing watch over the clearing and his brothers while they slept, the only sound to break the peace coming from Sigurd as his snores shattered the still morning air. The sound easily drowned out the songs of waking birds and the creek.

Rested and ready, he strung his bow and moved quietly to kneel by Toke's side, shaking him gently to wake him.

'Whaa?' he mumbled, sleep losing its grip on his tired body.

'Wake up, Toke. I'm going to go see what I can find for breakfast,' he said, shifting his bow hand slightly towards the forest. 'If the others ask where I went, tell them I'll be back in an hour or two.'

Toke nodded, letting out a loud yawn and rubbing his face to clear the sleep from his eyes.

'Get some sort of frame built. Something I can hang an animal on to bleed it. And get the fire going again – I want embers that I can cook in when

I return. Tell Sigurd or Olaf to make bread,' Bjørn whispered before standing and leaving.

'Last I checked, you were the *youngest* brother…' Toke groaned, yawning again.

'Gnnn, explains my energy, then,' Bjørn quipped, jabbing his bow stave into Toke's ribs. As he stood, he caught sight of their prisoner, his eyes red-rimmed with exhaustion, and full of hate. Bjørn smiled at him as he drew an arrow, nocking it to the flax string and drawing back to his cheek, sighting down the shaft as he had done a million times before. He watched the man's face change from fury to fear as he realised what was happening, the defiance leaving his exhausted face. One long, slow exhale to still his body and – *release*. The arrow crossed the space in less time it took for his heart to drum a beat, coming to rest a fingerbreadth above the man's head. He smiled as a dark patch appeared on the man's pants before turning and disappearing into the surrounding trees.

As soon as Bjørn entered the forest proper, the world changed around him. The silence of the woods was all consuming, broken only by occasional bird calls as they sang in the new day, and the gentle crunch of his own footsteps. The further into the woods he moved, the less he could see or hear of the clearing behind him, until eventually it was gone completely, the smell of woodsmoke replaced by the damp scent of centuries-old leaf litter.

'*As good a place as any,*' he mused under his breath as he began looking for signs of prey. As he went, he pulled long stalks of grass and wove them into loose plaits, tying them to branches as he went to mark his way back.

He came across his first signs of prey a rôst or so away from camp, the small pile of droppings still warm in the early morning chill.

'*Rabbit,*' he mused as he tied off another weave before taking his bow from his shoulder and drawing an arrow. It didn't take long to find the prints and he began following them through the clumps of virgin grass and thinning snow. As he moved he noted how the woods were slowly thinning out, letting more light leak through the canopy above him. Eventually the tracks led him to a small clearing a little larger than his father's hall. He spied the rabbit feeding on the edge of the glade, happily oblivious to his presence as it worked through the fresh virgin grass that had begun breaking through the receding snow. A small creek whispered its way through the clearing, its banks marked with barren patches of earth where animals had come to drink. He could see a few game trails snaking away from the broken earth into the forest and resigned himself to wait for bigger game to arrive. Moving as quietly as he could, he worked his way around the clearing, taking care to avoid dead branches and clumps of snow that could give away his position. Finding a concealed spot to watch from, he amused himself by watching a pair of early dragonflies as they darted to and fro between blades of grass, their erratic movements hard to follow from his seat in the shade.

He hadn't been waiting long when a small herd of roe deer appeared, their movements slow and hesitant as they checked for danger. One by one they stepped out into the small clearing, following an ancient buck as he led the way. Bjørn watched patiently as they entered the clearing, some bending down to graze at the patches of sweet green grass while others moved to drink from the small brook.

When the final doe emerged from the woods, the small herd had grown to twelve, spread across the clearing as they drank and ate their fill, as oblivious to his presence as the rabbit they shared their breakfast with. Calmly, Bjørn eased himself up on to his knees, moving as slowly as he could while he sought a target.

He was about to draw back on the bow and take a doe standing slightly aside from the group when a young buck raised its head from where it had been feeding. As he watched, he noticed that it walked with a slight limp, and he could see that its left hind leg was bleeding from a puncture. Likely it had challenged the stag for the harem and had been beaten down for his efforts. Watching the animal as it limped across the clearing to the water, he made his decision. As carefully as he could, he drew back on the bow, aiming for the flesh behind the left shoulder. As he exhaled to release, a crack came from the forest off to his right, causing the herd to freeze as their heads spun around to search for danger. Seeing his moment, Bjørn released the string, feeling it slide across his fingers and sending the arrow forwards with a vengeance. He had selected his shaft carefully, finding one that was perfectly straight and fletched with white owl feathers and a barbed iron hunting head. He watched as the arrow devoured the distance, crossing the clearing to strike the buck slightly above where he had aimed. The arrow hit like a thrust from *Gungnir* – the Allfather's spear – causing the buck to stumble slightly as it cried out.

Leaping forwards, it made for the woods with the rest of the herd as they scattered, but it was already losing blood and its injured leg betrayed it, sending it crashing to the ground. Bjørn was already moving as the buck fell with a painful bawl and by the time he arrived at its side the animal was almost dead. He reached it just in time to hear it breathe its last.

Resting his hands on the still warm chest, he drew Muninn from his belt and thanked the animal for its sacrifice before cutting along its stomach and pulling out the entrails, cutting them clean of the carcass. He watched as they lay steaming on a patch of blooded snow, the heat causing the slush to melt away in small rivers. They would quickly disappear down the gullets of foxes and ravens. The chest cavity empty, he extracted the valuable arrow and inspected it for cracks before cleaning it on virgin snow and returning it to his quiver. Pleased with his success he began the trek back to camp with the carcass across his shoulders, his mouth already salivating as he imagined the taste of fresh venison cooking over the embers.

Behind him, the first ravens had already spotted the feast he'd left on the ground and had begun to descend on the steaming pile of viscera, fighting over the scraps as he disappeared into the forest once again.

'The hunter returns.' Olaf smiled, spying his brother as he emerged from the woods with his grisly burden slung over his shoulder. 'And with breakfast no less. Toke…' Olaf trailed off, pointing behind him to their brother who was tying off the last piece of the frame, grunting as he pulled the rope tight.

'… is ready,' he beamed, finishing Olaf's sentence as he turned to face his brother. Bjørn noted the fresh blood on Toke's bandage from the labour but chose not to say anything.

Dropping the carcass, Bjørn drew Muninn and deftly sliced away at the skin on both hind legs, freeing the meat beneath before deftly removing the limbs from the body. He indicated for Toke to take the rest of the deer to the rack, his attention wholly consumed by the task at hand. Moving to the fire pit, he sharpened a stick of green wood before skewering it horizontally through the first leg to sit between muscle and bone. He set the leg to slowly cook above the glowing embers. The second he left hanging from a tree while he set to digging an earthen oven, leaving Olaf to slowly turn the meat over the coals.

He looked up while he dug, watching as Toke took his prized axe to the deer's head and chopped through flesh and bone in two strikes before tying the body neck-down on the frame and letting the last of the blood run out into a waiting bowl.

Comfortable that Toke had everything under control, Bjørn returned to his digging, listening contentedly as the crackle of the fire was joined by the occasional spit of fat as the meat began to cook. Once the hole was deep enough to fit the whole leg he began collecting stones from the creek, searching for flat rocks that would work as the base and walls of the oven. Once it was ready he used coals from the main fire to get a blaze going in the hole, building it up carefully before leaving it to burn down to the embers before returning to Olaf. Drawing his eating knife, he began slicing thin strips of meat from the slowly turning leg and put them into a rough wooden bowl while Sigurd put his dough in a pan and covered it with hot coals to bake.

'I had hoped that would be done by the time I got back,' Bjørn said with mock severity, offering Sigurd a strip of meat from the bowl. Sigurd smiled as he took a bite, the fat glazing his lips.

'I thought you'd take longer,' he shrugged, reaching for another slice.

Bjørn nodded, his mouth busy with a piece of his own as he cut more strips free from the slowly turning leg. When Toke joined them, the four brothers sat in companionable silence, eating the thin slivers of meat while they waited hungrily for the bread to finish baking.

'What are we going to do about him?' Toke asked through a mouthful of food, nodding vaguely in the direction of their prisoner.

'Hang him, for all I care,' Sigurd said helpfully, taking for another piece.

'He's not much use to us now, if we're here to hunt…' Olaf said, eyeing their prisoner dubiously.

'Why don't we half hang him?' Bjørn asked, turning to watch the man. 'We could hang him from a tree with a rope around his neck and place a log or something under his feet. We can tie each of his hands to separate trees on the edge of the clearing and then leave him there so that he's supported by whatever we put under him. He won't be able to escape for fear of knocking his support away and being left hanging, and we can all go hunting without having to leave someone behind to guard him,' he finished, shrugging as he put a final slice of venison in his mouth before moving to check his earthen oven.

'It's not a stupid idea,' Olaf mused, working a piece of meat free with his tongue.

'We have enough rope…' Sigurd added.

'What if he dies?'

'What if he does? Either way, he's living on borrowed time. Once Father hears that his sons were attacked in his own lands by him and his friends…' Toke said, trailing off.

They could all imagine what their father's reaction would be to the news.

'Let's just hang the bastard up and go hunting,' Sigurd muttered.

'Father will want to talk to him,' Bjørn insisted.

'Bjørn's right,' Olaf said, standing, and wiping his hands on his breeches. 'Sigurd, string him up how Bjørn suggested. Give him some water and a bit of the bread we brought from home. Then we'll eat properly – the new bread should be ready by then – and head out. Toke, if your hand is likely to bother you at all, you can keep an eye on the nithing. No one will think less of you.'

Toke clenched and unclenched his hand unconsciously, considering the suggestion.

They moved quickly after that, none of them keen to spend more time on the prisoner than they had to. Sigurd gave him a few gulps of water and a crust of bread while Bjørn chopped a rough stand for him to balance on.

'What's your name?' Bjørn asked as he placed the wooden block under an overhanging tree branch.

All he got in return was a snarl. Without a sound, he rose and shoved him over before kicking him in the side for good measure.

'I asked you your name,' he asked again, his tone unchanged.

'Rot in Helheim!' their prisoner snarled, ignoring the pain in his side as he spat at Bjørn's feet.

'I'm going to ask you one last time,' Bjørn said again, his voice calm as he bent down and slowly drew Muninn from its sheath. 'What's your name?' he asked, pulling the man's pinky proud of his clenched fist and tucking Muninn under the knuckle. He watched the resistance die in the man's face as he looked into Bjørn's unflinching eyes. A small stream of blood had begun running down his wrist from where the blade had already broken the flesh.

'Siv,' he muttered grudgingly, his eyes shooting daggers.

Bjørn looked at him properly for the first time since they'd captured him, ignoring Siv's filthy looks. He was shorter than most men, with a dirty mop of blond crusted hair and awkwardly spaced front teeth that gave him a simple look. Although his eyes betrayed the assumption, Bjørn noted, seeing a hidden intelligence there.

'Well, Siv,' Bjørn said, slicing a strip of cloth from the prisoner's shirt to clean his dagger, 'we're going to leave you here for a while and head out hunting. My brother may decide to stay and keep you company, but then again, he may not. But let me guarantee you one thing: if, by any chance, you do manage to escape, I will find you. And believe me, the arrow won't strike above

84

your head this time,' he said, gently tapping his dagger against Siv's exposed throat before sheathing the blade.

Siv gulped, unable to hide his fear in the face of Bjørn's threat. The message was abundantly clear.

'He's all yours,' Bjørn called before returning to his oven. The flames had burned down to the coals when he arrived, and he could feel the heat rising out of the confined space. Drawing an old knife from his pack, he made his way towards the creek, listening to his brothers' banter as they worked to make Siv secure.

'He looks like the White Christ,' Sigurd joked, standing back to examine his handy work while Olaf and Toke pulled the ropes tight to secure Siv's arms.

Bjørn knelt down by the bank and began cutting blocks of moss from the ground with the knife, slowly building a pile of the green-brown bricks. He smiled while he worked, listening to his brothers' banter behind him. Once he had enough, he added a few greenwood staves before carrying the pile back to his oven and set everything to one side.

Piece by piece he pulled the glowing coals and heated stones from the pit, the heat making sweat break out on his forehead. Once everything but the stones lining the walls and base were removed, he rubbed the second leg with salt pilfered from his father's kitchen and added it to the oven. The meat instantly began to sizzle and shrink away as it tried to escape the heat before he covered it with the remaining stones, sealing in the warmth. Finally, he added fresh coals from the fire before covering the pit with a lattice of greenwood and moss, and then a final layer of dirt. When they came back that evening they would have perfectly cooked, succulent venison waiting for them.

'You'll make someone a good wife,' Sigurd called from the fire as he ran a whetstone along the blade of his spear.

'At least I'll be married,' he shot back as he returned to the fire in time for Olaf to pull the freshly baked bread from the embers. While his brother saw to the bread, Bjørn sliced more strips from the leg over the flames. The smell was enough to make all of them salivate, and the few strips of meat they had already enjoyed were quickly forgotten in the face of the feast to come. Toke produced a small pouch of butter from somewhere in his saddle bags which they spread across the warm bread, watching it melt before covering it with warm venison and stuffing the whole lot in their mouths. There was near total silence as they ate their fill, mopping up the fatty juices in the wooden bowl with scraps of crust before washing everything down with a swig from an aleskin.

Taking up his bow and stringing it, Bjørn began to run a knot of beeswax along the string to protect it from grit. 'Are we all ready to go? Toke, what are you going to do?'

'I'll stay and keep an eye on our archer friend,' he said, nodding towards the hanging prisoner, his feet precariously balancing on the slightly-too-low stump of wood under his feet. 'Better to make sure he gets to enjoy Father's company, don't you think?' He smiled.

They all knew the real reason, but no one said anything.

'We'll be back at sundown,' Olaf said, nodding. 'Bjørn, Sigurd and I were thinking to head east. There's a small pond not too far away that is likely to be busy with animals looking for a drink. Do you want to come with us? Or do you prefer to head off on your own?' he asked, taking up his own bow.

'I'll head out on my own and see if I can track down the deer herd again. Toke, if you're going to stay, could you see about knocking together a few more frames so we can butcher whatever we bring back? There might already be a few staves in the cabin that you could use? And maybe get another loaf of bread ready?'

'Mhmm.' He nodded, spitting crumbs as he tried to speak around a particularly large mouthful. 'I can do that,' he said, swallowing.

'Let's get going then,' Sigurd said, taking up his spear.

Toke watched as they made for the forest with their weapons held loosely in their hands. It reminded him of a wolf pack the way they disappeared amongst the trees. He desperately wanted to go with them, but deep down he knew that he needed to rest his hand if he wanted to join the fleet when they sailed. Their father wasn't above leaving him behind if he thought he would be a liability to others, son or not. Shrugging, he cut off another piece of venison and wrapped it in a fresh slice of bread, deciding there was a silver lining to his wounded palm as he enjoyed the juicy meat.

# Chapter 5

They were blessed with warming weather and clear skies during their time in the hills. It was still cold enough in the evenings to see them huddled around the fire wrapped in their furs, but through the days they enjoyed crisp sun that often saw them head out each morning with just a cloak to keep them warm. They spent four days hunting together, their haul of meat slowly growing day-by-day as they harvested animals that were made slow and dumb after a long cold winter. Every day, Bjørn added a new piece of the first deer he had killed to his earthen oven, slowly working through the carcass so that, by the time they packed up to leave, all that was left was a pile of bones. What they didn't eat they took with them.

Toke only joined them on one of the days, preferring to keep his eyes on their prisoner and the horses, as well as ensure there was fresh bread and stacked firewood ready for when the others returned each evening. They all knew it was to rest his hand, but no one mentioned it. It took a lot for Toke to stay put while others worked, and they all preferred to have him with them on the whale road.

When the time came to break camp and return home, the pack horses were heavy with the meat from five deer and a boar, brought down by Sigurd's spear, as well as several rabbits.

The boar had been an unexpected surprise. They had come across it rooting through the undergrowth on their third day, the dawn light painting its dark bristles gold and reminding them all of Freyr's golden boar, *Gullinbursti*.

Toke's eyes had stood on stalks when they returned to the clearing carrying the giant, his excitement tempered by his frustration at having missed such a contest.

Once the final animal was loaded and ready to go, they had begun their trek home, the packhorses whinnying occasionally under the weight. With their grisly harvest loaded, Siv was forced to walk behind with a rope around his neck and his hands tied behind his back. He had gone ungagged for the first rôst or so, but his complaining had quickly become frustrating and Sigurd had gagged him. For four days, he'd survived under Toke's watchful gaze, strung up and left to consider his fate. None of the brothers had had anything to do with him beyond feeding him bread and water, and the occasional scrap of meat to keep him strong enough for the journey home.

Bjørn didn't ride either, instead staying in the trees, a short distance ahead of their small caravan. After what had happened when they arrived, they agreed that Bjørn should play scout until King's Leap to be sure there weren't any surprises. Armed with only his bow and his knife, he moved silently through the woods clad in a dark cloak that helped him to blend in with the surrounding forest and mask his movements. For his brothers lagging behind, they only occasionally caught sight of him through the trees. None of them really believed they would come across anyone else, but they were all keenly aware of how different the outcome could have been on their journey in and they didn't want to take any chances. As Bjørn moved through the woods, the conversation among the riders remained light, almost entirely taken up with theories about where they would sail. Olaf argued for Frankia, while Toke and Sigurd were for Ireland or Britain. In truth, none of them had any idea; only Erik knew his own mind. They could all admit that in the end it didn't matter, just so long as they got to go. Destination and organisation were their father's responsibility; rowing, fighting, and looting was theirs. They didn't much care who or where they raided, just so long as they did. They continued like this for some time, chatting easily amongst themselves as they retraced their steps through the forest before falling into an easy silence. The air around them was filled with the sound of the wind as it brushed through the trees, carrying whispers and the odd needle to cover the path and ground below.

'Enjoy it while it lasts,' Olaf smiled, closing his eyes and breathing deeply. 'As soon as we get home, life will be far from relaxed.'

'Good,' Sigurd said. 'The sooner we get home, the sooner we sail. That's the worst part about this time of year: the waiting.'

'Usually, I would agree with Sigurd,' Toke said from the back of their small convoy. 'But the waiting gives me time to heal, and I like being in the woods – it's calming.'

'Gnn,' Sigurd grunted from the front, unconvinced.

They rode in silence for the next half hour as they covered the final leg of the journey to King's Leap, each mulling over their own thoughts. At one point they heard a deer bark in the forest, catching a glimpse of it as it disappeared into the undergrowth.

By the time they broke the treeline and rode into the familiar clearing on the cliff, the sun was beginning its descent towards the west. They had passed the middle of the day.

Bjørn was already there waiting for them, sitting on a rock looking down on their home. 'Who's hungry?' He smiled, holding up two dead rabbits as his brothers broke the tree line.

The vote was unanimous.

Olaf climbed down from his mare with a sigh and patted its neck gently, earning a friendly shove as she nuzzled her nose into his shoulder. 'Sigurd, see if you can find some firewood. Toke and I can see to the horses and get them watered.'

Bjørn had already started cleaning his catch, throwing the guts and entrails into the blackened remains of their previous fire.

'We never heard a shot?' Olaf asked, sitting down with a contented sigh.

'I'm surprised you heard anything with all your blabbering about Frankia and forests,' Bjørn replied without looking up as he scooped out the innards from the second rabbit. Once the guts were free, he quickly whipped the skins off before crossing to the creek to clean the meat in the icy water.

Sigurd had a fire burning by the time he returned with the cleaned carcasses, the faggots crackling gently as he slowly fed in larger logs. 'Keep an eye on it,' he said as Bjørn sat down. 'I'll go get some more wood, and cut some skewers.'

Nodding, Bjørn handed the cleaned rabbits to Olaf before retrieving the small iron pot from his saddle and filling it with water from the creek. When he returned, he suspended the pot over the fire and began feeding in a handful of spruce needles.

'Something warm to go with the meal,' he said, looking up at Olaf as he fed another log to the flames.

'Good thinking.'

Toke was still watering the horses as the two talked, the sound of their gentle snorts blending with the crack of Sigurd's axe as he chopped wood.

Taking a pull from his waterskin, Olaf turned to his brother, watching as he stirred the brew.

'How are you feeling?' he asked suddenly.

'About what?'

'What happened at the clearing. About beating Father, sailing with us; a lot has happened in the last few days.'

Bjørn stopped his stirring, dropping the stick he had been using into the flames and watching absently as the water began to bubble gently.

'Fine,' he said at length. 'It's a lot to take in, but it's what I've always wanted, what I've been training for.'

Olaf didn't answer immediately, and Bjørn watched as he poked the fire, sending a stream of sparks into the darkening sky. 'It is,' Olaf said finally, lifting his eyes to meet Bjørn's. His gaze was serious.

'It shook me at first,' Bjørn admitted. 'Killing a man wasn't what I expected. It's not like killing an animal or training with a practice sword. But it was me or him, and I'm not ready for Valhöll yet. I've come to terms with it. I won't be found wanting,' he added with finality, meeting his brother's eyes.

Olaf nodded, satisfied. 'I just wanted to check,' he said, reaching over to grip Bjørn's shoulder briefly. He was remembering the first man he had killed, and his own feelings of confusion and guilt.

'Thank you,' Bjørn said, dipping his head briefly.

'What are you two whispering about?' Sigurd said, seeing Bjørn's face as he dropped a few more logs by the fire.

'Probably the thralls they'll bed first when they get back!' Toke joked as he found his own seat.

'It's hardly something we need to plan...' Bjørn smiled, glad for the change of subject. 'We all know they prefer me and Olaf.'

Olaf laughed as he took up one of the skewers and worked it through the fresh meat. Beside him, Bjørn began pulling coals from the main blaze. Once he had a glowing bed ready, they suspended the two rabbits over the forked sticks Sigurd had found and began rotating them over the embers, cooking them slowly and evenly.

Sigurd added another log to the fire to keep it going, while Toke took over responsibility for the brew Bjørn had started, stirring it occasionally as the water began to boil. The light breeze was lifting the veil of water from the creek high into the fjord, creating millions of rainbows as the evening light struck the droplets. All around them the trees whispered secrets to each other while gulls hung in the air, gliding and swooping in the afternoon breeze.

'We could stay one more night?' Bjørn suggested, looking at his brothers. 'Like you said, Olaf, as soon as we get back the calm period ends, and it will be all go getting the fleet ready to sail. One more night up here wouldn't be the end of the world.'

The brothers all sat for a few moments, the silence only broken by the crackle of the fire and the cries of the gulls as they waited for Olaf to speak.

'Why not?' Olaf said at last. 'Who knows when we'll next have a chance to do something like this together?'

Bjørn and Toke grinned in support, making Sigurd smile.

'Outvoted before I can open my mouth,' he grumbled good-naturedly before standing and stretching his back. 'I better get more firewood, then.'

'I'll help you,' Olaf said, following a few steps behind.

Bjørn and Toke talked quietly as their brothers disappeared into the trees, slowly rotating their dinner over the coals.

***

Carr watched the brothers quietly from the other side of the clearing, crouching on a bed of pine needles. For the past few days, he'd survived almost entirely on salted pork and stale bread, supplementing his diet with sips of water from the creek when he felt safe enough to sneak down. He'd watched as the brothers left each day to hunt, waiting for an opportunity to free his friend, but he was unwilling to risk confronting the brother who stayed behind. Even when they'd all left Siv alone one day to hunt, he'd decided not to risk capture or death without knowing they wouldn't return suddenly. One of them had to survive and make it home to Fótrfjord to report what they'd learned, he'd told himself. The six of them had spent weeks scouting Vágar and the land surrounding it, gathering valuable information about Erik and his men, for their jarl. They had been preparing to leave and return home when the brothers had arrived, and Carr had been forced to watch as his friends were killed or captured. He was determined to rescue Siv if he could, but not at the cost of his own life. In his heart of hearts, he knew that he was scared to challenge the brothers openly, even the injured one. He'd watched the ease with which they had shot and cut down his companions, laying them low as if they were made of straw. He wouldn't risk it in the open, not where they held all the advantages. So, he had watched, learning all he could from the sons of Erik while he waited. He knew that he should have escaped and returned to their small faering when the brothers had packed up to leave, but he couldn't bring himself to leave Siv without at least trying to save him. So, when the brothers had broken camp and made their way back through the forest, he'd followed them, avoiding Bjørn as best he could as he scouted ahead of the convoy.

He'd nearly blown it earlier that day as he followed them, focused as he was on staying out of Bjørn's sight. He'd watched as the youngest Eriksson headed out ahead of the riders to scout the route ahead, sticking to the right-hand side of the trail. Seeing this, Carr had made sure to follow behind on the left of the trail, hidden by the ancient forest and the carpet of needles beneath. He'd listened to the brothers as they discussed the raids to come and, needing to hear properly, he'd dared to move closer. He'd been so focused on the riders that he'd completely missed the deer as it grazed a few steps ahead of him. Stepping on a dead branch, the deer had been startled into life and he'd been forced to watch helplessly as it bounded away, drawing the eyes of the three horsemen. He had been sure then that they could see him, and he hadn't even dared to breathe for risk of drawing their attention. If he had had a bow or an axe, he might have felt a little more confident, but as it was, the only weapons he carried were his small hunting knife and dwindling pouch of dried meat he'd been forced to ration through the week. He had carved himself a makeshift spear from a long pine branch, but he knew that it was next to useless against the iron weapons carried by the sons of Erik. The only reason he had even survived the attack was that he had been out checking the snares when the brothers arrived. So now, he was resigned to watching, learning all he could before returning to his jarl, and rescuing Siv if an opportunity arose. '*He always was a sour bastard, anyway,*' he spat as he settled down into his bed of pine needles, wrapping his cloak around him for warmth. He knew now that Jarl Erik and his bloody brood would be away raiding for the spring and summer months. That was a journey of several weeks, if not months, giving his own jarl plenty of time to plan his own *raids*.

Tomorrow, he would either save Siv or kill him himself. He couldn't risk him giving anything away to save his own miserable skin.

Whatever the outcome, Carr's time in Vágar was at an end. Silently, he thanked the gods for sending the brothers to the hunting cabin, saving him the danger of sneaking into the settlement again. It had come at a high cost, but the information he had gathered from the brothers' evening talks would be invaluable to his jarl, and would more than make up for it. He soon fell asleep, his mind picturing the piles of thumb-thick silver ingots and arm rings his information would earn him.

\*\*\*

The brothers rose with the sun, quickly breaking down their makeshift camp and starting the final leg of their journey towards home. Bjørn took in the view one last time, his eyes drinking in the view as he breathed deeply, enjoying the crisp, fresh morning air.

They made good time descending from the heights, quickly passing through the narrowest part of the trail in single file before riding into the forest beyond. Behind them, the weather was slowly changing for the worse, and they looked back more than once with detached interest, commenting on whether they'd reach shelter before the rain reached them. Their woollen cloaks had been treated with both beeswax and fish oil to keep them soft and waterproof, and they would keep off the worst of the rain, however Siv was less fortunate and would be soaked through by the time they reached home, if the rain caught them. They continued in silence for the next few rôst, each lost in his own thoughts as they followed the path down. Being so close to the town walls and outlying farms, Bjørn no longer walked ahead of the group, but rode with them.

An hour or so after breaking camp, they came across a freshly fallen pine tree lying diagonally over the track, presumably pushed over by the growing winds. It hadn't fallen enough to warrant dismounting or leaving the path, but they were forced to ride single-file again to avoid the protruding branches, still heavy with needles. Toke went first, followed by Sigurd and then Olaf, leading the string of packhorses behind him. Bjørn came last, prompting his own mount forwards while leading Siv behind him, the rope held lightly in his left hand. As he was bending down to avoid a one of the branches, he felt a sudden, searing pain in his side, striking him without warning and forcing him to drop his grip on the rope and reins as he struggled to retain his seat in the saddle. He failed, but his grasping fingers managed to reach Huginn's leathered grip, drawing the blade as he fell. He landed with a thud, his head crashing into a broken branch that dazed him and sent stars dancing across his vision. Reaching for his side, his hand returned without blood, and he felt a moment of relief at the sight.

Regaining his bearings, he just had time to see a fur-clad man lunge at him with a sharpened stick, the tip slightly bent from the impact with his ribs. Rolling fast, he dodged the makeshift spear as it came for his throat, roaring for his brothers as he moved. His vision was still blurry, and he shook his head to try and clear it. Behind him, he could hear the disorder on the other side of the fallen tree as they tried to calm the panicking horses. Ignoring the sounds behind him, Bjørn watched as his attacker drew a knife from his belt and slit the ropes around Siv's wrists before handing him the blade. Grimacing, Bjørn reached behind his back for Muninn, holding the knife blade down in his left hand as he prepared to face the two men. He had the better weapons, but the makeshift spear had a longer reach, and iron tip or not it could still do wicked damage if it managed to pierce his unprotected skin. He was lucky it had only bruised him the first time, his cloak absorbing most of the impact.

He eyed the two men as they moved either side of him, trying to surround him. Behind him, the sounds of his brothers yelling as they tried to calm the horses and get back through to him sounded loud to his ears, and he blocked them out as he focused on the men before him.

'Careful with that toothpick, Siv,' he taunted, trying to force his hand. 'You wouldn't want to hurt yourself.'

'Shut it, *Bjørn*,' he barked, finding confidence in the blade as he moved it from hand to hand, trying to confuse him. 'Your thread is cut.'

'Gnnn,' he grunted disinterestedly, his eyes switching between the two.

Without warning, he turned on his left foot and swung diagonally upwards from left to right with his knife, forcing Siv to raise his own blade in defence to meet the blow. Without stopping, he quickly changed direction and pulled the blade back, forcing Siv to overextend his hand before slicing down with Huginn in a single sharp motion. Siv screamed as the metal sliced through bone and muscle, severing his hand at the wrist. Ignoring his cries, Bjørn kicked him viciously in the chest, forcing him onto his back amongst the dead needles and dirt from the fallen tree.

'Bjørn?' his brothers called, the worry in their voices carrying above the sounds of the horses.

'I'm fine!' he shouted, as he turned to face the would-be liberator. 'If you so much as touch me again with that *stick* of yours, I will shove it so far up your arse that it will come out your throat,' he snarled, pointing his sword threateningly at the make-shift spear.

Carr swallowed nervously in the face of Bjørn's unrestrained violence. He knew the rescue was doomed now. Already he could see the first brother running to his brother's aid with his axe in hand. '*Screw this,*' he thought as he took two rapid steps back before launching his spear like a javelin, forcing Bjørn to duck and deflect the projectile with his sword. By the time he straightened up, the spearman was already ten paces away and moving fast as he sprinted into the undergrowth, already a shadow. He would have made an easy shot with his bow, but the weapon was unstrung and stowed on his horse.

'I think that's all of them, Toke,' Bjørn sighed, forcing his eyes from the retreating figure. 'If there had been more, they would have attacked all at once.

This one must have been hiding when we took the others and risked a rescue for Siv *Half-Hand* over there.'

They both turned to take in the sight of the writhing man on the ground, covered with blood and gore as it spouted from the stump of his wrist.

'Get a fire going, Toke, we need to seal that wound and stop the bleeding, otherwise he will be no use to Father. We need to know what's going on. Sigurd, Olaf, have you got those bloody horses under control yet?' he yelled, turning his attention towards the fallen tree.

'Yes,' came the muffled reply. 'We'll keep them here for now – they can smell the blood and it's making them skittish.'

'Keep an eye out, just to be safe. I think that was the last of them, but we can't be too sure now. Our friend Siv has had an *accident*, so we need to seal the wound for Father.'

'Okay, be quick!'

Bjørn ran to his horse and grabbed a waterskin and his small pot, as well as a few strips of linen he kept in his saddlebags for bandages before returning to his brother. 'Boil these,' he said as he handed everything except one of the bandages to Toke. Then, without ceremony, he bent down and smashed his fist into Siv's head, dazing him long enough to stop his writhing so that he could wrap the strip of linin around the injured arm, just below the elbow. He pulled it as tightly as he could, slowing the blood flow. He soon heard the crackling of flames behind him and watched as Toke added more and more wood from the fallen tree, quickly turning the burning faggots into a raging blaze. Bjørn saw he had cut up the wooden spear and was feeding it piece by piece into the flames. Sheathing his sword, he took the wood axe from his saddle and buried the blade in the burning coals. Embers were still a good while away, but the flames themselves would soon burn hot enough to heat the iron. They both watched as the dull metal began to slowly change colour, drifting from yellow to orange to a deep, glowing red. They could hear Siv whimpering behind them as he returned to consciousness and realised what they planned, but neither had any sympathy for the man. He had been more than willing to kill both brothers at different times, and they all knew it.

'Toke, go and switch places with Sigurd. We don't want to risk your hand opening again.'

Standing with a grunt, Toke moved towards the fallen tree.

He was soon replaced by the hulking figure of Sigurd, his face furious. Before Bjørn could stop him, his brother had crossed the distance and smashed his own fist into Siv's face, shattering his nose with a fountain of blood.

'Sigurd!' Bjørn shouted, trying to calm his brother down. 'Sigurd! He's lost enough blood, already; we need to keep him alive for Father.'

'Try to kill my brother; my brother!' Sigurd raged, spitting fury at the trembling man.

'It's done, now,' Bjørn said, laying a hand on his brother's shoulder to calm him.

Grunting, Sigurd threw a final kick into Siv's ribs, spitting in his face for good measure as he calmed himself with visible effort. 'What do you need, brother?' he asked. His face was a deep crimson, and Bjørn could see that he was trying hard to keep his temper in check.

'I need you to hold him while I seal the wound. If we don't, he'll bleed out and die.'

'Gnn,' Sigurd grunted, turning to the prone figure and levering him onto his back. None too gently, he sat his considerable bulk on Siv, before grasping the wounded arm and holding it in a vice-like grip. Bjørn winced when he thought he heard a rib crack.

'Hold him tight, brother,' he said, briefly meeting Sigurd's seething eyes.

'Get on with it, before I change my mind,' Sigurd growled.

Ignoring Sigurd's fury, Bjørn forced a two-finger-thick stick between Siv's teeth before drawing the glowing axe from the flames. Holding the injured wrist to steady himself, he took a deep breath and pushed the glowing metal hard against the oozing wound, holding it tight as Siv tried to struggle against Sigurd's iron grip. The air was instantly filled with the sickly-sweet smell of burning flesh as the skin sizzled under the glowing metal. Siv's eyes bulged in his head as he bit down on the stick, his lungs bursting as he screamed through the wood. For a moment, Bjørn was convinced his eyes were going to pop from his head. He was relieved when Siv passed out from the pain, his energy spent. He quickly reheated the blade and pressed it against the wound once more for good measure before fishing out the boiled bandages with a piece of birchwood. Wincing as the boiling water scalded his bare hands, he began bandaging Siv's wrist as tightly as he could to keep the wound clean and fight off any infection. Siv didn't wake again.

'Okay, Sigurd. It's done,' Bjørn sighed, his own energy beginning to falter as the adrenaline began to leave his own body. 'Get him up on one of the horses and tie him down tight.'

Sigurd grunted in acknowledgement as he picked up the limp body and disappeared under the fallen tree.

Exhaling, Bjørn stood and poured the rest of the water over the flames, killing the fire before kicking dirt over the smouldering logs for good measure.

'Nithing,' he muttered, eyeing Siv's hand where it lay in the mud, still clasping the dagger. On an impulse he picked up the blade before leading his horse under the tree to reunite with his brothers, leaving the hand for whatever animal came along first.

He came through just in time to watch Siv's lame head slump over as Sigurd tied him firmly to one of the horses, tying the knots tight. 'He won't be coming off any time soon,' he grunted, looking up. 'Tighter than a tick on a dog.'

Bjørn nodded as he climbed onto his own horse, patting it briefly on the neck to calm it as it caught the scent of blood on him.

'Let's get out of here,' Olaf muttered, his breath steaming in front of him as the first drops of rain began to land around them.

Overhead, a crash of thunder tore the sky, its jagged edges bright against the heavy grey clouds.

'Thor's riding his chariot hard today,' Bjørn grunted, kicking his heels to set his horse walking. 'I for one would like to be under Father's roof before the worst of it hits.'

Before anyone could respond, Bjørn moved to the front of the small group and began riding down the path, heading for home.

# Chapter 6

Erik's sons returned to Vágar later that same afternoon, welcomed home by heavy rain and rumbling thunder as the heavens opened above them. They split up after riding through the gates, with Olaf and Sigurd taking the meat away to be smoked and salted, while Toke and Bjørn led Siv to their father. The curious gazes had started even before they reached Vágar's landward gate, with one of their father's húskarlar calling out as they approached the walls. Beyond a cursory explanation, they ignored his questions as they entered the town, preferring to keep the information to themselves until they saw Erik.

Siv's demeanour changed once they passed through the gates as the reality of his situation began to fully sink in. While he'd remained silent and disdainful since his capture, that was now replaced by physical fear. His eyes constantly darted from left to right as they walked through the town, suddenly aware of how many people were stopping and staring at their small caravan.

'Play your cards right, Siv *Half-Hand*, and you might get a quick and clean death at the end of Sven's giant axe,' Bjørn said, turning in the saddle to face the broken figure. 'Our father is a reasonable man, but he's not known for his patience. Tell him what he wants to know, and you might save yourself from a slow and painful death.'

'Or lie to him,' Toke said unhelpfully, smiling at the captured man. 'Our father's goði is well known for his zealous devotion to the gods but has been much starved of a blót sacrifice these past few months. If I recall, we even discussed it at the feast the night before we left and bumped into you and your friends. Funny old world, isn't it?' he said, shoving a strip of dried meat into his mouth.

'Let me go,' Siv said, his voice a whisper. 'Make me a thrall, set me free with naught but my clothes and my wits. Anything but that!'

Bjørn and Toke remained silent while the man begged. They both knew the man's mind would be conjuring images of sharp knives and shining axes, of burning coals and blood-eagles, the almost mythical act where a man's back was opened from shoulder to hips before having his ribs cut away from his spine with an axe. It only ended once the lungs were pulled out and resting on the victim's shoulders, with death arriving slowly through suffocation and blood loss. None in Vágar had seen a blood-eagle performed, but neither of them doubted that Gørm had the bloodlust to perform the act. They didn't dwell long on the thought. A man's fate was woven by the Nornir the day he came screaming into the world from their mother's womb. Wyrd.

Kicking in their heels, they raised their pace to a gentle trot, navigating through the crowds as they headed for their father's stables. They could see Sven waiting for them as they drew closer, his ever-present axe held lightly in his hand. Standing head and shoulders over even Erik, Sven was the largest man in Vágar, with deep red hair that even Thor would envy and dark blue eyes that reminded Bjørn of the fjords in winter. Of the four brothers, only Sigurd was able to handle a similar weapon, although he was still learning the skill and rarely chose it over his sword and shield – not yet, at least. The men who carried the giant Dane axes had to be incredibly strong and skilled, but also willing to stand unshielded in the melee, an easy target for arrows and spears.

'News travels fast,' Toke whispered to Bjørn as he drew alongside him to enter the stable.

'You've been busy,' Sven called as they approached, his face impassive as he pointed his axe towards Siv. The giant's voice seemed to cross the distance without conscious thought or effort.

'We found him skulking around in the bushes near the cabin up behind King's Leap,' Toke replied, sliding out of the saddle and rubbing his behind.

'Gnn,' Sven grunted, turning to face Bjørn with his eyebrow raised in question.

'There were six in total, including Siv *Half-Hand* here,' he replied, pulling sharply on Siv's rope.

Unprepared for the sudden yank, Siv fell unceremoniously from his horse into the muddy mire, barely managing to keep his wounded wrist from the filth that covered the ground outside the stable. A second scream escaped his lips as Toke helped him none too gently from the mud, putting pressure on the wound.

'Makes more noise than Olaf,' Toke observed, releasing his grip.

'What about the others?' Sven asked, ignoring the man's whimpering as he tried to stand.

'We killed four and captured this one,' Bjørn said. 'The sixth we missed until he attempted a rescue this morning. He escaped in the confusion and was gone before we could follow.'

Sven remained silent for a few moments, processing what he'd been told. Given his great size and strength, he was occasionally taken as dim-witted or slow, but the truth was quite the opposite. 'Are you sure only one escaped?' he said after a time.

'As sure as we can be. It stands to reason that any others would have helped in the rescue attempt, though.'

'Gnn,' Sven grunted again, eyeing the prisoner. 'Let's take him to your father and see what he wants done with him.'

Bjørn nodded, indicating for one of the stable thralls to come and take the horses from them after he had retrieved his sword from where it rested on the saddle.

They found Erik in his hall, engrossed in a game of *hnefatafl* with Yngvar. The board was one of their father's most prized possessions. Unlike the games his men would take with them on the whale road, made of coloured stones and marked scraps of leather or wood, this was a piece of art.

The board itself was beautifully carved from a single plank of elm and inlaid with fine lines of silver, with the central and corner squares framed and patterned in gold. The game pieces were equally beautiful, with the king and his cohort carved from walrus ivory, and their enemy out of black slate. At first glance, the game appeared to be tied between the attacking blacks and defending whites, but Yngvar was as cunning as they came, and looking more closely Bjørn could see that the game was very nearly over. His father's king would be captured within five moves, if the game finished the way he predicted. Hoping to avoid anything that might sour his father's mood, he coughed gently to try and get his attention. Erik ignored him and made his next move, his finger lingering over the piece to ensure it was safe. Bjørn shared a knowing smile with his brother while they waited for their father to notice them.

'You're back,' Erik said as he removed his finger at last, his eyes never leaving the board.

'Yes, Father,' they chorused, resigning themselves to a potentially long wait. They could cough as much as they liked, but Erik wouldn't be rushed when it came to hnefatafl. 'We brought back five deer and a boar, and a few rabbits,' Toke said, clearing his throat. 'But we also ran into some *complications* while we were away.'

'Do these complications have something to do with the man dripping

100

blood on my floor?' Erik asked, watching as Yngvar moved his own piece.

Before anyone could answer, Erik captured the exposed piece and slid it to the edge of the board to sit with its waiting companions.

'You could say that,' Toke said, his brows furrowed as he too tried to read the game.

Erik had demanded that his sons all learn to play the game to a high standard, viewing it as an essential element in their education and critical for men of their social standing. As a result, they were all strong players and had even beaten their father from time to time. None, however, had managed to beat Yngvar before.

They watched now as he moved another piece forward, one square away from the king, blocking any retreat for Erik's exposed soldiers.

Bjørn saw his father's eyes widen briefly as he too read the board. By closing the retreat for Erik's two exposed troops, Yngvar had effectively blocked any move for the king. His only option was to open his skjaldborg and take the offending blacks, but in doing so the king would be unguarded and exposed to the pieces left out of reach of his own soldiers. Growling in the back of his throat, he turned his attention to his two sons and their prisoner.

'He's a miserable-looking *complication*, wouldn't you say, Yngvar?'

'If I was feeling generous, perhaps,' Yngvar said, playing the game. '*Pathetic* might be a better word.'

'What happened to his hand?' Erik asked, leaning back in his chair and lifting a golden goblet to his lips.

'Bjørn chopped it off,' Toke said helpfully.

'So I can see,' Erik mused, staring at his youngest son expectantly.

'I can fill you in, Father,' Bjørn said, meeting his father's gaze.

'Does Sven know?'

'Yes. The short version, at least.'

Erik watched his son as he took another sip of his mead. 'I'm guessing there is a reason my youngest sons are here with the prisoner while my older two are…?'

'They're taking the meat to be smoked and salted.'

'Hmm,' Erik murmured, turning his attention back to the board in front of him. They all stood patiently while Erik surveyed the board, apparently forgotten by the jarl as his eyes danced from piece to piece, unpicking the battle being played out before him. After what felt like an age, Erik sighed. 'You win, Yngvar, as usual.'

'You nearly had me, though.' He smiled, reaching over to pack up the board.

'You're a poor liar, Yngvar,' Erik grinned, returning his attention to his sons. 'I'm glad to see that the complications didn't stop you from returning home,' he grunted. 'Come back before the evening meal, and we will discuss your time away further.'

He could see they wanted to stay and talk more, but neither argued the order. Instead, they both stood tall and nodded before turning to leave. He watched as the two young warriors disappeared through the open door. They had learned discipline and knew better to argue with their father's decisions.

Sometimes, Erik felt as if his heart would burst with the pride he felt for his sons, even Bjørn. He longed to hold them close and tell them how truly proud of them all he was, but he knew such an act would make them weak, and he wouldn't risk that. Smothering his emotions, he turned his gaze to the prisoner. Any signs of mirth or humour had disappeared, and Siv swallowed nervously as he met the glacial gaze of Erik's blue eyes.

'In my lands, MY LANDS!' Erik raged, the sound dampened by the rain as it thrashed the roof above. 'How did this happen?' he growled, turning to face the man who led his rangers.

Uffe stood tall and still as he faced the jarl, his golden eyes glowing in the dim light, adding credibility to his name – *wolf man*. 'My men found footprints in the hills a week or so ago, up near the cabin. They tracked them all the way to King's Leap, but lost them there. They must have doubled back when the rain set in before your sons left. Perhaps they used the creek to hide their tracks. My men never thought to return to the hut to look for another set entering from a different direction. I apologise, my jarl,' Uffe said, dipping his head. He was a short, powerfully built man with tattoos on his forearms depicting *Geri* and *Freki*, Óðinn's wolves, and a thick brown mane down his back to match, tied with a strip of rawhide. Aside from the seax at his belt, he was unarmed, but the danger radiating from the man was palpable. An expert archer, Uffe led the twenty rangers in Erik's hirð. Each man an expert with bows and throwing axes, as well as the hand axes and short seaxs they carried. Most Norsemen spurned bows except for hunting, preferring to fight up close and personal, but Erik had seen their value and formed the small elite band to patrol his borders, open engagements, and protect his flanks in battle. It was under Uffe's tutorship that his sons had learned to use the bow properly, although only Olaf and Bjørn showed any true talent with it.

Erik growled, settling into silence.

Uffe was well used to the jarl's moods, being one of the few men he allowed to bear arms when alone in his presence. He stood patiently as he waited for Erik to speak again, listening to the pattering rain and crackling fire as their songs surrounded him.

'I don't think our new friend has told us everything, yet,' Erik said after a time before standing as he called for Sven.

'Jarl Erik,' Sven answered calmly, his tightly corded muscles and heavy mane of thick red hair gaining definition as he came into the light. Across his back in a leather hoop lay his great Dane axe, the sharpened head gleaming keenly in the flickering light.

'Make him talk. I'm not convinced he's been completely honest with us yet. Give him one day to recover, then go to work. Do whatever you think necessary, short of killing him,' he growled, waving his hands to dismiss the pair. 'And send in my sons on your way out.'

'Jarl Erik,' they said in unison, turning and leaving the hall.

'Your father wants to see you all,' Sven said as he and Uffe left the hall, unconsciously pulling their cloaks tighter against the cold.

'Beware, though; there might be trouble, lads,' Uffe said, flashing his teeth as he punched Sigurd on the shoulder. 'The jarl's mood might just be fiercer than the storm brewing out there,' he added, nodding vaguely in the direction of the writhing seas.

'Shouldn't you two be freezing your balls off in the rain right about now?' Bjørn quipped as he turned towards the door.

'Better walking into the rain than a jarl's wrath.' Sven chuckled as he stepped onto one of the wooden planks that strewed Vágar's streets, keeping their feet from the worst of the muddy mire beneath.

'Boys,' Uffe said, dipping his head briefly before following the red-headed giant into the blackness.

'Jarl's wrath?' Sigurd asked sarcastically, an ironic smile playing on his lips as he pushed open the door. 'Never heard of it.'

They all followed him into the hall, their eyes naturally moving towards their father on his high seat as they adjusted to the light.

'You asked to see us, Father?' Olaf said, assuming the role of oldest as he moved to sit on Erik's right.

'Yes, come, boys, sit,' he said, indicating one of the tables as he moved to join them. 'Hoelun! You can tell them to start bringing the food and ale in when it's ready.'

'Yes, Lord!' came a shout from the darkness.

Bjørn started when he heard her voice, his eyes darting unbidden towards the sound.

The silence was broken by the rustle of chairs and benches as they settled themselves into their seats, drawing their eating knives from their belts as they did so. Erik remained silent for a while, watching his sons as he sipped ale from his goblet. Hoelun came and went twice, delivering heaped boards of bread and meat, with a second thrall bringing flagons of mead and ale to the table. It wasn't until the thralls had come and gone the second time and the table was set that Erik spoke again, stilling their chatter with his goblet as it clattered on the wooden surface.

'You've been busy,' he said, raising his brow. 'It would seem that not only have you helped supply my ships, but you've stopped a would-be assassination in the process.'

His words set their eyes dancing from one another in confusion, trying to make sense of their father's words. None of them could picture Siv as an assassin, from what they'd seen of him.

'First, tell me what happened. The whole story,' their father said, seeing the confusion in their eyes as he reached towards the table with his own knife to skewer a slice of meat.

Each brother told their side of the story, from Bjørn's battle at the cabin to Toke's capture of Siv, as well as the ambush at the fallen tree and the conquest of the boar. It took over an hour for the story to be told in full, and Erik remained silent throughout except to question or clarify certain points. By the time they had finished, everyone had eaten their fill, and the platters lay empty in front of them.

Erik belched quietly in contentment as the story ended before reaching again for his goblet. 'It would appear that our friend here was part of a group of disenfranchised nithings who had it in their minds to kill me in my bed. Something to do with revenge for a raid a few years back. I don't remember it personally, but they do – or did – and felt strongly enough to come for me in my own home, seeking recompense. The polite thing to do would have been to seek *weregild*,' he added, grumbling.

'Are you sure that's all it was?' Olaf asked, his face creased in concern.

'Sven got this much out of him before he passed out. I'm giving young

104

*Half-Hand* a day to recover before he resumes his questioning.'

'Where is Siv now, Father?' Bjørn asked, his expression mirroring Olaf's. 'I would like to speak to him one more time – something makes me feel this was more than simple vengeance.'

'He's being watched over by Gørm. He's begging me to give the man to him entirely. He swears a sacrifice to the gods will ensure our success when we sail. By the time Sven is done with him, death by Gørm will almost be a sweet release from this life, and I'm inclined to believe there is a shred of truth in what he's told us after everything he's already been through.'

'A man will say anything to make the pain stop,' Bjørn replied, meeting his father's eyes. 'I'm not convinced that it was an assassination attempt. Why else would we have been ambushed in an attempt to save the man? The final assassin could have simply made his way to Vágar without his companions.'

For a moment, Erik's eyes raged fire – he wasn't used to his sons disputing his decisions, but the moment passed. Bjørn was young, and the arrogance of youth was fast blooming in his youngest after his recent successes. If he was honest with himself, what he saw didn't displease him and he could see himself in the defiant young man. Under the circumstances, it was hard not to feel proud.

'Maybe' Erik conceded, dipping his head. 'We will see what Sven learns when he goes back to work on him,' Erik added with finality. Bjørn's brow remained furrowed in concern, but he remained silent. *'He knows when to stop,'* he thought, watching his son for a moment longer before turning his vision onto them all as a group.

'You have done well,' Erik continued, focusing on each son in turn. 'You acted quickly and have quite possibly kept me alive a little longer, and for that I thank you. But it has also made me very aware that we have never discussed what would happen in the event of my death. Brothers have gone to war over less than a Jarl's seat, and I would not see my sons – or my home – ripped apart over such a matter. We will decide this here and now, and seal it in blood.'

The four brothers looked to one another, shifting uncertainly from face to face before returning their gaze to their father. None of them had considered the ramifications of their father's death. It had always been assumed that Olaf would become jarl after Erik, but the conversation had never truly been laid bare. The silence stretched on the heels of Erik's words, and he watched their faces quietly, gauging their responses. He noticed how their eyes turned to Olaf more than any other, and the sight warmed his heart.

His sons would not fight his decision. In truth, he felt sure they had always known how it would have to be, but watching their reaction now had helped still his fears. A splinter could kill him just as easily as a sword or spear, and the sobering reality that would-be assassins had managed to enter his territory unnoticed had forced him to open the conversation.

'Should I die, Olaf will sit on the high seat and carry my sword,' he said finally. 'You will see to my burial – be it in the cold earth or the broiling waves – and lead the men of Vágar out into the world each year to build your reputation, and those of your brothers and men.'

Olaf nodded but otherwise remained silent, knowing his father well enough to know there was more to come. The action was mirrored by his brothers.

'Until such a time as your own sons are grown enough to take your place, or your weave cut short in the sword storm, you must name your own successor here and now from amongst your brothers. Whoever you name will name his own, until each of you has a place in the line of succession.'

Olaf eyed each of his brothers in turn, their faces betraying nothing of their emotions. Sigurd was the obvious choice being next in line, but they all knew he had little to no desire to become jarl, preferring to be the man swinging the axe where and when he was told, rather than telling others what to do.

'I name Toke as my successor, provided Sigurd has no objection and would sit in my place, should such a need arise,' Olaf said, fixing his brother with a questioning gaze.

Sigurd lapsed into thoughtful silence for a few moments, his face impassive as he leaned forward with his eating knife and pointed the meat-flecked blade at his younger brother. Images of gold and silver waterfalls flashed briefly behind his eyes, tempting him, but he blinked them away. 'I will support you, Toke, provided I am never put anywhere but the front of your skjaldborg, and at the prow of your ship. Promise me this, and I will support you as Jarl with my blood, sweat and tears, should such a time come.'

'You have it, brother,' Toke said without hesitation, reaching his right hand across the table to grasp his brother's forearm in the warrior's grip. They gripped one another's arm tightly, knowing that a world without Erik and Olaf was both unlikely and a long way away.

'Who do you name, Toke?' Erik asked as his two sons settled back into their seats.

'Bjørn,' Toke replied without hesitation, turning towards the youngest of

Erik's brood. 'In the event of my death, should my son be unborn or too young to claim the high seat, I would ask Bjørn to succeed me.'

Bjørn nodded seriously, knowing the unlikeliness of his ever sitting as Jarl of Vágar. 'I name Sigurd as my successor,' Bjørn said, nodding to his older brother.

'Well, it's good to know I sit somewhere in the hierarchy,' Sigurd grumbled with mock hurt in his voice, lightening the mood.

'Then it is done,' Erik said with a nod, facing each of his sons in turn. 'Before we sail, I will declare it in front of everyone, so they all know who to turn to should I die, and who to follow should they be lost. Before that, though, there is one last thing to do,' he said, drawing a knife from his belt. Pouring mead into a horn, Erik sliced his palm and let a few drops of his blood fall into the ale to mix with the golden brew, before passing both blade and drink to Olaf. He watched as each son copied the action, the knife and horn making their way around the table until they reached Erik again.

'As mead is the drink of the gods, created with the blood of Kvasir, swear on this brew that you will honour the words spoken here tonight, and that you will protect each other always, come what may,' Erik said solemnly, his gaze roving over his sons. Each of them swore their oath while their father watched, mixing the brew with the still bloody knife before, satisfied, he took a drink and passed it to Olaf.

The horn made its way around the brothers, each of them taking a sip of the draught before passing it to the next. When the remaining liquid returned to Erik, he stood and poured what was left over the flames, sending up a cloud of steam that caused the fires to hiss and spit at the intrusion. 'For the gods,' he said, his face briefly disappearing behind the rising cloud. 'Before the lords of Asgard, you have each committed to support and protect one another, and to protect our home, should anything happen to me, or anyone else at this table. This is your oath; do not break it,' he said seriously.

'Yes, Father,' they said in unison.

'Then, my sons, let us toast to the future, and the months we will spend riding the whale road together, seeking adventure and riches!' Erik said, his voice booming through the hall to shatter the solemn spell that had fallen over their small band.

'The whale road,' they all shouted in unison, raising their horns before tipping them back. For some of them, it was the last thing they remembered come the dawn.

# Chapter 7

It took another four weeks before the seas had calmed and the weather warmed enough to launch the ships. Every waking moment was spent finishing preparations, and by the time the ships were pushed into the gentle waves, they all but gleamed in the spring sunshine. The sight made Bjørn's heart race with excitement as he watched them rest on their moorings, patiently waiting. All three ships had newly woven sails and were freshly painted, with snarling prow beasts ready to be mounted so they could lead the way through the waves.

One hundred and forty-eight men had answered Erik's call, eager to sail the whale road and seek fame and wealth on distant shores. Another fifty-nine would stay behind under the watchful eye of Leif Geirsson to protect Vágar from ambitious neighbours and opportunistic raiders, not including the greybeards who had long since retired from the sea, and the young men not yet into their first beards. No one wanted to stay behind to protect the town, but for those that did, Erik always gave almost a quarter of the plunder, to be divided amongst them as Leif saw fit. The chances of Vágar being attacked in their absence were low, but Erik was a cautious man when it came to hearth and home.

The only thing left to do was for the men to bring their sea chests aboard, the valuable containers doubling as both personal storage and their rowing benches. For many of the young and inexperienced bóndi – the farm boys and young men of Vágar – their chests were mostly empty apart from clothes and essentials. Bjørn could well imagine the plunder and wealth they hoped to bring home with them that had inspired them to answer Erik's call. He felt it himself.

Arleigh watched the preparations with quiet anxiety. This would be the sixteenth time she had watched Erik sail away since coming to the North; but the first time she would watch her son sail with him. Possibly the last time. Her emotions were complicated when it came to Erik. She'd hated him at first, for the pain he and his men had caused her, and the upheaval they'd wrought in her life. A small part of her still did. No man could ever replace the hold

Torr had had on her. Even now, sixteen years later, she could still hear his voice whispering sweet nothings to her under their thatch roof in Shorewitchshire. But at the same time, she couldn't deny that Erik had been good to her, and that parts of her life were better than they ever could have been in Britain. More importantly, Erik had made her son into the powerful young man she watched now, moving easily and confidently amongst the crews as he joked and laughed with them. Because of Erik, Bjørn had a bright future ahead of him, full of more adventure, authority and influence than he ever would have known in Shorewitchshire. She had begged Erik in private to give her son a brynja as well as the shield when the time came to sail, but his answer had been the same as he gave Turid when Olaf had first joined the fleet: 'My boys will receive no special favours. They will earn their iron just as they had to earn their place in the wall. Let them capture it in war, or buy it in trade.' So, she had turned instead to Yngvar, seeking his help in keeping Bjørn safe. She knew the deep affection the man held for her son, and used that to her advantage. It had taken only four weeks for Yngvar to return to her with the piece, accepting only her simplest brooch in payment. Now, she held a simple but effective jerkin of hardened leather with overlapping iron plates sewn to the chest and back. The garment was lighter than a full iron brynja, but Yngvar had promised it was almost as good as the valuable iron-ringed shirts, and would keep Bjørn safe until he could find one of his own. It was the best she could do. She prayed it was enough.

She watched as her son turned and began walking towards her, an excited smile on his face as he tied his long hair back. While everyone blamed her English heritage for his difference in appearance, all she could see was Torr at sixteen, with broad shoulders, olive skin and a smile warm enough to melt ice. As her son stood out amongst the Northmen, so too had her husband amongst their own people.

'We sail tomorrow!' Bjørn said excitedly as he reached her, switching easily to English. 'I'm to sail with Yngvar in *Sleipnir,*' he added with pride.

'So I've heard,' she said, smiling despite herself as his excitement broke through her fears. 'I have something for you.'

'What more could I need?' He smiled, patting the sword at his hip with obvious pride.

'Something to bring you home to me again. Don't kid yourself, Bjørn Eriksson; war is a bloody business and many of the men who sail with you will die along the way. I have seen it and I know battle for what it truly is. Once the men are done swinging their swords and axes in their quest for glory and fame, mothers and women are left behind to bury and mourn our husbands and sons.'

Bjørn remained silent. He knew his mother had been married before his father brought her to the North – to a blacksmith, from what she'd told him. She rarely spoke of him, and never when Erik was around. From what he had pieced together, her husband had died in the same raid that had brought her to Erik.

'I know,' he said, his tone serious.

'I just want to see you home again,' she said, fighting to control her rising emotions. 'I asked Yngvar to make this for you' she said, forcing calm into her voice as she handed over the armour in its protective covering of oiled wool. She watched as he carefully removed the covering, handing it to her to keep it free of the mud at their feet.

'Mother, it's…I've never seen anything like it,' he said, holding it in front of him to examine it more closely. 'It weighs nothing?'

'Yngvar assures me that it will at least turn a dagger blow aside, and go some way towards bringing you back to me. He also gave me these,' she added, handing him a second package.

Bjørn quickly slipped his arms through the armholes and shrugged his shoulders to settle it into place. It fit like a second skin and he smiled at his mother as he became familiar with the weight. When closed, the armour would protect him from neck to waist. Opening the second, smaller package, he found five more of the iron plates, already riveted to hardened leather strips.

'You know how to sew,' she said when he looked up. 'The iron is strong, but the threads holding it is less so. A heavy impact, or even a strong yank could see them ripped off and lost. These are your replacements should that happen. It would be even stronger with a brynja worn beneath it…' she finished, trailing off as she cast her gaze over her son.

Bjørn smiled, looking up from the iron plates into his mother's eyes. 'A mother will always worry about her child,' he said, repeating the words that had accompanied every bruise and cut he had gained as he learned the warrior's craft.

'A mother will always worry about her child,' she repeated with a sigh, embracing him. 'Come back to me,' she whispered, savouring the precious moment together. The mayhem of the wharves continued unhindered, swelling past them like waves around rocks. Briefly, the story of Moses flashed

110

through her mind. Everywhere people were busy loading final supplies onto the ships and stowing their sea chests. Above them, the sky was dark with gulls as they swooped and shrieked at the activity, seeking the unguarded barrels of smoked fish or scraps of bread that had been lost in the chaos.

'I will,' he whispered, squeezing her tight. 'I promise.'

'The people are demanding blood, Jarl Erik,' Gørm said for what felt like the hundredth time. 'Their Jarl was at risk of assassination, a death that would deny you a seat in Valhöll!'

Despite their best efforts, news of the plot had gotten out, spreading through Vágar like wildfire. As truth became rumour, the story grew to include Erik's planned punishment of the captive: a sacrifice to the gods to win their favour in the coming months. Now, sitting in the dim light of the great hall, Erik sat and discussed the fate of the prisoner with his goði. They were alone but for a few of Erik's closest warriors and the fire burning in the hearth, with only the occasional thrall appearing to tend and stoke the flames or refill empty drinking vessels.

'I know, Gørm. But I will not change my mind simply because people want blood. You can kill the man, fine, but there is no need for a blood eagle. Such an act is reserved for the most heinous of crimes, and attempted assassination or not, the man was seeking vengeance, as was his right. He failed; it is enough.'

'Failure or not, the eagle will send a stronger message to others who would seek revenge than mere death. Your sons mentioned a sixth man who escaped into the forests, not to mention the favour you would earn from the gods,' he added, licking his lips hungrily.

Erik grunted, the sound deep in the back of his throat before he spat into the fire. 'It seems to me that the gods already favour us, having stopped the plot before it could start. Wouldn't you say?'

'Perhaps,' Gørm conceded. 'But if that is the case, shouldn't we thank them for their favour, and repay their kindness? You are about to leave your home, your high seat, and your people for months, perhaps even years – you cannot afford to spurn the gods at a time such as this!'

The goði's voice had grown in both volume and depth as he spoke until it seemed to be controlled by someone else altogether. As the final echo disappeared, the fire cracked and blossomed in an explosion of sparks, as a log split amongst the flames. Erik recognised the familiar feelings of admiration and disgust as he watched the man. Never had he met someone more in love with blood, or more devoted to the gods, than Gørm, and he had to admit that the man's devotion had benefited his own rule over the years. He was already feeling the pressure from his wife and Arleigh about taking all four of his sons with him. Perhaps such a sacrifice would help to put their minds at ease... that alone would be worth it.

'All right, Gørm,' Erik said at length, sighing. 'You can have the prisoner for your sacrifice. But it must be done tonight, so as not to interfere with our departure, and once the man is dead, that will be the end of it. Give his body to the fjord, and we will sail with the tide, leaving his blood to paint our sterns as we go.'

'As you command, Jarl Erik,' Gørm replied, dipping his head. 'Tonight, we will honour the Æsir, and tomorrow you will sail to foreign shores, war, and plunder.'

Gørm nodded excitedly, his fingers dancing over the omnipresent knife at his belt, seemingly oblivious to those around him.

'Tonight, Gørm,' Erik said, standing. 'And I will speak before you start. I have words to share with our people.'

'Jarl Erik.' Gørm nodded, his attention returning to the present as he bowed and turned to leave.

Erik watched the goði leave the hall, his black cloak flowing around him like the souls of Helheim. Despite the years he had known Gørm, the man still made his skin crawl through his sheer other-world-ness. His faith in the Allfather was complete, but Gørm's seemed to be on a whole 'nother level, as if the gods walked a step behind him, whispering in his ear. Shivering to himself, he reached for his sword belt. Darkness was still a few hours away, and he was already missing the softness of a woman's body. As much as he loved raiding, the lack of female company was something he missed keenly, and he felt himself grow excited as he imagined Arleigh's naked body alongside his own.

'*There are benefits to being jarl,*' he mused as he turned and headed for the back of the hall where his private apartments were. He knew he would find one of his women there, and he grinned happily at the thought.

\*\*\*

No one dared to speak while they waited for Erik to begin, the silence only broken by the hoot of an owl as it took flight and began hunting, and the gentle lapping of the tide. Erik stood dressed for war in his burnished brynja, the golden rings catching the light and standing proudly amongst their dull iron-grey counterparts. His raven helm sat atop his head and at his waist sat *Freki*, the new sword Yngvar had crafted for him. The blade was similarly designed to Huginn, although slightly longer and decorated in gold, as befitted a warrior and jarl of his stature. Flanked by both Yngvar and Sven, equally dressed for war, Erik looked every part the war god he was. For the first time, he was joined by all four of his sons, standing to his right with their own arms and armour gleaming in the flickering light.

Around them, the people of Vágar stood silently as they waited for their jarl to speak. From the iron-clad húskarlar and hirðsmen who dominated the front ranks, to the more lightly armed bóndi mingled with the townsfolk and craftsmen who would remain behind. Everyone was waiting for Erik. Only the half-naked figure kneeling in the middle of the clearing with his arms chained to posts dug into the earth could distract them, and the goði who stood behind like an avenging valkyrie.

'People of Vágar,' Erik boomed at last, lifting his helmet from his head as he spoke. 'Before you kneels Siv *Half-Hand*, who was captured by my sons in the forest behind King's Leap. Our *friend* here is the last but one of a group of would-be assassins who thought to kill me for a raid committed many years ago. My sons thought otherwise. Between them, they killed all but two of the killers. One sits before you now, while the other is even now hunted by Uffe's rangers. Through their actions, my thread remains uncut. Toke, Bjørn; step forward.'

Doing as instructed, Erik's two youngest sons took a step forward from Sigurd and Olaf, their faces impassive.

'If it wasn't for the quick thinking of Toke and Bjørn, there is a very real chance that men would right now be searching for the bodies of my sons. Instead, my youngest has been blooded, and I have been kept in Miðgarðr a little longer. In recognition of this, my sons will take home one tenth of the plunder we take in the raids this year, which they will divide between themselves. The rest will be distributed amongst those who sail with us, and those who remain to protect our homes and women. Does anyone question my decision? If so, you may speak without repercussion.'

There was a brief murmuring amongst the crowd, but after a while it died away to nothing. The people knew Erik to be generous and just, they would all end the season with wealth, regardless of how much went to his own brood.

'Very well,' he nodded, motioning for Bjørn and Toke to step back. 'Our goði has suggested we offer a sacrifice to the gods, both to thank them for my deliverance, and to beg their favour a little while longer. I agree. Gørm Goði will offer the ultimate sacrifice to our gods, and ensure smooth waters and wealthy targets when we set sail… for England!'

The people cheered at this. The lands of Britain had hardly been visited in recent years, as far as they knew, and were scantily guarded, offering easy wealth and little risk for a fleet of vikingr.

'Gørm Goði, Siv *Half-Hand* is yours,' Erik shouted above the noise, raising yet another cheer from his people. Off to the left, ten men began to beat drums in a slow rhythm, the sound drowning out and silencing the crowd. As the deepening rumble grew, Gørm began to walk, his black cloak swirling around him like smoke as he moved around the torch-lit square.

'Óðinn, Allfather, hear our prayers,' he began, his gravelly voice piercing easily through the beating of the drums. 'Accept this sacrifice and keep our warriors safe. Bring them wealth and success, and return them to us in victory, leaving only blood and death behind in your honour. *Njörd*, lord of the sea, carry our men across your domain, over *Ran's* writhing daughters and under Thor's lightning-ripped skies to the lands of Britain and back again. Bring them home with holds of gleaming metal and decks loaded with healthy thralls, fat and ready for market. Bring them home with stories of war and brotherhood, of trial and combat. Lords of Asgard, guard our warriors from deaths of straw and instead promise them a seat in the Allfather's corpse hall, should their thread be cut…'

Bjørn watched as Gørm worked himself into a fervour, drawing the small hand axe from his belt as he walked. As he moved around Siv's prone body, the bones and skulls that decorated his hair rattled together, adding to the seiðr that was beginning to surround the watchers. To his credit, Siv remained silent, his fear forgotten as he fixed the goði with a look of pure hatred. Beside him, a thrall bent to place a wooden bowl and pine bough below Siv's body, ready to collect his life's blood. Even then he stayed strong, his eyes straying from Gørm only long enough for him to spit on the unfortunate slave. It was only when Gørm finished speaking and pointed the axe straight at him that Siv cracked and his fear returned, his bladder releasing to darken the earth beneath him. None laughed at the moment of weakness, enthralled as they were by the seiðr that surrounded them. They could only watch as the goði moved to stand behind Siv, his movements wolf-like as he prepared to strike.

'Allfather! Accept our sacrifice,' Gørm cried, his voice guttural as he bent down and grasped Siv's shoulder tightly in his left hand, while his right raised the axe to the sky. Bjørn forced himself to watch as the blade came down. The dull impact of the blade biting into Siv's back was barely audible over the drums, and he watched as the sharpened metal broke the connection between rib and spine. Again and again Gørm struck, drawing spurts of red from Siv's broken back to paint his face and hands as he went about his bloody work.

Siv broke with the first strike, the pain so severe that it took away his ability to scream as his face twisted into a permanent grimace somewhere between agony and terror as he writhed and shook, trying to escape the relentless axe. Bjørn watched with his brothers as Gørm brought the blade down for the final time before sinking the blooded blade into the pole above Siv's missing hand. He winced as Gørm pushed the ribs aside before reaching in and pulling out Siv's lungs, inverting them to rest on his heaving shoulders.

In apparent ecstasy, Gørm turned his face to the sky and bellowed his lungs out, the cries piercing the still night. 'Óðinn!' he screamed, holding his arms out wide as if it would help carry his voice all the way to Asgard. In the distance, a sharp white light flashed as a storm built behind the hills, followed a few moments later by the strike of Thor's hammer. Silence followed the crash, the spell only broken by Gørm as he again shouted to the sky. 'Thor answers on the Allfather's behalf! He has accepted our sacrifice!'

Everyone's attention switched back to the ruined figure in the centre of the gathering as he struggled to breathe, his exposed lungs slowly suffocating him. Beside him, Gørm had collected the bowl, now red with Siv's blood and was moving through the crowd, flicking the grisly liquid over the onlookers with his pine-needle brush. Bjørn blinked when it was his turn. He could feel the spots of blood as they coated his face and he fought the impulse to wipe it away. It wouldn't do to offend the Allfather.

When he turned his attention back to Siv, he found himself staring into the man's eerily wide, bloodshot eyes. The wretched remains of Siv began to speak when their eyes met, each whispered word escaping his chapped lips with a gasp of pain: 'I... cu... curse... you... you and ev... everything you hold... you hold dear... from... from now until... until it is rippe... ripped from your hands...' Everyone watched as Siv fought for more air. Overhead, the skies flashed with lightening, as if in response to the curse. Bjørn stood and stared at the broken body, noting the slight tremors in his arms. He couldn't believe the man was still breathing, that he was clinging so desperately to life.

Overhead another lightning strike lit the sky, this one closer than the last, and Bjørn felt the first drops of rain began to fall, gently striking the muddy ground where they began washing away the blood surrounding Siv. As the thunder struck, Bjørn watched the man's bloodshot eyes open once more and fix him with a look of pure hatred.

'May you never reach Valhöll, Bjørn Eriksson,' he said with venom, his anger giving him a final burst of strength. On impulse, Bjørn drew the axe from his belt and crossed the ground towards Siv, placing the weapon's haft in his one remaining hand before driving his knife up through his chin, breaking the strange seiðr that had infected him. The remaining onlookers gasped as Bjørn withdrew his knife, but before anyone could speak the sky was ripped asunder by another flash of lightning. With it came the rain, lashing down on the onlookers with a vengeance and sending many to their homes. Within moments, the ground they had been standing on became a mire of mud as Siv's lifeless body was cleaned by the howling storm.

'May you find Valhöll,' Bjørn whispered as he reclaimed his axe. He couldn't help but admire Siv's strength, at the end.

'The Allfather is pleased by the actions of his loyal son, Bjørn Eriksson, and sends a storm to flatten the path ahead of our ships!' Gørm screamed into the pouring rain, his words whipped away by the growing howl of the wind as the crowd ran for shelter. The last thing Bjørn saw before returning to Erik's hall was Gørm kneeling before the prone figure of Siv, painting his face with the blood-soaked mud, his face twisted into one of demonic fanaticism.

\*\*\*

It took three days for the storm to blow itself out. The wind and rain lashed Vágar with a fury unseen through the winter months, confining the crews to land. Few people ventured out into the pouring rain to face Thor's wrath as he beat his anvil above their heads. Erik and his sons spent the time sharpening blades and burnishing armour. Leather was waxed and waterproofed and blades were oiled to make them ready for the journey ahead. The evenings were spent feasting and drinking with Erik's húskarlar, or playing hnefatafl. Erik and Yngvar played game after game on Erik's ornate board while the rest played on simpler sets, made from patterned leather and coloured stones or shaped wood and bone. A few even had glass pieces. They played for both fun and wagers, and by the time the storm had spent itself Bjørn had won a small horde of hacksilver and trinkets from Erik's warriors, and his brothers. He had even managed to best Erik himself, winning dark looks and a whale bone comb for his efforts. Yngvar however remained unbeaten and claimed the Mjölnir necklace Bjørn had looted at the clearing, after winning three straight games in a row. No one beat Yngvar.

'Patience, Bjørn. Hnefatafl is all about patience. I never beat you; you simply lose,' Yngvar said as he sat across from him, calmly watching the board between them while he sipped from an ale horn. After his defeat the day before, Bjørn wanted to win back the necklace, and had wagered half his winnings against it. Both knew that the wager was grossly unequal in Yngvar's favour, but neither mentioned it.

'I have patience, but it feels unbalanced against your Loki cunning,' he grunted.

'Anyone can win, Bjørn. Pay attention,' the older man replied, leaning forward to move another of his pieces, capturing one of Bjørn's in the process and adding it to the slowly growing pile. Without even moving his king, Bjørn had already lost three of his guards. Overhead, Thor struck again as if to emphasise the loss. Sigurd and Olaf were playing further down the table, while Toke nursed a horn of mead by the fire and lovingly sharpened his axe. Slowly, he moved another piece forward to capture one of the offending attackers, creating an opening for his king in the process. Without apparent thought, Yngvar leaned forward and moved a piece on the opposite side of the board, taking yet another defender from Bjørn.

'Try to think three or even four moves ahead, Bjørn. Not just one or two. Tafl is just like war and will be decided by the game in its totality, rather than the flickering moments of greatness in between.'

'Gnn,' Bjørn grunted, again watching the board and trying to read Yngvar's next moves. Already his warband was down to just eight warriors and his king, while Yngvar still commanded twenty-three of his twenty-four attackers.

'A smaller force can beat a larger one. Focus.'

Exhaling, Bjørn moved one of his *northern* defenders – those closest to Yngvar – forward to block the attackers, trying to draw attention away from the *Eastern* opening he had created for his king.

Quick as a snake, Yngvar moved into the *western flank*, preparing to capture another of Bjørn's beleaguered warriors. Again, Bjørn focused on the North, capturing his second piece.

Yngvar attacked the west again, removing another piece from the board.

With only seven men remaining, Bjørn adjusted his tactics and moved one of his *southern* pieces, moving towards Yngvar's so far untouched flank. Ignoring the move, Yngvar attacked west again, boxing in another attacker. The game continued in this vein for some time, with Bjørn moving into all sides of the board except for the *east*, using his moves to draw Yngvar's pieces away. When the time was right, he shifted tactics and moved his king east, reinforcing one of the defenders and capturing another piece in the process. Looking up, the slightest of smiles began to appear on his opponent's face as he moved a piece north to block the king's escape.

'Nice try, Bjørn,' Yngvar smiled.

Bjørn grunted, wearing a look of concern as he focused on the board, making Yngvar's grin grow even wider.

Putting his hand on the king, he looked up at Yngvar and smiled, slowly moving the king south into the corner of the board, and off the table, completing his escape and ending the game. Overhead, Thor struck his anvil once more, although from further away this time.

'Thank you,' he said with a smile, reaching across the table to claim back the necklace and drop it over his head. Yngvar remained still, watching the board as he replayed the final moves.

'Game,' he finally agreed, reaching across to grasp Bjørn's shoulder. 'Well done, lad, well done.' He winked, standing as he did to move towards Erik. 'I feel the storm is beginning to move away,' he said, settling next to him to watch his game with Sven.

Erik looked up from his own game briefly after capturing one of the giant's defenders. 'Perhaps,' he mused, turning his attention back to the board. 'But perhaps not.' Erik chuckled, moving another piece forward to surround and capture Sven's king completely, winning the game.

'I would have had you this time,' Sven growled as he reached into his beard to pull free one of the runed silver rings. 'If Yngvar hadn't distracted me.'

'Hmnnn,' Erik hummed happily, holding his hand up to block the wager from being passed over. 'Keep it, my friend. Next time I'll take two,' he said with a small laugh as he turned to face Yngvar. 'You may be right,' Erik said, looking up towards the roof and listening to the sounds of thunder and lightning as they moved away.

'Clearly my youngest pissed someone off when he decided to sheath his blade in our friend out there.'

'No… I think it is just the winter blowing itself out and preparing the winds for our sails. If anything, it is probably a good omen,' Yngvar said through a mouthful of stew.

'Gnn. Either way, I think you're right. Sven, I want you and Yngvar to muster the men first thing tomorrow and have the ships fully loaded and ready to go by first light the following day. It is time to leave.'

'Yes, Jarl Erik,' they said in unison as they moved away.

'And for everyone else enjoying the heat and comforts of my hall,' Erik boomed, his smile growing as he strode towards his high seat. 'Tomorrow, we will feast! Go now and prepare yourselves for our journey before returning here with the going down of the sun for a final night of food, revelry and women, if you're lucky! I myself will not be shy when it comes to seeking female company before spending weeks at sea with the likes of you!' he yelled.

Around the hall, men laughed and cheered as they raised their drinking horns before emptying them in giant gulps. Most of them made their way unsteadily out of the hall after Yngvar and Sven to make their own preparations. Those who didn't were either asleep or not far off.

'Turid, Arleigh! Tomorrow we feast! See to it that the thralls are ready!'

'Yes, Erik,' came the muted replies from the back of the hall.

Bjørn watched as his father settled on the great seat to watch as the cream of his men left his hall and walked into the dying storm. Half-blood or no, he felt nothing but pride when he looked at the warrior-jarl that was his father, and the power that he wore so easily.

'More ale here,' Erik shouted from his seat as he watched his men funnel out. Sigurd and Olaf were still locked in their game, neither willing to take any unnecessary risks, while Toke made the finishing strokes with his whetstone.

*'I don't think anyone will mind if I were to follow Father's advice a little early…'* Bjørn mused, already imagining Hoelun's shapely behind as he made his way towards the back of the hall, and the warmth waiting for him beyond.

# Chapter 8

Everywhere was chaos. Nothing had prepared Bjørn for the cacophony of sounds and sights that accompanied his father's fleet setting sail. Every year since he had been able to walk, he had watched his father sail away with the tide, off for adventure and glory while he stayed behind and learned the warrior crafts. Now, for the first time in his life, he was on the inside. He held an oar on *Sleipnir*'s starboard side and would sail under Yngvar's command. Sigurd and Olaf sailed with their father in *Fjord Ulf*, and Toke would sail on *Fjord Uxi*, under Halfdan's command.

Organised mayhem flowed around him as men secured their sea chests and loaded final supplies, teasing and boasting with easy confidence, or assumed bravado. Bjørn looked down at his own chest, a final gift from his father. It was nothing extravagant, a simple construction of oak and pine, with iron hinges and a *valknut* design engraved above the latch.

'I had this made not long after you were born,' Erik had said the previous night, handing it to his youngest son with an expression of pride and concern. 'If you look after the chest, it will look after you. Never put anything in here that you couldn't do without.'

Opening it later that night, he had found oiled sheep skins and sacking to protect his armour and weapons from the iron rot that infected war gear at sea. Lovingly, he had stowed his equipment, adding his embossed leather hnefatafl board and game pieces, his winnings from the previous few nights' gaming including the whale bone comb, two woollen cloaks, and some clothes. '*Only what I need; nothing more, nothing less,*' he whispered under his breath as he draped a sheepskin over the chest and tied it down to provide some cushioning for his backside. He could feel the excitement growing around him as the final preparations were made. Sails were secured and oars holes opened, and while warriors made final checks to their equipment or called out to friends, their children cried and women cheered as they held back tears. For some, it would be the last time they saw their loved ones. Standing amongst the crowd, Bjørn spied the three *úlfheðnar* warriors waiting impassively in their wolf skins. Bjørn couldn't help but compare them to islands in a storm as the rush of humanity swarmed around them. They had arrived the evening before in a small faering and their leader, a blue-eyed warrior called Hrolf, had sought passage to England with Erik and his men in exchange for a hefty sum of silver. All they'd asked for was a place to lay their heads until they reached land, so they could continue their journey to Dubh-Linn, and from there to Valhöll. Erik had accepted their offer and given them berths aboard *Fjord Ulf*, enjoying the irony. Looking at them now, Bjørn couldn't help but shiver at the mercilessness in their eyes, shadowed by the wolf-heads of their cloaks as they sat snarling atop their heads. It was with relief that he switched his gaze to find his mother amongst the crowd, standing on the beach slightly apart from the rest. Climbing back onto the wharf, he made his way along the seasoned timber towards her, barely keeping his excitement in check. For all her worrying and fear for him, he could see that his excitement was breaking through her defences as he drew nearer.

'And so we're off!' he said as he approached.

'And so you're off,' she agreed, smiling as she fought back her tears. For a moment she just embraced him, holding him tight as if the world would end if she let go. He held her back, savouring the moment. He wasn't so naïve that he thought his return was guaranteed. He knew all too well that a splinter or rogue wave could kill him just as easily as a sword or spear. The whale road was no place for weakness.

'Bjørn, be careful. What you're sailing for is nothing like what you've seen so far. Not even your successes at the hunting cabin will have prepared you for what's to come. You will experience death and destruction on a level unlike anything you can imagine. The glory comes after, but the action itself... the action is anything but glorious.'

'I promise,' he whispered, holding her close.

'Bjørn, before you go, there is something I must tell you. Something about your...something you need to know.'

Letting go, he looked down at his mother and waited patiently, ignoring the sounds around him. He could see the struggle on her face, and the concern in her eyes.

'Tell me,' he said, raising a questioning eyebrow.

Taking a deep breath to calm herself, Arleigh blinked away her tears and looked into her son's eyes. 'You know how I came to be here, Bjørn. That your father, Erik... that he saved me from his own men the year you were born, in a village called Shorewitchshire. There was a raid, and everyone was either captured and sold into slavery, or killed defending the village…'

Bjørn watched his mother struggle through her story, her voice breaking on the last sentence as her hand grasped the White Christ symbol she wore at her neck. Taking a deep breath, she began again. 'Your father was o…'

'Quiet down! Quiet down! Shut up, the lot of you!'

Erik's voice cut through anything Arleigh had been about to say like a knife through skyr, silencing everyone almost instantly. Bjørn saw his mother shrink as she swallowed whatever she had been building herself up to say, resigning herself to a lost moment.

He took her hand and squeezed gently, smiling as he felt her return the gesture while she wiped away her tears.

Overhead, even the gulls seemed to hang in silence for a few moments as they waited for the jarl to speak before they returned to their swooping and cawing, oblivious to the crowd below.

'Sixteen years ago, we raided a village in Essex. Since that time, those lands have lain untouched by our blades, its women and its gold hidden from my warriors, and kept free from our ships. Today, we sail for those long untouched islands, and the treasures they have kept safe for us all these years!'

The result was instant. Men began shouting and cheering, and those who hadn't yet stowed their weapons began beating them on shields, creating a din that would have woken the Æsir. More than a few of the watching gulls flew higher in surprise to escape the sudden noise, their cries adding to the cacophony of sound. Bjørn added his own voice to the chorus, raising his closed fist in excitement as he was caught up in the moment.

Unseen by his excited eyes, Arleigh fought to hold back her tears as memories of Torr and her old life came flooding back, returning as clearly as if it was yesterday. It was all she could do to stop herself from crying out loud.

'For too long, the English have guarded our gold and our silver! I think it is time we relieve them of the burden!'

The volume rose still higher as Erik stood tall on the abandoned barrel he was using as a podium, his sword held high as he cheered with his people.

'To the ships!' he shouted, jumping down with an agility that belied his size. 'Fix the prow beasts and release the dragons; it's time for them to fly!'

The men needed no further encouragement. Like a wave crashing on the tide, men ran for the ships, stowing final pieces of equipment and saying final hurried farewells before settling themselves for the voyage to come. At the prow of each ship, men stood with pride as they were given the honour of fixing the snarling beasts on the prow that would lead them across the seas towards English shores.

'Bjørn!' Arleigh shouted, struggling to be heard above the din. She watched as he turned and embraced her a final time, smiling down at her with those green eyes that were so achingly similar to her beloved Torr's. A hurried 'come back to me' was all she could manage before he released her and made his way towards the shore, and his seat aboard *Sleipnir*. She watched as he jumped over the gunwale and found his seat before taking up his oar.

*'Bring him back to me, O Lord. Bring him home safe and unharmed. Forgive him the sins he will commit, for he knows not what he does, nor who he is. Forgive him, and bring him back to me,'* she silently prayed, holding the silver cross tight to her, picturing Torr as she did so, and the sacrifice he made to see her safe. *'Forgive me, my love,'* she silently wept, before turning and making her way back to the now empty hall. Behind her, Erik's ships were already in the fjord, rowing towards open seas, and war.

'Oars in, lads,' Yngvar called from the helm. His voice carried easily over the calm water, echoed by Erik and Halfdan as they stood at the helms of their own ships.

Gratefully, Bjørn pulled in his length of pine. They'd only been under oar for a few hours and already his hands were blistered and raw. No matter how much time he had spent learning to sail the smaller faerings in the fjords around Vágar, nothing had prepared him for the labour of pulling an oar on a fully crewed snekkja for hours.

'Hold them over the edge,' Bjarni said, eyeing Bjørn's blistered hands. The older man was a veteran of several raids, and had crewed *Sleipnir* since his first summer on the whale road. It was often said that the quietly spoken warrior was as much a part of the ship as the horse-shaped prow. 'The salt water will sting like the ice of Hel, but it will dry the wounds and help them to heal,' he said, turning his attention back to his own oar and storing it properly.

Around them, seasoned warriors were busy readying the sheets that would raise the sail while others worked to unfurl the valuable red-and-white dyed wool that would harvest the wind. Leaning over the side, Bjørn dipped his oozing hands into the clear blue water, gritting his teeth against the sting. He wouldn't let the older men see any weakness. He might have earned his oar, and killed men in battle, but he was still a boy to those who had sailed *Sleipnir* together for years. He had to earn his place amongst them.

123

'Bjørn! Get your arse back here,' Yngvar yelled from the helm, his arm wrapped over the tiller to keep them on course. Behind them, he could see *Fjord Uxi* following in their wake, while *Fjord Ulf* led the pack on their starboard side, her bows sending great spumes of spray skyward as she sliced through the waves. Bjørn's place was in the middle of the ship, close to the mast. Over the days and weeks at sea he would learn how to handle the rippling sail as well as his oar, but for now the crew seemed content to let him find his sea legs, along with the rest of the younger warriors. Moving down the ship, he stepped over and around the men as those not working the sail relaxed on the deck, their time at the oars behind them for now. Some had pulled tafl boards from their chests and were beginning to gamble, while others mended holes in clothes or took knives to wood and bone.

'Yngvar,' he said with a nod when he reached the tiller.

'Take the helm, lad,' the older man said, proffering the great beam of wood that guaranteed all their safety. For a moment, Bjørn felt nothing but apprehension. 'Take it, Bjørn,' Yngvar said again, lowering his voice. 'You're the jarl's son. These men have sworn an oath to your father, and that oath extends to you. They will fight and die to keep you safe and see you home again; but they need to see what you're made of. Take the helm.' he repeated.

Taking a deep breath, Bjørn moved around to stand behind Yngvar and wrapped his right arm over the tiller. As soon as the older man stepped aside and relinquished his grip, he felt the power of the ship, and understood the strength needed to control her as they navigated the waves. He found himself again appreciating Yngvar's surprising strength. A few of the men looked up in mild surprise before going back to whatever it was they were doing. They trusted Yngvar's judgement.

'You hold the helm, Bjørn. From now until I take it back, the lives of all these men are in your hands. Now, as in battle, the decisions you make will have consequences beyond yourself – this is the price of privilege. See Red Orm there, standing to midships? He is the relay between you and the lookout at the prow; your life line. The man at the prow will call out any dangers to the fore, and old Orm there will relay them back to you.'

Bjørn nodded as he adjusted his grip on the tiller while he focused ahead, his eyes switching between what he could see, and Red Orm.

'Before we reach the open sea, and England, we must first cross *Moskstraumen*, the great tidal eddy that marks the entrance to Njörd's hall beneath the waves. Any sailor who lacks the skill and courage to cross that

124

stretch of ocean faces eternity with the sea-king. We'll be there before the end of the day tomorrow,' Yngvar said before sitting down against the gunwale behind Bjørn and closing his eyes. 'Just keep her straight, lad,' he said as Bjørn opened his mouth to speak. 'Keep her straight and listen to Red Orm.'

'Aye,' Bjørn muttered, turning his attention to steering. He could see his father's ship effortlessly cutting through the waves as the wind filled her sail and pushed her relentlessly forwards. The smaller *Sleipnir* and *Fjord Uxi* spent more time climbing over waves than slicing through them, but Bjørn quickly found he enjoyed the feeling of rising and falling with the swell. He knew without a shadow of a doubt that the sea was where he belonged.

The day passed without event, and Bjørn held the tiller for much of it, making occasional adjustments when Red Orm yelled back instructions. At one point, they were joined by a pod of orca, the giant black-and-white whales easily keeping pace with the ships as they played in the wakes before leaving them again to dive down to the depths. Above them, the sky was blue and clear, while the wind pushing them forwards carried the promise of fine weather and smooth seas for at least another day.

As the sun began its dip towards the horizon, with *Skoll* close on the great orb's heels, Yngvar stood and moved to stand beside Bjørn again.

'Well done. Now get back to your chest and rest up for a while. We'll be beaching the ships soon. There's an uninhabited island a few rôst ahead.'

Nodding his agreement, Bjørn relinquished the steering oar and made his way back down the ship to his chest, moving in time with the ship as she danced across the waves.

'Here,' Bjarni said as he sat down, passing him two strips of linen. 'Dip them in the water and then wrap them around your hands. It should help them to heal and stop new ones from opening. We'll be back on the oars in a little while.'

'Thank you,' Bjørn said, leaning over to do as Bjarni suggested. Looking around, he noticed that many of the men were sleeping and he quickly followed their lead. Laying out a sheep skin, he leaned back against the curved hull by his chest and began to doze, enjoying the sound of rushing water as it moved past the oak planks by his head, lulling him to sleep.

'Oars out! Lower the sail!' Yngvar boomed from the helm, his words transforming the ship from calm to chaos in seconds. Fumbling the wooden seal that holed up the oar port when under sail, Bjørn ran his length pine through the hole and held it ready, the blade skimming above the waterline as others followed suit. '*At least I wasn't last,*' Bjørn mused as he watched a few of the younger men manoeuvre their own oars into place.

'On my mark,' Yngvar's voice boomed again, his vision flitting between the crew and the sail. 'Three… two… one… pull!' he shouted.

Like an arrow, *Sleipnir* leapt forward as the men pulled their oars in time to Red Orm's cries of 'pull… pull… pull.' Stealing a glance to his left, Bjørn caught sight of his father's ship pulling away in the distance, all sixty oars moving in unison. He winced as his raw hands began to rub against their bandages. To his right, Bjarni pulled his oar relentlessly, sweat mingling with the ocean spray as *Sleipnir* charged over and through the waves.

'Come on! Pull! Not much longer now!' Yngvar called again. 'Row… row… row,' he chanted in time with Red Orm, their cries coming in unison as they sought to give a final burst of energy to the rowers as their muscles ached and strained at the long-forgotten exercise.

Listening closely, Bjørn could discern the slightest change in the sound of the water. Taking his eyes off Yngvar for a second time, he snatched a look to his left and could just make out the land they were making for, roughly a half-rôst off the starboard bow. *Fjord Ulf* had already reached the sheltered cove they would call home for the night, the combined power of sixty men allowing the great ship to quickly outstrip its smaller companions. Gritting his teeth together, Bjørn turned his attention back to the task at hand, his burning muscles pulling the great oar repetitively in time with his crewmates. Like Bjarni, the sweat burning on his head and face was cooled in equal measure by the spray that came whenever the oars were raised from the waves. Overhead, the cries of gulls and other sea birds grew increasingly louder as they drew closer to land.

'Bow oars up!' Yngvar called.

As one, the forward-most oars – five from each side – raised from the waves and were pulled back through their oar ports as their owners began to prepare the ship for land. On the stern, Yngvar's eyes were locked on Red Orm, who in turn was closely watching the bow lookout, Knud.

'Oars!' came the shout from the bow, repeated a moment later by Red Orm over the din of men stowing oars and preparing the anchor.

'Stern oars in! Anchors away!' Yngvar boomed, drawing in the tiller. Copying Bjarni, Bjørn raised the blade straight above the water and drew it back through its port, stowing the oar along the strakes by his sea chest. In the

126

stern by Yngvar, a wave of activity began as men raised the wood-and-stone anchor and threw it overboard where it landed with a resounding splash.

At a loss for what to do, Bjørn watched as the valuable walrus-skin rope followed the anchor over the side before turning his attention to Bjarni as he stood and stretched his back, easing the tension from his tired muscles. 'You'd best give yourself a few moments of peace, lad. Once we're on the shore, the work starts again,' he grunted, wiping the sweat from his forehead.

Nodding, he pivoted on his chest to watch as the beach drew rapidly closer, momentum and waves driving the ship to rest on the shore.

'Secure the ship!' Yngvar called from the tiller. To the fore, the second team of five men dropped the bow anchor overboard before carrying it into the shallows. Moving towards the bow, Bjørn watched as they carried it up the beach and buried it in the sand, making the ship fast. At the stern, the same was being done with the aft anchor before it was tied off and secured, allowing slack for the tides. Across the deck, men were easing tired muscles and lifting their sea chests, preparing to make their way ashore, while others dug out the spare sail. The woollen sheet would double as a make-shift tent for the night. Bjørn noticed a small group of men from *Fjord Ulf* heading into the forest with bows, most likely to hunt for whatever fresh meat could be found on the island.

'Torsten, Sune, Njal, Bo. You'll sleep aboard tonight and watch the ship,' Yngvar said, leaving the helm. 'Grab yourselves some food in turns from the fires once they're lit and the food's cooking. Tomorrow you'll sleep ashore with the rest of us,' he added.

Good natured grunts issued from the chosen men as they lowered their chests back onto the deck. Njal and Bo jumped overboard and disappeared into the forest, presumably to relieve themselves, while Torsten and Sune set about turning the sail into a makeshift shelter for the night.

'Follow me, lad,' Bjarni said, hefting his sea chest and making his way towards the bow. Lifting his own chest from its position, Bjørn followed the older man towards the bow where men were jumping overboard and making their way up the beach towards the quickly forming camp. He could hear his father's voice as it barked orders for fires to be lit, shelters erected and guards posted. Four men from *Sleipnir's* crew were heading into the forest to the left of the camp, armed with bows and arrows of their own. *Fjord Uxi* was easing into the cove alongside *Sleipnir*, the activity onboard achingly similar to what had happened around Bjørn just moments before.

'Pass your chest down, Eriksson,' one of the men called up, his arms held high expectantly. Passing the chest over the side with a heave, Bjørn quickly jumped down to land in the shallows, thanking the man before carrying his burden up the shore alongside Bjarni and Red Orm. Erik had chosen a sheltered cove with high cliffs on both sides that crawled their way back into the island that was filled with a forest of pine and spruce. The ships were protected by the spits of rock that pierced out into the waiting sea, while to the landward side they were protected by the forest. To the right, the remains of a small, long-abandoned hall was visible through the greenery on the edge of the forest, with a mature spruce growing where the roof would once have stood.

'*Whoever called this place home has been gone a long time*,' Bjørn mused, dropping his chest next to Red Orm's under the sail tent. 'Now what?' he asked, turning to Bjarni as he laid his own chest down.

'Get a fire going, eat something, sleep… whatever you like. This could be our last landfall before England, unless we stop at Storfjellet, or another of the southern islands. Enjoy it,' he said, pulling a small knife and whale tooth from his chest and settling down to carve.

Looking round, he could see the rest of the crew settling down to their own amusements, while others lit fires, gather wood, or headed up the shore to take first watch. He could see Yngvar crossing the beach towards his father and his crew, while Halfdan made his way up from his own ship. '*Likely discussing tomorrow's route*,' he thought as he turned back to the two crewmen. 'Tafl, Red Orm?' he said, pulling out his game pouch and purse of hacksilver, jingling it enticingly. Red Orm gave a sly smile as he dug out his own pouch of silver, his red eye glinting in the lowering light.

'We made good time,' Erik said, taking a deep draught of ale from his horn. 'I want to go faster tomorrow though and work the winter out of the men. We'll leave at first light, and get them back on the oars; that should keep the morning chill from their bones and put a little fire in their bellies.'

They were standing in the ruins of the hall on the edge of the camp. While the roof was long gone, the four walls were mostly intact and afforded them some privacy to discuss the next day's sailing.

'Aye, Erik,' Yngvar said, taking a draught from his own horn. Halfdan just nodded, listening patiently. Taciturn and cautious by nature, this was his first season as *Fjord Uxi's* captain, and he was happy to defer to the more experienced men while they made the plans.

'How did my sons fare today?'

Yngvar nodded to Halfdan, allowing him to speak first as he took another swig of ale.

'Toke was a testament to you, Jarl Erik,' Halfdan said. His injured hand clearly bothered him, but not once did he let go of the oar or slow his pace. 'I was proud to have him on my crew, as were the men he rowed with.'

Erik smiled at the image. Toke was nothing if not stubborn, and he could well imagine him dropping from blood loss before he would put up his oar and admit defeat. 'And Bjørn?' he asked, turning to Yngvar.

'Solid as an oak. He worked hard and had an instinct for what was needed of him. He sought advice and instruction when necessary and never had to be told twice. He spent most of the day holding the tiller. He was a testament to you. Bjarni and Red Orm seem to have taken him under their wings; they'll show him the ropes soon enough.'

'Gnn,' Erik grunted. 'Perhaps his English blood will be less of an impediment than I first thought, but I will reserve final judgement for Mokstraumen. You may guide him, Yngvar. But my son will hold the helm when we pass the entrance to Njörd's hall. The same goes for Toke, Halfdan; injured hand or not. They must earn their benches in the eyes of the crews, and I will not allow their positions as my sons to weaken them. Without challenge and trial, their courage will never grow.'

'Agreed,' both men chorused, emptying their drinking horns.

'Tomorrow, we make for Storfjellet, and from there, England,' he said, finishing his own horn before leading them from the ruined building. As they walked back into the light, they could see Sven calling challengers to wrestle, a rough square marked out on the sand with stones and driftwood. To the side of the improvised arena, Bersi, the defeated prow man of *Fjord Uxi,* lay sprawled in the sand, exhausted. A small crowd was gathering to watch the bouts, Erik's sons included. Few men ever bested Sven when it came to strength, but that never stopped people from trying. The three warriors watched as another man entered the ring, stripping his hooded cloak and tunic in the process. Yngvar and Halfdan looked first at each other, then at Erik, waiting to see his reaction to Sven's next challenger. His upper body bared, Sigurd's muscles rippled with strength, seasoned by training and raiding in equal measure.

'I have in my chest a seax with a whalebone handle. I wager it on my son,' the jarl said with a confident smile, his eyes on Sigurd as he stretched.

'Too rich for my blood, Jarl Erik,' Halfdan grunted, turning his attention back to the bout. He was unwilling to risk his favoured position on a simple wager so soon.

Yngvar, his eyes glinting with mischief, drew the axe from his belt and proffered it to his Jarl. A design of his own making, the weapon had a razor sharp blade that could cut through all but the best iron and was backed by a short, sharpened beak that grew thicker towards the haft, perfect for breaking apart the iron links of a ringed shirt, or piercing a man's helmet. 'I'll meet your bet,' he said simply as he twirled the weapon enticingly.

'Very well,' Erik nodded, taking his friend's hand before turning his attention back to his son. Sigurd and Sven had begun to circle each other in the ring, watching for openings that could yield an easy point. He could see the rest of his sons standing together amongst the crews as they watched the fight unfold. At least half the fleet had stopped what they were doing to come and watch their jarl's son take on the giant húskarl.

'Don't break him, Sven,' Yngvar called above the din. 'He'll still need to pull the oars come morning!' He was greeted by a spattering of laughter by those nearest to him, while in the ring the two wrestlers lunged at each other. It happened almost too fast for the eye to follow, but while the crowd was distracted by Yngvar's jokes, Sven leapt forward and grabbed Sigurd, putting his right leg behind the younger man's and pushing him onto his back. 'One!' the red-headed giant growled to the watching crowd as they cheered.

Smiling, Sigurd climbed back to his feet and brushed the sand from his arms, acknowledging the point with a good-natured nod before moving back to the starting position. Beside Yngvar, Erik grunted, his eyes fixed on his son. He knew that Sven wouldn't go easy on Sigurd, especially not while the jarl watched.

'Begin,' Bjørn and Toke yelled from the side of the ring, their excitement infecting those around them.

Sigurd and Sven slowly circled one another like caged beasts, each wary now that the first point was lost. Surrounding the two wrestlers, the cheering of the crowd slowly died down to a quiet murmur as the watchers waited for the next attack, all eyes locked on the two giants. It was Sven who finally broke the stalemate, lunging with the same speed as his first attack, only this time Sigurd was ready for him. Quick as an arrow, Sigurd stepped to the side and turned on his heel to face Sven's back as he charged past. Without giving the giant a moment to breathe, he stuck his foot between the man's legs and tripped him, before leaping onto his back and pinning him to the ground.

'One!' the young Eriksson yelled, helping the grounded warrior to regain his feet. Sven eyed him with a nod, his teeth briefly flashing white in his red beard.

Again, the wrestlers stood and took their places and began circling, more warily this time. The next point would announce the winner. Sigurd feinted to his right before coming in low towards the giant's legs from the left, but Sven wasn't fooled. Moving like smoke, he lifted his left foot out of the way and backed off a few steps while Sigurd corrected himself and turned to face him. Again, Sigurd lunged, this time going for Sven's right, but again the giant was too quick for him.

'He's tiring himself out,' Erik grunted as he watched Sigurd lunge and miss two more times, getting himself tripped and sent sprawling in the sand for his efforts on the third attempt. The two men watched as the jarl's son turned the trip into a roll, and came up with a roar, causing Sven to slow his advance rather than try to seize the advantage.

'Perhaps,' Yngvar grunted back, his eyes watching the bout. 'But perhaps not. He's younger and faster, just not stronger. He may yet prevail, Erik.'

Halfdan remained silent beside them, his own eyes as glued to the fight. All around the bout, the crowd had gone silent, the only sounds coming from the gentle clink of hacksilver as men placed or amended bets, and the gentle crashing of the tide.

As the silence grew, the two men settled into stillness, their eyes locked on one another, each willing the other to make the first move. Around them, everyone held their breath. In the end, Sven broke the stalemate. Years of wielding his giant Dane Axe had given him speed that belied his great size, and before Sigurd could react, the giant's arms were wrapped around his own. A heel tucked behind his leg sent him tumbling back towards the waiting sand before he had the air forced from his lungs by Sven's weight as it came crashing down on top of him, deciding the bout. The watching crowd cheered and groaned in equal measure as bets were settled around the ring.

'I'll have the seax sent to you, Yngvar,' Erik grunted, watching as his friend spun his axe once before returning it to his belt.

'Thank you kindly, Jarl Erik,' Yngvar smiled, nodding his head before turning to return to his crew. Throughout the camp, the smell of roasting meat and fish was beginning to fill the air, and the crowd was quickly dispersing, heading back to their respective cooking fires as they discussed the fight.

Back with the men of *Sleipnir*, Bjørn sighed as he eased himself down on his sea chest and began to slice meat off the venison steak he'd been given, folding it into a crust of bread before putting the whole thing in his mouth. Across from him, Red Orm and Bjarni were doing similarly, their game of tafl forgotten for the moment.

'I thought your brother might have had old red beard for a moment there,' Bjarni grumbled through a mouthful of meat.

'Aye,' Bjørn agreed, putting another slice in his mouth.

Red Orm watched the two in silence for a moment before speaking, his words coming quietly. 'He needs to pay more attention, your brother. Sven looks big and strong, and he is, but he's lightning fast as well. Sigurd should focus on more than the obvious strengths and weaknesses.'

'Gnn,' they both grumbled, focusing on their meals.

'He's right,' Yngvar grunted, coming up behind them and sitting down with his own meal. 'You should always look past the obvious.'

'So could you beat him?' Bjørn asked. Beside them, Red Orm and Bjarni listened in silence.

'I might surprise him,' he said after a while. 'But that's a conversation for another day. Red Orm, let's have a story.'

There were grunts of approval as others from the crew turned to face the small group in anticipation. Red Orm was known for his storytelling and sagas, and his listeners were never disappointed.

'Aye, Yngvar. What would you have?' the grizzled warrior asked, leaning back against his own sea chest with a horn of mead, his meal finished.

'Let's have the story of the Allfather, and the Mead of Poetry,' Yngvar said, nodding to Orm's drink.

More and more heads were turning to listen as word spread that Orm would share a story.

Sitting silently for a moment, Red Orm closed his eyes and focused his thoughts, untangling the threads from the numerous myths and legends that followed the gods wherever they went.

'It was the end of the war between the Æsir and the Vanir,' he began. 'The gods and goddesses of the two great tribes sealed the peace by spitting in a great cauldron, and from their spittle, they formed a being – Kvasir – who was the wisest man to ever live. None could pose a question to him which he could not answer, and he spent much of his life travelling the world and giving counsel. As a result, he soon became famous for his knowledge and wisdom.

But with this fame came jealousy and envy, and it wasn't long before others began desiring the knowledge of Kvasir. The *dvergr* – dwarves – Fjalar the deceiver, and Galar the screamer, invited the all-knowing Kvasir to their home, supposedly to share a meal together, so that Kvasir could share his wisdom and knowledge with them. However, upon his arrival, the manipulative dwarves slew Kvasir with their axes and drained him of his blood.' Orm paused to sip from his mead, nodding with his listeners as they groaned at the treachery.

'Moving quickly, the dwarves collected every last drop of blood in a great cauldron, and mixed it with honey, turning the grisly mixture into a powerful mead that contained Kvasir's ability to dispense wisdom. The mead became known as *Óðrœrir* – "Stirrer of Inspiration" – and anyone who drank it would become a great poet, or scholar.'

Around Red Orm, a few men muttered covetously about the ability to tell great stories. Everyone knew that to be a great and famous skald was a guarantee of wealth and comfort. Ignoring them, Orm continued the story.

'The murderous dvergr jealously guarded and kept their secret, telling the gods, and any others that came asking, that Kvasir had choked on his own wisdom. By all accounts, the two dwarves delighted in murder, and soon after creating the Óðrœrir, they killed the giant Gilling for sport. They tricked him into going fishing with them one day, and after taking him out to sea they tipped him over the side and left him to drown, laughing all the way back to shore as his cries for help were swallowed by the hungering waves. Gilling's death led to endless weeping from his wife, and it wasn't long before the desperate cries became too much to bear and the dwarves killed her too by dropping a great millstone on her head as she passed under their doorway. Unfortunately for them, this was the final straw, and when Gilling's son, Suttung, learned of his parents' murders he captured the two dwarves and threatened to kill them as they'd killed his parents, saying he would tie a millstone around their ankles and drop them deep in the ocean. The two dwarves begged and pleaded for their lives, offering everything they had until finally they offered the Óðrœrir mead. At this, Suttung agreed, and instead dropped them on a reef at low tide. Cursing his lies, he left the screaming murders alive but broken to await the coming in of the tide.'

'Ah, that's some Loki cunning, that is,' Yngvar said, earning nods of agreement from the surrounding listeners.

'After dealing with the dwarves, Suttung took the vats of mead and hid them under the mountain Hnitbjorg, telling his daughter Gunnlod to guard and protect his invaluable treasure. But by now Óðinn, the Allfather, had heard tell of the mead, and in his restless and unstoppable pursuit of wisdom, was displeased with the precious brew being secreted away beneath a mountain, and used by only one. Disguising himself as a wandering farmhand, the Allfather visited the farm of Baugi, Suttung's brother, where he found nine of his thralls cutting hay with their scythes. As he approached them, he drew from under his black cloak a whetstone, and offered to sharpen their blades for them. They quickly agreed, and were amazed at the difference, declaring it to be the finest whetstone they had ever seen. They all asked to buy it, and, after much feigned reluctance, the wandering stranger agreed to part with the precious stone.

'"But," he said with a sly smile, "such a stone comes at a high price," and in saying so, he launched the stone in the air, causing the nine men to kill themselves with their newly whetted blades as they struggled to catch the falling treasure. Soon after this incident, the Allfather went to visit Baugi, introducing himself as Bölverkr – worker of misfortune – and offered to do the work of the nine servants who had, as he told it, killed one another in a dispute earlier that day in the field. "But," he said, "such work would create a great thirst in me. A taste of Suttung's famous mead would go a good way towards allaying such a thirst."

'Baugi explained that he had no influence over the famous mead, but that if Bölverkr could indeed do the work of nine men, he would help him to obtain a precious sip of the Óðrœrir mead.

'By the end of the growing season, "Bölverkr" had fulfilled his promise to the giant, and Baugi agreed to uphold his side of the bargain, accompanying his new farmhand to the hall of Suttung. When they arrived, Suttung angrily refused, yelling at his brother to leave his hall, and take his thrall with him.

'Frustrated by the defeat, Óðinn reminded Baugi of their deal and convinced him to help him gain access to Gunnlod's dwelling, under Hnitbjorg. Honour bound, Baugi led his thrall up the mountain to a spot where he knew they would be closest to the underground hiding place. Óðinn, still disguised as Bölverkr, took an auger from his cloak for Baugi to drill through the rock. The giant did as he was bidden, and soon announced that he had drilled clean through the mountain to the hidden chambers below. The Allfather blew into the hole to verify the giant's claim, and when dust blew back into his face, he grew suspicious and bid Baugi to complete the hole. After a few moments, he blew again, and this time the dust blew straight through. Eyeing the giant with suspicion, Óðinn turned into a snake and slithered through the hole, narrowly escaping the auger that followed closely on his tail as Baugi tried to stab him in the back. Once inside, Óðinn changed shape again, this time assuming the shape of a charming young man, as he made his way towards Gunnlod, to seduce her. He won her favour and secured a promise from her that if he would sleep with her for three nights, she would grant him three sips of the mead. After the third night he went to the mead where it waited in three huge vats, consuming each in a single draught, thus keeping his honour intact. Without warning, the Allfather changed his shape again, this time transforming into a great eagle, flying for all he was worth as he set out for Asgard, with his prize sitting in his throat. Suttung, furious with his daughter, refused to be cheated of his treasure and chased after the great eagle as it fled the mountain hall, having himself taken the shape of an even larger, night-black eagle. As god and giant sped through the darkling skies, drawing ever nearer to the celestial stronghold of Asgard, the other gods noticed the race, and launched vessels from the edge of the fortress to protect the fleeing Óðinn. When he at last reached the hallowed hall, Suttung could only watch in furious frustration as the fleeing eagle took refuge amongst the gods, out of reach forever. With a final, despairing cry, Suttung turned and returned to his home in Jötunheim. Meanwhile, Óðinn regurgitated the mead into waiting vessels, securing the secrets of the Óðrœrir for all of Asgard. But, while he was doing so, a few drops escaped his beak and fell to Miðgarðr, becoming the source of inspiration for all poets and scholars. Those who are considered truly great are said to have had their gift personally bestowed upon them by Óðinn himself.'

Red Orm took a sip of mead to wet his mouth as he looked around the men with him. A few, including Bjørn, had fallen asleep where they sat, while others simply nodded in acknowledgement of a story well told. Smiling, he settled himself more comfortably by his sea chest to mull over the story again, happy with the thought that he might have been fortunate enough to have shared in the Allfather's gift.

# Chapter 9

Bjørn gasped as another spume of frigid water cascaded over the bow, covering him with the freezing liquid. None aboard *Sleipnir* were in a better state, and those that had them covered themselves with waxed cloaks to keep the worst of the water at bay. Overnight, the wind had picked up, pushing hard onto the shore and making it impossible to raise the sails until they reached open water, so all three crews were at their benches and rowing hard through the broiling seas around them. As on the day before, *Fjord Ulf* led the pack, her larger crew and size helping the great ship to slice through the waves and draw ahead of *Sleipnir and Fjord Uxi*. Yngvar eased his own ship into *Fjord Ulf's* wake to try and make the going easier for the crew, but this only did so much. It had taken them nearly half an hour of hard rowing to move the ship into the open water and allow the sail to be unfurled. Once they were free of the shore, *Sleipnir* had all but leapt forward under the weight of the heavy gusts, and Bjørn had wondered briefly if the mast would snap under the sudden pressure. The crew had released a collective sigh as they pulled in their oars and rested tired muscles, and Bjørn imagined their sighs adding to the wind as it filled the sail still further. More than one of the younger men were bent over their oars completely spent, the lengths of pine left hanging above the waves, forgotten for the time being. Leaning back on his chest with his spine up against the strakes, Bjørn took deep gulps from his waterskin as he fought to bring his racing heartbeat under control. Alongside him, Bjarni was doing the same, his chest rising and falling as air filled his lungs, between gulps of water.

'Well done, Eriksson,' Red Orm said, smacking his shoulder as he stepped up to his position amidships.

'Aye, you did well, lad,' Bjarni seconded, taking another giant gulp before dropping the emptied skin to the deck.

'Gnn.' He nodded, taking the compliments with another pull from the waterskin.

Yngvar stood calmly in the stern holding the tiller, his eyes tirelessly scanning the horizon. Behind them, two gulls tracked *Sleipnir* as she cut through the waves, and Bjørn watched as the birds dipped and rose with the swell, occasionally diving for fish as they were thrown about in the wake. He could feel his mind and body relaxing, and he allowed himself to drift back to the chaotic morning he had experienced prior to launching the ships. The crews had awoken before dawn and broken their fast on venison and stale bread from the night before, washed down with sips of ale and water from a nearby spring. Everywhere he looked, tired men had been rubbing groggy eyes with soot-stained hands as they grumbled and groaned while their captains called them back into the world.

From the first horn call, everything had happened so quickly that Bjørn barely had a chance to adjust to the new day before the make-shift shelter above his head was pulled down and bundled up, ready to be stowed again. All around him men were returning cloaks and sleeping sacks to sea chests, while others added wood to the smouldering embers and coaxed fires to life to beat back the early morning chill. Yngvar had been at the centre of the mayhem, cheerfully shouting commands through mouthfuls of food, while further up the beach his father and Halfdan did the same, their orders pushing the crews as they raced to be first back on the waves. Bjørn had hurriedly packed his own chest, mimicking the practised movements of Bjarni and Red Orm in a bid to not be the last one ready. Within the hour, the crew of *Sleipnir* were pushing their ship into the frothing waves and running out the oars, nipping closely at *Fjord Ulf's* heels while *Fjord Uxi* followed behind. Now, that same crew lay bent over and exhausted as they fought to recover their breath.

'Get up here, Bjørn,' Yngvar called, his voice shattering his calm.

Sighing, he worked his way along the swaying deck, adjusting his steps to the rise and fall of the ship as she moved through the waves. He was quietly proud of how quickly he had adapted to the rolling motion of *Sleipnir*, and the feeling of the water beneath her. Some of the younger men hadn't yet found their sea legs and were even now hurling their guts over the side to the good natured jeers of the older warriors.

'Take the helm,' said Yngvar, making space so Bjørn could grip the tiller. 'Today, we meet Mokstraumen,' he grinned.

Bjørn nodded as he took the helm, once again feeling the power of the giant oar that would guide them past Njörd's hall. He didn't want Yngvar or the rest of the crew to see any of the apprehension he was feeling and he forced himself to show nothing but confidence. Confidence, and fearless arrogance.

'I'll help you get us past, but you need to be the one to steer her through.

Everyone knows how hard and dangerous that passage is, and more than one will be less than thrilled to see you at the helm when our time comes. Do this right and your place on *Sleipnir* is assured. Fail, and you deny each and every man here their seats in Valhöll,' he said seriously before patting him roughly on the back. 'No pressure, eh?' He chuckled.

'How long until we get there?' he asked, hiding his concern. Silently, he thanked Óðinn for the permanent mask of sea spray that covered his face and hid the cool sweat that had appeared on his forehead. His attention was already locked on the horizon, and the numerous islands and islets that added colour and texture to the otherwise endless blue.

'A few hours yet, but the waves will prepare you as well as anything for what's to come.' Yngvar chuckled, leaning back against his own chest and closing his eyes to calm his young ward.

Sighing, Bjørn gripped the tiller more firmly and focused his attention on keeping their course true, taking occasional cues from Red Orm and Knud, but for the most part, trusting his own instinct as he followed along behind *Fjord Ulf*. He had gained a deep appreciation for *Sleipnir* and the way she responded to his touch. Aside from occasional corrections from Yngvar, who woke up every half hour or so to check the lay of the ship and their progress, he was left to his own devices. It didn't take long for their island camp to disappear in their wake, replaced by the same blues and greys that they were sailing towards, broken only by an occasional smear of green. He could see Toke manning the tiller on *Uxi*, his attention fixed firmly on the horizon. Ahead, *Fjord Ulf's* tall stern blocked any view of who was steering the great ship, but he guessed it was one of his brothers, most likely Sigurd. Erik had decided to test his sons.

The hours passed quickly as he steered the ship, unnoticed by the rest of the crew as those not working the sail played games or slept.

'Not much further,' Yngvar said suddenly as he rose like smoke to stand alongside Bjørn. 'We'll reach it within the hour. Now listen closely. You want to stay to the left of the waves. Keep the tiller pushed to starboard to keep our course true, and make sure you adjust it for the push and pull of the Sea King's door. The waves are strong and Njörd will be watching for the slightest mistake, hungry to pull us beneath the waves to join him in his hall. Listen to Knud and Red Orm and you'll be fine. We'll need to stow the sail and run out the oars. I'll take yours. Good luck,' he added before walking down the deck to take his place at Bjørn's oar.

Bjørn was momentarily struck dumb as the reality set in, and he forced himself to breathe deeply and calm his racing thoughts. '*The Nornir have already woven what comes next,*' he muttered to himself, briefly squeezing the silver hammer around his neck before tightening his grip on the tiller. '*What will be, will be. Wyrd.*'

For a while longer, he focused on guiding the ship to port, staying close to *Fjord Ulf* while he considered Yngvar's words and prepared himself for the coming trial.

When he saw the wind begin spilling from *Fjord Ulf's* sail as men began to work the sheets he judged the moment was right and bellowed his own orders.

'Stow the sails,' he called, startling the crew into action. 'Run out the oars!'

It felt like only a moment had passed since Yngvar had left his side, and already he could see the first signs of froth in the distance, as if the seas themselves were boiling like an enormous stew. Quietly he began to mark the distances as Knud and Red Orm called instructions to stern, slowly guiding the ship to avoid the writhing waves.

Once the sail was furled and stowed away, Bjørn's sightline was clear, revealing the trial he was about to face. Over forty souls would be in his hands as he steered them past what looked to be the passage of *Jörmungandr* himself, as if the great serpent was swimming just below the waves. The broiling water seemed to fill his entire vision as they twisted and turned ahead of the bow, pulling anything and everything that touched them to a watery grave. He could see the crews of *Ulf* and *Uxi* running out their own oars as they prepared for the gauntlet. Already the water around *Fjord Ulf* was a mess of whitewash as her crew drove the ship forwards against the sucking waves.

'Row... row... row... row... row,' he chanted, setting a rhythm for the men as he fought to keep their course true. He could feel the oceans pull on the tiller as Moskstraumen sought to claim them. The chants from the other crews carried across the water as they took up the call, keeping their own pace as they pushed tirelessly through the hungering waters. Before long, his arms began to burn as he fought to keep his grip on the tiller, with every ship-length seemingly adding to the weight he was holding.

'Steer her more to port!' Knud called from the bow, his left arm held out to act as a guiding arrow for Bjørn to follow.

Gritting his teeth, Bjørn pulled the tiller further over, guiding the snarling figurehead until it was in line with Knud's extended arm. Men were beginning to gasp for air along the length of the ship as they fought the waves, each of them trapped in their own silent battle as they worked to keep a steady rhythm on the oars.

Yngvar's gaze remained firmly locked on Bjørn as he guided the ship through Njörd's wrath, and he allowed himself a small smile whenever a call or order was given that he himself would have made. He knew Bjørn had it in himself to become a famous vikingr, just like his namesake.

Stealing a glance to port, Bjørn could see Toke fighting his own battle as he worked the tiller of *Fjord Uxi*. All around them the ocean was dancing its bizarre dance, full of rushing waves and swirling currents as the different tides crashed together. They rowed for what seemed an age, but after a while Bjørn began to feel a merciful lessening on his arms. It was slight, but it was there. Slowly but surely, Moskstraumen was giving up the fight, and before long he was able to pull the tiller back to true and remain on course. He kept the men at their oars for another few minutes – despite the sweat streaming down their faces – before finally giving the order to raise the sail and ship oars. They had passed the Sea King's hall. As the great lengths of pine were exchanged for water and aleskins, a cheer rose up from those still with air in their lungs, joined man-by-man as others recovered their breath: 'Bjørn! Bjørn! Bjørn!'

Smiling with pride, he raised his hand in acknowledgement before tightening his grip on the tiller and guiding the ship onwards towards their next stop, wherever it was to be. He watched as Yngvar pulled in his oar and stored it before taking a great gulp from Bjørn's waterskin and making his way back along the ship.

'Well done, Bjørn' he said, handing him the skin. 'There's many a would-be *styrisman* who would hand over the tiller rather than sail through Moskstraumen, especially on their first voyage with the wind kicking up a fuss.'

'Thank you,' Bjørn said, glad to relinquish the tiller in exchange for the offered waterskin. He felt a wave of pride wash over him at Yngvar's words and allowed another smile to cross his face before he nodded and returned to his bench, accepting the compliments from the crew he passed. Bjarni offered him a strip of smoked meat when he sat down which he gratefully accepted, chewing the hardened morsel until it had softened enough to swallow. Overcome with exhaustion, he rested his head against the starboard hull and let the sound of the waves rushing against the wood lull him to sleep.

\*\*\*

'You're positive they're gone?' Jarl Ake asked as he looked down from his high seat at the dishevelled and filthy figure standing before him. He hardly recognised Carr as he stood in his great hall, mud-splattered and bloody from weeks in the wilderness as he worked his way home from Vágar.

'Yes, my Lord Jarl,' Carr replied, ignoring his exhaustion as he forced himself to stand straighter in front of his lord.

'Gnn,' Ake mused, absorbing the information while Carr's questing eyes went unnoticed.

Not for the first time, Carr was struck by the difference between Ake and what he had seen of Erik. Where Erik wore the height and volume of most Northmen with ease, Ake was slight in stature with a bald head and small grey eyes that nestled in dark hollows above a thin black moustache. What he lacked in strength, he made up for with remorseless cruelty and wicked cunning, and the fear that preceded him and his loyal húskarlar and hirðsmen. Carr knew the rumours as well as anyone that Ake had led his older brother to a wolf den when they were children, before disappearing into the woods. His remains had been found days later, surrounded by wolf droppings and blood-stained snow. He shivered as he imagined the sounds of old bones clicking on the wind.

'I'm positive, my Lord. Three ships set sail six days ago, crewed by at least one-hundred-and-fifty men. It was an impressive display,' he added lamely.

Jarl Ake didn't care what the man looked like, so long as the information he brought him was useful.

'Were there any men left behind?'

'Yes. I saw a handful of men amongst the women and children cheering the ships off when they sailed, but I couldn't guess at their numbers accurately. Certainly not enough to be a problem for you, though...'

'Gnn,' Ake grunted again as he twisted his moustache around his finger, eyeing the filthy scout. 'The loss of Siv and the rest has been more than worth it for the information you've brought back,' he said finally, standing. 'You have done well, Carr, and deserve to be rewarded.'

He allowed a small smile to creep across his face as he saw the greed in the other man's eyes.

'Here,' he said, throwing across a pouch of hacksilver, watching as the filthy man caught it in his mud-stained hands and struggled not to count the precious metal through the leather. He could hear the silver clinking gently. 'Leave us,' he said as he turned to his first warrior, the scout forgotten.

Canute eyed the dishevelled figure with disdain as he moved forward from the shadows, recognising his jarl's order before it could be uttered. Blond-haired and huge, Canute stood first among Jarl Ake's húskarlar, and enforced his demands with a ruthless ferocity. More than a few men had left the realm of men under a blow from Canute's sword or his inseparable Dane axe, his piercing blue eyes the last thing they ever saw before passing from Miðgarðr forever.

'Take ten men and my war arrow and muster my warriors, Canute,' Ake said, his voice loud in the empty hall. 'I want all my full force assembled and ready to sail within the week! The saga of Erik *Golden Hand* is about to come to a sudden end.' He chuckled mirthlessly.

'Your will, Jarl Ake,' the giant said impassively, dipping his head.

'And take my son with you. It's about time Steinar did something more useful than screwing my thralls and drinking my ale!' he snarled venomously.

Canute dipped his head without a word, well used to his jarl's outbursts towards his son's slovenly behaviour.

'You have one week, Canute. Don't disappoint me,' the jarl growled with finality, standing to emphasise his point. Even on his raised dais he couldn't stand eye-to-eye with Canute.

'Jarl Ake,' Canute said again, before turning for the door, beckoning for warriors as he went.

As they left, Jarl Ake sat back down on his seat and began playing with his moustache, his men already forgotten.

\*\*\*

'Land ahead!' Knud called from the bow, his call carrying back to Yngvar at the stern by way of Red Orm. Opening his eyes, Bjørn saw the rest of the crew preparing the ship for an evening ashore. They were approaching a sheltered cove with cliffs on both sides that lunged out into the ocean from the heavily wooded forest that blanketed the shoreline. For a moment, he was sure they were returning to their first anchorage until he saw that the ruins were missing, and the cove was slightly bigger. He thought he could see the wreckage of a few ships piled together, but he couldn't be sure it wasn't just driftwood tossed ashore by the sea. Around him, men worked to stow the sail while others prepared their oars. Yawning contentedly, he stretched once before running out his own oar to rest above the waves. When the order came to pull, they heaved as one, driving *Sleipnir* on through the gentle waves. It felt like only a few moments before the order came for the stern anchors to be dropped overboard and they were covering the final distance before the ship came to rest, slumping slightly to one side. Bjørn heard the splashes from behind him as the men at the prow jumped overboard and began wading ashore, carrying the bow anchors with them. The crew of *Fjord Ulf* were already disembarking, while *Fjord Uxi* slid into the small harbour moments after *Sleipnir*. As Bjørn stood to hoist his own sea chest and make his way ashore, he thought he spied a metallic glint from the edge of the woods, gone before he could be sure it had been there. He began to feel apprehensive as the crew moved around him, oblivious to his searching eyes as he tried to penetrate the deeper dark of the trees. He was just about to shrug it off when the screams began, coming from the direction of *Fjord Ulf*.

'Shields!' Yngvar bellowed, his voice shattering the surprise as he hefted his own to cover himself. Within seconds, sea chests were dropped and shields raised as the men scrambled to obey the command. From the bow, Bjørn heard a cry as someone was too slow to raise their shield and they fell overboard with an arrow in their chest. He stole a glance across at the other ships and was relieved to see they too were similarly shielded.

'Cover me,' he said to Bjarni, handing over his shield so he could retrieve his bow and quiver. Stringing the bow by feel, he kept his eyes on the treeline through a gap in the shields as he searched for enemies. He could see them now, emerging from the woods to fire another volley of arrows that struck the shields and decking, but did no more damage than slicing across someone's arm. Once his bow was strung with an arrow waiting on the string, he nodded to Bjarni that he was ready before settling down for the next volley to arrive. When it came, the sound of arrows striking wood was loud in the confined space and Bjørn winced as an arrowhead came bursting through one of the shields to rest a short distance from Red Orm's face. As soon as the volley finished, he nodded to Bjarni who opened a space for him in the ceiling of shields. As fast as he could, he stood and sighted down the arrow, picking one of the ambushing archers as the man fumbled with his own shaft. He released on the exhale before disappearing back into the protection of the shield wall without waiting to see if he had struck true. He was rewarded seconds later with a scream from the shore, and he grinned at the sound. Two more volleys came in quick succession, stopping him from firing again.

'We can't stay here,' Red Orm yelled from under his shield.

'I know!' Yngvar growled angrily, his own shield pinned with three arrows.

'Rangers! String your bows and return fire. Pick two men a piece to cover

143

you with shields. The rest of you, prepare to go ashore!'

The men moved quickly to do his bidding, relieved to have someone take charge of the situation as they rearranged themselves so that the archers stood at the back of the group. 'Bjørn, drop that bow and come with us.'

Nodding, Bjørn stood and loosed two more arrows into the forest and was rewarded with two more shrieks before he ducked back under the shields and unstrung the valuable weapon. As quickly as he could, he donned his mother's armoured jerkin and his helmet before strapping Muninn onto his belt. When he was ready, he drew Huginn, but left the sheath behind. No one would remember him if he tripped and died a straw death because his sheath got tangled in his legs. Finally, he reclaimed his shield from Bjarni before pushing his way to the front of the waiting warriors. He wouldn't have the men say that the jarl's son had shirked from the danger.

'On my mark,' Yngvar yelled from the front rank. 'Over side, move forward ten paces, then form up!'

'Huuuh!' the crew replied.

'One... two... three...GO!' he yelled, leaping over the side.

The rest of them followed closely behind, their cries joining with those of *Fjord Ulf*.

Immediately, a smattering of arrows fell amongst them as they splashed through the shallows, and two more men fell screaming, although neither looked to be mortally wounded. Bjørn caught two more arrows on his shield as he leapt onto the shore and made his way forward to stand with Yngvar.

'You ready?' Yngvar asked, throwing him a piercing glance before turning his attention to the battle lines take shape around them. Further down the beach, Erik's men were forming their own shield wall in front of *Fjord Ulf*, while the men of *Fjord Uxi* had begun launching volleys of arrows into the trees, covering the assembling crews. Bjørn grunted in response while the crew took up position alongside him and Yngvar, and he soon found himself flanked by Bjarni and Red Orm, their shields overlapping his to create a single, impenetrable wall while the arrows continued to fly overhead.

'On my mark, move forward!' Yngvar cried.

'Huuuh!' the men chorused again, the sound echoing loudly in their ears as it bounced off their shields.

'Move!' Yngvar called, beating his axe against the side of his shield to set the pace. The beat was quickly taken up by the rest of the crew as they moved towards the waiting forest. The two crews moved diagonally towards each other until they met in the middle of the beach to form a single united front protected by shields both in front and above as the men to the rear raised their shields skyward. Behind them, the archers continued to rain arrows into the forest at anyone who dared to expose themselves while the warriors from *Uxi* formed up to protect the ships. Stealing a glance between the shields, Bjørn saw their enemies emerging from the forest. Except for a few, they were lightly armoured with simple leather or thick woollen jerkins and carried only spears and axes to match their battered shields. Less than five of them carried swords, one of whom was clearly in command. He wore a gleaming iron brynja and was waving his sword above his head as he bellowed orders.

Bjørn felt the first waves of nervousness in his gut as his first ever battle drew nearer and he glanced nervously at the men either side of them to see if they felt the same. Both Bjarni and Red Orm looked calm, and he took strength from their quiet confidence.

'Prepare to charge,' Erik bellowed, taking control of the unified force as he hammered his sword and shield together.

In front of them, the ambushing force had begun to form their own shield wall, presenting unified ranks of iron and wood on the rising ground where the beach and grass met.

Bjørn watched as his father inhaled slowly, preparing for the charge. His body tensed in anticipation before a gut-wrenching howl pierced the rising din. Men on both sides men stepped back in fear, searching for the source of the sound even as Hrolf and his úlfheðnar broke through Erik's shield wall, thirsting for blood. To the assembled warriors, they resembled wolves running like men, and Bjørn could only watch with the rest as the wolf-skins sprinted the final few feet towards the enemy wall, spitting death and blood as they fell amongst them. They fought like men possessed, spinning and swirling in a graceful mess of glinting iron and splintered wood, making the men they killed look slow and dim-witted in comparison.

Erik spoke first, shocking men on both sides into action as he called the order to charge before leading his warriors into the hole Hrolf's men had opened with their mad charge.

Bjørn tightened his grip on his shield and followed his father, reacting just in time to block a spear thrust that was aimed for his throat. Gritting his teeth, he pushed his shield down, dragging the man's weapon with it before flicking his sword forward. He felt, more than saw, the man's leather shirt give way under the weight of his thrust before he fell away dead or dying; Bjørn didn't care. Snarling, he began to search for another enemy, feeling the blood rage come over him in the tight crush of the shield walls. Within moments, his entire world had shrunk to an arm span on either side and the air had filled with the iron-tinged scent of blood and viscera as dead and dying warriors spilled red, painting the ground. All along the line, Erik's warriors were fighting with furious determination, protecting each other as they cut down their attackers with impunity. Bjørn watched as Yngvar drove his axe down on a man's unprotected head before driving his shield boss into another man's face, shattering his nose before his axe came down again, relentless in its thirst. To his right, Sven had broken loose of the shield wall and was swinging his great Dane axe with deadly effect, the blade cutting a path through all comers. Sigurd followed closely behind him with his own axe, taking advantage of the space Sven had created to bring his own blade to bare. The presence of the two axes, coupled with the mad charge of the úlfheðnar and deadly efficiency of Erik's warriors began to eat away at their enemies' morale. All along the line, the shield walls were breaking apart as warriors began to fight individual duels, while the weaker of heart began to turn and run.

Bjørn sliced his own path through his foes, wielding Huginn like a scythe through wheat as he silently thanked Yngvar and his father for the countless hours they had sacrificed teaching him weapons craft. As they pushed their way up the beach, Bjørn suddenly found himself with no enemies in front of him. Gasping, he wiped the sweat and blood from his brow and surveyed the battle. It wasn't going well for their enemies, and already a sizeable number of them lay dead or dying on the ground, or trying to retreat to the safety of the forest. As he prepared to re-enter the fray, he caught sight of an archer drawing an arrow and staring intently at the men from *Fjord Ulf*. Following the man's gaze, he could see his father's sizeable bulk as he stood amongst his men and gleefully cut his way through his enemies while Olaf followed behind, guarding his father's flank. Realising what was about to happen, Bjørn drew and launched the axe at his belt without thinking, watching with relief as the blade dug into the archer's temple, spoiling his aim as the arrow slipped from his dead fingers. He almost laughed at the offended expression on his father's face when the arrow struck his helmet harmlessly before pinging away. He saw his father raise his sword in thanks and raised his own in response before returning to the fight. A few spears and axes reached him, and he thanked his mother for the armour as he felt the metal stop blades that would otherwise have pierced his skin. Beside him, Yngvar had dropped his shield altogether and was fighting with a long seax in his left hand instead, the blade dancing alongside his bloody axe to leave death and destruction in his wake. The ground around Red Orm and Bjarni was equally coated in gore, both men having sent more than their fair share of warriors to the corpse hall.

From start to finish, the battle was decided in less than an hour, and the sun was beginning its descent towards evening when Bjørn drew his blade back from his final victim, pulling it from the man's throat with a sickening sucking sound. Across the battlefield, the survivors were already looting the dead and finishing the wounded. Their own injured were being carried back to the ships by their crewmates to be cared for. In all, they just lost ten men, with another seventeen wounded from across the three ships. Behind them, one hundred-and-eight bodies were left for the ravens.

'Nothing like a good scrap to get the blood running, eh.' Bjarni grinned, bending down to clean his sword on a dead man's cloak.

Bjørn nodded as he rubbed the gore from his arms. He'd survived his first experience in the steel storm, and he felt lightheaded as the numerous bumps and cuts he'd taken began to make themselves known. Further down the beach, he could see Sigurd and Olaf speaking with their father.

'It's been an eventful day for you,' Yngvar said, coming up alongside him.

His face and arms were covered in gore and his axe glared hungrily from his waist, slowly dripping blood.

'You could say that,' he grunted, looking around for something to clean his own sword on.

'Here,' Yngvar grunted, passing over a rag. 'You'll need to give it a good polish and sharpen later to get it back to normal.'

Nodding, Bjørn took the cloth and ran it along the still-red blade, staining the fabric. 'Who were they?' he asked.

'No idea. Some poor bastards who thought we looked like easy pickings? Or perhaps they've been wrecked here since last summer,' he grunted, motioning towards the wreckage on the shore. 'They probably hit a storm or were driven onto the rocks and couldn't fix their hulls. Most likely they were waiting for a chance to escape. Your father might know more.' He shrugged, motioning down the beach with his seax before taking the rag back.

'Shall we go find out?'

Yngvar grunted, his attention focused on cleaning his blade.

'We should counter-attack,' Olaf said, exhaling exhaustedly, 'or at least prepare for one.'

'Why?' Sigurd asked. Bjørn couldn't help thinking that his brother more

147

closely resembled a corpse than a living man, covered as he was with blood.

'Because there could be more of them…' Olaf said patiently, watching his brother. 'We need to rest the men, and we can't do that until we've gotten rid of the dead and sent our own on their way to Valhöll. But before we can do either, we need to be sure that the survivors won't return to knife us in the night.'

Erik listened while his sons spoke, absently scratching the bandage around his arm while he waited for them to finish. There was no immediate danger and he was content to let them speak while around them the rest of their warriors continued stripping the dead and tending the wounded. Sven stood impassively behind his jarl next to the growing pile of plunder, his vision switching between Erik and the surrounding forest.

'If more come, we'll send them the way of their friends and return to our beds.' Sigurd shrugged, pulling a piece of smoked meat from his pocket and taking a bite nonchalantly. Olaf rolled his eyes and turned to his father in silent exasperation.

'I could go,' Bjørn said, speaking before Erik could reply. 'I could take hunters and rangers from *Sleipnir* and the other ships and find their camp. If there are more of them, we can lead you there, or even set an ambush of our own? While we're gone, the crew from *Fjord Uxi* could set about making a grave for their dead and building pyres above it for our own. It only seems fitting that they have such a send-off, and the crew from *Fjord Uxi* will be better rested than the rest, relatively speaking. That would free up the remaining men from *Sleipnir* and *Fjord Ulf* to set up camp, secure the ships and prepare for another attack, in case we're overwhelmed while looking for them.'

Everyone remained silent as they considered Bjørn's words. As the silence stretched, he turned and waved to Toke as he and Halfdan reached the small conference.

'I saw what you did today,' Erik said finally.

Bjørn furrowed his brows in confusion, sending a fresh shower of bloody flakes to the ground as the skin creased.

'The archer. It was quick thinking to throw your axe; you likely saved my life. So, I'll give you this opportunity and trust your judgement. Take five men and find where they're holed up. The rest of us will prepare for a counter-attack and make camp.'

Try as he might, he couldn't keep the smile from breaking out on his face at the unexpected compliment. He could feel Olaf and Sigurd nodding their agreement at the plan, boosting his confidence further.

148

'Thank you,' he said, nodding quietly.

'One more thing!' Erik said, raising his voice to halt his son.

'Yes?'

'Sven!' Erik grunted, turning to where the giant stood impassively by the pile of plunder.

Everyone turned to watch as the giant bent to lift something wrapped in a cloak from the pile, his axe clasped tightly in his right hand. Inside, Bjørn felt a growing sense of excitement when he heard the ringing of metal within the package.

'You saved my life today, Bjørn. Whether or not the archer would have made the shot, you saw it and stopped it. Let no man say that Erik Golden Hand is not generous, or that he doesn't reward loyalty.' Turning to Sven, the jarl took the package and removed the cloth wrapping. Beside him, his brothers gasped. Lying within the folds of wool lay one of the captured brynjas, the iron rings tinged with blood. Smiling at his son's stunned silence, Erik offered the bundle forwards, clasping his shoulder as he took the gift. 'Something to return the favour,' he said seriously.

Bjørn accepted the iron-ringed shirt in stunned silence. He had never expected to even find such a valuable item so young, let alone receive one as a gift from his father. Remembering himself, he met the jarl's piercing gaze and nodded. 'Thank you, Jarl Erik,' he said formally before taking his father's forearm in the warrior's grip.

'Gnn,' Erik replied, still smiling. 'Toke?' he said, turning his attention to his third son.

'Father?'

'Halfdan tells me it was your idea to protect the ships and subdue them with arrow fire?'

Toke blushed under the sudden attention as the watching warrior's eyes swung from Bjørn to him. Nodding once, he eyed his father hesitantly. Such a statement could go either way with Erik, and everyone held their breath waiting for him to continue. Behind them, crows and gulls were beginning to settle on the most distant of the corpses, the bloody feast calling the scavengers despite the men walking amongst the bodies.

'Well done.' Erik chuckled, breaking the tension. 'You gave us the time we needed to prepare our lines and respond.'

There was a collective sigh of relief from the rest of the waiting men as Erik again reached for a wrapped bundle from Sven.

'Such quick thinking also deserves to be rewarded. The axe you carry already sits as a part of your saga, but it is time you carried a weapon befitting a jarl's son,' he said, drawing one of the captured swords from the second parcel. The sheath was simply designed, made of pine and leather with an oiled-wool lining, but the sword itself was fine quality, with a simply styled hilt and pommel that resembled Thor's hammer, Mjölnir.

'Thank you, Father,' Toke said quietly, eyeing the blade with unmasked excitement. Forcing himself to look away, he followed Bjørn's example and took his father's arm in the warrior's grip as he accepted the blade. None of them missed the pride on his face as he wrapped the leather belt around his waist, settling the sword on his left hip. 'Like a glove,' he said, beaming.

'Hmph,' Erik grunted, his mood changing rapidly. 'Enough now. We have work to do. Bjørn, you have three hours to find their camp and report back. Halfdan, Toke, direct your men to dig a pit for the enemy dead and construct pyres above them for our dead. Our men deserve a send-off we will all remember. Sigurd and Olaf, you're in charge of setting up the camp and a perimeter around us,' he said, nodding once before turning and walking back towards *Fjord Ulf*, the ever-present Sven following closely behind.

# Chapter 10

'Shhh,' Bjørn hissed, briefly eyeing the men behind him before turning his attention back to the trail ahead. They'd been following the footprints left behind by the survivors for the past half-hour, moving slowly through the woods towards the heart of the island. Along the way, they found a small spring and Yngvar had returned to the beach to bring men forward to replenish the water barrels and skins.

'You'll be fine with this lot,' he'd winked before disappearing into the forest, nodding towards the rest of the small scouting party. And just like that, he had been left in charge of the small group. Without Yngvar's guiding hand he had had a moment of doubt as the older men watched him expectantly, and he had swallowed his fears and pushed on, more determined than ever to succeed. The four of them were all lightly armed with bows, knives and axes, having left anything that could slow them or snag on foliage behind. Each of them was an experienced hunter and they wore dark clothing that helped them to blend in with their surroundings as they worked their way along the vivid trail their attackers had left behind. All around them, ancient pines brushed the sky, rising from the carpet of needles that muffled the sound of their passing. The smells of the pine forest conjured memories from home.

They hadn't gone more than a few rôst from camp when the wind changed, carrying with it the scent of woodsmoke and what sounded like the voices and moans of wounded men.

As one, the group moved closer together and knelt, awaiting instructions.

'We're close now,' Bjørn whispered. 'Uffi, you and Galti, move around to the right, while Sindri and I go left. Keep your eyes open for any sentries; try to kill them silently, but only if you have to. We don't want them knowing we're here, and chances are they're prepared for a counterattack. See what you can find out, then meet back here.'

The pair nodded once before moving away on silent feet. Bjørn and Sindri watched them go before following suit, tracking their own path. They made slow progress, stopping every few steps to check their surroundings. The closer they got to the voices, the stronger the smell of woodsmoke became.

They hadn't gone more than a hundred paces before Sindri stopped suddenly and put his arm across Bjørn's chest, nodding across the small clearing they were approaching. The space had been cleared by one tree falling into another, opening a hole in the ceiling of needles above their heads and leaving a wall of wood on one side of the space where the trees had fallen together and were slowly rotting away. It took a few moments for him to notice the bored-looking sentry that Sindri had spotted. The man was leaning against a tree and absent-mindedly picking dirt from under his nails with a short knife. He was dressed in a combination of homespun wool and animal skins and looked as though he belonged to the group that had attacked them at the beach. A spear was leaning against the tree next to him within easy reach. Risking a quick look, Bjørn raised his head above the bushes looking for more enemies, but the man was alone. He didn't look wounded so it was unlikely he had fought at the beach. More likely he had been left behind to guard their camp, and had been sent back out to keep watch when the survivors limped back in defeat.

The pair watched the man intently, marking the time by counting their breaths while they waited to see if the man would change position, or if anyone else would arrive to relieve him. The man didn't move beyond a single cursory glance around the clearing.

Neither Bjørn or Sindri could see a way to continue their mission without removing the guard from the equation. Crouching back down behind the bushes, Bjørn pointed to a tree a few paces away and mimed crawling towards it, passing a rock to Sindri as he did so. 'A distraction,' he whispered to the older man with a wink. Sindri raised an eyebrow sceptically but didn't say anything; he simply took the stone and hefted it once to gauge its weight.

'Count to fifty, then throw,' Bjørn whispered as quietly as he dared before moving away slowly, using the brush to hide his movements. He counted his breathes as he moved, waiting for the sound of Sindri's rock as it crashed through the undergrowth. As quickly as he dared, he moved around to the sentry's left, taking care to keep the bushes between. *Thirty-one… thirty-two… thirty-three,*' he counted, aiming for a tree that was wide enough to conceal him while he climbed to his feet. Stealing a glance back the way he'd come, he caught sight of Sindri watching him. They locked eyes briefly before the older man nodded and turned his attention back to the oblivious sentry.

'*Forty-two… forty-three… forty-four…*'

When he finally reached the tree, he quickly positioned himself against its trunk with his back against the wood before sliding himself onto his feet, drawing Muninn from his belt as he did so.

*'Forty-seven... forty-eight... forty-nine...'*

He just caught sight of Sindri's rock flying past him before it struck a low-hanging branch and disappeared into the undergrowth, shattering the silence. Out of the corner of his eye, he saw the butt of the sentry's spear lift off the ground. He could imagine the confused look on the man's face as he searched for a threat amongst the trees, deciding whether to sound the alert or return to his post. After a few heartbeats, he heard the tell-tale shuffle of pine needles and dead branches as the guard moved cautiously through the undergrowth towards the sound.

He watched as the spearhead slid slowly past him as the sentry inched towards the tree, the iron blade closely followed by the stave and then the guard's hand. The man was moving cautiously, and for a time the spear just hovered there, quivering slightly as the spearman searched for a threat. Bjørn tightened his grip on his knife, his attention solely focused on the man's hand as he waited for him to continue moving. He felt sure the man could hear his heart beating in his chest, and at any minute he would spin and drive the spear into him. To his right, he caught sight of Sindri as he himself moved through the bushes with his knife ready in case Bjørn blundered the strike. The sight only made him more determined. Exhaling as quietly as he dared, he turned his attention back to the lingering hand and waited.

With almost painful slowness, the spear began to inch forward again, revealing first an arm, and then a shoulder and torso. Bjørn struck as the man's head came into view, swinging the knife around and up to drive it through the man's lower jaw and into his brain. With his spare hand he quickly covered the man's mouth to muffle any sound.

The dying warrior struggled briefly in surprise before the light left his eyes and they greyed over in sightless death. Struggling under the sudden weight, he lowered the body to the ground as quietly as he could before withdrawing his knife, the open wound releasing a stream of blood that soaked the man's shirt and soiled breeches. Before he knew it, Sindri was by his side, whispering for Bjørn to grab the dead man's arms even as he lifted his legs. Working together, they carried the body back into the woods and hid it under the roots of the fallen tree, covering it with branches and leaf litter.

'Nice throw,' he whispered as he threw a final handful of leaves over the dead man's feet.

'Nice strike,' Sindri replied, returning Bjørn's bow and quiver. 'Let's keep going,' he added, heading back the way they'd come.

As they moved back through the now empty clearing, they stopped briefly

153

to cover the puddle of blood they had left behind, removing all trace of their passage. 'Might come in handy.' Sindri shrugged as he picked up the dead warrior's spear from where he had dropped it.

They continued through the undergrowth as they had before, stopping every few paces to check for threats. The smell of smoke had been joined by roasting meat, and both men began to salivate at the scent. Neither had eaten a proper meal since before they set sail that morning, and between now and then they'd taken the fleet past Njörd's hall and fought a battle. Feeling his stomach groan, Bjørn pulled a strip of smoked venison from a pouch at his hip and sliced it in two with his eating knife, passing half to Sindri who stuffed the morsel into his mouth and chewed gratefully. Above them, a raven perched on a branch and croaked, staring expectantly at them with its black eyes. Bjørn threw a morsel up to the bird and watched as it swooped down and caught it in its beak before disappearing into the forest.

As the foliage began to thin out the source of the smoke came into sight. They could see a sizeable cooking fire crackling away in the centre of a large clearing, dotted here and there with makeshift shelters made from driftwood, tattered sails and animal skins. Seven men were sitting around the fire slowly turning skewered rabbits and birds over the flames.

Bjørn and Sindri watched in silence as another three men appeared from one of the shelters and made their way to the fire. Behind them, an eleventh man with a bored expression guarded a group of women. Bjørn could see that they were chained together. All of them wore the same empty look and their faces carried the abuse they'd experienced at the hands of their captors. Their clothes were no better than rags and left little to the imagination.

'How many do you see?' Bjørn whispered, discounting the captives as he searched for more warriors.

'Eleven.'

'Same.'

'Plus the women,' Sindri added, wearing an expression of disgust. It wasn't hard to imagine the torment the women would have experienced at the hands of marooned and frustrated men.

'There are probably more sentries spread around the far side of the camp too, but I wouldn't say there are more than twenty of them left.'

'I'd agree.'

They stayed where they were for another ten minutes or so, but none came or left the clearing. They watched as a short squat man with an angry face rose from the fire and unchained a young woman from the group before roughly pushing her towards one of the crude shelters, chased by the half-hearted jeers from the men by the fire. She moved as if in a trance, her face showing no emotion other than a depressed acceptance of her fate. The fight had gone out of her long ago.

After the pair had disappeared into the shelter, Bjørn nudged Sindri and nodded back the way they'd come. 'Let's get going,' he mouthed before sliding back on his belly until they were far enough away to crouch again. 'Perhaps the others saw something we missed?' he whispered when they were out of earshot.

They kept their eyes locked on the camp as they retreated, only turning their backs when the fire was lost to sight completely.

It didn't take long to get back to the others.

'How many did you count?' Bjørn whispered as they came to rest alongside, breathing lightly.

'Eleven, minus a sentry we had to put down,' Galti said, drawing a finger across his throat.

'We counted the same,' Sindri nodded.

'And the women, too,' Uffi added.

'They're unimportant,' Bjørn grunted. 'I want to know how many other sentries there could be on the other side of the camp that we missed. You two stay here and keep watch while we go back and tell my father and Yngvar. *Sleipnir's* crew should be more than enough to finish this. Get back to the beach as fast as you can if anything changes.'

'And take this,' Sindri said, handing Uffi the captured spear.

The pair nodded and made themselves comfortable while Bjørn and Sindri returned to the waiting crews.


'We found the camp,' Bjørn said.

They had found Erik and Yngvar standing next to *Fjord Ulf* while the crews worked around them. Pyres were being built from washed up driftwood and the remains of the ruined ships, while dead men were dropped into the pits that had been dug below. Further along the beach, men were busy assembling shelters from spare sails, while others kept weathered eyes on the surrounding forest. They wouldn't be caught out again. Bjørn and Sindri had been challenged twice just returning to the beach.

'What did you find?' Erik asked, his eyes flicking from his son to Sindri.

'We killed two sentries and hid the bodies, and saw another eleven men in the camp, plus a handful of female hostages. It looks like they've been stuck here a while, judging by the state of their camp. It must be quite some time since their ships were holed.' Bjørn added, motioning to what remained of the wrecks. 'Our ships were probably the best opportunity they'd seen to escape since last summer.'

'I don't care why they did it – but they'll pay for trying to catch us with our breeches around our ankles,' Erik gnarled. 'Where are the other two?' he asked, noticing their absence.

'We left them behind in case anything changes,' Sindri said, watching the jarl.

Erik nodded once but didn't say anything, his mind running.

'I think we could easily finish it with *Sleipnir's* crew, Father,' Bjørn ventured after a time, pulling his father's attention back. 'Even accounting for any sentries we may have missed, I doubt there are more than twenty-or-so men left. There might even be plunder in it for us if they were shipwrecked on their return voyage. It would make sense given the captives: they were probably bound for slave markets.'

'Gnn,' Erik grunted, watching his son for a while. 'What do you think, Yngvar?'

'I think your son has done well, Jarl Erik. And I'm inclined to agree with what he's said. If there are captives, there could also be plunder, and the men would appreciate having something to show for their wounds, and their dead brothers.'

Above the small council, the crows and gulls were crying out in fury as they watched their grisly feast continue its progress towards the pit, hovering in the darkening sky.

'Very well. The two of you, take half the crew from *Sleipnir* and finish this. If you're not back before morning, I'll send the other half in after you with Sindri. I'll stay here with the rest of the men and keep the beach secure until you return. Bjørn, send Galti or Uffi back to me to report the success when you're done.'

'Yes, Father,' he said sharply, keeping a straight face.

'And, so we're clear: Yngvar is in charge, not you.'

'Of course,' Bjørn assured him.

'Gnn,' Erik grunted again, eyeing his son meaningfully before turning away and walking down the beach towards Sven and Halfdan, the problem

156

forgotten.

'Well done, Bjørn,' Yngvar said once Erik was out of earshot, clapping him on the back. 'See to your kit and we'll head out as soon as the crew is ready. Sindri,' he said, turning to the ranger. 'Stay a while. I want to talk to you before we go.'

Bjørn left them and navigated his way through the quickly forming camp towards his crewmates. He found Bjarni and Red Orm sitting under the sail-tent together, sharpening their weapons after the fight. His sea chest was sitting in the sand beside theirs and he quickly opened it to retrieve his new brynja. The iron rings gleamed dully in the low light under the sail, and he couldn't help staring at the shirt in wonder. A few weeks ago, he'd owned nothing more than an old knife, an axe, and his bow. Now he owned a full kit of war gear and was beginning to build his reputation amongst his father's men. Hiding his delight at the gift, he shrugged off his cloak and pulled the heavy iron rings over his head and onto his body. It was awkward and heavy to put on and after a few moments of struggling, he heard Bjarni and Red Orm burst into laughter. Shrugging the armour off again, he laughed with his companions.

'Can one of you help me?' he asked, regaining control.

'Aye lad,' Bjarni said, still chuckling as he took up the weight and helped him to shrug the iron shirt down his body. 'I'll show you how to do it yourself when we're not in such a hurry' he added, stepping away.

It fit perfectly, and he set about covering the brynja with his mother's armoured jerkin to keep it tight against his body, and to add another layer of protection. Finally, he fastened his weapons belt, pulling some of the iron rings over the leather to better distribute the weight before donning his helmet and taking up his shield. It was hard not to feel like a warrior from the saga tales he'd listened to around his father's fire.

'Easy there, *Ironside*.' Bjarni chuckled, mimicking his thoughts as he stood and retrieved his own brynja.

Bjørn smiled despite the teasing tone in the older man's voice. He could hardly contain his excitement as Red Orm and Bjarni donned their own war gear. All around them, the chosen men from *Sleipnir's* crew were donning what arms and armour they owned and preparing to follow Bjørn and Yngvar into the forest. Many of the veteran raiders carried axes and swords at their belts, and wore iron-ringed shirts, showing their worth and experience. They stood in stark contrast to the younger, less experienced warriors who mostly stood wrapped in thick homespun jerkins with a seax sheathed at their hip. All, however, carried a spear, and a red-and-white painted shield decorated on the inside with a yellow fist, marking them out as men of Erik Golden Hand. Every man who sailed or served under the jarl received the gifts in exchange for their loyalty and Bjørn watched with pride as they hefted those same shields, waiting patiently for the order to march. He fell into step alongside Bjarni and Red Orm, pushing himself through to the front of the raiding party. To his right, he could see Yngvar as he led the march, wearing a simple jerkin of woven leather with his axe and sword at his belt.

As they moved, Bjørn angled himself so he could walk alongside the older man and guide him through the woods.

'How far do we have to go, Bjørn?' he asked as they entered the forest. Above them, the sky was soon hidden from sight by the ceiling of dark leaves and pine needles, while underfoot their steps were muffled by generations-old leaf litter. The only sound was the men's breath and the quiet jingle of their weapons and armour as they moved.

'Not too far. We should meet Uffi and Galti in twenty or so minutes.'

'And if you were me, Bjørn, what would you do? You said you only saw eleven men in the clearing, but you couldn't tell how many more there might be. Given that we're only twenty men, how would you approach this?'

Bjørn didn't respond immediately, and instead focused on the gentle *one… two… one… two…* of the men's steps as they moved. He knew Yngvar was testing him, and he didn't want to rush his answer. All around them, the forest was silent, and he could feel the closeness of the woods as they passed through, causing the small group to lose cohesion as they flowed around the trees like the tide.

'I would send Uffi and Galti to different sides of the camp with their bows, along with two or three of the less armoured men to protect them. They'll be able to move quicker than those with heavy armour, and will be better able to protect the archers, if they're threatened. Once they're in position, they can begin firing into the camp from both sides, catching the enemy in a crossfire and forcing them to split their forces. That leaves us with fourteen men. When they separate, we can move into the camp and roll them up like a carpet, attacking them from in front and behind. While this is happening, Uffi and Galti can relocate and search out any remaining sentries and try to ambush them before they can return to the camp to provide support…'

He let the final words trail off as he waited for Yngvar's reaction. For a time, they walked in silence as Yngvar considered Bjørn's plan, while behind them the gentle *one... two... one... two...* of the men following them dogged their steps.

'All right, we'll do it your way,' Yngvar said at last, flashing an amused grin at the nervous smile that had spread over Bjørn's face.

Before Bjørn could respond, Yngvar held up a fist to halt the raiding party, bringing the repetitive *one...two...one...two* to an abrupt end. They could see the two scouts ahead and Yngvar motioned for the pair to join them.

Kneeling amongst the leaf litter, Yngvar quickly outlined the plan Bjørn had proposed, noting the eager faces of his men as they prepared to revenge their fallen crewmates. Guards were assigned to protect the archers, while the more heavily armoured warriors were broken into two groups of seven; one led by Yngvar, and the other by Bjarni. Once everyone understood the plan, they fell into formation and began moving forwards again, walking at a slower pace than before to reduce their noise. After a few minutes, they passed the tree where Bjørn and Sindri had hidden the sentry's body and he was relieved to see it had remained undisturbed. He could only hope the same was true for Uffi and Galti's man.

Yngvar held up a hand to stop them as the camp came into sight. In silence, Uffi and Galti led their small groups to the flanks while the rest of the men shuffled into ranks as quietly as they could. Bjørn winced every time he heard the gentle strike of metal on metal or the jingle of an iron-ringed shirt, but he knew the sounds were unavoidable. He just hoped they wouldn't carry far through the trees.

Bjørn felt the first waves of nervous excitement begin in his gut as they moved, coupled with a sudden need to empty his bladder. He ignored the urge and instead focused on his breathing, trying to calm his body lest the older men think he was scared and had to piss with fear.

When Yngvar judged they had advanced far enough, he again held up a fist to halt the men, giving the archers time to get into position. Final adjustments were made to arms and armour while they waited, and muscles loosened with gentle swings. Swords were drawn and axes slid free of belt loops, while those with spears tightened and released their grips on the shafts. Bjørn silently slid Huginn from its scabbard, allowing a little smile to cross his face as the patterned steel licked free of the wool-lined sheath to gleam dully in the dim light. He saw a few of the warriors eyeing the blade with a lust typically reserved for beautiful woman. Bjarni winked beside him as he drew his own sword.

The waiting was becoming unbearable when the first arrow struck, taking one of the unsuspecting men in the throat and dropping his body into the fire he was tending. Two more followed in quick succession from either side of the camp, followed soon after by another two, leaving one man dead and another writhing on the ground with an arrow through his arm. Shaking themselves from their stupor, the ambushed warriors ran for their weapons and shields, and Bjørn watched as they formed an iron ring in the centre of the camp, ready for the next attack. He saw two more sentries come running in with arrows nocked and ready, while still more warriors appeared from the makeshift shelters. Before long, seventeen or so men were huddled in the centre of the camp, waiting to do battle as the arrows continued to crash against them

Bjørn could hear them murmuring amongst themselves as they discussed their next move, ducking behind their shields every time a volley came from the surrounding trees. One unfortunate warrior was caught a glancing blow from an arrow that struck his shield rim and drove upwards into his eye, killing him instantly. As he fell on the ground, his own weight drove the arrow the rest of the way through his skull to emerge out the back of his head, flecked red and grey with all manner of bodily matter.

Bjørn clasped the Mjölnir pendant at his neck and said a prayer to Óðinn, willing the warriors to split up like they'd planned. Stealing a glance at Yngvar he found the older man looking at him with a raised eyebrow, as if saying, '*now what?*' He hadn't planned for this eventuality.

Grimacing, he returned his attention to the trapped warriors just in time to watch another fall, screaming with an arrow through his foot. He could still hear them talking amongst themselves, their voices becoming more urgent as they sought a way out of the trap. The arrows kept coming for another few moments until, at last, the group split, with half charging towards Galti's small band, and the rest moved towards Uffi and his men. Another quick glance at Yngvar earned him a satisfied nod before he focused his attention wholly on the task at hand. In his head, he counted to twenty before Yngvar gave the call to advance. When the order came, they advanced as quickly as they could, their shields overlapping to protect themselves and the men beside them as they pushed forwards. They had barely covered ten paces before they were noticed. One of the charging warriors called a warning to his companions as they emerged from the trees, stopping the charge as quickly as it started as they formed two small skjaldborgs. Within moments, Bjørn and Bjarni's men were faced with a hedge of shields and spears. Keeping the initiative, Bjarni began to beat his sword against his shield, creating a rhythm for the men following him. The air around them filled with the sounds of war as metal struck metal, the sound aided by the steady tramp of feet as their small band moved inexorably forwards towards their enemies.

Before he knew it, the first spear was licking forwards to strike at Bjørn's neck, the weapon's longer reach surprising him. He just had time to raise his shield before the blade struck. Years of practice guided his actions as he tilted his shield to deflect the below before stepping forward to drive Huginn through the spearman's throat with enough force that the blade emerged out the back of his neck. He died quickly with a gurgling scream, his face wearing an expression of barely registered surprise. Bjørn saw an axe-wielding warrior eye him up out of the corner of his eye as the warrior fell, his snarling face eager as he moved into the now vacant space in the shield wall. Growling, he yanked at Huginn to free the blade from the dead spearman but it was stuck fast, the blunted blade caught in the man's spine. In frustration, he yanked for all he was worth, snapping the leather blood knot that secured the blade to his wrist but unable to free the blade.

He barely had time to get his shield up in time to block the axeman's first strike as the man sought to take advantage of the situation. Bjørn quickly realised that the warrior facing him was vastly more experienced than the spearman had been, and he found himself on the back foot as the warrior struck again and again with terrible ferocity and speed, forcing him back step by step. Snarling, he angled his shield for the next strike, causing the axeman to stumble briefly and buying himself time to draw his own axe.

Bjørn knew a moment of fear when he saw how quickly the axeman recovered, turning his stumble into a slash as he brought his axe up against Bjørn's shield, aiming for his knee. He felt his arm go numb under the impact, and before he knew it the man was coming at him again, this time spinning around to strike at his head. He managed to get his shield up against the man's arm in time to deaden the blow, but the axe still managed to glance off his helmet and drive into his shoulder with enough force to have done serious damage, were it not for the armour he wore. As it was, he would have a hell of a bruise in the morning; he just hoped nothing was broken. Shaking his head furiously to clear it, he blocked the next strike with his shield before taking two rapid steps back to buy himself some space. The axemen grinned evilly at him as he followed. He could see that Bjørn was dazed from the impact and he could sense the kill.

Seeing the man's eagerness to end the contest, Bjørn played up his dizziness, moving his axe and shield with feigned sluggishness as he prepared to defend himself again. His opponent took the bait and stepped forward into the space Bjørn had created, bringing his axe down in a vicious chopping motion as he moved. As the axe descended, Bjørn suddenly lunged forward with his shield, pushing it up with all his might to catch the falling weapon even as he brought his own axe around in a wide arc, aiming to drive it into and through the man's ribs. He caught the man's weapon easily, but he could only watch in mute frustration as his own axe was easily blocked by his opponent's shield, the blade becoming trapped in the wood. He barely had time to register what had happened before he felt a foot against his chest and he was driven from his feet to land in the leaf litter behind. Winded, he felt more than saw his opponent follow up the attack. He found Muninn at his belt and drew the blade, but he knew it was too late. Resigning himself to Valhöll, he tightened his grip on the knife handle and prepared himself to meet the Allfather.

He opened his eyes in confusion after a few heartbeats when nothing happened. There was no flap of wings as the valkyrie came for him, nor the warm rush of blood as the axe drove into his body. Instead, he found himself staring at the equally confused expression on his opponent's face as he looked down at the gore covered spear blade that was protruding from his chest. Bjørn almost laughed as the man fell to the ground beside him and he realised what had happened. The warriors protecting Uffi and Galti had entered the fray, capturing their enemies in a pincer.

As the axemen fell to the ground, Bjørn caught sight of his saviour and was rewarded with a surprised smile when the man saw whose life he had saved. Climbing to his feet, Bjørn nodded his thanks to the unknown warrior before bending down to free his axe from the dead man's shield. He had to jiggle the blade left and right a few times to remove it and was rewarded with a small shower of wood chips for his efforts when it finally came free. He could see Huginn standing up in the dead spearman's throat a few steps away and he crossed the space to reclaim his sword. There was no immediate danger nearby, and the unknown warrior was still standing next to him with his spear at the ready while the final duels were fought around them. The blade was stuck fast and he was forced to put his foot on the dead man's chest to finally pull the sword free. He grimaced as the blade crunched against the dead warrior's spine, releasing a fresh flood of blood. Rearmed, he cast his gaze over the clearing, watching the last of the battle. Their enemies had crumbled with the flanking attack, and now only one man was left standing, slowly moving backwards to stand against a giant fir tree. Bjørn watched as the man covered himself with a shield and held his sword forwards and down, ready to meet his next attacker. Already two crewmen were screaming on the ground at his feet, although neither looked to be mortally wounded.

Bjørn leapt forward and attacked the swordsman, eager to wipe away the shame of his last duel. With unrestrained fury, he whipped Huginn across in a horizontal strike to force the warrior's sword wide before driving forward with his shield, knocking the wind from the man. Before he could react to Bjørn's ferocity, Huginn was coming back around to bury itself in the man's chest, ending the duel. The man crumbled as Bjørn pulled his sword free, the blade returning with surprising ease. He sliced a strip of cloth from the man's jerkin and ran the scrap of fabric along the length of his sword, cleaning off the worst of the blood before sheathing the blade.

Behind him, the rest of the crew were moving among the dead, gathering weapons, shields, and armour into a pile to take back to the beach. Bjørn retrieved the dead man's sword from where it had fallen among the leaves. It was a simple, unadorned blade with a plain guard and pommel, but it was a sword, and more valuable than anything most men could ever expect to own. He removed the sheath from the corpse at his feet and drove the blade home with a satisfying *thunk*. Behind him, a few of the men had drifted across to explore the shelters, while others moved towards the women.

Bjørn found his saviour working alongside a group of younger warriors as they collected the fallen weapons and armour from the dead, swapping stories from the fight; both exaggerated and true. He watched as the man lifted a small bundle of spears and saw that he was a little taller than the men around him, with a braid at his right temple that reached his shoulder.

Grasping the newly liberated sword, he moved towards the small group, arriving in time to hear one of them talking about how he'd thrust his spear into a man's calf, allowing Bjarni to bring his sword down on the man's head. Next to the speaker, Bjørn's saviour remained silent, listening intently while others spoke. As he drew closer, the voices died away as they realised who had joined their small company.

Nodding towards the spearman, he asked his name.

'Guttorm, my Lord.'

Bjørn laughed aloud, startling him. He saw a glint of metal woven into the warrior's braid.

'My Lord?' he asked nervously.

'How fitting that the man who saved my life should have a name meaning "to spare",' Bjørn said, still chuckling.

'Thank Thor it doesn't mean the slow one, then,' Guttorm replied, his lips parting to reveal a friendly smile.

'Aye, lucky indeed,' he mused, returning the smile. 'But you mustn't call me lord. My father is Jarl, I'm just Bjørn. And your name would be better defined as "poor aim" with a thrust like that. That spear clearly isn't the weapon for you,' he added, nodding to the length of ash the warrior carried. He watched as Guttorm's expression moved from pride to confusion and finally to anger at the accusation that he'd missed his mark. Smiling to cover any insult, Bjørn held out the sheathed sword. 'Perhaps you'll have better luck with this in the future?'

The warriors around them fell completely silent, watching in awe as Bjørn handed over the priceless gift. They could only look on in mute envy as Guttorm reached with a shaking hand to take the blade from Bjørn. With aching slowness, he drew the sword and held it, gauging its weight. From the way he held the weapon, it was clear that he'd never even come close to a sword before, let alone touched one.

Internally, Bjørn felt only pride at bestowing such a valuable gift on someone who had saved his life, as his own father had done for him earlier that same day. *Was that really today?* he wondered idly, before speaking into the silence. 'Have you ever held a sword before?' he asked.

'No, my lor– no, Bjørn,' Guttorm replied. 'We've never had the wealth to support such a weapon in my family – we're just poor farmers.'

'Well then,' Bjørn said, 'I'll have to teach you. We'll crew *Sleipnir* by day, and each night we'll work at your swordplay. Before you know it, you'll be swinging that blade as well as Tyr himself. You have my word,' he said, holding out his hand.

Guttorm's hand flew across the clearing to clasp Bjørn's wrist quicker than the arrows that had started the fight. They smiled as their eyes met, each finding something to like in the other. Nodding once, Bjørn turned and walked away, catching sight of Yngvar.

'That was a good thing you did,' he said as Bjørn drew near.

'He saved my life,' he replied, standing next to his teacher to watch as Guttorm swung the sword clumsily. He could see the hunger in his friend's faces as they admired the sword.

'You may have just cost him his.' The older man chuckled, watching as Guttorm nearly dropped the blade.

'I've promised to teach him.'

'Gnn,' Yngvar grunted. 'It went well. I'll tell your father when we get back. It doesn't look like there is anything worse than a few nicks and bruises on our end, and no one escaped. I think you were right, judging by the size of the camp: the wrecks on the shore were likely theirs and they found themselves marooned here over the winter. Bjarni and Red Orm have men searching for any plunder they may have taken, aside from the slaves,' he muttered, waving a hand vaguely towards the group of women still chained in the middle of the camp.

'What do we do with them?'

'We'll take them with us – we can either sell them ourselves or keep them with us... There are a few slave markets to the south,' he continued. 'We could send a ship through one of them on our way, but that's a decision for your father.'

The pair watched in silence for a time as men moved from shelter to shelter, adding useful and valuable items to the small pile in the centre of the camp. A few were replacing broken spears and axes from those captured during the skirmish, and overall the mood remained light as the men worked and discussed their own feats during the battle. A few had been dispatched as sentries to guard the approaches to the camp, but no one expected a counterattack. There was no one left to surprise them.

'Yngvar, Bjørn! I think you better see this!'

The two men turned and watched as the voice's owner exited one of the larger dwellings, carrying a small sack in his hand that jingled suggestively.

'I found it tucked under a makeshift cot in there,' he said excitedly, his hand waving back the way he'd come.

'And what exactly is "it?"' Yngvar mused, betraying nothing.

'Here!' he said, passing across the parcel when he reached them.

Bjørn saw a flicker of surprise flash across Yngvar's face as he opened the sack, before his usual stoic mask returned.

'Bjørn,' he said, passing over the sack before turning back to the other man. 'Was there any more in there?'

'There might be. This is all I've found so far.'

'All right, get back in there and see what else you can find. Take that young man over there to help you,' he said, pointing at Guttorm who had finally sheathed his new sword and was busy belting the weapon around his waist.

'Aye,' the man grunted before running towards Guttorm.

'Definitely shipwrecked, then,' Bjørn said, handing the sack back.

'Aye,' Yngvar muttered, pulling out a handful of hacksilver. 'Either way, your father will be pleased.'

'That he will,' Bjørn said, smiling.

'Uffi, Galti!' Yngvar shouted across the clearing. 'Head back to the beach and tell the jarl we will stay here this evening and bring back the spoils in the morning. Then bring back another ten men from *Sleipnir*. They can help us to carry everything back tomorrow.' He didn't wait for a response, instead turning to dole out more orders to the remaining men to better secure the camp, clear the bodies and get food cooked. Five of the women were unchained for the final task, and after they realised they were only being asked to help with the food they were happy enough to help. As one, they moved towards the rabbits the dead men had left cooking over the coals. This done, Yngvar made his way towards the shelter where the silver had been discovered, indicating for Bjørn to follow him.

'Let's see what else our friends left for us,' he said with a sly grin.

# Chapter 11

'You're back,' Sindri said as Bjørn, Red Orm and Bjarni ducked under the makeshift shelter and began shedding their war gear.

'Aye, and with a fine haul as well,' Bjørn said, sighing with relief as he slid off the heavy brynja, enjoying the sound of the iron rings as they sang together.

Further searching of the shelters had revealed two more sacks of hacksilver as well as three gold-and-jewel-encrusted Christian prayer books, a large golden cross, and various smaller pieces. Everything had been handed over to Erik for safekeeping until it could be divided between the crews upon their return home.

'Erik says that we're staying here for a few days so the injured can recover some of their strength,' Bjørn said, raising his voice slightly to speak over the sound of the iron rings as he wrapped them in an oiled sheep skin and stowed them.

'We're not going anywhere with this wind, anyway,' Red Orm added, nodding towards the breakers that were crashing against the shore. Overnight a heavy wind had sprung up off the coast, keeping the fleet securely bottled up on the island.

'A few men from *Uxi* and *Ulf* are heading back into the woods to check through the camp for anything else we might have missed, and to bring the best building materials to the beach. Erik wants to build a small longphort here that we can use as a staging post in the future,' Bjørn continued, fishing a whetstone from his chest.

'He's not concerned about building something that someone else could take over? Or destroy?'

'Uffe is taking a few of the rangers across the island to search for any other settlements, but I doubt there will be anything if that many men were shipwrecked here since last year,' Bjørn said, without looking up from his blade.

'Those of us who went into the woods last night have a few hours to rest before we have to go and help,' Bjarni grinned before wrapping himself in his cloak and lying down by his sea chest to sleep.

'You know what that means, Sindri?' Red Orm smirked as he donned his own cloak.

'What?'

'It means you get to go carry lumber and chop wood,' Bjørn finished for them as he ran the stone along the blade again.

'Gnn,' Sindri scowled, watching the two men close their eyes, while others around him made themselves comfortable. Sighing, he picked up his axe and tucked it into the loop on his belt next to his eating knife. Already men from the other ships were making their way into the treeline above the campsite carrying axes and shovels. Further down the beach he could see Erik and Sven directing the work crews and he made his way towards them.

'Sindri,' Erik called as he drew near, 'take the remaining men from *Sleipnir* and return to the enemy camp. There's a small team already there, but a few more hands wouldn't go amiss. Bring back whatever appears useful for the shelters here.'

Erik's instructions were punctuated by the sounds of axes striking wood as men began to clear the ground amongst the pine and fir trees at their back.

'Yes, Jarl Erik,' he said, motioning for his unbloodied crewmates to follow him.

Erik turned his attention back to Sven and picked up where he had left off. 'Get the rest of the men from *Fjord Ulf* into those trees to help clear the ground. I want it ready for us to begin work on the palisade by this afternoon.'

The big man nodded wordlessly before turning and walking along the shore to carry out his instructions, bellowing orders to the crew as he went.

'He really is a man of few words, isn't he?' Yngvar said as he drew near.

'It might be one of his greatest traits.' Erik chuckled, smiling as his friend came to stand alongside him. 'You did well yesterday.'

'Thank you,' Yngvar said, bowing his head humbly.

'I've heard my son's name mentioned through the camp? Something to do with a sword?' The question sounded innocent enough, but Yngvar could hear the curiosity in Erik's voice. He knew well the internal battle his jarl fought between pride and prejudice when it came to his youngest son.

Nodding, Yngvar recounted the story of Guttorm's spear thrust and Bjørn's own duel for the sword, allowing some of his own pride to enter the telling. 'Soon after killing the sword's previous owner, he gave the weapon in thanks to Guttorm. A strikingly similar gesture to your own actions yesterday, wouldn't you say, Jarl Erik?' he added with an ironic nod.

'Aye,' the jarl nodded. 'He did well, although I'd prefer he not know it. It wouldn't do for such thoughts to go to his head. Now, have you finished the plans?' he asked, changing the topic.

In answer, Yngvar handed across a square plank of wood that he'd used to draw a rough draft of the longphort Erik wanted built. With charcoal from the fires, he'd mapped out a rectangular design, with the longer sides facing the forest and shore, and two paths intersecting the camp through the middle where they circled around what would become the central hall. The site would be built back in the trees a few paces to keep it hidden from passing ships, and a small lookout post would be built on the taller of the two cliffs that hugged the cove. There was also space marked out for a small forge, should it become a more permanent settlement in the future. It was nothing grand, but it would easily accommodate the crews of the three ships when necessary.

Erik's eyes ran across the design for several minutes before returning the plans. 'How long will it take to build?'

'A week at most to get the walls up and a simple hall built, given the number of hands we have available. Another four or five days to build a few shelters,' he said with a shrug. 'Judging by the weather, we have the time, and a few of the men could use it to recover.'

Erik grunted in acceptance, his eyes drifting along the shore as men headed into the woods. Above them, grey wisps of cloud raced across the sky, pushed along by the same winds that kept their ships on the shore. 'It will give the men something to do while we're stuck here, at least, and help burn the winter out of them,' he said before turning his attention back to Yngvar. 'Get some rest, old friend.' He smiled, his mood changing again. 'You too had a long day yesterday. I'll send someone to wake you and the remaining men of *Sleipnir* a little after noon.'

'Aye, that we did. I won't say no to a few hours of shut eye. Jarl Erik,' Yngvar said, suddenly exhausted as he handed over the designs and made his way back to his own crew. He hadn't realised how tired he was until that moment.

*'Honestly, he gives one farm boy a sword and thinks he can sleep all day while the rest of us work,'* said the first voice.

*'Almost as if he thinks himself the jarl of the island,'* said a second.

*'And with three older, vastly more handsome brothers standing ahead of him for the high seat,'* the third laughed.

*'Well, two…'* chuckled the first voice.

The laughter broke into Bjørn's subconscious, pulling him back from a dreamless sleep into the world of men. Opening his eyes revealed the smiling faces of his three brothers as they stood over him. Sigurd was grinning like an idiot, and a quick glance at his right hand revealed the bucket of water he was preparing to upend over his youngest brother.

'I'm up, I'm up!' he said hurriedly, shooting upright and rubbing his eyes. 'How long have I been asleep?' he yawned, looking around for the rest of the crew.

'A few hours. Father sent us to wake the rest of the crew and we thought this the best bed to start with,' Sigurd said, still smiling.

'Hmph.' Bjørn yawned, taking a deep draught from his waterskin. 'Any idea how long we're likely to be stuck here?'

'A week, at least,' Toke replied. 'It's fine, though, the camp will give us a place to stage future raids from and provide shelter should we need it. Some of the men have seen signs of game as well. Nothing big, but plenty of birds and rabbits.'

Bjørn grunted as he took another drink. 'Well, now that I'm awake – thank you very much – what needs doing?'

'The ground has been cleared for the longphort, and now the men are starting to cut and shape staves for the palisade, and digging holes for the posts to sit in. Take your pick,' Olaf said.

'I'll cut and shape,' Bjørn replied, sliding his axe into the loop at his belt as he climbed to his feet.

'I'll come with you.' Toke smiled. 'Yngvar is already up there with Sven, directing everything.'

Bjørn saw that many of the beds were already empty, including Yngvar's. He shot a questioning glance back at his brothers.

'No, you didn't sleep longer than the others,' Olaf said quickly, reading his brother's thoughts. 'They just woke up sooner and made their own way up. We're the official wake-up party for the rest of you.'

'Gnn,' Bjørn grunted, mollified. 'All right, Toke, let's get going.'

Sigurd and Olaf watched as the pair made their way up the beach before turning their attention back to the rest of the sleeping crew. It didn't escape Bjørn's notice that they left the bucket behind as they began moving among the remaining sleepers.

The pair walked in silence for a time, the sound of waves striking the shore dogging their footsteps as they walked across the shingle.

'Why didn't you keep the sword?' Toke asked suddenly, breaking the silence. 'You could have given him silver, or the weapons from the man he

170

speared. Why the sword?'

Bjørn didn't answer immediately, instead shoving a slice of dried meat into his mouth as he turned the answer over in his head.

'He saved my life, Toke,' he said at length. 'I have a sword, but I didn't have Guttorm's loyalty. Now I do.'

'Father has his loyalty,' Toke said firmly.

'Aye, he does, and I'd never seek to take it from him. But I'm new to the crews, untested and unknown. More than that, I'm the half-blooded fourth-born son of their jarl. I need to earn their trust, to bind them to me the way Father has done. It's not about taking their loyalty from our father, but rather building trust and reliability in me.'

Toke nodded uncertainly, thinking over his brother's words as they continued walking.

'Do you want the high seat?' Toke asked after a few moments.

'NO! Never,' Bjørn said quickly. 'It should go to Olaf; he's the oldest, and I would happily pledge my sword and life to him without a second thought.'

'So why are you trying to bind men to you?'

Bjørn remained silent, considering his words carefully to ensure they couldn't be misconstrued.

'There may come a day when Father's prestige and name carry further than the lands around Vágar. There will be more land and men that rally under the Golden banners. Olaf will sit on a high seat, and you and Sigurd will likely end up with holdings of your own, and perhaps I will, too. But I'm not sure that's what I want. When my time comes, I want a ship of my own and the men to crew it, to write my own saga and make my name known on Father's behalf, or perhaps for Olaf. That's why I gave him the sword.'

Toke stayed silent as he mulled over Bjørn's answer, his brow furrowed in concentration. He knew that his father took issue with Bjørn's mixed blood, despite the pride he showed in him, and he could see where the sentiment came from. To Bjørn's credit, he held no resentment towards Erik, just a cold acceptance of his fate.

Sighing, Toke opened his mouth to speak. 'When that time comes, if it comes, I will pledge men to your ships, Bjørn. You have my word.'

Bjørn smiled. 'That day may never come, Toke. And if it does, you will have your own worries and concerns to deal with, as will I.'

It took a few moments for him to realise that his brother was no longer walking alongside him, and he turned in time to watch Toke draw the seax from his belt and slice the blade across his right palm, opening the skin. A smile crept across Toke's face as the blood began to swell in the wound and he handed the knife across to his brother, handle first.

Feeling the strange seiðr that had sprung up between them, Bjørn took the blade and sliced his own skin before clasping his brother's bloody palm.

'I, Toke Eriksson, swear, before Óðinn and the Æsir, that should a day come where you find yourself in need of land, men or ships, you will find them in my hand, and support in my heart,' Toke said, his eyes locked on Bjørn's as he uttered his oath.

Emotion welled in Bjørn as he digested the oath before taking a breath to speak his own vow. 'I, Bjørn Eriksson, swear to always defend my brother's name, his land and his honour, should such a time come when he is in need of my sword and shield, my spear and my axe. I will answer the call. This I swear before Óðinn and the Æsir.'

A grin crept across Toke's face as he met his younger brother's serious gaze. Bjørn's eyes were prickling with emotion.

None of his brothers had ever shunned him for his mixed blood, nor teased him about it. But Toke's oath secured him beyond any familial bonds. It bound them in the eyes of the Allfather, and no man of the North would break such an oath lightly.

'Thank you, Toke,' he said quietly, his eyes locked on his brother's.

'You'd do the same for me.' He shrugged, suddenly embarrassed. 'Now, let's get up there and get chopping before Father sends someone to find us.'

'Here,' Bjørn said in reply, producing a strip of cloth and slicing it in two before binding one around his palm to close the wound.

Erik set fire to the funeral pyres the night after the battle. The crews from all three ships stood in silent ranks dressed in their war gear as their jarl spoke over the dead, honouring them even as he touched his burning torch to the dry kindling at the base of the pyres. The fire took instantly, fanned by the same winds that kept them locked on the shore as it sent their warriors high into the sky, their bodies turning to spark and ash as they drifted ever higher. Their enemies burned in a pit beneath the pyres, and Erik called on them to serve his own warriors in the afterlife. Bjørn watched with the rest, standing silently as their men burned. Already, they would be sitting in the corpse hall, drinking and fighting to their hearts' content as they prepared for Ragnarök, their lives in Miðgarðr forgotten.

The warriors maintained their vigil until the pyres began to collapse under the flames, each falling beam sending great clouds of sparks into the sky where they joined with the stars above.

It took far longer than expected to complete the basic structure of the camp, with the men working in shifts to build walls and shelters. The buildings were dug into the earth to keep them warm and dry during the winter months, and cool during the summer, and crude drainage ditches were dug to carry water under the walls towards the beach to avoid flooding. Only Erik's hall, located in the centre of the camp, was able to be called complete, and it would be the job of those staying behind to finish the rest over the coming months while they waited for the fleet to return. Uffe and his rangers had scouted the entire island, confirming they were alone. During their search they found a freshwater spring a few hundred paces inland which Erik ordered connected to the camp. A dozen men had laboured to dig a crude channel for the water, guiding it beneath the walls where it came to rest in a central cistern next to the finished hall. It would likely be filled in by the time they next visited on the island, but it could easily be cleared out to provide them with fresh water.

The wind had remained strong, keeping the crews trapped on the island for far longer than planned, but the time had allowed most of the wounded to recover from their injuries, while the rest remembered their summer strength through the labour. Seven of the wounded were still too weak to sail, and two had died from their wounds. Yngvar had ordered strong onion soup to be brought, and as the two men drunk the severity of their wounds had been revealed as the sweet smell mingled with their blood. They were gut-wounded. Both had asked to die with weapons in their hands so they could feast with their fathers in Valhöll, and Erik had personally dispatched them, honouring their service and loyalty.

It was another two days after the final piece of palisade was driven into the ground that the wind died, and the time was spent building basic furniture for the dwellings, and storing wood for fires should they need to stop there on their return journey. Bjørn directed a handful of the younger crew members to cut and shape offcuts of wood into rough piping that they then buried underground, concealing the route of the spring water as it made its way into camp. Erik also reached a decision on the women they had captured, deciding to leave them in the longphort and turn it into a working staging post. He reasoned that there was no escaping the island other than on another ship which would see them sold into slavery, or used as pleasure objects by frustrated crews. This way they could keep developing the camp and preparing it for future raids, and work to regain their lives in some small way. The seven

173

wounded warriors would also remain, both to finish work on the camp and to recover from their injuries.

Uffe led his rangers on multiple hunts through the surrounding forests to provide food for those staying behind and to replenish the ships' stores. The women had quickly come to recognise that their rescuers were different from those who had captured them, and some of the younger ones began selling their favours to the men in exchange for useful tools and spare cloaks that would see them through on their island home. Few of the men ignored the offer of a woman's touch, and more than one of them had turned a pretty profit by the time the crews left.

For Bjørn, every evening ended teaching Guttorm the sword. Although the progress was slow, he was pleased with his friend's skills and determination, and the friendship they were building. The bouts soon became something of a spectacle for the land-locked crews, and within a few days he had found himself teaching a small band of men from across the fleet, swinging and thrusting with weighted spears. On occasion, Yngvar, Bjarni or Red Orm would join in and help with the lessons, whiling away the time as the days continued to lengthen.

By the time the wind had finally died down enough for the ships to be launched, the fleet had spent close to three weeks on the island, and the men were itching to hold their oars again, and return to the whale road. Those left behind could only watch in mute jealousy as the dragons were once again loaded and made ready to sail, their only consolation being the women that would be left behind with them.

Bjørn felt the familiar flutter of excitement in the pit of his stomach as he grasped his brother's hands before joining the crew aboard *Sleipnir*. He'd smiled when he saw that Guttorm had shifted places with one of the other young warriors to sit nearer his new friend.

'Keep the sword stowed tight in the oiled sheep skins to avoid the iron rot,' he said as he stowed his own weapons in his sea chest.

'Aye,' he replied, watching what Bjørn did before copying him.

'You've got yourself a new dog, Bjørn,' Bjarni laughed, stowing his own gear.

'And I'll bite just as hard,' Guttorm shot back, bristling.

Bjarni held his hands up placatingly. 'Peace, Guttorm. You may have a shiny new sword, but it'll take more than that toothpick to scare me. Pick your battles, lad,' he said, extending a hand in peace.

'Gnn,' the young man grunted as he clasped the older man's wrist before turning his attention back to the oiled skin he was wrapping awkwardly around his sword.

'Like this,' Bjarni said, crossing the deck and taking the sword and skin from the younger man. Guttorm watched intently as the oiled skin was expertly wrapped fleece-down around the sheathed blade before being tied off with strips of leather to keep the package tight.

'Here,' he said, handing it back before returning to his own chest.

'Thank you.'

Bjørn watched the exchange in silence before turning his attention to his own kit. He'd managed to stow the new brynja with his mother's jerkin to keep it safe from rust, and still have room in his chest for plunder along the way. Sitting back on his chest to wait for instructions, he watched as Red Orm drew his whale-bone comb through his hair and beard, a routine he had observed most days of their journey so far. There was something soothing in the simple motions, and his mind started to drift as he waited for the rest of the crew to finish their preparations. On the shore, he could see the final pieces of cargo being lifted onto the other ships, while those staying behind watched from the treeline as the fleet made ready to sail again. He could just make out the small group of women nestled back in the treeline behind the men, watching as their saviours prepared to leave.

'All right, lads, I hope you enjoyed your holiday!' Yngvar cried as he climbed aboard, earning a cheer from the crew. 'This was our last landfall until Britain!' he called as he made his way to the stern. 'Stern oars! Pull!' he cried as he grasped the tiller. 'Pull, pull, pull!'

Slowly, *Sleipnir* eased herself back out into the open sea, with more and more men adding their oars as they gained searoom. Off to starboard, *Fjord Ulf* and *Fjord Uxi* were doing the same, and within a matter of minutes, all three ships were free of the small cove and turning their bows to the open sea beyond, the snarling figure heads angled towards the west. Only the scars of their bows remained as they slipped into the waves, and they too would soon disappear, eaten away by the hungering tide.

Once they were free of the island's shelter, the sails were run up and the three ships flew across the water in a loose arrow formation, with *Fjord Ulf* leading the pack as always. Onboard all the ships, men entertained themselves as best they could as they sliced through the waves, the unseen shores of Britain locked firmly in their sights. The mood had subtly changed on board, and all were now looking forward to the adventures yet to come, the newly claimed island already forgotten as they left it in their wake.

# Chapter 12

The four ships moved slowly through the mist, the heavy white shroud masking their progress from unwelcome eyes on the shore. The great walls of the fjord stood like ranks of silent sentinels, blocking the wind and forcing the crews to drive their ships forward under oars alone, the bows slicing cleanly through the eerily still water. Only the repetitive song of the oars as they rose and fell, and the occasional cry of a startled gull, broke the entombing silence.

Across the decks, men sat at their chests and worked their oars, lost in their own thoughts as they drove the ships onwards, waiting to begin the attack. Jarl Ake cast his gaze over the warriors as they worked, his húskarlar easily discernible from the hirðsmen and bóndi by the heavy iron ringed brynja and helmets they wore, and the swords many of them carried. Most of the hirðsmen also were equipped with simple iron helmets, although only a few could afford the valuable iron-ringed shirts, and those that couldn't were instead armoured in layers of hardened leather or thick woollen jerkins. The bóndi, the poorest of his warriors, made do with leather skullcaps and homespun jerkins, if they could afford it.

A small grin appeared on Ake's face as he turned his attention back to the gleaming húskarlar. Their loyalty to him was total, recognised and secured by their valuable weapons and armour, all of them gifts from his own hands. They would fight and die at his bidding, as they should.

He allowed the smile to reach his eyes as he lifted his gaze to the fleet he had assembled, taking in the racks of shields crowding the gunwales, each bearing his sigil of a snarling snake poised to strike. And strike he would, right at the heart of Jarl Erik's hearth and home.

'Not far now, Canute,' Jarl Ake whispered, his eyes twitching up to face the giant warrior beside him. Dressed in a burnished brynja with a decorated sword at his hip and a silver-and-gold-detailed helmet under his arm, Jarl Ake gained some credibility as a warrior jarl, but even he paled in comparison to Canute's giant frame. With his great Dane axe held effortlessly in his right hand and his face hidden by the iron rings that hung from his helmet to protect his neck and lower face, Ake looked more like a boy playing dress-up than a man

176

of war.

'Not much further,' the giant agreed, the rings singing as he turned his head to face the jarl. Ake could see the gleam of Canute's eyes through the iron-rimmed eye hole; for many warriors it was the last thing they would see on this earth.

'How can you tell?' whined a voice from behind the jarl, shattering the near-silence they were maintaining. 'All I can see is fog and water, and it's soaking me.'

'Silence, Steinar!' Ake snapped, whirling around. Unlike his father, the jarl's son was tall and handsome, but a life of luxury and slothful habits had made him weak, and even in the brynja his father had gifted him, he looked nothing like the warrior he was expected to be.

'The sound of the water has changed, Steinar,' Canute whispered quietly. 'If you listen very carefully, you can hear it striking the shoreline off the bows.'

'Gnn,' he grunted unconvinced as he pulled his fur cloak tighter over his armour. The rest of the army had forgone their cloaks long ago in preparation of the assault, but the jarl's son had simply sneered and pulled his own furs tighter.

The jarl sighed in frustration before pushing his son from his thoughts and turning his attention back to the fog ahead. He had bigger things to worry about. Months of planning were about to be realised, and it all depended on catching the men of Vágar unaware. Carr had mentioned that a sizable garrison remained, and he was thankful for the heavy weather that was hiding their approach. The fog especially was an added bonus, removing any chance of a confrontation against the ships Erik had left behind. They wouldn't sail in this weather, or have enough warning to launch before Ake's fleet was upon them. They wouldn't even have time to leave their beds before men with axes were knocking on their doors, Ake mused.

For the thousandth time Ake looked across the fleet he had assembled, checking and rechecking every detail. Two hundred-and-thirteen warriors had answered his call, coming in twos and threes to his hall at Fótrfjord until the full force was assembled. He hadn't been surprised by how many had come, given the legendary wealth of Erik Golden Hand, and the opportunity to conquer and claim new land and pastures for themselves. They would all be wealthy men by the end, those that survived. Ake imagined he could already hear the metallic clink of silver and gold falling from his hands as his men chanted his name in victory.

Ahead, hidden by the mist, Vágar slept soundly.

***

Leif was walking slowly along the shoreline below the settlement. Sleep had escaped him as it often did on cold mornings. The chill always sunk into his bones and set his wounded knee aching, reminding him of better days and the arrow that had buried itself there years before. He could still run and fight as well as any man, but after the injury, Erik had quietly told him that he would no longer stand in the front of his skjaldborg, instead offering him command of the garrison instead. The jarl wasn't willing to risk Leif's knee weakening the rest of his lines. At first he had resented the offer, but over time he had come to accept it and even enjoy the position, not to mention the wealth he gained at the end of every successful raiding season. He had also come to realise the honour Erik had paid him, and he now took pride in the position every time he watched the fleet slip their moorings and disappear into the fjord. From the day Erik left to the day he returned, Leif was jarl in all but name, answerable only to Turid.

Every morning, he ran his men raw for two hours to make sure they could defend their home against any challenger, and this morning would be no different.

'Come on, Fen,' he said excitedly to Yngvar's dog, picking up a stick and throwing it along the beach, smiling to himself as the dog disappeared into the mist after it. He was back a moment later with his prize locked in his jaw, his tail wagging excitedly as he dropped it at Leif's feet and sat patiently. He threw the wood into the mist a second time, following slowly behind. The only sounds around him were his own feet as they scrunched through the pebbles, and the gentle lapping of the tide as it sucked the small stones down to Njörd's hall. If he was honest with himself, he could admit that old age would have stopped him from raiding sooner or later anyway, and there was a quiet pleasure in spending his later years at home with his wife, rather than on distant shores.

He was just beginning to wonder where Fen had gotten to when he found him, almost tripping over the dark shape as he loomed from the thick fog. He was staring straight out into the fjord, his dark eyes fixed on the still nothingness.

'What is it, boy?' he whispered, following the dog's gaze. He couldn't see a thing through the blanketing whiteness. Fen looked up momentarily before returning his focus to the waters beyond the mist. A slow feeling of unease was beginning to creep up Leif's spine, setting the hairs on the back of his neck to stand tall. He thought he could hear the distant sound of sloshing water above the rise and fall of the tide.

'What is it, boy?' he asked again, opening his mouth slightly to improve his hearing. Again, he heard it, closer this time. '*Shit*,' he whispered under his breath. 'Come away, boy,' he said, turning and beginning to run back up the shore towards the palisade. 'Fen, COME!' he shouted as he ran, turning in time to see the dog pull its attention away from the water and chase him up the shore, easily reaching and passing him. Around him, the sound of metal striking stone began to dog his footsteps, and it took him a few moments to recognise it for what it was. '*Arrows!*'

'We're under attack!' he yelled at the top of his lungs, his voice piercing the fog. 'To arms!' he bellowed as he sprinted for the palisade. The watchmen already had the gate open for him and he bolted through, following closely on Fen's heels.

'What's going on?' one of the guardsmen asked, unable to see through the mist in the bay.

'We're under attack. Strike the bronze and call out the men!'

Nodding urgently, the warrior turned and climbed back up the ladder to the walkway above the gate before Leif had even finished his sentence. He nodded briefly to himself, pleased at the man's calm before turning to bellow more orders. Overhead, the sounds of iron on bronze began to toll, the deep *clang* filling the air. The 'bronze' was a *liberated* bell from an English church Leif and Erik had raided many seasons ago. The jarl had taken such a fancy to the piece that he'd had it brought back to his home to decorate Vágar's entrance. It was only rung in times of danger or celebration. At this time of day, there could be only one reason.

Leif had just over forty men within the settlement, with the rest on rotation to their farms. Young boys would soon be running for the stables as the bell tolled to bring them in, but for now, he would have to make do with those he had on hand.

'Ensure that the first ten men who come in are up on the walls are armed with bows or slings, and have plenty of ammunition brought, regardless of how prepared they are for combat. And get those gates barred!' he barked as one of the guardsmen dropped his hammer. 'I'm going to find my sword,' he grunted before sprinting for Erik's hall. Beyond the gates, the arrows had fallen silent, replaced by the drums of war as the dragons drew closer.

*** 

'They're onto us,' Jarl Ake called, raising his voice for the first time. 'It was bound to happen sooner or later. Archers, blind fire!' he bellowed, watching with satisfaction as men on each ship extracted themselves from their benches and ran to the bow, raining arrows down in the general direction of the settlement and the watcher's cries. Beside him, Canute was turning his giant bulk and staring at the remaining rowers. 'Row, you lazy sons of dogs, row!' he boomed, before climbing onto the bow and wrapping his left hand around the snarling serpent's head, oblivious to the arrows flying past him. From the slightly higher vantage point, he could just see the peaks of roofs poking through the mist.

'First ten!' Canute bellowed across the fleet, watching with satisfaction as the chosen men gave three final pulls on their oars before drawing them in and stowing them. The air was briefly filled with the sound of wood on wood as the chosen warriors lifted their shields from where they waited on the gunwales. His order sent ten of the most heavily armoured húskarlar from each ship forward to crowd the bows, holding shields and swords ready as the archers stepped back and shouldered their bows. Blooded in countless battles, these were the elite among Jarl Ake's warriors, and each of them had earned the right to be first ashore.

'Spare no man!' the jarl shouted across the decks, drawing his own sword, and hefting his shield. 'Steinar, on your feet,' he snarled, kicking his son's shin viciously when he didn't respond quickly enough. 'You'll march with them,' he grunted, nodding towards the heavily armed men at the bow.

He watched with disgust as his son's face blanched, the fear clear in his eyes. 'Father, I don't think I can,' he stuttered, suddenly unable to meet his gaze.

'You'll go or you'll die. You'll have no land or wealth from my hand if you can't prove to me and the men you can keep it!'

Before either of them could say more, they felt the hull strike the shore, the impact unbalancing them. As one, the men waiting in the bows cried 'Ake!' and leapt overboard.

'Shields!' Canute yelled as the elite warriors formed a small skjaldborg around him, oblivious to the incoming arrows and slingstones. Beside him, one of the warriors fell noiselessly to the ground with an arrow though his helmet's eyehole. He was the first man to fall.

'Go!' Ake snarled at his son, pushing him towards the bow and watching with frustration as he leapt over the side, barely managing not to stumble as he landed.

'In here, Steinar!' Canute roared as he watched the boy look for instruction.

Steinar didn't need to be told twice, sprinting towards the waiting men and huddling down behind his shield in the second rank.

'Get to the front!' Jarl Ake roared at his son as he watched him hide behind the older men. Before Steinar could protest, the front rank parted and he was pushed forward by one of the warriors, filling the dead man's space.

'Forward!' Canute roared, driving the small skjaldborg up the beach. As one, they began beating their weapons against their shields as arrows and stones continued to strike them. Another man fell with an arrow through his throat, the gurgling sound of his final breaths accompanied by fountains of blood as the valkyries came for him.

'With me!' Jarl Ake yelled to his remaining warriors, leaping over the side of the ship and running forward ten paces before planting his shield in the sand, waiting for the rest of his warband to form up around him. His entire force would assault the settlement, leaving only the ship's boys to guard the ships should they need to escape quickly.

By the time the rest of the crews had formed up around him, the warriors with Canute and Steinar were already half way towards the gates, ready to begin chopping into them with axes and hammers while the Jarl's men covered them with arrow and sling.

The threads had been woven, and Jarl Ake would conquer, or die.

\*\*\*

'It's Jarl Ake! The snake!' Leif shouted, recognising the device on the approaching shields as they appeared out of the mist. He was dressed in his brynja and helmet, with his sword on his hip and a Dane axe leaning against the palisade beside him, waiting to reap its grisly harvest. 'Archers!' he shouted, looking along the wall. Bowstrings were charged and released, the shafts arcing through the mist into the approaching men. Already he could see one body lying on the shore behind them.

'Volley fire on my order!' he cried. 'Ready! Fire!'

He watched with satisfaction as the arrows flew and fell in unison, whistling through the air like a flight of swallows as they struck man and shield with a vengeance. He allowed a stiff smile to play across his lips as another warrior fell with a shaft through his throat. He gave the order again, setting the pace for his men before leaving them to their work.

Before long, he had twenty-three men on the walls raining arrows and slingstones into the approaching force. By the third volley, two more men lay dead on the shore, while four more fell from the ranks clutching their wounds.

The rest of the garrison was forming up behind the gates, hurriedly shrugging on armour and lifting shields and weapons, while women and children ran back and forth from the waiting storehouses with sheaves of arrows and spears. Two more men were manoeuvring a cart filled with skins of pitch into the path of the gate, ready to release it if the enemy broke through, while thralls worked to light braziers for burning arrows. Vágar would not fall without a fight.

'Keep firing!' Leif bellowed, his voice rising above the growing battle din as the air filled with the screams of wounded and dying warriors. The fog was rapidly disappearing with the rising sun, and he could see the full size of the force arrayed against them. Beside him, the first of his own men went down with an arrow in his shoulder, wincing as he tested the wound.

'Get down below and help with that cart, if you can,' he ordered, lifting the man's fallen javelin as he did so. Carefully, he raised his left hand to aim and drew back the length of wood until his hand was level with his right ear. Below him in the front rank, he could see a youth carrying a sword and sighted on him. Exhaling slowly, he drew the spear back a fraction further and launched, watching with satisfaction as it travelled straight and true. He snarled in frustration as the swordsman stumbled at the last moment, and his spear flew into the gap he left behind, driving into an axe-carrying greybeard. The grizzled warrior carried on for another two steps before crumbling to the ground, his iron shirt unable to prevent the heavy blade from piercing his heart. Leif was moving before the man hit the ground, ducking back behind the palisade as two archers turned their aim towards him, the first of the shafts slicing through the air where his head had been a moment before. Risking a glance over the wall, he could see the small stream of dead and wounded men that littered the ground behind the advancing warriors. He was still heavily outnumbered and could already hear the sounds of axes and hammers as they began striking the gates.

'You ten, stay here and keep firing! The rest of you, with me!' he shouted before jumping down and taking his place amongst the men forming up on either side of the gates, ready to follow the burning cart through once it was released. Another of his archers fell back off the wall with an arrow through his eye, his screams dying before they started. Above the gate, he saw a group of boys too young to fight begin dropping rocks on Ake's men as they began beating the gates, slowing their progress.

'You!' he said, grabbing at a boy who couldn't be more than ten or eleven winters as he made to climb up to the walls. 'What are you doing here?' he asked incredulously.

'I want to fight,' he said, unsure of himself as he met Leif's furious gaze, frightened by the blood on the man's helmet.

'No!'

Another archer fell to the ground beside him with an arrow through his jaw, and Leif watched detachedly for a moment as he breathed his last before returning his attention to the boy. The youth was staring at the dead body in horror, unable to tear his eyes away from the blood gushing out of the warrior's mouth. Leif looked away as the boy doubled over and vomited into the mud at their feet, waiting for the sound to stop before speaking again. 'No,' he repeated, placing his hand on the boy's shoulder as he hung his head in disappointment. 'I have more important a job for you,' he said, smiling as the boy looked up hopefully. 'Run to the jarl's hall and find Turid and Arleigh. Tell them that the enemy is already at the gates, and that they will break through soon. Tell them that I sent you and that I need them to gather whatever they can carry and flee into the mountains with the rest of the women and children. I'll send word when it's safe.'

The youth nodded seriously, fear and pride plastered on his face in equal measure as he repeated the orders carefully. Behind them the sounds of hammers and axes striking the gates intensified.

'Go,' Leif said when the boy finished, nudging him towards the centre of Vágar. 'We're all counting on you!'

Nodding seriously, the boy turned and sprinted up the path towards the hall, turning back briefly to face the palisade when he reached the top of the path. Maybe he wanted a final glimpse of the fighting, or maybe he hoped that Leif was still watching him and would remember him to Erik, when he returned. Whatever it was, the pause killed him, and Leif could only watch in frustration as he crumpled to the ground with an arrow in his chest, dead.

'They'll have to figure it out for themselves,' he thought as he listened to the ominous sounds of splintering wood coming from the gates. 'Spearmen forward! Ready the wagon!' he barked, the youth forgotten as he watched four lightly armoured warriors run towards the gates with spears clasped tightly in gloved fists, ready to stab through any gaps that appeared in the wood.

*** 

'Keep going!' Canute heaved as he brought his great axe down on the gate once more, grunting with satisfaction as the blade bit clean through, creating a gap in the thick wood. He leapt back as a spear shot through the opening, piercing the now vacant space where his head had been. A slower man would have died on the spot. Steinar quickly brought his own axe down on the exposed spear shaft, shearing the head clean off and earning a nod from the stoic giant. Behind them, they could hear Ake directing his archers to increase their rate of fire, while the rest of the men formed ranks and awaited the order to charge. By now the archers' shoulders would be starting to burn and their fingers ache, Canute mused as he brought his axe down again, widening the gap in the gate and striking the locking bar behind. Three more strikes smashed through the same space in quick succession, with the last severing the beam behind.

'On me!' he bellowed, pressing his shoulder against the heavy wood and pushing. Three warriors rushed to join him at the gate, adding their weight to the task, but the thick wood refused to budge.

'Axes here! There must be another beam!' he shouted, raising his axe again and bringing it down below the first hole. Beside him, Steinar screamed as an arrow struck his helmet, the fear blinding him to the fact that he was unharmed. Canute saw the veterans among them snarl in disdain at the cowardly display.

'Steinar, use your axe!' he growled, watching as he registered his lack of injury. Shaking, the youth brought the weapon down against the wood, adding another tooth to bite at the wooden barrier. 'Keep going!' Canute called, pushing the men to work harder before shouldering his axe and taking up a dead man's shield, covering his back as he walked towards the jarl.

'We can't stay here, Jarl Ake,' he said as he approached, swinging his arm across his body towards the dead and dying warriors around them.

'I know!' the jarl snapped. Already they'd lost more men than he'd expected, and he silently cursed Erik's preparedness as he surveyed the ground around them, counting the fallen warriors. 'Tell your men to double their

184

efforts on the walls. I'll send a small force around the settlement to try and draw some of their archers away.'

'Jarl Ake.' Canute nodded before turning and running back to the gate. The jarl watched him go while arrows flew from behind him. Already the walls looked like a stuck pig, filled as it was with his men's arrows. He grunted as another shaft buried itself in his shield before he turned to call up another man from his hirð. 'Take twenty men and break left. Try to draw off some of their archers. If you can see an opportunity to break into the town, take it.'

The man nodded once before running to the end of the line, taking men from the formation as they went. Ake watched as four of the defending archers broke cover and sprinted along the wall to follow the departing force, watching with satisfaction as one fell with an arrow through his neck. A cheer from Canute's warriors pulled his attention back to the gate in time to watch as they broke through the second locking bar.

'You men,' he shouted, pointing his sword towards the right edge of his line before running towards the gates. 'On me!'

***

'Arleigh, take this. We need to get to the stables. If the gates fall, we don't want to be anywhere near here when they get through,' Turid said as she thrust one of Erik's axes into the younger woman's hand.

'Who are they?' Arleigh asked, gripping the haft to gauge the weapon's weight.

'I don't know, and I don't intend to find out. The more men they lose, the more frustrated they'll be, and we'll be the ones to suffer for it,' Turid grunted as she lifted Geri down from the wall and belted it around her waist. 'Grab that pack and follow me,' she said, taking up her own bundle and running for the stables. All around them, women and children were making their way towards the landward gate, their valuables clutched tightly in their arms, or on their backs as they fled the sounds of battle. The air was filled with the sounds of screaming children as they clung to their mother's skirts and tried not to get lost, while unbloodied boys clutched what weapons they could find and tried to look brave.

The stables weren't far from Erik's hall and the two women covered the distance in just a few moments. The animals were shifting uneasily at the unexpected commotion, and they lost precious time calming them down enough to saddle them and secure their bundles. In her mind, Arleigh saw the events of sixteen years ago when Torr marched to war and she was forced to flee her home. She couldn't help shivering at the memory, made all the more real by the retired warriors who ran past hefting ancient war gear in gnarled hands, a cruel memory of Old Manton and his last stand against some of these very men.

'Arleigh, come on!' Turid shrieked, already in her own saddle. Climbing quickly onto her own horse's back, she grasped her reins and kicked in her heels, guiding the horse through the flowing crowd of women and children.

'Follow us!' they cried as they moved through the sea of soon-to-be refugees, their voices rallying the crowd as they looked for someone to follow. It didn't take long to reach the gate, and they arrived just in time to watch as the three archers guarding it went down in a single volley, their arrow-riddled bodies landing in the mud with a collective thump. Without thinking, Arleigh jumped from the saddle and ran to the nearest body, taking up his bow and quiver and throwing them over her shoulder.

'I don't intend to be captured a second time,' she said, answering the question in Turid's eyes.

Unseen, they heard the axes begin to fall against the now unguarded gate, and Turid quickly copied her sister-wife and picked up a second bow, drawing the arrows and driving them point-first into the earth beside her. Arleigh stood next to her and planted her own arrows before drawing one and placing it on the string, surprised at how steady her hands were. Around them, the crowd watched in nervous anticipation as their jarl's women prepared to defend them. Taking strength from the sight, they took up whatever weapons they could find and began forming a makeshift skjaldborg of their own. Hoelun walked out from amongst the crowd and took up the final bow from the dead warriors before moving to stand next to her master's women, calmly drawing her first arrow. She looked completely at home with the weapon in her hands, and Turid and Arleigh exchanged questioning glances to each other, briefly wondering at the woman's own history before she came to live amongst the sword-Norse.

'Fire in volleys,' the thrall said quietly, her gaze remaining deferential. 'It will be more efficient and make it harder for them to come through the gate.'

Arleigh and Turid nodded in unison, their eyes locked on the rapidly splintering gates. Without Leif's warriors standing on the platform above, Ake's men were able to attack the gates with impunity.

'You and you!' Turid shouted, catching the attention of two boys nervously gripping their spears. They were too young to even carry the hint of a beard and she winced inwardly at the command before she gave it, steeling herself. 'Get up to that gate and thrust through any breach that appears. We have to hold them back for as long as we can.'

The pair turned at the command, standing in mute surprise when they realised who was speaking to them. Under ordinary circumstances, Turid would have been amused by their hesitation, but not today. 'MOVE!' She ordered, raising her voice.

The older of the two reacted first, shaken from his stupor as he gripped his shorter companion's shoulder and pulled him towards the gate. Turid watched them go with mixed emotions. She'd never imagined having to organise the defence of her home, and the sight of the boy's gangly limbs as they ran for the gate brought their situation into harsh reality. She stole a glance at the people surrounding her, realising that most of them were watching her, waiting for her next command. *'This is what Erik lives for,'* she realised, feeling a heady combination of excitement and apprehension rush through her system as she steeled herself to speak again. She would do what she could.

'Whoever comes through that gate, we will stand and we will fight!' Turid cried, casting her furious gaze across the grey-bearded warriors and townspeople around her. 'We will fight, and we will kill, and we will protect what is ours!'

There was a smattering of cheers through the small crowd, although many were too focused on not dropping their weapons to listen properly. *'Thor, Óðinn, hear me now. Accept our offering of these men and cast their damned souls down to Hel!'* Turid snarled, taking strength from the greybeards as they stood taller at her words. One of them stepped towards her, throwing her a conspiratorial wink as he pushed his hood back. 'Begging your pardon, Lady Turid,' he said. 'If anyone is going to take the first passage to meet the Allfather, I reckon it should be those who have spent their lives foiling the valkyries.'

'I couldn't agree more.' She smiled back, eyeing the grizzled warrior, his weathered skin telling its own stories. 'What's your name?' she asked, raising her voice to above the growing cacophony of axes as the attackers became more excited.

'Bo, Lady Turid.'

'Well then, Bo, please lead the charge,' she said, stepping aside so he could move to stand between her and the gates. 'You will be our front line.'

'Aye, my Lady,' he said, flashing a gap-toothed grin before pulling his thick homespun hood back over his head. 'Come on, you grey-bearded maggots!' he growled, striding forward a few paces to block the path to Turid and her companions before planting his feet firmly in the mud and hefting his spear. Behind him, ten more grizzled warriors marched forwards bearing similarly scarred and battered shields and armour. Unlike the women and children behind them, they carried their spears and axes in practiced hands, moving with a confidence earned through a lifetime of war.

***

'Prepare to open the gates!' Leif called, sending four of his lightly-armoured warriors forward at his order. 'On my mark! One...'

Behind him, he could hear the blazing fires in the braziers as they danced and spat, ready to play their part in the grisly task to come.

'Two...' he called, nodding as the waiting warriors grasped the final locking beam and prepared to pull.

'Three! Open the gates!' he cried, forcing his voice above the spear din. With one quick, well-practiced motion, the gates were opened, revealing the surprised faces of Ake's men as they registered the suddenly open portal. One of them stumbled forward into the mud as his hammer struck empty air. It took them only a moment to realise that they were through before they started tripping over themselves in their desperation to be the first in the town, and to claim Erik's legendary treasure for themselves and their jarl.

'Push!' Leif cried, motioning for the blocks of wood holding the wheels in place to be kicked free before the cart tumbled down the hill, straight into the enemy warriors as they pushed through the gate. 'Archers!' he bellowed, raising his sword and dropping it, aiming at the rolling cart.

As one, the waiting bowmen stepped forward and held their pitch-tipped arrows in the flames before drawing the shafts back smoothly and releasing. The arrows cut a flaming arc through the air, leaving a trail of black smoke in their path as they dropped to pierce the skins of oil loaded on the wagon, transforming it into an unstoppable rolling inferno in seconds.

'Close the gates!' Leif shouted, watching as Ake's men took in their rolling doom and began screaming in terror. He saw more than one drop his weapon or shield in their desperation to escape the rolling flames even as their oblivious comrades pushed forwards, desperate to enter the town. It was chaos, as expected.

As soon as the gate was clear, Leif's men sprinted forwards and leaned against the heavy gates, bringing the two doors together before slamming down the beaten locking bar. As the gates closed Leif caught a glimpse of the flaming cart knocking two of Ake's mail-clad warriors from their feet before they were hidden from his sight. He smiled grimly as Ake's warriors began screaming in agony, the flaming cart spilling its treacherous cargo over them as it barrelled through their ranks. On the walls above, Leif's archers began firing again, raining shaft after shaft into the disorganised warriors as they fled the flames.

'Well done, lads!' he shouted, casting his gaze across his warriors. 'They'll be back soon enough. Get food and water, tend to your wounds and restock the ammunition. And secure that gate!' His men cheered as they moved to obey his commands.

Above the wall, an orange glow danced in the last of the mist as the air filled with screams, and the sickly-sweet smell of burning flesh.

*** 

'What the fuck just happened?' Jarl Ake raged incredulously, his eyes glued to the sight of at least fifteen of his warriors disappearing under the mess of flames and fire that bellowed forth from the open gates. He could only watch in mute fury as he registered the losses. Already he had seen almost a quarter of his force carried away to the corpse hall, or left lying on the ground too wounded to go on, and now he had to watch his carefully laid plans go up in literal smoke.

'Fall back! Fall back!' he shouted, fighting to create order from chaos as he retreated out of arrow range. 'Canute!' he barked, forcing his voice above those of his men while they formed around him, holding their shields high towards the settlement to protect themselves from any lucky shots. 'Are you tickling the gate? Or were you planning to break through in the near future?' he growled dangerously when the giant appeared before him.

'They are better prepared than we expected,' Canute replied impassively. He had suffered a wound to the neck which had sheared through the iron links protecting him, scouring the skin. Ake was sure it hurt, although the giant seemed unaware of the pain. Behind him, Steinar sulked sullenly, wiping his mud-covered hands on his breeches. Many of the men carried some wound or injury, and several were wincing from burns to their hands or knuckles.

189

'We're going again,' Ake snarled, ignoring Canute's response. 'Front rank, hold your shields forward. Second rank, hold them high! When you reach the gates, hold them up to cover the axemen. I doubt they have a second cart waiting for you. We're nearly through. I will not be defeated by the *dregs* of Vágar,' he added furiously, his gaze flickering across the assembled warriors. None dared to meet his vengeful gaze. 'Do not disappoint me again. Go! And archers, fire faster!' he spat. He watched as his men sprinted back up the hill towards the besieged settlement for a few moments before he became aware of a presence lingering beside him. He grimaced when he saw who it was. 'What are you still doing here?'

'Where do you want me, Father?' Steinar ventured lamely, unable to meet his father's gaze.

Ake could see the fear in his son's eyes, and he felt a wave of loathing wash over him at the sight. The feeling was compounded further when an arrow struck the ground by Steinar's foot, and he winced visibly as his son jumped in fright. It was a long shot, with little power in it, yet still the boy started like a rabbit.

'Front and centre! I don't want to see you again unless you're behind the walls of Vágar, or dead!' he said dangerously, shooting a withering look at his son before spitting on the ground. 'Go.'

Steinar looked briefly as if he would argue, but thought better of it and instead turned and followed on the heels of the retreating warriors, stumbling in the mud as he went. Jarl Ake followed more slowly, watching as his men came under fire again as they came back into range. His son was struck twice, but both arrows buried themselves in his shield, more out of luck than anything else. Two more men fell with arrows protruding from their shoulders, dead.

'*Is that twenty-nine? Or thirty?*' he mused. '*The Golden Hand had better have piles of silver hidden away in this shit-pit of a settlement.*' With a sigh, he hoisted his shield and followed his men into battle. He could see Canute raising his giant axe to attack the gate again, bringing the blade down in a mighty swing before leaping back as a spear shot through the newly created window. Two more strikes followed in quick succession.

'Nearly there!' the giant boomed as he brought the axe back for a fourth strike.

'Let's see what you've got tucked away, Erik,' Ake muttered as he heard the gate break, finally yielding to Canute and his húskarlar as they pushed their

190

combined weight against the shattered wood, exposing the town within.

***

'They're through!' Turid called, watching as the axe blade sheared through the wood and drove into the locking bar behind. Immediately, the taller of the two boys she'd sent to the gate rammed his spear through the gap and Arleigh saw the pride flash across his face at the answering scream as he turned to the crowd behind him.

Beside him, the second boy screamed as an answering spear flicked through the opening and wedged itself in his companion's throat. Arleigh and the rest could only watch as the boy's pride was replaced by surprise and fear before he fell to the ground, dead.

As the body hit the ground, the air was split by a heart-rendering cry and Arleigh felt her blood run cold as one of the women dropped her pitchfork and forced her way through the grey-bearded warriors, tears pouring form her eyes as she sprinted towards the broken body. Beside him, the second boy stood rooted to the spot, frozen, his spear useless in his hand as he gazed down at the dead body as the woman arrived and threw herself over the boy. He could only be her son. Beside them, the sound of axes began again, the sound of splintering wood shaking the boy from his daze. Arleigh and Turid shared a horrified glance as he moved to stand between the crying woman and the disintegrating gate, preparing to protect her even as the spear licked forward again to bury itself in his ribs. Even the greybeards, well versed in the art of violence, cried in fury at the sight and took a step forwards as the woman's cries grew even louder. Arleigh could only watch as the second body hit the ground with a thud, the spear stuck in the boy's body as he breathed his last. Blood was pouring from his mouth. Arleigh's heart broke as he reached for the woman, crying 'Mother' over and over. She couldn't imagine the pain of watching two perfect sons die in as many seconds. Mercifully, the woman's anguish didn't last long as the axe came down a final time, splitting the locking bar and revealing a tall, thin warrior with a short beard who pushed through the broken gate and ripped his knife across her throat without breaking his stride.

'Fire!' Hoelun screamed, launching her first arrow a heartbeat before Arleigh and Turid. All three shafts buried themselves in the warrior's breast, avenging the woman and her son. 'Nock. Draw. Loose,' Hoelun called, her thralldom forgotten as she reached for another shaft, setting the pace. The

191

three women fired two more volleys before the enemy struck, downing two more warriors before they could reach the line of greybeards waiting for them. Unlike Old Manton, these men welcomed death, and Arleigh watched with the rest as they launched themselves at their enemies with such ruthless abandon that they were forced to retreat in the face of their ferocity. 'No man wants to grow old in the North,' Turid said, seeing the question on Hoelun's face. Beside her, Arleigh launched another arrow, taking a running warrior in the neck and tripping the man behind.

Throwing her bow over her shoulder, Arleigh drew the axe from her belt and unsheathed her eating knife, holding it in her left hand. Already their enemies had recovered from the unexpected ferocity of the greybeards' attack and had thrown themselves back into the fray.

Despite their eagerness to defend their home one last time, the grizzled veterans couldn't escape the realities of age and they were soon overpowered and killed by their younger, faster opponents.

'For Vágar!' Turid cried, drawing Geri from her belt as she charged forwards with the blade held high. Arleigh followed closely on her heels while Hoelun walked behind them, drawing and loosing her arrows with terrifying accuracy. Erik's people fought furiously, but none amongst them had the skill or the equipment to stand up to Ake's warriors and already Arleigh could see the less stout-hearted amongst them beginning to flee under the assault.

Pushing their way through the melee, the two women swung their weapons wildly, working together to keep the attackers at bay as they fought. Between them, they managed to kill one last warrior, but Arleigh's axe stuck fast in the man's skull, leaving her open to the club that struck her ribs, winding her. Gasping, she lost her grip on the axe and fell back, holding her hands up in surrender. She could only watch in dismay as Geri was wrangled from Turid's grasp before she too was beaten to the ground with a punch from a man's shield, the iron boss smashing into her face and shattering her nose. Arleigh screamed with rage as her friend was knocked to the ground where she lay still. Painfully, Arleigh crawled through the mud towards her. All around her, the survivors were dropping their weapons and fleeing as the attackers streamed down the hill towards the fighting by the shore, leaving only two behind to guard the gate. She watched in horror as one of the men ripped the bow from Hoelun's grasp and threw her roughly on the ground. Wincing, she closed her ears to the girl's screams as his hands tore at her clothes and skin as he sought to vent his frustration in her. Arleigh was transported back to her last night in Shorewitchshire and the memory lent her strength as she quietly crawled through the mud towards the struggling girl. Hoelun shrieked and struggled against the man's grasp, clawing at his eyes and neck as he fought to grip her breasts and force her legs apart, his intent clear. Arleigh could see the fear in the girl's eyes.

She moved as quickly as she dared, a discarded knife held firmly in her fist. She watched in silent fury as the man slapped Hoelun twice across the face, dazing her so her resistance faltered. Taking advantage of her stupor, the man pressed her down with his left hand and pulled his manhood from his breeches. Seeing what was coming, Hoelun began to struggle again, earning another resounding slap for her efforts that knocked the fight out of her completely.

Arleigh's anger drove her on, and as the man prepared to enter her friend she leapt on him, screaming like a harpy as she pushed her knife through his neck from the right and punched it forwards through his windpipe. Gasping, she fell to the ground, exhausted. She barely noticed the flood of blood that exploded over Hoelun, nor did she see the girl take up the bloody blade and slice clean through the man's deflating member and stuff the bloody trophy into his ripped throat. Arleigh focused on the young woman's face, her tears cutting lines through the mud and blood on her face as she began stabbing the body repeatedly. There was no mercy there.

'Hoelun, get... get to Váli! Tell him to... to find Erik...' she said, sighing as her wounds carried her into unconsciousness.

The last thing she remembered was seeing Hoelun climb to her feet and stomp down on the man's face with all her might, crushing his skull before taking up her bow and running.

Arleigh never saw the men Hoelun killed as she rode through the ruined gates, or the knife she had thrust through her belt to accompany her bow. If she had, she might have thought one of the corpse maidens had come to wreak vengeance for the dead.

***

'Fight, men of Vágar!' Leif shouted, forcing his voice above the sounds of battle as he yanked his sword free of a warrior's throat, spitting as the dead body was replaced with a live one. The two forces had clashed in the open gateway, the shattered wood lying in ruins under their feet as it was pushed deeper into the churning mud. Behind the attackers he could see a fully armed and armoured warrior patiently watching the fighting, his unbloodied sword still in its scabbard. It could only be Ake.

'Coward,' he bellowed as he ducked behind his shield, narrowly avoiding the spear that had been aimed at his head. His sword licked under the rim of his shield in response, slicing through the man's thigh and the vein waiting there. He too was quickly replaced and dispatched before Leif took a step back, relinquishing his spot at the front for a sip of water. His men were making a good account of themselves, taking two of the attackers for every one of their own, but still the numbers didn't add up. They would all be dead by the time the sun reached its zenith. Already he thought he could hear the beating of wings as the valkyries moved among the dead, choosing those worthy to sit at the Allfather's table.

Glancing along the battle lines, he was just in time to watch the largest warrior he had ever seen bring his giant axe down on one of the defenders, slicing through the man's shield and arm with apparent effortlessness. Leif winced as the hapless warrior screamed in agony, the blood curdling sound penetrating the confined battle lines. Leif could only watch as the giant brought his weapon around again, cutting the man's screams short as he added another body to the carpet he was weaving at his feet.

He took another gulp of water from a waiting bucket before moving determinedly along the line towards the giant, watching as another of his men fell to the axe. Just as he was about to attack, Gørm leapt into the fray, his blót knife in one hand and an axe in the other. Bellowing the Allfather's name, Leif watched as he began slashing and chopping in short, controlled motions, forcing the axeman onto the defensive. It was like watching a wasp fight a bear. Despite the speed and fury of his attacks, he couldn't do more than irritate the giant. Snarling, the goði darted forward again, aiming his axe towards the giant's shoulder even as he drove the knife towards his midriff. The attack happened in slow motion for Leif, and he could only watch in frustration as Gørm's foot slipped on a mud-covered scrap of wood, sending him sprawling in the mud. Before the goði had even hit the ground, Leif knew his thread was cut, his premonition confirmed a moment later as the giant buried his axe in Gørm's guts.

'Wyrd,' Leif grunted before pushing his way through the struggling warriors blocking his path. The axeman hadn't seen him yet, and he thought to end the contest before it could begin. He imagined the death of such a warrior would demoralise Ake's men enough that his own men could regain the initiative.

194

Pushing through the front rank, he drew back his sword and threw a furious lunge at the warrior as he struggled to free his axe, aiming for the man's crotch. He could only growl in frustration as the man leaped backwards with surprising agility, pulling both axe and corpse with him. The blade came free with a sickly squelching sound as he moved. Ignoring Gørm's ruined body, Leif attacked, his sword and shield moving in unison. The movements came unbidden to him, ingrained in his muscle memory after a lifetime of war. Yet even as he moved, some small part of him recognised that this was his last sword song. For every lunge or thrust he made, the giant countered or blocked before responding with terrifying accuracy. Within a matter of moments, Leif's shield arm was completely numb, and he was convinced something in the limb had broken. He couldn't move his shield as he had, and just tightening his grip sent sparks of agony up his arm. It didn't matter. He knew that he would be with his forefathers soon. All he cared about now was having a story to share with them when he finally claimed his seat amongst the Allfather's *einherjar*. If he was going to die, he would die on his terms. With a cry he attacked again, stepping forward to add power to his thrust as he tried to drive his sword through the axeman's armour and into the soft flesh behind. He felt a moment of hope as the giant slipped in the mud, but at the last moment the warrior twisted his body, letting Leif's sword slide harmlessly across the iron rings, forcing Leif to overextend. Leif cried out in rage as his bad leg gave way and he himself slipped, falling into the quagmire at his feet. Tightening his grip on the sword, he imagined the beating of wings overhead and smiled. He would see his father soon.

Like the striking snake on Ake's banner, Canute spun on his heels and brought the axe around in a great arc, slicing straight through Leif's armoured side and deep into his body, shearing through brynja, ribs and spine before the blade became stuck in the bones on the opposite side. Leif was dead before he even knew the giant had struck. He never saw the warriors who attacked his men from the rear, spearing and stabbing them with the cruel efficiency of warriors too long denied victory. Vágar had fallen.

\*\*\*

Jarl Ake covered his nose against the smell as he walked through the shattered gates of Vágar, trying to ignore the mingling odours of piss and shit that lingered there. The skalds never mention the smells of battle when they sing about the glories of war. The dead lay in a thick carpet beneath his feet, the corpses barely two steps back from the broken gates; the warriors of Vágar had sold their lives dearly, refusing to yield even a step. There were no survivors, and already the flies were beginning to swarm. Overhead, the ravens cawed.

Only one warrior had survived the battle, holding on long enough to point out the ruined body of their leader before he too succumbed to his wounds.

'Who killed him, Canute?' he asked as he stared down at the ruined corpse the man had indicated. The body was nearly cloven in two and Ake knew the answer before he'd asked the question. But he wanted to honour his first warrior in front of the rest.

'I did,' Canute grunted impassively, barely looking at the ruined body.

'His sword is yours, then,' Ake said before moving on. Behind him, the giant bent low and picked up the sword, testing the weight briefly before cleaning it on the dead man's cloak and sliding it through his belt, alongside his own. Ake didn't see him close the dead man's eyes and bow his head briefly before following his jarl. The man had fought well and deserved his respect.

Ake's warriors were moving through the settlement, rounding up women and children and putting them in the stables and byres behind Jarl Erik's great hall. He would deal with them in time.

In his hand he held *Geri*, the Golden Hand's famed sword, and an unexpected treasure. '*It is beautiful*,' he admitted to himself as he looked again at the blade. The balance was perfect. One of his men had found it beside the unconscious body of a woman who could only be Turid, Erik's wife. No one else would have dared to take up the jarl's sword; she too would be dealt with in time. For what felt like the hundredth time he cast his gaze across the captured settlement, considering the price of his victory. '*Fifty-two dead, another eighteen wounded, some of whom will also die*,' he thought, spitting on the ground as if to rid himself of a foul taste. He could barely contain his temper as he moved through the field of corpses. The capture of the jarl's wife and bed thrall did little to allay his temper. He knew that the job was only half done, that there were still men loyal to Erik in the lands around his new home. He would deal with them in due course, but first he had to secure what was his. Already his men had begun repairing the gates to secure the town.

'*Ake The Landed. That will be my name,*' he mused, throwing his gaze over the battlefield once more. 'Bring my son to me,' he said to the nearest man, refocusing his thoughts. He sat on a stack of firewood while he waited, gazing up at the ravens as they circled overhead, no doubt watching the feast below as his men separated friend from foe. He could see Canute directing the work, loading the dead onto carts or thrown over shoulders as they were carried to the shore.

'You sent for me, Father?' Steinar asked, his voice breaking into his father's thoughts. He hadn't heard his son approach. Now that the killing had stopped and the danger passed, Steinar had regained his usual arrogant swagger, and Ake briefly reconsidered his decision before speaking.

'Yes,' Ake said, eyeing his son. He had been disappointed with the boy's cowardice when the attack began, but he had found some semblance of courage before the end and fought as hard as the next man. Perhaps in time his courage would grow, and he would become a leader of men. He wasn't confident in the thought, but neither was he rich in choices. Steinar was the only son he had. He watched as the boy shuffled his feet, his confidence melting as the silence stretched between them. He let the boy squirm a few moments more before speaking again. 'You did well today,' he said, 'but I *never* want to see you hang back like you did today. When I'm gone, you will lead these men, but they will not follow a coward. You must earn their trust, Steinar. Or they will choose to follow another.'

Steinar nodded, biting his tongue on whatever response had been cooking in his head. Above them, the ravens continued to circle, waiting for their cue to feast, and Ake watched as a few of the braver ones swooped low enough to peck at the dead before they were chased off by his men.

'Here,' Ake said suddenly, focusing on his son as he unbuckled his sword belt and handed it to him. 'Next time you wield a sword, let it be this one. May it give you courage and strength in the skjaldborg.'

'Thank you, Jarl Ake,' Steinar said formally as he wrapped his fingers around the hilt. Clasping the scabbard, he slowly drew the blade, eyeing the wicked sharpness of the iron as it rasped free.

'You have earned this, but never let me see you dishonour it,' Ake said in a low voice, his eyes dangerous. Steinar's gaze hadn't left the blade, and he only nodded as Ake spoke, lost in his own thoughts.

For once, Ake allowed a brief smile to cross his face as he watched his son before he stood and strapped Geri around his own waist. The weight felt right. 'Now, get to work,' he grumbled, his voice hardening. 'I want the enemy dead out of the settlement by nightfall, and our own on pyres by noon tomorrow at the latest; you're in charge of that. Get it done,' he said with finality. Out of the corner of his eye, he spotted what he assumed was the blacksmith, by the anvil and forge that sat alongside to the rough home. Through the open door, he could see the fearful eyes of a beautiful woman as she hid from the invaders behind her husband's frame.

'Bring that woman to Erik's hall,' he said to one of his waiting warriors before walking towards the towering building. 'My hall,' he corrected himself, smiling. 'Bring her to my hall.'

Behind him, the warrior laughed to see his jarl in such a joyous mood as he drew his sword and walked towards the blacksmith, ready to do his lord's bidding.

# Chapter 13

The rain and hail felt like a thousand tiny needles as they raked across *Sleipnir's* decks, blinding the crew as they guided her through the furious seas.

In the dim light, visibility was almost zero and they were only able to catch sight of their sister ships when sparks from Thor's hammer lit the sky. They'd been sailing for two days, one of which had been spent battling the storm. It had crept up on them from the west, the dark ominous cloud staining the horizon as far as the eye could see. During a brief conference between the three captains Yngvar had pushed to turn back and run before the storm, rather than risk the waves, but Erik, supported by Halfdan, had argued that they had suffered enough delays already. So now here they were, battling Ran's daughters as Thor raged overhead. They'd been lucky so far in that none from *Sleipnir* had been swept overboard, but they had no idea how the other crews were faring. Each ship could only continue forward in their own misery. Only the Nornir knew if they would survive another day, or find themselves sucked below to join Njörd in his sunken hall. Bjørn had no idea how Yngvar was navigating through the endless grey and black around them, or if he even could.

'*Fjord Ulf* ho!' Red Orm cried from his position by the mast, his arm pointing off to starboard as the storm stole the volume from his words.

'Right you are!' Yngvar called back, adjusting the tiller to avoid a collision. From his bench, Bjørn could just make out the looming outline of his father's ship as she slid into view, her snarling prow beast spitting defiance into the waves as they thrashed around her.

Bjørn could make out snippets of shouted conversation as Yngvar and Erik bellowed at each other through the storm, but from where he was sitting, their words were mostly stolen by the wind. '*Tu... ck! We m...t tu...n ba...! Fjo... U...i has al...dy turn... arou...*'

Bjørn watched as Yngvar listened intently before shouting a response across the gap. The message became clear a few moments later when *Fjord Ulf* turned about, narrowly avoiding a wave that would have swamped her.

'All right, lads,' Yngvar shouted into the wind, his arms bulging on the tiller as he fought to keep *Sleipnir* under control. 'We're coming about! It seems Ran's daughters have won this round!'

Bjørn watched as Yngvar pushed his weight against the tiller, causing the ship to falter and then pivot as she completed her one-hundred-and-eighty-degree turn. As they came abreast of the waves, the port gunwale dipped briefly, taking on buckets of water in seconds. With a roar, Yngvar ordered the water to be bailed as *Sleipnir* began to leap forwards again. Men and ship's boys were already moving before the order was out, throwing the water back over the side with anything and everything they could find as they bent their backs to the task.

Despite the greased cloak wrapped around his shoulders, Bjørn was soaked to the bone and freezing, the combination of saltwater, rain and sweat making a mockery of his attempts to stay dry. He was sure he looked a sorry sight. They all did.

When the storm had hit, Yngvar had ordered the spare sail rigged as a makeshift shelter to keep the crew protected from the worst of the rain and hail. But he had soon changed his mind as the wind continued to grow and the risk of losing the valuable wool became too great. Now, with freezing skin and burning muscles, the order to turn about was a blessing greeted with a cheer from the crew. Throwing another pail of water overboard, he sent a silent prayer to the Æsir that all three ships would survive the return to Storfjellet.

Wyrd.

\*\*\*

*Sleipnir* limped exhaustedly back into the harbour she had so recently left, embracing the cove's calmer waters while the tempest continued to rage beyond. Amongst the trees they could just make out the reddish-orange glow of campfires as they lit the trees above them from within the newly created longphort. *Fjord Ulf* was already waiting for them, listing badly to port, and Yngvar calmly steered *Sleipnir* into the harbour to rest on the drakkar's starboard side. The space beside her was ominously empty; there was no sign of *Uxi* yet. With the storm still thrashing the waves behind them, they had no choice but to wait. They all knew it was a miracle they had made it back at all.

As the anchors were thrown sluggishly overboard by exhausted men, Bjørn collapsed across his oar, too tired to even pull it onboard. The rest of the crew were similarly positioned, their backs heaving as they struggled to move leaden arms. Even the unstoppable Yngvar was bent almost double over the tiller, his hands still wrapped hard around weathered wood as if they'd fused together. Bjørn wouldn't have been surprised to find his handprints ground into the wood's surface after such a battle they'd just fought.

Mercifully, they had made it back without losing anyone to the waves, but it had been a near thing. More than once, Bjørn had been sure they would break their spine as they crashed down into a trough between waves, or that they would run aground, but in the end Yngvar had seen them through. Bjørn was amazed they'd even found the island again, and his appreciation for his friend had grown substantially.

*Fjord Ulf* hadn't been so lucky. Three men had been claimed by the waves, their bodies sucked down to the impenetrable depths of Njörd's hall before anyone could even try to save them.

Judging that the crew had rested long enough, Yngvar gave the order to disembark, earning himself groans and grunts in response. Moving like *draugr* risen from their burial mounds, the crew half-limped, half-dragged themselves into the fortified camp where they were greeted with thick broth and warm ale.

As soon as *Fjord Ulf* had been spotted, the men and women who had been left behind had thrown wood on the flames and begun preparing for the rest of the fleet to return, they were told. Within an hour of entering the camp, everyone was asleep, trusting the men who had stayed behind to keep watch while they slept. They were only too happy to oblige, eager to show their worth in the hope of earning back their seats in the fleet.

The storm continued to rage, thrashing the shore as it wasted its anger against the cliffs, unable to claim the ships that nestled within their rocky embrace.

The sun was high in the sky when Bjørn finally exited the shelter, the bright light bathing the world around him a stark contrast to the nightmare he had fallen asleep to. There was still no sign of *Fjord Uxi* in the harbour, but Bjørn could see men on the cliffs, no doubt scouring the calming sea for her.

'*Where are you, Toke?*' Bjørn whispered to himself as he cast his tired eyes over the water.

'Bjørn! Over here!'

Recognising the voices, he turned to find Bjarni and Red Orm sitting with

Yngvar beside one of the communal fires, an iron pot suspended over the flames. The thought of hot food made his stomach growl and he strapped Huginn around his waist as he crossed the short distance to his friends. Around him, he could hear the sounds of construction as men continued to work on the camp and surrounding palisade.

'Here,' Red Orm said as he drew near, packing a rough wooden bowl with porridge from the pot. He could see a few berries colouring the mixture and his stomach growled hungrily in anticipation.

'Still no sign of *Uxi*?' he asked, pushing a heaped spoon into his mouth. He closed his eyes briefly, savouring the taste of the fruit as he bit down and felt the warm juices in his mouth. He thought he could also taste the slightest hint of honey.

'Not yet,' Yngvar said, refilling his own bowl. The exhaustion was written clear on his face, the shadows under his eyes deeply etched. 'Your father has ordered the crews to rest and recover their strength. If there is no sign of her within three days, we're to head back out and see if we can find any sign of her while *Ulf's* strakes are repaired. They struck a rock as they came into the harbour which ripped a hole in her bows. It's nothing major, but she'll be landlocked for at least a week while they repair the damage. We'll pull her further up on the shore when the tide comes back in and beach her for repairs.'

'And *Sleipnir*?'

'Her hull is solid and there's nothing wrong with her keel. We could go straight back out today and take on Njörd himself,' Red Orm replied with a tired smile. Bjarni grunted noncommittally beside him as he stirred the flames with a stick. He, too, looked exhausted.

Bjørn grunted wordlessly, his mind on Toke as he took another mouthful.

They sat in companionable silence after that, each lost in his own thoughts as they considered the fate of the missing ship. The air around them was filled by the gentle hum of conversation as men from both ships intermingled, eating and talking in small groups as they recovered from the ordeal, their energy spent. Bjørn could feel his stomach relaxing as it received the incoming food, the grumbling dying away 'How is my father? And my brothers?' he asked, looking as Yngvar.

'All fine,' Yngvar replied, softening his gaze briefly. 'Sigurd took a decent hit on his arm when they struck the rock and has a bruise the size of Bjarni's arse, and Olaf got a small cut above his eye when he struck a gunwale, but they're both fine. Your father came through unscathed.'

'Good. I'll go find them now,' he said, spooning the final scraps of food into his mouth. Sighing contentedly, he smiled at his companions before standing with a nod and handing back the empty bowl and turning to make his way through the camp towards his father's hall.

The three men watched him go, exchanging greetings here and there as he passed through the different groups.

'He's a good lad,' Bjarni grunted after a while, taking a swig from his waterskin.

'Aye,' Red Orm agreed, unstopping his own skin.

Yngvar just smiled, his eyes following the young man he had spent so many hours with over the years. In the brief time they'd been away from Vágar, Bjørn had already achieved far more than he could have expected, and his chest swelled with pride every time he heard the young man's name mentioned around the fires at night. His saga was being written without him even knowing it.

'We will wait for them,' Bjørn heard his father say to Sigurd and Olaf as he approached. The three of them were standing outside of his father's hall. It was the only fully completed structure in the camp, although, in its fury, the storm had ripped some of the recently laid roofing off and deposited it a short distance away. Bjørn could see the bloodstained bandage around Olaf's head. *'A little more than a cut,'* he mused.

'Of course,' Olaf replied before throwing a smile at Bjørn as he approached. 'You're alive, then.'

'Aye,' Bjørn grinned, 'Njörd had no interest in me lying about in his halls and drinking his salty ale. You've seen better days,' he added, nodding at the bandage.

Olaf shrugged, touching a hand to the bloody bandage.

'He'll be telling everyone it was a sword wound by the time we get home.' Sigurd laughed. Olaf ignored him.

'It does me good to see you alive and unharmed, Bjørn,' Erik said seriously, eyeing his youngest. 'Are you injured?'

'Not a scratch.' Bjørn smiled, holding his arms wide.

'Good.' Erik smiled, recognising the familiar internal battle his youngest always stoked in him and pushing the feelings down. He had never truly faced a risk to his youngest's life before, and the experience had raised unexpected emotions.

'Yngvar will have told you by now that we're going to wait here for *Fjord*

*Uxi,* and your brother?'

Bjørn nodded as he reached for Sigurd's proffered waterskin. 'And that *Sleipnir* will seek them out if they're not back within three days.'

'Aye,' Erik said quietly. He could see his sons trying to hide their worry behind confident nonchalance and he felt a moment of pride. He hadn't raised weak men. 'The Nornir haven't claimed your brother yet, I can feel it. He's out there somewhere, and we'll find him. All of them.'

None of them replied as their eyes flicked towards the conspicuously empty waters, willing *Fjord Uxi* to appear. For a moment the four of them stood in silence and watched the endless blue beyond the bay, as if their shared willpower could draw the lost ship to them. Nothing happened.

'All right, no point wasting our time staring at the waves,' Erik said, snapping them back to reality. 'Olaf, get yourself and half the crew down to the shore. The tide will soon be high enough to get *Ulf* drawn up on to the shingle. We'll begin repairs once she's properly beached. Sigurd, you can take the other half and get them working on the camp – I want at least two more of the buildings completed, or as close to it, before we leave here. If we're going to be stuck here, we may as well be comfortable while we wait.'

'What about me, Father?' Bjørn asked.

'Seeing as you've already started training your new friend in the use of the sword, you may as well do so for the rest of the younger warriors. When they're not training, they can join Sigurd.'

'Yes, Father.' Bjørn nodded.

'Good,' Erik said with finality, smiling at each of his boys in turn before turning and walking into the hall. For a while, the three brothers stood in silence, their individual fears for Toke flooding into the void their father had left. Death was a reality for all of them, and despite their father's words, they knew it well. Ships disappeared all the time, never to be heard from again. Life without Toke was a strange concept, as was the idea of his not reaching Valhöll if the waves had claimed him. Overhead, two ravens crossed the grey sky, croaking into the horizon. Bjørn shivered.

'We should get to it,' Olaf said quietly, speaking into the silence. 'Father won't thank us for standing around doing nothing, and nor would Toke.'

'Aye,' Sigurd grunted, forcing a smile as he hefted his axe and headed towards the waiting crew. 'Come on, Olaf,' he called over his shoulder as he walked.

Bjørn watched them go for a few moments longer before turning his eyes back to the horizon. *'Come on, Toke. Njörd doesn't want your sorry arse crowding his hall.'* As if in answer, the wind picked up and blew hard against Bjørn's face forcing him to turn his face from the lashing tide before he too turned and walked back towards his own men.

\*\*\*

Toke was in a world of pain. His shoulders were burning and his lungs were heaving from the hours spent pulling the oar as *Uxi* defied the raging tempest. The wood had reopened the wound on his left hand, wearing away at the scar to leave a trail of blood along his oar that gummed his palm to the handle. And still he pulled. They had soon lost sight of the other ships after coming about, and had quickly been blown off course by the surging ocean and screaming winds as they struggled in the dark grey light. At one point, a piece of debris had struck the steering oar, shearing a great bite from the blade and reducing Halfdan's ability to keep their course true. Not long after, a log had been swept over the ship and struck the mast halfway up, snapping it. Miraculously no one had been hurt, but there had been an audible moan from the crew as they watched their ruined mast be swept away. It was down to oars alone from that point on. Halfdan had taken it in his stride, snarling at the sky and challenging Óðinn and Njörd themselves to do their worst. Toke had taken strength from the sight, watching as Halfdan tirelessly fought to turn the ship into the oncoming waves with gritted teeth. After a few hours, when it had become clear that the storm wouldn't blow itself out, he'd ordered every fourth man to help the ship's buoys bail. From that point on, they had worked in shifts in the battle against Ran's daughters. Unfortunately for Toke, he had been one of the men left at his oar while around him his crewmates began relieving *Uxi* of her water weight. Up and down the length of the snekkja men were using buckets, bowls and even their helmets to empty the ship and lighten her load as quickly as they could while those left at their oars struggled to lift the heavy wood again and again, fighting to keep their bow pointed into the waves. They were no longer concerned with reaching any sort of destination, they just wanted to survive. The sky had filled with sparks as Thor struck his anvil again and again, turning night into day. At one point, a rogue wave had swamped the deck and carried two men overboard, their screams drowned before they could begin as they were pulled below to a watery grave. 'Allfather, spare me a straw death,' Toke grunted as he tugged his oar again. The order to change places came soon after, and it was with begrudging relief that he shipped his oar and took up a bucket. 'If Ran tries to catch me in her net, I'll fight her myself for a seat at Valhöll's table,' he muttered as he tossed another bucketful of water over the side. The crew was beyond exhaustion, their teeth gritted as they fought their own private battles to keep going.

It wasn't until *Skoll* and *Hati* changed places and the sun crested the horizon that the tempest finally blew itself out, miraculously claiming no more lives. As the waters began to calm, the crew slumped against their oars or the hull, too tired to even try and hide their exhaustion anymore. The storm had taken even that from them. Toke watched Halfdan relinquish the tiller as he too slumped exhausted against the hull, defeated.

For almost an hour, the crew lay where they fell, completely spent, while *Uxi* drifted where the ocean carried her. Not a man among them moved to take the tiller or try to control their passage. Overhead, the gentle winds pushed the final wisps of cloud away to reveal blue skies and sun which beat down on their heads, slowly drying their sodden clothes.

It was the cries of gulls that eventually woke Toke, their harsh screeches drawing him from sleep and making him aware of every knotted muscle in his battered body. His left hand ached and he cut away the remains of the bandage with his seax before leaning over the side and bathing it in the cool water. He winced as he rubbed his thumb against the wound to wash away the dried blood and clean it. The sound of his oar striking wood when he moved had woken the men nearby and gradually the rest of the ship woke up from their reprieve in a ripple effect of yawns, groans, grunts and farts. The sun was still low in the east by the time everyone was fully awake and stretching their tired muscles. Up and down the ship, men were relieving themselves over the side while Halfdan ordered the ship's boys to distribute food and drink. Miraculously, most of their stores had survived the storm and they all enjoyed a feast of dried meat, hard bread, and a horn of ale each; it may as well have come from Óðinn's table after the night they'd been through, and Halfdan didn't worry about rationing. He was as hungry as the rest. Toke watched as Halfdan and Bersi worked to replace the damaged tiller with the spare they carried below the deck planks. The two men pulled in the damaged oar and, after a quick examination, threw it overboard with a splash before heaving its replacement into position, the blade sliding into the water with barely a sound. Once the tiller was fixed, the ship immediately felt more stable in the water, and Halfdan pushed the oar over to slowly bring *Uxi* around to point south, keeping the sun on their left. Toke put the final piece of meat into his mouth before washing it down with the last of his ale, dunking the horn over the side to clean it. The rest of the crew were doing the same, preparing for the order to run out the oars.

'All right, lads!' Halfdan shouted, his hands once again wrapped around the tiller. 'We put old Thor in his place last night, although it cost us two good men and a mast. By my reckoning, the storm blew us further east, back towards Vágar. We'll make for either home, or the first island we stopped on, and organise a new mast, then it's on to Storfjellet to reconnect with the rest of the fleet. We just have to hope they haven't sailed off to have all the fun without us!'

Halfdan was met with a chorus of cheers and laughter. They were battered and beaten, but they weren't finished. Not by a long shot.

'I want every second oar manned, and the rest of you resting. We'll work in shifts until we're back at full strength. To your oars; we're coming about!'

The men quickly hustled to their chests and ran out the oars, the lengths of wood sprouting from the gunwales like spears in a shield wall.
'Row!' Halfdan called as the men fell into the rhythm they knew so well. After a few strokes, he pushed the tiller over and turned the great ship back on itself to face north, and hopefully familiar waters. Those not at an oar sunk back into sleep while their shipmates rowed. Toke was one of those resting and he stood at the prow for a while watching the infinite horizon. His lips moved wordlessly, sending prayers to Óðinn that would return him to his father and brothers.

# Chapter 14

Bjørn barely moved as the sword descended, the sharpened steel drawing a clumsy arc in the air as it aimed for his unarmoured head. At the last moment, he sent Huginn to answer the attack, swatting the blade aside before rapping the flat of the blade none too gently against his opponent's unprotected ribs. 'Argh!' Guttorm grimaced, dropping his sword as he grabbed his bruised side. It was the second time he had felt Bjørn's blade against his ribs and he was sure he would have a bruise come morning.

'Again,' Bjørn said, flicking Guttorm's discarded sword onto his foot and kicking it back to him, watching as his friend awkwardly caught the blade. 'But this time, don't leave yourself so open like that; you won't last two minutes. Your shield and sword should work together, with one attacking and the other defending. Like this,' he finished, drawing his shield across his body and bringing his sword up and down in a smooth motion, stopping the blade an inch from Guttorm's head. 'Look how I've finished,' he said, turning his head to face the circle of men surrounding them, his sword steady. His body was entirely covered by the shield, presenting Guttorm with an impenetrable wall of wood and iron that prevented any counterattack. 'Again!' he shouted, returning his attention to Guttorm. 'Those of you with an axe or spear, as I showed you before. Pair off!'

There were twenty-seven of them, twenty-eight including Bjørn, all standing in a clear patch of ground beyond the walled encampment. Surrounded by tall trees on three sides, with the ocean on the fourth, it was a perfect place to train the least experienced of Erik's warriors. Young men had come in twos and threes to learn warfare from the jarl's son, honing what skills their own fathers had given them, if any. Almost to a man they had joined the fleet in search of fame or fortune, hoping to return to their farms rich men. For many, it was a chance to win enough silver to pay a bride price or buy a farm of their own; for others an opportunity for adventure that they would never find at home. Only four had swords, Bjørn and Guttorm included. A further fifteen had axes, while the rest had come with nothing but their seaxes. One didn't even have that. Now, they stood and trained with the spears and shields they had been gifted by Erik.

The sounds of *battle* had soon drawn spectators from amongst the veterans. Most of them were seasoned campaigners who had sailed with Erik before, and they had quickly added their jokes and jeers to the sounds of metal striking wood. The silver had started flowing soon after as they began betting on certain fights. Erik himself had come with Yngvar to watch for a while before continuing his rounds of the burgeoning longphort, leaving with a subtle nod of approval. He didn't want too many idle hands while he waited for *Uxi* to return. Idle hands quickly became bored hands, and bored hands grasped for ale and mead. Drunkenness itself wasn't a problem – it was a common enough pastime amongst his people – but it was the inevitable brawling that came with it that he wanted to avoid. As much as possible, he wanted to minimise unnecessary injuries. For as long as they were in port, his men would work and train through the day so that by night they would all but drop from exhaustion every evening, too tired even to reach for their horns.

All of this passed through Bjørn's head as he eyed Guttorm, waiting for him to attack again.

Guttorm was taking to the sword quickly, but he still viewed it as a sharpened length of iron to be swung wildly, rather than a weapon to be handled with finesse. No matter. He would learn soon enough, or he would die trying. Wyrd.

Guttorm released a breath of air, raising his sword to strike from above, but Bjørn was quicker. As soon as the blade reached the peak of its ascent, he lunged forward and rested Huginn under his friend's chin, the blade pushing hard enough to dent the flesh without drawing blood.

'Use your shield,' he said again, miming the same action Guttorm had just tried to create and raising his own shield to protect his torso and throat. 'Otherwise you're open to a counter strike.'

'Gnn,' Guttorm grunted, stepping back to try again.

The two watched each other, Bjørn slowly circling around to face Guttorm's shielded left side while he waited for him to attack. It was an unfair manoeuvre as footwork was still foreign to Guttorm, but fighting wasn't fair in the first place, and he continued to move gracefully around his *foe* as he shuffled awkwardly to protect himself. Bjørn's last lesson was likely ringing in his ears as he focused his attention keeping his shield up. The training area around them was filled with the ring of iron striking wood as men trained, and Bjørn could see Guttorm's eyes darting distractedly from left to right as he took in the other battles around him. He heard a cry come from behind and watched as Guttorm's eyes flicked towards the sound, widening when they took in the sight. In the moment of inattention, he lowered his shield, opening himself to attack. Bjørn struck, raising his shield high to block Guttorm's hurried lunge before rapping the flat of his blade against his friend's ribs. Guttorm yelled in pain and surprise, jumping back and grasping his side.

'You need to be aware of your surroundings without losing focus of what's in front of you,' Bjørn said calmly, stepping back and sheathing Huginn. 'Let the older warriors worry about the bigger picture; your attention should be the man in front of you, and the one that fills his place when he falls.'

Guttorm nodded, breathing heavily as he dropped his shield to the ground and rubbed his injured ribs. Satisfied that the lesson had been absorbed, Bjørn turned his attention to the growing commotion behind him. He couldn't see clearly what was causing it beyond a figure lying on the ground screaming, and he quickly crossed the ground towards the growing crowd. He pushed his way through the group of men and soon arrived at the edge of the ring where he found one of the bóndi on the ground, a wound bleeding freely in his right side. He was one of those who had arrived with nothing but his knife, and the spear and shield Erik had given him. Arne was his name, Bjørn remembered. He had never held a spear before this voyage, but had taken to it with eagerness and tenacity, and had quickly endeared him to many of the older warriors. Coupled with his open and excited personality, charismatic smile and easy nature, he had become a popular figure among crews. Standing over him was Knut Troelsson, the blood-stained spear answering Bjørn's unasked question. He was everything Arne wasn't, and Bjørn had taken an instant dislike to him. He'd recognised him amongst the men as the crews had boarded, but hadn't made the effort to meet him. The story of Knut's family was well known in Vágar. Knut's father, Troel, had fallen from grace with Erik years earlier after being caught keeping plunder for himself rather than sharing it with his crew, and his jarl. It was a serious crime and in doing so, he had broken his oath to Erik. In punishment, he had been forbidden to raid with Erik ever again, and died years later in poverty. Few had been willing to deal with him due to his dishonesty, and later ill luck. Erik's only concession had been to allow his son, Knut, to join them on the whale road when he came of age, but the family's reduced finances had forced him to arrive at the muster with nothing more than an aged shield, and a chipped sword his father had refused to sell. Knut's dislike of Erik's sons was clear to all, and his position on *Sleipnir* had made it Bjørn's problem. Knut was sullen and difficult, with a surly nature. He had challenged Bjørn on two occasions already during the previous days' training sessions, once over his being paired with Arne in the first place, who he viewed as his social inferior.

'Guttorm, get the wound dressed as quickly as possible. Send for onion soup, ale, gut and needle, and something to bandage it,' Bjørn said quickly, his eyes locked on Knut's. Guttorm ran back to the camp for the soup while others bent to tend the wound and staunch the blood flow. One of the older men drew a knife and made a makeshift bandage from Arne's ruined tunic.

'What happened, Knut?' Bjørn asked quietly.

'The fool didn't cover himself quickly enough,' Knut said defiantly.

'And you didn't have the skill or ability to stay your blade?' Knut didn't reply, his eyes full of contempt as he focused on Arne instead. Around them, the men waited in silence to see what would happen next. Men got hurt training with weapons almost as often as they did in battle, it was how they learned. But at the same time, most had the sense to stay their hand before any real damage could be done.

'Answer me!' Bjørn growled, letting some of his anger show. He knew that he had put Knut in an impossible situation, but there had been enough defiance of his authority already. Erik had told him to train the young warriors, and he took the role seriously. Any admittance to being unable to stop his blade would tarnish his reputation and see him known for his poor weapon skills and damage his reputation. Yet, if he admitted to striking Arne deliberately, the result would be the same; likely worse. He'd become a pariah.

Knut was saved from answering by the sound of running footsteps as Guttorm returned with the soup.

'I'll expect your answer soon, Knut. For your sake, you better hope it's not a gut wound,' Bjørn said dangerously before turning to Guttorm. He was kneeling on the ground next to the injured Arne, already feeding him the pungent onion broth. Bjørn joined them on the ground and watched as Arne took a third strained gulp of the liquid before motioning for Guttorm to take the bowl away. Obediently, the young man stepped back and Bjørn nodded for the men pressing against the wound to remove their blooded hands before putting his nose by the bleeding flesh. He took a few deep sniffs and was welcomed by the iron-tinged scent of fresh blood. After a few more explorative breaths he nodded, satisfied.

'It's not a gut wound. Sew him up and get him back to the camp. He'll survive.'

'Aye, Bjørn,' one of the older men said, his voice emotionless as he took up the pitcher of ale Guttorm had brought with him and poured it over the wound, the golden liquid mixing with the blood to stain the soil at his side. To his credit, Arne barely made a sound as one of the older warriors began knitting his skin back together, stitch by agonising stitch. More than a few of the men watching nodded appreciatively at his bravery.

Bjørn stood and turned in one smooth motion, smashing his fist into Knut's face, feeling his nose smash under his balled fingers. What had once been a structured mass of cartilage and skin instantly blossomed into a flattened mess of red. The impact sent Knut sprawling with a scream, his hands covering his bloody face. Several men laughed at the sound, but most remained silent, watching. One or two placed bets, but on what, Bjørn neither knew nor cared. After a few seconds, Knut leapt to his feet and wiped his sleeve across his face. His eyes were watering from the blow, the involuntary tears mixing with the blood to cut rivers through the red mess. He didn't dare draw steel on Erik's son, not surrounded by so many loyal warriors. But the murder in his eyes was clear.

'Learn to stay your hand!' Bjørn growled. 'Or it will be *my* sword in *your* ribs next time. Now, let this be an end to it,' he said, extending his hand in an offering of peace. 'There need be no feud here.'

Knut stared at the outstretched hand for a few moments before spitting pointedly at Bjørn's feet and shoving his way angrily through the watching crowd and running back to the camp. No one followed him. Bjørn had acted quickly and honourably, and everyone watching knew it. It was up to Knut to take it or leave it, as he had chosen to.

'Pair off!' Bjørn shouted, Knut forgotten as he motioned for Guttorm to follow him back across the clearing, drawing Huginn as he moved. Behind him, he heard the sounds of a sword being drawn and knew that Guttorm had followed suit.

Men came and went through the rest of the afternoon as their work duties allowed, but it wasn't until Bjørn called an end that the weapons were sheathed for the final time. He spent a few minutes more with Guttorm offering advice about his foot and sword work after the session while others tiredly nodded their thanks and headed back to the camp in twos and threes. He was happy with his friend's progress, and proud of the part he was playing in it. He would write a good saga for himself one day, if he survived long enough.

The sun was still in the sky as he made his way back to the camp, the orange orb dropping towards the west as it painted the world with a golden glow. He could see wisps of smoke hanging above the camp like a fog as it played in the gentle breeze before being carried away to the north. He was frustrated at being confined on the island while they waited for *Uxi* and her crew to return. His great adventure had gotten off to a far rougher start than he had planned. Lost in his own thoughts, it took him a moment to register the sound of the stick snapping behind him. Instinctively, he drew his sword and turned to face the threat, bending his knees slightly in preparation. There was nothing. Just the dimming forest as the light leaked out of the day, and the occasional clipped conversation carried on the wind. Shrugging his shield from his shoulder, he gripped the handle tightly as he slowly turned, searching for threats amongst the trees as he forced his eyes to pierce the growing dark. He could feel the hairs on the back of his neck rising slowly and he opened his mouth slightly to improve his hearing as he listened for the tell-tale sound of cloth on cloth that would precede an attack. As he continued to turn, he began counting his breaths, tracking the time as it passed. When he reached sixty he stopped counting and stood upright. Overhead a bird had begun singing and he grinned at his own cautiousness. *'It must have been a branch falling,'* he thought, shouldering his shield. It was as his sword was sliding back into its sheath that he heard the swish of fabric as someone lifted their sleeve to lunge. His body screamed at the sound and he dropped to one knee and turned, sweeping his sword in a wide arc that drove the blade into the incoming spear shaft, the sound of iron meeting wood loud amongst the trees. 'Almost,' Yngvar said with a grin as he drew the spear shaft back and rested the butt on the ground, idly examining the fresh gouge in the wood.

'Gnn,' Bjørn grunted, standing again. 'What are you doing here?'

'I came to find you,' he said, motioning back towards camp before stepping forward to walk alongside him. 'I saw Knut coming back into the settlement dripping blood...' he said, leaving the question unfinished.

'He got what he deserved,' Bjørn grunted, briefly turning to face Yngvar. 'He nearly killed Arne; a broken nose is a light punishment for such foolishness.'

Yngvar nodded but said no more. He knew well Knut's heritage and could guess at his feelings he harboured towards the sons of Erik. He wasn't surprised to hear he had challenged Bjørn, nor was he fazed by the outcome. Their progress was punctuated every second step by the gentle tap of Yngvar's spear as it struck the ground. They walked in companionable silence with nothing but the soughing of the wind as it described its path through the branches above for company.

'We're heading back out tomorrow,' Yngvar said after a while. 'There's been no sign of *Uxi*, and if they haven't found their way here, there's every chance that they've returned to Vágar.'

'We're going home?' Bjørn asked without turning.

'We need to know where they are. The loss of a whole crew – plus the ship – is enough to keep the rest of the fleet here for a few more days while we head out and see what we can find.'

'When do we leave?'

'First light.'

\*\*\*

Hoelun's face was numb from the slaps she had received. She could still feel the man's ringed hand where it struck her with enough force to daze her vision. She knew that her cheek was split by the searing pain and the constant dribble of blood that ran down her face, but despite that she kept going. It had been easy to get through the gates after the victors took control of Vágar. The sounds of victory had mingled with those of defeat, sending her mind back to her youth as the laughter of men blending with the screams of women and the crying of children. Two more men had died by her hand before she escaped Vágar, their bodies turning cold as she sliced Arleigh's knife through their throats and stole a horse before making for the hills. The feeling of the horse between her legs and the drumming of its hooves on the hard earth was a freedom she hadn't felt since her enslavement years before. The same went for the bow she now carried in her left hand, which sang a final time as she rode past the lone sentry left to guard Vágar's ruined gate, the arrow's iron tooth ripping through his throat before he could even register she was there. And then she was free. Free of the Northman's yoke, of Erik and his people; free to make her way home to the sea of grass. Except she wasn't; not by a long shot. Between her and home lay an entire world she didn't know, through which she would have to travel alone, with a face and complexion that didn't belong in any of the lands she would pass through. Reality soon drowned her idealistic hopes as she acknowledged that her only way to survive was as a thrall to Jarl Erik. In her heart of hearts, she also knew that she couldn't

214

abandon Bjørn, or the love that had started to grow between them. There was a chance – however slim – that she could earn her freedom by helping him to win back his father's territory, but to do that she had to rally men loyal to Erik, and warn them of Vágar's fate. They would know what to do, she hoped. Váli's home was only a short ride away, she remembered. She had accompanied Bjørn and Toke there the previous year to help them bring back livestock owed to Erik as part of Váli's annual tithe. His small ring fort, and the farms of the men loyal to him, were only a day's ride from Vágar, if she moved fast. Turning, she took a final look at the captured town and the smoke beginning to rise above the settlement, before kicking her heels in and riding for the hills, leaving death and fire in her wake.

The cries from Vágar carried high into the surrounding mountains as if the gates of Hel had opened beneath it, the screams chasing her relentlessly. She sat and took a final look at the captured town from high above, the wind whipping her hair as it rose up around her. Hoelun had made it as far as King's Leap before exhaustion broke her and she stopped for the night. She'd forced herself to keep going long enough to water and hobble her horse and get something of a shelter made before settling down with a waterskin by the fire, slowly turning a young rabbit over the flames. The critter had ended up on the fire more by chance than design. It had bolted from below her horse when she was halfway up the mountain and followed the path she was on into the woods. A lifetime in the saddle with bow in hand had made her fast and accurate, and it was a reflex to draw and shoot the fleeing animal before she'd formed the conscious thought. Now, it was her only food and she still had another half-a-day in the saddle ahead of her before she reached Váli's territory. Behind her, a few strips of the gamey meat were hanging above the coals of her make-shift smoker. There wasn't much to smoke, but it would keep her going and see her through to Váli, and safety. Wrapped in her horse blanket with the familiar equine smell mixing with the pine smoke, she allowed some of the tension to ease from her body as she processed everything that had happened. Turid and Arleigh were both captured, with a fate similar to her own facing them unless she could get word to Erik and his fleet. Leif and his warriors were dead or captured, likely bound for Frisian slave markets. Not for the first time, Hoelun's thoughts wandered to the women and children of Vágar. It was for them Hoelun feared the most. She'd come to know some of them well during her time in among the Northmen, like Arleigh and Turid, who had

215

treated her fairly despite her lower status. It was the women who would suffer the most as men who'd been confined on ships and then fought a battle sated their frustration and lust. A lust Hoelun knew all too well. If she closed her eyes and listened, she imagined she could still hear their cries. Thrall or not, Vágar was her home now, and she wept for the survivors below as she stoked her fire and lay down to sleep, exhausted.

She woke early the next day, breaking her fast with water from the creek and a few strips of the smoked rabbit. It was leathery and tough, but it was all she had. Stowing the rest in the crude pouch she'd fashioned from a strip of cloth ripped from her hem, she saddled her horse and kicked it forward, keeping an arrow on the string as she went, remembering the man Bjørn and his brothers had brought back from the mountains. Aside from a small herd of deer she startled as she emerged on the far side of the forest, the ride was uneventful. Lost in her thoughts, she hadn't even realised she was leaving the wooded shade until a young buck barked once and bounded away, startling her. As she emerged from the shadows and readjusted to the full light of day, she spied Váli's home a few rôst away. Seeing the smoke rising lazily from the hall nestled in the ring of earth and wood that surrounded it, she allowed some of the tension to leave her body as she replaced the arrow in her quiver. At last, she could pass the responsibility off to someone else. Sighing, she leaned forward to pat the horse's neck, whispering her thanks for having carried her this far. She felt the wind above her change briefly before she registered what had happened. It was the *twang* behind her that brought her back to reality, followed by the frustrated shouts of a failed shot. She turned in time to see three men racing from the forest behind her on horseback, their mounts white-flecked with foam from the ride while the archer scrambled back into the saddle. *'They must have followed my trail,'* she thought, kicking her heels in and spurring her own horse forward. 'Chuh' she cried, feeling the animal's muscles bunch and release as it surged forward, whinnying at the sudden exertion. Her pursuers yelled out in surprise and she heard their horses cry out as they kicked their heels in and gave chase. She threw a gaze over her shoulder, watching as the warriors spread out behind her in a line. One drew back awkwardly on his bow and released it on the fly, but it was clumsily executed, and the arrow went well wide of her. They were not born to the saddle and bow as she was; no Norseman was. She would show them the error of their ways, she thought, gritting her teeth in determination. In one fluid motion, she drew and aimed her own arrow, feeling the movement of the horse beneath her. She waited for the moment of perfect stillness, when all four hooves left the ground, before releasing her arrow. The shaft disappeared against the dark of the forest behind her pursuers, but she watched with satisfaction as it took the archer under his chin, lifting him from the saddle. Her bow had none of the power and grace of the small, double curved bows she'd grown up with, but she adapted quickly. After the rabbit, a man made an easy target.

Her second arrow was on the string before the first had finished its flight. Again she drew and loosed in one smooth motion, yelling into the wind as the shaft embedded itself in a man's shoulder. She heard him cry out in surprise and pain as he yanked back on his reins, his wounded arm hanging uselessly by his side. The final two pulled their shields from their backs and held them across their fronts. They were safe from direct arrow fire, but their shields made riding awkward, slowing them considerably. Letting loose a final arrow for good measure Hoelun kicked in her heels again and gave another loud "chuh!" coaxing a burst of speed as she made for the distant buildings. Behind her, she heard one of her pursuers swear as her arrow pinged off his helmeted head. The chase moved from a sprint to an endurance race as Hoelun was chased rôst after rôst, the remaining warriors following her tenaciously while their companion trailed behind, his injury slowing him. Occasionally, Hoelun would turn to send another arrow at the pursuers to keep them at bay, but her quiver was already dangerously empty. She knew she could kill their horses, but she couldn't bring herself to do that, not yet. The safety of Váli's was drawing closer by the minute, and she knew that she would reach it within the hour if she could keep her horse going. Despite the circumstances, she felt a small smile forming on her face. This is what she loved, what she'd been born to do. What she'd lost among the Norse. This was home. The constant thrum of hooves beneath her feet and the wind whipping through her hair. Like the bow, her horse had none of the endurance or fire of the horses she had known as a girl, but it had heart, and was only now beginning to foam at the mouth. Stealing another glance behind her, she watched one of her pursuers open a gap between himself and his companions, drawing closer to her. Noting his position, she tugged on her reins and adjusted her angle slightly, allowing him to draw closer as she carefully drew an arrow from her quiver, keeping her empty bow clearly visible. She heard him yell in excitement, expecting the end of the chase, thinking she'd made a mistake in changing direction. Snarling, he drew his sword and pointed it at her, lowering his shield enough to allow the length of iron past. Seizing the opportunity, Hoelun brought her right hand around and laid the arrow across the string, drawing and shooting in a single smooth motion that sent the iron-tipped shaft into the man's neck. He was on his way to Valhöll before he hit the ground. Behind him, the final man pulled back his reins and relinquished the chase, watching in frustration as Hoelun turned her horse and rode the final rôst towards the ring fort, and safety.

# Chapter 15

Arleigh had been here before, bound and abandoned in a lord's hall while the world around her was plundered and raped by violent men carried to her in dragon ships. The only difference this time was that she wasn't alone. Beside her lay an unconscious Turid, equally bound but as of yet unmoving. She had no idea how long they had been in the annex at the back of Erik's hall, forced to listen to the drunken debauchery of Jarl Ake's men as they celebrated their conquest of Vágar. The room had been looted by warriors seeking Erik's legendary wealth, but they had been unlucky. Few knew where Erik's hoards were hidden, and the frustration of Ake's men was written clearly in the ransacked chamber. The floor around Arleigh and Turid was covered in ripped garments, flipped chests and the straw stuffing that had filled the mattresses. In one day, Jarl Ake had doubled his land and power, and had claimed Vágar for himself, but as of yet he had been unable to double his silver wealth. In that, at least, he had failed.

The two women had been dropped in the room soon after their capture. Ake had smirked cruelly when he realised who they were and instructed that they be tied up and left in the annex to listen as his men caroused and celebrated their victory, but beyond that he had shown less interest in them than one would a chair. He could talk to them whenever he wanted; they weren't going anywhere. Arleigh had spotted the terrified face of Revna, the blacksmith's wife, as she was forced to kneel before the jarl, his dirt-stained hands grasping her cheeks roughly before his men closed the door to the annex, the fates of their people heard but unseen by either of them. The sight of Revna's terrified face as their eyes met briefly had thrown Arleigh into her past, and she'd allowed herself to weep silently for the women of Vágar once they were alone.

Arleigh had spent the first few hours of her captivity wondering about their fate. She doubted they would be bound for slave markets like many of the surviving warriors would be, if there were any left alive, but the thought didn't make her any less fearful. Freedom in the north only lasted for as long as it could be held, and for all intents and purposes they were as much Ake's property as Erik's legendary golden horde. If Ake ever found it. The thought made her shiver. Erik had treated her fairly and kindly since the day he had captured her, and was a good and honourable man, despite the conditions surrounding their meeting. Ake was not. She had seen it in his eyes. Despite his outward show of strength and arrogance, there was a weakness behind the bluster, a lack of certainty and a cruel streak that nestled just below the surface. Arleigh feared for herself and, more importantly, for Turid. She was just a bed-thrall, but Turid was a prize, and Ake's key to completing Erik's humiliation. For her sake, Arleigh hoped she remained unconscious for as long as possible. Like Erik, she was a good and kind woman who had always treated her fairly, and she was loath to see her in pain.

She shivered when she thought back to those cruel eyes, and the giant man who stood at the jarl's back with his giant axe at the ready, as if expecting the fighting to begin again at any minute. His son had been there as well, as weak a man as Arleigh had ever met. Unlike Ake who at least held the respect of his men, the same clearly couldn't be said of his son. There was a deep cruelty behind those eyes that Arleigh had never before experienced. Her only hope was that Hoelun managed to reach Váli. But for now, she needed to look to her own resources. She began searching for any sort of blade or tool that she could use to cut the cords around her wrists. Erik had always kept several swords and other weapons in the annex, but Ake had claimed them quickly, presumably to bolster his own armoury, or to reward loyal men. But there was always a chance one had been missed in the search. Ignoring her aches and pains she crawled towards the bed, thanking God under her breath that she didn't need to worry about making noise with the celebrations in the hall. Ake hadn't even thought them worth guarding, leaving them bound and alone in the room. For some reason, she'd found the lack of a guard deeply insulting, as if mere women couldn't pose a threat to him. Beyond the door, she could hear the men raising another toast and her thoughts flew unbidden to Torr, and the memories of Erik and his own men celebrating their victory in Shorewitchshire. 'Not this time, my love,' she whispered as she crawled. 'I won't be captured a second time.'

The sound pushed her to move faster as she crawled awkwardly on her elbows towards the head of the bed. She knew that Erik kept a small seax there above his head, and she prayed that the looters' greed had drawn them to the beautiful swords, axes, and spears that had decorated the walls, keeping the simple blade from being found. Behind her, she heard a groan and froze.

After a few seconds, she turned and saw that Turid was beginning to stir. Turning back to her task, she levered herself up onto the bed and ran her hands along the wall where the two met. She could feel her heart beating in her throat as she searched. After a few moments of awkward scrabbling, her fingers felt the cold wood of the handle and she almost squealed with excitement as she drew the blade. She quickly sliced through the cord around her ankles, gasping as the blood rushed back into her deprived feet before turning her attention to her wrists. Grasping the blade awkwardly between her feet, she began to slide her hands up and down against the iron, careful not to slice her skin in the process. It took a few fumbled attempts, but eventually the cord tore through and she gasped in relief as the blood returned to her fingers. Shaking her hands to speed the flow, she turned to Turid. No one had come to check on them, but that didn't make her feel any safer. The longer they took to free themselves, the more Ake and his men would drink, increasing the chances of them bringing the women out to parade like trophies, or worse.

Looking around the room, her eyes settled on a discarded aleskin lying in the corner and she felt a surge of relief when she picked it up and heard the sound of liquid sloshing within. She took a deep swig before dumping the remainder unceremoniously over Turid's head, covering her friend's mouth as she did so. The liquid mingled with the dried blood around her shattered nose and Arleigh felt a moment of pity for the beautiful woman. The sight reminded her of her own injury, and the pain there. Before she could focus on it, Turid's eyes began to flicker and she began coughing as some of the ale entered her ruined nose. Arleigh pushed harder on her mouth and whispered for silence, waiting for Turid to regain full consciousness. After a few moments, she nodded her understanding, pushing Arleigh's hand away with her bound wrists before holding them out to be cut. Arleigh sliced through the cords before handing her the aleskin. 'Drink this,' she said. There were still a few dregs swimming at the bottom and Turid hungrily swallowed them.

While Turid regained herself, Arleigh began searching the room. She fished the sheath from behind the bed and tied it around her waist before sliding the blade home and crossing to one of the chests sitting against the wall. Praying silently, she reached behind it and ran her hands along the smooth wood, grinning when her fingers closed around another small knife, which she tossed to Turid. The older woman caught the blade awkwardly before tying it to her own belt. Arleigh silently thanked Erik for his preparedness, and his love of knives. He had always known that his immense wealth would breed jealousy amongst his enemies, and had prepared as best he could to protect what was his. It was the reason the walls had been built around the town and a garrison created in the first place.

Opening another heavy oak chest to the left of the first, she drew out two rucksacks and began filling them with whatever warm clothes she could find. It would take them over a day to reach Váli, and they would need to spend at least one night sleeping out of doors. She also found a few coins that had been missed during the looting that she secreted into one of the bags. Behind her, Turid had drawn her knife and was standing guard by the door, leaning slightly against the frame as she watched for anyone moving towards the annex while Arleigh searched for Erik's hunting supplies. Most of it was away with him on the whale road, but she managed to find an old flint and a whetstone, as well as a few lengths of gut and some needles. Snatching up the discarded aleskin, she tucked it into one of the bags with the rest of their kit before throwing it over her back, tossing the lighter one to Turid. She watched with satisfaction as Turid caught it with more dexterity than she had the knife. They were ready. 'Help me with this,' she whispered, moving towards the largest of the three chests and gripping the cowskin it rested on. Turid sheathed her knife and hurried across the room before taking a strong grip on the opposite corner. Arleigh quietly mouthed counting to three before heaving back on the leather, tugging the heavy chest away from the wall, into the room. The chest was immensely heavy, but they managed to free it far enough to reveal the small opening beneath, and the ladder leading down into the darkness.

'Go,' Arleigh whispered hurriedly,

'Thank you, Arleigh,' Turid whispered, grasping her bicep meaningfully before climbing down into the darkness.

Arleigh watched as Turid's yellow hair was swallowed up by the blackness before following behind. Once her head was below the opening, she reached up and grasped the edge of the cowskin. Whispering another silent prayer, she leaned back as far as she could into the space behind her and pulled. Slowly but surely, the chest slid back into place, sealing the tunnel entrance. She was sure that the passage would be found eventually; Ake would be furious when he found them missing and would have his men search the room from top to bottom looking for them. The passage only needed to remain hidden long enough for them to escape.

Once the entrance was sealed, Arleigh climbed the rest of the way down, finding her way awkwardly with no light to guide her. When she finally felt solid ground beneath her feet again she found Turid waiting at the bottom. They shared a quick embrace and Arleigh felt how fast her friend's heartbeat was racing, sure her own felt the same. Despite everything, she felt alive.

'We need to get to Vali,' Arleigh whispered, reaching into her bag for the flint. 'I imagine that Ake and his men will be celebrating their victory long into the night, so we have until sunrise to be gone from here.'

'What about the rest of the survivors?' Turid asked, grabbing her other arm and spinning her back around. 'We have to save them!' she whispered urgently.

Their voices were muffled by the cloying dampness of the earth walls around them. The smells of dirt and decay were strong and Arleigh took a few deep breaths before replying, trying hard to ignore the feeling of being swallowed by the earth. The only light visible to them came through a tiny slit above, shooting through a crease in the cow skin, but it offered nothing in terms of visibility.

'No!' she hissed. 'We can't do anything for them now. Our best chance is getting to Váli and warning him. With any luck, Hoelun has already told him what happened and he's even now preparing to set sail with his own warriors. Trust me, Turid,' she said, softening her tone. 'I've been here before. The only thing to do is escape and find help. If we stay and try to save the others, we'll be caught again, and what good would that do anyone?' She couldn't see her face, but Turid's silence was enough agreement for the time being. It wasn't hard to imagine the feelings of guilt and failure that her friend would be experiencing, but there was no other choice.

Reaching for where she thought Turid's shoulder was, Arleigh squeezed once to reassure her before turning and striking the back of her knife against the flint, releasing a shower of sparks that briefly banished the darkness. Erik had stashed a chest of torches somewhere by the ladder in case the tunnel was ever needed, but Arleigh had to find them first. It took a few strikes, but eventually she spotted the glint of metal, revealing the chest.

Arleigh withdrew two torches and struck her flint again, briefly lighting the tunnel as the sparks rained down on the torches. They took after the third strike, banishing the darkness and revealing the flickering tunnel around them. The shaft stretched away into blackness, revealing an unbroken hole of glinting earth that reflected the dancing flames. Nestled in the chest were a few extra torches and both women took two, stowing them in their respective bags. Arleigh also found a fresh flint and a small axe which she slid into her belt. The only thing they didn't have was food. '*One thing at a time,*' Arleigh thought.

The tunnel was low, and both women had to walk hunched over to avoid hitting their heads.

Erik had ordered the tunnel built a few years earlier after watching a fleet of ships appear out of the mist and make for Vágar before turning away at the last minute, leaving as suddenly as they had arrived. They'd never returned, but their sudden appearance had made him realise how exposed they were and had triggered a flurry of defence work, including the construction of walls and watchtowers. Hidden amongst the construction, he had secretly asked Yngvar to build the tunnel. Outside of the family, only Yngvar and Sven knew of its existence.

Above them they could hear the muffled sounds of celebration, the noise dampened in the crypt-like shaft. In contrast, their own footsteps sounded loud in the confined space, but they knew there was no chance of their being heard by the men above. The tunnel emerged in the back of a store house near Erik's hall, the entrance hidden behind sacks of grain and furs. As Arleigh remembered, it was just under one-hundred steps from Erik's room to the store house and she silently began counting her steps to push back the feeling of being swallowed. As they went, she had a moment of panic at the idea of some thrall covering the exit with sacks or crates, trapping them in the tunnel and she unconsciously quickened her pace. Behind her, she heard Turid's footsteps pick up speed.

Just as it was beginning to feel like the tunnel would never end, they spied the ladder, the light wood seeming to glow amongst the infinite blackness around them. Arleigh dropped her torch into the dirt and covered it with a thick cloak, smothering the flames. It wouldn't do for the light to be spotted by an eagle-eyed sentry exploring the warehouse for hidden riches. The tunnel became noticeably darker with only Turid's light to banish the darkness.

'Wait here,' Arleigh whispered before grasping the first rungs of the ladder and beginning to climb. She could feel her heart beating in her chest and was almost surprised Turid hadn't said a word about the noise. She carefully reached up and placed her hand against the trapdoor, the rough wood a welcome change from the dampness of the tunnel walls. Gently, she pushed against the wood, feeling it shift as it slowly opened. She had opened it to about the height of her hand when it creaked, the sound loud in the surrounding silence. She waited for what felt like an age, expecting to be heaved out of the tunnel at any second by one of Ake's warriors. Only when spots began to dance before her eyes did she realise she had been holding her breath. Deciding the coast was clear she continued pushing, opening the portal fully as she took a deep breath of the fresh, clean air. Carrying scents of fur and grain, the air tasted as crisp as the clearest of fjords after the tunnel's cloying darkness. Motioning for Turid to wait below, she climbed through the opening and drew her knife, creeping silently around the bales to check there was nobody lying in wait for them. Her back clicked as she straightened and she sighed quietly in relief. After the damp silence of the tunnel, the cries of drunken warriors and screaming women sounded loud to her ears. She knew the sound well, and she gritted her teeth to calm herself as the blood ran hot in her veins. Grimacing, she continued to make her way around the stacked bales and crates, her eyes constantly on the move for anyone who could give them away, or anything useful they could use. She had already noticed a small pile of recently tanned sheepskins when she emerged from the tunnel and had decided to take two to use as bed rolls.

After several minutes scouting, she decided the coast was clear and was just about to return to Turid when she heard a cough. Stopping instantly, she tried to isolate where the sound had come from. The warehouse was completely still, apart from the motes of dust floating around the room, visible in the beams of moonlight breaking through cracks in the walls. Listening carefully, she could just make out the gentle sound of someone breathing near the entrance. Slowly, she moved closer towards the door, keeping her knife hidden in the folds of her dress so the metal wouldn't catch the light and alert anyone to her presence.

Lying on his back by the open doorway was one of Ake's raiders, a strung bow leaning against the wall beside him. He was unarmed but for the knife at his waist and appeared to be fast asleep. Moving as carefully as she could so as not to cause a creak beneath her feet, Arleigh drew closer to the prone figure. In her mind, she could already see what she would do. Her left hand would cover his mouth and nose while her right drove the knife straight into his windpipe and pulled upwards, ripping the blade through the soft flesh of his throat. With each step she felt the blood surging through her veins in quiet anticipation. Arleigh was just a few steps away when some sixth sense warned him of her presence and he opened his eyes. He froze when he saw her, both of them unsure what to do as their eyes met. Arleigh moved first. Lunging

225

furiously, she drove her blade straight into the man's throat, driving him back against the wall to hide their struggle. He was stronger than her and she could feel he was threatening to break her grip on the blade, but her fear drove her on, and after a few seconds his strength began ebbing away as his life's blood gushed out to cover her arm. As suddenly as it had begun, it was over, and Arleigh was left struggling under the man's sudden weight. Gasping, she lowered him to the ground as quietly as she could and withdrew her knife, releasing a sluggish flow of blood in the process. She cleaned the blade as best she could on the man's tunic before returning it to her sheath and dragging his body back into the warehouse towards the bales of grain and furs, ignoring the bloody trail that followed his limp body. She relieved him of his possessions, including his knife, a small purse of hacksilver, and an extra bowstring, before covering the body under some loose sacking and returning to collect the discarded bow. She noted the quality of the weapon when she picked it up, and the craftsmanship that had gone into its construction. It was bigger than she was used to, and made from what looked like yew wood, although it was hard to tell in the dim light. Shrugging on the quiver of arrows, she moved back through the warehouse and found Turid already above ground with her own knife drawn.

'What was all that noise?' she hissed, sheathing the blade when she saw Arleigh return alone.

'There was a man sleeping at the entrance,' Arleigh whispered without further explanation. 'Let's go.'

She turned and wove her way back around the bales and sacks towards the entrance without waiting for an answer, taking up two of the sheepskins as she went. Behind her, Turid moved to the opposite side of the opening and drew her knife, the blade shining in the light.

'Turid,' Arleigh hissed urgently. 'Turid! Your knife! Hide the blade in your dress.'

She watched as the older woman followed her instructions before turning her attention back to the space ahead of them. In her head a plan was forming, but it depended on crossing the open ground between the storehouse and the next bank of buildings; roughly the length of *Fjord Ulf* from stem to stern. She could see the wall behind, and once they reached them, all they had to do was follow it around towards the rear gate. About halfway along the wall there was internal scaffolding where men had been repairing a weakened section. If they could reach that then they could climb over and be lost to the night and make good their escape. The problem was the drunk and sleeping men in the clearing, eating and drinking beside a small fire. She had no clear plan as to how they would cross without being spotted.

'We need to get across there,' she whispered to Turid, nodding her head towards the lurking darkness between the buildings. 'Do you have any ideas?'

Turid remained quiet for a few moments, her eyes flicking rapidly across the space. Just as Arleigh was about to break the lengthening silence a shadow flicked across her vision and she caught sight of white wings reflecting the firelight as it flew above the drunk men. '*A snow owl,*' she thought absently as she continued searching for a plan.

'Look,' Turid whispered, gripping her arm and making her turn to face the men again. One of the drunker warriors had also noticed the owl and was failing miserably to aim his spear at it as it flew away. Around him, his companions were jeering him on as he swayed unevenly before launching the projectile. He cheered in surprise as the owl dipped suddenly, thinking he had struck true, before one of the sleeping men let out a cry of pain. The spear had gone straight through his leg, pinning him to the ground. Without missing a beat, another of them turned and drove his balled fist into the failed hunter's face before he too was hit from behind. Within seconds, the warriors had fallen into free-for-all of flying limbs and bellowed curses as they began to brawl drunkenly.

'Now's our chance!' Turid said quietly before crouching and making her way across the clearing without waiting for a response. Arleigh had little time to think before following her across the open ground, keeping as low as she could. She was halfway across when she heard the cry and turned in mute horror to see one of the drunken warriors pointing directly at her. Before she could even think to launch her arrow the man was struck from behind by one of his companions with a lump of firewood he was swinging like a club, rendering the man unconscious Sighing in relief, she sprinted the rest of the distance to reunite with Turid. The two women embraced briefly when she reached the darkness, their hearts beating.

'Now what?' Turid hissed.

'Follow me,' Arleigh said, making her way deeper into the darkened streets. Twice they had to duck back into the shadows as patrols made their way around the length of the wall. Clearly Jarl Ake wasn't as stupid as they had assumed and had managed to keep a few of his men sober. On one point, they had been caught with nowhere to hide and had only been saved when Arleigh's knife flashed out from the folds of her dress to rip away a man's throat, giving Turid time to bury her axe in his surprised companion's skull. Working together, they dragged the bodies behind another building and left them in shadow to be discovered later, looting what they could before leaving them for the crows.

Dawn was breaking by the time they reached the scaffolding, a wolf grey light creeping over the eastern horizon. They only had a few hours left to make good their escape before their absence was discovered.

'You go first,' Arleigh whispered, turning to watch for any potential pursuers.

'Don't be stupid,' Turid hissed. 'We'll go together; we don't have time for caution any more. It's only a matter of time before someone discovers that we're gone, or one of the bodies we've left behind is found. It's a miracle we've made it this far.'

Seeing the logic Arleigh sheathed her dagger and the two women climbed as quickly as they could up the beams of wood, reaching the top a few moments later.

That was where their luck ended.

Just as they crested the top, a horn began to blow, the deep notes echoing from the direction of Erik's hall.

'Quickly,' Arleigh hissed. 'Jump!'

Turid didn't need to be told twice. Taking a deep breath, she stepped off the platform and over the wall, landing with a gentle thud in the packed earth below. Taking a final glance behind her, Arleigh caught sight of armoured men beginning to move through the streets below, and she quickly followed Turid's lead, landing in a heap next to her.

'To the trees,' she hissed before sprinting the hundred-or-so steps between the walls and the protection of the waiting forest. Behind her, she could hear Turid's footsteps as they struck the hard ground as she struggled to keep pace. It was still cold enough that they could see their breath as it misted in the dim light. By the time they reached the edge of the woods they were both breathing heavily.

'Here,' Arleigh said, taking a sip from a liberated waterskin before passing it across to Turid. 'The water will cool your mouth and hide the mist.' It wasn't impossible that an eagle-eyed sentry would notice their steaming breath.

Turid nodded her thanks as she took a deep gulp before corking the top. Meanwhile, Arleigh had drawn an arrow from her quiver and nocked it.

'Can you even shoot that thing?' Turid asked, handing back the skin.

'Oh aye,' Arleigh said with a mischievous wink. 'When Erik and his men tried to capture me, there were a few less to put the ropes on me than set out to try.'

Turid gave her a curious glance as she processed the information, but remained silent. It wasn't hard to imagine after the battle at the gate. 'We should move. It won't take them long to realise we're not in the town.'

Arleigh watched the walls intently for a few moments longer, waiting to see if anyone would follow them over the scaffolding, but nobody came. Satisfied, she returned the arrow to her quiver and unstrung the bow, stowing the valuable cord. She only had one spare and she didn't know how well the previous owner had cared for them. Already this one looked dry and could have used a coating of beeswax.

'All right, let's go,' she whispered. 'But not directly along the paths. After the town, it's the first thing they would expect us to do. They won't expect two women to take to the woods rather than follow the roads.'

'Agreed,' Turid said before turning and marching resolutely into the forest.

Arleigh took a final look at the walls, listening to the shouts and confusion coming from within the town, before turning and following her friend into the trees. Behind her, the sun's golden light was beginning to shine on Jarl Ake's new settlement, Vágar.

# Chapter 16

*Sleipnir* danced across the calm water like a stallion released to the fields after a winter spent inside. Despite the purpose of their voyage, the mood onboard was light as the crew shrugged off the confines of land. Storfjellet was almost lost to sight as they flew across the waves leaving swirling bubbles in their wake. Bjørn stood on the aft deck beside Yngvar, watching silently as the older man gently guided the ship while the crew entertained themselves, enjoying the break from the oars. Red Orm was trailing a fishing line overboard. There was little else to do, driven as they were by the wind. Smiling to himself, Bjørn took a deep breath of fresh salty air as he felt the labours of land slip from his shoulders. Knut had been shooting bitter glances at him ever since they had pushed off from shore, but it did little to dampen Bjørn's mood.

Overhead the sky was as calm and clear as the ocean beneath their hull, and there was no evidence of the storm apart from the wind filling their sails. Vágar was only a few days sail away and their aim was to get there and back again within the week, returning with *Uxi* in tow.

'We'll be coming up against Moskstraumen again in no time,' Yngvar said after a time, breaking the silence.

'Would you have me hold the helm again?' Bjørn asked.

'Aye, if you're willing.'

'Aye. Let's just hope old Njörd doesn't mind us passing his front door so often without saying hello.' Bjørn chuckled.

A smile flickered across Yngvar's face briefly before they lapsed back into companionable silence. Near the mast, Bjørn could see Guttorm playing hnefatafl with Bjarni, his sword resting proudly against his sea chest rather than in it, like the rest of the crew's weapons and armour. His pride was clear, but Bjørn knew he should warn him again about the iron rot when on the salt water. *'He'll learn soon enough,'* he thought, his attention moving across the rest of the crew. Towards the bow he caught another glimpse of Knut sitting alone, his snarling face a mess of black and blue blotches as he sat and brooded in sullen silence. Their eyes met briefly before Knut averted his gaze. Bjørn knew he had made an enemy there, but he didn't let the thought worry him. *'Wyrd,'* he mused. Grunting, he made his way back to his own chest, telling Yngvar to call him if he wanted to be relieved.

Yngvar watched him go, the familiar sense of pride settling over him as he watched Bjørn move easily amongst the crew. Like his father, he was a natural leader.

Taking a seat beside Bjarni and Guttorm, Bjørn pulled a strip of dried meat from the pouch at his belt before settling down to watch their game. Guttorm's attacking pieces had the king and his brave band in a tight spot, with only a few defenders left. But Bjørn had played with Bjarni enough times himself to know he hadn't lost yet. Behind him, he heard Red Orm shout in surprise, and turned in time to see him tugging his line back into the ship with an excited grin on his face. A few of the men moved closer to watch the show and he smiled contentedly before turning back to the game. Sure enough, Guttorm's lapse in concentration had cost him, and Bjørn watched as Bjarni moved one of his pieces into a space between two of Guttorm's, taking them both and opening an avenue for the king to escape. Without thinking, Guttorm moved one of his attackers into one of the vacant spots and Bjørn watched as his face fell in dismay as Bjarni's king moved to the edge of the board, coming to rest in line with two of the tables four corners. Bjarni won on his next turn and Guttorm passed across the agreed wager in resignation, ignoring his opponent's victorious grin.

'Will you play, Bjørn?' Guttorm asked, placing two more pieces of silver on the makeshift table before resetting the pieces.

'Of course,' Bjørn said, pulling a few pieces of hacksilver from the pouch at his hip and adding them to the scales. They weighed the silver quickly, adding and subtracting pieces until the wagers were as even as they were going to be on the gently rocking ship. Beside them Bjarni pulled out his knife and whale tooth and began to carve, gently scratching a pattern into the bone.

'You start,' Bjørn said with a nod.

Immediately, Guttorm sent an attacker forward and blocked one of Bjørn's defenders.

Without expression, Bjørn slid one of his own men across to capture the attacker.

*Scratch… scratch… scratch… scratch.*

Guttorm attacked again, this time coming at Bjørn's pieces from the other side. Again, one of the white defenders broke formation to capture the wayward attacker, the darker piece disappearing into the leather pouch next to the board. Bjarni snorted as he watched the second piece be defeated in four moves.

'What?' Guttorm said, raising to the bait.

'You're too aggressive,' Bjarni offered. 'Hnefatafl is a game of patience and strategy, not reckless aggression.'

'But isn't boldness always the best strategy?' the younger man replied as he slid another piece forward to block two of Bjørn's, coming again from the original side. Again, Bjørn calmly slid a defender back across, removing a third piece.

'No,' Bjørn said. 'Like the sword, hnefatafl is about patience and cunning. The more you swing your sword, the more tired you get. The wilder you cut, the more you open yourself up to attack. The same applies here. In less than ten turns you've lost three pieces, while my own formation remains solid.'

Bjarni nodded wordlessly beside them.

*Scratch... scratch... scraaaatch... scratch...scratch.*

Taking a breath, Guttorm surveyed the table before sliding another piece forward from an untouched edge of the board.

'Good,' Bjørn said before moving a piece of his own, opening an avenue for the king to enter the fray.

Guttorm's shallow grin gave away his excitement at Bjørn's manoeuvre and he again moved quickly to capture the exposed defender, removing it from the board.

Keeping his expression neutral, Bjørn moved another defender forward to flank the offending attacker, blocking any further encroachment. Beside them, they heard Bjarni's carving slow as his attention flicked between the tooth and the game.

Four more moves passed in quick succession, costing Guttorm four more pieces to one of Bjørn's. Again, Guttorm rushed his turn, moving one of his pieces forward to block the king's retreat and leaving his own piece exposed to retaliation. It too left the board.

*Scraaatch... scraaatch... scraaatch... scraaaaaatch.*

'Think, lad,' Bjarni muttered. 'Bjørn is playing with you and you're letting him do it. You started with the superior force and already you've lost a quarter of it. Think. Look at how he's playing and learn from it.'

Bjørn subtly shook his head when Bjarni finished speaking, meeting his friend's eyes. The message was clear: *let him figure it out.*

Bjarni picked up his carving again with a shrug.

Guttorm slowed himself down with a grimace and surveyed the board.

Moving more cautiously this time, he shifted a piece forward and blocked Bjørn's line towards one of the corners, removing the king's escape for the time being and earning an approving grunt from Bjarni.

*Scratch… scratch… scratch… scratch.*

Ten more moves and Guttorm had taken two more of Bjørn's at the cost of one of his own and blocked two escape routes in the process.

Just as it was beginning to look desperate for Bjørn, he shifted focus to the opposite side of the board, pulling his king straight across to the under-defended edge.

Guttorm's face was his undoing and Bjørn could see him becoming flustered as he moved to block one of the remaining avenues of escape, leaving the second wide open.

Two more moves and it was over, and Guttorm could only watch as Bjørn slid the king off the board and won the game, losing only four pieces in the process. Victorious, he picked up the pieces of silver with a grin and slipped them into the pouch at his belt where they landed with a metallic ring.

'Focus on the bigger picture, Guttorm. Not just what's happening immediately in front of you. Otherwise, you'll lose every time,' Bjørn said, jingling his money pouch meaningly to emphasise the point.

Guttorm nodded silently, his eyes still dancing across the board as he took in the remaining pieces. He didn't say anything.

'Bjørn's right,' Bjarni said, his deep voice breaking into the silence. 'A good warrior knows what's happening in front of him; a great one knows what's happening around him.'

'I understand,' Guttorm said with a nod.

'Will you play again?' Bjørn asked, moving to reset the board.

'Aye, but not for a wager. I think my purse has suffered enough for one day,' he said, smiling resignedly.

'Fair enough.' Bjørn laughed, resetting the board.

'Also, before you start, I'd get that blade covered and put away. You don't want it getting infected with iron rot,' Bjarni said motioning towards the sword at Guttorm's side. Bjørn smiled to himself as Guttorm nodded and moved to store the blade.

Several more hours passed this way, with grunts of victory and defeat temporarily drowning out the constant scratching of Bjarni's knife as he carved away beside them, making occasional comments on the game. At one point, Red Orm joined them with his prize and began gutting the fish alongside the starboard strakes, throwing the guts and frame overboard. Soon after that, he was dipping the fillets into a bucket of salt water, sharing around succulent strips of raw fish which did much to add to the mood aboard ship.

'Moskstraumen ho,' Knud called from the masthead, drawing the eyes of the crew first up to his precarious perch overhead, then towards the bow, and the broiling seas.

'Bjørn! Get back here,' Yngvar called from the stern, his eyes serious. The crew had already begun preparing for the rougher waters ahead, stowing games and lose equipment in sea chests and opening oar ports, ready to run out the oars.

Bjørn made his way quickly down the ship, moving easily with the motion of the waves as he made for the aft deck. Yngvar nodded as Bjørn stepped up and took his place beside him, wrapping his arm over the tiller. He felt the weight intensify as Yngvar relinquished his grip, along with the responsibility. Bjørn could feel the pull on the ship as Njörd tried to pull *Sleipnir* down to his feast below the waves. 'Drop sail and run out the oars,' he shouted, watching with satisfaction as the crew ran to answer his command. Bjørn could feel that he was slowly winning the trust of the men on board, but that could only go so far against his inexperience and youth. Gritting his teeth, he pulled the tiller towards himself to turn the ship and give the danger ahead a wider berth.

As they drew nearer to the tidal eddy, he heard the collective intake of breath as the men aboard felt the pull, and several clasped the Thor's amulets at their necks or made warding off signs with their hands.

Once the danger was passed, the crew released a collective breath, making it feel as if *Sleipnir* herself was breathing a sigh of relief. As the crew began to smile and Yngvar gave the order to run up the sail again, Bjørn released his own breath, unaware that he had been holding it in the first place.

'Well done,' Yngvar grunted from beside him. 'Keep her on this course and we'll haul up and make landfall where we stopped our first evening. With any luck, we'll find *Uxi* and her crew already there with fires blazing and food cooking. If not, we'll haul up and plan what to do next.'

Bjørn nodded, his eyes dancing across the waves as he sought out the island on the horizon. The skies overhead remained clear for the rest of the afternoon and the ocean continued to calm itself as the storm clouds retreated before their bows. In the distance, Bjørn could make out the island they were aiming for, the imperceptible dot slowly taking shape and becoming discernible from the horizon itself. The shadows were lengthening when they were finally close enough to make out the cove they had camped in on their last visit.

The crew was well used to the routines of the ship, and the sail was quickly lowered and stowed while others slid out the oars and drove *Sleipnir* up onto the beach. Bjørn braced himself for impact as the bow carved through the sand, shifting slightly as she struck solid ground. Beside him, Yngvar called forward the order to secure the ship, sending men over the prow and into the shallow waves. The rest of the crew moved quickly to stow their oars and unload what they would need for a night ashore. Uffi, Galti, and Sindri were already disappearing into the woods above the shoreline to gather firewood.

'No sign of *Uxi*,' Bjørn said, casting an accusing eye over the abandoned beach as if the cove itself was to blame for their absence.

'Aye,' Yngvar said with a sigh. 'We'll wait here for a day while we search the island. It could be that they're hauled up on another stretch of shore. Hopefully, they'll show up while we wait. If not, we'll continue on towards Vágar. We might even find them hauled up on one of the small islets between here and home. There's no telling what condition *Uxi* was in after the storm,' he added.

'Meaning?'

'Meaning they could be holed with broken strakes, or they could have lost their mast or sail, and can only move under oars.'

Bjørn nodded gloomily. 'We'll find them,' he said before moving down the ship to carry his own chest ashore.

Yngvar stayed where he was on the deck, shifting his gaze to the distant horizon as the light slowly leaked out of the day. Behind him, he could hear his men relaxing after a day on the waves, their laughter mingling with the sound of water hitting the shore.

\*\*\*

It took three days for Arleigh and Turid to reach Váli's hall. They made much slower progress than they'd hoped and had been constantly on edge as they moved. Several times they'd been forced to lie in the dirt as riders passed them, not daring to breathe as the warriors flitted through the trees less than an arrowshot away. It had been an enormous relief to finally exit the forest on the other side and reach the open lands at the edge of Váli's territory. They could see newly sown fields surrounding the small ring fort, with the roof of his hall standing proud above the wooden palisade. For the first time, they allowed a feeling of safety to take root in their bellies.

Váli was an independent landowner, with his own warriors, who owed allegiance to Erik, paying him an annual tithe of livestock and silver in return for protection from raiders, and support in hard winters. More than that though, he was Erik's friend. Oversized in both stature and volume, he had an enormous brown beard that was fading to grey and deep green eyes that made him instantly recognisable. He was immensely popular amongst the people of Vágar and had spent many evenings drinking and eating in Erik's hall with the jarl and his sons. The pair had raided together in their youth, with Váli's small thirty-oared snekkja, *Hrafn*, joining Erik's ships to raid both the British Isles and Frankia. He had joined Erik in the attack on Shorewitchshire, Arleigh remembered, and had always treated her well. After a life on the whale road, he had retired a wealthy man, choosing to spend the rest of his days as a farmer. Nowadays, *Hrafn* was used more as a trading ship than a raider, and was used for travel between his farm and settlements along the coast like Vágar. As far as Arleigh knew, Váli and his warriors only drew their weapons these days to settle disputes with other landowners, and the occasions were few and far between. Few would risk Erik's ire, and his favour of Váli was well known.

The sun was shining overhead, bringing warmth into the day as Arleigh and Turid crossed the open fields. In the distance, they could see several riders leaving the homestead and kicking their mounts in their direction. Arleigh drew an arrow and knocked it without breaking stride.

'What are you doing?' Turid asked, turning at the sound. 'We're safe now.'

'We're not safe yet, Turid,' Arleigh said, eyeing the riders. She hadn't missed the glint of iron as the sun danced off their weapons and armour.

Turid didn't say anything, but after a few moments she too loosened her knife in its sheath and drew her axe, carrying it discreetly in her right hand. They continued moving in silence, watching the approaching horsemen and stealing occasional glances behind them to make sure that none of Ake's men had picked up their trail. They'd both noted the recent hoof prints in the ground near the path where they exited the forest. If Hoelun had been followed this far, it was likely that Ake's men would make the connection between her escape and their own. As the riders drew closer, they began to pick out individual forms and Arleigh counted thirteen riders and two extra mounts. She knew there was next to no chance of surviving if things turned sour, but she was a survivor, and would fight until the last breath left her tired lungs. Discreetly, she loosened her own knife as she again caught the glint of iron. They could hear them now, and Arleigh imagined that she could feel the dry ground trembling beneath her feet as they drew closer.

The riders were a little over a rôst away when they heard a voice shouting from behind them. 'There!' Several more acknowledged the cry, and as the two women turned, they watched in horror as at least twenty riders broke the treeline behind them, spilling from the forest like a swarm of furious wasps.

Arleigh didn't hesitate.

'Run,' she screamed before sprinting towards Váli's riders, suddenly confident that that was where safety lay.

Turid didn't need to be told twice and the pair sprinted for the approaching horsemen.

Váli's men had seen the threat too and were kicking their horses into action, their distant shouts reaching the two women as they spurred their mounts on. One of them, lightly armoured and with a slight figure, was quickly drawing ahead of the main party, rapidly closing the distance between Váli's warriors and the fleeing women.

Arleigh could hear Turid's feet drumming the earth behind her, the sound muted by the growing thunder of approaching hooves. Risking a glance over her shoulder, she caught sight of the closest rider, less than three-hundred paces from her and closing fast. At his current pace, he would be on her, or more likely Turid, in moments.

'Turid, move to my left,' Arleigh gasped, refusing to break her stride for even a second more than she had to. Turid had learned to trust Arleigh's judgement over the previous days, and she moved without question. 'No matter what happens, you don't stop,' Arleigh panted, raising her voice to be heard above the thundering hooves. It sounded as if they were right on top of them, and images of a spear being driven through her back flashed briefly through her mind. 'Do you understand?' she shouted when Turid didn't answer.

'I... I understand,' she gasped.

'Good,' Arleigh grunted before digging her foot into the ground and spinning, drawing back on her bow as far as she could and launching the arrow at the closest rider. Behind her Turid kept running, the sound of her footsteps swallowed up by Váli's approaching warriors. The bow was heavier than Arleigh was used to, and she had to fight to bring it to full draw, although even if she hadn't been able to it wouldn't have mattered at so short a distance. The

237

closest rider was less than forty alnir from her. Straining against the string, she forced herself to ignore the charging rider as he bore down on her, and the spear held towards her that somehow filled her vision completely. Taking a final deep breath, she released, watching with satisfaction as the shaft flew straight and true. The arrow took the rider in the stomach, his own momentum driving the shaft deeper into his body and forcing him to the ground where he writhed in screaming agony.

'*If he isn't dead now, he soon will be,*' Arleigh thought as his companions shouted in rage, slapping their swords and axe hafts against their horses flanks to coax more speed. Moving as fast as she could, she sprinted for the now-empty saddle, loosing precious seconds as she calmed the horse which had become skittish at the scent of blood. She ignored the splotches of red gore that had painted the saddle, throwing herself onto the horse's back as quickly as she could.

'Yaaah,' she cried, using her bow as a whip. She wheeled the spirited beast and aimed straight for Turid's fleeing form, now fifty paces ahead of her. 'Turid,' she cried, her eyes flicking between her friend, the approaching riders, and the men chasing her. She slapped the horse again, gaining an extra burst of speed. 'Turid,' she called again, struggling to be heard above the approaching horses. 'Turid, stop!'

Mercifully, she heard her, and Arleigh pulled up alongside, helping her swiftly into the saddle behind her. The entire manoeuvre had taken less than twenty seconds, but in that time both groups of warriors had drawn frighteningly close and she imagined she could see the whites of their eyes. 'This is going to be close,' she gasped, kicking in her heels. She could feel Turid's arms wrapped tightly around her waist as she drove the horse towards Váli's men. They were now less than half a rôst from her, but the men behind were closer, and Arleigh could almost feel their breath on the back of her neck as they raced away. Foam was flicking from their horse's mouth as it pounded the ground, and Arleigh could feel it flagging under the extra weight.

She heard a cry from behind her and turned in time to see one of Ake's men go flying from the saddle, followed closely by a second. It took her a moment to find the archer, her eyes finally finding the warrior who had ridden ahead of Váli's warriors. She was surprised to find the man still mounted, and she watched in fascination as he took aim a third time while guiding the horse with his knees. She'd never seen anything like it, and she watched in awe as a third arrow found its mark, burying itself in another man's shield and knocking him from the saddle. With three well-placed arrows, the unknown warrior had evened the odds for Váli and his warriors. The archer raised his bow in salute before breaking off from the main group, drawing two more of Ake's warriors away from the fight as they followed in pursuit.

Arleigh's heart was in her throat as she watched the horseman turn in the saddle and loose two more arrows in quick succession, downing one of their pursuers while the other caught a shaft on their shield. The second warrior decided against the chase and turned back to rejoin the main force.

'Lady Turid,' a booming voice called from the approaching riders as they pulled up on the reins and dismounted.

'Váli!' Turid cried, struggling to compose herself. 'We would appreciate your aid for a moment.'

'Of course. Ragnar,' he said, turning to one of his warriors, 'take the women back to the *borg* and protect them with your life. Don't open the gates for anyone except myself, or my men.'

Nodding, one of the younger men climbed back into his saddle and rode towards the two women while the rest of the warriors finished hobbling their horses before forming a skjaldborg in front of them.

'Lady Turid,' Ragnar said invitingly, indicating towards the distant farm buildings.

Before Turid could speak, Arleigh took the axe from her belt and dismounted. 'Take Turid to the borg, I will stay and fight. Your men are outnumbered, and an archer in the rear could stop your flank from being broken.'

'Arleigh?' Turid asked, turning in the saddle, her brows furrowed in concern. 'Are you sure?'

'Completely. If Váli falls, we're dead anyway. Go,' Arleigh said, softening her voice and looking up at her friend. They had never been close before. How could they be, both being Erik's women? But their recent ordeal had forged a bond between them that wouldn't be easily broken.

'I will be fine,' she added as she drew her first arrow and moved to stand behind the shield wall. Behind her, she heard Ragnar make a *chuh* sound and kick the horses into a gallop, the sound joined by Turid's own horse.

Despite his history on the whale road, Váli was now a farmer first and a warrior second. Only he and four of his men wore brynja and helmets, the iron shining brilliantly in the sun. All five of them carried swords and axes at their hips and carried long spears that jutted forwards from behind their shields. The rest of his men carried spears and shields, and while many had an axe or seax at their belts, though they were armoured only in leather or thick homespun.

Ake's men were similarly armed, but they outnumbered the defenders and many wore gleaming iron shirts, tipping the balance in their favour. In the distance Arleigh spied the mysterious horse archer disappearing into a small copse of woods behind the skjaldborg. The air around her was filled with the thuds of iron on wood as the shields locked together and the two lines of men faced one another, waiting for someone to make the first move.

'Who are you to enter my lands unannounced, armed and armoured for war?' Váli challenged from the front rank. Silence greeted him. 'Answer me!' he snarled, taking a step forward from his own line. Behind him, his men slowly moved forward to protect their lord, reabsorbing him into the wall.

'We come on Jarl Ake's bidding,' one of the men said, standing tall from the ranks as he lowered his shield slightly. The warriors around him remained hunched down and ready as he continued speaking. 'Lord of Vágar and the lands around. I am Ottar Svensson, húskarl to the jarl.'

'Jarl Erik, who they call the Golden Hand, is the only lord of Vágar,' Váli growled, dangerously. He was met by a resounding *thump* as his men beat their weapons once against their shields.

'There is no need for you and your men to die here today,' Ottar said, continuing as if Váli hadn't spoken. 'Yield the women to us and my jarl will surely look on your actions with favour as he consolidates his new territory.'

Arleigh felt a brief moment of panic as Váli turned to gaze at her, as if pondering the proposition, but the emotion was quickly replaced by amusement when she saw the look of surprise that had plastered itself across Ottar's face. Váli had burst out laughing at his words, the sound enveloping the men in both shield walls, soon infecting several of his own men. The sound was so out of place among the spears and shields of warriors preparing to kill one another that more than a few of Ottar's men stood straighter to watch the spectacle.

When Váli finally regained control and spoke again, there was no mirth in his voice, and Arleigh shivered at the coldness of his voice. 'I've bought and sold thralls whose favour I would rather earn than that which your snake of a jarl can give me,' he said, reaching under his helmet's eye-guard to wipe a tear from his eye. 'Nor will I tarnish my reputation, or those of my men, by bantering further with one of his lap dogs.'

Ottar's face grew red at the insult, but Váli continued speaking without pause. 'If you want the women, come and take them, Svensson. But know this, Erik's byname wasn't just earned for the rivers of gold and silver that flow from his hand. Your *jarl* will learn soon enough just how *generous* Erik can be,' he growled, hunkering down behind his shield. 'You have no idea the storm you've unleashed on yourselves,' he added ominously.

'There's no arguing with farmers,' Ottar said, his face red with fury as he struggled to compose himself and regain the situation. 'We will take the women, and leave you and your *thralls* as carrion in this field. If you see my father in Valhöll, tell him Ottar sent you,' he added, before ducking behind his own shield. 'Forward!' he called, leading his warriors towards Váli's.

Arleigh shivered involuntarily as the snake-painted shields moved slowly towards them, their steps falling in a constant rhythm as they drew closer. She had never stood so close to a battle before, let alone in the shield wall, and she found that the experience both thrilled and scared her. Unconsciously, she ran her fingers over her arrows' fletching, taking strength from the feeling as they slid over the feathers before coming to rest on the bow string. '*I won't be found wanting,*' she thought determinedly, steeling herself.

'On my command,' Váli said quietly, his voice easily hidden by the sound of the approaching warriors, 'form a *svinfylking* around me.'

A memory flashed through Arleigh's head at the mention of the svinfylking formation, bringing an image of a six- or seven-year old Bjørn as he rushed into Erik's hall after a day spent learning from Yngvar. He had proudly laid hnefatafl pieces on the table, showing her how the wedge-shaped swine array, or boar snout, could be used to drive through an enemy shield wall to disrupt their ranks. From what she remembered, the tip of the wedge was the most dangerous place to be, but also the most honourable.

Váli and his warriors waited in stoic silence as Ottar's ranks continued to advance, their bodies angled slightly forward to support their shields when the walls clashed.

Arleigh's heart was racing in her chest as the lines met, the air filled with the crash of shields and the grunts of struggling warriors as they lunged and blocked, straining to maintain their ranks. Váli's men held strong, resisting Ottar's as they waited for the call to attack. Standing at the rear, Arleigh's eyes moved constantly, flicking from left to right as she watched for someone trying to whip around and attack Váli's flanks. She was so engrossed in her vigil that she almost jumped in surprise when Váli's thundering baritone rose above the fighting, bellowing out a single order: 'Svinfylking!'

Like a wave striking the shore he charged, leading with his shield. Those clad in heavy iron-ringed shirts followed closely on his heels, two on each side, protecting his flanks and helping to drive the wedge through Ottar's wall of iron and wood. If it was possible, the sounds of iron striking wood intensified as the warriors pushed deeper into the enemy ranks.

On her left, Arleigh watched as one of Ottar's spearmen whipped around the flank and prepared to bury his spear in the stomach of one of Váli's warriors. Acting instinctively, she drew her bow back and released, the arrow crossing the distance in a heartbeat to bury itself in the warrior's armpit before the arrowhead burst out of his back near his spine. A look of surprise crossed his face as he dropped his weapons, suddenly unable to grip them as his strength fled. Arleigh ignored his strangled cries for help as she drew another arrow and turned her attention back to the battle, watching closely for more warriors trying the same manoeuvre.

Already several warriors had fallen on either side, their screams adding to the war cries of the living as the air filled with the metallic tang of blood and viscera. On her left, another man tried to turn the flank and write his saga. He was young, barely into his first beard. 'He'll never grow one now,' she thought as her arrow found his throat, the impact driving him from his feet. Arleigh became vaguely aware of a faint drumming sound drawing closer, the rhythm at odds with the sounds of battle that seemed to surround her. Risking a glance, spied a lone horseman approaching Ottar's warband from the rear and she felt a moment of horror that reinforcements were arriving to relieve them. She quickly nocked another arrow and began to track the horseman as he drew closer, ready to drop him before he could do any damage. She was just about to draw back on the string before she recognised the rider as the horse archer who had disappeared before the battle. In less time than it took for Arleigh to take a breath, the archer drew and loosed two arrows, sending more of Ake's warriors to the ground with arrows in their backs. Váli's warriors were quick to fill the holes in the line, reaping a bitter harvest among Ottar's men. Seeing the opportunity, Arleigh ran around the flank and began pouring arrows of her own into the exposed flanks, winnowing away at the enemy warriors like so much chaff as her arrows struck with ruthless abandon. One man fell with an arrow through his neck, another fell screaming with one in his buttock, the shaft snapping as he landed in the dirt. It was too much for the attackers. As if by some unseen signal, they turned and ran, making for their horses. Váli's men pursued them for several paces until they were called back by a long, mournful horn call. The battle was over. From her position slightly forward of Váli and his warriors, Arleigh continued firing arrows until her fingers clasped only empty air, her arrows spent. Frustrated, she lowered her bow and watched as her final arrow struck the horse of one of the retreating warriors. She felt a moment of guilt as the animal reared up in pain, its cries loud against the eerily quiet battlefield. Only nine of the saddles were filled as the retreating warriors made for the treeline, their escape closely followed by Váli's mysterious horse archer who chased them relentlessly. Arleigh watched with the rest as the rider loosed arrow after arrow like a stinging wasp, bringing down two more warriors before giving up the chase. The sounds of battle had been replaced by the cries of injured and dying warriors. Ottar wasn't amongst them, Arleigh noticed. Váli's men were already moving among the fallen, separating friend from foe as they began administering to their wounds. Three of Ottar's men were still alive, although their injuries were grievous. Váli gave the order for them to be put out of their misery, and Arleigh watched detachedly as one of his warriors moved amongst them, placing weapons into hands before dispatching them with quick thrusts to the heart or throat. Their bodies were quickly looted for valuables, weapons, and armour by practiced hands.

Ottar's warriors had suffered the worst, attacked in the rear and split in half by the swine array, but they had managed to down several of Váli's men. One of them nearest to Arleigh was sitting on the ground gritting his teeth through the pain in his arm, where a spear or sword blade had split the skin along the length of the limb. Arleigh shouldered her bow and moved towards him. She saw with satisfaction that the wound wasn't fatal, and she quickly emptied her waterskin over the injury, ignoring his sharp intake of breath as she did so. Drawing her knife, she sliced the undamaged sleeve from the man's tunic and bound his arm, unable to do more. 'Keep the arm up to slow the blood flow,' she said. 'I can stitch it when we get back to the borg.'

He did as she said, nodding his thanks as he supported his injured arm with the good one. Behind her, Arleigh could hear the sound of hooves approaching, and turned in time to see the mysterious archer dismount and pull off their leather skull cap, releasing a waterfall of raven-black hair.

'Hoelun!' Arleigh cried in surprise. The whole time she'd known the girl she'd never been more than a quiet thrall, and more recently her son's infatuation. The skill with horse and bow were completely unexpected. 'You're alive!'

Snow-white teeth greeted her as the younger woman smiled and embraced her. Arleigh paused briefly at the unexpected sign of emotion before returning the embrace, wrapping her own arms around the younger woman. 'Yes,' she said simply, before turning to Váli. 'We need to go. Seven of them escaped, and it's only a matter of time before Ake sends more.'

Váli laughed at her words, the sound drawing all eyes to him. 'I never thought I would live to see the day a thrall gave me instructions!' He chuckled, his mirth becoming infectious as the survivors saw the humour in the situation. Hoelun blushed briefly, allowing a small smile to creep across her face as she recognised the absurdity of the situation.

Regaining control of his emotions, he nodded. 'Aye, lass, you're right though. Gather up our dead, and get them onto horses. Strip theirs and leave them for the ravens,' he added as he climbed into the saddle. 'Arleigh,' he said, smiling down at her kindly, 'will you and Lady Turid join us for dinner?'
Arleigh just smiled, suddenly overcome with exhaustion as the realisation that she was safe sunk in.

# Chapter 17

'This could never have happened if Erik was here,' Váli grunted as he angrily speared another slice of meat with his eating knife.

Turid, Arleigh and Hoelun were eating with Váli in his hall along with several of his warriors, his wife, Astrid, their son, Ragnar, and their daughter, Signy. Both Arleigh and Turid had met Astrid in the past, and had cherished the kindness and warmth she had showed them when they arrived, bringing them food and drink after their journey. The table before them was laid with haunches of beef and pork, as well as bread and plenty of ale and mead. Váli was a generous host.

Compared to Erik's hall in Vágar, Váli's home was modest. It stood taller than the surrounding buildings and had a similar design, looking much like an upturned ship, but that was where the similarities ended. Everything about Váli's hall was more subdued and humble, which gave it a cosy feeling, rather than working to exhibit his power and influence as Erik's hall did. Arleigh saw that the beams supporting the roof were decorated with both Váli's and Erik's banners, which swayed gently as the smoke rose from the central hearth. The sight of Erik's banner still standing gave her a feeling of hope.

'I still can't believe that Vágar has fallen,' Astrid said quietly. She was the polar opposite of her husband, with a slight frame and long blonde hair that fell down her back in a single thick braid. 'I'm so sorry for all that you've suffered, it must have been terrible.'

'You said they struck almost immediately after the fleet left. Jarl Ake must have known when they would leave and been waiting for them. He's probably been planning the attack for months.'

'The prisoner,' Turid gasped, surprising everyone as Váli's words sunk in.

'Prisoner? What prisoner?' Váli and Astrid asked together.

'The boys went hunting a few weeks before Erik sailed,' Turid explained, 'and found a group of vagrants up in the hills. The one they brought back said they were there for simple vengeance; something Erik had done years ago. Bjørn told us that one escaped and fled into the woods but Erik's warriors never found him. He must have been Ake's man.'

'I would guess you're right on that count,' Váli said, shaking his head, 'but there's nothing we can do about it now. What happened in the attack? If I knew Leif at all, he wouldn't have gone down without a fight. He always was an unshakeable bastard.'

'As far as we know, Leif and his men fought to the last man,' Turid began, taking a sip of the rare Frankish wine Váli had opened for them. 'They held the front gate against overwhelming odds and beat them back at least once, but Ake sent men around the rear of the settlement who overwhelmed our defences. It was a miracle that Hoelun was able to escape when she did; even more so that we could follow. If not for Erik's forward thinking, we'd still be tied up in the hall. I doubt any more will manage to escape now that we've gone,' she added mournfully.

Arleigh watched her friend as she spoke. She had become sunken and withdrawn towards the end of their journey together, but some of her confidence and strength had returned after bathing and changing into the clothes Astrid had given them. One of Váli's men had reset her nose as well, although it was still a mess of blue and purple, and she was still recovering from the shock of having everything she knew taken away from her. Hoelun and herself had recovered much faster; they knew what it was to see their world stolen from them by violent men.

'What's important now is what we do next,' Arleigh began, speaking into the silence. 'Erik has barely left, and with a fast ship we can surely catch the fleet and warn him of the news. The fact that your ship hasn't already been sunk, stolen or burned shows that Ake doesn't consider you a threat, or that he didn't. I doubt he still feels the same way.'

'Gnn,' Váli agreed, chewing on the last of his meal. Arleigh watched as he swallowed the mouthful, aided by a deep gulp of the wine. 'No, I'm sure you're right. But no matter, *Jarl* Ake was never any friend of mine to begin with. The man is an untrustworthy coward, he always was.'

The sarcastic way he pronounced *jarl* wasn't lost on his guests, and they took strength from his defiance. None of them underestimated Jarl Ake, or the punishment that he would rain down on Váli and his men. They wouldn't stand a chance. Like it or not, Váli was firmly invested in Erik's fight. The conversation lapsed into silence for a time as everyone contemplated the severity of their situation, the only noise coming from the crackling flames, and the sounds of people quietly eating and drinking.

'As to your idea of sailing to find Erik,' Váli said as he threw another log on the flames, 'that is no small request. I have just over thirty men able to bear arms and crew *Hrafn*, and only a few of those are warriors like the ones you saw today. Along with yourselves and Astrid< the bird would be full. I would be leaving the women and children of my men – not to mention my land and wealth – undefended.'

The three women knew it was a steep request to ask Váli to leave his home so unprotected. The hall and buildings were surrounded by a ring of earth, topped with a wooden palisade, and was more than adequate to repel an attack from a small raiding party coming up the fjord. But an attack from Ake and his warriors would be something else entirely. Against the numbers Ake could bring, the defences were little better than a livestock pen.

Another silence followed as everyone weighed the options while unseen thralls filled curved horns and looted chalices with mead and ale. Turid and Astrid finished the last of the wine.

'So hide it,' Hoelun said after a while. If once she might have hesitated to speak in such company, that hesitancy was gone, replaced by the confidence of a warrior. 'Your wealth and your herds will be worth nothing if Jarl Ake seeks vengeance,' she said, realising no one was going to stop her. 'He will take them from you, along with your life and the lives of your men. Tell your people to leave, to hide in the forests and hills beyond your walls where they will be safe. His position in Vágar is precarious as it is, not to mention the danger to his own lands given how many warriors he's brought with him. Halls and houses can be rebuilt, wealth re-earned, but lives cannot be restored once they are lost. If you stay here to defend what is yours, you will lose everything. Send the women and children, along with your herds and any food you have left from the winter, into the hills with any warriors you can spare. Bury your wealth in a hidden place, and pray Jarl Ake isn't smart enough to know how to dig. Erik is the only hope we have now,' she finished, looking around the table once more. Realising that all eyes were on her she remembered her place and became hesitant again, lowering her gaze, briefly catching a nod from Arleigh as she did so.

'Hoelun is right, Váli,' Turid said, resting her hand briefly on the woman's shoulder. 'Erik is not known as the Golden Hand for nothing; he will repay both your loyalty to his family, and your losses at Ake's hands, with interest,' she said, her voice laced with venom. 'But to do that, we must find him. Set *Hrafn* free. It's our only chance.'

Beside them a log burned through in the fire, sending a cloud of sparks up towards the roof of the hall.

'You have given us much to think about,' Váli said at length, dipping his head in thought as he rose from the table. 'I must sleep on all you've said. I will give you my decision in the morning. In the meantime, you are all welcome to enjoy the comforts of my hall, such as they are. My thralls will see to it that you have everything that you need.' Astrid stood and nodded once to their guests before following her husband towards their sleeping chamber at the back of the hall.

'That was well said, Hoelun.' Turid smiled once they were gone.

'I agree,' Arleigh added. 'Váli knows there is only one choice left to him, but it will not make it any easier.'

'I only told him the reality that I know from my own world. Amongst my own people, when the danger is too great, there is no shame in fleeing and returning when you're stronger. To us, all that matters is that you are the one still standing at the end.'

'Is that where you learned to ride and shoot like that?' Arleigh asked, filling a horn with mead. The question had been burning in her head all day and she could see that she wasn't alone in her curiosity. Váli's warriors and children had fallen silent at her question, eager to hear the story of the mysterious warrior woman. By now, everyone knew about Hoelun, and her skill with the bow.

Hoelun shyly took a swig from her own drinking horn, the silver decorations on the rim dancing in the flickering fire light.

'Tell us, please,' Turid prompted, filling a horn of her own. Around them, there were murmurs of agreement and support from the rest of the listeners.

'I was born on the sea of grass,' Hoelun began. 'As you find wealth and freedom on the whale road, mine find it on the endless steppe, where we move with the seasons to follow the green pasture for our herds. We don't build halls as you do, but rather live in round homes made of felt called a *ger*, in my language. They too move with us, as do all our belongings. Once our animals have grazed the land so that the bones of the hills are revealed, we move again.'

A few of the listeners tried to mimic the foreign word, but none could replicate the sound and they again lapsed into rapt silence. Around the table, all eyes were glued to the beautiful, wolf-eyed woman as she took another drink before continuing her saga.

'My people, the *Borjigin*, are one of many tribes who live on the sea of grass, raising our herds in times of peace, and raiding our neighbours in times of war. The winter is long in my home, and when the years are leaner, or there isn't enough food to feed the tribe, we will take what we can't produce. There is only one true rule: the strong survive.'

A few of the listeners murmured their approval now, the talk of raiding and war stirring memories of distant shores and plunder, as well as the harsh realities of survival in the north. The whale road, like this mysterious sea of grass, was not a place for the weak or the soft.

'We are taught to ride before we can walk, often tied to the backs of sheep so we can become used to the motion of an animal beneath us, and we train with the bow and arrow as soon as we can stand. By the time they are adolescents, most of our young men can take a bird on the wing at full gallop and hit a target a hundred paces away nine times out of ten. We do not fight war the way you do, standing shoulder to shoulder in the shield wall, but rather ride in and out releasing torrents of arrows to weaken our enemies before finishing them off with sword and mace, or the axe.'

The listening warriors murmured between them as they imagined war on horseback, and a life spent using bow and arrow instead of spear and shield. They'd all seen the skill with which Hoelun had effortlessly brought down Ake's warriors earlier that day. It wasn't hard to imagine the impact a swarm of riders would have.

'One of my father's favourite tactics was the feigned retreat, where he would withdraw from his enemy in disorder with his men, letting his foes think they were routed, before he would turn around and fall on their disorganised pursuit. By your standards this would appear dishonourable, but for my people, cleverness in war is the mark of a great warrior. Winning is winning, in our eyes.'

A few warriors nodded their agreement at that, but none spoke.

'I was the daughter of a *khan* – what you would call a jarl – and was taught to ride and shoot alongside the men. My father insisted I would be a strong match for my future husband and I was happy to learn. It was during an enemy raid that I was captured. My betrothed took an arrow to the eye moments before my horse was killed under me, and I was taken as a slave while our men were regrouping, preparing to attack again. I can still remember my mother's screams as I was thrown over my captor's saddle and carried away. I never saw my family again after that day, nor do I know what became of my people. From there began my long journey from east to west, traded from person to person along the ancient silk road, until I found myself in Vágar amongst your people. I hadn't held a bow for many years, until Jarl Ake's ships came.'

Hoelun fell silent as she finished her story, a solitary tear running down her face. It wasn't lost on Arleigh or Turid that the bow she had claimed for herself was leaning against the bench beside her.

'I will see to it that Erik makes you a free woman, once all this is done,' Turid said suddenly, leaning over to embrace Hoelun. 'You could have run and found freedom, but instead you came to Váli, and today you saved us from Ake's riders. I won't forget this, and neither will Erik.'

'Thank you,' Hoelun said quietly, returning the embrace.

Arleigh smiled quietly to herself at the sight, understanding Hoelun's pain.

***

'We have to go, Váli,' Astrid said. 'You know this.'

They were lying in bed while their guests finished their meal in the main hall. They could hear whispered snatches of Hoelun's story filtering through the door, but neither of them were listening closely. Váli was focused entirely on what his next move would be. He knew that he was now committed to Erik's cause, and part of him yearned to leave the land in his wake and once again free *Hrafn's* wings, to feel the wind whip his face with the promise of danger and adventure. The other part knew that doing so exposed his people to the full wrath of Ake's anger.

'Either way I'm stuck in the middle,' he grunted, rolling onto his side to face his wife. He could only just make out her silhouette against the light from the hearth burning low behind her. 'If I stay, Ake's men will overrun mine within an hour, two at the most, and we will all find ourselves on the way to Valhöll, while the women and children are taken as slaves, or worse. But if I sail, the women and children we leave behind will be even more exposed.'

'They must do as Hoelun suggested,' Astrid said with fire in her voice. 'Our hall can be rebuilt. The buildings, our belongings and the walls can all be replaced. We can resow fields and replace livestock. But the lives of our people are irreplaceable and if you stay and fight, all will be lost. The risks to our people are high if we leave, but if we stay they will have no chance at all. We have no choice, Váli. We must leave.'

'I know,' he said with firm gentleness, resting his hand on hers to calm the storm that was brewing alongside him. 'Tomorrow, I will order the lands around to be evacuated and pick ten good men to guard our people. The rest will sail with us to find Erik. There is no other choice.'

Beside him, he heard Astrid exhale in relief. He was used to a life of blood and war but this was all new for Astrid, yet she was taking it all in her stride. He was proud to have found such a strong wife with as much fire in her blood as she had. He felt her weight shift beside him in the bed and smiled as she came to rest on top of him, the swell of her chest pushing against him as she kissed him. There were no more words that night.

When Arleigh and Turid left the hall the next morning, they walked into a hive of activity. Everywhere, warriors were darting to-and-fro while riders were sent to the outlying farms and fields to warn the people there of the evacuation. Thralls and freemen worked side-by-side to prepare the wagons and carts that would carry the women and children, and their guards, into the woods. The mayhem raised a cacophony of sounds, filled with lowing cattle and bleating sheep, crying children and shouted instructions. And yet, Váli's booming voice could be heard above everything else, the deep baritone piercing through the chaos to manage the operation. The two women caught a glimpse of him clad in a gleaming brynja with his sword at his hip as he moved from group to group.

'Arleigh, Turid,' Astrid called as she crossed the empty ground in front of the hall. A silver-wrapped seax rested on her left hip, opposite her keys and eating knife. She was carrying two bowls in her hands.

'What can we do?' Turid asked, watching as another crate was loaded onto the wagon nearest to them. The man sighed in relief as he dropped his load before turning back for another. He was streaming with sweat.

'Eat,' she said with a soft smile as she handed each of them a bowl. They were filled with thick, creamy white *skyr* mixed with oats, and covered with berries and honey. 'You must be famished.'

'We are,' they said in unison, taking a bowl and laying into the contents with gusto.

'This is delicious,' Arleigh said between mouthfuls as she smiled through the merging flavours of sweet and sour. She didn't think anything had ever tasted so good before. Unlike the night before, where her only focus had been replacing the energy she had lost during their escape, she could now appreciate her food.

Astrid smiled again as Turid made an appreciative sound of her own. 'Váli keeps bees, and we eat what we don't trade. A pot was dropped this morning, so we rescued and shared what we could so it wouldn't go to waste.'

'Whoever dropped it should be thanked,' Arleigh said appreciatively, scooping out another spoonful.

When they were finished, Astrid took the bowls and stacked them. 'Váli has already begun sending provisions to the docks to prepare *Hrafn* to sail,' she said. 'He asked me to collect you and your belongings and bring you both down to the shore.'

'Surely we can help in some way?' Turid asked.

Arleigh nodded beside her.

'Of course. Váli asked if you could help me and Ragnar to oversee the loading and provisioning of *Hrafn*. He wants to be on the water as soon as the people are evacuated and the last of the men arrive from their farms. This evening, if possible.'

'Lead the way.'

Turning, Astrid beckoned to a thrall coming out of the hall and handed her the bowls before motioning for the women to follow her. The dancing water in the fjord came into view as they exited the walls, and they could see the hive of activity below as supplies were carted to the small harbour from Váli's rapidly emptying store houses.

'It's beautiful here,' Arleigh said as she took in the view. The small harbour was hemmed in on either side by natural walls of stone that created a deep avenue of blue that was surrounded by green forest and grey stone. Sitting in the distance, where the fjord met the open water, she spied a small islet with a single pine standing on its crown like a beacon.

'It is,' Astrid said in agreement. 'I often forget just how beautiful until someone reminds me.'

They walked in companionable silence, following the well-worn path down the hill. They could clearly see the scars of recent wagons in the dirt. Overhead, the sun was shining brightly and for a while they forgot the danger following them and simply enjoyed each other's company. The sounds of activity behind them were slowly drowned out, replaced by the gentle buzz of bees as they darted from flower to flower.

'Where is Hoelun?' Turid asked after a time, breaking the silence.

'Váli sent her back towards the woods to keep an eye out for a counterattack. He doesn't really expect anything to happen so soon, but she's the best rider we have and her skill with the bow will make Ake's scouts think twice before leaving the safety of the forest.'

'Her home sounds so different to ours,' Arleigh said, remembering the story from the night before.

'To fight with a bow instead of the spear, and to fight entirely from the back of a horse!' Turid added, picking up the conversation. 'It feels so cowardly,' she added, almost to herself.

'You had no idea?' Astrid asked.

'No,' they chorused together. 'We knew she was from the East, but we didn't ask more than that; why would we? There are hundreds of thralls in Vágar after all.'

'That makes sense, I suppose. We know so little of their lives before they come to us. It is the way of the world,' she agreed quietly.

'I'm glad she came when she did,' Arleigh added. In her mind, she was remembering the skill Hoelun had shown as she drew and loosed her arrows from the back of her horse. She had always been quietly proud of her own skills with the bow, but they paled in comparison. Hoelun made her look like a child.

'I will speak to Erik and see that he grants her her freedom. She's earned that and more for saving us yesterday, and for warning Váli.'

Astrid and Arleigh nodded in agreement. Arleigh didn't dare entertain her own hopes for freedom. In her heart, she knew that even if she was granted it, she would stay with Erik. Her old life was long gone.

'I've also noticed a connection between her and Bjørn,' Turid said suddenly, throwing Arleigh a mischievous smile.

Arleigh smiled at the question. 'I caught them together before they sailed. He was a little embarrassed about it,' she said, giggling suddenly at the memory.

It didn't take long for Turid and Astrid to share their own stories of catching their sons with their pants down and their reactions, or of being caught themselves when they were younger women. By the time they arrived at the shore, they were laughing so much they struggled to stand upright, and more than a few of the men stopped what they were doing to watch as the women drew near. It was only when Ragnar broke through the crowd and began walking towards them that they collected themselves again.

'For all that they strive to be honourable warriors, they're still our little boys in the end!' Arleigh whispered, nudging Astrid before bursting out laughing again. The three of them were nearly bent double by the time Ragnar reached them and had tears running down their faces.

'What's so funny?' he asked with a bemused smile on his face.

'Just womanly things,' Astrid said innocently while her friends quieted their own laughter.

'How can we help?' Turid asked at last, regaining control of herself.

Around them, the men had resumed their work, unloading barrels from a waiting cart and stowing them alongside *Hrafn*.

'We've unloaded a few carts now, but we need to begin bringing them aboard ship and stowing them. I can take charge of that, but if you could organise them into different piles so we can store it all depending on weight, and what we will need to access most frequently, that would be helpful.'

'We can do that,' Astrid said enthusiastically before Ragnar turned to begin organising the work crews to load the ship.

'Sometimes they do grow up to become warriors.' Arleigh chuckled as they moved towards the piles of supplies.

It took them until just before sundown to load the final barrel on *Hrafn* and ensure she was evenly weighted and floating true, and to complete the evacuation. In the end, Váli decided that it was too late to set sail, declaring that they would spend a final night ashore. Turid and Arleigh stood with Váli and his family as the men they would sail with kissed their wives and children goodbye, trusting their safety into the hands of the few men that would guide and protect them through their own ordeal. Everyone knew there was a very real chance that the goodbyes were permanent, and the light mood of the day had been banished by the cries of children and the stoic tears of women as they led the carts into the hills. It took over an hour for the entire convoy to be lost to sight amongst the trees, and as the final light flickered out of sight, the reality of the situation sunk in. Those left behind had a simple dinner of bread and mead with a roast pig the thralls had put on the fire before they too had left with the convoy. Everyone knew the risks they were taking. Váli had made it clear that everyone except the sentries were to sleep in the hall that evening so no time would be lost the next morning rounding up errant warriors. Arleigh briefly caught sight of the tireless Hoelun when she returned from her lonely vigil to quickly eat and drink, but the young woman left again to resume her post without speaking to anyone. Arleigh marvelled at her endurance but was too tired to suggest someone else take a turn watching the forest, and it wasn't long before she fell into a deep slumber, surrounded by snoring warriors as they tossed and turned in their war gear.

It felt like Arleigh had hardly closed her eyes before she was quietly shaken awake with a hand covering her mouth.

'They're coming,' a voice hissed in her ear. It took a few moments for Arleigh to recognise Hoelun's voice and register what she was saying as she banished sleep from her body.

'Have you woken anyone else yet?' she said, snapping upright.

'Not yet, you were the first person I saw.'

'We need to warn them. Now. Go and wake Váli, I'll begin waking the others.'

Hall burning was not an uncommon practice, and if Ake's men caught them sleeping, it would be all too easy for them to be trapped inside. She shuddered as she pictured the options that would leave them with: burn to death, or run onto the spears that would inevitably be waiting outside. Moving quickly, she began shaking people awake, quietly telling them to take up their arms and prepare to move. It wasn't long before Váli stormed from the annex, tightening his sword belt around his gleaming brynja. His helmet was under his arm and seeing him standing like a warrior of legend, Arleigh knew a moment of panic that he would order his men into battle, rather than to the ship. But she needn't have worried.

'Hoelun tells me that at least fifty men are on their way here, possibly led by Ake's son. Gather what you can and make for the ship. We leave in ten minutes.'

Váli's words transformed the hall from a quiet den of slumbering warriors into a storm of activity as the men rushed to pack their supplies and don their war gear.

'How did you get away?' Arleigh asked as Hoelun moved through the crowd towards her.

'I was on foot and had my horse hidden in the trees a ways behind me. They had no idea I was there. I stopped counting at fifty and came back to warn you all.'

'Well done.' Arleigh nodded as she took up her own bow and quiver. She and Hoelun had raided Váli's personal supply of arrows, and each of them now had twenty beautifully fletched shafts a piece at her disposal. Arleigh wrapped her belt around her waist with her knife sheath attached before sliding her small hand axe through the loop she had attached the day before.

Turid stood opposite her similarly dressed with an axe of her own at her hip. Váli had gifted it to her the day before when he came to check on the loading of *Hrafn*. Turid had argued that Váli had already done enough for them, but he had argued that he wouldn't see Erik's wife unarmed and defenceless while she was in his care.

Hoelun waited patiently for the two women, and the rest of the crew, to finish their preparations. She was already armed and ready, with her own bow strung in her hand and a large seax at her hip.

'Time's up, lads,' Váli's voice boomed. 'Make for the ship, now. Ragnar, take five men and go on ahead; make sure everything is ready to cast off immediately. The rest of you, with me.'

Watching Váli as he moved through the crowd reminded Arleigh of Moses parting the red sea and she quickly joined the rest of the warriors as they began filing out after their leader. Once they were all outside, Ragnar and the men he'd chosen quickly ran ahead to prepare the ship, while Váli led the rest of his warriors and the women at a slower pace behind him. Hoelun was again lost to sight as she sprung back into the saddle and galloped through one of the gates, a sack of unlit torches thrown over the saddle.

'There is an abandoned barn a few rôst away,' Astrid explained, seeing Arleigh's confusion. 'Váli is hoping that if she lights the torches close enough together, Ake's men will get confused in the dark and march there. It should buy us some time while we're boarding the ship and making our final preparations to sail. She won't be far away.'

Before Arleigh could reply she was separated from Astrid as the column marched through the gate that led to the water, and she had to focus on not tripping up on the men in front or behind her. It wasn't long before the land dipped and the awaiting fjord revealed itself to them, glinting with a thousand different stars while the moon's light danced over the water. She could see Ragnar and his men already moving across *Hrafn*, illuminated by the light from their torches. Hidden down the hillside as they were, there was little chance of Ake's men seeing the lights.

By the time they reached the shore, the ship was ready to sail, and all that was left to do was embark.

'Ladies,' Váli smiled, his voice calm as he indicated for them to board first. Astrid, Signy and Turid moved across the gangplank and made their way forward to the bow, standing as far out of the way of the men's sea chests and the oars as they could get. As Arleigh moved to climb over last, Váli gently grabbed her arm, stopping her.

'The other day, your arrows protected my flank and saved my men from being enveloped. Could you do the same today from the stern of the ship?' he asked, nodding briefly at the bow in her hand.

'Aye,' she said, flashing her teeth as she drew an arrow and set it on the string. 'I could do that.'

Váli nodded once before turning around and motioning for the rest of his men to begin boarding and take their positions. 'Hoelun will join you when she gets here,' he added before moving back down the wharf.

It didn't take long to get the rest of the crew on board, and they quickly moved to their places and took up the oars, ready to run them through the oar ports when the order came. Last to board was Váli, who moved to the stern and took up the tiller, preparing to guide the ship into open water. Mounted along the sides of the ship were the men's shields, their round shapes and the rearing prow beast of *Hrafn* casting a Jörmungandr-like shadow on the water next to them.

'We can't wait here much longer,' Váli grumbled quietly, eyeing the path back towards his home.

'Hoelun will be here,' Arleigh replied, her eyes locked on the shoreline. Unseen, she was running her fingers along the arrow's fletching, the soft feeling of the feathers calming her.

The night was completely still but for the occasional gentle breeze and the constant lapping of the small waves as they pushed and pulled the pebbles back and forth.

'We have to leave,' Váli whispered quietly so only Arleigh could hear. 'It's becoming too dangerous, and it's not inconceivable that there isn't a ship making its way here from Vágar to head us off…'

'Hoelun will be here,' Arleigh said firmly. She heard Váli take a breath to respond, but before he could speak, they heard the sound of hooves on the earth. 'There!' she gasped, feeling relief flood through her body as she pointed towards the sound.

She heard a low cheer rise from the crew as they too heard the drumming of hooves drawing nearer. They watched with tension as Hoelun threw her horse down the slope and galloped full tilt towards the waiting ship, closely pursued by three mailed horsemen, the moon glinting off their armour.

'There is no end to these maggots,' Váli growled, his own eyes as glued to Hoelun as those of his men as she turned and shot in a fluid motion, dropping the nearest rider. His cry as he fell to the ground was drowned out by the cheers of the watching warriors. The second two were more cautious after that, closing in on the retreating Hoelun in a swerving pattern. Arleigh watched as they split apart before coming back together again, disrupting her aim. It made no difference, and Váli's men watched in awe as one of the riders drew too close before he too was sent to the ground with an arrow through his arm. Again, the watching warriors cheered as the stricken warrior's sword went flying from his grip.

Arleigh had been watching the pursuit closely, and as the final warrior came into range, she too drew and loosed her own arrow, watching with satisfaction as her shaft flew across the gap to pierce the final rider's throat. Without turning or slowing, Hoelun rode her horse straight onto the jetty and came to a stop alongside the waiting gangplank before gracefully leaping from the saddle.

'They fell for it,' she gasped, whipping out her seax and slicing the horse's saddle free before pushing it from her horse's back to strike the wharf with a heavy thud. 'Those three noticed me escaping and gave chase instantly,' she said motioning back the way she had come, 'but the men on foot were already on their way towards the barn. They won't be here until we're well away.' They could all hear the hoofbeats as the injured man galloped back up the hill, groaning in agony.

'Good!' Váli exclaimed with a smile. 'Come aboard, girl! The whale road beckons!'

Hoelun grinned at him, her white teeth flashing in the dark as she slapped her horse on the rump to send the mare galloping into the darkness before she climbed aboard *Hrafn*. Still smiling she quickly made her way to the stern to stand alongside Arleigh and the towering Váli.

'Good shooting,' she said quietly as she unstrung her bow. Arleigh flashed her own smile as she removed her own bow string.

'Starboard oars, push off!' Váli boomed next to them.

As one, the starboard rowers ran out their oars and set them against the wharf, pushing *Hrafn* free while men at the bow and stern cast off the ropes holding them in place.

'Port oars at the ready,' he called as they drifted free, the shackles of land falling away from them. 'ROW!' he boomed, releasing *Hrafn* from her winter prison. Like a loosed arrow, *Hrafn* began to beat her wings and fly across the gentle waves, leaving the land behind her. High on the hill, they could see Ake's injured rider as he turned his horse to watch them disappear into the dawn, leaving only whooping insults in their wake for him to take back to Ake, the *jarl* of Vágar.

# Chapter 18

'What!' Ake roared, hurling his drinking horn across the empty hall. The vessel trailed an arc mead behind it as it flew across the room to crack against one of the carved roof supports. Ake was alone but for Canute and Steinar, and a few of his most trusted warriors. The mood in Vágar had been muted since Arleigh and Turid had escaped, stealing total victory from Ake's grasp. The discovery of the empty room and the hidden tunnel had sent Ake into a rage, and in one motion he had drawn his sword and taken the head off one of the guards set to watch the two women. He was the lucky one. The other had been stripped naked and chained to the rocks at the high tide mark where he was just able to keep his head above water. Steinar had gone to see the punishment for himself and was horrified by what had awaited him. Crabs and other marine life had begun eating the man's flesh while he still lived, stopping only when the tide receded. However, his agony didn't end there. As soon as the tide went out, the ravens, gulls and other small animals arrived to begin the feast anew. Steinar had almost vomited at the sight. The man's pathetic begging for a quick death had only made it worse.

Now he was again faced with his father's rage, this time at Váli's escape. The news that they had escaped almost unhindered had only enraged Ake further. In his mind, he imagined the single ship sailing to find Erik, and while they were more likely to find a needle in a haystack, it had planted the first seeds of worry in his gut. Erik's byname came from his near-infinite wealth, but also for the vengeance he brought down on his enemies. Ake's grip on Vágar wasn't nearly secure enough for such a confrontation. Not yet.

'What could be easier than stopping a *farmer*?' Ake shouted again, directing his rage at Steinar. Beside him, Canute stood impassive as always, his giant axe loose in his hand. Sometimes, Ake wondered if it was part of his body.

'They tricked us,' Steinar responded lamely, unable to meet his father's glowering eyes. 'They used torches to draw us away from the fort, and we couldn't tell the difference in the dark…' Steinar let the story trail off under his father's furious gaze. Even to his own ears the story was weak and he sought desperately for an ally amongst the watching warriors. He spied Ottar and hoped he would speak into the silence, having also been foiled by Váli, but he remained silent, his eyes downcast.

Despite the glowing fire, Ake knew the room would feel cold for his son, and he let him squirm for a few minutes before speaking again. 'You failed me, Steinar,' he said quietly, his voice almost a whisper. 'I needed the women here. Without them, I have no leverage over Erik! So, what do you suggest we do now?'

Steinar shuffled uncomfortably before responding, his voice low and quiet with none of its usual arrogance as he struggled to meet his father's eyes. 'Put extra men on the walls? Maybe put a ship in the fjord to give us an early warn...' he started before trailing off under the jarl's contemptuous gaze.

Not for the first time, Ake found himself wishing for a son with more intuition or bravery, rather than the arrogant weasel he'd sired. Enviously, he thought of the reputations Erik's brood were already earning for themselves. Giving Steinar a final look of disgust, he turned his fiery gaze onto his prow man, knowing already that his next order was useless before he gave it.

'Canute.'

'Yes, Jarl Ake.'

'Take *Slatra* with enough supplies for two days. Sail light and sail fast, and catch them if you can. They will be overloaded with supplies if they plan to find Erik; you may have a chance. Take whoever you want. If you haven't caught sight of them within two days, return here immediately and we will prepare for Erik's return. You're to leave immediately.'

'Yes, Lord.' He nodded, dipping his head briefly in acknowledgement before gesturing for three of the waiting warriors to follow him out of the hall.

'Leave us,' Ake said into the ensuing silence that followed the warrior's departure.

Steinar almost jumped at the audible sigh that escaped from the remaining men as they left the hall, and Ake's wrath. Neither of them spoke as the iron-clad warriors trailed out of the hall, the giant oak doors closing with an ominous boom.

The silence stretched as Steinar continued to wither under his father's unwavering glare. Even the fire seemed to have lost its warmth against Ake's smouldering rage.

'Father, I—'

'I'm prepared to give you one last chance, Steinar,' Ake said, interrupting him. 'But bear in mind, if you fail me again in so much as retrieving a mead horn, I will find another man to rule Vágar when I return home. One able to succeed. And know this,' he continued, speaking over Steinar, 'if you fail me again, you will be exiled from my realms, and I will find another man to adopt and call *son*. One able to sit in my high seat when I'm gone and be called Jarl.'

'What?' Steinar stammered, shocked. 'Father, I—'

'The men are beginning to whisper that you're unlucky,' Ake said, continuing as if Steinar hadn't spoken. 'They're saying that you're cursed. A coward. Don't think it escaped their notice that you shirked from danger when we took the town, that you only returned to the front lines under threat from me. And now you were given the simple task of capturing a few women from a farmer, and you failed.'

'But, Father, I—'

'Had horsemen with you!' Ake snarled furiously. 'Three of them who could have been sent ahead to scout the land, to survey Váli's men, to harry their escape, even to burn the ship! I've spoken with the men who marched with you. They told me the three men rode with you the entire way, that they didn't leave even once to check the path ahead. And, when you finally deigned to deploy them, they were sent in pursuit of that cursed archer who's already emptied too many saddles.'

Steinar remained silent, but Ake could see the thinly veiled anger on his son's face at the realisation that he had been *betrayed* by the men he had led.

The silence stretched again as both of them considered their next words carefully. It was Steinar who spoke first, unable to handle the silence any longer.

'What would you have me do?' he asked, trying to add steel to his voice.

Ake let his son squirm a few moments longer before replying.

'Take twenty men and return to the farmer's home. Burn everything. You have four days,' Ake grunted, his temper finally cooling. 'Go.'

The sight of his son as he all but ran from the hall made him grimace in disgust, doing nothing to dispel the sickening feeling in his stomach. He knew his position had become all the more precarious now that Erik's women had escaped his grasp. If they reached their husband – however unlikely that was – he would not only turn back to retake what was his, but he would have another ship full of warriors at his command.

'*Let him come*,' he thought, his eyes blazing as they reflected the dancing flames in the hearth. Out of the corner of his eye he spotted Revna, the blacksmith's wife, as she entered the hall. He had forgotten that he had summoned her in his rage, but the sight of her lithe curves under the tight-fitting dress he had ordered she wear drew his gaze from the fire, and he felt himself grow excited as he remembered her visit the night before. Ignoring the tears that welled in her eyes, he motioned for her to wait for him in the annex. He was vaguely aware of her sobs as she walked past, the sound barely audible over the crackling flames. He smirked at the sound, and the power he felt at having another man's wife in his control. It was his right as jarl, he mused, returning his attention to the fire as an unnoticed thrall brought him a fresh horn of ale.

***

'Sail ho!' Toke called to the stern, his eyes locked on the horizon.

*Uxi* and her crew had been rowing almost non-stop since the storm, stopping just once on a small island when they thought they saw suitable wood for a new mast. When they landed to investigate, they found the trees either too young, too crooked or too dead, but Halfdan had recognised the need for a proper night's sleep and gave them a night ashore. They had celebrated their dead there, collecting driftwood and creating a giant fire to serve as a funeral pyre, to which they'd added barrels of ale and salted meat, as well as possessions from the sea chests of their lost crewmates. Led by Halfdan, the crew had prayed to the Allfather for their companions to be accepted into the corpse hall, asking Óðinn to look on their deaths with favour. Otherwise, they were destined to an eternity aboard the *Naglfar*, waiting for Ragnarök. Wyrd.

The next morning, Halfdan had set them to hew two of the largest trees they could find and jerry-rig them to stand upright either side of the prow. The idea was to tie what they could of the spare sail between them and try to harvest some of the wind to reduce their reliance on the oars.

The result wasn't pretty, but it worked. The progress was nothing like what they'd experience under sail normally, but the men were able to stow their oars for the first time in what felt like an age. The downside was that Halfdan's visibility from the stern was greatly diminished, so now someone had to stand watch at the prow at all times while the *sail* was up. This was where Toke stood now, his eyes locked on the horizon.

'Do you recognise her?'

'I can't tell at this distance. I'd say she's at least thirty oars, though. Maybe forty.'

They had re-entered familiar waters now and had started charting a course back to Vágar to resupply and repair before putting to sea again to try and reconnect with *Fjord Ulf* and *Sleipnir*. The mood had grown lighter as they returned to the waters they knew, leaving feelings of uncertainty in their wake.

Toke kept a weathered eye on the horizon, eyeing the unknown ship with suspicion. Something about it was familiar, but he couldn't place it in his memory. Nothing about it seemed threatening; if they'd spotted *Uxi* they made no indication of it. Their course remained true as they sailed towards the west, and after a few hours they were lost to the horizon and Toke forgot about them. Despite the frustration at having to turn back, his spirits lifted as he sighted landmarks he recognised. On a sound ship, he knew they could be hauled up below Vágar by the end of the day, but given the state of *Uxi*, they would have to stop for the evening and make the rest of the journey tomorrow.

'Anything ahead?' Bersi asked, ducking under the makeshift sail and breaking Toke's train of thought.

'Nothing. Just empty fjords and calm water.'

'Gnnn,' Bersi grunted.

He'd never been one for talk and was perhaps the most stoic person Toke had ever met, but he'd found he enjoyed the older man's company. They stood silently together for a few minutes, watching the horizon.

'Head on back,' Bersi said suddenly. 'I can take over until we make landfall.'

'Thanks,' Toke yawned, suddenly realising how tired he was after spending hours on watch. '*I suppose I've stood here for the better part of a day,*' he thought as he patted the big man in thanks before ducking under the sail. The prospect of food and ale, and perhaps a game of tafl, made him smile as he walked back along the deck towards his own chest. He had to move carefully to avoid the outstretched ankles and arms of sleeping crewmen.

He was just sitting down on his chest and nodding for Orm to set up the board when Halfdan called him, his deep voice causing a few of the sleepers to stir and grumble incoherently. 'Toke, get back here!' he called.

'No rest for the wicked, eh, Orm?' he grunted as he climbed back to his feet with a sigh and worked his way back to the stern. He missed his brothers and wished they could sail together. He knew why his father spread them across the fleet, grim as the reasoning was, but he would have enjoyed their company now. Other than that he enjoyed sailing with Halfdan. The man was tireless and had a wealth of knowledge to pass on despite his relative youth.

'Aye, Halfdan?' he asked, climbing up to the small aft deck, after the older man had nodded his consent.

'Your father's friend Váli has a hall near here, doesn't he?'

Toke turned and re-evaluated where they were, taking in the walls of rock and the small islets that dotted the waves around them. After a few moments he had oriented himself. 'Aye, Váli lives near here. See where those birds are circling,' he asked, pointing ahead off their starboard bow.

Halfdan searched for a few moments before nodding.

'If we follow that inlet for a few rôst we will come to a small island with a single pine growing on it. When we reach the island, we want to turn hard to starboard. We will be able to see his home and harbour from there.'

'And do you think he would allow us to haul up there for the night?'

'Of course,' Toke said with a smile, his mind flicking involuntarily to Váli's daughter, Signy. They had met the year before when he had ridden with Hoelun and Bjørn to collect livestock for their father, and the connection between them had been instant. They'd met once or twice since then, but he hadn't yet picked up the courage to ask his father to approach Váli for her hand. *Perhaps when all this is done,* he mused.

'Okay,' Halfdan said, oblivious to Toke's running thoughts. 'Call out when we need to make the turn. From here it's only a day or so sailing until we reach home.'

'Aye,' Toke grunted, nodding once before making his way back along the crowded deck towards the prow. He stopped by Orm and explained briefly what was happening, smiling apologetically at the disappointment on his friend's face as he began packing up the tafl board he had just finished setting up. He grabbed a few strips of smoked meat and tucked them between the two least-stale pieces of bread he could find along with a half-full aleskin before moving back to the bow.

'Can't sleep?' Bersi asked as he ducked back under the makeshift sail.

'Gnn,' Toke grunted, holding up a hand as he finished his mouthful. He washed it down quickly with a gulp of ale before handing the skin across and explaining what Halfdan had said.

'Váli, eh? There's a man I haven't seen in a few years.'

'Did you know him well?'

'Oh aye,' Bersi said without turning. 'We were young men together, along with your father. He did well during his years on the whale road and settled down to the farmer's life some years ago. A waste of a life if you ask me, but he was always one to plan for the future.'

'I heard something similar from my father. I've only met him a handful of times.'

Toke waited for a response from Bersi, but he had lapsed back into his usual stoic silence, leaving Toke alone with his thoughts. Unperturbed, he returned to his meal, making short work of the remaining bread and meat while *Uxi* staggered her way through the darkling fjord. It didn't take long for the small islet to come into sight, and Toke ducked back under the sail to indicate the inlet Halfdan was looking for. A nod from the aft deck was enough to see the ship turn into the shallow fjord towards Váli's land. Blocked as their vision was by the sail, the first Bersi and Toke knew about the oars being run out was the familiar splash as *Uxi* leapt forward with new energy. The men knew they were nearing the end of their ordeal and were eager to put it behind them. A night ashore eating proper food and sleeping in a proper hall was a good enough reason to pull hard at the oars. At the bow, Toke and Bersi worked together to remove the prow beast from its mount and stow it safely, showing those watching from the shore that they came in peace.

'Toke, come back here, will you?' Halfdan called from the stern. There was a strange edge to his voice now, and Toke moved quickly to reach the stern.

'It appears that Váli may not be in residence. I see no sign of his ship, nor smoke or movement at the farm.'

'Perhaps his people turned in early for the day?' Toke said, trying to dispel the feeling of unease that was creeping into his own gut. Soon the walls and buildings would be lost from sight as they drew closer to the land, but at this time of day there should be men on the dock, fishermen returning with their catch, or even a passing trader unloading their cargo.

'Perhaps,' Halfdan muttered, sounding unconvinced. 'We have no reason to worry, but pass the word along the ship that we're going ashore with shields in hand.' There was no need to mention weapons. No Northman worth his salt would go anywhere unarmed.

'Aye, I'll do that.'

The eagerness of the crew to reach land was written clear in *Uxi's* race to the shore, and Toke was only halfway along the deck relaying Halfdan's orders when Bersi's voice boomed back from the bow warning of impact. Toke quickly took hold of the ruined mast stump moments before the sound of pebbles scraping *Uxi's* hull reverberated through the ship like arrows striking a raised shield.

'You six, stay aboard ship and secure her to the beach,' Halfdan said, pointing to the men closest to him. 'The rest of you, with me!' he called, springing overboard with his shield in hand. Toke winced, feeling that Halfdan's actions were closer to those of a raider than a guest.

The rest of the crew grumbled about the need to bring the heavy shields as they too leapt over the sides, but they did as ordered and within moments the exhausted crew was transformed into a lightly-armed warband as they made their way up the dirt path towards the waiting walls.

Behind them, the six remaining men were fixing the ship to the shore with long lines of walrus hide, the thick ropes tied to stakes they drove into the pebbled beach with the backs of their axes.

It didn't take long for the ship to be secured, and the hammering of axes on wood and the shuffling of pebbles was soon replaced by the steady beat of nearly forty pairs of boots rising and falling on the dirt path. Halfdan was in the lead, easily recognisable by the metal helmet he had donned despite their peaceful intentions. Only a few of the men who owned helmets had followed suit. For the most part they had been left tied to their belts, or aboard ship. To his right, Toke stole a glance at Bersi as his giant frame loped up the hill, taking one step to every one-and-a-half of the rest of the crew. He'd ignored Halfdan's order for shields, instead carrying his giant Dane axe loosely in his right hand. His helmet was hanging from the sword at his waist by its chin strap, the metal ringing dully as it struck the leather-bound sheath.

They were about halfway up the slope when the first building burst into flames, lighting up the sky. One minute all was quiet and then suddenly the air above Váli's home was aflame, the fire and smoke turning the sky a deep, dull orange.

'Shields!' Halfdan whispered urgently, raising his own. As one the crew followed suit, forming up in a wedge of painted shields and glinting weapons. Those who had brought their helmets quickly pushed their way to the front line, and Toke cursed himself for leaving his behind. He hated fighting anywhere but the front. *'Perhaps there won't be any fighting,'* he thought grimly.

Seeing that the men were ready, Halfdan gave a hushed order to march, leading them slowly towards the flames. Voices began to reach them as they drew closer, rising above the sounds of crackling wood. They couldn't make out what was being said, but they could hear laughter filtering through. There

266

was something strange about it, though. Something was missing, but Toke couldn't put his finger on what it was.

It was only when they were less than a hundred paces from the walls that he realised what it was, the thought ringing in his head like alarm horns in the night. *'There are no screams, no crying women or children.'*

Like a madman, he shoved aside the men in front of him to reach the front, ignoring their irritated grunts as he grabbed Halfdan by the shoulder and pulled him around to face him. He was met by furious eyes and gritted teeth. 'Whaa…'

'Shhhh!' Toke whispered urgently. 'Something's wrong.'

'Yes, Váli and his people are being attacked!'

'Then where are the screams?' Toke said hurriedly, waving his sword for emphasis. 'Why are there no women crying or children screaming?'

Halfdan's face slowly changed from anger to realisation as Toke's words sunk in. Regaining control, he indicated for two of the rangers assigned to the crew to come forward.

They moved like wraiths, wrapped in their dark cloaks with their hoods pulled over their heads. Both had strung bows with arrows nocked and ready.

'Bergathor, Odd. Scout ahead and see what you can see. Climb over the walls if you need to.'

The two men nodded in acknowledgement before trotting forward on silent feet. Toke's words were spreading through the rest of the crew. They all knew what the absence of crying could mean for Váli's people, and a few of the older warriors like Bersi, who had raided with him in their youth, were showing signs of anger at the thought that he might be dead.

Without speaking, Halfdan motioned for the men to move off the path and into the longer grass that flanked the dirt road, concealing themselves from hostile eyes. The knowledge that something more than an out-of-control fire might be amiss had made them all acutely aware of how exposed they were. Toke watched as one of the young bóndi warriors moved to Halfdan's side briefly for a whispered exchange before making his way quickly back down the path towards the ship, presumedly to warn those left behind to prepare for a rapid escape if the need arose.

After he left, the remaining men settled into a tense silence as they watched Odd and Bergathor creep towards the looming palisade. The flames had well and truly taken hold now, and even the closed gate facing the path was beginning to smoulder ominously as the flames licked at it from the other side.

The mountains of smoke climbing upwards from within the walls made Toke imagine one of the great forges used by the dvergr to craft weapons and armour for the gods. Despite the circumstances, he found himself smiling at the poetic thought and made a mental note to remember it for his brothers.

As the wait began to stretch, his mind began conjuring darker images, and he had a vision of Signy lying dead in her own blood while those who had killed her laughed at her corpse, or worse, carried her away as a slave. His stomach clenched at the thought, and he felt his hands tighten around his sword hilt, as if he would grind it to dust. Slowly, he calmed his breathing and focused his attention on the two rangers as they reached the walls and began to climb. A collective silence surrounded the crew as they held their breath in apprehension, watching as the pair crested the palisade.

Their two heads were raven black when silhouetted against the glow from the flames, and the waiting crew watched patiently as the two men surveyed the inside of the fort. Slowly, Odd began to move around the crest of the wall to the left, while Bergathor moved to the right, occasionally ducking their heads down to keep out of sight. Toke began silently counting his breaths as the two scouts disappeared from sight. He had just passed two-hundred-and-twenty when Bergathor came back into view, freezing suddenly. It wasn't the slow, considered movement he had used earlier, but the sudden stop of a doe when she hears a hunter. There was a collective pause as everyone held their breath, waiting. It was Odd who broke the silence, leaping onto the wall with his bow in hand, drawing and loosing in a single motion at some unseen target before shouting for Bergathor to jump. All hell broke loose as Bergathor leapt from the wall seconds before a volley of arrows pierced the sky where his head had been. Odd followed a moment later, firing another arrow before jumping from the wall and sprinting towards the waiting crew.

'Here we go,' Toke muttered as the men around him began to shake their muscles to loosen them and prepare for combat.

'Skjaldborg!' Halfdan ordered as he moved to the centre of the path and waited for his men to form around him. It took all of two breaths for *Uxi's* crew to snap into action and form up behind and around to their captain. Meanwhile the gates to the small fort were pushed open, spewing smoke and sparks as the scorched timber disintegrated. Armed warriors began pouring out of the ruined gates, shoving the flaming wood aside with spears and axes as they marched out to face the offending crew. As soon as the doors were open, three men sprinted ahead of the advancing warband and began loosing shafts at the retreating rangers. Two had bows while a third set a sling singing above his head. Bergathor and Odd started running in erratic patterns as the arrows and stones began to dog the ground around them in an attempt to confuse their attackers' aim. Toke held his breath with the rest as the pair moved, willing their luck to last and see them to safety.

They had almost reached the shield wall when Odd took an arrow through his calf. He cried in agony as the shaft knocked him off balance and sent him sprawling in the dirt, snapping the arrow as he fell. Without thinking, Toke broke ranks and sprinted forward with his shield raised. 'Keep going!' he bellowed at Bergathor, who had turned at his friend's cry. 'Keep going, I'll get him!'

Running as fast as he could, he reached Odd just in time to block an arrow that would have hit the back of his skull. Sheathing his sword, Toke threw his arm around the injured man and half carried, half dragged him back towards their own line of advancing warriors, covering them both as best he could with his shield. He watched with relief as Bergathor reached the advancing warriors before turning on the spot and launching two arrows in quick succession at the advancing enemy. He heard a gurgling cry from behind him as at least one of the arrows found a mark in human flesh. The arrows and sling stones were still striking Toke's shield and the ground around them, but the rate of fire had slowed as a few of their own men added their own bows and slings to Bergathor's. It didn't take long to reach the advancing skjaldborg and deposit the injured Odd behind the line before finding his place in the ranks, next to the impassive Bersi. His casual movements made it feel more like they were going to collect firewood than marching into combat, and Toke took strength from his calm demeanour. It didn't take long for the gap between the two warbands to shrink to just twenty paces, and Toke was preparing himself to charge when Halfdan raised his sword to stop the advance. A man in the front rank of the opposing warband followed suit and an uneasy silence settled around them. Toke noted with some relief that the arrows and stones had also stopped falling. Halfdan's force more than doubled that of the men in front of them, although none of them wore armour and only a few had helmets. The front rank facing them on the other hand was centred around ten iron-clad warriors staring menacingly back, their armour glinting in the firelight.

They stood in silence facing each other for several moments until Halfdan's patience snapped and he tired of the games. 'Who are you to burn the home of Váli and greet us so armed for war?'

Silence followed the question, and the men waited impassively for the leader of the smaller force to step forward and respond. Only the sounds of shifting men as they bumped weapons on shields broke the silence. That, and the crackling of flames as Váli's home was consumed by fire.

'I won't ask again,' Halfdan grunted, twisting his sword so it flashed in the dying light. Behind him, bows bent ominously once again.

Toke watched silently with the rest as Halfdan's patience wore out and he tensed himself in preparation to charge.

'Who is this Váli you speak of?' one of the warriors said at last. 'He owns no territory here. These lands are the property of Jarl Ake, lord of Vágar and the surrounding territory.'

Toke felt the ground open beneath him at the words, confusion and anger mingling as he tried to comprehend what had been said. The men around him began to grumble angrily as they too processed what had been said, and Toke was about to march forwards in contestation when he felt Bersi's steadying hand on his arm. He looked up and saw the man shake his head once before looking forwards again, waiting to see what would happen next. Taking a deep breath, Toke remembered his place in the crew and trusted in Halfdan to deal with the situation.

'And who are you to make such bold claims?' Halfdan asked, his voice surprisingly calm.

'I am Steinar Akesson, conqueror of these lands,' he replied arrogantly, waving his sword back towards the burning buildings.

Toke thought he saw a few of the men around Steinar nudge each other at the statement, although he couldn't be sure it wasn't a trick of the light as smoke drifted lazily on the evening breeze.

'Oh aye?' Halfdan asked, spitting contemptuously on the ground. 'Last I heard, Jarl Erik the Golden Hand ruled Vágar?'

'No longer. Vágar is ruled my father, Jarl Ake, and under his command I have claimed these lands. Even as we stand here, the rest of my men are preparing to join us, and they would be more than happy to help you and your men find a seat at the Allfather's table, if you make the wrong choice here today.'

This time, Toke was sure he saw the men behind Steinar roll their eyes, and one of them visibly took a deep breath resembling something close to frustration.

Something wasn't adding up; Steinar was lying, but Toke wasn't sure about what. Taking a deep breath, Toke broke ranks once again and moved to stand beside Halfdan. The older man turned his furious gaze on him, but Toke spoke before he could say anything, leaning in quickly and whispering his suspicions in the captain's ear. He watched as Halfdan's face switched from incredulous anger to sly calculation as he processed the information, before settling into a grin. He nodded subtly to Toke to show he understood before motioning for him to return to his place in the shield wall.

Steinar watched the exchange impassively, but Toke was sure he caught him shoot a questioning glance towards the men either side of him.

'So… Váli is dead, then?' Halfdan said. 'His men have been slain, his women raped and enslaved alongside their children? Or are they dead as well?'

'Aye, Váli is dead, along with his kin,' Steinar said confidently. Beside and behind him the men were beginning to stir.

'I see,' Halfdan muttered, spitting another gob of phlegm onto the ground between them. 'Prove it,' he said, a wicked smile spreading across his face.

'Prove it?' Steinar said, confused. 'Feast your eyes, old man, if you can still see that far. His home burns and the land is mine. Váli is done.'

'Oh aye, I can see you figured out how to flick a flint and make a little campfire – and good for you, *boy*. But I want to see his body. Make sure the bastard is good and dead before we leave this place.'

'Make sure he is good and dead?'

'Aye. We came here to take what was Váli's today. Years ago, the bastard killed my brother and abandoned me and my men in England,' Halfdan lied. 'We've been searching him out ever since and finally caught word that he had a holding hereabouts. If you've gone and slain him like you say, then power to you. But I'll spit on his corpse before we sail from this place to make sure he is as dead as you say.'

Toke chuckled when he heard Halfdan's ploy. Steinar had unwittingly backed himself into a corner and been exposed as a liar. That wouldn't bode well with the men at his back, and already a few more were beginning to shuffle uncomfortably. He watched as Steinar's entire demeanour changed, the confident youth from earlier replaced by someone far less cocksure as he spoke to the men beside him, waving his hands furiously to emphasise whatever he was saying.

'I will count one-hundred breaths, lad. Then we're going through those gates, either with you, or through you, unless you can produce a corpse. Your choice.'

# Chapter 19

Steinar eyed the men before him with apprehension. They easily outnumbered his own small force, and apart from himself and the few men wearing armour, none of them had come prepared for a fight. There was an air of barely restrained violence emanating from the men facing him and for the first time he wished he'd asked his father for more warriors. He had no idea where this mysterious crew had materialised from, and their sudden appearance had made the simple job of burning an abandoned hall infinitely more complicated. He could feel the whispers at his back as his men mumbled about his ill luck, bringing unwanted images of his father's fury if he failed again.

It had all started so well. He had led his warband out on the same day that Canute set sail, aiming to return the same day as the bumbling giant with a success to share with his father. He was confident that Canute would fail in his task, and he looked forward to basking in the man's failure. Canute was far too self-assured around his father, and it would do no harm to remind him of his place, and who the Jarl's son was. Then, his luck restored and his reputation intact, he planned to spend several days in a bed warmed by the captured women of Vágar. Willing or not, it didn't matter.

They'd even managed to capture an old man when they returned to the abandoned borg. They had found him hiding in one of the abandoned store houses, but one of the more overzealous, younger warriors had skewered him with his spear before they could question him about the rest of Váli's people.

Everything had been going according to plan, until now. In less than an hour, he'd been surprised by an enemy warband and one of his men lay dead with an arrow through his throat, while another had been injured so badly that Steinar doubted he would last another hour. Even now he lay in a pool of his own blood amongst the burning rubble.

'Perhaps we can stall them until the sun sets,' he whispered subtly to the man next to him, 'and make an escape back into the walls once the light is gone?'

Aven turned to him and was silent for a few moments before speaking, considering his answer. Only his eyes were visible, glowing in the afternoon light while the rest of his face remained hidden by the iron rings hanging from his helmet's nose and cheek guards. 'We could, but what good would that do? We would be stuck in there with no supplies and surrounded by a superior force.'

'I doubt they could surround us,' Steinar grunted. 'But I take your point. We could attack them by surprise? Try a svinfylking and break their formation apart?'

'Aye, but we'd run the risk of being flanked and surrounded ourselves.'

From across the gap, Steinar heard the enemy leader call out again, the growing frustration clear in his voice. They were running out of time.

'What about the old man?' Aven offered. 'The one that we found in the barn?'

'What about him?' Steinar grunted absently, his eyes running over the waiting band for the hundredth time.

'They said it's been several years since they last saw Váli,' Aven murmured, motioning towards Halfdan. 'Perhaps we could pass the old man off as him, and they won't notice the difference?'

Steinar's eyes stopped roving suddenly as the words sunk in, the beginnings of an idea taking shape in his head. 'That's brilliant, Aven. Send one of the men back to find the corpse and have them bash the face so it's harder to recognise. We'll pass him off as Váli, and while they're distracted, we can make a break through the farm buildings and out the other side. Pass the order along for the men to retreat very, very slowly, taking quarter step backwards every time I cough, to widen the gap. We break on my signal.'

'Aye.' The taller man nodded before moving to the rear to relay the instructions.

'Hold, hold!' Steinar called across the gap, stretching his hands out in a mollifying gesture as he watched a few men take a half-step forward. 'One of my men is going to retrieve Váli's body. Then we can go our separate ways, no harm done.'

The enemy leader nodded imperceptibly, his eyes glowering.

While they waited for Steinar's man to return with *Váli's* corpse, he studied the mysterious warriors more closely, coughing every few moments to widen the space between the two forces. The men before him stood in organised ranks and were well armed, although none wore armour beyond a few helmets. As far as he could see, there was an even split between younger, likely less experienced bóndi, and seasoned raiders. To a man they carried spears, seaxes and good shields, and the veterans amongst them carried swords and axes as well. Several also sported iron helmets. Steinar didn't doubt that if his men were to search their ship, they would find more than a few iron ringed shirts sitting in their sea chests.

They were clearly tired, and he wondered idly if they'd been caught in the recent storms. He was just beginning to imagine what being caught in such a tempest would be like when his eyes fell on a giant of a man wearing a bear skin and carrying a Dane axe. He was standing in the second row, speaking quietly to a younger, blond-haired warrior. He too was tall, standing well above his neighbours and carrying his sword and shield with the easy confidence of someone well versed in their use.

If it came to a clash of arms, Steinar didn't feel confident in the outcome. Aside from his own small hirð of armoured warriors, the men at his back were pulled from his father's bóndi, and while many carried axes and swords, it was with the clumsy hands of men who were not born to war. Most, if not all of them, had looted the weapons from the hands of those who had died defending Vágar, and even these were the leavings Ake didn't want. Unlike Erik, Steinar's father was not a generous jarl and, with the exception of his húskarlar, his men had to provide for themselves.

*They came for blood, expecting a fight… why aren't they wearing armour?*' he mused, watching them closely. As the silence stretched on, his mind began to turn and explore the question from different angles. '*Perhaps they don't have any other armour? Or they didn't think they would need it? Surprise attack? No, they marched right up the road. Perhaps they didn't expect any resistance…? Perhaps they didn't expect any resistance.*'

'Aven, does something feel off to you?'

'This whole situation feels off to me,' Aven grunted.

'No, something about them specifically,' Steinar said irritably, his mind running.

'Off? Off how?'

'Wrong. Something's not right here. Why are they so lightly armoured? They said they came for blood. And if they don't have more armour, then why did they march right up the road, rather than wait for darkness and burn Váli in his hall? Something's wrong.'

Aven stood silently for a moment, his eyes flickering across the men as he processed the information.

Ignoring him, Steinar spoke into the silence. 'Where have you come from?' he called across the gap. Beside him, Aven grunted in frustration, realising that their previous plan to withdraw was being disrupted before it could even begin.

***

'Get ready,' Bersi grumbled, sensing blood.

Toke watched as he pulled the bear's head of his cloak over his head before taking a firmer grip on his axe. Along the line, those men who hadn't yet fitted or secured helmets were doing so, and Toke took a moment to tighten the blood knot around his wrist to better secure his sword. He didn't want to lose it in the frenzy to come.

He could see several of Steinar's men doing the same, and a few more helmets appeared, but not many. If they'd come from Vágar as he suspected, they'd travelled light and fast to catch Váli by surprise, if he'd even been here in the first place.

'Where do you come from?' Steinar asked again, the suspicion clear in his voice. His men were growing restless behind him.

Halfdan stood impassively for a few moments, considering his options before answering. 'The Faroe Islands,' he lied.

'Oh aye, where in the islands? Traders from there often visit my father.'

Toke tightened his grip on his sword. As far as he knew, Halfdan had never even been to the islands before.

'Toftanes,' Halfdan said through gritted teeth. 'I have a small holding there, and the men at my back work my land, or own farms of their own alongside mine.'

'Ah Toftanes!' Steinar said with forced mirth. 'My father raided with the blacksmith in his youth, I'm sure you know him. He visited us just last summer, although his name escapes me now. Can you remind me?'

To Toke's surprise, Halfdan smiled, although there was nothing cheerful about the expression. 'Enough of the games,' he growled. 'I am Halfdan, Captain of *Fjord Uxi*, and húskarl to Erik Golden Hand, the true Jarl of Vágar,' he said proudly, shedding the lies like a cloak. 'And you, *boy*, you and your men are thralls to a tainted jarl, fit only to become food for the crows.'

Halfdan gave the order to attack before Steinar could respond, lifting his own shield and marching forward, leading with his left foot. Along the line, his men slid their weapons between the overlapping shields and marched with him while the rangers whipped around to the flanks and began loosing arrows into Steinar and his men with a furious vengeance.

Toke showed his teeth, eager for the fray. He wasn't one for duplicitous tactics and deception; that was best left to his Loki-cunning brothers. He preferred to draw steel and let the Nornir decide the outcome.

Beside him he heard Bersi growl, the sound coming from deep within his throat, and Toke took a step to his left to give the giant – or more specifically his axe – more space. He had seen Bersi fight once before, and he didn't want to be anywhere near him when the enormous blade started collecting heads. The two men in front of Bersi also took subtle steps to either side, making space for the skin-clad warrior to join the front rank. Without warning Bersi roared, emitting a deep, gut-wrenching, inhuman sound that made the men facing him take a step back in fright as the beserkr rage boiled his blood. Snarling like a cornered bear, he leapt into the enemy ranks, completely oblivious to the spear blade that sliced along his ribs and split the skin there. He was unleashed.

Bersi fought like a man possessed, swinging his axe in a great arc that freed two heads from their bodies and opened a space in the enemy wall for *Uxi's* crew. Seeing the opportunity, Toke charged into the gap, ready to protect Bersi's exposed flanks as he reaped his terrible harvest. Stealing a quick glance to his left, he watched as the two lines met, briefly catching sight of Halfdan as he lunged straight for Steinar, only for the attack deflected at the last moment by the tall warrior beside the jarl's son. That was all Toke saw before his world shrunk to the small ring of struggling men around him as he battled to keep iron out of his and Bersi's bodies. Ducking and weaving, he used his sword and shield in unison and was soon sprayed with blood as he ended a duel with a young axeman, burying the blade deep in the man's ribs. Before he could draw the sword back out, an axe came for his arm and he had to rip hard to sever the blood knot and free his hand, rather than see it freed for him. Looking up, he saw a young warrior of about his own age preparing to attack again, swinging his weapon with more fury than form. Before the strike could land, Toke drove the iron-rimmed edge of his shield into the axeman's teeth, shattering them as he yanked his axe from his belt and swung upwards, burying the blade in the man's jaw. He kicked hard, freeing the weapon before turning to find another enemy. There were none. The few men who had survived the skirmish had disengaged and were sprinting for the relative safety of the burning walls, Steinar among them. Toke made to follow, but Halfdan called them back, blowing once on the horn at his hip. 'Let them go,' he heaved. 'Váli's not here, and we need to return to Erik and warn him about what's happened. Bring our dead and wounded; kill theirs. We're leaving.'

Five men had died in the battle, with another five lightly wounded. It was a small price to pay compared to the thirteen bodies they left to cool on the ground around them. Halfdan allowed them to liberate arm rings and other small valuables, but he stopped them from taking weapons and armour. Stripping a heavy brynja from a dead body was far from quick, and he didn't want the extra weight aboard ship slowing their progress.

Toke came to stand alongside Halfdan, watching as Steinar and one of his armoured warriors watched them from the burning remains of the gate, eyeing them with murder in his eyes.

'Bergathor, come here to me,' Halfdan called, slicing a strip from a dead man's tunic to clean his sword.

The tall ranger moved silently to stand next to the captain, his ever-present bow ready in his hand.

'Put an arrow through the runt's throat,' Halfdan grunted as he sheathed his sword with a *clack* before turning away, motioning for his men to finish up and follow him. Toke pocketed a gold ring from one of the fallen before following his captain, throwing a final longing look at the gleaming iron ringed shirt he was forced to leave on the cooling body. Behind him, Bergathor subtly drew three arrows and inspected them closely before returning two to his quiver. Exhaling, he drew back on the string and sighted down the shaft, waiting for total stillness before releasing. The arrow flew across the gap faster than any of them could follow. Toke watched as Steinar stood impassively between the ruined gate posts, either ignorant of the incoming missile or arrogant enough to believe Bergathor would miss. Whichever it was, the warrior next to him was aware of the danger, and Toke watched with grudging admiration as he stepped in front of his captain and raised his arms to block the projectile.

He died silently as the arrow flew past his armoured limbs to pierce his eye, leaving a mist of blood in the air where he had stood moments earlier, the red cloud bright against the flames. Steinar's nerve broke and he disappeared into the burning chaos and was lost from sight. Toke spat disgustedly towards the burning buildings before turning to follow the rest of the crew.

\*\*\*

Steinar wiped the blood from his face as he looked over the tattered ruins of his warband, a sorry replica of the buildings they had come to destroy. Only four of the twenty men he had led out from Vágar were still standing. Five, if he counted himself. All of them were wounded in some way. The arrow-injured warrior they'd left behind had died from his wounds during the battle.

Looking more closely at the men around him, Steinar saw that Ottar too had survived the battle. Ake had ordered him to join Steinar in the hall burning after his failed attempt to capture Arleigh and Turid, giving him a chance to redeem himself. Now that was gone, and Steinar could barely hold the man's furious gaze, forcing himself not to wince at the loathing in his eyes. Twice now Ottar had failed his jarl, and it was clear that he blamed Steinar for stealing his chance at redemption.

Forcing Ottar from his mind, Steinar began processing everything that had gone wrong, casting about furiously for an excuse or explanation he could tell his father. The survivors were watching him with thinly veiled anger, waiting for him to take charge of the situation. Already he knew that two of them wouldn't survive the journey back to Vágar. One was limping with a deep gouge in his leg that was oozing dark blood, his skin almost translucent as he remained standing by sheer willpower. The other had been pierced by an arrow, the wicked head gleaming dark red in the fire light as it showed through his back. If Aven had survived, he would have felt more secure in his role as leader, but the final arrow had ended his life just moments ago. Even now his body was cooling by the gates while his blood dried on Steinar's face. He didn't dare to retrieve the body.

'I need to warn Father. He will know what to do. And now that they've escaped, it's only a matter of time before Erik returns, with or without Váli.'

Spitting, he realised Ake would ask the other survivors what had happened, as he had after Váli's escape. Silently he cursed Halfdan and his men for what he was about to do.

Taking a deep breath, he barked an order for the two least wounded of his warriors to guard the gate in case Halfdan and his men decided to finish the job. He felt calmer with Ottar out of sight, and once the pair were gone he turned to the two injured warriors lying next to him, telling them to catch their breath while he found something to bind their wounds. Moving quickly, he sprinted around the back of the byre beside them to come around the other side. Steeling himself, he crept forwards silently, his progress muffled by the sound of crackling flames as he drew the seax from his belt. The first man died without a sound, the blade slicing cleanly through his windpipe to unleash a torrent of red. The second man, already weak from blood loss, turned lethargically at his companion's gurgled gasp. Before he could cry for help, Steinar drove his knife into his throat, feeling the blade grate against his spine before the man slumped lifelessly to the ground. *'They're dead anyway,'* he thought shakily, justifying his actions to himself as he withdrew his knife.

Taking up their abandoned spears, he moved towards the gate as quietly as he could, heading towards the two warriors standing guard. He could hear them muttering between themselves, but he couldn't make out the individual words over the crackling of the flames. It didn't matter. Taking a step forward, he launched the first spear as quietly as he could, aiming for what he hoped was Ottar's back. It struck true, and he watched with mixed emotions as the hardened tip drove straight through the man's armoured shirt to pierce his skin. He fell with a gut-wrenching scream as the impact drove him to the ground where he lay writhing in agony as he arced his body, trying furiously to reach the offending weapon. Seeing his companion fall, the second warrior turned in surprise and Steinar felt his heart drop at the sight of Ottar drawing his sword. Remembering himself, Steinar pulled his arm back and launched his second spear, desperate to end the man before he could get within striking distance. He could only watch in frustration as Ottar caught the spear on his shield with contemptuous ease before dropping the useless pile to the ground. Fury raged in his eyes as he drew his seax and held it easily in his left hand, replacing the discarded shield as he roared in wordless anger.

Spitting his own challenge, Steinar drew his sword and charged straight at the man, batting his first strike aside with his shield before driving his sword over the shield rim and into his left wrist. Ottar snarled as the blade bit and his knife fell from his now useless hand before bringing his sword around in a wild swipe, aiming for Steinar's unarmoured head. Steinar barely had time to get his shield up to block the blow before a second attack come, unleashing an explosion of agony in his legs. While he had been fumbling to protect his head, Ottar had dropped to one knee and pulled his sword back around, slashing it across both of Steinar's unprotected shins. Steinar screamed as the pain registered, feeling his boots fill with blood. His body was in agony as he stumbled once before the strength left his legs entirely and he fell to his knees, the impact jarring him. He forced himself to look up, meeting Ottar's furious face as he towered over him, his merciless eyes full of furious anger. 'Nithing coward,' he spat, drawing his sword back over his shoulder to strike.

Steinar watched the sword descend towards his neck as if in slow motion, the metal glinting red and orange in the flickering fire light. At the last moment, just before the blade struck, he let his body go limp, leaving Ottar's sword to slice the air where Steinar's head had been a moment earlier. Before Ottar could react, Steinar drove his own sword straight up under the man's armour, pushing as hard as he could to drive the length of iron through his body and out the top by his neck where it emerged in a spray of blood. Ottar was dead before he hit the ground.

Struggling to his feet, Steinar spat on the corpse before ripping his father's sword free of the cooling body, wrinkling his nose at the smell of voided bowels.

He cut strips from Ottar's tunic to bind the wounds around his shins, stemming the blood flow as best he could. Stealing a furtive glance through the open gate, he saw the road was empty. Halfdan and his men were gone, leaving like wraiths with only death behind them. The ravens were already landing, cawing greedily to the sky as they began their grisly feast. Ake had to be warned. There were no witnesses to tell how he'd blundered into the superior force, nor could anyone expose him for fleeing the battle rather than die with his men. As he stood to leave, his eyes lingered on the half-looted corpses of his men lying outside the gates, inspiring the first strands of a story he could spin for his father. By the time he returned, he would have a tale to tell. A sword and some armour was a fair exchange, he thought grudgingly, as he shrugged off his armour and hid it with his father's sword beneath some burned rubble.

***

'Sail ho! Sail ho!'

Guttorm's call raced up the beach with the wind, stirring *Sleipnir's* crew to action as curious eyes drifted to the horizon while focused hands took up weapons and shields.

The crew had been on the island for a full day already, re-establishing their camp from the outward voyage. Without the rest of the fleet anchored up alongside them, the mood had been sullen and for the most part the crew had stayed on the beach while a few ventured out for food. Yngvar had made it clear they would sail again the next day, giving *Uxi* the chance to reconnect with them before they continued on towards home. If they couldn't find her back in Vágar, they would return to Erik and hope that they were already

280

waiting for them on Storfjellet. Otherwise, they would continue on to England and hope *Uxi* would be waiting for them in port when they returned home again. It was the most they could do.

Across the temporary camp men were appearing from their shelters with weapon belts half attached, or spears held casually over shoulders as they moved towards the shore, searching for the speck that had triggered Guttorm's call.

'Where?' Bjørn asked, standing next to his friend.

'About three fists to the left of that small islet,' Guttorm replied, pointing.

Bjørn followed Guttorm's finger and instructions, estimating the distance of three fists side-by-side as he searched the horizon for a speck of sail. It took him a few moments to find it, his eyes roving carefully over the endless blue. The ship was still several rôst offshore and likely hadn't sighted *Sleipnir* yet, pulled up as she was on the beach with the woods behind her.

'Well done, Guttorm,' he said without turning, his eyes locked on the distant sail. Occasionally, he lost it to the swell as the waves rose and fell, but for the most part he was able to keep it in sight.

'*Come on, Toke,*' he mumbled, his words snatched away by the wind and carried to the gods.

In the time it had taken for Bjørn to reach his friend, Yngvar had located the ship on his own and begun to prepare the beach should they come this way. Already, some of the younger warriors were building up a signal fire on the shore to guide the ship in, dragging firewood and kindling along the shore to the slowly-growing pile. Further up the beach, the rest of the crew had begun knocking together a make-shift barrier of driftwood and fallen logs in case they were forced to offer their guests a less hospitable welcome. Bjørn caught sight of Red Orm and Bjarni working alongside the other warriors, their giant frames moving tirelessly as they lifted and placed the felled logs into place, giving the wall height and length. The final barrier wouldn't be much, but it would give them somewhere to retreat to, if they needed it.

'You coming?'

Turning, Bjørn found Sindri standing behind him with Uffi and Galti. All three had bows in their hands and full quivers of arrows over their shoulders.

'Where?'

'There,' Sindri said, motioning towards one of the small rocky crescents that made up the sheltered bay. 'Yngvar wants some archers on that point to ambush them from behind if they turn out to be hostile.'

'Four bows are better than three,' Galti added, knocking his bow against

Bjørn's suggestively.

Nodding, Bjørn turned back to Guttorm and told him to keep his eyes glued to the ship before following the three archers along the coast.

'He doesn't waste time does he, our Yngvar.'

Sindri grunted in acknowledgement but otherwise remained silent as they walked along the shore, their passage marked by the gentle sigh of the waves as they pulled the beach down into the depths. The spit of rock they were aiming for had a small lip that raised up against the cove, hiding a small space where the four men could huddle comfortably. It was mostly dry except for a few small puddles where the waves had splashed over, and Bjørn set to work with Sindri to fill them in with pebbles and sand from the beach before covering them with pine boughs. While the pair worked to make the space more comfortable, Uffi and Galti soaked a few logs below the water line and began collecting pine sap in a small metal container. By the time they had filled the container and returned with it and their soaking logs, the hide was mostly finished. Bjørn and Sindri had managed to fill the worst of the puddles, and the ground was covered with fresh boughs, adding the scent of pine to the salty tang in the air.

'Grab some firewood, would you?' Uffi grunted as he set about arranging the soaked logs on the ground next to them, while Galti stood more pine boughs upright to hide the flames from unwanted eyes.

Bjørn and Sindri set about their work quickly, and returned to find a platform of soaking logs set snugly against the rock, ready and waiting for their collection of driftwood.

'Here,' Galti said, handing an old shirt to Sindri who quickly set about cutting the front from the back before passing half to Bjørn.

'Do as I do,' he said by way of explanation before slicing long strips from the fabric. Bjørn had a suspicion as to what they were doing, but he didn't want to look foolish in front of the others so kept his thoughts to himself. He doubted there would be a fight; something in his gut told him that the incoming ship wasn't a threat; however, Yngvar wasn't taking any chances. By now, Bjørn could recognise the signs of combat in the crew, and in his gut he felt the now familiar tingling as his body tensed expectantly. The mood had become serious along the shore, and the air was tinged with apprehension as the men worked. Even Knut's ruined, usually sullen face was one of determination as he hauled logs towards the makeshift barricade.

Bjørn watched as Sindri expertly transformed the fabric into several long strips of cloth, each roughly a half-a-hand thick. Nodding once, he followed

282

the older man's example and began slicing up his own scrap of fabric. While they worked, the others built up the fire and began drawing embers out to where the cup of pine resin was sitting, stirring it occasionally. It didn't take long for Bjørn's half of the shirt to go the same way as Sindri's, and before long they had a small pile of twenty uniform strips of fabric.

'Now,' Galti said, 'we tie them around the arrows.' Bjørn watched as Galti's experienced fingers rolled a length of the fabric expertly around one of the arrows from his quiver, fixing the scrap just behind the arrowhead. 'We do five per quiver,' he added, looking up as Bjørn drew an arrow of his own. Sindri joined them, leaving Uffi to stir the resin as it liquified.

'We're ready,' Uffi grunted from the fire, carrying the burning metal between two pieces of wood. As soon as the cup was on the ground, Galti leaned forward and dipped three arrows in the resin, stirring them briefly so they would soak up as much melted sap as possible. Working in batches, he soaked the arrows, turning the lengths of wood-and-iron into ship-killers, as Bjørn had suspected. Each of the arrows was placed tip down on the lip of their little hide so the gentle breeze would help the sap to dry faster, while the cup was placed back in the coals to keep the remaining resin from setting. Overhead, the sun was continuing to descend towards evening, and Bjørn could see the signal fire on the shore had been lit, casting bright flames on the surrounding beach. He could smell food cooking on the campfires further up amongst the trees and his stomach made itself known as the smell of roasting meat reached them.

Once the arrows were dry, Galti recoated each arrow with another layer of the resin, repeating the process several times until he had emptied the container. Uffi silently tended the fire beside him.

'Leave the fire to die down to coals,' Sindri said after a while. 'We don't want the flames to give us away once the sun is gone, and coals will be easy to bring back to life while the ship comes into shore. I'm going to find some food. Galti?' he added questioningly before standing and walking towards the blazing fires of the main camp.

Galti grinned wolfishly as he stood and followed Sindri, and his nose, towards the waiting food. The pair returned shortly after with meat and bread, and a half-full aleskin which they passed around while they ate, talking quietly amongst themselves. Soon after, Bjørn was left alone on watch while the others lapsed into sleep.

'*Come on, Toke.*' Bjørn sighed again, his eyes locked on the unknown vessel as it made a beeline for the safety of the sheltered cove.

# Chapter 20

Váli had been standing at *Hrafn's* prow when the flames first sparked into life on the small island. His son, Ragnar, was at the stern holding the tiller. It had taken all of an hour for him to decide that the boy would steer the ship on their journey to find Erik. He had little-to-no expectation of his son wanting to return to a life of farming after their time on the whale road; he was in no doubt that the time aboard *Hrafn* would awaken a craving for adventure in his son, just as it had in himself. He may as well make up for lost time now that adventure had found them. Since leaving their home waters, the young man had guided *Hrafn* under his father's tutelage, and now held the helm alone while Váli stood watch at the bow. Váli knew the island he was searching for, having used it many times in his youth, but he was suspicious when he first spied it that someone else might have beaten him there. It was hard to be sure at that distance that what he was seeing wasn't just a fallen tree or piled flotsam cast ashore by a storm, but he was unwilling to take any chances, and he kept his eyes glued to unknown shape as they drew nearer. When flames burst into life on the shore he gave the order to don weapons and armour, bidding the women to take shelter by the mast. He and Torsten had removed the figurehead and stowed it below the sweep of the bow strakes, plunging the flying raven into darkness. For anyone watching from the shore, that would be as good a sign as any that they weren't coming for blood, while the donned armour and weapons would make it clear they were willing to defend themselves, if necessary.

Ragnar brought the ship about and angled the bow for the distant shore and the beacon of light on the shingle beach, turning the tiller over just a little too fast so a few of the standing men stumbled. Váli grinned. He remembered his own excitement the first time he held the helm and guided a ship towards an occupied stretch of beach. He had been eager to prove himself in the eyes of the other men, as Ragnar clearly was now. He chuckled at his son's nonchalant expression, broken only by the eager gleam in his eyes. He had discussed it with Torsten when he joined him at the prow, sharing stories of their own youth and the men they had dined and raided with who now feasted at the Allfather's table. Torsten had been by his side for almost as long as he could remember, as loyal to Váli as Sven was to Erik. It was hardly surprising, given their shared blood. The two brothers had raided alongside Váli and Erik in their younger years, but when Váli had hung up his sword and shield in favour of a hoe and plough, Torsten had followed him. Váli had never asked why, and Torsten had never shared his reasoning, but to recognise his unwavering loyalty he had given him his old brynja and named him his first warrior. Like Sven, Torsten was a giant of a man, with long blond hair and a thick plaited beard that reached down to his stomach. Váli grinned as the giant lifted his iron-ringed shirt over his shoulders and let it drop onto him, the metal rings bunching briefly on his stomach before falling like so many hailstones hitting the shore.

'You've grown fat.' Váli laughed, poking his friend's belly with the pommel of his sword before wrapping his weapons belt around his waist. He felt the weight lessen on his shoulders as he pulled the belt tight.

'Aye, Váli. I've followed your example in all things.' Torsten chuckled, tying on his own sword belt.

Váli punched his friend's shoulder gently before turning his attention back to the growing speck of light. Friend or foe, they had to make landfall there or risk sailing through the night, and no one liked to do that. Too much could go wrong sailing in the dark, and Váli was unwilling to take such a risk given the importance of their mission.

'Who do you think they are?' Torsten asked, his own eyes equally locked on the distant fire.

Farmer or not, Váli tended to know more than most about what happened in the lands and waters around his home, and who did or didn't have power.

'It could be anyone,' Váli said, rubbing his beard idly. 'Erik and his ships are already well on their way to England, while Ake's ships are clearly not raiding this season, at least not abroad,' he added. 'Perhaps Jarl Gorm has come down from the north? I heard a rumour that he was bound for Frankia this year, but that could just as easily be hearsay...'

'I guess we'll find out, soon enough.'

'Aye, soon enough. Make sure everyone has something to eat, will you?'

Torsten nodded once before making his way down the ship to where Astrid and Signy were sitting with Erik's women. The five women had assumed a combined role of camp mother to the crew and were already preparing food when Torsten arrived.

Despite everything that had happened, Váli felt calm. He had not grown fat after his years on land, nor had Torsten, not really. It was more of a thickening as his body adapted to the demands of farming, instead of raiding. Being back on the water – and killing Ake's men on his doorstep – had awakened something in him that had lain dormant for too long, he realised. The summer was rising in his blood, and the feeling of *Hrafn* beneath his feet and the danger of an unknown ship waiting for them was combining to make his heart beat faster in excitement. Part of him relished the idea of another fight, but his first duty was to the men and women aboard his ship. They had to come first, and he sent a murmured prayer to the Allfather to keep those they had left behind safe and hidden from Ake's wrath.

'I've only ever sailed on a ship once before,' Arleigh said suddenly, startling him.

He'd been so lost in his own thoughts he hadn't heard her arrive.

'Oh aye?' he asked, collecting himself. 'When was that?'

'Sixteen, maybe seventeen years ago? Before my son was born.'

Váli nodded, not sure how to respond. He had only met Arleigh a handful of times before their adventure had begun, and he didn't know her well despite all they had been through.

'Erik and his men raided my home in England,' she continued, her eyes glazed as she looked back into the past. 'My husband, Torr, was killed defending our home along with the rest of the men, while the women and children were carried off as thralls, myself included. Most of the others were sold off in Frisia on the voyage home, but Erik kept me for himself. It was only after Bjørn was born that my position became more… certain. I can see the appeal of it,' she whispered, watching the island grow larger as *Hrafn* danced over waves.

'There's nothing like it,' Váli muttered, focusing on the distant flames rather than the woman beside him, unsure how to respond.

Arleigh chuckled mirthlessly as she handed him some food before turning to walk back down the ship towards the other women.

Váli watched her go for a few moments before turning his gaze back to the rapidly growing flames. He trusted Ragnar to guide them in and he was familiar enough with the cove they were heading for to know there weren't any hidden rocks waiting below the surface to rip out their hull. There was nothing left to do but wait.

***

Bjørn watched the ship as it continued its unwavering process towards the shore. The closer it drew, the more individual features began to materialise out of the growing gloom. He could see that the prow beast had been removed, and the glint of armour was clearly visible in the dying light. He assumed they also had weapons close to hand. He would have done the exact same thing, and his respect for the unknown captain went up a notch. Only a fool would arrive on an occupied beach without preparing his ship.

'Not long now,' Galti grumbled as he briefly lifted his gaze above the lip of rock they were huddled behind.

Bjørn nodded silently, his gaze flicking over the shoreline for the hundredth time at the fifteen-or-so men there, caring for the fire and keeping visible to the incoming ship. The last thing they wanted was for them to think it was a trap, if they turned out to be hostile.

'Reminds me of the Frankia raid,' Uffi muttered. Beside him, Sindri and Galti nodded their agreement. Sindri chuckled.

'The Frankia raid?' Bjørn asked, looking away from the ship briefly. The wind had died away completely and they were coming in under oars alone, the rising and falling of the blades creating a ring of whitewash around the hull.

Behind him Uffi took a pull from the aleskin before he spoke. 'Your father sent ten-or-so of us rangers out to scout an area of coast before we set up camp for the night. We'd only gone a few miles when we caught sight of a small band of warriors on horseback coming our way. They hadn't seen us yet, but the sun glinting on their helmets and armour had shown them to us.'

'It wasn't so different from the men yonder,' Galti added, nodding his head in the ship's general direction.

'Aye. Anyway, some of the younger men wanted to fall back to the shoreline, but Uffe was adamant we could handle it ourselves. So, we moved quickly into a small copse of trees and set about lighting a fire to draw them in. Uffe told four of the youngest men, those most in favour of withdrawing, to sit by the fire and make sure they could be clearly seen, while the rest of us climbed into the trees and bushes around the flames and remained completely still.'

Uffi paused and took a deep pull on the aleskin, leaving the story hanging in the cooling night air.

Sindri grunted and took up the tale, ignoring Uffi's disgruntled gaze. 'It didn't take long for the riders to spot the flames and ride in. There were eight of them, if I remember correctly, and they rode straight into the clearing like the lords of Asgard themselves. They started yelling and hollering at our men who did their best to mollify them before the rest of us sprung our trap.'

Galti chuckled, nodding as Bjørn sat down to listen to the rest of the story, raising his head occasionally to check the ship's position. 'It didn't take long. Five went down in the first volley with arrows through their throats or chests, while the final three fell under blades as men leapt on them from the trees above.'

'And Erik ended up with eight pretty horses to scout with, and a shiny new sword,' Uffi finished, grinning.

'That's where your father's Frankish blade, *Geri*, came from,' Sindri added helpfully. 'Turned out that one of the men we killed was the son of some local lord, who paid three times his son's weight in silver and gold for the body back, and for us to leave his lands. Erik agreed, but he kept the sword. I remember his laugh when the lord asked for it back, saying anyone foolish enough to lose such a fine weapon didn't deserve to carry it in the first place.'

'Clever,' Bjørn smiled. 'Was Yngvar there?'

'Oh aye. It was his blade that killed the young pup,' Galti grunted as he stood up again to check the ship's position. 'Eye's up, lads, she's coming in fast now.'

Like mist, Bjørn, Galti and Uffe stood upright and knocked the first of their resin-soaked arrows, while Sindri quietly blew on the coals, adding a few finger-thick faggots to build up a small flame.

The ship swept past them like a wraith with only the repetitive rise and fall of the oars to mark its passing. The world itself seemed to hold its breath as the four archers watched the ship. She was clumsily handled, and the helmsman left it too late giving the order to ship oars, causing the front few to dig at the ground as the curved keel was driven up onto shingle.

'Disembark! Skjaldborg!' a voice boomed from the bow, pushing the crew into an eruption of activity as armoured men rushed over the side and formed a curved barrier between the island and their ship.

Bjørn felt a flash of recognition at the voice, but he couldn't put a finger on the memory. Shoving the thought aside, he watched with the others as the ring of men in front of the ship continued to grow as each man crouched behind his shield to protect himself from attack. Once the ring was formed, each man in the shield wall raised their right hands, showing they were unarmed.

By the flames, the young men who had been tending the fire retreated to the forest and joined the rear of Yngvar's waiting shield wall as it marched forward from the tree line and into the light, weapons drawn but held low.

For a time, no one spoke, both waiting for the other to make the first move in a silent battle of wills. Bjørn watched as silently as anyone, ignoring Uffi's frustrated whispers for action. He flicked his eyes across the beached ship, noting the small group of people standing by the mast, but he couldn't discern their features against the glow of the fire. He thought they might be women, by their figures, but he couldn't be sure. It was almost completely dark now, and the light from the flames was drawing all eyes there.

He counted almost fifty breaths before the silence was broken. It was the same familiar voice that spoke first, and Bjørn watched as a tall man stood upright in the centre of the unknown warband, lowering his shield as he did so. 'Who are you to challenge our landing?' he boomed. 'We come in peace with our prow beast removed and weapons sheathed, yet we are greeted with drawn swords and bared shields.'

Again, Bjørn searched his memory for the voice's owner, but no matter how hard he tried he couldn't place it. Alongside him the three rangers bent their bows slightly, the creaking sounding loud in his ears.

'I am Yngvar, húskarl to Erik Golden Hand and master of his ship, *Sleipnir*. Who are you?'

Bjørn imagined the surprise on Yngvar's face as the unknown warrior burst into laughter, the belly-deep sound smashing the tension on the beach. After a few moments, he regained himself and wiped the tears from his eyes as he responded.

'Then we have found you!' he said. 'I am Váli, lord of my own lands, and loyal ally to Erik Golden Hand.'

'*Váli*,' Bjørn smiled to himself, placing the voice at last. '*Of course.*'

'Váli!' Yngvar laughed, sheathing his sword and walking forward from the wall of shields and blades.

Váli too marched forward from his own men and the two met in the middle, clasping hands to forearms as they greeted one another as friends.

'You are most welcome,' Bjørn heard Yngvar say as he released the tension on his bow, his actions mirrored by the men alongside him.

'Gnnn,' Uffi huffed, throwing water over the coals and releasing a hiss of steam as they died. 'Wouldn't have minded a good fight.'

'If only you knew what that looked like.' Sindri chuckled, taking up his resin-soaked arrows and putting them in his quiver. 'Come on, let's head back.'

By the time, Bjørn and the three rangers reached the beach the young men from *Sleipnir's* crew were stoking the bonfire while others dragged burning logs away to create new blazes, adding to them from Yngvar's makeshift wall. Both crews were intermingling as men shook hands with friends and past comrades, or helped to make *Hrafn* secure. The four archers had expected to walk into a festive atmosphere, but when they arrived, it felt more like a wake than a party. Bjørn made a beeline for Yngvar and Váli, clasping the older man's outstretched arm when he arrived.

'Bjørn.' Váli nodded, dipping his head in acknowledgement. 'Where did you come from?'

'Your flank,' Bjørn grinned, flashing his white teeth before turning and pointing with his unstrung bow back towards the rocks. A small wisp of smoke was just visible against the darkness beyond and as he turned back he saw realisation crept over Váli's grizzled face.

'Up to your old tricks again?' He chuckled, turning his attention back to Yngvar.

'We might have surprised you.' Yngvar smiled, shrugging nonchalantly as he lifted a wineskin to his lips.

'How is it that you're here?' Bjørn asked, his curiosity bursting beyond any sense of manners. He knew as well as anyone that his father's neighbour had hung up his shield years ago. He watched as a concentrated frown came over Váli's face, furrowing his brow.

'Walk with me,' he said quietly to the two of them before turning and making his way through the crowd.

Bjørn saw him whisper something to another young warrior and point along the shore towards his ship, sending the man darting back towards *Hrafn*.

Once they were out of earshot, Váli turned and faced them, his expression uncomfortable. 'What have you heard of home, since you left?'

'Of Vágar?' Bjørn asked, a sense of unease creeping into his gut. 'Nothing?'

Yngvar nodded uneasily in agreement, laying a calming hand briefly on Bjørn's shoulder.

'I thought as much,' Váli said with a tired sigh, his shoulders slumping slightly. 'There is much to tell, but you should not hear it from my lips.'

Behind them, the crunch of several sets of feet on the shingle became increasingly audible, and Bjørn turned to see several cloaked figures walking towards him. It was only once they were a few steps away that the darkness revealed them for who they were. 'Mother?' he asked incredulously, the surprise clear in his voice.

Arleigh threw herself forwards and wrapped her arms around him, her familiar scent filling his nostrils.

'Mother! Why are you here?' he asked as her grip loosened, but before she could reply another figure grabbed him, this one pressing her lips to his in a fierce kiss that stole the breath from his lungs.

'If only we all got such a greeting.' Yngvar chuckled.

'Hoelun?' He smiled.

She slapped him gently on the shoulder before stepping back. It was only then that he noticed the unstrung bow in her hand and the knife at her belt.

Behind them, Turid nodded her greeting to them both, and on instinct Bjørn stepped forward and embraced her, sensing her fragility. Even in the dying light, he could see the bruises on her face and he felt a moment of rage rush through him at the sight.

'I think you better tell us what happened,' Yngvar said seriously, seeing the turmoil written on their faces.


The sun was beginning to crest the horizon by the time the three women had finished telling their stories, and Váli had shared his part. Yngvar and Bjørn had been the perfect listeners, only interrupting to clarify certain points or ask the occasional question.

'So, Ake has captured Vágar,' Yngvar said calmly, summarising the stories.

Bjørn couldn't help but admire his friend's stoicism in the face of such news. While he could feel safe in the knowledge that his mother and lover had both managed to escape Ake's clutches, he knew that most if not all of the men who followed Erik had families now trapped in Vágar. Their blood would boil when they heard the news. There would be no talk of England, not now.

'We need to return to Erik,' Bjørn said seriously. 'Halfdan and his crew will have to wait for the time being.'

By unspoken agreement, Bjørn and Yngvar had kept their reason for being away from Erik quiet. They could both see Turid was holding on by a thread, and the news that one of her sons was missing would break her. That was Erik's news to break.

'Aye,' Yngvar grunted, nodding his agreement before turning to face Váli.

'You've already done more than we could have asked or expected, old friend, but I must ask more of you. Sail with us to Erik. Undoubtedly, he would like to thank and reward you for all you have done.'

'I have nowhere else to go.' Váli chuckled. 'We reaped quite a harvest among Ake's men when they came to claim the women; I doubt I have much of a home to return to. If Erik will have us, we will fight.'

'Oh, he'll have you,' Bjørn said. 'Of that, I'm sure.'

Beside him, Yngvar grunted his agreement, motioning for everyone to follow him. As one, they rose and walked down the beach towards the waiting crews.

'Váli, I would be most thankful if the women could remain with you onboard *Hrafn* for the time being?' he said while they walked. 'I'm sure they're more than comfortable with you, and I would prefer to protect them from the questions of home that my crew will undoubtedly ask, and that they may be unable to answer.'

'Of course.'

'Good. Then let's get to it. Bjørn, go on ahead and wake the laggards up. We leave within the hour.'

Bjørn could feel his blood rising as his mind filled with images of Vágar in flames, with the bodies of men and women he had known all his life filling the streets, left as food for crows. It was hard to imagine that men like Leif and Gørm were gone, grizzled warriors that they were, but if the attack was anything like what the women and Váli had described, the chances of them having survived were slim. It was a relief when he reached the sleeping figures and could begin shaking them awake, shouting orders to light fires and eat quickly so they could return to the whale road.

'*I'm sorry, Toke,*' he whispered, searching the horizon for the millionth time before pushing his brother from his mind.

It took them the better part of a day to return to Erik and the crew of *Fjord Ulf*, despite the strong wind filling the ship's sails. Like hunting eagles, *Sleipnir* and *Hrafn* had flown past Moskstraumen, barely pausing in their haste to reach Erik as their bows carved deep furrows through the waves. Bjørn hardly even thought about it as he guided the ship past the tidal eddy for what felt like the hundredth time, confident in his abilities as Yngvar stood stoically beside him. The whole crew was eager to return to *Fjord Ulf* as quickly as possible, and those not working the sails were already making preparations for the return voyage home. Armour was being cleaned and burnished, weapons oiled and clothes repaired. There was no doubt whatsoever as to their destination now: they were sailing to war.

By the time Erik's small raiding camp came into sight, *Skoll's* hunt for the sun was nearly finished as the giant orb dipped below the western horizon, casting a final golden glow across the world. Off their starboard stern, a pod of orca had begun to chase them, and Bjørn smiled at the omen as they played in their wake before disappearing below the surface. He could see his mother aboard *Hrafn* a few ship lengths to port, speaking with Hoelun who stood alongside her. So much had changed in such a short time, including Hoelun. She stood taller now, and since *Hrafn* had arrived the evening before he hadn't seen her without her bow. Part of him was beginning to doubt he ever would.

'They did well to escape,' Yngvar said, breaking into his thoughts as he followed his gaze across the water.

'Ake must have been watching for us to leave,' Bjørn replied, shifting his attention to Yngvar. 'My guess is that our friend Siv *Half-Hand's* rescuer managed to return with news that we'd set sail.'

'That's what I've been thinking as well. He timed it perfectly,' Yngvar grunted grudgingly, acknowledging the thoroughness of Ake's planning.

'How many of the men left behind do you think survived?'

Yngvar sighed. 'If Ake has half a brain, any of the men who survived are already on ships bound for Frisian slave markets. Good fighting men fetch a high price as farm thralls, and it destroys any chance of rebellion. And that's assuming he left any of them alive. I expect most of our men are now dining in the Allfather's hall,' Yngvar said mournfully.

'Gnn,' Bjørn grunted, absorbing the information as he adjusted the tiller slightly. 'What do we do about *Uxi*?' he asked after a few minutes.

'I don't know, lad, that's for your father to decide. Drive her up there,' he grunted, pointing to a stretch of beach alongside *Fjord Ulf*. Bjørn could still see the faint shape of their bow from where they had beached previously.

'Stow the sail,' he roared, sparking a hive of activity as men stowed weapons and armour in chests as they moved to obey his order. 'Oars!' he called, the order echoing from *Hrafn* a heartbeat later as Váli's crew aped *Sleipnir*.

He could feel the crew's eagerness to reach land as *Sleipnir* sliced through the waves, her bow lunging forward eagerly with every pull. They covered the final rôst between them and the island in a matter of minutes, and before they knew it *Sleipnir* was driving up the beach. Men were waiting ready at the prow,

293

and leapt overboard with tough walrus skin ropes to make her fast.

'Come, let's find your father,' Yngvar grunted as he moved past him. 'Bjarni, Orm. See her settled, will you?'

'Aye, Yngvar,' they chorused, before turning to bellow orders. Bjørn followed Yngvar over the side, carrying his sword belt in his hand to protect it from the splash. They crossed the distance to *Hrafn* and helped the women climb down before leading them and Váli up the shore towards the burgeoning longphort. Erik met them at the gate with Olaf, Sven and Sigurd, his expressions unreadable.

'Come with me,' was all he said when they reached him, his eyes flickering briefly in surprise as he registered the unexpected presence of the new comers. None of them missed the flash of rage that crossed his face as he took in his wife's bruised face, and he wrapped his arm around her protectively as he led the small party inside. Safe at last, Turid began to weep softly.

It was a sombre mood inside Erik's rough hall as the twelve of them sat around the central table while the rescued women brought food and drink. Bjørn was famished despite the seriousness of the situation, and he realised that he hadn't eaten anything since the night before while he lay in ambush. The plate before him already had one deer bone picked clean and he was partway through a second. Yngvar wasn't far behind.

'Why are you here, Váli?' Erik asked once everyone had eaten their fill.

The question filled the room and everyone stopped what they were doing to watch Váli as they spoke, the seriousness of the situation taking hold of them all.

'Jarl Erik,' Váli said formally, dipping his head. 'I, we, bring news from home.'

'Tell me everything,' Erik said, his voice icy as he emptied his horn.

'Vágar has fallen,' Váli said, bowing his head briefly before beginning the story.

# Chapter 21

*Uxi* cut a sorry sight as she limped through the waves, tracking a course back to the burgeoning longphort. Halfdan's best guess was that the crews would be waiting for them there, and now that returning to Vágar was no longer an option, he'd set a course for the west. Their jerry-rigged sail barely held the wind and Halfdan ordered every second man to run out their oars to speed their passage through the waves. The mood aboard ship was dark, and after they'd left their dead burning on the small islet opposite Váli's fjord they had rowed with a single-minded focus, their minds entirely focused on finding *Fjord Ulf* and *Sleipnir*. Many of the men aboard had women and children in Vágar, and none doubted the retribution that Erik would bring down on Ake when they brought him the news.

They had been sailing for less than an hour when one of the lookouts called the warning, marking a sail on the horizon. Toke's eyes followed the gaze of the older warriors as they turned to Halfdan for instructions, while the younger men scanned the horizon. He could see Halfdan gritting his teeth as he held the tiller, and Toke's heart began to beat in anticipation. None aboard were under any illusions that *Uxi* could escape anything more than a small faering, and perhaps not even that. While the young men sought out the sail, the more seasoned among them looked to Halfdan, waiting for the order to prepare to fight, or to run for land. They had no other choice available to them, and the growing breeze seemed to mock them with its certainty.

For a while Halfdan stood motionless at the tiller as he considered their options, his eyes darting across the horizon and all points of his ship. Toke could guess at the thoughts running through Halfdan's head as he tried to estimate the size and number of fighting men aboard the unknown vessel, as well as their ability to reach land before they were caught.

Stealing a glance over his shoulder, Toke watched as the unknown ship turned slowly before settling on its new course, its bow pointing like an arrow directly at *Uxi's* heart. He gritted his teeth in challenge, ready for the barked order to prepare weapons when it came. He felt calmer once he had his sword and axe beside him, placed within easy reach so he could snatch them up at a moment's notice and defend *Uxi* and his crewmates.

'Row, you sons of whores!' Halfdan's voice echoed from the aft deck, his decision made as he threw the tiller over and made for land. 'Row for Erik and your wives, for your sons and your daughters. Row!'

Toke felt his blood begin to boil as he worked, adding to the rage that had been building since they first left the burning ruin of Váli's home. The sons of Erik Golden Hand did not run, and while he understood the logic, he felt a flash of anger at the twisted thread the Nornir had woven for him and the crew. On the rowing bench beside him, Bersi had rested his giant axe where he could take it up easily, the haft glowing warmly in the morning light.

*Uxi* lunged forward under the power of their arms, the hard work a trifle for men who lived in the cold north where every day was a battle for their very survival. They expected no less.

'Mount the prow beast,' Halfdan snarled, the steel in his voice sending the ship's boys running to obey the order.

Toke risked fouling his oar to steal a glance behind him as the snarling figurehead took its place on the prow, its twisted face spitting the crew's defiance.

Halfdan's men were determined, and after an hour at the oars every man was pouring sweat, unwilling to give up their seat and let another man work while they took their rest. Two of the ship's boys worked tirelessly to tend the makeshift sail, their hands raw from the effort as they struggled to add what speed they could to the rower's strokes, while a third sat on the ruined mast and tracked the pursuing ship's progress.

Everyone aboard knew there was no hope of outrunning their pursuers on the waves, but every pull of the oars drove them one step closer to land and safety. It was clear that the unknown ship was making a beeline for *Uxi*, its sail full as it chased their wake. The only escape left to them was to make for land and cut the strangers down when they disembarked. On the water, they had no chance.

\*\*\*

Canute glared at the young man before him as he suggested breaking off the chase and returning to Ake. They were expected to return that evening and chasing the unknown vessel was an unnecessary use of the jarl's men and ship now that the chance of Erik returning early had become a reality. In his heart of hearts, Canute knew he had missed his chance to catch Váli and that he should push the tiller over and return to his jarl, but after Steinar's blunder trying to subdue the errant farmer, he was determined to bring his jarl a victory, if he could. If he was lucky, the distant ship belonged to Váli himself, and he could return in triumph and show Ake's snivelling pup what success looked like. Their prey moved sluggishly despite its sail, and he felt the risk was worth the potential reward. No raider worth their salt would handle a longship so poorly and he felt safe in his decision, despite the misgivings of some among the crew. *'Let them have their concerns,'* he thought, feeling his mouth twist into a jeering snarl. *'The wolf doesn't seek the opinions of sheep.'* A piece of him was relishing the chase. The battle for Vágar had fired his blood, but the inactivity that followed had bored him beyond words. Being on the waves again made him feel free, away from the statecraft and decision making that followed Ake wherever he went.

'Lord?' the voice asked again, breaking through Canute's thoughts like an axe through ice.

Canute cracked his hand backhanded across the young warrior's face, knocking him from his feet to land sprawled amongst the sea chests and feet of the watching crew. A few of the men glanced nervously at him, but none would meet his eye. He chuckled to himself as he watched the young man pick himself up and spit blood on the deck, the red-tinged globule landing close enough to Canute's feet be directed at him, but not enough to warrant another slap.

Having made his point, he returned his gaze to their prey, his grin widening as he saw the distance between them was closing rapidly. He could make out the sail more clearly and wondered at the odd shape and its position so far forward, but he didn't let it bother him. They would be on them well before the sun touched the horizon. The rest was in the hands of the Nornir. Wyrd.

\*\*\*

'They're going to catch us,' Bersi grunted, his voice breaking through Toke's drifting thoughts. He had been remembering a summer years ago when he and his brothers had all been too young to raid with their father. The four of them had sailed to an uninhabited island, pretending they were raiders. Bjørn had been little more than a child then, his first knife slapping proudly against his thigh as he raced to keep up with the rest of them. He could still remember Olaf's pride in the axe Erik had given him as he cut wood for their fire while the rest could only watch in mute envy as they themselves used their knives to slice thin slivers of wood to use as kindling.

Bersi's grim prediction shattered the memory like ice on a pail as he pulled his attention back to the horizon, easily finding the rapidly approaching ship. The chase couldn't last much longer, and the spit of land they were making for was still several rôst away. His shoulders burned, and the injury in his palm was bothering him more than he wanted to admit. The wound had never fully closed after pulling an oar every day, and the almost-healed scab had worn away under the hard-wood, causing a thin trail of blood to run along the shaft and down to the oar port. He watched it idly as he grunted, acknowledging Bersi's matter-of-fact statement. He had his weapons close to hand, and his shield rested next to him on the top strake. It was enough. Wyrd.

As soon as they had left Váli's fjord in their wake, they had pointed the bow straight at Erik. The crew had discussed the possibility of Váli escaping and already being on his way to the jarl, as there had been no sight of *Hrafn* on the shore or below the waterline. But the reality was they had no idea where he was, and speculating did them little good. Váli and his men could have escaped just as easily as they could have been captured or killed, and *Hrafn* taken back to Ake as a prize.

With their broken sail they would rely on the power of their arms more than any of them liked to acknowledge, but none would be found wanting in the eyes of their crewmates. They knew that if they could make it to their jarl, they would have achieved something incredible, and few doubted that Erik would frown on such sacrifice to reach him. In his private thoughts, Toke had made a mental note to commend Halfdan's leadership to his father. The man deserved his place at *Uxi's* tiller.

Before long, Toke let his thoughts drift back to memories of past summers, loosing himself in the repetitive motion of driving *Uxi* forward. It wasn't until one of the ship's boys came by with an aleskin and a slice of dried meat that he snapped back to reality. Out of habit, his eyes darted across all points of the ship before aligning on the not-so-distant ship following in their wake. They were close enough to make out the shapes of individual faces now.

'Will you eat, Lord?' the boy asked, awe struck as he spoke to the jarl's son.

Toke nodded his agreement before a mouthful of meat was put between his teeth. Halfdan had ordered that the men keep the pace without slowing, and the ship's boys had worked hard to keep their strength up by feeding them from their own hands. Each man had been given a mouthful of meat and a sip of ale. It was enough, and Toke felt his strength return as he pulled back on the oar again. Only one man was left to feed, and Toke watched the young lad move further back to make the same offer to Halfdan, who lowered his head briefly to have a handful of dried meat shoved into his mouth.

He heard Halfdan tell the lad to get his sling ready through his mouthful, sending him running to the forward-most sea chest the three boys shared together. Toke remembered begging his father to go raiding with the crews as a ship's boy when he was a similar age, but his father had always refused. Erik had always said that he had no need for boys on his ship, getting in the way of his warriors, nor would he have his sons sail as anything but raiders in his fleet. So, Toke had trained, and waited for his turn to fight Erik in the ring, and earn his seat in the fleet.

The three boys were quick to return to the stern, their slings ready in their hands while pouches of pebbles and stones bounced on their waists. Toke didn't doubt their aim, but he knew that the stones from three boys would do little to no lasting damage to the men waiting at the prow, unless they struck eyes or throats.

'Bergathor, Odd. Bows to the stern!' Halfdan called.

Toke watched as the two rangers pulled in their oars before rising like smoke. Their shoulders would be burning when the time came to draw their bows, and Toke's appreciation of Halfdan went up a notch at the thought. They would lose a tiny bit of speed, but the two rangers would have a moment to rest their shoulders, and be better able to pull their bows and disturb the pursuing rowers when the time came.

The two men moved to the stern with quivers and bows in their hands, swaying easily with *Uxi's* motion as she cut through the waves. Toke watched as they belted their quivers onto their waists, adjusting them slightly so the arrows would be within easy reach of grasping fingers before they strung their bows.

'Aim true, boys,' Halfdan shouted when their pursuers came into range, raising his voice so all aboard could hear him. 'Let's leave these dogs as chaff in our wake!'

'Huuh,' the crew boomed, the cry carrying across the water before being replaced by the humming of slings. As one, the three boys had begun spinning their leather slings, creating halos of blurred brown above their heads before releasing them with a resounding snap which was closely followed by the crack of stones striking wood. Bergathor and Odd's arrows followed close behind, the twang of their bows acknowledged by a cry and splash as someone fell overboard. Toke grinned at the sound as he pulled back again on his oar. *Uxi* kept up a consistent stream of fire from that point on, occasionally answered by a cry or scream as an arrow or stone found its mark. For the briefest of moments, Toke felt hope that they might escape and return to Erik with the news, but it didn't last long. Despite the barrage they were coming through, their enemies were still gaining on them. Toke's eyes flicked briefly across the deck to where the grappling hooks waited, lying patiently with their coils of rope for eager hands to grab them and throw. Beside him, Bersi was scanning the deck, his face wearing a mask of fierce determination while his axe waited patiently alongside him. The blood would flow before long. At the stern, Halfdan was snatching his eyes back more and more frequently to check the distances, gauging when the time was right to ship oars and fight. All aboard knew they wouldn't reach land now, and the vibe had become calm as the men prepared for the sword storm to come. Overhead, two ravens landed briefly on *Uxi's* shattered mast and looked down with something resembling curiosity before cawing once and flying off again. Toke took strength from the omen, sure that one of them had met his eye.

'The Allfather is watching, lads!' Halfdan roared, as if reading Toke's thoughts. 'Ship the oars and prepare the grapnels. Let's send these bastards down to Njörd!'

Across the deck, the crew cheered their support as they exchanged wood for iron, and began donning their armour. Toke was among the first to be ready, quickly stowing his oar and shrugging on his padded leather armour. Bersi was already prepared, his great axe leaning against the strakes while he tightened and loosened his grip on the grappling hook in his hand. Toke picked up his shield and moved to stand alongside the giant beserkr, waiting for the enemy ship to come alongside. At the stern, Halfdan had tied off the tiller and moved to stand alongside his crew while Bergathor and Odd fired off their final arrows. Toke noted that the rate of fire had slowed as each man took their time to choose their shots more carefully, earning more screams for their efforts. He could see them now, the warriors standing stoically while a few remained at the stern oars to bring them alongside *Uxi*. At the tiller stood the largest man he had ever seen, taller even than Bersi or Sven. Like Bersi, he too fought with a giant axe, the weapon waiting ominously against the stern strakes.

'Ever fought on the water before?' Bersi grunted suddenly from beside

300

him.

Toke pulled his attention back to his immediate surroundings before answering, eyeing the grappling hook in the giant's hand again.

'Never.'

'It's no skjaldborg,' he said seriously, 'you can be sure of that. No matter what happens, don't fall in the water. Armed and armoured as you are, that's a one-way trip to Njörd's hall and there will be no dining with the Allfather after that.'

'Wyrd,' Toke grunted, refusing to show fear or concern before the stoic warrior. To his surprise, Bersi began chuckling.

'Aye, wyrd. But that doesn't mean you shouldn't fight against the three bitches and twist the thread a little.'

'Let's keep the Spear-Shaker waiting a little longer then, eh,' Toke said with a grin as he met the giant warrior's gaze.

'Aye' Bersi growled, showing his teeth as his grip tightened on his grapnel.

The time for words was past. Two more men went down screaming as Bergathor and Odd's final arrows found homes in their flesh before the pair sprinted back to their chests. Toke snatched a glance behind him as the two archers dropped the valuable weapons and threw on their leather armour, the hardened tunics pressing tight against their chests. Both men drew axes and seaxes before moving to stand behind the *Uxi's* iron-clad warriors.

'We go straight over, lads,' Halfdan muttered, his words travelling easily as the crew waited for the order to attack. 'I'll not have a single one of them set foot on *my* deck! Understood?' he growled.

The crew grunted their acknowledgement, showing their teeth as they watched the ship drawing ever closer.

Time seemed to stretch on forever before *Uxi* rocked suddenly, her stern hit by the incoming ship as she slid against her hull, filling the air with the sound of wood scraping wood before being driven apart again by the impact.

'Grapnels!' Halfdan called, pointing with his sword moments before the iron hooks flew across the enemy decks.

'See you on the other side,' Bersi grunted before heaving the iron hook across the ship as she passed, pulling hard to make the iron teeth bite deep into the strakes. One of the teeth caught behind a man's leg and Toke watched the man's eyes widen in horror when Bersi pulled the rope tight, driving the sharpened point straight through the muscle and fixing him fast against the side of his ship where he stayed, his agonised screams filling the air.

Along the decks of both ships, men began to shout their challenges and Toke added his voice to the cacophony of chaos as warriors heaved, pulling the vessels together.

He marked a target on the enemy ship, spotting a warrior who kept raising and lowering his shield as he screamed, giving Toke a clear shot. Moving his sword to his shield hand, he picked up a spear leaning against the mast, gripping it easily. He fixed his gaze on the man, waiting for an opportunity to throw.

The water between the two ships had turned white with froth as the crews pulled, feeding the ropes behind them into the waiting hands of ship's boys who coiled them neatly out of the way.

At the stern of the enemy ship the giant helmsman bellowed an order to his crew, and Toke watched as his target turned his head to listen, lowering his shield and exposing his shoulders and neck. It was enough. As quickly as he could, he drew back on the spear and launched it across the gap, throwing it with all his might. The length of ash-and-iron crossed the space between the two ships in a heartbeat, slicing through the man's throat before coming to rest in the shoulder of the man behind, pinning the pair together. Toke chuckled mirthlessly at the sight as the man behind screamed in agony as his companion's dead weight fell to the deck, wrenching the spear from his shoulder. A flood of red began to blossom over his leather armour, the spear doing as much damage on the way out as it had on the way in, rendering his arm useless. A few more men took up spears and began to launch them across the gap, scoring a few hits even as an answering volley came across to strike against their raised shields. Toke heard a scream behind him, and turned to see Tolstan, the ship's boy who had been coiling Bersi's rope, doubled over with a giant gash along his ribs. The spear was still quivering in the strake next to him; a finger's width to his left and the boy would be pinned fast to the side of the ship.

'Here!' he grunted, tossing across the mead skin at his feet. 'Pour this on it and bind the wound as best you can.'

The skin landed with a sploshing sound and Toke glimpsed the boy lean forward with a wince to pick it up before he turned his attention back to the fight, the boy forgotten. The enemy was less than a sword length away and *Uxi's* crew were bracing themselves for impact, preparing to leap across the gap and begin the slaughter. Toke shifted his sword back to his right hand, aping the men on either side of him. Next to him Bersi ducked down to make his rope fast before taking up his axe, and Toke took half a step to his left.

302

A final, hard tug on the ropes made their enemies stumble at the unexpected speed right before the two ships hit, the crunch of wood loud as men on both ships struggled to keep their balance. *Uxi's* crew recovered first, and with a roar they began flooding onto the enemy ship. Bersi all but flew across the gap to land among the enemy, taking two men down with him in a stumbling mess of flailing limbs and weapons. Toke swelled into the gap his friend had created, driving his sword straight through an upturned mouth. He felt his blade crunch against bone as it severed the man's spine. He would have lost his sword then, if not for the blood knot around his wrist. For a moment, the deck before him was clear, and he snatched a glance across the battle, catching sight of Halfdan as he ducked below a wild blow before driving his sword up under his enemy's armour and into his ribcage.

The fighting had devolved into a mess of duels, filling air with the screams and shouts of struggling warriors, and the smells of voided bowels and iron-laced blood. Ducking a wild thrust, Toke smashed his shield into his attacker's face, knocking him off his feet before stepping down hard on the man's throat, crushing it. Beside him, Odd ripped his seax across a man's thigh, severing the artery there before spinning gracefully to bring his axe down on another man's head.

The giant who had steered the enemy ship was almost walking through the mêlée, swinging his giant axe in well-practised arcs that took limbs and heads with something like disdain. Toke watched two men fall under the flying blade before he had to raise his shield and re-enter the fighting himself. The duel with his assailant ended quickly, and as Toke withdrew his sword from the man's chest, he caught sight of a ship's boy from the enemy crew creeping through the fight with a drawn seax, making for Bersi. Aware of his friend's unprotected ankles, Toke moved fast to remove the threat. Growling, he shoved his shield into an enemy warrior's side, forcing him to stumble and fall onto the boy's back before he brought his booted foot down on the would-be assassin's fingers, crushing them between his knife and the decking. The boy screamed, the high-pitched sound bouncing around in Toke's helmet as he ducked down to avoid a wildly swung axe from a bearded warrior. The blade skimmed across the top of his helmet before coming to rest in the mast, causing the man to stumble. Toke moved before the axeman could recover from his surprise, ripping his sword across his unprotected thighs and sending him screaming to the deck to fall alongside the whimpering boy. Toke eyed him for half a second before driving his sword through his throat, ending the contest. The boy's screams lapsed into horrified silence as the dead man's blood exploded over him, oblivious to Toke's presence as he bent down to pick up his discarded knife. Toke tossed the discarded blade across the deck, aiming for another of the enemy and was rewarded with a resounding *ding* as the handle struck off the man's helmet, distracting him long enough for one of Halfdan's men to put him out of the fight.

'Get out of here,' he snarled at the boy as he tugged his sword free from the man's throat, unleashing a sluggish stream of blood. The boy nodded, his courage failing him as he ran to the far side of the ship and hid between two sea chests. Around him, the enemy ship was slowly being covered with a blanket of dead and dying warriors, the deck slippery with spilled guts and viscera. Toke allowed himself a moment of hope as he felt the tide of the battle begin flowing in their favour, but the moment was shattered seconds later as he watched Halfdan's head fly from his shoulders. Time seemed to slow as the giant styrisman shoved a dead man straight into Halfdan, knocking him off balance as he was forced to brace against the unexpected weight. As *Uxi's* captain struggled to regain his footing the axe came down faster than Halfdan's shield could rise, severing his head in a single sweep. A moment of dumb shock settled across the deck as *Uxi's* captain fell, the news spreading fast among the crew. It was Bersi who finally broke the spell, uttering a furious, animal-like roar as he brought his axe down vertically on the man before him, splitting his head in two. Like a dam breaking, the rest of the crew resumed the attack, furiously striking down the men before them in their rage. Across the deck, men fell and died in twos and threes as they sought to avenge their fallen captain, but they had lost the upper hand. Toke felt the shape of the battle change as he took his first step backwards and then another, madly swinging his sword and shield to block attacks from two men at once. He only stopped when his foot struck the strakes behind him, ducking just in time to avoid a chopping strike from a sword. He sprang forward with his shoulder tight against his shield and shoved one of his attackers off balance before driving his sword down through the foot of the other. Before either man could recover, he withdrew his sword with a vicious twist and rammed it up through the second warrior's chin, stopping only when he felt the blade grate against the inside of the man's skull. Along the deck, the rest of the crew were fighting with their backs against the side of the ship. With Halfdan gone, no one was leading the crew, and without thinking he gave the call to return to *Uxi,* seeing that their situation had become hopeless.

He rolled backwards across the strakes to land safely aboard his own ship, his shield raised and ready once again. He was horrified to see only half of the crew return, most carrying some sort of wound. Bersi stood tall and gore covered amongst them as they formed a small shield wall around their ruined mast and prepared to push back any pursuers.

To their surprise, they were allowed to escape unhindered, and Toke watched with the rest in confused suspense as their enemies resisted the urge to pursue and instead stood gazing at them with murder in their eyes. They too had suffered heavy losses, he noted, although less than *Uxi*. Toke and the crew stood together in a loose skjaldborg, their breathing heavy as they held their shields at the ready and waited to see what would come next. Only the giant styrisman seemed unperturbed, and Toke watched as he moved calmly through his men to face the crew of *Uxi*.

'Enough,' he said, his voice steady and commanding. 'It is enough. You can't win here today. If you choose to fight, we will kill you to a man, but I don't doubt you will take many more of my men with you before we do, and I would prefer to return to my jarl with them alive. Surrender now, and you have my word you will live.'

Toke watched as the crew looked dumbly from man to man, unsure what to do without Halfdan to lead them. Before despair could destroy them, Toke took a deep breath and stepped forward, shrugging aside the uncertainty that threatened to bubble up as he moved.

'What you ask is not unreasonable, and it may well be our wryd to surrender now. But the Nornir may have woven a different story for us here today. What you say is true. If we continue fighting, all of us here will die and tonight feast in the corpse hall, but so will many of you; perhaps even all of you. What you suggest may save more unnecessary blood. Would you allow us time to discuss what you offer?'

The giant nodded once.

'Who is your jarl?' Toke asked before the man could speak again.

'Jarl Ake, lord of Fótrfjord and Vágar. I am Canute, his first warrior. Who are you?'

'Sven Halfdansson,' Toke said without thinking, Canute's words crossing the distance like a slap. 'The man you slew was my father,' he added, pointing to Halfdan's headless corpse.

'He fought well,' Canute said, dipping his head briefly in respect. 'You have until I complete a single lap of this ship to decide, Sven Halfdansson. Then we will board you and finish this.'

Toke watched as the man began to move amongst his men, checking their wounds and giving whispered orders, struggling to hide the internal struggle that had begun the moment he heard Jarl Ake's name.

Seeing the flickering emotion on Toke's face, Bersi turned him around and motioned for the rest of the survivors to join them. The act of being moved shocked Toke from his stupor and he took comfort from Bersi's presence as he registered the men around him, looking for leadership.

'I am Jarl Erik's son,' he whispered, not daring to be overheard. 'This Canute cannot know this. If we continue fighting, our deaths will serve no purpose to my father, or your families. If, however, we surrender and return to Vágar with this man, we can find a way to break free and fight from the inside. I will not make this decision for us and if you choose to fight, I will be first amongst you to go back over the side. The decision is yours, and there will be no judgement. Every man willing to fight, take a step back slightly. Those of you willing to surrender and trust me, place your weapons with mine.' As he finished speaking, Toke placed his sword point down into the deck in the middle of the huddle, his eyes moving from man to man. A stolen glance at Canute showed he was almost three-quarters of the way around the deck. Time was running out. As one, the men added their own weapons to Toke's, their eyes locked on the young man before them. Toke could see their determination, and the fierce loyalty they had for him, through his father.

'Do you trust me?'

Bersi spoke for them all, placing his heavy hand on Toke's back and staring into his eyes. After a few seconds he nodded, answering an unasked question before adding his gore-stained axe to the pile. 'We're with you, lad. Whatever you decide, we will follow you.'

'Thank you,' Toke said, touched by their loyalty as he struggled to control his rising emotions. 'Then from here on in, I am Sven Halfdansson, and I swear I will see Halfdan, our warriors and our home avenged, when the time is right,' he whispered fiercely, already hating the duplicitous role he would have to play.

Around him, the watching warriors nodded, their own resolve clear.

'*Where is Bjørn when I need him?*' he thought as he turned to face Canute. He'd just finished his lap and was facing Toke expectantly with a questioning expression on his face. Discreetly, the crew around him had formed a solid line of shields and weapons, ready to face another attack if *Uxi's* crew charged.

'Canute. I have a third proposition for you. One with no bloodshed, and that benefits both you and your jarl.'

'Oh aye?' the giant grunted, raising his eyebrows. 'I'm listening.'

306

# Chapter 22

Bjørn had experienced his father's anger before, but the icy fury he saw now was something else entirely. He had expected tables to be flipped, ale horns to be thrown or an axe to be driven into something, at the very least. Instead, Erik had sunk deeply into himself, remaining silent as the rage consumed him. Bjørn could see the anger smouldering below the surface like an undying coal. He wouldn't have traded places with Ake for all the gold and silver in Miðgarðr. Around them, the silence continued to stretch as Erik absorbed the story in its fullness. The heat of the fire did little to warm the room around them under the weight of Erik's frozen stare, and even the women who had been serving them had fled rather than stay a moment longer in the tense atmosphere. No one had tried to stop them.

'It is a fífl of a man who thinks I will not answer this slight with fire and iron,' Erik whispered finally, his voice like a knife through gravel. 'A fool, I tell you. Mark my words: blood will flow through the streets of Vágar before the summer has ended, and I will see *Jarl* Ake's head on a spike before my hall.' Erik's voice stayed level, but his tone carried fire and ice through the crude hall, and none at the table doubted the vengeance he would bring down on their enemies, when the time came.

'Váli, my friend,' Erik said, pulling his attention back from the flames. 'You have shown me great loyalty by bringing this news, and my family, to me. But I must ask more of—'

'There is nothing to ask, Jarl Erik,' Váli said, cutting him off. 'My men will sail with or without you to reclaim Vágar from Ake. There is a price to be repaid for all things, and the attack on my home is yet to be answered.'

Erik nodded once, a slight smile breaking through the stoic mask he had worn since their arrival. 'Thank you,' he said simply.

'You have a plan then?' Yngvar asked, speaking for the first time.

'Aye, Yngvar. I have a plan.'

'And Toke?'

A loaded silence filled the room as everyone pulled their gaze from Erik to his wife. The news that one of her sons was missing had been the final straw for Turid, and her resolve had broken as she began to weep uncontrollably. Sigurd had put a comforting arm around her shoulder as she fought to regain control of her emotions. She knew that Erik had done everything he could to find their son, but the reality of calling off the search had been the final straw after everything she had been through. Erik ruled because of his strength and generosity, and his ability to keep his men and their families safe. If they stayed on the island waiting for a crew that may never return simply because the jarl's son was onboard, he could lose more than just his home.

'I will leave those too injured to sail here with the women we rescued, along with enough supplies to last them a month. After that, they will have to hunt or fish. If Halfdan can bring *Fjord Uxi* here, those left behind can tell him where to find us.'

'So, you will abandon him?' Turid asked quietly, her eyes glistening with fresh tears.

'I can do no more for Halfdan and his crew. Whatever fate the three sisters have woven for them... it is not in my power to undo the weave.'

At Erik's words, the Turid's last vestiges of strength snapped and Bjørn watched with the rest as his mother stepped up and squeezed her tight before guiding her away from the men, her sobbing disappearing as they moved through the hall. She nodded for Hoelun to follow with Astrid and Signy, but the young thrall shook her head and resolutely turned back to the men. Bjørn grinned with pride at the sight and made room next to him on the bench so she could join them before turning back to his father.

'She's more than earned a place at this table, Father,' Bjørn said, speaking before Erik could disagree. 'Wouldn't you agree?'

'Aye,' Erik grunted, eying Hoelun. 'My wife mentioned something about granting your freedom. Would this please you?'

Bjørn felt Hoelun tense beside him, her body becoming rigid at his father's words. He knew his own mother had accepted her fate, but he had never spoken to Hoelun about it. He could only imagine what it was like living so far from her home, your life and freedom completely at the mercy of another person's whims.

'Yes, Jarl Erik,' she said quietly. The men watching could almost taste the eagerness in her voice.

'I suppose now is as good a time as any to discuss it. I will honour the promise made in my name, and even give you a good horse and a pouch of silver, as well as a full quiver for that bow you've managed to glue to your hand.'

A few of the men chuckled at that, their eyes flickering to the bow leaning against the bench she now shared with Bjørn. 'You will be free to return to the lands of your youth. Or you can find your place amongst us as a free woman, and build a new life for yourself in the North,' Erik added, his eyes briefly flicking over Bjørn.

Hoelun opened her mouth to respond, her eyes shining at the reality put in front of her, but before she could say anything Erik spoke again.

'But,' he said. 'I must ask you to fight for us again. Everything I have promised, I will provide. But I can only do that as the Jarl of Vágar, and I cannot afford the time it would take to drop you at another settlement. So, what do you say? Will you sail with the Golden Hand and help us to free our home?'

'It seems I am left with little choice, Jarl Erik,' she said after a few moments, her yellow, almond-shaped eyes meeting Erik's. 'I will fight for you, and help you reclaim your home. But then I will accept my freedom. I will decide later what I do with it.'

Under the table, Bjørn gripped her knee tight in support.

'So, it is done,' Erik nodded. 'Once we have reclaimed Vágar, you will have your freedom. This I promise, with those here as our witnesses.'

The men around the table nodded encouragingly at Erik's words, smiling as Hoelun's eyes began to well with tears, while Yngvar left to chase down the serving women, calling for food and drink as he went. Both Olaf and Sigurd came and patted Hoelun encouragingly on the back, thanking her again for saving their mother.

'Come! Let me share my plan as to how we will attack our home,' Erik said, allowing a hint of mirth into his voice at the irony.

Bjørn watched as life and energy came flooding back into his father, and for the first time since Váli had arrived he felt a flare of hope flow back into his body.

They spoke long into the night, as Hoelun and the men added their thoughts and opinions to the conversation.

The crews had found shelter where they could for the night. Some had slept in the half-constructed buildings while others had stretched spare sails between trees or slept aboard ship. Bjørn took it all in as he left his father's hall and set off down the beach, aiming for *Sleipnir's* patterned spare sail, where he knew he would find Bjarni and Red Orm. He could see his brothers seeking out *Ulf's* crew, with Olaf going building to building waking men up while Sigurd made for the anchored ship. Váli's son, Ragnar, was walking alongside him on a similar mission. The four of them had left Erik, Yngvar, Váli and Sven in the hall to finalise the plan while they woke the crews and got them moving.

'Bjarni, wake up,' Bjørn grunted as he ducked under the spread sail and nudged the sleeping man with his boot. The giant groaned once before rolling over. Bjørn spied Red Orm sleeping further under the sail and gave Bjarni another, harder kick before moving on to the next man, angling towards his sleeping friend. Behind him, he heard Bjarni grunt a stream of good-natured abuse at him and he laughed as he leaned down to shake Guttorm awake. 'Help me rouse the crew,' he whispered, stopping his friend's hand as it shot for his sword. 'There are no enemies here, my friend. Help me wake the men and tell them to gather on the shore before the walls; my father will speak to them shortly,' he added. Guttorm sat up and yawned, noticing the pale light of the wolf dawn. Proper dawn was still an hour or so off. Absently, he stood and belted on his sword before moving through the rest of the sleeping crew, nudging men into the new day as he went. Bjarni and Red Orm had followed his example, and it didn't take long for the space under the sail to fill with the yawns and groans of waking men.

Those who had been shaken from sleep were dragging themselves tiredly after Bjørn as he led them towards the open ground between the walls and the waiting ships where they were joined by the crews of *Fjord Ulf* and *Hrafn*. More and more men were streaming from the walls as the word spread that they had been summoned by Jarl Erik and, once the crew was awake, Guttorm hurried through the gates as quickly as he could to avoid being the last to arrive. He spied Bjørn standing in front of the crew from *Sleipnir* and hurried to join them, nodding briefly to his friend and Yngvar as he passed before joining Bjarni and Red Orm.

'Is that everyone?' Yngvar asked, raising his voice slightly to be heard above the hum of conversation as he approached Bjørn.

'They're the last,' Bjørn said, spitting on the ground in disdain as a group of younger warriors came through the walls with Knut at their centre.

Yngvar didn't miss the way Bjørn's lip curled when he saw Knut, or the sneer that was returned, but he didn't have time to worry about that now.

'Your father will begin his speech soon. Make sure the crew is ready,' he said before moving back towards the longphort.

Bjørn nodded at the command before turning and calling the men to attention. Half-finished conversations trailed off as he moved along the lines and before long the crew was standing in silent ranks as they waited to see what came next. Beside them, the crews of *Fjord Ulf* and *Hrafn* followed their example and before long the only sounds that could be heard were the occasional cough and the gentle sigh of the waves. Overhead the sky was growing increasingly brighter as a red glow spilled across the horizon, banishing the grey. The tension was palpable in light of the news *Hrafn's* crew had brought with them.

Lost in his own thoughts, Bjørn only looked up when Bjarni nudged him gently, pulling his attention back to the gates of the longphort. Erik had emerged and was walking down the slope, armed and armoured like Tyr himself. His raven helmet glinted on his head, matching the gleam from the gold rings woven among the iron of his brynja as they caught the early morning light. At his waist sat the sword Yngvar had made for him, the fist-shaped pommel swaying in time with his gait. Yngvar and Váli walked on his right, equally dressed for war with burnished armour and gleaming weapons, although neither came close to Erik's grandeur. They were matched by Turid and Arleigh, who walked calmly on Erik's left wearing freshly laundered gowns. Turid wore a vibrant red gown that matched her husband's gold-pinned cloak while Arleigh wore a more subtle white dress with red stitching. Both women carried knives and keys at their hips and Arleigh also carried her bow, the length of shaped wood comfortable in her clenched fist. When Erik came to a stop he turned and nodded to both men, acknowledging them in front of the assembled warriors before motioning for them to return to their crews, leaving him alone with the two women. The silence was total, and Bjørn felt as though the world itself was holding its breath in anticipation, waiting for his father to begin speaking.

'As you will no doubt have heard, Vágar has fallen,' Erik said, his voice carrying easily on the still morning air. A murmur flooded through the crowd as rumour became fact, and Erik raised a hand for quiet, stilling them instantly.

'Our friend, Váli, risked everything to bring this news, and my women, to me. His sacrifice, and that of his people, will not go unrewarded,' he said, pausing to pass his gaze meaningfully over *Hrafn's* crew. Bjørn saw several of them stand taller as the jarl's gaze passed over them. 'I will begin now by cancelling the tithe owed by Váli.' Erik continued, 'From this moment on,

311

there will be no debt between us, other than the debt of friendship.'

Váli nodded his acknowledgement from where he stood among his men, dipping his head meaningfully but otherwise remaining silent, unwilling to interrupt the jarl.

'My friends,' Erik continued. 'The call of England is still strong, and I long to lighten the burden their priests surely feel in caring for so much treasure. But the call of home is now stronger. This jarl, this Ake,' he spat, as if banishing a foul taste from his mouth, 'has been a thorn in my side in the past, but now he oversteps. He thinks to take my home? Our home? This will not stand!'

Erik all but roared the final words, and Bjørn felt his blood begin to boil, the rage building in his chest clearly visible on the faces of the men around him. He saw his brothers wearing the same expressions as the men beside them, a violent combination of anger and frustration.

'This... crime. I will repay it with iron. I will wash the streets of our home with the blood and viscera of *Jarl* Ake and his men, and when I am done, none will doubt the vengeance of Erik Golden Hand, or dare to take what is mine, again!' he snarled, drawing his sword and holding it aloft, the blade pointing straight towards the sky as his face contorted with rage and fury.

The roar of the crews must have been heard all the way back in Vágar, and Bjørn added his voice to those of the men around him, drawing Huginn as he shouted. Around him, weapons blazed like flames as the early morning light kissed the iron, the flaming light joined by the shouts of warriors as they bellowed their support to their jarl, and the liberation of their home.

Erik let the men shout themselves ragged before sheathing his sword and raising his hands for silence. It took a few moments, and Erik let a small smile creep onto his face as the final voices died out. It took time to calm three boatloads of warriors and he wouldn't deny them their war fervour.

'Captains and my sons to me. Men, prepare the ships,' he said when they finally silenced themselves. 'We're going to war!'

Impossible as it seemed, the answering roar was even louder than before, and Bjørn found himself grinning as he walked towards his father.

***

Toke held fast to the tiller as he worked to keep *Uxi* in the wake of Canute's ship, *Slatra*, ignoring the nagging feelings of guilt as he stood where Halfdan had only hours earlier. Only eighteen of the crew had survived the battle, killing fifteen of Canute's men in the process. Toke knew they couldn't fight again. The men were exhausted after the chase, and the loss of their homes coupled with Halfdan's death had pushed their morale to an all-time low. In the distance, he could see the outline of Vágar, resting in the shadow of King's Leap as it always had. Above the palisade and rooftops hung a blanket of smoke, drifting lazily in the slight breeze, and he could just make out Ake's snake banners flying proudly above the newly repaired gates. The sight made his stomach curl in anger and he let the emotion run briefly before squashing it. They couldn't help Erik if they were dead. He could only hope that Váli's disappearance was in search of his father, but even then, it could be months before ships appeared on the horizon, and that was assuming they survived the season. Until then, the crew of *Uxi* were on their own. He had spoken with Bersi, and the two of them had come up with the plan of embedding themselves and their men amongst Ake's, seeding dissent and fear from the inside. Bersi stood stoically alongside him now, his eyes fixed on their home as they drew ever closer. Only the white knuckles wrapped around the handle of his axe revealed the battle raging inside his head. They both knew that there was no honour in their plan, but neither of them, nor the crew, had objected, accepting that some occasions called for Loki cunning rather than brute strength. Two men from Canute's crew had joined them on board to guide them in, but ale from the ship's boys had kept them busy in the bow while Toke's plan spread from man to man in hushed whispers. Not for the first time, Toke found himself wishing for Bjørn's company. His younger brother had cunning to rival the trickster god himself.

In the distance a war horn blew, the mournful sound echoing across the silent waters as their arrival was announced. From the stern of *Slatra*, Canute indicated that they should head for a position to his left, and Toke raised his hand to acknowledge the order before adjusting the tiller slightly. 'See to the tow rope, Bersi,' he muttered quietly. 'Prepare to secure the ship,' he called, hearing Halfdan's voice in his ears as the words left his mouth. While the crew rushed to do his bidding, he focused his attention on the shoreline as it drew ever-nearer, and the men waiting for them there.

'It seems Canute was successful, Steinar,' Ake grunted without turning as they watched the incoming ships. The giant húskarl could be seen clearly standing at the helm as he guided *Slatra* towards the shore.

313

Steinar sneered sullenly, his eyes burning bright with anger and humiliation as he too watched the ships draw closer. He'd told his father his story, about being knocked unconscious and looted by a band of raiders, before being left to die among his men. Ake had taken in his son's dishevelled appearance in silence as he told the story, letting the words wash over him without even deigning to comment on the loss of his sword or armour. It wasn't until Steinar finished his tale that Ake's anger materialised, his fury unleashed like a flooding river smashing through a dam. Yet again, he had lost warriors under his son's command, and with every loss, his hold on Vágar became increasingly strained. Just that morning, he had had two men and a woman hanged after they were found with a stash of stolen spears, their bodies left to rot on the shoreline as a warning to the rest of the citizens. They would learn what happened to rebels, and the return of *Slatra* with her crew would go a long way towards quelling any further signs of rebellion. Canute knew how to enforce his law, even if his son didn't.

The sound of *Slatra* and her prize driving up onto the shore disrupted his thoughts, bringing him back into reality. He watched as Canute jumped easily overboard and waded through the ankle-deep water towards them, his ever-present axe held loosely in his right hand. If Ake was surprised to see Canute indicate for one of the men on the unknown to join him ashore, he didn't show it.

'You've brought guests, Canute,' he said, honouring him by speaking first.

'In a manner of speaking, Jarl Ake.'

Toke froze for a second at the name, his body tensing as he took in the jarl. Thankfully, no one noticed the momentary slip, their attention wholly focused on Canute.

'Explain.'

'We couldn't catch Váli, my Lord. His head start was too great, and we didn't even catch sight of him. We thought we had found him,' he said, motioning towards *Uxi* with his axe, 'but it wasn't until we were within boarding range that we realised it wasn't Váli. By then it was too late to withdraw; arrows had been fired and lives claimed. We killed several of their crew in the exchange, including their captain, but we lost fifteen of our own in the fighting. This is Sven Halfdansson, the captain's son,' Canute added, motioning towards Toke. 'He has pledged himself and his crew's service to you in exchange for their lives and their ship.'

Ake's iron gaze turned to Toke, as if seeing him for the first time. Beside him, Steinar was oblivious to the newcomers, his loathing gaze wholly fixed

314

on the giant axeman. Canute too turned his attention on Toke, ignoring Steinar's furious glare. He served the wolf of Fótrfjord; he wasn't going to worry about the yapping pup.

'Is this true?' Ake asked, his voice cold as he cast a critical eye over Toke and his men, judging their war gear and the state of their ship. His gaze lingered briefly on the makeshift sail before returning to Toke.

Toke had studied the jarl while he spoke with Canute, taking in the man who had usurped his father's high seat. He had recognised his son immediately, the coward from the skirmish at Váli's recognisable in the light of day. He just hoped the recognition didn't go both ways. He could sense a hardness in Ake that Steinar clearly hadn't inherited, and a thinly veiled cruelty that lurked below the surface. He hadn't missed the hanging corpses of people he'd known on the shore, or the sword Ake wore on his waist as if it was his own. Geri was his father's blade, and it hurt to see it sullied by the hands of a lesser man. They were just two more crimes to be repaid.

'Aye, Jarl Ake' he said, proud to hear no sign of nervousness or hesitation in his voice. 'Word has spread of your name and when your man here told us who he serves, we offered our swords in exchange for our freedom. I have sworn to not seek revenge on Canute for the death of my father, Halfdan, nor will I or my men seek *weregild* in compensation. My father died fairly in combat and is even now dining in the Allfather's hall with my grandfather. All I ask is the lives of my men. If that comes at the price of service, then we will gladly pay it.'

Ake fixed Toke with a penetrating stare, his piercing gaze seeking the slightest hint of deception. It took every ounce of self-control for Toke to meet the gaze calmly, rather than draw his sword and start slashing. Only the presence of Canute's axe at his back held him in place.

It was Ake who broke first, satisfied. 'If you speak true, I would be glad to accept your men into my ranks. War is coming to my home, and I will need every sword and axe I can find. Serve loyally, and you will be rewarded with arm bands and plunder. Betray me, and you will face a death far worse than our friends here,' he said, nodding vaguely towards the hanging bodies. Toke nodded as he took the offered hand, forcing himself not to wince at the touch.

'Steinar, find them a place to sleep.'

Oblivious to the battle of wills between the two men, Steinar finally tore his gaze from Canute and focused on the man before him. Something about him was familiar, but he couldn't put his finger on it, and given his current standing with his father, he was unwilling to say or do anything that would see him fall further from favour.

'Yes, Father. You and your men can come with me when you're ready,' he said, eyeing Toke curiously.

Toke nodded once before returning to *Uxi*, eager to get away from the jarl and his son. The sound of his feet crunching on the shore sounded loud in his ears as he walked towards the ship, nodding subtly to Bersi to give him the all-clear. He could almost see the tension leaving his friend's body at the signal, although he doubted Bersi would be hanging up his blade any time soon.

'It seems we're to stay,' he said quietly as he climbed back aboard. 'Tell the men that the jarl's son, Steinar, survived the fight at Váli's and is here. We need to keep a low profile. We're not walking back into the Vágar we know.'

'Aye, Toke.'

'It's Sven from here on in,' Toke growled, stealing a furtive glance behind him to make sure none of Ake's men had followed him to the ship. Satisfied, he moved towards his sea chest, passing along the word as he went. They were home, but they were far from safe.

\*\*\*

'Moskstraumen holds no mystery for you now,' Yngvar grunted, standing alongside Bjørn as he guided *Sleipnir* past the tidal eddy for what felt like the hundredth time. From his position in the stern he could see *Fjord Ulf* and *Hrafn* strung out behind them like a pack of hunting hounds. Only the women they had rescued had been left behind when the order came to sail, and three of the warriors who were still too injured to fight. The rest were aboard the ships, sailing for war.

'Aye,' Bjørn smiled. 'I think I have it tamed for now.'

Overhead the sky was a blazing blue, and the three ships were being pushed forwards by a steady wind, the snarling beasts at their prows eating the distance. The fine weather hadn't helped the mood aboard ship, however, and there was no light-hearted banter amongst the crew as they sailed. No one sat playing games of tafl or telling stories, or carving bones or tusks. Instead, weapons were being obsessively sharpened and armour repaired, the sounds of whet stones on iron mingling with the water as it rushed along the hull. Guttorm had borrowed Bjørn's stone before they set sail and he could see him sitting with Bjarni as the grizzled veteran showed him how to work the steel

316

to give his sword a razor edge and grind out any chips and dents, his brow furrowed in concentration.

Bjørn was the only one aboard not preparing his equipment, having taken a turn at the tiller so Yngvar could prepare his own war gear. Bjørn found the constant ringing of stone on steel calming and he felt himself relax, enjoying Yngvar's presence as he worked silently beside him, his tongue poking between his lips in concentration.

Erik's announcement had left no doubt as to their destination, or what came next. All that was left now was to follow the threads. His attention slipped briefly as a pod of orca appeared and began swimming alongside them, their graceful bodies sliding easily through the waves. A few of the younger men watched nervously as the oily black bodies danced around *Sleipnir*, no doubt remembering stories of ships breaking their backs when they struck a whale. Bjørn chuckled at the thought, feeling no fear himself. Somehow, he knew that Njörd wouldn't stand in the way of their vengeance, nor would the beasts that roamed his domain.

'It is a good omen!' he shouted, startling a few of the more nervous among the crew. 'Njörd looks on our voyage with favour and has sent his friends here to guide us to our next anchorage as we pass by the doors to his hall!'

His words were rewarded by a spattering of nervous laughter and good-natured jeers as those who had worried at the sudden appearance of the orca were ribbed by their crewmates. Laughing with the rest, Bjørn returned his attention to the horizon as the small pod of orca suddenly disappeared below the waves, banished to the depths by the crew's sudden eruption of noise. In the distance, he could see the island they were making for and called an order forward to have one of the sheets adjusted, trying to capture every drop of wind that he could in the sail. Yngvar rose silently to stand beside him.

'I'll take the tiller from here, lad. See to your gear. We don't know what tomorrow – or even this evening – will bring.'

'Aye,' Bjørn said without argument, sliding to the left to make space for Yngvar before relinquishing the oar. Yngvar took the length of wood easily and settled in to guide them the rest of the way, leaving Bjørn wondering at the sudden burst of speed he was able to coax from the ship as he walked towards his sea chest.

Seeing him draw close, Guttorm stopped running the stone along his blade and offered it across, mid-stroke. 'I can see to my armour first,' Bjørn said, shaking his head. Guttorm smiled and returned to his sword.

'There'll be naught left if you keep running that stone on it,' Bjarni grunted. Bjørn saw Guttorm turn red out of the corner of his eye and smiled without saying anything. He remembered learning to sharpen a blade years ago, working by the light of Yngvar's forge. He'd been younger then, and more than once he'd felt the sting of an un-tipped arrow shaft on his knuckles if he made a mistake, like forgetting to wet the stone, or grinding the edge unevenly. Sighing, he pulled the armoured vest his mother had given him from the chest and began to inspect each strip of iron individually, checking every thread to ensure they were tight and secure. Two were coming loose, and he set about reattaching them with a thick thread his mother had given him for that purpose. Once they were secure like the rest he began oiling the leather and iron scales to protect against wear and rot. He did the same with his brynja, covering it with oil until it gleamed before turning to his weapons. He retrieved both Huginn and Muninn from where they lay in his chest, sheathed and wrapped in their oiled sheepskins, as well as his axe. He accepted the stone from Guttorm then, and started first on the knife, spitting occasionally on the stone as he worked. He took his time with each of the blades, talking quietly with his companions without looking up from his work. All but a few had finished their preparations, and they now sat in small groups eating and discussing the days ahead, the mood sombre. Bjørn heard more than a few of them discussing their families and homes, and he again felt a surge of guilt-tinged relief that his mother and Hoelun were both safe. He couldn't imagine having a family under the control of another man, and his blood seethed for those around him.

He realised that his mother knew this pain all too well, and he began imagining what she must have gone through when Erik first took her. For the first time, he truly appreciated how hard it must have been for her to have come to live amongst the Northmen, and to start a new life that she'd never wanted after losing everything she had. He had no misconceptions about the way she had come to live amongst them, nor his own conception. But despite it all there was a genuine fondness between Arleigh and Erik.

'Hoelun must feel the same,' he thought, hoping not for the first time that she would stay in the north after earning her freedom. He smiled to himself as he worked, realising that he might be in danger of falling in love. His father was unlikely to object, given his mixed blood, and her status as a freed thrall. Nor would his mother. He'd seen the way the two women were together, although

318

given his limited knowledge and experience with women, the thought made him oddly uncomfortable.

He was almost finished honing the blade on his sword when *Fjord Ulf* drew alongside them. He could see Sigurd standing in the stern, expertly handling the ship while his father stood alongside him, guiding. Olaf was at the prow with Sven, working on his own sword. He would have already taken his turn at the helm.

'We will rest here for the night!' Erik called over the wind, once they were within shouting distance, indicating the island ahead.

Yngvar raised his hand in confirmation, already forgotten by his jarl as *Fjord Ulf* peeled off to share the orders with *Hrafn*.

Everyone onboard had heard Erik's words; there was no need for Yngvar to repeat the order.

Bjørn passed the stone across his sword a few more times before returning it to its scabbard, wrapping it lovingly in the oiled sheepskin. He caught sight of Knut staring daggers at him as he worked on his own blade, his face twisted with barely concealed loathing as he watched Bjørn return his weapons to his sea chest. Knut's nose was still a bruised and broken mess, underlined by purplish-yellow swelling that reached up to hang below his eyes, and Bjørn found himself wondering if he could breathe properly before deciding he didn't care. Knut had gotten what he deserved.

Bjørn met the stare until Knut was forced to look away under his unflinching gaze. He knew they would likely come to blows one day, but he didn't let the thought worry him now. Small men like Knut were just that, small men. Guttorm watched the exchange but remained silent, giving Bjørn a meaningful shrug before setting about packing his own gear away. As Guttorm lifted the lid of his sea chest, Bjørn flicked his gaze to the man behind him, recognising gap-toothed smile and mop of shoulder-length blond hair. It was Arne, the spearman Knut had stabbed during training.

'You didn't leave Vágar with us,' Bjørn asked, smiling at him, 'how is it you've come to be on *Sleipnir* now?'

Arne grinned awkwardly at the sudden attention before staring sheepishly at his feet as Bjarni, Red Orm and Guttorm all turned to look at him in turn.

'I asked Yngvar, Lord Bjørn, when you returned to the camp the other day. One of the bóndi who sailed with you was eager to join the jarl's ship, so we traded places,' he explained, his eyes flicking between Bjørn and *Sleipnir's* suddenly fascinating decking.

Bjørn smiled kindly at him, trying to ease his nerves. 'The only lord here is my father. I'm just Bjørn. But why the trade? Surely the opportunity to sail with my father, and gain recognition in his skjaldborg, is the dream of any man?'

'Aye... Bjørn,' he said tentatively, testing the name. 'I did think of it. But you stepped in and avenged me when I was injured.' Bjørn saw his eyes flicker briefly to Knut, lowering his voice when he saw the ruined face staring back maliciously. 'I'm sure it was deliberate, and none could miss the hatred he displayed towards you. So, I changed ships, to keep an eye on him, and make sure he doesn't come for you like a thief in the night.'

Bjørn blinked at the humble bravery of the man. There was no doubt that Knut would cut him to ribbons without breaking a sweat if it came to a real fight, yet still he had come. He glanced at Guttorm, noting the smile there as he no doubt remembered his own introduction to the son of Erik.

*'Men can be bought, Bjørn, but true loyalty is earned, and priceless,'* he heard his father say again, the words coming unbidden.

'Welcome aboard.' He chuckled, seeing his own smile reflected on Arne's face as they shook hands.

# Chapter 23

'It's decided. Váli and I will stay here for the next three days and drill the bóndi. I have no qualms about yours or my hirðsmen, Váli,' Erik said placatingly, nodding to his friend, 'but the bóndi need work. This will be no hit-and-run raid on an unguarded monastery. They need to be prepared for the fire we will have to walk through as we charge the walls, and that's before we even get within a sword length of the bastards hiding behind them.'

'Agreed,' Váli grunted. They'd both seen less experienced men break in the face of an armoured hirð or an English shield wall. Fighting Ake would be no different, and the unbloodied youths in the fleet needed to be trained as best they could be, even if they only had three days in which to do it.

'You will sail at first light tomorrow, Yngvar. We attack in five days. I'm trusting you to be in position and ready to fall on their rear when you hear the battle begin. I will look for you.'

Yngvar nodded, keeping his own council. He had devised this part of the attack strategy himself, with the exception of Bjørn's suggestion to take the rangers from *Fjord Ulf* with them on *Sleipnir*. He knew what he had to do, as did they all. The small council of captains had grown to include the jarl's sons, as well as Sven, Uffe, and Ragnar. The rest of the crew had been ordered to eat and then start work on simple defences around the camp. It wouldn't be anything fancy, just a simple ditch encircling the camp leading to the water on either side where the ships were hauled up, with the earth shovelled up into low walls. It was enough for a temporary camp, and would form a defensible redoubt for them, should they need it. Unlikely as it was, Erik wasn't taking any chances this close to Vágar. They didn't know who else was sympathetic to Ake's attack, and may be helping him.

The nine of them had been talking for well over two hours while the sun worked its way across the sky and the walls slowly took shape around them. Turid and Arleigh had worked as hard as any man there, directing the women and ship's boys to light fires and get food cooking for the warriors.

Other than the suggestion to trade men between *Ulf* and *Sleipnir*, Bjørn too had kept quiet, content to listen while more experienced heads spoke. His silent mask had only broken when Yngvar named him as his second-in-command and he'd felt his face grow a shade redder as he forced himself not to let his pride show at his friend's words. He would lead ten men from *Sleipnir*, including Guttorm, Arne, Red Orm and Bjarni. He knew the older warriors were there to ensure he didn't make any mistakes, but he didn't let the thought trouble him.

Sigurd and Olaf had also been assigned warriors to command, as had Ragnar. Between the sons of Erik and Váli, as well as their fathers, Yngvar and Uffe, the army had its captains. Each of the younger men would lead ten men apiece, except for Olaf who would command twenty, while the rest of the force was led by more seasoned warriors. The only man amongst them who hadn't been given a command was Sven, but they all knew that asking him to leave Erik's side was a pointless venture. All told, Erik would lead a warband of over a hundred-and-thirty warriors to reclaim his home. Despite the size of their combined army, Bjørn knew that the presence of *Fjord Uxi* and her crew would have tipped the balance heavily in their favour.

Lifting his horn, Erik downed the contents in a single gulp before fixing the men around him with his iron gaze. 'Get to it, we have work to do.'

Each of the men bowed their heads briefly to the jarl before making their way across the beach to their respective ships.

'Bjørn, stay a moment,' Erik said suddenly, speaking impulsively as his youngest made to leave with Yngvar.

He watched with mixed emotions as the young man nodded once to Yngvar before turning back to face his father, his gaze calm and expectant. Erik knew that their relationship had been strained at times, the factor of his son's blood hanging over them like a cloud that would never go away. But he couldn't ignore the swell of pride that rushed through him as he watched his son, standing tall and confident as he waited for his father to speak. From his recent conversations with Yngvar, he had been forced to admit that his fears about Bjørn's mixed blood had been unfounded. He had proven himself more than once since they had set sail and, in this one instance, he was happy to have been wrong.

Erik refilled two of the ale horns from a skin at his side before passing one across the table. Bjørn took it in his right hand and waited for his father to speak. His sons had learned patience.

'The men will look to you now, Bjørn,' he said at last, letting the words linger as he took a sip of his ale.

'I know,' Bjørn replied, raising his own horn.

Erik grunted, taking a moment before replying. His mood had been sharper than usual since Váli had arrived with the news, and he had struggled to find calm since that moment. 'You must show them that your word is iron and bind them to you. Their lives are yours; spend them wisely.'

Bjørn remained silent as his father spoke, and Erik could see he was following the words closely despite his outward show of confidence. It dawned on him that this was the first time he'd spoken to Bjørn in this way. Both Sigurd and Olaf had commanded men before, as had Toke the year before. For Bjørn, this was entirely new, and despite the seriousness of the conversation, he found he was enjoying the moment alone with his youngest son.

'You must put them first above all things,' Erik continued. 'Show them that you can think and adapt to situations, that you can lead, and that you will not waste their lives needlessly. Lead from the front, but only after you've stood at the back and made your plans. Any man can swing a sword, but few can think ahead of the sword storm. Those men will follow you because I've told them they must. Now make them follow you because they want to; because they're eager to fight under your command. Bind them to you, Bjørn,' he repeated passionately.

'I will, Father,' Bjørn said seriously, without any trace of false confidence. 'I promise.'

Erik studied him in silence, letting the sounds of men working fill the space for a few moments before nodding to himself, satisfied.

'Good. Go now and prepare your men. I will see you in five days,' he said, the finality in his voice ending the meeting as suddenly as it had started.

Bjørn nodded to his father, and Erik was briefly tempted to say more, but the moment passed. Instead, he took Bjørn's proffered hand in a firm grip and grinned, meeting his son's serious eyes. 'Thank you, Jarl Erik. I won't let you down,' Bjørn said seriously before turning and walking back towards *Sleipnir*.

'I know,' Erik said quietly to himself as he watched his son disappear into the hustle and bustle of the camp, weaving easily between the different groups as he headed towards his own crew. He had almost told his son to be careful, but he'd held his tongue. Such words did little good and would only encourage a failure of courage. Bjørn would find his own path, as would his brothers. Red Orm and Bjarni would guide him, just as Yngvar had over the years. He suspected that *Sleipnir's* captain may have been a better father to his youngest than he had himself at times, but he was unfazed by the thought; Bjørn was stronger for it. He was unlikely to sit on Vágar's high seat, and when Erik's thread was finally cut, Bjørn would have to bend the knee or make his own way in the world. Erik had given him the tools he would need for either path, it was enough. Pulling his attention from Bjørn, he turned and made his way back to the crew of *Fjord Ulf*. He could see Sigurd and Olaf amongst the men as they slaved away in the ditch, digging ever deeper. On an impulse, he threw off his own coat and tunic and took up a shovel before joining his men in the pit. Let them see their jarl amongst them and take heart. War was coming, and many of the men there would die in the coming days. Perhaps he too would fall and travel to Valhöll to be reunited with his own father and brothers. The thought made him smile as he buried the shovel in the ground again and scooped out a heaped load of dirt and sand, finding calm in the simple labour. Whatever happened would happen. Wyrd.

'Here they are,' Yngvar said as Bjørn returned to *Sleipnir*. Behind him, Red Orm and Bjarni stood silently in front of eight young warriors, including Guttorm and Arne, trying to hide the excited grins they both wore. Bjørn smiled to himself when he realised that all but two of the men he was to lead were bóndi. *'Of course I wouldn't lead the cream of the crop,'* he mused, eyeing the men carefully. He was relieved when he saw Knut was not amongst them. Yngvar had saved him that frustration at least.

'Thank you,' he said to his friend.

Smiling, Yngvar patted him on the back with a nod before returning to the rest of the crew and began issuing orders. Unlike the men of *Fjord Ulf* and *Hrafn*, they had stopped work much sooner than the other crews given their early departure. Bjørn watched him leave before turning his attention back to the men before him.

'Return to *Sleipnir* and bring me all the war gear you own,' he said, trying to instil strength in his voice.

There was shuffling as the men left to obey his order, and Bjørn moved quickly to his own chest, where it lay resting near the mast. As fast as he could, he threw his brynja over his head, shrugging the iron rings down over his body before covering it with the armoured jerkin his mother had given him. His helmet followed, tied loosely under his chin, before he re-tied his sword belt around his waist, the familiar weight resting comfortably on his hips and taking some of the weight from the iron rings. Lastly, he slid his axe into the loop at his lower back before taking up his shield and returning to await his men, leaving his bow and quiver behind. It didn't take long for the rest to return, each carrying what equipment they could afford, or that their fathers had handed down to them. Aside from himself, only Red Orm and Bjarni wore the coveted iron ringed shirts and iron helmets. He noted the gash in Red Orm's brynja but said nothing. Neither of them would thank him for what he had in mind. The pair both carried swords at their waists, as did Guttorm, but aside from them, none of the waiting warriors owned such a weapon. One carried a long seax at his side, and two more came with axes, but the rest carried only the spear and shield that Erik had given them, and a short knife or seax that they'd provided themselves. Only Arne carried a bow, but Bjørn had yet to see the man shoot, and he doubted he would be able to given his wound. As for armour, two wore thick leather jerkins, while the rest stood in homespun wool. It would have to do. If they were successful in defeating Ake, Bjørn would see to it that they were better equipped, if he still had the power to do so. And if he survived.

'We're not the best equipped of Jarl Erik's men,' he began, his tone light as he eyed the men before him and raising a few chuckles. 'Nor are we the most experienced!' More joined in the merriment, the warm sound loud underlined by the deep baritone of Bjarni's laughter.

'We're not the biggest, nor the most fearsome and we certainly don't have the most experienced leader,' he continued, bringing forth more laughter and a spattering of conversation as he spread his arms wide and took a mock bow. He let the laughter and conversation continue for a few moments before speaking again.

'This puts us amongst the weakest here,' he said, suddenly serious as he washed the humour from his voice and swept his arms around him, gesturing vaguely to the surrounding camp. The laughter trailed off at his words, and Bjørn caught more than one of them stealing nervous glances to the men either side of them.

All men knew their fates were written by the Nornir at birth, the three bitches chuckling as they wove the stories of men's lives. However, such knowledge didn't mean that they were eager to rush into their graves. Red Orm and Bjarni nodded subtly to Bjørn as he spoke, reassuring him. He could see his words had hit the younger warriors, curbing their enthusiasm.

'If we want to survive, we must fight as one cohesive unit, where every man here can trust those standing beside of him. You have all learned to fight in the skjaldborg, but not necessarily with the men standing beside you now.

325

When we fight to reclaim our home, these men will be your sword brothers, warriors you can trust and rely on.' He paused then, knowing his next words would be unpopular. 'And if you're to fight together, you must know what the men next to you are made of. Follow me now, and let's see what I can make of you.'

So saying, he turned and began to run through the camp towards the small plank bridge that had been placed over the rough ditch without looking back to check they were following him. He knew they would.

Bjørn and his small troop returned over two hours later, red-faced and winded. He had led them to the far side of the small island and back again, the small warband thumping across the rough-hewn bridge as the sun disappeared below the western horizon. After the first few rôst, Bjørn had fallen to the back of the group to make sure no one was left behind, setting the pace and keeping them together. None had stopped, each of them eager to prove to the others that they could be relied upon and trusted, that they wouldn't fail them. Even Arne, injured as he was, refused to stop despite his obvious pain, returning only when Bjørn ordered him back to camp. Even then he argued for another rôst before giving in to reality and turning back.

They were met with good-natured jeers from the men in camp when they returned, including some of their own shipmates, but none complained. Their young captain had shown his willingness to endure with them and had undoubtedly carried the heaviest load throughout. They were met with fresh cooked fish porridge and bread, served to them by Bjørn's mother and Hoelun, that they washed down with horns of frothing ale and mead.

Yngvar noted the way the small group sat together over their meal, rather than breaking up to sit with their usual shipmates. He had no doubt that Bjørn would bind them to him in the same way his father did. He hoped for their sake that they would survive the fight to come.

*Sleipnir's* crew were up before dawn as they loaded the ship and made their final preparations before launching. Hoelun had come to Yngvar the night before and asked to sail with them and join the rangers, under Uffe. He had no objections, having heard of her prowess with the bow from Erik's women and Váli. He watched as a few of the men turned to follow her with their eyes as she came aboard, her dress doing little to hide her lithe figure and natural curves despite the fur cloak she wore. He chuckled when a few looked guiltily to where Bjørn sat with Guttorm and Bjarni before calling for the final pieces of equipment to be stowed so they could push off. He could see Erik and Váli watching them from the shore, along with their sons and Sven. Sigurd and Olaf both raised their hands before the small group turned back to the camp.

'Oars!' Yngvar boomed, his hands instinctively finding the tiller. Bjørn would row with his men today. Time was not on their side, and they had to reach their destination as soon as possible. Erik would accept no less. 'Starboard oars, forward! Port oars, backwards!'

With speed that spoke to her purpose, *Sleipnir* gracefully pirouetted on the spot, the crew feeling the moment to reverse oars and settle her once she was pointed forwards towards open water. At Yngvar's command they began to pull, pushing *Sleipnir* into deeper water until the sail could be unfurled and the wind harnessed. They were going home.

*** 

'You can sleep here,' Steinar grunted, motioning towards an empty byre with a surly gesture. The sight of the bearskin-clad giant, and the younger warrior who now led the crew, had triggered his memories from the battle at Váli's as he suddenly recognised the men Canute had returned with. He watched the young leader now as he indicated for his crew to make themselves as comfortable as they could amongst the hay piled in the empty byre. After they'd secured *Uxi* at her usual berth on the shore, unbeknownst to their hosts, they'd followed Steinar through their home with the eyes of strangers. Behind the gazes had been a hunger for information, each of them searching with subtle desperation for a sight of their loved ones, along with anything that could help them destroy the men who presumed ownership of their homes. It had been all Toke could do to keep calm and not draw his sword and start swinging when they had passed his father's hall. His father's banners had been ripped off and shoved into the mud, the golden fists stained and ruined from the passage of men's feet as they entered and exited the hall. It was just one more insult to repay.

'My father will speak with you this evening,' Steinar continued insolently when no one acknowledged him. 'You will find him in *his* hall,' he added, emphasising the word.

'Thank you,' Toke said, refusing to rise to the challenge as he fixed the shorter man with a cold gaze. 'I'm sure he will be curious about our *adventures* over the previous weeks, given the state of our ship.'

Steinar sneered again, trying and failing to hold Toke's icy stare. The rest of the crew had dropped their sea chests and were fixing Steinar with the same unflinching gaze. Toke knew it was foolish to bait the jarl's son in the middle of a town full of his warriors, but he couldn't resist. The tension built until Steinar could take it no longer.

'Bah,' he grunted with forced nonchalance as he spat on the ground between Toke's feet before turning and walking back towards the harbour with as much dignity as he could muster.

Toke laughed. It wasn't much of a victory, but after the events of the previous days it had made him feel better to clip Steinar's wings and show him they wouldn't be intimidated by him, or his father. He saw that many of his men wore the same smiles on their own faces as he turned to face them and he felt his smile grow, enjoying the feeling of camaraderie. The crew had accepted his right to lead without question, helped in part by Bersi's unwavering support, but he still felt the need to earn their trust.

'Stack your sea chests in a line here,' he said, walking forwards and marking the space. 'We will sleep at the back there. It won't do much, but it will slow anyone down if they try to attack or surprise us in the night. I think Steinar lied to the jarl about what happened at Váli's, so for now we're safe. But better to be sure.'

There were grunts of approval as the crew worked to create a barrier across the byrne, stacking their sea chests end to end to form a low wall that would slow or trip attackers in the dark.

'Frode, get out there and see what you can learn. If anyone stops you, say you're looking to buy food. And keep your hood up,' he added as Frode's hand snatched the small pouch of hacksilver Toke threw to him, the metal clinking warmly in his hand. Short and slight, the young man nodded once before digging into his chest and pulling out a curved hunting knife which he strapped onto his weapons belt opposite his axe as he slid out the door.

'The rest of you, get some rest as best you can. I'm sure someone will come to find us soon. We will discuss everything we've seen this evening, while the town sleeps.'

Like the seasoned raiders they were, they quickly settled into the ordinary routines of camp. A few found a discarded crate which soon had a hnefatafl board rolled out on it, while others dozed. Bersi took up a position by the door, keeping his eyes glued to the small crack to keep watch on the world outside. Satisfied, Toke crossed the byre to where Tolstan lay. All of the bóndi had died during the fighting, along with the ship's boys, with the exception of Tolstan. Canute had allowed *Uxi's* crew to mourn their dead on a small islet a few rôst from Vágar, where they had laid them to rest. Only the wound to Tolstan's ribs had kept him safe, having barred him from entering the fray. Frode had stitched the wound as best he could, and Toke had poured ale over it to keep it clean before binding it. He would live, but he would carry the scar for the rest of his days as a memory of his first time on the whale road.

'How are you?' Toke asked, kneeling next to the prone boy.

Tolstan climbed up onto his elbows, struggling to keep a brave expression on his face as the wound pulled at the stitches. Toke smiled at his strength and motioned for him to lie down again.

'I'll live,' he said, wincing.

'Aye, I'm sure you will. I have a job for you,' he said, grinning at the excitement that flashed across his face. He'd been subdued and grim since learning that all the other boys had died in the fight, and Toke was happy to see the spark return.

'Anything, Lord. To—'

'Shhh,' Toke hissed, his eyes glowing. 'No one here can know who I am,' he whispered conspiratorially. 'I am Sven Halfdansson, remember?'

Tolstan nodded furiously, the fear of disappointing or exposing Toke written clear on his young face. Toke smiled again, softening his expression before continuing.

'Good lad. Now, I need you to sleep up there with Odd,' he whispered, pointing at the raised floor above the resting men. 'There is a loading window there and I need you to keep watch for anyone coming for us during the night.'

'Shall I go now?' he asked eagerly, unable to cover a wince as he sat up too fast.

'Not yet. For now, get some sleep and heal. We'll be summoned to meet this jarl soon enough and I want you to stay here and sleep when we go. You climb up when we return.'

'All right, Sven,' he said quietly, leaning back onto the soft hay.

'Good lad. We'll be counting on you,' Toke said before returning to Bersi, oblivious to the look of pride on the boy's face as he moved away.

'Anything?' he asked, approaching his friend.

Bersi was silent for a few moments, his eyes flicking tirelessly across the open ground beyond the doorway. Toke was just about to ask again when he finally answered. 'Nothing. I saw Frode cross the clearing a few times, and Steinar came past, glaring at the building as he went. Other than that, we're alone, at least from this side.'

'Tolstan will sleep above us with Odd this evening and watch the rear. We'll take turns at the front through the night. I'm sure this Jarl Ake will reveal his plans for us this evening.'

'Gnn,' Bersi grunted, returning to his vigil. 'Get some rest, *Sven*,' he added quietly. 'I can keep an eye on things.'

Toke hadn't realised how tired he was. Only a few of his men were still awake. He knew they were all eager to find out the fates of their families, but he had made it irrefutably clear that they had to avoid contact with their people. They couldn't risk being recognised by anyone.

Toke could guess at what his men's wives and lovers would have faced at the hands of Ake's men. He'd seen it before on his first raid and he'd kept the thought to himself. They had all ridden the whale road before; they knew what would have played out here in their absence.

'You're sure?'

'Aye, lad. You'll need your wits about you when we're summoned to meet Ake, and give him our *pledge* of loyalty.'

'Gnn,' Toke yawned. 'Perhaps you're right. Wake me if you need anything.'

Bersi nodded before continuing his quiet vigil through the gap in the door. Toke spied a vacant spot amongst the men and moved towards it, yawning as he went. He wondered idly if Halfdan or his father had ever felt so completely exhausted at having to think of everything all the time, always trying to look one step ahead. Neither of them had ever mentioned it; both were tireless. *'There's a lesson there,'* he mused before promptly falling asleep, his dreams filled with images of Signy, and Jarl Ake's head on a spike.

# Chapter 24

'So, Sven Halfdansson,' Ake said, raising a drinking horn to his lips. 'Canute tells me your men put up quite a fight.'

'We only did what was needed to defend ourselves and our ship, *Jörmungandr*,' Toke replied, watching as the jarl's horn was refilled by a passing thrall. He didn't recognise her, which both comforted and worried him. Ake went silent for a time, watching them all while they stood patiently and confidently under the glare.

'Gnn,' Ake grunted as he moved his eyes from man to man. 'I'm curious, Sven, where you've come from to find yourself in my fjords with a ship so broken? It can't be from around these parts. If you were, I'd have heard of you, or your father.'

Toke and the rest of his men had been summoned before the jarl a few hours after Steinar had shown them to the byre. All of them had entered Erik's hall, except for Tolstan and Odd who had remained behind due to their injuries. For the crew of *Fjord Uxi*, it had been a trial in itself to keep the fury from their faces as they crossed through the doors they knew so well and into the familiar space. For Toke, it had been an immense battle of wills to stand on his father's banners and push the yellow fists deeper into the quagmire as he entered the hall. It was even harder to see Ake sitting in his father's seat. He was surrounded by his warriors, all of them dressed in gleaming brynjas with good swords on their hips. Toke's men had been permitted to retain their weapons, but the threat wasn't lost on them. They were unarmoured and outnumbered at least two-to-one. Now was not the time to attack Jarl Ake. Steinar was not amongst them Toke noticed, storing the information. '*Clearly, there is no love lost between father and son.*'

'We were heading west, my Lord,' he said, meeting Ake's piercing gaze as he begun the story he and the crew had created together. 'We set out from Borg with one other ship, having wintered there. Just a few days onto the whale road, we were caught in a storm even the Sea King himself would have struggled to survive. We did all we could to stay with our companions, but they broke apart on the evening of the first day. We think she broke her back on a whale; we saw the great tail break the waves at the same time as our companion ship came apart. There was naught we could do for our friends, and we were forced to press on. On the second day, our steering oar was sheared away by something in the water, and our mast was smashed by a log, carried over the side by a rogue wave that claimed two of our crew mates. All we could do was keep rowing and hope no other lives would be lost. By the third or fourth day, Thor put his hammer away and we were safe, although far off course with nothing but the sun to guide us. We found ourselves in these fjords more by chance than design, but when we saw your man bearing down on us with his prow beast set and shields mounted, we had no choice but to run, and then, when it was clear we couldn't outrun them, to defend ourselves.'

Jarl Ake watched him for a time, chewing idly on a piece of meat as he considered the story. Borg was a major settlement, and two ships being caught in a storm was as common as the sun chasing the moon. Toke was confident in the story, but all the same he took a deep swig of his ale to hide any signs of unease as the silence filled the room. He had led the crew into the mouth of the beast, and everything now depended on the perceived honesty of his lies. Beside him, he felt Bersi tense subtly, preparing for a fight, and he gently bumped his foot, willing him to relax. If Bersi berserked now, they would all die, and while it may claim Ake as well, there were more than enough men to hold the town under his son.

'You and your men are lucky to be alive,' Ake grunted at last. 'The Allfather isn't one to suffer weak men in Miðgarðr, and it seems that only the strongest amongst you were destined to remain amongst the living, and a good thing, too. War is coming to my home. If you were sincere in your offer to my man,' he said, motioning towards Canute, 'I will accept your swords and axes into my service, and pay you well for it. Furthermore, any man who distinguishes himself to me may make the oath and live amongst my people should he choose, once the war is won.'

Toke said nothing for a while, pretending to consider the offer as he emptied his drinking horn. 'We will fight for you,' he said at last, holding his empty vessel out for a thrall to refill. 'It would be our honour.'

Where Erik would have grinned and called for a toast, Ake remained cold and impassive, his eyes like flint as he spoke again. 'I am no merchant, and I will not haggle on the price. I have here an armband weighing exactly one *eyrir*,' he said, removing the thin band and holding it between his thumb and forefinger so everyone could see it. 'Your payment will be balanced against it.

332

If you have scales, you are welcome to verify the weight,' he added, offering it towards Toke. 'Otherwise, I will provide a set.'

'That won't be necessary, Jarl Ake,' Toke replied, raising his hands. 'I will trust you.'

'Hmmm,' Ake hummed, eyeing him. 'Thank you, but I would not have it said that you were cheated by Jarl Ake when you eventually leave my shores. Canute,' he said, turning his head.

Canute came forward without speaking, carrying a small set of scales and an iron weight, which he showed to Toke. While everyone watched impassively, he took Ake's ring and placed it on one of the small scale plates, before balancing it with the weight on the other. Once the scales were settled he held them up for everyone to see. The balance was perfect.

'Thank you, Canute,' Ake said before turning back to Toke and his men. 'I will pay one eyrir of hacksilver per day for each man from tomorrow until the first snowfall of winter. In addition, I will provide food, ale and shelter. As captain, you will take two eyrir, and after victory is assured, you will also take a tenth share of any plunder that is captured, after my tithe is removed. Do you accept?'

Ake could have offered Toke a sack of gold a day for all he cared. He was busy imagining his sword driving between the arrogant jarl's ribs and out through his back, and he let the thought distract him for a few moments to give the impression of considering the offer before nodding his agreement.

'We accept, with one exception. I would also ask permission to refit and repair our ship. She has taken a beating, and none of us can stand to see her so broken. We will of course pay for anything we need.'

In his mind's eye, Toke could see the sheds on the shore where he had skewered his hand. They were packed full of supplies, or at least they had been, when they first set sail. Ake remained silent, and Toke saw again the contrast between him and his own father. Where Erik was loud and boisterous, and generous with all men, Ake was cold and calculating. There was little joy in the man.

'When you arrived, you said that you will not seek weregild for the death of your father, or those of your men,' Ake replied, his voice questioning.

'Aye,' Toke agreed. 'He died well and is surely even now in the corpse hall with his father. I will miss the old man, but I will not begrudge the honour of his death,' he added, nodding briefly at Canute.

Canute dipped his head in response, but remained silent.

'Be that as it may,' Ake continued, 'I will allow you to repair your ship in compensation, and to avoid any bad blood between your men and my own. I'm told that the buildings on the shore near where you anchored have the supplies you may need. You may begin tomorrow.'

'Thank you,' Toke said, dipping his head.

'I will give you two days to make the necessary repairs, then I will need your men. Come to me then, Sven. I will tell you what you must do.'

'Your will,' Toke grunted, raising his horn and downing the remains in a single gulp to hide his relief. He could feel Bersi uncoiling beside him.

Toke and his men stayed for a few more hours with Jarl Ake and his men, quietly gathering all the information they could while outwardly showing the joyous faces of sailors who had finally found safe harbour. They all knew the dangers of the whale road, and the relief of reaching solid ground again. It wasn't until the central fire was down to the embers that Toke and his crew returned to their lodgings, leaving the smiling masks they had worn at the door as they were swallowed by the dark. The wolves were among the sheep.


'Find out what you can, Canute,' Ake said quietly as he watched the last of Toke's men leave the hall. 'I'm prepared to trust this Sven Halfdansson for the time being. It is *convenient* to have men to replace those they killed, not to mention those my useless son lost. Bandits in the hills, my arse,' Ake growled, spitting the words like they were poison. Their position wasn't precarious, yet, but between the men lost dealing with Váli, and those killed by Halfdan's crew, Ake had lost close to a fifth of his remaining warriors, if not more. Canute knew the mettle of the new men, having fought them first hand, but he understood his jarl's caution. Strange ships packed with warriors rarely appeared in Nordic fjords for no reason during the summer months, although they had all seen the storm. He winced involuntarily at the thought of being caught in such a tempest, hoping his own weave wouldn't lead him to a watery grave. That was no way to go.

'I will ask amongst the men and see if they know of any such man from Borg,' he said, pulling his attention back to the jarl. 'Although they have no reason to be anything other than what they say they are...' he added, letting his words trail away.

'Hmm,' Ake grunted, unconvinced. 'See what you can learn all the same.'

Canute grunted his confirmation, knowing it was easier to agree than argue. He had served his jarl long enough to read his mood, and he could see the desire for anything but blind obedience was gone this evening. The new men would be accepted only because he needed them.

The crew spent two days working tirelessly on *Fjord Uxi*. During the trips from their lodgings to the shoreline it became clear that, for the most part, the people of Vágar were forbidden from travelling further than the palisade. Toke had watched from a crack in their doorway on their first morning in the town as a small group of men and thralls were guided towards the landward gate by a group of armed guards. He recognised a few of the men from the outlying farms, and assumed they were being taken to work the land for the new lord of Vágar.

To keep from being seen by anyone they knew, Toke had the crew up and outside the walls just as the sun peaked over the horizon where they worked on the ship until dusk. Only Odd and Tolstan were excused from the work, being left behind to tend to their wounds while the rest repaired *Uxi* as best they could. She would need at least a week's repairs to get her ready to sail again but they did what they could with the time they had, shaping the new mast, caulking her hull with horsehair and tar, and replacing damaged or lost oars. It wasn't until torches were burning on the walls that Toke would lead the exhausted men back through the empty streets to their temporary home. He knew there was still a chance someone would recognise *Uxi*, so he had ordered her prow beast removed and stowed below the loose planks in the bow. On the evening of the second day, he went with Bersi to meet with the jarl, as requested.

'Have you been here before?' Ake asked as Toke stood before him. The jarl was again surrounded by several heavily armed warriors who stared impassively at Toke and Bersi.

'To this town, Lord?' Toke asked, feigning confusion.

'Yes, to my town, Vágar.'

'Never; this is the furthest north I have ever been. As I said, we had hoped to sail west and spend the season raiding.'

'Hmm,' Ake grunted, his hands fingering the pommel of his sword, the bronze glinting warmly in the fire light. Toke's eyes flashed briefly when he saw his father's blade in the man's clawing hands, but he remained silent.

'To the rear of my town is a path that leads into the hills that eventually arrives at an outcrop above us known as King's Leap. Before you reach the landing, you will find a narrow and easily defendable path that can be held by a small force. You will guard it and protect my flank from a surprise attack over the hills.'

Toke knew the exact spot the jarl was talking about. He could picture it clearly in his head, a brief stretch of path on the trail to King's Leap that was barely wide enough for three men to stand shoulder to shoulder. The path had fallen away years ago in heavy rain, leaving a vertical drop on one side, and a sheer cliff on the other. With enough food and water, they would be able to hold it indefinitely.

'This is where I would have you make your stand,' the jarl continued, oblivious to Toke's thoughts. 'I will provide you with food and water, shelter and anything else you may need to spend the summer there. Your ship will be kept safe for you here,' the jarl finished, the unspoken threat hanging in the air between them.

'If you could provide horses for our supplies and a man to guide us, we will leave at first light, Jarl Ake. We will hold the ground for you until the first snows of winter arrive, as agreed.'

'Yes, yes,' Ake said impatiently. 'You'll have whatever you need. My son will guide you into the mountains along with some of the boys from my ships who will lead the horses. It's all I can trust my son with these days,' he added to under his breath, his lip curling briefly. 'Make your preparations, Sven Halfdansson. You leave at dawn.'

***

*Sleipnir* had done everything but take flight in her rush to reach familiar waters. Yngvar had stood tirelessly at the tiller guiding her over the waves as they ate away at the hours, leaving the rest of the fleet in their wake to train and prepare. The strong wind at their back pushed them tirelessly forwards and Bjørn heard more than one of the men whisper that Thor and Óðinn were with them on their journey. When the familiar lonely islet that marked the entry to Váli's lands finally appeared on the horizon, Bjørn couldn't help but look back at Yngvar in appreciation. It seemed impossible they had travelled so fast. Letting his eyes wander across the ship, he eventually settled on Hoelun, watching her as she sat by the mast. She had her own memories of that place, and he could see the tension in her body as she watched the horizon. There was a fire in her belly that had been awoken by Jarl Ake's attack, and he couldn't help but smile at the thought. He had found himself a she-wolf, he realised, pleased with the thought.

Within an hour the orders came to run out the oars and guide the ship into shore. Few had missed the whispers of smoke leaking into the sky from the top of the hill, and more than one fingered their weapons in preparation for a fight. It wasn't until Uffe called them ignorant fools that blades slid back into their sheaths. 'White smoke means the fires are finished; black smoke would be something to worry about,' he grunted, telling them to keep their eyes on the work at hand. Yngvar drove the ship up onto the shingle and held her there while the crew unloaded their supplies. Bjørn and his small command went first, working as a vanguard with the rangers while Yngvar followed behind with the rest. As they assembled alongside the ship, Bjørn made his way to where his friend was overseeing his own men as they saw to their own equipment and supplies.

'Will she be safe in their hands?' he asked, looking at the five ship's boys who were to guide her back out to the small cove on the islet. The oldest was just fifteen. In another year, he would be old enough to raid with the men. Bjørn watched him with amusement as he ordered the other four around with a puffed-out chest. Yngvar himself had given him the seax he now wore with such obvious pride, the single-edged blade as long as his forearm. Neither *Fjord Ulf* or *Hrafn* carried ship's boys who could get in the way during the assault. All of them had sailed in *Sleipnir* and would now work as her guards until someone came for them, after the battle was won. They had plenty of food and water and they could fish and scavenge from the rocks if they needed to. They would survive.

'As safe as she would be anywhere else,' he answered briefly.

'Gnn,' Bjørn grunted before turning to face Yngvar. 'I'll see you at the cabin,' he said, holding out his hand.

'Aye, the cabin. Make sure to get the rangers out as scouts. We need to know everything we can get our hands on. Information will win this war as much as a strong right arm.'

'I will. Go well, Yngvar.'

'And you, Bjørn,' Yngvar said, taking his arm and gripping hard in the warrior's grip. 'I'll see you soon.'

'Aye.' Bjørn nodded, allowing a slight smile to cross his face before turning and making his way along the shingle, moving easily in his armour as he walked towards his waiting men. Erik's words bounced around in his head as he walked, but he refused to let them cloud his excitement.

'With me,' he grunted as he took up his shield and bundle of supplies and threw them over his shoulder. Armed and armoured as he was, it was a heavy burden to carry, but he carried it easily after a lifetime of building and honing his muscles. 'Uffe, take your rangers and scout ahead. We're making for the hunting cabin.'

Uffe nodded once before turning and whistling to his own men to get their attention. The rangers responded instantly, falling into a loose skirmish formation behind their grizzled leader as he began dogtrotting up the path. All had their bows strung and ready with arrows on the strings.

Bjørn watched them for a few moments, unsurprised to see Hoelun among them as they moved quickly up the well-worn path, before turning and giving the order for his own men to march. There was nothing silent about their progress and the air was soon filled with the ringing of helmets and shields bumping together, and the repetitive *stomp stomp stomp* of their leather boots as they struck the dirt path. It was the sounds of war, and Bjørn felt his blood begin to flow in excited anticipation as they made their way up the slope. He stole a glance to his left and saw his excitement mirrored on Guttorm and Arne's smiling faces, the expressions a stark contrast to the stoic indifference Red Orm and Bjarni showed. Bjørn just hoped that Arne could keep up with his injury, but for now he looked willing.

They were over halfway up the hill when Sindri came jogging back down the slope, his bow held low. At the sight of him, Bjørn gave orders for the men to unhook their shields and form a small skjaldborg across the path. He could see Yngvar's men doing the same, forming a circular wall of shields around the front of *Sleipnir*, ready to protect her.

'There's been a fight here, only a few days ago,' Sindri said as he drew closer. 'Come,' he added, before turning and walking back up the path.

Remaining in formation, the small group made their way up to the top of the slope, struggling to keep pace with the lightly armed archer. As they neared the top, Bjørn began noticing the tracks, and the way they folded out of the grass on either side. Perhaps thirty or forty men had come this way, and recently. Gritting his teeth, he tightened his grip on his sword hilt and continued up the path.

It was the smell that revealed the bodies first, filling the air with the bittersweet scent of putrefying flesh and voided bowels. It didn't take long after that for the corpses to come into sight; warriors clad in iron rings and homespun jerkins left to rot in the sun while their bodies fed the crows. More than one wore a brynja, he noted as he moved closer, fighting the urge to hold

338

his nose and defend it from the beating it was taking. A few of the younger warriors were going green in the face, and he moved fast to stop any from becoming unmanned. He gave four of them the grisly job of stripping the dead of their war gear and piling it all by the entrance of the settlement, away from the bodies. As the chosen men moved to follow the command, he ordered the rest to guard their surroundings, sending three men to either side of the walls to watch the distant forest. He doubted anyone would attack them given how old the bodies were, but he wasn't taking any chances. Satisfied, he turned and followed Uffe through the burned-out gates.

He saw the bodies almost as soon as he stepped through the gates, being forced to step over a man clad in burnished iron rings who lay face up in a pool of dried blood, his throat pierced by an arrow. Beside him lay another whose throat had been ripped open, and he ducked back through the gate quickly, calling to Guttorm not to miss the dead inside. He tried to read the battle as best he could as he returned to Uffe. By his count, at least eighteen warriors had been left to rot in the sun, all of them facing towards the fjord but none facing the other way. Either the victors had carried their dead with them, or there hadn't been any, but that didn't explain why they didn't loot the corpses. They had left behind a hoard in weapons and armour, whoever they were.

'Here,' Uffe grunted, breaking through his thoughts. He was holding a gleaming brynja and a good sword with rune-carved hilt, carrying the weight easily.

'His?' he asked questioningly as he nodded towards one of the bodies.

'I found them hidden over there,' Uffe replied, pointing towards one of the burned buildings. 'They'd been abandoned. There was no body.'

'Hmm,' Bjørn grunted, processing the information. 'So, we have defeated men who lie unlooted, an enemy with no dead, and a warrior's war gear hidden or abandoned.'

Uffe blew air through his nose but said nothing as he too looked over Váli's burned out home. They let the silence stretch as they surveyed the ground together.

'It doesn't matter,' Bjørn said finally. 'We need to keep moving, and whoever was here is long gone. Send Sindri, Galti and Uffi along the path and into the forest to scout ahead with Hoelun; she's been there most recently. You go with them.'

Uffe handed him the iron shirt and sword with a brief nod before leaving to give his orders.

Bjørn followed him through the ruined gates in time to watch Arne deposit a pair of spears on the growing pile of war gear. Following his friend's example, he added the brynja to the pile, listening to the metal sing as it slid across the rest of the equipment before coming to rest against a pair of axes. He kept a grip on the sword for the time being, ignoring the hungry eyes of his men as they stared at the unimaginable wealth before them.

'It seems that the Allfather has been watching our struggles, and decided to take pity on us,' he began, drawing their reluctant eyes away from the pile. Only Red Orm and Bjarni seemed uninterested in the wealth, their own war gear already more than what most men could hope to own in a lifetime. 'I do not know for how long you will fight for me,' he continued, 'but while you do, I will see you properly equipped. Red Orm, Bjarni, step forward,' he said.

'*Bind them to you, Bjørn,*' he heard his father say in his head, the words coming unbidden as the grizzled warriors stepped forward from the ranks.

'You accepted me when I was green on the oars and unknown in the fleet. You took me in as a friend and showed me the ropes and you've remained loyal to that friendship since the day we left our homes, knowing there was no promise of reward. If you would have anything from my hand, take it now,' he finished, nodding to the pile.

Bowing their heads briefly, the two men stepped across the dry ground and began inspecting the equipment. With ease Bjørn could only wonder at, Bjarni wrestled his brynja from his shoulders and dumped it on the pile, replacing it with one made from smaller rings, promising greater protection. Red Orm too took a new brynja, leaving the damaged one on the pile. Beyond that, neither man took anything more.

'Thank you, Bjørn Eriksson,' they said seriously before moving to stand aside from the main group to watch what would happen next. They too could see the hunger in the eyes of the young warriors and were amused by it. Unlike Bjørn and his brothers, neither Bjarni or Red Orm had been born into wealth, and both had begun their journey on the whale road as fresh-faced farm boys like those they stood watching. Through spit and blood, they had risen in Erik's fleet to stand where they stood now, earning and looting their war gear along the way. They knew well the hunger that would be feeding the young men standing there, waiting with thinly veiled patience.

'Guttorm. To you, too, I owe a debt,' Bjørn continued. 'You saved my life once, and an old sword does little to repay it. Take what you desire, along with this,' he said, handing across the sword Uffe had found. 'I think you'll find this a much finer blade.'

He allowed a smile to creep across his face at his friend's sudden speechlessness as he accepted the blade. More than one of those watching eyed the sword enviously as it glinted in the sunlight.

'Thank you, Bjørn,' he said as he slid the new sword into the sheath at his hip and dropped the old one on the pile.

'Take what you will,' Bjørn said again, his smile growing as he motioned towards the gleaming pile. He watched happily as his friend selected a shining brynja and helmet from the pile, as well as a new axe and knife. One or two of the men groaned as pieces they had hoped to claim were taken by Guttorm, but Bjørn didn't let the thought trouble him. He had enough here to equip each and every man under his command as if they were húskarlar, but proven loyalty would be rewarded first and send a message to the rest. Secretly, he also hoped that the equipment would boost their confidence in the fighting ahead.

Satisfied, Guttorm nodded and moved to stand next to Red Orm and Bjarni, asking them to help him into the heavy iron shirt while Bjørn turned his attention back to the rest of his men.

'Take what you desire, but hear this before you do,' he said, holding his hands up to stop them as they began to rush forward towards the pile. 'There will be no debate or argument over any piece of equipment. Do not fight over anything; not sword nor knife, nor axe nor armour. If I hear a dispute, both men shall go without. Do not test me on this,' he said seriously.

The remaining men nodded in unison before moving hungrily to the pile, quickly filling the air with the ringing of metal as men began pulling swords and axes from the pile, or helping each other into iron-ringed shirts.

Red Orm and Bjarni shared a look of approval as they watched their young leader move back to the lip of the hill to watch the ship below. Bjørn was proving himself a man to follow, and they had both discussed their position as part of his small troop. They were proud to serve under the jarl's youngest son.

The men were still holding formation around *Sleipnir*, and Bjørn moved back into their sightline and raised his shield to give the all-clear. At his signal, the crew shifted out of formation and continued their preparations while Bjørn returned to his own men to find all but two of his men dressed in their new armour. He was about to comment before they too fell into line, where they helped each other into their new iron shirts. As the men dressed, he spied Uffe moving back through the burned-out farm, his restless eyes flicking over the ranks of newly equipped men. 'Guttorm,' Bjørn said quickly, 'run down the hill and tell Yngvar there are weapons and armour here waiting for them. There is no need for them to go to waste. I will leave Uffe here to guide you in.'

'Yes, Lord,' the young man grunted before turning and sprinting down the hill, his steps heavier with the armour he now carried.

'They at least look the part,' Uffe said gruffly as he drew near, his attention switching from the men to Bjørn. 'There is nothing on the forest path. I have sent Sindri ahead into the woods with Galti. Uffi is waiting at the edge of the forest with Hoelun and the rest of the troop.'

'Good, I'll lead the men in. You wait here for Guttorm, then catch up with us. Take what you want from the pile, and anything for your men,' he added, motioning to the weapons. 'Guttorm can help you carry them.'

'Very well.' Uffe nodded before moving to examine the pile of plunder. Bjørn watched the wolf tattoos on Uffe's arms writhe as he selected an axe from the pile, imagining the men who had died under the wolves' snarling gazes.

Pulling his thoughts back to the mission at hand, Bjørn gave the order to march as he walked to the front of his small *hirð*, allowing himself a small smile at the sound of jingling armour behind him. One or two glanced back at the abandoned wealth behind them, but none complained.

They found Uffi and Hoelun at the edge of the forest, and Bjørn and his men followed the pair further into the woods to connect with Galti and Sindri. The rest of the rangers were sent out in a screen on either flank to watch for unwanted visitors. Overhead, the arms of trees touched gently like long-lost lovers, surrounding them with a hushed silence that dampened the sounds of their passage. The sun disappeared from view after just a few steps as they were swallowed by the deepening darkness of the forest, and surrounded by its ancient smells. To Bjørn's ears, their footsteps still sounded impossibly loud, but he knew there was little risk of them being noticed with his screen of rangers shielding them. Uffe's men could move like smoke when they needed to, and they wouldn't be caught unawares by any of Ake's men lurking in the woods.

It didn't take long for Guttorm and Uffe to catch up with the main group, but the squat ranger only stayed long enough to confer with Bjørn before he too disappeared down the trail, following in Uffi's barely visible footsteps. Bjørn found himself relaxing into the silence as they marched, and he allowed his thoughts to drift as he walked. He kept part of his mind alert for danger, but another part he let wander over everything that had happened. It seemed impossible that in just a few weeks, Toke and the whole crew of *Uxi* had disappeared without a trace, that their home had been captured by Jarl Ake, and that they had barely managed to leave the familiar waters of home.

It was the smell of smoke and the sharp angle of the sun's rays flickering through the canopy above that brought him back from his daydreaming. He carefully drew an arrow and placed it on his bowstring, motioning for his men to slow their pace. Arne moved forward to stand alongside Bjørn with his own bow while Red Orm and Bjarni ordered the rest of the men into a small skjaldborg behind them.

'On me, *quietly,*' Bjørn hissed before slowly edging forward through the growing dark as the sun edged towards the west. They were deep in the forest now, and their visibility was greatly diminished by the ancient tree trunks and thick foliage that littered the forest floor. There was no sign of the rangers, but occasionally snatches of quiet laughter or conversation would filter through the trees. Hissing quietly to get Arne's attention, he motioned for him to move off the path to the left and walk parallel to the main group while he did the same on the right. Reading his thoughts, Bjarni moved forward to assume the lead. Bjørn slipped amongst the trees and moved with his men. The deeper woods would better hide him and Arne from any enemies, and allow them to protect the flanks with arrows if they were attacked by a larger force.

They had barely gone ten paces when he suddenly realised his mistake. Arne was still injured and wouldn't be able to fire his bow quickly or well. The blood was roaring in his ears as he turned to whisper a hushed order for Red Orm to guard the left flank, but he calmed just as quickly. Orm was already there, having realised the danger. His father and Yngvar had given him good men to guide him, and Bjørn found himself quietly thanking Red Orm for his foresight even as he kicked himself for not realising the mistake sooner.

Forcing the thoughts from his head, he opened his mouth slightly to improve his hearing, listening for the telltale clink of armour or tread of leather boots. After another few steps, he felt a tingling experience on the back of his neck, as if someone was standing near him, watching. Without warning, he dropped to one knee and spun in an explosion of movement, pulling his arrow back to his cheek as he moved. Just as he was about to release, he caught sight of an arrow pointing directly at his own face, staying his hand.

'You should be more careful, Bjørn Eriksson,' Uffe whispered, his face breaking into a mischievous grin. 'Scouts are mortal men, too. They could easily have been killed, leaving you deaf and blind to the dangers lurking in the forest.'

'Gnn,' Bjørn grunted, accepting the lesson as he eased his bow string back and climbed to his feet.

Chuckling, Uffe motioned for him to follow him back to the rough path. Bjarni saw the movement and quickly spun on his heel, crouching behind his shield with a bellowed order for the rest of the men to follow suit. Bjørn winced at the untidy line they struggled to form, realising that he would have to keep training them when they stopped each night if they had any chance of surviving the fighting ahead.

'We've made camp by a stream a little way into the forest,' Uffe said. 'This way.'

Bjørn grunted and walked back to his men, ordering them out of the lines before turning and following Uffe towards the camp.

'Don't shed your gear when we get to camp,' Bjørn said as they marched, raising his voice to be heard over their footsteps. 'We've got work to do.'

# Chapter 25

Bjørn worked his men to the bone when they reached the small camp. Splitting in two groups of five, they spent over two hours practicing charging and breaking shield walls and retreating in formation. They were too close to Vágar to risk injuries, so they had fought with sheathed blades, the weight allowing them to become used to their weapons without the risk that came from swinging swords at one another. All the same, more than once a man had been struck a hard blow that would be black and blue come sun up. Bjørn only called an end to the exercise when the light failed completely and the cries of pain became too regular to continue. The men dropped their weapons and shields with a collective sigh of relief when the order to stop finally came, exchanging them for waterskins filled in the nearby stream. For a while after, the air was filled with the sounds of slushing water and heavy breathing, and the gentle crackle of the fire.

The camp was far enough into the woods that they had lost sight of the trail completely. Measuring roughly twenty steps by thirty on one side of the stream, and twenty by ten on the other, there was plenty of room for them to train and sleep, with little chance of their being spotted by passing eyes, although guards would still be set throughout the night. Uffi had even found a stump of wood that they placed in the small stream to act as a stepping-stone so they could cross without getting their boots wet.

Sindri had disappeared almost as soon as Bjørn and his men arrived, vanishing into the woods with his quiver and bow. He had returned partway through the drills with a young doe over his shoulders, the neck still dribbling blood. While Bjørn and his men trained, the rangers and Hoelun dressed and quartered the small deer and set it to cook over the flames while others stood guard around the perimeter. Uffe's men knew their business; they didn't need more practice.

By the time they had drunk their fill and their breathing had begun to even out, the small clearing was filled with the scent of roasting meat. Many of them dug hungrily into the supplies they had carried with them while they waited, their hunger getting the better of them after their march and training.

*'True leadership is putting others' needs before your own, Bjørn,'* he heard his father

345

say in his head. Ignoring his own gnawing hunger and exhaustion, he dug a slice of dried meat from his pack before joining Galti where he was trimming thin saplings by the cooking fire. Together, they set about creating a small pyramid out of the wooden staves before tying shorter lengths of green wood horizontally across them at intervals. They used their axes to cut pine boughs from the surrounding trees which they used to cover the top two thirds of the structure, the smell of fresh pine sap mingling with the scents of cooking meat and wood smoke. By the fire, Uffi had seen what they were doing and was working to trim thinner staves of green wood that he slid thin strips of meat onto. Patiently, the three worked to fill the makeshift smoker with the loaded skewers, the strips of red flesh shimmering in the flickering light. Finally, Bjørn dug up the earth beneath the meat, using the dirt to make a small wall around the exposed area before filling the space with embers and fresh pine boughs. The smoke would work to preserve the meat through the night and by morning, it would be smoked and dried, supplementing their limited rations.

Only once this was done did Bjørn accept a steak of roasted venison from Uffe, wrapped in the last of the bread they had carried with them. He felt the meal replenish his energy reserves and he realised how exhausted and hungry he was as he sank gratefully next to the fire to eat, watching the men around him. Many of the youngest were trying and failing to hide their excitement at their new war gear, and more than one was running a whetstone across their new weapons under the watchful eyes of Bjarni and Orm. Never in their wildest dreams would they have imagined carrying such equipment, and Bjørn knew he had bound them to him with his generosity. Sighing, he stood and crossed the small camp to sit next to Uffe. 'We made good progress,' he said, sitting next to the ranger and earning a grunt for his troubles. Uffe was lost in concentration as he sharpened his arrow heads. 'I will set my men to watch through the night,' Bjørn continued unperturbed. 'Your men can guard tomorrow. They have more experience and I would prefer to have them keep watch the closer we get to home.'

Uffe stopped working briefly to consider the suggestion. Bjørn knew the logic was sound. Apart from Bjarni and Red Orm, none of his men, including himself, had campaigned before. The rangers on the other hand were well versed in guarding Erik's borders and camps. After a few moments, Uffe grunted his confirmation and went back to his arrows, spitting on his stone occasionally as he worked the iron heads.

Leaving Uffe to his task, Bjørn called Guttorm, Bjarni and Red Orm to him as he walked across the small camp, using Uffi's stump to cross the stream

346

to the smaller clearing on the opposite bank. The three men came quickly, stepping on the wooden stump to keep their boots dry as they crossed the water. Only Guttorm still wore his armour, and the older men smiled knowingly to each other at the sight.

'We made good progress today,' Red Orm said, stuffing a piece of meat into his mouth.

Bjarni nodded in agreement.

'Aye, but the men need more work,' Bjørn said. 'New weapons and armour will only get them so far when we face Ake's men.'

'There's not much we can do in just a few evenings,' Bjarni said seriously. 'We'll give them the best instruction we can, but learning to fight in a skjaldborg, clad in iron, isn't something they can learn with just a few evenings' practice, Bjørn. The best option is for us to continue training them to fight as a cohesive unit, and to stay together during the fighting. It's their best chance of survival,' he added.

'Yngvar's men will also support us in the assault,' said Red Orm.

'I agree,' Bjørn said. 'We'll do the same tomorrow evening and focus on fighting together, as you say Bjarni.'

'It is harder than I expected,' Guttorm admitted awkwardly, lifting his iron-clad arm as he spoke.

'You'll get used to it, lad,' Red Orm said, giving him a friendly nudge.

'Gnn,' Guttorm grunted, his expression unsure.

'You will,' Bjørn said, eyeing his friend. 'We will train more tomorrow, you will become used to the weight, as will I,' he said, smiling meaningfully at his friend. In truth, Bjørn was already familiar with the weight of a brynja, having learned how to fight wearing the heavy iron ringed shirts from Yngvar.

'Our men will keep watch this evening,' Bjørn said, changing topic. 'Guttorm, you and one other will take the first shift. In two hours, wake Red Orm and another man, and then two hours after that, Bjarni with another. I will go last with Arne and remain until dawn.'

'Very good,' Bjarni grunted, speaking for the others. Beside him, Orm nodded his agreement, his red eye catching the light.

'Let's get to it, then,' Bjørn said, rising to his feet and making his way back across the stream towards the camp fire where his men were lounging and eating the last of their meal. Some were already asleep by the looks of it.

'All right, lads. Let's get some sleep. If you're woken to take a watch, do it quietly, and make sure to add embers to the smoker and logs to the fire.'

Around him, the air filled with grunts of acknowledgement as men began rolling out their sleeping sacks, laying out cloaks and furs, or anything else they'd brought with them to make the evenings more comfortable. Bjørn kicked himself silently for leaving his own sleeping sack on board *Sleipnir* before shrugging and laying down on his cloak by the fire. He would survive.

'How did Red Orm get his name?' Arne asked quietly as he walked alongside Bjørn. It was their turn on watch, and the only sounds to disturb the night's silence was the gentle crunch of their steps and the occasional sound of a creature hidden among the trees, or the snores of their companions. The faintest hint of light was leaking through the woods around them, and they would soon have to wake the men to continue their march.

'From the stories I've heard, it happened when he was very young, back when my grandfather was jarl,' Bjørn answered without breaking his stride, his eyes watching the forest around them. 'Raiders came out of the fjord and attacked Vágar while most of the men were away on the whale road. This was before the walls were built, or a garrison created. The only people left behind to defend against the raiders were grizzled greybeards too old to stand in the shield wall, or beardless boys who were too young. Still, they put up a fierce resistance and ultimately beat the raiders back, but during the fighting young Orm took a nasty wound. The way I heard it, he was trying to slash his knife across a fleeing man's heels and earned a shield rim to the eye for his efforts. If you look closely next time you speak to him, you can see the faded scars where it split the skin. Luckily, his eye survived undamaged, but it has been red ever since,' Bjørn said, finishing the story.

'How old was he?' Arne asked, noticing they had made a full circuit of the camp while Bjørn spoke.

'Eight or nine, maybe ten?' Bjørn answered. 'Old enough that the name stuck,' he added. In the time they had been speaking, the wolf dawn that had begun to light the sky had been replaced by the first true light of day.

'I hope I can earn a by-name for myself one day,' Arne said hopefully, his voice quiet.

'I think we all hope for that,' Bjørn agreed, turning his head briefly to face his friend. 'It's a worthy goal, but for now we have to settle with waking the men.'

Nodding, Arne followed his lead and began moving amongst the sleeping figures, nudging them into the day with their boots or the butts of their spears.

Uffe was already awake and was busy stirring the embers back to life with Galti, banking the glowing coals with fresh wood. Both men already had pots of porridge on the coals for their breakfast, beating the rest of the men to the task. Following their example, Bjørn added a handful of barley and water to his own pot and placed it in the coals before moving to pull apart the smoker. Guttorm rose to help him and together they removed the thick covering of pine branches to reveal the darkened and shrivelled strips of smoked meat beneath. They quickly cleared all but two of the branches of their burdens, stowing the strips of meat in a small sack. The rest they brought to the fire for men to add to their day rations. Around them, the sounds of men stretching, farting, and groaning filled the air as they banished sleep from their bodies. Bjørn wanted to reach the hunting cabin by day's end and secure it for when Yngvar joined him with the rest of the crew. He knew it was ambitious, but if they arrived early enough he planned to send a few of the rangers ahead to scout the way to King's Leap.

'We leave in twenty,' Bjørn shouted across the clearing, kicking the slower among them into action as they realised, they needed to cook, eat, and stow their kit quickly. 'I want waterskins filled, the fire doused and all of you fed by the time we break camp. Get to it.'

The men started moving as if they'd been struck, setting food to cook or disappearing into the undergrowth to relieve themselves while others stowed bedding and donned their armour. Around him, the bluster of his men couldn't hide the sounds of the forest as it woke from its slumber and he smiled at the sounds as he began spooning hot porridge into his mouth.

\*\*\*

'We leave in twenty,' Toke said into the darkness, the sounds of his men as they prepared to march amplified in the closed space of the byre. The work on *Uxi* had been exhausting, and he was as reluctant as the rest of them to leave their precious ship in Ake's hands, but there was nothing for it. The march would be a challenge for Tolstan and Odd, but Toke wouldn't risk leaving them behind where they could be recognised. He had already decided that if they couldn't keep up, he would order them to ride the pack horses, and the rest of them could carry the supplies themselves. Both men were healing well and Odd had argued against the offer of a horse, swearing he could make the climb. Toke had held his hands up and accepted it, admiring Odd's

349

determination and pride, but he also knew the climb they faced today. The option was there if he needed it.

'Steinar will be here soon to guide us up the trail. Give no clue to whoever he has with him that you already know the way,' he added, lowering his voice to a whisper. 'We've come too far now to risk that.'

He took the sudden mixture of grunts and the jingling of iron as nodded agreement. Satisfied, he made the final preparations to his own gear, making sure his sword was properly secured and supporting the weight of the unfamiliar brynja. After Halfdan's death, Bersi had pushed Toke to take his armour, arguing that he would need it more than Halfdan in the weeks ahead. Initially Toke had argued against the idea, but Bersi had convinced him in the end. He still felt slightly uncomfortable wearing it, but he reasoned that Halfdan wouldn't want it to go to waste.

Toke and Bersi had seen to the supplies the night before with Bergathor, ensuring they had everything they would need to last them a week in the hills until Ake sent the next delivery. With their departure drawing closer, Toke felt a weight shift from his shoulders. It had been hard keeping the men from being seen, and from searching out their families, and he was relieved to finally be putting the town behind them.

'Toke,' Odd whispered from the door. 'There are men coming.'

He crossed the byre with his hand ready on his sword, his actions mimicked by the men around him. Odd moved aside so that Toke could put his eye to the small peep hole they had drilled into the wood and saw Steinar approaching the byre with several ship's boys in tow.

Toke watched as he drew near, quietly removing the locking bar from the door as he waited patiently for them to arrive. He saw Steinar stop and take a deep breath, ignoring the questioning eyes of the boys as he paused. Toke took a pleasure in the internal conflict that took place on Steinar's face as he prepared himself to knock. He *knew* they were Erik's men, but he was stuck in a lie and his cowardice was keeping him quiet. Toke had learned from Ake how his son had returned with stories of bandits in the hills who had killed his men, and how he had barely managed to get away with his life. Doubtless, Steinar was eager to see Toke and his men removed from the town as quickly as possible.

Unaware that he was being watched, Steinar took a deep breath to prepare himself before stepping closer to the door and raising his hand to knock. Toke waited for his hand to fall before pulling back sharply on the door and causing

Steinar to stumble on the threshold. He hid his smile at the embarrassment that flashed across the other man's face, instead staring into his eyes and waiting for him to speak. The ship's boys Steinar had brought with him were less practiced at hiding their emotions however, and several of them chuckled at the sight. Toke knew there was a danger in toying with Steinar, but he didn't care. He wanted to humiliate the man as much as possible and make it clear that Toke *knew* he was a coward and a liar.

Steinar stared daggers at Toke as he righted himself awkwardly, his voice coming out as a sneer when he spoke. 'Are you ready yet, *Sven Halfdansson*?'

'Aye, we're ready. We're glad to have such an experienced guide to lead us up the trail. Your father mentioned your *adventures* up that way and we wouldn't want to run into any trouble ourselves,' Toke said with an innocent smile, his teeth flashing white in the early light.

Anger and shame flashed across Steinar's face and Toke watched with amusement as he fought to bring his emotions under control. 'We've had the horses packed and they are ready at the landward gate. Follow me,' Steinar said in a clipped tone before turning and walking away, the smirking ship's boys dogging his footsteps.

Toke laughed quietly as he turned to pick up his kit, his expression mirrored on the faces of his men as he motioned for them to follow him through the open door. They quickly fell into formation behind him, walking side by side in two ranks as they made their way through the sleeping town. More than one looked hopefully towards their homes, hoping to catch a glimpse of a loved one as they passed. Toke couldn't begrudge them that, but he had to be strong, and he was just about to give the order to stop them looking around when Bersi's rough voice pierced the silence. 'Eyes forward,' he growled from the rear, his tone understanding but irrefutable. Toke silently thanked him even as his own thoughts flew to his mother and Signy for the hundredth time. He had no idea of their fate, or that of Arleigh's, and the lack of information was eating away at him. Sighing, he pulled himself back from the edge before he sunk too deeply into the morass of uncertainty, instead focusing his attention on the way ahead. They had almost made it out of the town, and he couldn't risk a lapse in his caution now. He had formed his plan after hearing their orders from Ake, and now knew exactly what he and his men must do, even though it would likely end with them travelling to Valhöll together. They had all seen Ake's ships with their prow beasts and shields removed, lazily tied to the shore and made to look more like traders than raiders. Vágar was a popular trading port, and Toke knew exactly what his father would see as they rowed quietly up the fjord when they came home. Their only chance of surviving the trap was for Toke and his men to attack and draw some of Ake's men away from the fjord, giving Erik a chance to fight his way into the settlement while Ake was distracted, but the timing had to be perfect. Bergathor and Odd had already offered to camp at King's Leap and watch for the returning fleet. Provided they weren't recognised between now and leaving Vágar, they had a chance, however small.

As they neared the stables, Toke heard the first whicker of a horse and the jingle of harnesses. They were close, and the sounds set his heart pumping in anticipation. He could see the stable building towering over the structures either side of it and he felt hope stir that his father's horses had survived the fighting, and that they hadn't been eaten or sacrificed. He could only imagine what Erik would say if Steinar had decided to use his prized horses as beasts of burden.

The sun crested the horizon as they rounded the corner, and Toke was greeted with the sight of six ponies packed and ready to carry them high above the town towards King's Leap. He released the breath he had been holding as he saw there was no trap or armed party waiting to see them off. He had half expected Ake to betray them, but the only other people there were two more boys who had been left to ready the ponies. Toke didn't break his stride when Steinar stopped, instead marching straight past and on towards the wall where two of Ake's hirðsmen were opening the gate. Steinar had no choice but to run ignobly to catch up, or risk losing face by letting Toke take the lead. The boys quickly pulled the ponies into file and took up position behind the warriors. Tolstan was already sweating from the exertion and the wound on his side, and Toke indicated for Bersi to get the boy onto one of the mounts. As he passed through the gate, Steinar came to walk sullenly alongside him, his frustration tangible. Toke could feel the slowly-building fury radiating from the man like heat from a forge, bringing his father's advice to mind as he studied the man discreetly. *'Never let another man see your weakness, your frustration, your anger. Bury the emotions deep and hide them from the world, otherwise they will own you and you will lose everything.'* Clearly Steinar hadn't benefited from such sage advice. 'Is something wrong?' Toke asked innocently without turning as they walked along the well-trodden path.

Beside him Steinar spat angrily on the ground beside him before marching meaningfully ahead of the group to lead the way towards the forest. They had

352

a few hours yet to go, and he planned to pass the time chipping away at Steinar as they went.

***

Bjørn led his men along the forest path as the sun continued its tireless passage across the sky, every step taking them further away from Váli's land and *Sleipnir*, and closer to home. The familiar path brought nostalgic memories of riding the same route with Hoelun and Toke, and he lost himself to the past for a while as they walked. He felt like a completely different person to the boy who had travelled these paths to collect livestock for his father. Since then he had killed and led men, lain in ambush, and sailed the whale road. And now he was leading men to war.

A cough from behind pulled him back from his thoughts and he turned his attention to their current mission, and the battle ahead. He had begun trying to view it as a raid, as if they were attacking a town in Frankia or England rather than liberating his home. Otherwise, he risked becoming bogged down in a mire of emotions. He did the same with Toke. His brother was tough and resourceful, as was Halfdan, and he was confident that they had survived the storm and would find their way to safety, but he couldn't afford to dwell on *Uxi's* fate until Ake was defeated.

Part of his brain was constantly alert as they walked under the ancient trees, and he didn't miss the semi-fresh tracks that marked the trail they were following. There were too many to ignore and he had ordered the men to march in full armour and keep their weapons close to hand as they went. From what he could see, the tracks were several days old at least and were softening on the edges, but he still walked with his bow strung and ready, and it didn't hurt to keep the men alert.

A pair of ravens had followed them for a time, flying from tree to tree as they moved through the silent forest and more than one of the men had commented that Óðinn was watching their progress. Bjørn had commented his agreement, although secretly he thought it was more likely that the birds had picked up the scent of the deer's legs Bjarni and Sweyn were carrying from the night before. Still, it didn't hurt to have the men thinking that Huginn and Muninn would share their story with the Allfather. Other than the two ravens, their trek was uneventful. At one point some of the younger warriors claimed they heard wolves howling in the distance, but Bjørn ignored them. Men

353

always spoke of wolves in the lands around their home, but no one alive could claim to have actually seen them. Bjørn thought they were more likely stories that had been thought up to frighten children in the dead of winter to stop them from wandering off in the dark.

The sun was setting by the time they arrived at the cabin, the fire already bursting into life as the waiting rangers patiently fed dried wood into the flames. Bjørn was transported back in time as he walked into the clearing, remembering his first real fight, and the time spent with his brothers hunting and drinking together. None of them could have predicted the changes that would be wrought in their lives in just a few weeks. Shaking his head to banish the memory he called Uffe, Bjarni and Red Orm to him while the rest of his men dropped their packs and began to relax, taking deep pulls from their waterskins or pulling tafl board from their packs.

'Uffe, I want eyes on Vágar as soon as possible. Send Sindri and Uffi further down the track towards King's Leap so we can get an idea of what Jarl Ake has done since taking control.'

'Aye. I'll go with them,' Uffe said.

'Very well, go now while there's still light,' Bjørn said.

Uffe nodded to Bjørn and the others before standing and leaving the small conference.

'As for the rest of us,' he said, turning back to Bjarni and Red Orm, 'we need to keep working the men. Get them up and training.'

'Aye, Bjørn,' they said together before moving away to begin organising the warriors into groups, ignoring the groans and dirty looks that were shot their way. Bjørn stifled a laugh when Bjarni silenced the protests with a look, the younger warriors wilting under his cold, flint-like eyes.

Seeing that Bjarni and Orm had everything under control for the time being, he crossed the ground to where Galti and Hoelun were sitting and talking quietly, interrupting them to address the ranger. 'I need you to go back down the path and connect with Yngvar's scouts. Tell them that the way forward is clear.'

Galti rose smoothly without a trace of the exhaustion. 'Would you have me return here afterwards?'

'Aye, but rest with them for a few hours first. We won't be going much further tomorrow.'

Nodding once, Galti took up his bow and disappeared back the way they had come without a backwards glance.

Without meaning to, Bjørn realised he had bought himself a few precious moments alone with Hoelun, the first he'd had since before the fleet set sail.

'I got you something,' he said awkwardly, suddenly nervous.

'Oh aye?' she said coyly, tilting her head to one side so her hair slid off her shoulder and exposed the smooth skin of her neck. 'A pretty ring, or a brooch of gold?' she asked with a teasing smile.

'Aye.' He smiled, growing excited as he shrugged off his pack. 'Something like that.'

Bjørn saw her eyes widen briefly as he withdrew a small, beautifully engraved axe from his pack, handing it to her haft first. He had taken it from the abandoned weapons they had found, thinking it would be perfect for her shorter reach, should anyone come too close to her. The axehead was razor sharp and light as a feather, with a hooked beak and a stylised wolf etched into the blade.

'I took it from the bodies we found,' he said lamely, suddenly feeling foolish for offering such a gift. It was hardly a sign of affection to give a woman an axe and he wished he'd thought to find a ring or brooch to give her instead, as she'd said.

To his pleasure and surprise, Hoelun's eyes began to water slightly as she held the weapon, studying the curling patterns that flowed across the blade. It was a weapon fit for one of his father's húskarlar, hardly something for a thrall to carry, yet Bjørn had made it clear that Hoelun was under his protection. She would be safe carrying it, and it comforted him to know she could defend herself.

Still smiling, she drew her own axe from her belt and buried it in the wood beside her, abandoning it. 'Thank you,' she said as she ran her thumb over the engravings once more before sliding it into the vacated loop on her belt, alongside her seax. 'I will treasure it,' she added before kissing him quickly.

Bjørn smiled, reaching out to cup her cheek briefly in the palm of his hand before groaning audibly. The sound of men fighting was beginning to fill the once-quiet camp and he knew he couldn't be seen to sit and talk with a woman while his men swung their swords and stabbed their spears.

'Something to keep you safe.' He grinned, before taking up his own sword and shield and walking across to the small group to take his place in the centre of Bjarni's skjaldborg. Several of the men teased him good naturedly as he approached and he laughed easily with them.

'All right, you laggards, that's enough. Shields up!' he called as he hunkered down behind his shield. 'Winners eat first,' he called before giving the order to attack and throwing himself against the *enemy* line, filling the air with the sounds of battle.

Hoelun watched him joke easily with his men as she ran her thumb over the axe at her hip, considering her own future. She only drew her attention away from the tall handsome warrior when a spark cracked from the fire and landed on her arm, scalding her.

Uffe, Sindri and Uffi moved quickly along the well-trodden path, their feet barely touching the ground as they ran back to Bjørn. They had made good time in reaching King's Leap, and the sight of Vágar far below had stilled their breath when they finally arrived. The invaders' ships rested arrogantly on the shore as if they hadn't a care in the world, and Sindri couldn't resist commenting on the careless way they had been secured. Uffe had found himself unconsciously clenching his fists as he looked down on their home, relishing the battle to come even as he felt the frustration of being so close yet out of reach. They had remained at the clearing long enough to check the coals of a long dead fire and learn what they could from their position on the cliffs. It wasn't easy, but from the ships alone they could roughly estimate the number of men under Ake's command. The numbers didn't match what they had heard from Arleigh and Turid, but it was entirely possible that they had missed a ship in their hurry to escape. From what he could see, there were six ships moored on the quiet shoreline. Two he assumed were Erik's, *Jörmungandr* and *Fjord Elg*, resting where they always did, which suggested the four unfamiliar vessels were Ake's. All told, he could have brought anywhere from one-hundred-and-eighty to two-hundred warriors with him to Vágar, if not more. It was more than enough to compete with the hundred-and-thirty-something Erik could bring. Their only hope was surprise, and Uffe redoubled his efforts to learn everything he could for Bjørn, and Yngvar. Uffe measured the sun's passing with two sticks stuck in the ground, and when the shadow of the first hit the second, he gave the order for them to return to the forest, and Bjørn. As they were turning to leave, Uffe thought he heard the sound of horses' harnesses carried on the wind. A quick glance at Sindri and Uffi showed they had heard it as well and he returned his gaze to the trail that led to Vágar, opening his mouth slightly to improve his hearing. Behind him, he heard the gentle click of wood as Sindri and Uffi fitted arrows to their bows.

After a few heartbeats they heard the sound again, the jingle of harnesses joined by horses whinnying to one another. Without wasting any time Uffe waved his hand to get Uffi's attention, motioning for him to return the way they had come to warn Bjørn while he and Sindri sank into the forest to watch and wait.

Uffe could hear them loudly now, the chorus of armoured footsteps and horses hooves silencing the forest around them. He clicked once in the back of his throat to get Sindri's attention before motioning towards a deep green bush growing on the far side of the stream. From their new position they could see further down the trail, but would be harder to spot with the sun shining directly into the eyes of whoever was coming.

When the newcomers broke through the cover of the forest, Uffe noted the age of the man who led them. He was roughly the same age as Erik's sons and carried an axe on his hip, and was leading a group of boys and mounts loaded with supplies. Behind them came the warriors, each of them heavily armed and prepared for war, their iron-ringed brynjas and helmets glinting in the failing light. They carried their weapons with the confidence of professional warriors, and were followed by two hooded figures at the rear, who carried only bows and axes, one of whom walked with a bad limp. There was something familiar about the men, but with their faces hidden by helmets and hoods, he couldn't put his finger on what it was.

He felt Sindri twitch beside him and turned to find the same confused recognition on his face. As they watched, the leader spoke with one of the helmeted men, waving his arms around in the general direction of the clearing behind him, but they were too far away to hear what was being said. It was clear from his posture and stance that he was used to leading, but there was no submission from the man he spoke to. If anything, he stood taller as they faced one another, which only seemed to infuriate the leader more. Uffe and Sindri shared a glance briefly as they watched the exchange. Abruptly, the order was given for the horses to be unloaded and young boys began dumping sacks and bags on the side of the path while the young axeman glared at the armoured man. Without another word, the young warrior turned and walked back down the path, leaving the boys and their ponies to catch up once the supplies were unloaded. Uffe and Sindri continued watching patiently as the small caravan of horses and boys disappeared back down the path, their footsteps swallowed by the forest as they went.

'They've been sent to guard Vágar's flank,' Uffe hissed at Sindri, his voice barely a whisper. A subtle grunt was all that Sindri offered back. He wouldn't waste words unnecessarily. To their surprise, the leader of the small band burst out laughing once the last of the ponies had disappeared into the undergrowth, the sound taken up by the men around him.

'Get the tents set up and fill the waterskins. Bergathor, head back down the path and make sure we're alone.'

'*Bergathor?*' Uffe mused. '*If Bergathor is here, then…*'

His thoughts were cut short as the leader of the small band removed his helmet and gazed over the clearing at the top of the cliff, his face a mixture of emotions that Uffe couldn't understand. '*Toke?*'

'We need to go, now!' he whispered urgently to Sindri. Beside him, the man nodded and step by silent step, they eased deeper into the dark security of the forest. Once they had gone two-hundred paces, they abandoned caution and ran.

# Chapter 26

'Toke's alive? You're certain? You saw him?' Bjørn asked excitedly. He hadn't even given Uffe a chance to catch his breath after he had all but thrown the words at him. Both he and Sindri were running rivers of sweat and breathing heavily, and Bjørn motioned for Guttorm to bring them food and water while they reported on what they'd seen.

'Yes, we saw him, with about seventeen or eighteen other men. They came up to King's Leap with men from Vágar who left them there,' Uffe said, struggling to control his breathing. 'We thought the men were sent there to guard Ake's flank, but when we saw Toke amongst them, we weren't so sure... we didn't know if we should show ourselves or not...'

Bjørn could see the concern on Uffe's face. He refused to believe that Toke, or Halfdan, would sell out their father and betray their home to Jarl Ake, but he also couldn't ignore the possibility. For the briefest moment, indecision ruled his thoughts before he squashed his doubts, showing only confidence to his men as he reminded himself that the next move rested on his shoulders. Many had friends who had sailed with Halfdan aboard *Fjord Uxi* and they were no doubt just as curious about their fates.

'Break camp,' he said, snapping the men into action. 'Arne, you wait here for Galti. The pair of you can join us at King's Leap together. Come through with Yngvar and the rest of the crew, he will know the way. The rest of you, we leave in ten minutes. Be ready.'

As one, the men set about breaking the camp they had so recently finished making. They were exhausted and worn out from trekking and training, but the possibility of seeing lost friends, or fighting new enemies, fired their blood and put strength back into their tired bones. Bjørn didn't notice Uffe's presence beside him until he felt the man's hand on his shoulder. His breathing had evened out, and Bjørn found himself admiring the man's endurance.

'Are you sure this is a good idea?' Uffe asked quietly, his voice low. 'The men Toke had with him were all professional warriors, armed with swords and axes, and good shields to a man. It's unlikely they happened to come across such wealth lying in a field,' he added meaningfully, casting his gaze over the men around them. 'If your brother has changed sides, this rabble won't stand a chance,' he added seriously.

Bjørn stared at him for a few moments before replying, his voice heavy. 'No, they won't. If *Uxi's* crew are alive, we need to know. But you're right in your caution. Position yourself and your men on our flanks. If it comes to a fight, you can pin them down and give us room to manoeuvre. From that high up, the sound of fighting won't reach the people in Vágar, and I doubt their guides will still be within earshot.'

Uffe could feel the determination emanating from the younger man and opened his mouth to try one more time to make him see reason. Yngvar would join them in less than a day, and their combined force would have little trouble destroying Toke's men if there had been a betrayal.

'I know my brother, Uffe,' Bjørn said softly, stopping him before he could speak again. 'He is loyal to my father; I'm certain of it. I understand the need for caution, but I refuse to believe that men who fight for my father would betray him for a man like Ake.'

'Gnn,' Uffe grunted, relaxing his stance. 'No, I suppose you're right. It will be as you say. Approach in formation and let us cover your flanks.'

'Thank you, Uffe,' Bjørn said, grasping the older man's shoulder meaningfully. He knew that Uffe could have overridden his decision if he wanted, and that Yngvar would have supported him in it. Uffe returned the grip briefly before moving away to pack his own equipment, and Bjørn again found himself marvelling at the man's stamina. He had hardly sat down all day and yet he moved as if he had just woken up.

It would take the better part of an hour to reach the clearing, and it didn't take long to get the men underway and hit the trail again. Everything was packed up and carried with them including the uncooked deer legs, but Bjørn left some of the dried meat with Arne to see him through the night. The young man nodded his thanks and wished them well, before turning his back on them to stoke the fire. He had never spent the night alone in the woods before, but he refused to show any sign of discomfort or fear to his companions. He stood as nonchalantly as he could while he built up the flames, apparently oblivious while the rest of the men were swallowed by the forest. '*No need to be cold,*' he mused.

Bjørn pushed his men hard, covering the distance between the cabin and King's Leap in a little under an hour. It was only when Uffe held up a closed fist that the column stopped, the sounds of stomping feet and jingling armour replaced by heavy breathing and slurped water as the men regained their breath, awaiting instructions.

'We're close,' Uffe hissed as Bjørn came to stand alongside him.

The light was running from the world as the sun dipped closer to the horizon, painting the woods around them a vibrant golden-red. Bjørn and Uffe had laid their plans with Bjarni and Red Orm as they marched, deciding how best to approach Toke and his men. Now, within reach of the Leap, Bjørn gave whispered orders for the men to form up into their assigned positions. As quietly as they could, they shuffled into two equal ranks, leaving space in the front for Bjørn to join them if things went wrong. Uffe nodded to the armoured men before leading his rangers around the edges of the clearing and back towards the bushes they had hidden in earlier, their cloaks disrupting their shapes and helping them to fade into the undergrowth like wraiths.

'Whatever happens, listen to Bjarni and Red Orm,' Bjørn hissed. 'Have your weapons ready, and if it comes to blows, don't hesitate for even a second. The Allfather values bravery over all else, and only those who die a warrior's death will find a seat in his feasting hall.' He focused on each of the watching warriors individually as he spoke, trying to fire their blood and instil confidence in them. When he reached Red Orm and Bjarni, the pair nodded reassuringly to him and he took strength from their support. They hadn't disagreed with the plan, and Bjørn knew that Bjarni's support was in part because of a desire to know Bersi's fate. Like Bjørn, he too wanted to know what had happened to his brother.

Satisfied everything was clear, Bjørn turned and began walking towards the clearing, counting his steps as he walked. When he reached twenty, he heard the tell-tale sound of armoured feet as his men followed behind, their steps loud in the silent forest. He felt his heartbeat quicken in anticipation of seeing Toke again, and the uncertainty of what would happen, and he gripped his sword hilt tighter to calm his nerves. His left hand covered his body with the shield his father had gifted him, the god-runes exposed for all to see in the orange light. Before long, he began to hear the low hum of men speaking and he soon caught sight of the small group sitting around a fire. None wore armour, and there was no sign of a sentry or guard watching the waiting forest, but that didn't mean there wasn't one. Shrugging off his nerves, Bjørn crossed the final few steps into the clearing, trusting that Uffe and his men had arrows on their bow strings, ready to protect him at a moment's notice. He stopped when he was five paces from the treeline, leaving room for his men to assemble behind him while he waited for someone to notice his arrival.

'Toke!' he roared, shattering the calm when no one responded to his sudden appearance before drawing his sword and ducking down behind his shield, his breath loud in the sudden closeness.

By the fire, men scrambled to draw weapons and raise shields, quickly forming a skjaldborg that showed their veterancy. Bjørn admired the rapid response, even as he recognised the very real danger he had potentially led his own men into. He swallowed his indecision, taking strength from the sounds of his own warriors as they arrived and formed ranks behind him.

From where he stood behind Bjørn, Bjarni had watched as Toke's warriors formed ranks against his captain with growing concern. In the dying light, with the fire silhouetting their ranks, it was impossible to discern facial features on the men at the fire. He thought he could pick his brother's bulk among the assembled men, but he couldn't be sure in the dim light and was unwilling to risk Bjørn's life on a whim.

'We need to move, now!' he hissed across the ranks to Red Orm. He saw his friend's red-eyed gaze turn to face him as he grunted his agreement before standing slightly taller and giving the order to move forward. As one, the warriors began edging forwards, their feet crunching down on the dry earth in unison as they crossed the distance between themselves and Bjørn to envelop him into their armoured wall.

Toke's men took an involuntary step backwards in surprise as the small warband emerged unexpectedly from the forest, their armour blazing in the golden light.

'Toke,' Bjørn said again, quieting his voice. 'It's Bjørn. If you are there, come forward now.'

Time seemed to slow as the silence stretched between the two war bands, although Bjørn knew that in reality it was less than a minute since he first emerged and called out to his brother.

Growing tired at the answering silence, Bjørn strode forward and lowered his weapons, trusting his armour to protect him from any unseen arrows. 'Not three months ago, we sat here with Sigurd and Olaf, hearing the story of the Loki-tricked king and his wish for immortality. It is me, Toke. You need fear no trickery. But if you do not reveal yourself to me soon, I will have no choice but to assume you now serve Jarl Ake, and blood will flow. My archers have arrows pointed at the hearts of your men, and my warriors have already fought off one band of raiders on their march here. This can only go one way,' he finished, adding bravado to the lie.

The sound of Toke's belly-aching laughter filling the clearing was the last thing Bjørn had expected. He watched as a tall figure detached itself from the skjaldborg before him and strode forwards, revealing his brother's gleaming blue eyes as they caught the final light of day. 'Put up your sword, little brother.' Toke chuckled, grinning from ear to ear. 'You'll find no enemies here.'

'Toke?' Bjørn asked, hope and surprise hanging in the air.

'Aye, Bjørn. It's me.' He laughed, banishing the tension from the environment as he strode forward and pulled his brother into a giant bear hug. The rest of the men followed suit at the sight of Bjørn and Toke embracing, and the air was soon filled with the sounds of laughter and conversation as they began swapping stories and news. Bjørn caught sight of Bjarni and Bersi as they embraced, and overheard Bergathor explaining Odd's injury as he led Uffe to him.

'We thought you were dead,' Bjørn said, releasing his grip, 'or at the very least still lost and roaming the whale road.'

'So did we, for a time. We lost many of our men during our trials; we're all that survived,' he said, spreading his hands wide to indicate the men around him. 'Proudly employed as mercenaries to the great Jarl Ake of Vágar.' He chuckled.

'I will want to hear the rest of this story, brother,' Bjørn said, releasing his grip on his arm. 'But now is not the time. Váli reached us while we were searching for you and told us everything. Our mothers managed to escape and reach him, and...'

'And Signy? Did she also escape?' Toke asked suddenly, interrupting him in his haste to know her fate.

'Aye, brother, she's safe,' Bjørn said, wondering at Toke's concern.

'Ake is prepared, Bjørn,' Toke said seriously. 'He knows that Father may return any day. He's lost men securing the town, but his army is nothing to laugh at, especially behind the town's walls. He will not come out and meet Father to fight shield to shield. The only way to end this is within the walls themselves.'

'That's what we thought. Father will row straight up the fjord, drawing as many of Ake's men to the wall as he can, distracting them; he may even burn their ships,' he added. 'Once the attack has begun, we will attack the rear, doing exactly what Ake's men did to Leif and the garrison. The flank attack will distract them and force Ake to split his forces, allowing Father and our brothers to climb the walls and join the storm. The úlfheðnar who joined us on the outward journey have also offered to fight with us,' Bjørn added. They'd both seen what the wolfskin clad warriors were capable of.

As he was speaking, a look of understanding spread across Toke's face. 'What is it?' he asked.

'Jarl Ake hired us to guard against just that; against an attack on his flanks,' Toke said conspiratorially. 'We're to stay here and protect the path down from King's Leap. I assume he's worried about Váli returning with his men, although he never mentioned him.'

'But why you, and not his own warriors?'

'I don't think Ake commands the same loyalty Father does. There is one warrior – Canute – who seems entirely devoted to Ake whom he trusts implicitly. He's a giant of a man, perhaps even bigger than Sven. He killed Halfdan,' Toke added quietly.

'We will avenge him, all of them,' Bjørn said, gripping his brother's shoulder as he waited for him to speak again.

'Ake's son is there also,' Toke continued, pulling his attention back to his brother. 'But from what we've learned, he has fallen far in his father's graces; a nithing through and through, that one. Ake won't entrust the guarding of his flank to a man he can't rely on, and I feel he prefers to keep Canute close, for the most part. So, here we are. Paid men can be relied on, apparently. Although, in this case, he may find that we've found a more appealing offer than a few eyrir of silver a day,' Toke added with a sly expression on his face.

'Indeed.' Bjørn chuckled. 'Yngvar is on his way to join us with the rest of our crew. Between the three of us, we should have the better part of fifty or sixty men.' In his mind, he pictured the look of horror and surprise on Ake's face having sent a handful of men into the forest and seeing nearly four times that number return. He smiled at the thought as he began picturing ways of getting their men behind the walls before their enemies could respond. Ake wasn't going to leave the rear gate unguarded. So how to get in…

'You will need to stay deeper in the woods; by the cabin,' Toke said, breaking through his thoughts. 'We can't risk Steinar returning with supplies and discovering you before the attack begins.'

'Gnn,' Bjørn grunted, pulling his attention back to his brother. 'I agree. But we can do that tomorrow. For now, we're young and alive, and we're reunited. Let's have a drink.'

Toke's teeth flashed white in the twilight as he threw an arm around Bjørn's shoulder and led him back to the flames. 'Now that, little brother, is something we have an abundance of.'

Bjørn woke early despite his headache. Around him were the combined crews of *Sleipnir* and *Fjord Uxi*, many of them lying where they had fallen after celebrating together long into the night. Climbing to his feet, he saw Sindri already awake, patiently stoking one of the fires back to life and made his way towards him.

'You're up early,' he intoned, gratefully accepting a mug of pine tea.

'I couldn't decide what was worse, the snoring or the farting,' Sindri said matter-of-factly as he drank from his own mug.

Bjørn laughed quietly at the answer as he blew on his drink, his eyes focused on a small bird that was scratching at the cold earth. Around them, the quiet snores of the men filled the air.

'So, what do we do now?' Sindri asked after a while.

Relishing the feeling of the warm liquid as it spread through his body, Bjørn took another sip before answering. 'I need you to go back to where we left Arne and connect with Yngvar. Tell him what happened, and to stop there. I'll follow behind with the rest.'

'Do you want me to go now?'

'Finish your drink first,' Bjørn said, slurping down the rest of his own before climbing back to his feet. 'I'll wake the men.'

He heard Sindri add another log to the flames as he began walking amongst his hirð, gently shaking them back to life. He couldn't remember when he had started thinking of them as *his hirð*, but he liked the idea that they were the men who would join him from now until his thread was cut, or theirs. Whether or not that would be the case he didn't know, but the thought pleased and excited him all the same.

It took longer than usual to get the small band ready to travel as the calm morning was shattered by more than the usual amount of grumbling groans as men awoke to dry mouths and thumping heads. They had finished the last of the ale they had carried with them as well as drinking a good amount of the supply Toke's men had brought. It took the better part of an hour to get them all up and into lines ready to leave, and only then did he shake his brother back into the world of the living. 'See you in two days, brother,' he whispered. Toke groaned a mumbled goodbye before rolling over again, leaving Bjørn to lead his men back through the forest, relishing the darker light as the canopy fought back the sun's rays. Yngvar would be glad of another eighteen heavily armoured fighting men, and Bjørn already had the makings of a way back into Vágar turning over in his head. It could have been his imagination, but he thought he heard a sly laugh rising on the wind as it blew over the cliffs to his rear.

\*\*\*

'How do you know you can trust these men?' Steinar asked his father, hiding his own guilt behind the question. They were alone but for Canute in Vágar's great hall, the remains of their meal scattered on the table before them. Steinar was desperate to expose the men his father had hired, but he couldn't do so without destroying his own lie, and himself. And what was worse, Toke and his men *knew* he had lied. It was maddening, and he was caught between the need to protect himself from his father's wrath, and the need to protect his father. It had been two days since he had led Toke and his men into the hills, and he hadn't seen his father since then. The invitation to dinner had come as a surprise, given everything that had happened in recent weeks, and his stomach had sunk at the prospect. His father's anger was legendary, and he doubted his past failures had been forgotten; they certainly hadn't been forgiven.

Jarl Ake's eyes reflected the flickering light as he watched his son, not deigning to answer him immediately. The jarl sat at the head of one of the long tables, with Canute and Steinar facing each other on either side of him. The giant prow man was using a small bone to pick scraps of food from his teeth, blissfully ignoring the tension between father and son. He had little love for the welp his jarl had sired, and their conquest of Vágar had taken the last hopes he had that Steinar would improve with age. Failure was failure, plain and simple, and it was clear the boy's luck was as useful as a blind archer or a wooden sword.

'Because they dealt honourably with Canute and his men,' Ake finally said, his voice breaking into both men's thoughts. 'Because they could have sought vengeance, but instead chose peace. Because they accepted my rule and my law without argument. And because I have no choice!' he finished, raising his voice so that it echoed around the hall. Steinar flinched visibly at his father's sudden anger.

'More than once I have entrusted men, *my* men, to your command, and every time you have come back with far less than you set out with. Some deaths are to be expected, it's the nature of war. But not to the extent of your ineptitude. I can't even spare men to collect and bury the bodies that now lie rotting in the farmer's field. Thanks to your failures, I no longer have the men I need to protect my flank, Steinar. So, I am forced to hire them, and hire what I can get, with money that will come from *your* chest,' he finished, pointing at his son with a pork bone like it was a knife. 'Instead of questioning my ability to read a man,' he continued, ignoring the flash of anger that crossed his son's face, 'you might instead thank the gods that these men arrived when I needed them.'

Steinar stared furiously at his father, letting the silence grow before speaking, his voice low and his eyes murderous, despite the alarm horns howling in his head. 'My chest? I'm to pay for them now?'

'Yes. *You* lost the men *I* needed to guard the mountain path, just as you lost the sword I gave you. So *you* will pay Sven Halfdansson and his men. There is a price for all things, Steinar. Be thankful that in this case it is only silver. Fail me again, and it will be blood.'

Steinar closed his mouth, swallowing the retort he had ready on his tongue. He could feel the ruthless fury bubbling below the surface and he had no doubt that his father meant what he said. In a single sentence, the risk of exile or death had become very real. There was no possibility of admitting who the men were, not now. '*Let them come,*' he thought angrily, staring at his father with a rage he hadn't felt since he was a child. '*Let them co... Yes, let them come...*' he surprised himself at the thoughts as they came to him. Rapidly, he began turning them over and over, exploring them from every angle until he was sure. He felt the beginnings of a smile as the corners of his mouth started to curl and he fought to bring it back into an ugly sneer before replying. 'It would be my pleasure, Father,' he said through gritted teeth.

'Gnn,' Ake growled, eyeing his son. 'Then let that be an end to it.'

'Yes, Jarl Ake,' Steinar said placatingly as his mind continued to race.

\*\*\*

'They're alive, then,' Yngvar said, looking at Bjørn over the rim of his bowl.

'Aye, some of them, anyway. They lost several of their number on the journey home, and during a skirmish with some of Jarl Ake's men. Halfdan didn't survive their fight.'

'Now that is a shame,' Yngvar said, swallowing his mouthful. 'He was a good man. I have no doubt he was carried up to the corpse hall to dine with his forefathers.'

'He was,' Bjørn agreed. 'Luckily for Toke – or Sven Halfdansson, I should say – the jarl needs warriors and took them on as mercenaries, provided they didn't seek vengeance. He has no idea who they are.'

'That was clever,' Yngvar agreed, taking a pull from his aleskin.

The crew had reunited at the hunting cabin at more or less the same time, each seeming to materialise out of the forest. After the men had pitched camp Bjørn and Yngvar had sat together to discuss Toke's re-emergence, and the plan Bjørn had been mulling over in his head during the march.

'It could work,' Yngvar said again. 'The timings would need to be perfect though. Any mistakes, and we lose both the advantage and your brother's men, not to mention Toke himself.'

Bjørn nodded silently, casting his eyes across the men around them to make sure they were out of earshot. They only had one day left before Erik attacked, and they had made the decision to reconnect with Toke's small force that evening, rather than lose a march and wait for morning.

'If Toke falls, he goes to Valhöll,' Bjørn said at last. 'It's what he would expect; he's not one to shirk from danger. I would take his place in a heartbeat with my own hirð if I could, but the danger has to be Toke's.'

He saw his friend's lips curl into a small smile at the word, but he didn't comment. Instead, Yngvar fell silent and considered their options, and Bjørn had no choice but to wait. He was used to Yngvar's silences when he had to consider something in detail; he wasn't one to rush needlessly. Idly, he found himself eyeing the dirt-stained wrinkles on his friend's face, and the grizzled determination that lay below.

'I don't disagree,' Yngvar said at length, shifting his eyes back to Bjørn. 'But I will need time to make a final decision. Leave me now and you will have my answer when we march.'

Bjørn might have said more, but he knew Yngvar well enough not to ignore the request for solitude. Nodding once, he turned and made his way through the small camp to where Guttorm was leaning against a pile of firewood, running a looted whetstone across his new axe. His seax gleamed next to him, the spots of water hinting at its new sharpness.

'We'll leave in a few hours,' he said, breaking into his friend's thoughts.

Guttorm nodded once but continued sharpening, his eyes fixed on his task. Bjørn smiled to himself before drawing his own sword and wetting it with water from the skin at his side and digging for his own whetstone. Huginn was already razor sharp, but he needed to do something to distract himself from the inactivity. Bjarni had once told him that the worst part about fighting was the waiting, and he didn't disagree. It didn't take long for the repetitive rasp of stone and metal to slow his thoughts as he settled into the monotony of the task, stopping to check his edge every few strokes, or wet the stone. All around them, the camp had sunk into a calm buzz of activity as idle hands kept busy preparing weapons and armour, cooking food or mending damaged clothes and kit. The distinction between seasoned campaigner and first-time raider was clear to see, and Bjørn wondered idly where he sat in the mix. He had only just begun to earn his oar amongst the bearded warriors who crewed his father's ships, yet his sword was already well-blooded compared to his peers. He found his mind turning the thought over as he worked, wondering occasionally if other men looked at themselves in such a light. He wasn't scared; he knew that from the stories his brothers and father told of past campaigns, when men would compulsively piss or talk to cover their nerves or hide their fear. He wondered at that, his complete lack of fear. He could only assume it came from his father, and the blood that ran through his veins. He had worried as a boy that his English blood would make him weak and lower him in the eyes of those around him. More than once, he had heard his father express the same concerns when he thought Bjørn wasn't nearby. Maybe that had caused the disconnect, the need to prove that the blood running through his veins was as worthy of a seat in his father's fleet as that of his oar brothers. Whatever the case, it had hardened him like the folds in Huginn's blade. Next to him Guttorm swore suddenly, pulling Bjørn back to the present as his friend's knuckles bloomed red with blood.

'Will you live?' he joked, wiping Huginn clean on a rag before returning it to its sheath.

Guttorm scowled as he stuck the sliced knuckles into his mouth, the blood turning his mouth red as he sucked on the wound. 'Aye, I'll live,' he grunted, spitting a bloody stain on the ground.

Bjørn reached into the pack at his feet and pulled out a pouch of waxed seal skin full of fresh bandages. 'Here,' he grunted, pulling his friend's hand across to him. He didn't think it would need stitches, but to be safe he bit the stopper from his aleskin and poured what little remained of the golden liquid over the wound, ignoring his friend's discomfort as the alcohol burned. Fresh

369

blood blossomed as the ale hit, which he quickly covered and held tight with a boiled rag, waiting for the blood flow to slow. Guttorm grunted again at the pressure but otherwise remained silent, instead pulling a rag from his own belt and using his left hand to awkwardly wipe the blade clean. After a few minutes, Bjørn began wrapping and bandaging the cut with a fresh bandage before tying the cloth off on the back of his hand.

'We should call you Guttorm Hand Taker.' Bjørn chuckled when he finished, putting his supplies back in his pack. 'Men everywhere will tremble at your approach, and women will swoon at the stories they've heard.'

'If you're not more careful, they'll begin to know you as Bjørn sword-in-the-arse,' Guttorm growled, holding his injured hand high to slow the blood flow.

Bjørn laughed quietly but didn't respond, instead drawing Muninn from its sheath and going to work on the blade. He knew that it wouldn't be long now before the sounds of stone rasping along iron were replaced by the sword storm.

# Chapter 27

Spumes of frigid water crashed over the bows of *Fjord Ulf* as she sliced through the waves, covering her crew in mist-woven blankets of salty spray. Alongside her, *Hrafn* cut her own path, the crying raven at her prow matching *Fjord Ulf's* snarling wolf.

Since the two crews had watched *Sleipnir* disappear below the horizon, Erik and Váli had pushed their men to exhaustion every day, training them from dawn to dusk to get them ready for the fight ahead. It had taken immense willpower for Sigurd and Olaf not to pass out where they stood when Erik finally called an end to the exercises. By the end of each day, their muscles were completely spent, and their bodies were left gasping for water and rest. Around them, their companions sought sleep as if their lives depended on it, stopping only to eat their fill before crashing onto their bed rolls. The sons of Erik enjoyed no such respite, instead spending several more hours planning and strategizing the assault on Vágar each night with their father and Váli, and their senior warriors. Both had commented on their father's tireless endurance. Their only respite was the swim they ran for at the end of each day. Olaf thought fondly of the first day when Sigurd had all but thrown himself into the water, shocking his body back into life and banishing the exhaustion. It had helped, and it became their ritual to swim together in the still-cold waters of their island-home before the evening council. Erik had only raised an eyebrow at their sodden appearance the first evening, but he didn't object. Tempers were high in the camp, and he hadn't begrudged his sons a few moments of peace amidst the preparations for war.

Even that simple memory seemed a lifetime ago, Olaf mused, his eyes on the horizon as they pushed towards home. In the end, they had decided unanimously that they would keep the plan simple and obvious, charging straight up the fjord and making a combined push for the walls, hoping to find the gates open and securing them as quickly as possible. If that failed, they would use the ladders they had built, or raid the supplies of mast wood drying in the buildings on the shore to build a ram. Erik had made it abundantly clear to them all that Ake's attention needed to remain fixed solely on the seaward gates so that Yngvar and Bjørn could attack from the rear. It was their only hope of success.

'Tomorrow then, brother,' Sigurd said, breaking into Olaf's thoughts as he came to stand alongside him at the bow.

'Aye,' Olaf grunted, eyeing the small islet that marked the entrance to Váli's fjord. He thought he could spy *Sleipnir's* mast behind the young stand of trees, bobbing gently on the water, but he couldn't be sure. They planned to spend the evening in the quiet fjord and then set off before dawn the next morning, hoping to catch their enemies asleep in their beds. 'Tomorrow,' he added, turning to face his younger brother. Like himself and Toke, the line of Erik was strong in Sigurd, and it felt right to have his brother stand alongside him then. On an impulse he reached out and clasped his brother's shoulder, squeezing tightly before turning back to the horizon.

Sigurd smiled at the touch but said no more. Like Olaf, he knew well what the next day would hold. Heads would roll before the sun set the following evening, and neither brother pitied the men who would survive the swinging blades. Death in battle would be a mercy compared to the vengeance of Erik Golden Hand. If the survivors were lucky, they'd find themselves bound for the slave markets.

Without conscious thought, both brothers adjusted their stance as *Fjord Ulf* turned to starboard, the prow beast fixing its snarling gaze on the empty shore and the well-worn path up to Váli's home. Wisps of smoke still hung in the air, and both brothers turned at the cries of outrage that came from *Hrafn* as she too made the turn, revealing her ruined home as they passed the headland. The trench that had marked *Sleipnir's* resting place was still visible above the tideline, and Olaf saw that their father was aiming straight for it. *Fjord Ulf's* larger bulk was guaranteed to override any trace that *Sleipnir* had ever been there in the first place. Without speaking, Olaf turned and made his way back down the ship towards his sea chest, ready to run out and drive the great ship onto the beach. Sigurd followed soon after, holding back long enough to be sure there was no one watching for their arrival.

*Hrafn* had barely settled on the beach alongside *Fjord Ulf* when Váli leapt from the prow and made his way towards the sloping ground, and the path that led to his home. Ragnar and Torsten followed close behind. All three men wore their iron shirts and carried swords and shields with murderous intent.

'Go with them,' Erik grunted, motioning for his sons to follow the small troop up the hill. 'I'll get the crews settled here.'

Nodding, the two brothers took up their shields from where they rested on the racks and followed the small group up the hill, hands ready on their swords. Erik watched them go for a moment before bawling orders for Sven and the crew to gather firewood and set camp.

Olaf and Sigurd caught the small group easily, unburdened by their iron-linked shirts, and quickly fell into step behind them. The five of them cut a silent path up the slope towards the burned-out buildings. The footsteps left by Yngvar and Bjørn were still clear, but Olaf couldn't help feeling that there were more footsteps than there had been men aboard *Sleipnir*. His brows furrowed as he surveyed the ground before turning to share the thought with Sigurd, but his brother's eyes were locked on the charred walls ahead of them. Some of the prints were clearly older than the others; he could tell by the way the grass was bouncing back in places, suggesting that whoever it had been, they were long gone now.

'Swords,' Váli snarled, his pace unyielding as he drew the blade, eager to discover the fate of his home. The sound of blades licking free of scabbards filled the air briefly as the accompanying warriors moved closer to Váli and continued forward in a loose line. Olaf doubted anyone would be waiting for them, but he couldn't shake the feeling of foreboding as they drew closer to the top of the path. A few moments later, he caught the scent of putrefying flesh on the wind, the foul smell making him want to gag. He looked to the others and saw that they too had smelled it, their faces wrinkled as they continued up the path. It didn't take long before they found the source of the smells. The ground before Váli's home was littered with bodies, each stripped and blackened in the sun. Many of them had viscous wounds where beasts and birds had torn flesh from bone, and there were several ravens hopping lazily among the corpses, too fat to fly. Sigurd snarled and broke formation when he saw there was no danger; the birds would be long gone if there had been men around prior to their arrival. With frustration he kicked a particularly fat bird out of the way as he bent to check a body, gagging at the scent as he searched for familiar faces. The raven glared indignantly at him, and Olaf almost laughed at the look on the bird's face.

'They're not ours,' Sigurd said with relief.

'No,' Váli confirmed, 'these are Ake's men,' he said, stepping through the burned-out gateway. 'I recognise this one from the battle to rescue your mother and Arleigh; Ottar was his name,' he said, kicking the body out of his way.

'Gnn,' Olaf grunted from behind Váli as he followed him through the ruined gates. There were more bodies waiting inside, but none were familiar to them. Either they had walked into a mass suicide, or the victors had carried away their own dead with the loot.

'He's losing his grip before he's even grabbed a hold,' Váli muttered as Olaf came to stand beside him. 'This isn't an insignificant number of men. Coupled with those they would have lost in the initial assault, and the tussle in my fields. His rule is weaker than we thought.'

'Suits us fine,' Sigurd grunted as he pushed over another body.

Olaf nodded vaguely as he surveyed Váli's ruined hall. The pair stood in silence as they took in the ruins that had so recently been a home. A small part of Olaf thanked the gods that Jarl Ake had come to conquer Vágar, rather than destroy it. He could only imagine the frustration and pain that Váli must feel seeing his home destroyed by such reckless hate. He couldn't help but feel a degree of guilt at the sacrifices that Váli and his family had made for his own.

'We will help you rebuild, Váli,' he said, squeezing the older man's shoulder. 'You have my word on that.'

'Thank you, Olaf,' he said, sighing resignedly. 'At the end of the day, it is just wood and straw. It is only a home when it is filled with the voices and laughter of my people. They will return and we will start again. This… this doesn't matter,' he said quietly, putting his hand briefly on a blackened beam. 'Come,' he said at last. 'Let's leave this place to the ghosts, for a while longer.'

Olaf nodded, pretending not to notice the water pooling in the corners of Váli's eyes as the older man turned and began walking back down the hill, his back straight and strong. Olaf watched him go before motioning for Sigurd and the others to follow. After they left, the ravens returned to their feast.

'Everything is gone, Father,' Olaf said later that evening as he lowered his drinking horn to wipe rogue drops of ale from his moustache. 'I promised that we would help him to rebuild, once Vágar is ours again,' he added hesitantly.

'Calm, Olaf,' Erik said, sensing his son's uncertainty. 'You were right to do so, and I will not forget the loyalty Váli has shown me. Had you not made the offer, I would have done so myself.'

Erik smiled inwardly as Olaf subtly exhaled in relief. Always eager to please, Olaf was the spitting image of Erik, and had more than a few of the qualities he hoped to see in the son who would one day take his high seat.

Beside him, Sigurd was sitting lazily on his father's sea chest, repetitively running a stone along his sword, his own drinking horn lying empty on the ground beside him. The three of them were enjoying a moment of peace together, the first since Bjørn and Yngvar had left, where there were no orders to give or questions to answer. Erik knew the moment would be fleeting, and already his mind was running across the myriad of tasks that needed to be completed before the sun set, but he wanted to prolong the moment a little longer. It was extraordinarily rare to have time alone with his boys. He was proud of them and the men they were becoming. It pained him to hold the emotions so tight, rarely speaking of the pride he felt, to never embrace them. But he wouldn't risk them becoming soft or coddled. He needed warriors to continue his line, and the offspring he had been given did nothing to disappoint that need, he thought happily as his gaze flicked between Olaf and Sigurd, proud of the calm confidence they both exuded. He let the moment of peace last a few moments longer, enjoying the repetitive rasp of stone on steel, the sound mingling with the quiet hum of the crews as they sat down to drink and eat their evening meals.

'You best see to your men,' Erik said after a while, laughing gently as Sigurd jumped in surprise and dropped the stone as his father's voice shattered the calm. 'We need to leave before the sun touches the sky, and I want them ready to fight, with sharpened weapons and plenty of food and water in their bellies.'

'Aye, Father,' they said in unison, standing together to leave and carry out his orders. Once they were gone, Erik realised he had bought himself a few blissful moments of complete solitude, standing alone for the first time since they set sail. Unfortunately, it didn't take long for his head to begin conjuring darker thoughts as he moved from his sons to the fight ahead, and the vengeance he would rip from Ake's cold, dead fingers. He would have the man's head on a spear before the sun set the following day, leaving his blood to gum the wooden shaft as it fed the hungering earth below. By sundown tomorrow, all debts would be repaid, and Ake would discover just how *generous* Jarl Erik Golden Hand could be.

Before his thoughts spiralled too far, he caught sight of Turid walking towards him, her damaged nose just one more debt to repay. Banishing his thoughts of revenge, he forced a smile onto his face as she began walking towards him. Turid didn't need reminding of the horrors she had seen, nor the realities yet to come. Not yet, at least.

'Not long now,' Bjørn said, passing his brother a carved wooden cup full of steaming pine tea as he sat down beside him on the ledge at King's Leap, their legs dangling precariously over the edge as they looked down on Vágar. The air was still frigid so high up, but neither brother could resist the view of their home from the precipice at King's Leap.

Toke grunted as he took the steaming cup, feeling the warmth flow into his chilled hands.

Bjørn and Yngvar had decided to connect with Toke's forces early, moving *Uxi's* surviving crew further down the path to where they could guard the narrow pass. Anyone coming from the town could be equally held there, and it made it easier for the leaders to coordinate their attack. Toke too had agreed to Bjørn's plan, despite the risk it exposed to him and his men. Together, they had explored opening the gates from every perceivable angle, but they couldn't think of another way to open them without alerting Ake's men to the presence of Bjørn and Yngvar's men.

'Do you think we can do it?' Toke said suddenly, pulling his eyes from the view below to look at his brother. 'Ake has been preparing for us since he took the town. He won't give it up easily, brother.'

Bjørn didn't answer immediately, instead focusing on his breath as it misted and danced in the cold night air. He hadn't explored the possibility of failure in any close detail; it wasn't something they could afford, so beyond considering the risks to his strategy, he had ignored it. If they failed, it meant they were all dead. Wyrd.

'I do,' he said, turning to meet Toke's gaze. 'We have the element of surprise, made stronger by the presence of you and your men, and all of Ake's attention will be focused on our father, thinking his rear is protected. He won't be expecting a third crew to appear suddenly from the mountains.'

Toke grunted his agreement as he took a sip of the steaming brew, wincing as he burned his tongue.

'Aye, you're right,' Toke agreed, blowing on the liquid. 'It's all in the hands of the three bitches, anyway,' he added, almost as an afterthought.

'Aye,' Bjørn said, giving his brother a small smile before turning his attention back to the town below, enjoying the brief moment of peace. Behind them, the crew of *Sleipnir* slept, except for a few of the younger warriors who were sitting together by one of the fires, talking quietly amongst themselves as they nervously sharpened already sharp weapons. Bjarni and Red Orm had bunked down with Yngvar and several of the older veterans, chatting nonchalantly or drifting off to sleep as if the following dawn brought nothing more worrying than another training session. The younger men however were all bluster and nervous energy, and only a few had managed to find sleep. Despite his best efforts, Bjørn fell into the latter group, although for different reasons. The opportunity to write his saga in an actual battle had filled him with a nervous energy that made it almost impossible to sleep.

'I best be off, brother,' Toke said, climbing to his feet. 'I want to get a few hours of shut eye before tomorrow.'

Heaving himself up, Bjørn stood with him. 'I'll see you tomorrow,' he said, reaching out his right hand to grasp Toke's forearm. He saw the almost healed scar on his brother's palm and took strength from the sight, remembering the oaths they had sworn. It felt like a lifetime had passed since then.'

'Tomorrow,' Toke agreed, smiling as he squeezed his brother's arm before turning and making his way back down the track to his men. Bjørn watched him go until he was lost to sight, hidden by the trees that lined the trail.

Uffe would send a runner as soon as Erik's ships were sighted, and then they were in the hands of the gods and at the mercy of fate. Bjørn pictured them sitting in Asgard as they looked down on the waiting men, passing wagers from hand to glowing hand as they bet on the outcome. Pleased with the image, he spat a stream of burning tea over the cliff face, watching as the trail of steam spun away into the star-pierced sky.

Instead of seeking his bedroll, he sat back down on the cliff and returned his gaze to Vágar, watching as tiny sentries passed from flame to flame along the wall's fighting platforms, briefly blocking the light from view as they marked their passage. 'Not long now.'

If all had gone to plan, Erik and Váli would right now be catching a few hours' sleep on the same stretch of coast that they had used to disembark from *Sleipnir*. He could picture his father sleeping alongside his mother or Turid, probably enjoying a few hours of passion before the harsh reality of war sunk in the following day. None of the other men would enjoy such an evening, and he began to feel himself grow excited at the prospect of a similar evening with Hoelun. He knew she was sleeping slightly apart from the men, and with a happy sigh he eased himself up to seek her out amongst the shadows, already picturing her soft skin and golden eyes as he walked. Either one of them could die tomorrow, or both of them for that matter, so why not enjoy the night while they had it, he thought cheerfully as he made his way between the sleeping figures.

Knut watched with red-rimmed eyes as Bjørn made his way through the sleeping camp, following as he wove his way between snoring men towards his eastern whore. Ever since his beating at the hands or Erik's bastard, he'd been nurturing a slowly burning ember of hatred, eager for revenge. Bjørn was a popular figure amongst the fleet, despite his tainted blood, and the few young men Knut had drawn to him had all abandoned him as soon as they realised how deeply he despised their jarl's fourth-born. None of them had joined with any ambition beyond possibly challenging the warrior son to make a name for themselves. None were willing to risk killing him. Knut had realised that their absence had brought a sense of relief, promising him revenge his own way, hard won and unshared. As soon as the three leaders had shared their final strategy with the crews, Knut had begun forming his own plans.

He assumed that Jarl Ake would want information about a considerable warband waiting in the hills ready to fall on his flank; information he would happily share for the right price. He didn't think it was greedy to ask for the head of Bjørn Eriksson when the entirety of Vágar was at stake, along with the wealthy trade routes it controlled. Knut had no loyalty to Erik after what he had done to his father, and if he could see the arrogant jarl dead as well as Bjørn, he wouldn't miss the opportunity.

His wandering thoughts were disrupted by the sound of rhythmic breathing as the English bastard and his foreign slut began to couple, the sound mingling with the snores and farts of the sleeping warriors around him. Slowly, Knut released his breath and slipped out from under his blankets. Moving as quickly as he dared, he rolled his bedroll tight and secured it with a length of cord wrapped around the bundle before throwing it over his shoulder with the rest of his belongings, leaving only his shield behind; it would only slow him down.

Slipping away from the sleeping crew was easy, having laid down in a spot on the edge of the clearing, close to the forest, and sentries were no concern either. The only eyes watching were facing outwards, looking back the way they had come or down the hill towards the sleeping town, and he wasn't going either way – not yet, at least. Stealing a final glance at the sleeping figures, he disappeared into the trees and was swallowed by the darkness, relishing his sudden invisibility. As fast as he could, he angled himself through the woods towards the small deer path he had scouted the day before with Guttorm. The pair had been sent out to look for other routes into their small camp they would need to guard against, but he'd soon left the weakling in his dust as he went ahead, searching for a potential escape path. What he'd seen had filled him with glee, and he'd quickly retreated back up the path to tell a different story, working hard to hide his nervous delight. While Guttorm returned to report Knut's story of a landslide, the reality was a small, unobstructed game trail that connected with the main path a few hundred steps further down from where Toke's men were waiting. In the depth of night, he'd be all but invisible. By the time anyone realised he was gone, he would be sipping warmed mead in his new jarl's hall, putting paid to the saga and family of Erik Golden Hand, and hopefully damaging Guttorm in the bastard's eyes as well. At long last, the fates were smiling on Knut Troelsson. Tomorrow would be a good day.

# Chapter 28

Steinar hoiked and spat a wad of phlegm from the fighting platform that clung to Vágar's walls, watching as the yellow-green globule twisted and spun through the flame-ringed halo that surrounded the palisade. The gentle splat as it hit the ground was swallowed by the constant crackling of flames as they danced and writhed around him. Ever since it had become clear that Jarl Erik may return sooner than expected, his father had ordered the town gates surrounded by an almost unbroken blanket of golden flames. He had done the same for the major paths leading into the town, marking them with torches on either side for a hundred paces so that they glowed like flaming arteries in the night. He wasn't going to be caught unaware like they had caught Erik's men. Steinar could do nothing but scowl as he followed one of the paths into the darkness. More than once he'd allowed his eyes to wander towards the dim glow he imagined he could see high in the hills where the *mercenaries* were camped. He was still unsure what to do about the problem, but he knew he couldn't leave them there. His father had finally relented in his rage and given him command of the men guarding the gates at the rear of the settlement. He'd turned a nearby byre into makeshift barracks and split the men into two watches of nine. No one really expected to be attacked from behind, not while Erik was on the whale road, and it showed in the quality of men his father had put under his command. Steinar couldn't help feeling sorry for himself when he looked at them, compared to the warriors he'd led previously. Almost all of them were poorly armed farm boys without a sword amongst them. Armed with looted spears and shields, they were ill-equipped and unlikely to repel the attack Steinar was sure would come. He had managed to find three bows and had put them into the hands of those best able to use them, watching with a small degree of satisfaction as five men stepped forward when he'd searched for worthy owners. He'd tested them and had the most proficient armed with the valuable weapons, hoping to keep attackers at bay with long shafts until help could arrive. The other two had been given slings and pouches of stones and told to make do. He thought again of the men he had lost burning Váli's pathetic hall. They had been properly armed and fed, with battle experience

380

that his new command sorely lacked; he wasn't even sure where his father had found the men standing next to him now. His father's forgiveness hadn't extended to the loss of his old sword; that was clear from the axe he now carried in its place. 'You'll not see another sword from me, *boy*,' he'd snarled furiously when Steinar had asked for a replacement blade. 'You'll get one when you can take it for yourself or buy it from the smith.'

Steinar hadn't missed the ironic way his father had handed over the axe as if it was some great treasure from a saga hero, or an heirloom. Steinar spat again, resting his hand on the axe head. All would be repaid, he mused as he stared into the darkness beyond the ring of flames. He was just about to descend the steps and make his way to the private nook he'd made for himself out of storage crates at the back of the *barracks* when one of his men spoke, interrupting his thoughts. Jungulf was wire thin, and lanky, with a mop of dirty blond hair resting on top of a head that looked as though it had never been within thirty paces of clean water before, encrusted as it was with dirt and grime. Despite appearances, Steinar had found he could rely on and, to a degree, trust him. From the others under his command, he'd learned about Jungulf's ruthless streak. More than one had shared stories about him slicing the fingers from wounded warriors' right hands before killing them when they took the town, ensuring that if they met in the next life, the outcome would be the same.

'What is it, Jungulf?' he asked, stopping midstride to turn back around.

'I said there's someone out there, or something. I saw movement,' he added, placing an arrow on his bow string as he gazed beyond the walls unwaveringly. He was one of the three who had proven they could use a bow, and he handled the weapon comfortably.

'A lost goat or sheep perhaps,' Steinar grunted, moving across the wooden platform to stand alongside him. Jungulf shook his head, his eyes locked on the darkness beyond with the patience of a hunter.

Relieved to see that his other two archers were on the walls with them, he signalled for them to follow Jungulf's lead, the sound of arrows meeting bow staves briefly filling the air.

The only audible sound was the wind as it brushed the grass and caused the torches to crackle, sending sparks into the waiting sky. After counting a hundred breaths, Steinar spoke, his voice surprisingly loud as it shattered the loaded silence around them.

'Whoever is out there, show yourself if you don't want an arrow through your throat. I've no mind to play games this night, not when there's a pretty wench waiting for me on a bed of hay that I'll not be kept from any longer than necessary.' He ignored the chuckles from his men as he raked the ground with his eyes, seeking the slightest sign of movement, knowing the others were doing the same. He was just about to give up and stand the men down when a voice replied from the darkness.

'I'm a friend and ally to Jarl Ake,' said a voice from the darkness, drawing all eyes to a point just beyond the ring of light to the right of the path.

'If you are a friend to the jarl, then you have nothing to fear,' Steinar said, searching the darkness in vain for the voice's owner. 'Step into the light and show yourself,' he added, making his voice as commanding as possible.

After a few moments, a young man materialised from the darkness, stepping confidently onto the path with a spear in his hand, his eyes meeting Steinar's. They were close in age, Steinar saw as he looked the stranger up and down, his eyes lingering hungrily on the sword on the man's hip.

'Then I have nothing to fear,' the stranger said, standing straighter.

'And what's to make me believe you're not a spy, come to kill us in our sleep?' Steinar asked, drawing his axe nonchalantly. 'Better we put an arrow in you now and put an end to the matter,' he said, motioning towards Jungulf with his axe who then drew back on his bow, the wood creaking ominously. The other two archers followed his lead a second later.

To the stranger's credit, he didn't flinch at the creaking bows, but Steinar saw his eyes flick briefly between himself and the gleaming arrow heads.

'You could,' he agreed calmly. 'But then you would deprive Jarl Ake of a victory that could echo through the ages. Spare me or kill me; the choice is yours, but so too are the consequences,' he said, leaning confidently on his spear.

Steinar spat in irritation as the man raised his voice louder to ensure all those listening would hear what he had to say. Jungulf's arrow strayed true, but Steinar saw the other two dip uncertainly out of the corner of his eyes at the stranger's words. They were unwilling to tempt the jarl's wrath, Steinar noted, curling his lip into an ugly snarl. The fear of failure sat heavily on his shoulders, constantly pushing him down even as he forced himself to keep his head held high. He was secretly happy to have command of the rear gate, knowing that the *mercenaries* his father had sent to the hills would fall on their flank at the first sign of fighting, but that too was tinged. Any *betrayal* by the men Canute had brought in would help dim his rising star, but Steinar wasn't confident in the ability of his men to put down an attack from Toke's warriors. In a straight fight they would be cut to ribbons with impunity.

'Well?' the stranger asked.

Ignoring the creeping feeling of guilt in his gut, Steinar made his decision. 'If he moves, kill him,' he said loud enough for the stranger to hear, the threat clear in the glinting iron at the end of Jungulf's waiting arrow. 'Open the gate,' he grunted to two of his men as he climbed down the steps.

'Weapons – throw them down now and take five paces back,' he said as he walked through the open gate. 'Left-handed,' he added quickly as the stranger began drawing his sword. He was impressed by the man's calmness as he dropped his sword, spear and seax on the ground before him, moving awkwardly with his left hand.

Steinar kept his axe ready as he drew closer, throwing a critical eye over the man's weapons, noting the chipped sword. It had seen its share of combat, that much was clear.

'Who are you?' Steinar asked, speaking first.

'My name is Knut, a bóndi in the fleet of Jarl Erik,' Knut said. 'Jarl Erik destroyed my family name and all but killed my father himself,' he added quickly, seeing the alarm rise in Steinar's face. 'I would join you if your jarl would have me. I have information he must hear,' he finished, exhaling as the words left his mouth.

'And what might that be?' Steinar replied, motioning for his men to lower their arrows, ignoring their groans of relief as they released the tension from their bows.

'The warning I bring is for the jarl's ears alone,' Knut said, raising his voice again so those on the walls to hear him. 'Will you take me to him?'

Steinar stood still for a few minutes, eyeing the stranger while his head raced through the possibilities. Knut wasn't one of those Toke had come in with. That knowledge alone blew warning horns in his head as he realised Erik must have a whole nother warband hidden somewhere nearby.

'Where are they?' Steinar asked, flicking his axe threateningly. He could imagine the thoughts running through Knut's head as he watched the man's eyes flick briefly towards his weapons, calculating whether he would be able to reach them before Steinar's axe came down on his head, or an arrow struck him.

'Take me to your jarl,' Knut replied finally, tearing his gaze back to Steinar as the first beads of perspiration appeared on his forehead. 'The news I have is for his ears alone.'

'I am his son, and trusted in all things,' Steinar announced, motioning towards the walls behind him to emphasise the point before continuing, speaking before Knut could evaluate the quality of the men, or their numbers. 'Tell me the news, and I will decide if it is good enough for the jarl to hear. My father is not a forgiving man when men waste his time,' he added.

It was Knut's turn to weigh his options. He couldn't reach his weapons without an axe to the head or back, and he had the distinct feeling that one of the archers was angry at having to lower his bow. At that range, a child could have hit him, let alone a trained warrior. He was left with no choices.

'All I can tell you is that there is another warband of warriors that are ready to attack as soon as Erik returns. That is all I will say until I meet the jarl,' he added, before pointedly closing his mouth.

'Gnn,' Steinar grunted. Nearby, an owl hooted in the woods, the sound conjuring memories of his father's warriors telling him that the night birds were warnings to be heeded.

'Come with me,' he said at last, shoving the axe back into his belt. 'Rune! Collect the man's weapons and follow us to my father's hall,' he ordered, motioning Knut back as he bent to retrieve his sword. After a few steps, Steinar changed his mind, turning to face Knut and causing him to stop abruptly. 'Bring that piece of metal with you,' he said, pointing towards the sword in Rune's hand. It could just as easily be reclaimed later, and his father's men would no doubt take it from him before letting him in front of the jarl. They made their way silently through the sleeping town, the rest of the inhabitants long since confined to their homes under the curfew that Ake's men ruthlessly enforced. Just the day before, an elderly man had been cut down for objecting, his body left staked to the shoreline for the crabs and the crows, his family unable to do anything but watch in silent misery. Steinar imagined he could hear the birds as they fought for scraps of the bloody feast and shivered involuntarily. He'd gone down to look just once, arriving in time to watch as an eagle arrived and tore a great strip from the man's liver before disappearing into the sky. The jarl's word was law, and the inhabitants of Vágar were slowly learning to bend the knee.

'When we reach my father's hall, let me do the talking,' Steinar said without breaking his stride. Beside him, Knut grunted something resembling agreement, but said nothing as his eyes flickered across the sleeping town.

It didn't take long to reach Ake's hall, the giant structure looking like an upturned boat as it towered over the surrounding buildings. Flaming torches danced all around it, their flickering light glinting off the silent, armour-clad húskarlar that guarded the entrance. As they approached, one of the guards motioned for Knut to hand over his sword. Steinar noted the reluctance with which Knut relinquished the weapon, and the way his eyes followed the guard as he casually ran his thumb along the chipped and worn blade before leaning it carelessly against the wall, showing its worth. Steinar laughed at Knut's quickly hidden anger at the perceived insult before motioning for him to follow him into the hall. A wave of heat from the fires burning within hit them as they crossed the threshold, and Steinar noted with satisfaction that Canute was sitting alongside the jarl, his eyes devoid of emotion as he watched them approach. His giant axe was within easy reach, as always, the haft visible above the table's edge.

'Steinar, what a pleasure to see you at my table,' Ake said, the smile on his face failing to reach his eyes. The words were for the benefit of the unknown stranger, Steinar knew, but at that moment he didn't care about his father's petty games. He could bear one more insult; in a few moments, Knut's words would change everything.

'Thank you, Father. Let me introduce Knut, a stranger to our town and a valuable ally to you and your hirð.'

'And what value is that?' Ake asked as he turned his flint-like gaze on Knut.

Steinar faltered for a moment as he saw Knut through his father's eyes, seeing the sullen and bruised face, broken nose and the worn and ripped clothes. He was little better than a farmer turned warrior and Steinar felt a moment of doubt at the thought before steeling himself to continue, pulling himself up to his full height to meet his father's gaze. 'Knut was formerly a bóndi in the fleet of Jarl Erik Golden Hand, former lord of Vágar,' he said, his voice echoing around the empty hall. His father's gaze flicker from his son back to the man beside him, curiosity flashing across his face briefly before he masked his emotions again.

'Gnn,' Ake grunted. 'So, we thin my enemy's ranks by a single man? Hardly valuable enough to interrupt your jarl while he dines, but I suppose every man helps. Thank you, Steinar,' he said sarcastically. 'Canute, take Knut outside and remove the lad's head from his shoulders,' he added nonchalantly, spearing a piece of fish with his eating knife.

Steinar felt like he had been struck. Had his trust fallen so far that his father wouldn't even hear him out? He watched in a mute daze as Canute stood and took up his great axe, his movements and expression as casual as if Ake had asked him to refill his drinking horn. As Steinar stood dumbfounded, struggling to regain control of his racing thoughts, Knut stepped forward and spoke, his voice calm despite the axe-wielding giant approaching him.

'Kill me now, Jarl Ake, and you will lose the valuable information I have risked my life to bring you. You will never know when the *pirate* Erik Golden Hand will attack your town, nor where he has hidden an entire crew of men, ready to attack you when you least expect it. You will never know about the traitors in your ranks, nor the stratagems they will employ to bring you low.'

Regaining his wits at Knut's words, Steinar took a step forward and continued where he had left off, forcing the confidence back into his voice.

'He speaks the truth, Father. He came to us in good faith and stood under drawn bows to bring the news to us. From what he tells me, he has no loyalty to Jarl Erik, having seen his father and family shamed beyond recompense, and seeks only to help us in the battle to come. I urge you to listen to what he has to say,' he said, letting his outstretched arms fall as the words landed in his father's ears.

Canute had stopped his ominous advance and was standing silently as he waited for instructions. All three men waited as Ake stared at his son and Knut, his face unreadable as he considered what had been said. Steinar felt a hot flush of impatience creep across the back of his neck as he waited for his father to speak, forcing himself to keep the emotion from his face as they waited. Instead, he watched as a thrall added wood to the flames, sending sparks heavenwards in a brief spray of colour.

Finally, Ake spoke. 'Tell me what you know,' he said, his voice carrying a dangerous edge as he sat back in his chair and called for ale and food.

It took over an hour for Knut to tell everything he knew of Erik's plans, including the ruse played by the *mercenaries* Canute had brought back with him. To Steinar's silent delight, Ake had stared murderously at his prow man when he heard these words, his face flashing red in a wordless fury that forced Canute to look away in shame. Steinar had listened just as closely as the others while Knut told his story, filling in the blanks from what he had already deciphered while thralls came twice to refill ale horns and stoke the fires. 'If you would have me, Jarl Ake,' Knut said, taking a deep breath as he came to the end of his story, 'I would pledge my sword and my life to you here and now. All I would ask in return is the opportunity to kill Erik's fourth-born, Bjørn.'

'My son has not proven himself the most reliable of men, of late,' Ake said, ignoring Steinar's glare as he stood and walked around the table towards the fire where he held his hands over the flames to warm them. 'At first, because of this, I was disinclined to listen to your story, or to trust you; but I can feel the hatred coming off you just as I feel the heat in these flames. I will accept your oath, Knut Troelsson, and give you more than the bastard half-caste son of a *pirate* for your services. For this information, I will give you gold and hacksilver, an iron brynja and a shield to keep you safe in the coming battle. If you live through the clash, you will join my hirð under the command of my son. Is this acceptable to you?' Ake asked, turning his flint-like eyes on Knut.

Knut beamed at the news, the added wealth an unexpected bonus. He'd heard stories of Ake's ruthlessness and greed, but already he was proving a more generous jarl than Erik had ever been. 'It is, my Jarl,' Knut said, remembering himself before bowing his head towards Ake.

'The let it be so, Knut Troelsson. In the eyes of the Allfather, I accept your service and your sword. Do you swear to serve me loyally and faithfully until old age take you, or the Valkyrie claim you?'

'I swear it, Jarl Ake,' Knut said seriously, bowing again.

No one noticed the anger that flashed across Steinar's face at the news. He too had expected to be recognised and thanked for bringing the man to his father in the first place, and he struggled to keep a straight face as he listened to the exchange.

'Then it is done,' Ake said, nodding his head towards Knut, the slightest of smiles creasing his face. 'Wait outside, both of you,' he said, turning his eyes briefly towards his son. 'I will call you back shortly. And Knut, don't you dare show yourself in my presence again without your sword.'

Surprised into silence by his change in fortunes, Knut bowed once before turning and walking with Steinar towards the exit. Ake watched them leave, considering whether or not he should reward his son for bringing the man to him, his mind flashing to the sword he had given to him only to see it lost almost instantly. He had carried the blade for most of his adult life after inheriting it from his own father. The memory brought a rush of irritation that he quickly smothered. No, he decided. Steinar would have a brynja for the simple reason that Ake needed an heir and for the time being he was all he had, but he could find his own sword. He wouldn't reward him for merely doing his duty, he thought, before turning his cold gaze onto Canute.

'Erik's son,' he said dangerously. 'You captured Erik's son and let him go! I could have used him as leverage, ransomed him, or any number of things! And now he sits on my flank with his bastard brother and a small army, ready to fall on us the second his father sails up my fjord!'

Canute stood in silence while Ake raged, his face impassive as the jarl spent his anger. They both knew that he couldn't have known who he had captured, although Canute wasn't sure that would count for squat in light of what Knut had revealed. His mind wandered while the jarl's words washed over him like a wave, soaking through but never breaking him.

After a few minutes, Ake paused to sip from his horn and Canute took the opportunity to speak for the first time, his voice calm and sure. 'My jarl, the fault is mine and so is the responsibility. If you would have it, I will fall on my sword now and end this shame, or if you—'

'Oh, shut up, Canute,' Ake snapped irritably, cutting him off mid-sentence. 'Your death won't change what's been done, and you still have your uses,' he grunted. 'There will come a time where I call on you for this failure, and the debt you will incur through my leniency, but that time is not now. For now, I need you. There may yet be a chance for redemption, given what we now know,' he added.

Canute grunted once, accepting his fate. '*Wyrd,*' he thought to himself.

'He did well keeping his men away from the townsfolk. They would have given them away in an instant,' Ake mused absently, remembering Sven's, no, Toke's insistence on working on their ship from dawn to dusk.

In silence, he brooded over everything he had learned, feeling his blood cool as he stared into the flames. He watched detachedly as a log burned through and crashed onto another, sending a shower of sparks skyward.

'You will command the rear gate now,' he said after a time. 'I won't trust my son with the responsibility, although he did the right thing in not killing Knut. They will both serve under you in defending the gate. Take fifty men with as many bows as you can find. Erik's men *must not enter the town*, Canute. Succeed, and I may just forgive you for this mistake.'

'It will be done, Jarl Ake,' Canute grunted.

Ake eyed him for a while before nodding, closing the conversation as he beckoned for a woman to come forward from the shadows, Canute forgotten for the moment.

'Lord Ake?' Revna asked, her eyes deliberately downcast as she approached the jarl. Before his arrival she had helped her husband in his forge, polishing and cleaning the weapons and armour he produced for the warriors of Vágar. The jarl had seen her beauty and promised to let her husband and children live, provided she obeyed him in everything, without complaint. The memories of his sweaty hands on her bare skin made her flesh crawl, and only the knowledge that her husband and children were safe had gotten her through the ordeal, and kept her in his chamber each evening.

She tried not to shudder as he reached for her, sliding his hand up her skirt to grasp her smooth buttocks, the motion revealing her thighs to Canute who stood silently alongside. She winced slightly as he squeezed tightly, pinching her flesh before he spoke. 'Tell my son and this Knut to come back, then wait for me in the annex.'

'Yes, Jarl Ake. May I also run home and check if my children are settled for the evening?' she said quietly, trying to keep the tremor from her voice.

'Gnn,' he grunted. 'Put a log on the fire. If it is burned through by the time you return, your husband will pay for your tardiness.'

She nodded once before dropping the largest log she could find on the flames, hoping it would roll away and burn slowly before she all but ran for the door, stopping only to tell Steinar and the traitor to return to the jarl. She had recognised Knut when he entered, and it was everything she could do not to slap him for the betrayal as she left.

Ake chuckled as he watched her leave, thinking briefly about what he would do with her after dismissing his men. His mellow mood disappeared as soon as he caught sight of his son re-entering the hall with Knut in tow, this time carrying his battered sword proudly on his hip.

Seeing them enter, Ake called for one of his men and whispered quietly into his ear, motioning towards the exit. Steinar's eyes flicked briefly over the warrior as he hurried from the hall before returning his gaze to his father and Canute. Internally, he seethed at the sight of the giant still standing alongside his father, clearly forgiven for his mistake. Anger coursed through him briefly as he remembered his father's fury and unforgiving response to his own failures, while his second-in-command had brought his enemy's son to their very gates and stood unpunished! None of the internal battle showed on his face as he stood calmly before his father, waiting.

'It seems we owe you a debt, Knut,' Ake began, sipping again from his horn. Steinar could see red on his lips and noted absently that his father must have found a stash of wine amongst the plunder they had found. The valuable alcohol was rare this far north, and it was unlikely his father would let a single skin of the precious liquid escape his grasping fingers.

'It was my pleasure, Jarl Ake,' Knut answered, a glimmer of pride appearing on his face. 'As will fighting alongside your warriors when the usurper comes to take what is yours,' he added.

Ake didn't answer immediately, instead turning his attention to the warrior he had sent off as he returned to the hall. Another man had returned with him, their faces straining under the weight of the chest they carried between them. 'Put it down here,' Ake said, ignoring the confused expressions on Knut's and Steinar's faces.

'As promised,' he said with a slight smile as he stood and opened the chest to reveal the gleaming iron-ringed shirts within. 'Knut. Steinar. Take your pick.'

He watched as both men stepped forwards and pulled brynjas from the chest, examining each until they found ones that fit. Steinar was well-practised and easily manoeuvred his body to let the armour slide down his back before wrapping his weapons belt around his waist. Knut on the other hand revealed his inexperience, and Canute had to step forward to help the boy, and Ake chuckled as he staggered under the weight, fighting to keep his balance.

'Your belt will relieve some of the weight,' Canute grunted, pointing to his before showing Knut how to adjust his own.

Once they were dressed, Ake threw a clinking pouch across to the young man, watching as Knut tried and failed not to count the valuable metal through the leather.

'I have made good on my promise,' Ake said, facing the pair. 'Tomorrow, Canute will lead the defence of the rear gate, and you will both answer his commands without question. I will fight the ships as they come and, Norn's willing, Erik and his band of pirates will be dining in Óðinn's Hall, or Hel, come sundown.'

Steinar gritted his teeth and bowed at the reality of serving under Canute, but he knew better than to argue. The arrival of Knut had helped him to regain a fraction of his father's favour. He eyed the giant prow man from under his brow, thinking about how accidents could happen in the heat of battle. Arrows and spears could find themselves buried in friends just as easily as foes, often without anyone knowing where they came from. It wasn't impossible that Canute would meet with such an accident in the coming battle. The thought warmed Steinar as he nodded to his father before sitting down with him to plan the defence. None of the men looked up as Revna slipped through the hall and made her way back to the annex at the rear of the building.

\*\*\*

Fafnir clambered over the wall closest to the forests that framed Vágar. He winced as the pouch of sling stones at his hip clinked when he reached the ground, the sound loud in the night as he landed on the cold earth. At ten years old, the leap from the top of the wall was a sizeable feat, and he stumbled as he landed. He looked around furtively, thanking the Allfather that no one was there to see his poor landing. His mother had appeared at their house and started speaking before Fafnir or Ulf, his father, could even register that she was in the room. Without stopping to catch her breath she told them everything she had heard in the great hall, whispering the message he was to carry to the sons of Erik and Yngvar before disappearing again into the night, saying something about flames and burning logs. Ulf had looked pensive at the risk to his son, before making up his mind. He'd told Fafnir to run for his sling while he packed him a waterskin and small pouch of food. He would have to run through the night to reach King's Leap before dawn.

Now, as he ran through the silent dark, he thanked his father for his endless talk about a warrior needing to be fit and strong when he dragged him from his bed every day to work the forge, and the land around their home. He was both those things, and the adventure ahead excited him. Showing his teeth to the night, he collected his bearings and set off, disappearing into the darkness like a ghost as he repeated his message over and over again under his breath like a mantra.

# Chapter 29

Fafnir Ulfsson ran as fast as his young body would carry him, constantly alert for the imagined arrow in the back that would snatch life and adventure from him before it had even properly started. As soon as he left the flames of Vágar behind he'd allowed himself to relax a little, dropping his shoulders as the stress lessened. He'd all but inhaled the food and water his father had given him before abandoning the pouches on the trail to lighten his load, determined that nothing would slow his progress. In his haste, he had only allowed himself to stop twice; once to empty his bladder and the second to climb a tree as an unseen beast, made invisible by the darkness, made its way through the forest, panting and snarling as it passed beneath him. It had taken everything he had not to give in and sleep for just an hour under a tree as exhaustion threatened to overwhelm his young body, but he had persevered. When he finally saw the warriors waiting on the path, he had all but fallen onto the shield wall that greeted him, his tiny chest heaving as he swallowed giant gulps of air and asked to speak to the sons of Erik. He didn't recognise Toke when he arrived at first, focused as he was on simply remaining conscious as he battled through his exhaustion. It was only when the grinning face looking down on him spoke that he realised who he was, and he found himself suddenly shy in the presence of the jarl's son.

'Relax, lad,' Toke said gently, a kind smile on his face visible through his beard. 'You're safe now. What message have you brought?'

'I need to speak with you and your brother, and Yngvar as well. I bring news from Vágar you must hear.'

'Can you walk?' Toke asked, wondering how he knew that Yngvar and his brother were nearby as he eyed the boy's heaving chest and sweat-plastered face. He could see the lad was close to collapsing, but he didn't want to demean whatever trail he had been through by offering to carry him. 'Yngvar and my brother are a way up the trail at the Leap. Can you make it there?'

'Aye,' Fafnir nodded, fixing his face in a mask of fierce determination as he climbed to his feet and began up the path, not bothering to check if Toke was following. He had already spent the day working with his father in the forge, hammering a scrap of iron that would one day become his first seax knife. When his mother had burst through the door, he had been settling down to sleep, already exhausted. After the run through the woods, and the sweet moment of peace when he found Toke and his men, the final few steps to King's Leap were too much and his small body betrayed him. He didn't see the affectionate smiles that flashed between the watching warriors when he collapsed from exhaustion, nor did he hear their compliments about his endurance and bravery. His heart would have swelled with pride if he had.

They had recognised Ulf's son instantly; he could have only come from the town. Grinning with the rest, Toke bent down and picked Fafnir up off the ground, throwing him gently over his shoulder as if he weighed nothing. The boy didn't stir.

'Come on, little warrior.' He chuckled as he began walking up the path. 'Let's hear what news you've brought us. Uffe, you come with me. Bersi, you have the watch,' he added, turning briefly to find his friend among the crew.

Bersi nodded in confirmation before turning to reorder the sentries and motion the rest back to sleep. Daylight was still a few hours off.

Fafnir couldn't remember food having ever tasted so good. He was sitting next to the main fire with two sons of his jarl and one of his most trusted warriors while their warband slept around them. In his hand was a hunk of rabbit, the gleaming juices running over his small fingers as it steamed in the cold air. Fafnir felt very important with so many eyes watching him work his way through the meat, and he could feel the food restoring his energy. He had tried to deliver his message as soon as they arrived, Toke having woken him before they entered the camp so he could walk in unaided. He had thanked him for that, splashing water from Toke's waterskin over his face before strolling into camp with as much confidence as he could muster. Bjørn had seen right through him, insisting that Fafnir should eat and drink his fill first, and recover his strength. He had worn the same amused expression as Yngvar and Toke as they watched Fafnir devour first one and then another rabbit leg, waiting patiently while the boy ate. It was only when Fafnir pushed the final piece of flesh past his juice-stained lips that Bjørn nodded for him to begin his story.

'My Lords,' Fafnir began, suddenly shy as he climbed back to his feet. Toke could see that the boy's legs were still shaky and motioned for him to sit back down. 'This is no jarl's hall, Fafnir,' he said gently with a friendly wink.

'My Lords,' Fafnir continued, swallowing as he reclaimed his seat. 'You have been betrayed,' he said, forcing authority into his young voice. 'My mother – Revna – bid me tell you that one of your men, Knut Troelsson, has turned traitor and revealed your presence to Jarl Ake. Additional warriors are being positioned at the landward gate to strengthen the defences there,' he finished, watching to see how the news would be received.

'I knew we couldn't trust the nithing coward,' Bjørn grunted after a few moments, spitting into the fire. In truth, the loss of Knut was of no real concern to him. They would have come to blows sooner or later and now he could kill him without fearing repercussions from his father.

'Aye,' Uffe grunted, his face dark. 'His father wasn't one to be trusted either; the ship doesn't sail far from the fjord, it seems.'

'Hoelun,' Yngvar asked, seeing her step into the light, 'could you take the boy and see he gets whatever else he wants, then find him a place to sleep until morning. Then check to make sure Knut really is missing from his bed.'

'Of course,' she said quietly, placing her hand gently on Fafnir's shoulder as he climbed tiredly to his feet.

'Thank you, Fafnir,' Yngvar said. 'We won't forget what you've done here tonight.'

Fafnir bowed tiredly and made to follow Hoelun but Bjørn stopped him suddenly.

'Wait a moment,' he said, digging into the pack at his feet. Fafnir watched in enthralled silence as Bjørn drew a small hand axe from the pack, the iron head glinting warmly in the light of the fire. His eyes doubled in size as Bjørn handed the valuable weapon to him, haft first.

'A weapon fit for a warrior,' Bjørn said seriously, hiding his smile as the boy's hand dipped under the weight. Fafnir held the axe in stunned silence for a few moments before remembering himself and tucking it carefully into his waistband alongside the pouch of sling stones.

'Thank you,' Fafnir said proudly, standing tall among the ring of warriors, his hand resting on the axe head.

Bjørn nodded for Hoelun to take the boy away.

The four of them watched as Hoelun led the boy away, laughing quietly amongst themselves when Fafnir drew the weapon from his belt and began chatting happily about his adventure. He more than deserved the reward.

'This changes everything,' Toke said, turning back to the fire.

'I agree,' Uffe growled, earning a grunted agreement from Yngvar as he repetitively drew and released his sword so it fell back into its sheath with a resounding *crack* each time he dropped it.

His words were greeted by silence as the four of them considered their next move. The only interruption was Hoelun briefly returning with her shoulders raised and hands empty, confirming Fafnir's story. Knut was gone.

'Maybe it doesn't?' Bjørn said cautiously, speaking slowly as if he was weighing each word individually.

'Of course it does,' Toke grunted. 'It was already a risk for me and my crew before we were betrayed, and that was when we thought the gates would open for us when Father attacked. There's no way they'll let us in now, let alone even approach the gates. As soon as they catch sight of us, they'll set shaft to string and darken the sky with arrows and sling stones, or break us with rocks as we approach the walls.'

'True,' Bjørn said unhelpfully. 'But that's exactly what Knut will have told them to do; or if not, what Ake will have thought to do.'

'Oh, well in that case, I guess we'll just go ahead as planned and hope to meet you all in Valhöll while you and your men watch from the treeline,' Toke grunted, picturing the arrows and spears piercing his skin, leaving him to cough blood into the cold earth. It wasn't a straw death, but it wasn't far off.

'No, because you won't step into range,' Bjørn said, eyeing his brother.

'You have a plan?' Yngvar said, speaking before Toke could respond.

'Aye, I have a plan. One that lessens the chances of an arrow ending up point-first in my brother's arse.' He grinned, reaching across to grip Toke's shoulder.

Toke grunted unconvinced before leaning forward to add another log to the embers, sending a cloud of sparks up into the sky.

'Here's what we'll do,' Bjørn said, leaning forward conspiratorially to lay out his plans.

\*\*\*

The sun hadn't even crested the horizon as the crews of *Sleipnir* and *Uxi* roused themselves and stirred the still glowing embers from the night before. Logs of dew-kissed wood were dropped into the gently glowing pits, hissing and spluttering until the flames caught. Men grunted and groaned, farted and burped as they pulled themselves from sleep and climbed out of their sleeping sacks to prepare for the day to come.

Down the trail, Toke and Bersi had already roused their own warriors and the sound of their footsteps sounded loud to Bjørn's ears as they entered the quiet clearing to break their fast. The crews mingled easily as friends and brothers sought each other out while Toke sat with Yngvar and Bjørn, as well as Bersi, Bjarni, and Red Orm. There was little talking as their warriors prepared for the coming sword storm, and more than one ran whetstones over already sharp weapons, or made final adjustments to their armour. Bjørn could feel the nervous energy that had crept through the clearing and understood it. He felt the same. For many of them, this would be their last sunrise, their final day in Miðgarðr.

From where he sat, he could see Hoelun, sitting and eating with Uffe and his dark-cloaked rangers by their own small fire, her ever-present bow by her side.

Toke noticed the stolen gazes his brother cast towards Hoelun and smiled to himself, imagining he would be much the same if Signy was here.

As if by an unspoken agreement, both brothers returned their attention to the older warriors with them, grinning to each other before focusing on the task at hand. Men would bleed and die before the day was out, and they couldn't afford to let a woman distract them. Toke nodded in agreement at something Red Orm and Bersi were discussing about the best way for him to approach the gate with his men, adding their thoughts to the formations he had been considering.

Bjørn was sharing his own opinion when Uffe crossed the clearing to briefly confer with them. Between the four of them, they had refined and improved Bjørn's plans until they were happy, only then sharing them with their seconds in command. Now, the first phase was being put into play as Uffe murmured his whispered farewells to the small group before motioning for his men to follow him towards the forest path.

Bjørn watched them leave, making eye contact briefly with Hoelun as she followed the rest of the hooded figures. She was wearing a homespun cloak from his own chest and carried her bow and a full quiver of arrows, as well as the axe he had given her. The dark wool would make her harder to spot against the dim light of the trees. A soft smile touched her face as their eyes met and Bjørn felt a warm feeling rush through his body as she touched her hand briefly to her heart before donning her own hood and disappearing among the trees.

'That's part one,' he grunted, motioning for Toke to begin calling his own men to attention. The disappearance of the archers had dulled the quiet hum of conversation that filled the camp as men turned expectantly to watch their leaders. As Bjørn and his companions climbed to their feet, they set off a flurry of activity as men copied the motion and began preparing to march. In no time at all, the air was filled with the sounds of metal and wood as shields were lifted, weapons belts cinched tight, and iron-ringed shirts ran down bodies like metal waterfalls. The younger warriors, filled with nervous energy, tried to match the calm indifference of the veterans as they prepared themselves. Bjørn caught himself watching Red Orm and Bjarni as they donned their brynjas with practiced ease, trying to copy their example.

'This is it,' Yngvar said, coming to stand alongside him. Unlike the ironclad veterans around them, Yngvar wore only hardened leather armour, sacrificing protection for mobility. Bjørn noted the streaks of ash he'd pulled across his face, giving him a fearsome visage, and felt a brief moment of pity for anyone who found themselves within reach of Yngvar's sword.

Bjørn grunted as he pulled his own brynja over his shoulders, accepting help from Yngvar as he sent the iron rings hissing down his body. With practiced ease he wrapped his weapons belt around his waist to lessen the weight before throwing his armoured jerkin over the top. Only his head remained unencumbered, choosing to leave the iron helmet looped over his sword hilt for the time being. At his back sat his knife, the blade sharpened to a keen point that would slice through all but the toughest leather. He felt the sheath knock his axe haft when he moved and he shifted the loop on his belt further around to rest on his hip before taking up his shield. He decided to leave his bow in the clearing with the rest of the gear that they wouldn't be bringing with them.

Bjørn grunted as he tightened the belt an extra notch, feeling the leather constrict around his waist. 'Aye, this is it,' he said, turning to face Yngvar. 'Keep your head down today, old man,' he added, wearing a cheeky grin as he put his hand on Yngvar's shoulder and squeezed briefly.

'The arrogance of youth,' he grunted kindly, his brow furrowing as a smile crossed his face. 'Watch your own head, Bjørn,' he said, the smile fading as he grew serious again. 'Many a man, in their eagerness to earn fair fame and a saga tale of their own, would happily see it mounted on the end of their spear. A son of Erik Golden Hand is a worthy trophy.'

'Aye, Yngvar. I'll remember it,' he said, nodding in acknowledgement. 'Well then, let's see what the three bitches have woven for us,' Bjørn added, speaking with what he hoped was casual nonchalance. Yngvar's warning wasn't enough to wipe the grin from his face as he pictured the fighting to come. This would be his first real battle, and a chance to win fame and glory for himself and his family, and revenge themselves on the pretender jarl. The threat of death did little to temper his excitement.

With a final nod, Yngvar turned and began bellowing orders. His words carried easily across the clearing, and within moments nearly sixty warriors were falling into formation, shields resting on their shoulders while spears and axes waited patiently to be called to task. Bjørn stared in awe for a few seconds before following behind Yngvar to find his own men. They had done everything they could to prepare. The rest was in the hands of the Nornir. Wyrd.

***

Sigurd pulled his oar again, his strokes perfectly in time with those around him as they pushed *Fjord Ulf* ever closer to home. *Hrafn* flew alongside them, her crew, like *Ulf's*, already wearing their armour as they prepared to bring war and death to Ake's feet. Erik stood tall at the stern, his brynja gleaming despite the dim early-morning light that shone down on them, the golden rings bright amidst the iron. Behind him rested his famous raven helmet and sword, the pair lying at ease against his shield as they waited to do their master's bidding. Looking at his father now, it was hard to imagine any of the gods looking more battle hungry than Jarl Erik Golden Hand. Across the decks of both ships, men worked the oars at a steady pace that they could maintain for hours, the motion warming their blood and loosening muscles, preparing them for the battle ahead. Stealing a glance between strokes, Sigurd saw Olaf pulling his own oar, his shield mounted on the rack alongside him while his sword and helmet rested within easy reach at his feet. Most of the sword-armed men had chosen to forego their sheathes to avoid the risk of them getting tangled between quickly moving legs and tripping them. Sigurd, however, wore his sword diagonally across his back, ready to be whipped out and paired with his hand axe or seax, or with a stolen shield, should he lose his Dane axe in the fighting, or the haft break.

To a man they looked fearsome and hungry for vengeance and retribution, but after Erik, it was Sven who caught his attention the most. The giant carried a great axe with practiced ease and murderous intent. He had seen him swing the blade on more than one occasion, and he aspired to do the same with such easy skill and balance. Few could hope to best Sven in battle as he wrote complicated patterns through the air with the giant weapon, and Sigurd hungered to see such battle-won skill again that day. Sven had donned his brynja and helmet, the helms skirt of iron rings concealing all but his eyes. Sigurd showed his teeth as he imagined the maelstrom they were rowing towards, taking comfort from the men with him. Wordlessly, he offered a prayer to the Allfather that Bjørn would succeed in his mission, and that Toke would survive the whale road and return to them once the battle was won. It was all he could do.

They had been up since first light, eating quickly before loading the ships and setting sail. Against Erik's best efforts, both Turid and Arleigh had climbed aboard *Fjord Ulf* as the great ship was shoved off the shore and into the waiting waves, while Váli's own women mimicked the action. Sigurd chuckled to himself as he remembered the helpless expressions that had flicked across both Erik's and Váli's faces before they shrugged and accepted that their wives were coming with them.

They'd caught sight of *Sleipnir* anchored and calm against the islet as they passed, but Erik had done little more than raise a hand in recognition to the ship's boys as they cheered his passage.

'Vágar ho!' Sven called, his voice carrying easily along the length of the ship and across to *Hrafn*, where it was acknowledged by his brother, Torsten.

The oars were fouled briefly as men spun their heads to catch a glimpse of their home, and Sigurd caught the worried glances that crossed the faces of those with wives and children who had spent the previous weeks under Jarl Ake's thumb.

'Eyes to stern,' Erik growled, his voice firm but not unkind as he gave the count and set the oars back into motion. Turid and Arleigh both stood ready beside him, dressed in poorly fitting leather armour that had been looted from the marooned crews they fought. Both women carried axes and knives at their belts, and Arleigh still carried her bow and a quiver of arrows on her hip, although Erik had made it clear that neither woman was to leave the safety of the ship and join the fighting. Sigurd doubted his mother would defy Erik's command, desperate as she would be for revenge, but he wasn't so sure about Arleigh. He had heard the stories about her skill with the bow, and how she had led his mother out from Vágar. His father had once drunkenly confided in him that Arleigh was Freyja kissed, and that was why he had saved her all those years ago. To look at her now as she stretched her arms with the bow in her hands, he didn't doubt the claim. Beauty and war incarnate.

'One rôst,' Sven called, picking up his axe and bracing himself to leap from the prow.

'Fifteen count, first ten rowers!' Erik and Váli called in unison, their words joining across the water, although Váli, with his smaller crew, only called for eight. Sigurd began counting the strokes in his head, preparing to take up the strain as the ten forward-most warriors traded oars for weapons so they could leap overboard with Sven and claim a beachhead with their shields.

'Together, brother!' Olaf shouted over the rising din of water and wood, his teeth flashing white as he threw his brother a fearsome grin. Like many of the men, he had marked his face with soot and ash from the fires the evening before, the black mixture giving him a fearsome visage for the coming fight.

'To Vágar or Valhöll!' Sigurd called back, his voice coming out in a husky growl as he strained at the oar. The men around them took up the chant, the cry rising higher and higher into the early morning air as it was taken up by *Hrafn*'s crew.

'To Vágar or Valhöll! To Vágar or Valhöll! TO VÁGAR OR VALHÖLL!' they roared, their voices carrying across the waves to crash against the walls of their home. If Ake didn't know they were coming, he knew now.

'Fifteen!' Erik boomed, raising his voice above the chants of his men to be answered moments later by the sounds of wood on wood as oars were drawn in and shields grasped by practiced hands. Behind him, Sigurd heard the familiar sound of swords licking free of sheaths, the lengths of sharpened iron thirsting for blood as the sheaths were dropped to the decks below. From the walls they could hear the warning horns blowing, their mournful calls joined by the resounding *toll* of Erik's bronze bell.

Pulling as hard as they could, those left at their oars drove the great ship up onto the shore, the bow biting deeply before coming to a grinding stop. Roaring like beserkrs, the first ten men leapt overboard with Sven and charged twenty paces up the shore, matched step for step by the men from *Hrafn* before coming to stop with a resounding cry.

Sigurd all but threw his oar to the deck in his haste to join those already on the shore. He briefly locked eyes with his father and brother before taking up his axe and leaping over the side and running to join Sven and those around him, bellowing for his own warriors to follow him. He watched with pride as Erik strode forward with calm indifference to take his place in the centre of the front rank, his helmet and armour making him easily recognisable.

'To Vágar or Valhöll!' he bellowed, his voice carrying easily in the still morning air as he motioned his warriors forward with his sword, leaving only the women behind to guard the ships. 'We feed the raven this day!' he roared, sending his sword high into the air. His warriors erupted around him, bellowing his name as they shouted their challenge at the walls of Vágar. 'Golden Hand! Golden Hand! Golden Hand!' they cried, cracking weapons against shields, as they raised a din fierce enough to wake the dead.

Sigurd emptied his lungs with the rest, raising his axe high as he bellowed his father's name. He could hear their cries echoing off the surrounding fjords, sure the Allfather himself would have been roused from his rest by the sounds of approaching battle.

'Forward!' Erik ordered, pointing with his sword. The men fell smoothly into three lines of thirty, the days of training taking effect as they began marching towards the waiting gates of Vágar. Behind them came the úlfheðnar, their silent steps ominous against the cries of Erik's warriors. Sigurd couldn't resist stealing a glance behind him, watching as they chanted quietly under their breath and carved strange patterns with their bodies, their blackened skin gleaming as they pulled the wolf heads over their helmets and pledged their lives to the Allfather.

They could hear the cries of alarm from behind the walls as those guarding the palisades watched Erik and his men draw near. A few inexperienced sentries released their arrows well before the approaching warriors were in range, and there was a spattering of laughter and jeers from Erik's crews as the shafts fell uselessly into the ground.

Sigurd remained silent as he marched. Positioned as he was in the front rank with the brynja-clad húskarlar and hirðsmen, he was eager to set an example for the men around him. The sounds of booted feet striking the ground caused the blood in his veins to run hot, filling him with adrenaline, and he felt the familiar pressure on his bladder as it tightened in nervous anticipation. Behind him the sound of war drums grew louder as *Hrafn's* ship's boys redoubled their efforts, the resounding booms enveloping the marching warriors.

It wasn't long before they were in range and the arrows began to fall in earnest. Sigurd watched as the barbed shafts arced high into the air before coming down almost vertically among them. The air filled with the familiar *thwt-thwt-thwt* of shafts striking wood, the sound amplified by the confines of their protecting shields. One pierced right through the wood-and-linen covering of his shield, the barbed arrowhead coming to rest a few finger-widths from his right eye. Grunting, he whipped his axe up and over the shield, the whetted iron shearing through the shafts as they prepared for the next volley to fall.

'Archers!' Erik roared over the rising din around him. At the order, ten lightly armoured volunteers from amongst his bóndi shouldered their shields and ran forwards ahead of the ranks in a loose skirmish line, drawing and loosing as fast as they could. Sigurd counted roughly fifteen heartbeats between volleys, surprised to find it was only slightly slower than what he would have expected from Uffe and his rangers, although he questioned their accuracy.

As another volley rained down on them, a sharp, agonised cry pierced the air, briefly drowning out the sound of the drums. Snatching a glance beneath his shield rim, Sigurd saw one of the archers go down screaming, a red-tinged arrowhead blossoming on the underside of his thigh. 'He won't be the last,' he thought bitterly as their ranks flowed around the crying figure like the sea around a rock. One of the men broke ranks to help the injured archer free his shield, catching an arrow in his own for his efforts that sent him sprawling in the mud. Sigurd chuckled mirthlessly at the sight before returning his attention to the looming walls.

Erik had promised each of the archers a dagger's weight in hacksilver for volunteering to stand unshielded ahead of the ranks, and their bravery had brought the crews the respite they needed to get below the walls, forcing Ake's bowmen to take cover between volleys. But, for all that, Sigurd doubted they had downed a single man, and he found himself wishing for a few of Uffe's rangers.

'On my mark!' Erik's voice boomed, the deep baritone bouncing off the waiting palisade as they marched the final steps towards the walls. 'Ladders!' Erik bawled, setting men rushing to obey.

'Ladders!' Sigurd echoed with the other captains. From behind him, men passed forward the roughly hewn lengths of pine, spitted at intervals with steps that would allow them to flow up and over the walls of Vágar like a winter mist. The sound of wood striking wood briefly filled the air as the great lengths fell into place, but was quickly replaced by a far more terrifying sound. Men on both sides of the wall froze at the howls that arose from the rear of Erik's ranks, the blood-chilling sound bouncing off shields and invading the confines of helmets.

Prepared as he was for what would come next, even Sigurd found himself frozen with the rest, and was almost bowled off his feet by the blood-crazed *úlfheðnar* as they shoved past him in their rush for the wall, and their eagerness to meet the Allfather. Recovering himself, he watched as they lunged up the walls in their wolfskins as if Ragnarök itself had come, throwing caution to the wind in their mad dash for the sword storm. Sigurd silently thanked Óðinn that he wasn't waiting at the top of that palisade as the wolf-warriors all but flew up the final few rungs, drawing axes and swords as they went before leaping down onto the men below where they transformed the fighting platform into an orgy of blood and death. The cries that came down to the men waiting to ascend the ladders gave pause to even the most resolute amongst them, and Sigurd snarled, banishing his own apprehension before leading his men up and over the walls.

The battle for Vágar had begun.

***

From the abandoned deck of *Fjord Ulf*, Arleigh and Turid waited with Astrid and Signy as their men walked deeper and deeper into the swords storm, the cries of dead and dying warriors growing louder with every passing minute.

Erik and Váli's strategy had been to rush the walls and flow straight up and over them before establishing a foothold on the other side which they would hold until Bjørn and Yngvar could reach them. The biggest problem had been achieving this without a huge loss of life. It hadn't been until the night before they left their island camp that Hrolf had approached them from the fire he was sharing with his úlfheðnar and offered himself and his men for the task. Arleigh could still picture him crossing the camp to talk with them, his back straight and his blue eyes gleaming. She shivered at the thought and thanked God that the blades they carried would be turned towards their enemies. With the capture of Vágar came the opportunity for a glorious death in battle, just as they had hoped to find in Ireland, and Hrolf and his men had willingly offered to be first into the fray, giving Erik his foothold. Arleigh watched as those same warriors flew over the walls and began painting the world with sweeping arcs of red as they laid into their enemies, the grisly liquid bright in the early morning light. She could imagine the fear and mayhem they would spread through Ake's men, giving Erik and Váli a brief window to lead their own warriors up onto the walls. She shook her head at the sight, amazed at how some things in this strange Northern world could still surprise her. Quietly, she sent a prayer to God for the safe delivery of her son and Erik,

403

before snatching up her bow and leaping over the side, following in the wake of the warriors.

'Arleigh!' Turid called incredulously. 'What are you doing? Erik told us to stay here!'

'Aye, he did, but if Erik and his men fall, we're as good as dead anyway. I'd rather die and find my way to heaven, or even your Valhöll, than spend the rest of my days a thrall to a man like Ake.' She didn't wait to see how her words landed, or the expressions the three women shared as she ran up the shore to join the faltering line of archers. They were firing arrows into the wings of Ake's defenders where there was less risk of hitting their own men.

Nocking her first arrow, she aimed and released in a single motion, the shaft whistling away to bury itself under the arm of a warrior as he drew back on his own bow. Arleigh thought she heard him cry as the arrow knocked him from the battlements, his place quickly taken by another. He too fell with an arrow through the throat.

'Aim for their armpits, or the neck!' Arleigh cried as she reached the remaining archers. 'Their armour will be weakest there.'

One of the young men almost fell over himself to see a woman beside him, and took a breath to protest that a battle was no place for her before she sunk two more arrows into an archer in quick succession. Throwing a knowing grin to the young archer, she sent another shaft sailing towards the walls, watching in satisfaction as it struck a man's shield and sent him stumbling from the walls. She caught sight of Turid as she walked up the shore with Astrid, and Signy, shields and axes ready in their hands. None would be excluded from the battle for Vágar, it seemed.

Drawing another shaft, she imagined the Valkyries weaving through the battle to choose the glorious dead for the Allfather's table, and she took strength from the thought. She had come a long way from her Christian roots she realised, as she fixed her cold gaze on another man and released her shaft.

404

# Chapter 30

*Drums in the deep announce war on the shore, and above us all, the gods clamour for more.*
The words came unbidden to Toke as the sounds from the harbour grew
louder and louder, setting his heart racing in anticipation. He'd sat with Bjørn
and Yngvar to finalise their plans, deciding on the perfect moment for Toke
to lead his men from the woods and approach the walls. Since the first report
reached him that Erik's fleet had arrived, he had begun counting his breaths,
waiting for the perfect moment to emerge.

'*One-hundred-eighty-seven, one-hundred-eighty-eight, one-hundred-eighty-nine...*'

They couldn't return to Vágar so quickly that it would appear suspicious,
but neither could they leave it so late that Erik's forces would be overwhelmed,
leaving Ake to deal with the men from *Sleipnir* and *Uxi* in detail. They had
settled on three-hundred breaths, compensating for the time it would have
taken for them to run down the hill and support the town. Uffe had briefly
come and found them where they waited, confirming the plans and marking
the count as Toke crossed two hundred breaths before returning to his own
men, and Hoelun. Yngvar and Bjørn wouldn't be far behind him, waiting for
their own moment to strike.

'*Two-hundred-forty-six, Two-hundred-forty-seven, Two-hundred-forty-eight...*'

With fifty breaths to go, he indicated for his men to make their final
preparations and move into position. A pair of ravens flitted briefly through
the trees, their black bodies speckled by the dappled light. The pair circled
once before disappearing again, cawing into the forest as they flew towards
where Yngvar and Bjørn waited. 'Huginn and Muninn are watching,' he
whispered, nodding towards the birds as they disappeared into the forest.

A few of the men smiled or nodded in response.

'*Two-hundred-seventy-one, Two-hundred-seventy-two, Two-hundred-seventy-three ...*'

Bersi stood a few steps away from the main group, moving slowly as if in
a trance as he mixed unknown powders and mushrooms in a rough-hewn
bowl. Toke watched as he added ale to the mixture before swallowing the brew
in a single gulp, drawing his lips back in a grimace at the taste. Toke had always
known Bersi fought as a beserkr, but he had never actually seen what happened
when he drank the semi-mythical brew and fully gave himself to frenzy.

'*Two-hundred-eighty-three, Two-hundred-eighty-four, Two-hundred-eighty-five...*'

Toke watched curiously as his friend shrugged off anything that could get in the way, throwing his sword belt over his back where the handle jutted above his right shoulder before pulling the snarling bear skin over his face to rest on his helmet. Toke had heard stories about beserkrs going into battle wearing nothing but the tanned hides of the bears they embodied, throwing themselves into battle with ruthless abandon, but from the armour he wore, he could see Bersi took a more reasoned approach. He was thankful for that; he enjoyed the man's stoic company, and his advice.

Exhaling his three-hundredth breath, Toke climbed to his feet, moving through his waiting warriors as they stuffed final bites into mouths, emptied ale or waterskins, and drew their weapons.

'This is it,' he said, turning to face the men as he hefted his shield. 'Stay together, move fast, and we *will* see the pretender jarl dead by sundown. That, or we wait for the bastard to join us in the corpse hall,' he added, drawing dark chuckles from the crew as he dropped his empty scabbard on the ground with the rest of his kit.

'Let's go,' he said, turning to lead them along a little-used deer path that cut through the undergrowth towards the well-worn trail that ended at the walls of Vágar, keeping his men hidden until the last possible moment. Judging the moment was right, increased the pace, his men moving with him. The chorus of jingling iron and leather soon covered the sounds of the forest, joined as it was by their exaggerated breathing as they ran. They had been ordered to breathe as if they had sprinted all the way down from the Leap to add credibility to their ruse. Beside him, he briefly met Bersi's eyes and immediately wished he hadn't. The beserkr brew had begun taking effect, and his friend's eyes had become red and bloodshot, and his teeth showed in a perpetual snarl. Toke half expected him to grow fangs and begin charging forwards on all fours, running with the ambling gait of a bear. He took an involuntary step to his left to give the giant more space, earning himself a disdainful scowl.

Ahead, the forest was beginning to thin, revealing the open fields that lay before Vágar's walls. 'Pick it up,' he growled as the first drops of sweat begin to creep across his forehead and neck. They were nearly there.

Like spray cascading over *Uxi's* bows, they emerged into the light and turned onto the path towards Vágar, crossing the final few hundred steps until they stood before the gates, standing just outside of arrow range. Gasping,

Toke surveyed the men guarding the walls, noting the bows that each of them carried, although he couldn't see any arrows on strings, yet. The sight of the archers confirmed Fafnir's warning, and Toke wordlessly thanked the boy and his mother for their bravery as he motioned his men to form a loose skjaldborg around him.

Above the gateway, he watched as a brynja-clad figure that could only be Steinar stepped onto the walkway, walking with what looked like forced confidence as he spoke to someone below the walls, hinting at hidden warriors behind the walls.

'*Fool,*' Toke thought as he took a deep breath in preparation for the next phase of the plan.

'Steinar!' he bellowed, taking a step forward. 'Steinar! We saw the ships coming up the fjord and even now hear the drums of war. The mountain path is clear. We've come to your aid. Let us in.'

Silence greeted his words as the jarl's son swaggered arrogantly along the wall, talking to his men as if oblivious to the presence of Toke and his warriors. In the distance, the bang of drums and clash of weapons grew louder as Erik and Váli assaulted the walls, their war cries carrying clearly on the morning breeze.

'Steinar!' Toke tried again, taking a few steps forward from his men, ignoring the feeling of uncertainty as he stepped within arrow range. 'Did you not hear me? We have come to support you against the invaders, as your father hired us to do!'

Still silence, the seconds stretching slowly into minutes as they waited for a response. Beside him, he could feel Bersi straining at the bit as the beserkr brew took full effect, and he was about to throw caution to the wind and send a runner back for Bjørn and Yngvar before Bersi lost control completely and charged the walls on his own. Between their two forces, they would wipe Steinar's men aside with ease.

Just as he was opening his mouth to give the order, Steinar spoke. 'No, I heard you, *Sven Halfdansson*. I was relaying your message back to my father to await his instructions. He bids you bring your men to the front to aid him in the fighting there. We will hold the rear gate in case you have been premature in your *abandonment* of the mountain pass,' he added with a sneer.

Toke ignored the jab at his honour as he beckoned his men forward to join him. To an untrained eye, they looked prepared but relaxed, but he knew the shields would be up and in formation before arrows could be set to strings.

None of his men would die a straw death to a coward's arrow, he swore.

Hoelun watched from the tree line as Toke led his men forward towards the town walls, waiting patiently with the troop of rangers who had sailed with Bjørn and Yngvar. They were hidden among the trees a few hundred paces to the left of Toke's men, facing an unprotected section of wall. Seeing the empty walls, Hoelun realised just how precarious Ake's grip was on the town.

'The boy was right,' Uffe said as he surveyed the empty walls, his words slightly muffled as he picked his teeth with a piece of whittled wood.

'A trap, perhaps?' Sindri ventured from beside him.

'I doubt it,' Uffe grunted, throwing the toothpick away. 'I don't think Ake has enough men to guard both gates *and* set a trap for us.'

She had found Uffe likeable despite his gruffness and enjoyed the stoic nature of the men she marched with. They were solitary and silent, comfortable in each other's company without the need for idle chat. In certain ways they reminded her of her own people, although in others they couldn't have been more different. She waited patiently in a pair of borrowed breeches from one of *Sleipnir's* smaller warriors, the homespun wool made tight by the winningas she had wrapped around her lower legs. Despite this, they still itched terribly, and she scratched idly as she waited for the order to move. She knew the discomfort would be worth it when their time came, but for now it was all she could do was remain patient. Each of the men with her had a bow and full quiver at the ready, as well as an assortment of axes and knives. None of them carried anything longer than a forearm-length seax, relying on mobility rather than brute strength, although she knew that wouldn't make them any less fearsome. The Norsemen were raised with weapons in their hands, much like her own people, and she had never seen one even relieve themselves without an axe or knife within easy reach. In her own belt was the axe Bjørn had given her and a wicked sharp hunting knife.

'Tss,' Uffe hissed, catching their attention. 'This is it. Sindri, Galti, go!'

Without a backwards glance, the two rangers broke cover and sprinted for the walls. Each of them carried coils of plaited walrus skin rope in their hands, the lengths of cord ending with gleaming grapnels that had been taken from *Sleipnir*. Hoelun thanked Bjørn under her breath for the idea as she watched the two men expertly throw them over the wooden palisade. Testing their bite, they scaled the walls without hesitation, stopping only once they were at the top where they awaited their companions with armed bows. Uffe gave the order for the rest to follow, sending them running towards the walls in pairs until only he and Hoelun were left.

'Let's have some fun, eh?' he grinned, flashing his teeth before sprinting after the rest to begin his climb. Hoelun snatched a final glance across at Toke and his men before she too ran for the walls, feeling her start to race as she gripped the rope and began to climb.

'It will take us no time at all to get to the rear gate,' she heard Uffe whisper as she pulled herself over the battlement. 'There is a byre there that we can use as a shooting platform and cover behind. No one shoots until the gates are opened. Uffi, Sindri – shoot anyone who tries to close those gates again. The rest of you, kill anyone holding a bow, then move onto the rest.'

Whispering their agreement, they descended from the walls as quietly as they could and made their way through the town towards the byre Uffe had chosen. Two men ran forward to scout the path ahead while another two fell behind to guard their rear. There would be no surprises. Hoelun was shocked by how quiet the town was as they passed between the buildings. Usually, Vágar was full of people but now there was nothing but silence, and for a moment she had a sinking feeling that Ake had sold them all into slavery, until she caught sight of a woman peeking through a quickly slammed doorway. '*Of course they're hiding,*' she realised.

Ahead Sindri and Uffi were already climbing up the side of the byre, using a stack of crates and barrels as makeshift stairs until they were on the softer thatch of the roof. If anyone thought to fire the building they would be in serious trouble, but she didn't let the thought trouble her. '*Wyrd,*' she mused, startling herself as the Norse word slid easily into her thoughts.

Within moments, the roof of the byre was covered with bow-wielding archers, each of them crouched low with arrows ready on their strings. The building was used to shelter cattle and other livestock in the colder months and was built parallel to the wall. There was more than enough room for the score of rangers, and they would be all but invisible from all angles except from the walls directly behind them, but Hoelun saw that Uffe had that covered with a man watching the rear.

Silently, she shifted some thatch to distort her shape as she peaked over the lip of the roof, watching from their elevated position as Toke and his men drew closer. A feeling of consternation crept over her as she looked down on the men Ake had stationed behind the gates. From where she sat, she could see at least forty spear-and-shield armed men spread evenly on either side of the gates, ready to fall on Toke's men as soon as they were through. The creaking of the gates seemed enormously loud as they began to creep open, and Hoelun felt the blood rush to her face as Ake's trap began to close. She was so focused on the men waiting behind the gates that she was almost oblivious to the battle raging less than a rôst away as Erik and Váli attacked the main gates. It was only when the mournful howls of wolves drowned out the boom of drums and screams of men that she briefly tore her gaze from the men below her. Whatever it was, it was Erik and Váli's problem, she thought, turning her attention back to the slowly opening gate.

'As soon as the gate is fully opened, fire the first volley and kill the bastards working the doors,' Uffe said, breaking through her thoughts. 'Then pick your shots well; we'll only get a few off before they start firing back.'

'What about that giant with the axe or Ake's son, Steinar? Or Knut, for that matter?' Sindri whispered, snarling as he eyed the traitor in his gleaming new brynja. There were murmurs of agreement when they spied Knut strutting arrogantly among Ake's men.

Uffe was silent for a few moments as he considered the question, casting his eyes across the three men before reluctantly shaking his head. 'None of them have a bow. Kill the archers and the gatekeepers first. Then the spearmen. I don't want Toke's men getting bogged down and those spears are the most immediate threat once they're through the gates.'

If Sindri disagreed with the order he didn't say anything, instead choosing to spit the foulness from his mouth as he sighted down his arrow. The air filled with the familiar rattle of arrows on bow staves as the rangers followed Sindri and Uffe's lead, and Hoelun felt herself grow calm as she knocked her first shaft. Ignoring the sudden pressure on her bladder, she focused her attention on the ranks of spearman waiting to fall on Toke's flank, seeking her first target.

It seemed to take an age for the gates to creak open, and she watched apprehensively with the rest as the lines of spearmen formed ranks either side of the gate, ready to fall on Toke's unprotected flanks. It didn't matter that they were clearly young bóndi. Positioned as they were, they would be able to strike before Toke's men could form up to defend themselves.

'Fire,' Uffe said, the single word greeted by a withering storm of arrows as the rangers released their first volley into the backs of unsuspecting men. Several went down screaming, and Hoelun watched with satisfaction as her shaft embedded itself in the throat of a spearman standing beside the axe-wielding giant.

'Keep firing,' Uffe snarled, launching another arrow.

Climbing to her feet, Hoelun began drawing and loosing her arrows in a continuous flow, relishing the familiar feeling as her muscles began to strain against the bow string. She sent arrow after arrow to pierce skin and armour, punching the men from their feet as the shafts struck. Ignoring Uffe's order, she launched a single arrow at Ake's giant húskarl, watching in frustration as the arrow pinged off his helmet and into another man's shield. Hoelun cursed in frustration as the giant raised his shield ready for another shaft and she instead turned her bow back onto the hapless spearmen. She had only just begun reaping the harvest that would grant her her freedom.

\*\*\*

Ake had barely left his bed when the horns began blaring, shattering the calm like ice on the top of a water bucket. The deep, resounding cry carried easily in the silent fjord, creeping into his bones as sentries on both gates responded in kind. He blinked once or twice to clear the sleep from his eyes before splashing water on his face from the waiting pail. A thrall was already rushing into the room with a bowl of food for him. He considered the irony of one of Erik's former slaves dressing him for war with his former master as he began shovelling the food into his mouth, barely tasting it. He felt the warmth seep into his bones, giving his waking limbs energy while the thrall pushed his heavy boots onto his feet. 'Get my sword,' he said through a mouthful, letting the now empty bowl drop to the floor as he stood and pulled on a thick homespun jerkin which he covered with a padded leather overshirt. Between them, they would make the heavy brynja more comfortable and defend against bruising, and any blades that slipped past the iron rings. He eyed the iron-ringed shirt while the thrall fastened the leather tresses that would keep the garment closed. He heard the thrall grunt under the weight of the brynja as he helped him to don it, shrugging it down his body with his shoulders. A snarl from Ake was enough to make the thrall move faster as he quickly tied the sword belt around his waist. Briefly, Ake considered leaving the sheath behind, but decided against it. He didn't know how long it would be until he needed the weapon and he preferred not to carry the naked blade all day. An axe and seax followed into the belt before he took up his helmet and held it under his arm. 'Bring my shield,' he grunted before marching out of the annex

411

and into the hall. There was already a buzz of activity in the main room as ship's boys darted to-and-fro carrying messages from both gates to the table where Canute was standing, the cool eye of the storm.

'Report,' Ake grunted as he came to stand alongside the bulking prow man.

'Two ships, Lord,' Canute said without hesitation. 'From what we can see, there is a fifty or sixty oared drakkar and a smaller snekkja. It must be Erik and Váli.'

'Who else?' Ake grunted. 'And Steinar's gate?'

'Nothing yet. We know that Toke and his mercenaries will already be on the move now that the ships have appeared. We assume they will arrive at some point after Erik launches his attack, based on what Knut told us.'

'Gnn. That's what I'd do,' Ake agreed, thinking deeply. 'Get yourself back there, Canute. Keep my fífl of a son from doing anything that will get him or any more of my men killed unnecessarily. Keep your bows ready, but if it is just Toke and his men, then let them come through the gates before you spring the trap. We can save their arrows for Erik when he flees,' Ake said, grinning maliciously.

'Your will,' Canute said, briefly clasping the jarl's wrist in the warrior grip before leaving the hall. Ake watched him go, wishing not for the first time that his son had half the courage and strength of his first warrior. Sighing, he spied Trygva, another of his húskarlar, speaking with two other warriors. Crossing the hall to where they were standing, he interrupted their conversation as they turned to face the jarl, bowing briefly.

'You,' he grunted, pointing at the closest of the bóndi. 'Who are you?'

'Skarde, Jarl Ake,' he said, averting his eyes.

Ake took in the man's weapons and armour, eyeing the dented shield and chipped spear, the scars telling the stories of battled past.

'Skarde. Stay here, and tell any messengers who arrive to find me at the front gate. Trygva, you're with me,' he said, turning on his heel and leaving without a backward glance as he called for the rest of the warriors to follow him to the wall.

Behind him, Skarde stood taller at the honour as he moved to stand by the table.

Ake created order from chaos as he collected warriors on his way towards the seaward gate. By the time he had climbed to the top of the walls he had assembled over eighty warriors, each armed and ready to fight. Fifteen archers waited on the fighting platform that clung to the walls, intermingled with warriors carrying axes and swords, ready to rain iron on Erik's men as they drew close. *'There will be no surprises from the Golden Hand. His weave is woven, and will soon be cut,'* he thought, spitting over the wall before taking his shield from the hapless thrall. He was already picturing the bloodletting to come. Wyrd.

'Steinar, get your archers on the wall. The rest of you, form two ranks either side of the gate, here and here,' Canute ordered, pointing with his axe. 'You!' he shouted, pointing to two of the young bow-armed bóndi idling by the wall. 'Take those buckets of water up to the fighting platform.' Canute was on the warpath, bellowing orders left and right as he shuffled the inexperienced bóndi into ranks, all the while ignoring the snarls Steinar shot his way as he took control of the lazy chaos he'd walked into. He didn't have time for a *child's* wounded pride, not with his jarl's territory under attack. He spied the traitor Knut standing beside Steinar in his gleaming brynja, awkwardly adjusting the unfamiliar weight. Beyond a subtle nod, Canute ignored the boy. As far as he was concerned, once a traitor always a traitor, and he would be watching closely for anything that suggested Knut was still loyal to Erik. He hadn't missed how Steinar had taken him under his wing, but that made sense. Cowards and traitors were drawn to each other like flies to shit.

Behind him, he could hear the sounds of battle beginning to flood through the town as Erik's men began assaulting the main gates. He was surprised to hear the sword song so soon and a part of him yearned to be with his jarl, but he knew where he was needed and he wouldn't fail, not again. The waiting was always the worst of it, and now that he found himself with no orders to give, Canute began to feel the familiar twitch of frustrated impatience in his gut. It was made all the worse by the growing sounds of battle coming from the main gate, and he was just about to call for a runner to check on the jarl when Steinar turned and looked down on him from his position on the wall.

'They're here,' Steinar called, the contempt clear in his voice.

'You know what to do,' he growled before moving into position with the spearmen on the left side of the gate. He began breathing deeply, pushing aside the feelings of impatience as he calmed his body for the fight ahead. It was only when he heard Steinar order Toke and his men into the town that he hefted his great axe and began to swing it experimentally, loosening his muscles. 'Take a few steps back,' he grunted to the waiting spearmen. 'It wouldn't do for them to see us too early,' he added, resetting the lines so that they formed a 'V' that ended at the gate, with the wide ends opening onto the town. Satisfied, he waited for Steinar to give the order to open the gates and spring the trap. Once Toke and his men were far enough through the gates, he would give the order to close formation and trap them, skewering them with spears or with arrows in the back as they fled. Cowardly as the tactic was, he grudgingly accepted its effectiveness, and Ake's men were spread thin as it was.

'Now,' Steinar said, looking down briefly at Canute as he stood among the spearmen.

'Open it,' Canute growled, sending four warrior forwards to open the gates, the iron hinges creaking despite the oil Ake had ordered applied to them. They moved slowly at first, but it didn't take long for them to be wide enough for five men to come through five-abreast, revealing the open ground beyond. 'Ready yourselves,' he whispered, motioning for one of the more eager spearmen to step back into position. *'It wouldn't do to spoil the ambush prematurely,'* he thought, tightening his grip on the axe.

Without warning, the warrior beside him jerked awkwardly and let out a gurgled cry as blood blossomed from a wound in his throat, the sticky liquid spraying across Canute's armour. He watched in surprise as the man fell to the ground and began clawing at the arrow as the air around him began to fill with screams of agony as whining shafts fell among them. Lunging into action, Canute took up the fallen man's shield and covered himself, desperately searching for the source of the arrows while the inexperienced spearmen struggled to hide from the stinging shafts. He could see Toke and his men charging towards the gates and began bellowing orders for Steinar's men to fire on the archers at their back while pushing the spearmen back into ranks. The shock of the ambush was wearing off, and he knew that if he could get the spearmen back into ranks in time, they could recover the situation. He spied Steinar crouching awkwardly behind one of the water barrels and snarled again for him to take control of the archers, briefly meeting his eyes before an arrow pinged off his own helmet, dazing him. Bellowing in fury, he raised his shield and eyed the archer, blinking in surprise when he saw a woman draw a fresh shaft from her quiver. He barely had time to turn and face Toke's men before the two lines crashed, the impact knocking him back a step in his unpreparedness. Spitting in fury, he crashed his axe over his shield and attacked, struggling in the familiar press of the skjaldborg.

Bjørn and his men waited amongst the trees, almost directly in line with the gate as they watched Toke lead his men towards the slowly opening portal. He could feel the men around him begin to grow agitated as the exchange between Steinar and Toke dragged on, now that the moment had finally arrived. They had agreed that as soon as Toke's men charged, Bjørn would lead his men through seconds later to help them secure and hold the gate, staggering the attack to avoid flooding the entrance with bodies. Yngvar would follow close behind once Steinar's men were dealt with, keeping his men fresh for the assault on Ake's rear.

Red Orm and Bjarni stood calmly under the trees, talking easily between themselves as they set an example for the younger warriors who were fidgeting with their kit and talking quickly to cover their nerves. Bjørn tried to follow Red Orm and Bjarni's lead as he pushed down his own nerves, instead securing his helmet with a leather strap under his chin and picking up his shield, the god-runes and Erik's golden fists standing proud in the dappled light. He was so focused on remaining calm that he almost missed the screams as the arrows began to fly. Beside him, Bjarni subtly cleared his throat to bring him back to the present. Blinking once, he turned to his men and grinned, lifting Huginn as he did. 'Shall we?'

They chuckled as they lifted their own weapons and shields in support, taking courage from one another.

'On me!' he ordered as he charged out from under the trees, his shield held across his body to protect himself from arrow fire. They crossed the hundred-or-so paces between the forest and the gates at a run before lunging through the portal where Toke's men were alternating between fighting the remaining spearmen, and defending themselves from the archers at their back. Bjørn spied Hoelun as he took in the scene, watching briefly as she raised herself to loose an arrow into the back of one of Ake's warriors. Relief at seeing her alive briefly flitted through his head as he turned to begin bellowing orders, raising his voice to be heard above the chaos. 'Bjarni, Red Orm, Guttorm – clear the archers from the platform above! The rest of you, with me!' he shouted before leading the remaining seven men to join Toke's besieged skjaldborg, evening the numbers.

Ducking to avoid a wild spear thrust, he quickly returned the attack, sliding Huginn along the length of the spear's shaft to sever the spearman's fingers, forcing him from the line with a mangled cry. Another came forward to take his place and Bjørn feinted high, forcing the snarling warrior to raise his shield before shifting his footing and driving his sword straight down through the man's unarmoured thigh. He felt the blade grind against the bone, causing the man to scream in agony and drop his weapons as he fell thrashing to the ground. Huginn licked free of the wound as the man fell, releasing a fresh spurt of wine-red blood. He bought himself a precious moment of calm as the man fell, quickly stepping back from the line so he could survey the battle around him. Another man stepped instinctively into his place, the intensive training over the previous days making him move without orders. Bjørn caught sight of Bersi's bearskin flailing as he raged and spat fury at Ake's men, swinging his great axe in mesmerizing patterns as he sliced through spears and cracked shields before bringing the blade down on exposed flesh. Beyond him was another axe-wielding giant that he didn't recognise, and Bjørn was about to charge towards him when he caught sight of Guttorm duelling with an armoured warrior on the walkway above out of the corner of his eye.

'Knut,' he snarled, recognising the aggressive chopping strokes the traitor favoured. Abandoning his charge for the axeman, he threw his shield over his shoulder and leapt onto one of the ladders, quickly scaling it to the walkway above. He crested the lip in time to watch Knut batter aside Guttorm's awkward sword stroke with his shield before raising his sword over his head ready to strike. Powerless to stop it, he watched as the sword came down in a vicious strike, crashing onto Guttorm's helmet and filling the air with the ring of iron on iron. Guttorm crumbled under the impact, and Knut callously kicked his body from the walkway to the ground below. Bjørn winced as his friend landed on a shattered spear, the blade bursting red and shining through his thigh. With a snarl, he flew up the final few rungs and bellowed his challenge at the top of his lungs as he shrugged the shield from his shoulder and took his position, causing Knut to turn in surprise at his own name.

Neither of them said anything at first as they faced each other, their swords held low and ready as they sought weaknesses in their opponent.

'You found me, *half-caste*,' Knut snarled at last, adjusting his stance slightly.

'Aye, the scent clued me in,' Bjørn growled. 'Few men smell so keenly of shit as you, Knut *Nithingsson*.'

Knut's face twisted at the insult, the anger at his father's fate stinging like vinegar in an open wound. With a roar, he charged, lunging forwards with his shield as he tried to punch Bjørn from his feet and end the contest with a single strike. Ducking low, Bjørn punched forward and up with his own shield, using Knut's own momentum to roll him over his body to land on the platform behind him. Spinning, he slashed his sword from low to high, ripping it across Knut's body as he struck the ground. His patterned blade made short work of the rough iron links of Knut's brynja, shearing through them like a knife through butter to bite deeply into his hip. He waited as Knut struggled to his feet, watching as the blood flooded from the wound to paint the iron rings around it. Snarling, Knut raised his sword and brought it down in a serious of furious chops, striking Bjørn's shield again and again in his fury. Bjørn caught the blows with ease, walking slowly backwards to lull Knut into a false sense of comfort as he blocked the strikes.

'You're a nithing, Knut,' he said quietly, ducking another wild swing as Knut's eyes flooded with rage, before continuing. 'An argr nithing – a coward – just like your father, and his father before him. The Nornir wove a twisted weave through your family, tainted with cowardice and deception. This betrayal is just the latest thread in an already broken cord.'

'You lie!' Knut cried, roaring to be heard above the fighting below.

'You know it's true, Knut,' Bjørn continued, his voice goadingly calm as he blocked another blow with ease. 'And once my sword slices through your flesh and banishes you to Hel to sit with the rest of your argr forefathers, your name and that of your family will be forgotten. There can be no glorious feast in the corpse hall for people like you; the Allfather has no time for cowards and traitors.'

Knut roared wordlessly, spitting fury at Bjørn as he brought his blade down again in another furious chop that numbed Bjørn's arm. He let his shield twist slightly under the impact so that the blade slid off and carried on towards the walkway, forcing Knut to overstep. Off balanced by his own momentum, his sword bit deeply into the wood at their feet. Before he could react, Bjørn stomped his foot against the flat of the blade, landing with enough force to snap the blood-knot around Knut's wrist and force the weapon from his grasp. Taking two rapid steps backwards, Knut yanked the axe from his belt, his face twisted in fear. Bjørn followed him, punching his shield against Knut's with all his might to send him sprawling onto the walkway. Unable to stop his fall and hold on to his shield at the same time, Knut could only watch in frustration as it flew from his hand to land on the churned ground below.

'Take up your axe, Knut,' Bjørn said quietly. 'I'll not deny you an honourable death, though I doubt the corpse maidens will waste their time with the likes of you. As I said, the Allfather has no time for cowards.'

Resignation blanketed Knut's face as Bjørn's words hit him. He had gambled and he had lost. For a heartbeat, he saw Bjørn in a new light and felt a moment of regret at his betrayal, but his anger quickly resurfaced and he smothered the thought. His wyrd had been written from the moment he drew his first squalling breath.

Silently, he gripped his axe and looked up at Bjørn, nodding once. Below them, the sword song filled their ears as Bjørn drove Huginn down through Knut's body, striking where his neck and shoulders met. The blade cut through muscle, bone and organ with ease.

'Nithing,' Bjørn grunted as he pulled his sword free, releasing a heavy stream of blood that spilled across the walkway as the body slumped wetly against the wood. He felt only relief as he looked down on the ruined body, but he didn't linger on the thought. Already the sounds of battle were returning to him, and he could feel the dull ache in his arm from Knut's repeated strikes against his shield.

Bjørn realised with a start that he was alone on the walkway. The rest of Ake's archers lay dead in pools of their own blood where they had been struck down by Bjarni or Red Orm, or felled by arrows. He spied the pair below as they stood together in the skjaldborg, anchoring the line. From what he could see, seven of his men were still standing, with two lying dead behind the shield wall, and Guttorm severely wounded and out of action.

Toke's men were pushing hard against the remaining spearmen, their superior quality and equipment tipping the balance as they scythed through Ake's men like farmers reaping their harvest. He watched from above as his brother smashed his shield against an iron-clad warrior, sending him sprawling in the mud before turning to drive his sword down through the neck of another. Further along the line he saw that several of Toke's men had fallen to the axe-wielding giant he had spied earlier, and he was about to climb down and make his way towards him when he saw Bersi tear his axe free from an axeman he had almost split in two and lunge at the giant. As fascinated as he was by the duel, he couldn't afford to stand around and watch. He could see Yngvar approaching with the rest of the crew and they needed to clear the way through for them as quickly as possible. The byre where Hoelun and the rangers had fired their volleys from was now empty, and Bjørn felt a moment of fear before he saw them emerge from the far side of the building. Like a wave breaking, they charged into the unprotected backs of Ake's remaining warriors and began laying about them with their axes and knives, thirsting for blood as they severed hamstrings and throats or slipped their blades between ribs. Seeing the battle was decided, he dropped down the final few rungs of the ladder and crossed to where Guttorm lay in a crumpled heap.

He was still unconscious, but his chest was rising and falling in a gentle pattern, and the blood flow had slowed from the injury in his leg. He was alive, for now at least, and Bjørn took comfort from the knowledge as he sliced a strip of cloth from a dead archer's cloak and tied it around the wound, just above the spearhead. He didn't have time to dress the wound properly and he could only hope that he would survive long enough for it to be properly tended to. Grimacing at the injury, he lifted his friend's leg up to rest on the body of a dead warrior, keeping the wound elevated. He spied Guttorm's sword lying in the mud a short distance away and retrieved it, shoving the grip into his limp hand and rolling the fingers around the grip. If he did die, Bjørn was sure they would meet again in the corpse hall.

Behind him, he heard the screams of Ake's men as they were attacked in front and behind, and he turned in time to watch as the final warrior was cut down. Uffe drove his knife into the man's back, forcing him to arch around the blade while Red Orm drove his sword through his chest. The sounds of clashing steel and screaming warriors was suddenly replaced by the repetitive tramp of feet as Yngvar and his men drew nearer, and the moans of the injured. The ground was carpeted with the dead, and Bjørn became acutely aware of the stench of death that filled the space. Blood and shit and mud filled the air, and he felt a sudden urge to vomit as the sights and smells mingled in his nostrils. He could see several of his men wore similar expressions and felt better knowing he wasn't alone in the feeling. Squashing the emotions, he looked for his brother and found him struggling to pull Bersi from the ground. The giant beserkr looked shaken and dazed, but he was alive, although Bjørn could see he was leaking blood from at least half a dozen wounds. He whistled to catch his brother's attention before nodding towards Yngvar.

Compared to Toke and Bjørn's men, Yngvar's warriors gleamed, in the morning sunshine, untouched by mud and guts and blood.

'A bloody day, brother,' Toke grunted as he drew up and removed his helmet to revealing a mess of blood and sweat.

'Aye, bloody but successful, so far. I saw the mailed one you sent sprawling escape moments before Uffe's men fell on their rear, and I see no sign of the giant Bersi was fighting?'

'Steinar,' Toke said, spitting the name with a mouthful of mud and blood. 'Argr swine. His time will come. The giant's name is Canute, Ake's right-hand man. He dealt fairly with us, although he is blindly loyal to Ake. He hooked his axe behind Bersi's ankle, tripping him so he hit his head on a shield boss when he fell. His helmet and thick skull saved him from any real damage. There's fight left in him yet.'

'Gnn,' Bjørn grunted, eyeing their men. They were all breathing heavily and there were several with serious wounds. 'Do what you can for the wounded,' he said, raising his voice to be heard above the moans of the wounded. 'Drink or eat what you have, or what you can find. Ake's men were sure to have supplies nearby.'

They didn't need to be told twice and the gore-covered warriors drank thirstily from waterskins and ate whatever food they'd thought to bring. Bjørn kicked himself for not giving the order to hold onto something for after the first fight. Nothing fired an appetite like a brush with death. He spied Hoelun and Uffe where they were working with their men to recover spent arrows, cutting them from the dead bodies with short, quick slices. He wove his way between the bodies, aiming for where Uffe and Hoelun were working. He passed Uffi as the ranger tugged a shaft free with a sickly squelching sound not unlike pulling a boot from the mud.

'The flanking attack was well done,' he said, speaking to Uffe while subtly running his eyes over Hoelun to make sure she was uninjured.

'Thank you,' Uffe said, nodding briefly in acknowledgement as he tugged another arrow free. 'It looks like Ake's men planned to pin Toke, and you, with the spears while filling you with arrows from behind,' he said as he rose, pointing towards the walkway with the bloody shaft to where his men were emptying the quivers there. 'They didn't expect us at all,' he added.

'Whatever they planned, it failed,' Bjørn grunted before turning to Hoelun. 'I'm pleased to see you're alive and unhurt,' he said lamely, aware that he himself was covered in the blood of at least three other men.

Uffe rolled his eyes and turned away to continue hunting for shafts.

'You too,' she replied shyly. The fighting had awakened a sudden urge to grab her, but he pressed it down, instead allowing himself to lean forward and kiss her awkwardly. The nosepiece of his helmet bumped her cheek, leaving a bloody smear on her unmarked skin. She let out a small laugh, the warm sound breaking the awkwardness between them as she shoved back his helmet and kissed him passionately on the mouth.

'I need to go,' he said after a few moments, flushed in the face and grinning wolfishly. 'Stay clear of the fighting to come. There will be no mercy on either side and a beautiful woman will fire more than one man's blood.'

'I will,' she said, meeting his gaze. 'You be careful as well, Bjørn Eriksson. A beautiful woman is one thing, the son of a jarl is another...' she replied, trailing off. She knew Yngvar had given him a similar warning.

Bjørn squeezed her wrist tightly before taking up his sword and trotting to where Toke was waiting. He arrived just as Yngvar came through the gate with the last of his men, his face stern as he approached them.

'Are your men ready?' Yngvar asked, stopping long enough for his men to close and secure the gate.

They both nodded.

'Then let's go,' Yngvar said simply, clapping his hands on their shoulders. 'The fun's just getting started, and I'll be damned before I let your father and Sven have it all to themselves.'

Grinning at Yngvar's bravado, Toke and Bjørn refastened their helmets and ordered their men into ranks, silencing the nervous conversation that had sprung up as the combined crews stepped off together. They could hear the clash of arms in the distance, the ring of steel intermingled with war drums and battle cries as men fought to delay their journey to Valhöll.

# Chapter 31

As Erik crested the walls to his home, he was met by the carnage the úlfheðnar had wrought amongst Ake's men. Óðinn's wolf warriors had all but devoured those that thought to stand against them, ripping through them like a winter blizzard. There was nothing but death and gore and twitching bodies for as far as Erik could see. He cast his battle-hardened gaze over the bloody scene while his warriors flooded around him to secure the gates below, while others formed a skjaldborg facing the town to protect their flanks. He could find no sign of the three wolf-skinned warriors amidst the carnage, although their presence on the walls was written with the arcs of blood and viscera that described their passage.

He was distracted from carnage around him as the gates groaned below him, earning a roaring cheer from his warriors as they poured through the portal. From his position on the walls, he could see where Ake and his men had retreated to form a shield wall of their own, anchoring their flanks against the nearby buildings.

It was only when he turned to descend the walls that he spotted the úlfheðnar, their bodies twisted together in a mess of oozing blood and shattered bones that was sure to have earned them their longed-for seats in the corpse hall. Erik counted eight more dead warriors around them, and wordlessly he thanked the zealous wolf-skins for their sacrifice as he rejoined his men.

Behind him, the remaining archers were charging for the rough-hewn ladders, their bows over their shoulders as they raced to claim the high ground. Among them, unbeknown to Erik or Váli, came their women, chasing hard on Arleigh's heels as she raced with the men towards the ladders, her dress whipping behind her as she ran.

'Jarl Ake!' Erik boomed, pushing himself through to the front of his shield wall. 'Ake! It is over for you. Lay down your arms and I will let your men go free. You will die here today, I will broker no alternative there, but I will spare the lives of your warriors. And I will see that sword you wear as if it was your own returned to me,' he added dangerously, spying the familiar blade with fury.

Behind him, his and Váli's warriors stood in silent, disciplined ranks as they waited for orders, presenting Ake with a wall of iron as those with brynja's stood patiently in the front ranks. Around them, the sword din had been replaced by the cries of the wounded and dying as their pitiful moans filled the air. Thanks to the úlfheðnar, most of Erik's men had made it up and over the walls unscathed, reducing Ake's advantage even more. Even so, he could see that Ake still outnumbered Váli and himself and he tightened the grip on his sword in anticipation.

'It *is* my own!' Ake snarled, thrusting the sword towards Erik. 'It is *you* who must lay down *your* arms, Erik *Golden Hand*!' He spat contemptuously, taking a step forward from his own ranks. 'You are outnumbered and betrayed. One of your own revealed the men hidden in the hills behind me, and even now they are falling to biting arrows and piercing spears as my warriors spring their trap. Listen closely, *Jarl* Erik, to the sounds of battle as you lose not one, but two sons!'

As Ake spoke, Erik became aware of the sounds of battle in the distance, previously covered as the men around him heaved and regained their breath after capturing the walls. The realisation that their plan had failed swept through his ranks like a physical blow as the warriors around him heard Ake's words. The sounds of death coming from the rear gate were proof enough for many, especially among the less experienced warriors, and Erik heard several of the veterans snarl to keep them in the ranks as they began edging away. Erik worked hard to calm his racing thoughts. '*Two sons?*' he heard Ake say, raising his head in confusion.

Eyeing Ake again, he felt his confidence return; the man knew nothing of his sons. 'You lie, snake. The warriors at your back are led by only one of my boys. Two others stand here alongside me today, while my fourth travels the whale road. You lie!' he said again.

Ake's grin grew wider as Erik spoke.

'I am no liar, Erik,' he said maliciously. 'Your son Toke came limping into *my* town like a lame duck barely a week ago, his ship as broken as its crew. Eighteen survivors came with him. The rest were cut down by my first warrior as they hunted the coward whose farm my son raised to the ground. Your sons are dead, Erik,' he said with finality, the words punching into Erik's chest like arrows.

At Ake's words, the air was shattered by a piercing scream like a dying Valkyrie, the sharp sound causing superstitious warriors to make warding signs against evil, or clasp at medallions. The distraught cries were infinite, and heads spun on tops as warriors urgently sought out the source, fearing that Hel herself had arrived on the field.

Erik's heart broke when he found the source of the screams, and he could only watch as his wife fell to her knees in agony as tears began coursing down her face in rivers, her mournful cries filling the stunned silence. Arleigh dropped her bow and moved to comfort her, her tears mingling with Turid's as she fought to accept that her own son had also fallen. She held the older woman close, whispering to her while fixing Ake with a gaze of such tear-stained hatred that he was forced to look away. Seeing Turid and Arleigh in such agony, coupled with the knowledge that two of his sons were gone, was more than Erik could bear. Breathing deeply, he tried to focus his thoughts, fighting to conceal the hateful rage that was growing in his gut.

Turning coolly back to Ake, he stood straight and tall as he took two steps forward from his men, his eyes showing nothing of the battle raging within. All Ake saw was the ice-cooled fury that blazed in the depths of Erik's raven helmet, the sight forcing him back into the safety of his own shield wall. Erik's men erupted in a chorus of jeers at the display of cowardice, and one or two of Ake's own men shook their heads contemptuously at the sight.

'If what you say is true, and the bodies of my sons lie cooling in the mud of Vágar,' Erik said icily, 'then all you have done is send them and their men on their way to Valhöll. But you, Ake, you will not see such honour. Before the sun falls beyond the horizon, you will be dead, and there will be no golden feasting hall with Óðinn for you. No glorious death or saga tales. Only the icy nothingness of Hel, and a forgotten name.'

Olaf and Sigurd led the crews forward to stand alongside Erik while their father spoke, tears staining their cheeks as over ninety pairs of boots shattered the heavy hanging silence. At the sound, Erik began marching forwards, his men shifting pace easily to absorb the jarl back into their ranks as they advanced on Ake's forces. The men around Ake took a step back in the face of their unmasked fury before remembering themselves shamefacedly raising their shields in preparation of the sword storm.

'Come to me, carrion,' Erik snarled, pointing his sword at Ake before sprinting the final few paces and driving his shield into Ake's, all but bowling the shorter man from his feet.

Surprised by Erik's sudden burst of speed, his men rushed to match his pace, and for the briefest of moments he stood alone against the full weight of Ake's warriors. Years of training and war came unbidden to his arms as his sword and shield carved blurring patterns through the air, knocking axes and spears aside with ease as they licked out from Ake's ranks, thirsting for his flesh. Erik killed two before his men reached him, making children of the brynja-clad húskarlar as his sword slashed through necks and groins.

Yanking his sword free of the second man, Erik barely had time to raise his shield before the lines met, the crash of wood and the screams of warriors blending with the ring of steel to fill the air with the blood-soaked cacophony of war. The sounds fuelled him, burning away any hint of fear or caution in his body as it fired his blood and set his sword dancing.

Behind them, Erik's archers began loosing carefully placed shafts, trimming the wings of Ake's men as they sought to encircle Erik and Váli's smaller force. Arleigh squeezed Turid's shoulder once before taking up her own bow to add her arrows to the storm, ignoring the tears that streamed down her face as she plucked men from life with merciless precision, avenging her son. Taking strength from her friend, Turid forced herself to her feet and began screaming for the gods, begging them to strike Ake and his men from life and send them crippled and blind to Helheim, depriving them of the Spear Shakers hall. 'Let them ride the *Naglfar* as the nithings they are!' she shrieked.

Ducking a spear as it flicked from between two shields, Erik caught sight of Ake slinking between his warriors, a mask of fear covering his features as he disappeared into the third rank. Snarling in contempt, he ignored the argr jarl and drove his sword up and under the spearman's shield, burying it in the man's guts before ripping it free and releasing a grisly soup of blood and viscera. On either side of him stood two sword-armed húskarlr, their blades protecting him from unseen attacks as they ripped through armour and flesh with zealous fury, protecting their jarl from all comers. He felt he hardly needed them as he reaped his bloody harvest among Ake's men, as if the Spear Shaker himself controlled his sword arm, eager to choose his own einherjar for the final battle.

After the initial rush the fighting took on a slogging rhythm as arms became leaden and bloody hands became gummed to the weapons they grasped. It felt like they had been fighting for days, but Erik doubted more than fifteen minutes had passed since the lines met. Grimly, he acknowledged that he was no longer a young man able to fight from sunrise to sunset, even as he cut down a warrior half his age. The Allfather might have lent his sword arm strength for a while, but even old One Eyed couldn't deny the realities of time.

'Two step in three,' he bellowed, hearing the order repeated by his captains.

*One.*

He lifted his right foot and brought it crashing down against the shield before him, sending the man stumbling into the man behind him with the force of his blow.

*Two.*

Erik lunged forward and tangled Freki between the man's legs, severing the vital hard-pumping vein at his groin and adding fresh paint to the blade. The man screamed as the cut burned like fire, dropping his weapons as he struggled to staunch the unstoppable flow.

'Three!' he bellowed, his voice booming like the Thunderer's hammer before he took two sharp steps backwards, the rest of his men moving with him. It was neatly done and several of Ake's men fell forwards to be skewered on long spears as the weight they pushed against suddenly disappeared.

'Second rank!' Erik bellowed, the call taken up by his sons, Sven and Váli as they barked to their own men. As one, what had previously been the first rank took another step backwards, flowing between the men behind them as they in turn moved forward to take their places. In less time than it took to open a water skin, Erik's entire front rank had been replaced by fresh warriors, eager for the fray. A final order saw the whole line charge forward again to continue the killing, giving Ake's stunned warriors no time at all to adapt their own formations.

Gasping, Erik ripped the stopper from a waterskin and took deep gulps of the liquid, feeling it cool his body under the weight of his armour. His right arm was on fire and he could feel the bruises forming under the iron links on his left forearm from the countless impacts on his shield. He was bleeding freely from a wound on his left knee, but beyond checking he could still stand and move, he ignored it. He could see their position was hopeless. They were killing scores of Ake's men, but the weight of numbers was beginning to tell, despite the lives they were harvesting. He quickly found his sons and captains among the gasping warriors who had stepped back with him and motioned for them to join him. Váli grabbed another warrior before crossing the ground to the jarl, and Erik recognised him as Ragnar when they drew closer. Their sons were already breathing at a normal rate, Erik noted grimly as he ignored the rapid beating of his own heart.

'We can't defeat him,' he said, his voice dry and raspy. 'Not like this,' he added, drinking deeply from his waterskin.

No one said anything as they stood together drawing deep breaths into tired lungs as they considered Erik's words.

'We need to turn his flank,' Erik continued. 'On the next change, I want every third man to shift to our right. The added weight should be enough to punch through the men on his left. Then we can roll him up like a carpet.'

The men nodded silently, each standing straight and tall as they fought to hide even an inkling of weakness or exhaustion, despite their wounds. Not one of them was unmarked, and Erik noticed that both his boys were bleeding freely from different wounds. He was about to say something before he stopped himself. He wouldn't shame them by showing concern in front of the other men. If they were too wounded to fight, they would withdraw – he knew that. And if they died, they would join their brothers at the Allfather's table. Wyrd.

'I can do this thing,' Olaf said, his brows locked together in concentration. 'Let me take the right wing and drive the wedge through. The men in the centre and our left flank will need strong leaders then to keep them together and give the order to push when the time comes.'

'I agree with Olaf,' Sigurd said, speaking before Erik could reply. He was seconded by Váli and Sven. Ragnar too nodded but didn't deign to speak, unsure of his place amongst the others.

'I have another suggestion, Father,' Sigurd added, taking a gulp from his own waterskin. Erik nodded for him to speak, his eyes ranging briefly over the fighting to check the lines. They were holding.

'Let me hold the far left flank with Sven. When the moment is right, we can clear a path through with our axes and lead a band of the more heavily armoured warriors there. We can roll them up from both ends.'

Erik thought quickly, loathe to put both of his remaining sons in the most dangerous positions, but he forced the emotion down. He had an army of warriors to think about.

'Do it,' he said finally, his eyes meeting Sven's meaningfully. The giant dipped his head subtly, the action unnoticed by the others. He would guard Sigurd with his life. 'Váli, call the change, and send someone to warn the archers so they know what's coming. We don't need them hitting any of our own men. Sigurd, Olaf, choose your men and do what you must. With the change, the bóndi will make up the front rank. We won't have long.'

The message was clear. None of them expected the inexperienced and lightly armed warriors to last long against Ake's horde, no matter how big their hearts may be. Erik watched silently as they ran to find their places before hefting his sword once again, swinging it as he moved to loosen his tightening muscles.

Ake was furious. One of his front teeth had shattered under the impact of Erik's shield, and the broken fragment had split his lip. Even as he snarled orders to the men around him, he was spitting blood in a near constant stream, trying not to choke as the iron-tinged liquid mixed with his saliva to form a thick paste in his mouth. Erik's men fought with a fury he hadn't expected, working themselves into a rage as they all but bit the rims of their shields in their desperation to kill him and his men. There was no doubt in his mind that the day would already be lost if Knut hadn't betrayed Erik's plans to him. Mercifully, the weight of numbers was beginning to tell. Beside him, Trygva jerked suddenly, blocking Ake's field of view for a moment as he threw his shield in front of the jarl before returning to his silent vigil. Ake ignored the motion, but he couldn't resist a quick sideways glance at the shield Trygva carried, seeing the arrow embedded there. His eyes flicked beyond the fighting to the archers on the wall, their shafts keeping his men hemmed in on the wings, unable to bring their superior numbers to bear. It was galling to have no archers of his own left to bring them down. He could only hope they were running low on shafts, and that the threat would eradicate itself. Otherwise, he would send Canute and Steinar's men around the flank to end the archers once and for all, when they were finished with Toke and the half-blood.

His attention was yanked back to the fighting as Erik's men suddenly broke off entirely, taking two sharp paces backwards before bringing fresh warriors to the front. Like the tide, his own warriors rushed forwards to claim the now vacant ground, failing to grasp what was happening. By the time they reached Erik's lines again, they came face-to-face with ranks of fresh warriors that were champing at the bit to begin the slaughter anew.

'Fools' he growled, spitting at the stupidity of his own men as a score of them fell to the unbloodied spears and axes of Erik's warriors. He watched with suspicion as Erik and a few of his other warriors moved to the rear.

Not for the first time, he found himself frustrated by his lack of archers as he watched Erik and his men talk within arrow-range. 'The day could be decided once and for all with a single, well-placed shaft,' he thought to himself, spitting a fresh mouthful of saliva-laden blood to the ground. As if the Nornir had heard his thoughts, Trygva jolted suddenly beside him, throwing his shield forward to

428

snatch another arrow meant for the jarl. Ake turned in time to watch as his húskarl fell to the ground with a second arrow through his throat. He grimaced at the sight, before motioning for another warrior to step forward and take the man's place. Behind him, Trygva's son leapt forward from the group of waiting messenger-cum-ship's boys, his eyes watering as he clasped his father's cooling fingers around his sword hilt, ensuring his seat in the corpse hall.

Keeping his eyes locked on the battle, Ake barked for one of the boys to run to the rear gate and order the spearmen there to return to him, leaving only the archers behind. 'And see that my son and Canute come with them,' he shouted after the boy. 'It's time we end the Golden Hand's saga once and for all.'

The spear din was as loud as it was inescapable, and more than one quickly-hidden face had peered at Ake through a half-opened door as the sounds of death and pain echoed through the town. The sounds of struggling men began to prick at his pride as he imagined judging eyes watching him stand behind the battle lines, safe and sound while his men fought and died for him.

'Come,' he said suddenly, drawing his sword as he turned to spit another bloody wad on the ground. 'Let us dull our blades in the flesh of Erik's men.'

The warrior beside him drew his sword and stepped forward with the jarl, shifting position to protect Ake's right-hand side. He motioned for the ship's boys to mark them as they entered the fray, making sure they could be found when Steinar and Canute arrived. The men before them began to split apart like water under the prow, making space for their jarl and his guard until eventually they again stood face-to-face with Erik's front rank. Snarls and spit greeted him as Erik's warriors realised who he was, and before he could bring his shield to bear an axe came sweeping out from their ranks, aiming for his head. Like a shot arrow, his guard threw his own blade up to block the blow, protecting Ake as he slid Geri under the man's arm. The blade lacerated flesh and muscle with ease, leaving his would-be killer to fall back into the rear ranks in screaming agony, his axe falling harmlessly amongst the bodies at their feet. With the effortless skill of one raised with a sword in his hand, he began laying waste to the men ahead of him, culling Erik's front rank of bóndi with careless ease, trusting that his guard would stop the blows he missed. It wasn't until he began to meet the armoured bodies of Erik's húskarlar and hirð that his confidence began to waver, and he found his sword blocked or deflected more and more regularly. He could feel the sweat prickling his face as he fought, the press of struggling bodies claustrophobic as he struggled against the man before him. Time and again, he found his sword flicked aside by the warrior's shield, forcing him to raise his own to block the broken-backed seax that licked forward in return, seeking an opening. He could see the hunger for saga-fame in the man's eyes, his blade thirsting for a jarl's blood, and Ake was hard pressed to keep it from his flesh. Struggling to keep his footing in the press, he stepped forward as if he had stumbled, dropping his shield slightly as he did so. It was enough for the fame-hungry seax-man. Like a snake, the seax lunged over the rim of Ake's shield faster than the eye could follow, and he was hard-pressed to spring the trap. At the last second, he twisted his body so the blade slid harmlessly along the iron rings before bringing his shield up against the man's elbow, snapping it with a resounding *crack*. He saw the man's eyes widen in pain and horror as he realised his mistake before they glassed over forever as *Geri* slid through his throat. Ake risked a glance at the walls behind Erik's men, his front briefly protected by the broken corpse. He breathed a sigh of relief when he saw that the archers had finally run out of shafts and were descending the walkway to join the fray.

A sudden searing agony exploded in his hip, and Ake screamed as he felt something grind against the bone there, releasing a flood of warm blood down his leg. Distracted by the archers, he was too slow to block the spear that spat from Erik's ranks and shattered the iron rings of his brynja. A fresh scream escaped his lips as the blade was torn free, causing him to stumble awkwardly on the weakened leg. Fear consumed him as his head dipped below the rim of shields, the terror of being crushed by the boots of struggling warriors and left to drown in the mud threatening to overwhelm him. By sheer power of will he forced himself to stand straight and drive his sword forwards, skewering the spearman before allowing himself to be guided to the rear. News that the jarl had been wounded spread along the lines like wildfire, and Ake heard the fighting intensify behind him as he was carried to safety.

Ake felt like his hip was on fire, and it was all he could do not to scream as one of his warriors helped him to sit on an overturned barrel. Beside them, another was trying fruitlessly to wipe the blood from his hands as he prepared to examine the wound. He grunted when he saw it. 'You'll live, Jarl Ake. But you'll not rejoin the fighting again any time soon.'

'Just fix it,' Ake snarled through gasping breaths. 'Find needle and thread and make me whole again.'

Deciding it was clearly better to obey than debate, the grizzled warrior dug into a pouch at his hip and produced a length of cat gut and a curved bone needle. A nod from Ake was all the approval he needed to begin, his tongue poking from between his lips as he started stitching the skin together, ignoring the jarl's gasps as the needle pierced his flesh.

Another warrior produced an aleskin from somewhere and Ake drank deeply, his eyes glued to the fight. He could no longer see Erik or his companions, and he began searching for them among the mass of struggling bodies. Taking another swig, he looked down as the final stitch was made, wincing quietly as his skin was pulled tight. He poured the rest of the aleskin over the wound, watching as it bloomed red as the alcohol hit it.

'Father! Father!'

Ake turned from the battle in time to watch as Steinar sprinted towards him with Canute close behind. The giant axeman was covered in blood, his axe dripping red as he came to a halt behind Steinar who, by comparison, was conspicuously unbloodied. The warrior who had stitched him up looked up from stowing his needle and thread, and Ake saw his eyes narrow in thinly veiled contempt as he looked Steinar up and down. Ake didn't blame him.

'You were successful, then?' Ake asked, ignoring his son as he locked eyes with his prowman.

Canute's voice was gravelly and dry when he answered, and sounded more like a rasp on metal than the usual fjord-deep grumble Ake was expecting. Both of them ignored Steinar's poorly concealed anger at being overlooked; Ake knew Canute would rather have died than retreat, unlike his son. Whatever Steinar had to say, it was unimportant.

'We are surrounded, Jarl Ake,' Canute said, unable to hold the jarl's gaze as the shame overcame him. 'Erik's son Bjørn and the one they call Yngvar have taken the rear gate with Toke and his men. Close to fifty warriors are marching this way to fall on our rear, if not more.'

'Father, it's not as simple as the fool tells it,' Steinar blurted out. 'They had archers behi—'

'Why have you not joined the fighting, Steinar?' Ake asked, turning his icy gaze on his son. His voice carried all the cold disdain he had struggled to contain since they first arrived in Vágar. 'The news has been delivered, and Canute will be able to answer any questions I have. Your arm would be better used in the fray,' he added, jerking his thumb towards the screaming maelstrom behind him.

Steinar stood in shock, his head shifting from man to man as he desperately sought an ally among the watching warriors, but their cool eyes

431

were as unflinching as his father's. Finally, Steinar snapped, the tension pushing him to breaking point as he clenched his fists and met his father's flint-cold gaze, willing him to look away first. 'Where would you have me?' he snarled, struggling to control his anger as he took a step closer to the jarl. Behind him Canute drew the seax from his belt, ready to defend his jarl even from his own son.

'I don't care, *son*. But you have failed me for the last time. Find your place in the skjaldborg while better men try to solve the mess you've created. Go!' Ake barked suddenly, his temper breaking as he pushed himself painfully to his feet and shoved his son towards the battle lines. Unprepared for the sudden violence, Steinar lost his footing and slipped, falling face first into the churned mud at their feet. Ake winced in shame at the sound that escaped his son's lips as he fell before reclaiming his seat, his hip burning. He heard the warrior beside him make an irritated sound in the back of his throat when he saw Ake had torn the stitches and began unpacking his supplies again.

'Leave it,' he growled, waving the man away irritably. 'We have bigger problems than a gashed hip. Canute, take the rear-most ranks and form a line across the street here,' he said, motioning towards two buildings. 'We have to fight on two fronts, it would seem, but the numbers will be even, albeit slightly in the *usurper's* favour.'

Canute didn't have to be told twice, motioning for one of the guards to join him as he ran for the skjaldborg to follow the jarl's orders. Ake watched as he began pulling men from the rear rank with bellowed orders, pointing to where they needed to go with his axe.

Left alone for a moment, Ake closed his eyes and exhaled, cursing the Nornir for weaving him such a twisted cord before forcing himself back to his feet, ready to re-join the fray. If his thread was to be cut, he would see it dyed red with Erik's blood.

Arleigh could hardly believe the carnage that greeted them when they reached the mass of struggling and dying men. The archers who had stood with her had long since disappeared into the skjaldborg to fight alongside their sword brothers, but armed as they were the women couldn't join the fighting. They'd be cut down in seconds. Sheathing her weapons, Arleigh began to heave a wounded warrior further back from the maelstrom of struggling men, forcing his fingers to close around the hilt as she did so. Seeing what she planned, Turid sheathed her own weapons and ran forward to help. Together, they manhandled the armour-clad body further back from the fighting before kneeling over him to examine the wound. He had a cut the length of his forearm that was bleeding freely and staining his breeches, and Arleigh worried he was already too far gone. Moving instinctively, she drew her knife and sliced a strip of cloth from a dead warrior's breeches before dipping it in a nearby water barrel. If they survived the battle, it would need cleaning with mead and honey, but for now they just needed to stop the bleeding. Working together, they wrapped his arm tightly above the wound, both sighing in relief when the blood flow slowed to a trickle. Behind them, Signy and Astrid had followed their example and were working on a warrior with a blood-soaked boot.

Arleigh couldn't resist glancing towards the battle every few minutes, unable to block out the sword din while she worked. Already several wounded men were making their way towards the four women, their bodies covered with blood and grime. While she watched, Erik's ranks began to thin in the centre and subtly thicken on the wings, especially the right. She couldn't make sense of what was happening and didn't have the capacity to dwell on it; the men in her care needed her full attention and she would gain nothing by trying to understand battle tactics. Erik knew his business. Banishing thoughts of the battle from her head, she turned her attention back to the warrior she was caring for. The young archer who had thought to question her right to shoot with them was lying on the ground before her with a vicious wound in his left shoulder. Pulling a curved needle from the cuff of her tunic, Arleigh drew threads from a dead man's cloak and began to spin them together on her knee before using the crude weave to stitch the wound. The boy winced under her touch, clasping his axe hard while trying to hide his pain behind a warrior's mask. She moved quickly to sew the skin together, his blood covering her fingers and hands as she worked. Turid rushed over with a pilfered aleskin and poured the contents over the wound, cleaning it enough for Arleigh to make the final stitch before blood blossomed again. Looking up in thanks, Arleigh noted the tear-cut paths on Turid's cheeks, dividing the blood and smoke stains that covered her face. She imagined she looked similar.

Leaning forwards as if to kiss the boy's throat, Arleigh bit through the crude thread and sat him upright against a ruined crate, slapping him gently across the face to wake him. 'Don't fall asleep,' she said, 'or all my hard work will have been wasted on a dead man.'

'I would... wouldn't dream of it,' he whispered, smiling weakly.

She returned the smile, watching as the bleary eyes focused on her. 'You fought well; now rest and recover. Erik has this in hand,' she whispered before standing and following Turid to another. Astrid and Signy were equally bloody, working with whatever was at hand to care for the wounded warriors as they found them. Sighing tiredly, Arleigh felt the dried blood crack on her forehead where she had wiped her hand previously as her brow furrowed. Instinctively she turned to look at the fighting, as she had every time she finished caring for someone, but this time she couldn't look away. Instead, she stood frozen in surprise at the sight that greeted her. Rank after rank of fresh warriors were charging towards the rear of Ake's ranks, and she felt hope stir her aching heart as her eyes locked on one shield in particular. Only one of Erik's warriors bore such a rune-marked shield and she cried for joy at the sight. 'Turid! Turid! Look!' she cried, lunging for the older woman's hand and yanking her around so fast she almost pulled her arm from the socket. 'Look!'

'Wha—' Turid began as she spun around, the question dying on her lips as she too took in the sight. 'It can't be,' she whispered, fresh tears coursing down her face.

'It is.' Arleigh grinned, unable to keep the smile from her face.

Erik's men let out a fjord-shaking cheer as they recognised the familiar banners and shields of the men charging to join them. Bjørn and Yngvar had come, charging forwards in tight ranks with Toke and the lost warriors from *Fjord Uxi* at their side.

The two women embraced tightly, their tears mingling with the blood and grime that painted their faces as they cried with relief to see their sons alive.

Ake's defeat had been carried on the wings of their sons.

# Chapter 32

Bjørn flashed his teeth in a triumphant snarl when he saw the surprised faces peeking back at him from behind the hastily built shield wall guarding Ake's rear. He could almost taste their fear as the combined crews of *Sleipnir* and *Fjord Uxi* came roaring down on them like water through a pierced strake. With less than twenty paces to go, he could hear the bellowed orders as grizzled veterans, their beards shot through with grey, urged those around them to stand strong and protect their jarl.

Uffe and his rangers had already scouted the path ahead for them and found the way clear. They had resisted the urge to loose arrows into Ake's thin shield wall, fearful of hitting Erik's men struggling just paces away.

Uffe had briefly returned to confer with Yngvar and the others before leading his men deeper into the town to root out any hidden forces Ake may have hidden in reserve. Bjørn was happy to see them go, knowing it would keep Hoelun further from danger, although he'd never admit as much.

As he was raising his shield, ready to crash against the black-bearded veteran he had singled out among the enemy ranks, an almighty roar broke from somewhere behind him. Stunned by the ground-shaking ferocity, he was completely unprepared for the sight of Bersi as he spewed from among Toke's men to fall on Ake's warriors, his great axe swinging. Growling and snarling like a cornered bear, his mouth a frothing mess of white foam, he began laying about himself with ruthless abandon, severing limbs and splintering shields as easily as if he was chopping wood. The sight of Ake's men trying fruitlessly to bring Bersi down reminded Bjørn of the time his father had taken him to watch a bearbaiting. Try as they might, the dogs couldn't get near the giant beast, and one by one the pack was culled by its giant claws and razor-sharp teeth. It seemed that anyone who came close to Bersi ended up on the ground, either dead or rapidly dying as they were bitten by his ravenous axe. Bjørn watched in mute fascination as the beserkr sent two heads went flying with a single strike, the axe only stopping when it bit into a third man's shield, the wood splintering under the impact as the blade bit through the linden, trapping it. Bersi roared in anger as the axe was ripped from his grasp by the quick-thinking warrior. Before the advantage could be seized, Bersi leapt at the man who had dared to declaw him, bearing him to the ground in a snarling mess of flailing limbs and muffled screams as he buried his teeth in the man's throat and ripped.

The sight of the bear-clad beserkr spitting one man's throat against another's shield, his chin and beard painted black with blood, was the stuff of nightmares, and Bjørn felt the bile rise in his throat at the sight. Oblivious to the fear he was causing, Bersi lunged to his feet, ripping his sword free from his back and marrying it to the axe from his belt before beginning his rampage anew.

Bersi had been fighting for less than twenty heartbeats, but it was all the distraction Bjørn and the rest needed, and with a roar he reclaimed his wits and ordered the charge before barrelling into Ake's warriors. He punched forwards with all his might, savagely driving his shield into Black Beard's face before following up with his sword, the blade shearing his lower jaw from his skull with a single strike. Before another could take his place in the line, Bjørn stepped forward into the hole he had created and began fighting in earnest, Yngvar's lessons coming unbidden as his sword was painted red. Smashing another warrior from his feet, he risked a glance either side of him, seeing that Red Orm and Bjarni had followed him in to form a V with him at the head, driving a wedge into Ake's lines for others to follow.

He could see resignation in the eyes of the men he fought, their movements frantic as they hacked and slashed against his shield with an urgency that belied their fear. They were dead men fighting on borrowed time, and the realisation was replacing their earthly ambitions with the sole desire to die well and meet again at the Allfather's table.

It took no time at all for the shield wall to collapse under the combined weight of Erik's crews, the pressure to the front and rear of Ake's ranks turning the structured ranks into a maelstrom of private duels. With a grunt, Bjørn drove his sword into the belly of a red-bearded axeman before taking two sharp steps backwards, to refresh himself from his pilfered waterskin. Along with Bjarni and Red Orm, he had driven a wedge straight into the centre of Ake's men, while Yngvar had destroyed the left flank and Toke the right, the three points biting like scythes as they reaped their bloody harvest.

He caught sight of Yngvar as he described his way through the battle, spinning and twisting in a bloody dance that sent arcs of blood high into the air as he sent warrior after warrior to the corpse hall with careless ease. His brother on the other hand fought with a cold determination, an unstoppable force as he cut down his enemies with short, measured strokes before moving on to the next.

Swallowing another mouthful of the brackish water, Bjørn prepared to step back into the fray when something caught his eye. Weaving between the individual duels was a black cloaked figure, his sly movements and clothing at odds with the shining, blood-covered steel that swum around him. A feeling of unease crept into Bjørn's gut as he watched the figure bend himself around a warrior's backswing, the sword slicing through the black fabric to reveal the steel shirt beneath, and dagger he held close to his chest. Trusting his instincts, he began to move, weaving his way hurriedly between the fighting as he drew a beeline on the black-clad figure whose eyes he now realised were firmly locked on Toke.

'Toke!' he screamed, his throat burning as he struggled to be heard above the ring of steel, knew it was useless before he started. 'Toke!' he screamed again, his voice ragged as he shoved two of Ake's men out of his way with his shield before bringing Huginn down on the neck of a third. He looked up in time to see the cloaked figure putting his arm around his brother's neck, yanking him off balance before shearing through the iron links of Toke's brynja where it covered his ribs.

As the iron shirt erupted in an explosion of shattered rings and glistening blood, a dead warrior fell against the assassin, knocking both him and Toke to the ground.

At the sight of his brother's body crashing to the ground to leak blood into the muddy earth, a deep, guttural howl escaped Bjørn's lips, causing the men around him to step back in surprise and fear. His vision turned red and he felt an Óðinn-sent rage take over him as he began describing viscous patterns with his sword and shield, leaving three dead in his wake as he cut his way to his brother's side. He saw the assassin scramble to his feet and force his way back towards Ake's disintegrating lines, a sword clasped tightly in his hands. Their eyes met briefly and Bjørn snarled, before turning back to his brother. He could feel the rage eeking from his body, leaving him tired and dazed as he looked down on his brother.

'Toke! Toke!' he shouted, raising his voice to be heard above the fighting while Toke's warriors formed a circle around their fallen leader. 'Toke!' he cried again, slapping his face for good measure.

Toke opened his eyes and grinned weakly. 'I can hear you, I'm not deaf,' he grunted, wincing sharply as he tried to sit.

'Don't you die on me,' Bjørn said, holding his brother's gaze. 'It would be a crime to bore the Allfather with your presence so early,' he grunted, rolling him over to examine the wound. The dagger had slashed through Toke's brynja to pierce his back below his lower left rib. It had been a poor strike and hadn't gone deep enough to hit an organ, but Toke was bleeding freely, and could still die of blood loss if they didn't see to it soon.

'You'll live,' he grunted, patting his brother on the shoulder before realising his words had gone unheard. Toke had passed out.

Groaning under the weight, he hefted his brother onto his shoulders, beckoning for another of his warriors to take up his and Toke's weapons and follow him. Once he was clear of the fighting, he lowered his brother as gently as he could onto an abandoned cart and turned to the warrior beside him, casting about for the man's name. He was from *Uxi's* crew.

Like a spark, the name burst through the fog as he took Huginn from him. 'Finnir, do you have a needle and gut?' he said quickly.

'Aye,' the warrior said, pulling the items from a pouch on his hip.

'Good. Stitch my brother up and guard him with your life. Find ale or mead to clean the wound. Toke cannot die, not so close to the end.'

'I will,' Finnir said, gentling his voice. He could see the fear in Bjørn's eyes and laid a reassuring hand on his shoulder before dropping his sword and shield on the cart and began pushing Toke's clothes up above the wound. Bjørn waited by Toke's side long enough for Finnir to begin sewing before turning to return to the fray. Movement out of the corner of his eyes made him stop, and he caught sight of Hoelun and Sindri as they appeared from between two buildings, their bows shouldered. Making his mind up in an instant, he turned his back on the battle and sprinted towards them, ignoring Finnir's question as he ran. Hoelun and Sindri flicked bows from shoulders and fixed arrows to strings when they saw him running at them in full war gear, only lowering them again when they recognised his shield.

'Toke's been badly wounded,' he said through gasping breaths, pointing back towards the cart where his brother lay. They could see Finnir rapidly sewing his brother's skin back together, sealing the wound as best he could. 'Find honey and mead, and take it to Finnir,' he added, forcing iron into his voice as he struggled to rein in his rushing emotions. He wouldn't let his brother die.

Sindri stood dumbly for a moment, his mind running through the town wondering where they would find what they needed before Hoelun nudged him and pointed to Erik's hall. 'There's a store room there. It will have all we need and I doubt it's guarded.'

'Go,' Bjørn said.

They turned and left without a word, their steps throwing mud into the air behind them as they ran for the abandoned hall.

'Thank you!' he called after them, watching as Hoelun's hand flew above up behind her in acknowledgement.

For the first time all day, Bjørn found himself completely alone. With a heaving chest he surveyed the battlefield, trying to catch a glimpse of his brothers or his father. The carnage being wrought by both sides was terrible to behold. Erik's warriors were fighting with the vengeance of men whose families had been taken and tormented while Ake's fought only for a seat in the corpse hall, knowing now all was lost.

From his elevated position, he could see the stacked ranks of his father's men as they crashed against Ake's left flank, chipping away at their defences like a runesmith on stone. On his father's left, two axe-wielding warriors sliced great chunks from the shield wall with their giant axes, carving an avenue that was quickly flooded by those coming behind. The taller could only be Sven, but he wasn't sure of the second. A few of Erik's men carried the great axes, and it took a moment for him to recognise the warrior's helmet as Sigurd's, covered as it was with blood and grime as he matched the giant húskarl blow for visceral blow. Bjørn turned his attention back to the centre where his own men were fighting. He'd quietly asked Yngvar to let him and his men hold the position the evening before, arguing that it would help bind them to him, and give them battle experience for the future. Grudgingly, Yngvar had agreed, bolstering Bjørn's ranks with ten more of his own men to make up the numbers. From what he could see, they were making a good account of themselves, slashing into the gap he had created with Bjarni and Red Orm as they drove ever deeper into Ake's men. He began walking forwards to rejoin the fray when he spotted a flicker of black moving through the struggling bodies, now armed with a sword and shield. Gritting his teeth, he flicked his eyes to where his brother lay unconscious as Finnir's stitches made him whole again. Hoelun and Sindri had reached them with jars of honey and alcohol. Seeing his brother safe, and feeling his breathing return to normal, he started marching back towards the battle, gently swinging his sword and shield to loosen tired muscles. He could feel the blood returning to his numbed shield arm, the ache in his left shoulder from a barely blocked axe, and the myriad of small cuts and slashes he had sustained in the fray. None of it distracted him from the black-robed assassin, who filled his vision like a snekkja appearing out of a greying mist. He didn't so much as blink as swords and spears swung around him, his own blade held low by his side, shedding the blood of previous victims to reveal it the wave-like patterns beneath, ready for a fresh feast. Something of his cool, vengeful energy infected the struggling warriors around them as they parted to let him pass, as if the Allfather himself had warned them of his passage.

'Halt!' he barked, stopping one of his warriors from driving his length ash-and-iron spear into Black Robe, the blade coming to rest a mere handspan from his neck. His enemy turned at the sound, noting the spreading stillness around him as warriors broke off their private duels to watch what would happen.

'He's mine,' Bjørn snarled coming to rest a spear length from his target, ignoring the spearman as he returned to the safety of his own men.

'Who are you to strike at my brother like an argr thief in the night?' Bjørn snarled, his sword twitching hungrily in his hand.

To his frustration, the man just sneered arrogantly. 'Who are you to assume the right to challenge me?' he said. One or two of Ake's watching warriors rolled their eyes at the comment.

Bjørn spat, sending a wad of phlegm to land inches from the man's foot. 'Bjørn Eriksson, son of Erik Golden Hand,' he snarled, lifting himself slightly onto the balls of his feet. Around him, his own warriors burst into a roar of support as they heard their jarl's name. 'Who are you? I won't ask again,' he added.

'I met a friend of yours recently, *Bjørn Eriksson*,' the man grunted, again ignoring the question. 'A promising warrior named Knut. Ring any bells?'

Now it was Bjørn's turn to grin, but there was no mirth in his expression. 'Aye, he lies as a corpse on the walls of my home. Perhaps I can reunite you? Help you write your own saga together? *The Argr Traitor and the Nithing Coward*,' he added, flicking his sword menacingly as he took a step forward.

'Steinar. Steinar Akesson,' the man blurted suddenly, earning nothing more than a few grunts and half-hearted cheers from his own men. 'Your brother tricked me and manipulated my father. All I was doing was seeking revenge for the slight,' he stammered, tripping over his words as fear took over. 'Surely you would do the same?'

'This is not the place to seek sympathy, Steinar *Snakesson*,' Bjørn said dangerously, his voice devoid of sympathy. 'Raise your sword and let us end it.'

Steinar took an involuntary step backwards, watching as Bjørn adjusted his grip on his blood-stained sword, his movements confident and graceful. Had he been facing one of Erik's poorly armed bóndi he would have been confident of the outcome, but his sons were something else entirely. It had felt good to drive his knife into Toke's back, and repay even a small part of the misfortune and ill luck that had haunted him ever since arriving in Vágar. He had hoped that it would go some way towards repairing his relationship with his father and redeem himself in the jarl's eyes. But now, facing one of Erik's sons over the length of a sword, he felt his hopes melt away like winter ice. Swallowing dryly, he raised his own shield and tried to fake a confidence he didn't feel as he swung the unfamiliar sword he had pilfered from a dead warrior.

'Very well, Bjørn Eriksson,' he said with forced bravado. 'Come to me and let us feed the ravens.'

Bjørn charged, his face contorted in a vicious snarl as he swung his sword, throwing everything into a single overhead strike that would take Steinar's head clean off.

Steinar staggered under the force of the blow, feeling his arm go numb under the impact, barely managing to get his shield up in time. He saw a rain of splinters fall to the ground below his shield rim as the blow carved into the linden wood. He brought his own sword around as quickly as he could, aiming for Bjørn's ribs, snarling in excitement when he heard him grunt and drop his shield into the mud with a splash. As he brought his sword around to the left, ready to follow up, he felt a sharp, searing pain as something drove into the flesh above his right hip, ripping the skin. He screamed when he saw Bjørn withdrawing a curved knife from the wound, unleashing a torrent of dark blood as to stain his breeches.

Bjørn returned Muninn to the sheath at his back while Steinar struggled to regain his balance. It had made his grip on the shield clumsy, holding both it and the knife, but the sight of Steinar's blood made it worth the risk. Dodging two awkward thrusts from Steinar, he stepped in on the third, battering his sword aside before bringing Huginn down to slice through the soft flesh above his knee. A sharp cry escaped Steinar's lips as the blade bit, and he brought his own sword back around in a wild strike, again aiming for Bjørn's unprotected ribs.

Bjørn danced back from the attack, curving his body around the blade before bending to retrieve his discarded shield. He managed to bring it up just in time to cover himself from Steinar's return swipe, but the impact smashed his shield rim against his helmet and set stars dancing across his vision, dazing him.

Taking two sluggish steps backwards he crouched behind his shield, shaking his head to clear his vision. A small trickle of blood was seeping down his face beside his ear and he angrily wiped it away. Rising again he saw that Steinar had regained his feet, but his wounds greatly restricted his movement, forcing him to make short, staggered hops to keep Bjørn in sight. He was bleeding freely from both wounds, the ochre liquid pumping down his breeches in grisly waterfalls.

Bjørn lunged again and again, forcing Steinar to turn left and right as he struggled to block the flurry of blows Bjørn rained down on him. The mud around his boots was turning to a reddish-brown slurry as his blood mingled with the earth, weakening him further with each staggering step. Bjørn could see his face growing whiter with every breath as blood continued to flow from him. Sensing the end was near, Bjørn shifted his shield slightly, exposing his stomach as he drew back his sword arm.

Steinar, his body screaming in agony, saw the opening and seized it, forcing energy back into his weakening limbs as he drove his sword towards Bjørn's exposed guts. His excitement quickly turned to horror as Bjørn twisted his body at the last moment, allowing the sword to slide harmlessly along his armour before his own sword came down in a chopping motion. The scream that escaped Steinar's lips was blood chilling and several of the surrounding warriors stepped backwards at the sound, making warding signs or clasping amulets. Steinar shrieked as his sword hand fell to the ground, the fingers still curved tightly around the handle. Screaming, he fell to his knees and struggled to staunch the flow of blood from the mangled stump, the explosion of blood making it difficult to grip.

Bjørn circled around to stand behind him, his back to Ake's watching warriors, trusting his own men to skewer anyone who dared disrupt the impromptu holmgang. Such an act would destroy any hope of their reaching Valhöll and would more likely see them wander the earth as cursed draugr rather than be remembered as heroic *drengir*.

'This is for Toke,' Bjørn snarled, watching as Steinar looked up through the pain to meet Bjørn's unflinching gaze. 'Pray he lives to seek his own vengeance in the corpse hall,' he said as he drove his sword down through Steinar's shoulder, pushing until the blade could go no further. Grunting, he kicked the body to the ground, freeing Huginn before stepping smartly back into line with his own men.

With a roar the fighting began again as the two sides, locked shields and snarled, heedless of their footing as they struggled across Steinar's broken body. Suddenly exhausted, Bjørn made his way back to Toke, the wound under his helmet running freely. Hoelun was still there, watching over his brother, and he saw a look of concern flash across her face when she saw him. He imagined himself through her eyes, with blood running freely down his face, and the gore and grime of dead warriors staining his armour, and he held up his hand to show he was unhurt.

'He's dead?' Hoelun asked as he approached.

Bjørn nodded, laying his sword and shield on the cart before unstrapping his helmet. His shield was battered and beaten, the painted runes wearing their battle scars with pride. He smiled when he saw Toke looking back at him, eyes open and his breathing settled. His face was still covered in sweat and his skin was deathly white, but he was awake.

'I thought you were done for,' he said, wincing as Hoelun pressed an ale-dipped rag against the cut by his temple.

'Gnn,' Toke grunted weakly, his voice like gravel. 'Did you kill him?'

'Steinar Akesson is food for the ravens. Whether or not he makes it to the Allfather's hall is out of our hands.'

Toke nodded once. 'It would be more than he deserves,' he mumbled quietly before closing his eyes again and drifting back to sleep.

Turning slowly so he could sit on the cart, Bjørn looked at Hoelun and smiled. 'Thank you,' he said, nodding towards Toke. She smiled back at him before dipping her head and kissing him hard on the mouth. 'This will hurt,' she said as she drove a needle into his head and began to sew. He grimaced as he felt his skin pulled back together but otherwise remained silent, instead focusing on the battle raging below. Sven and Sigurd had driven a wedge right into the heart of Ake's warriors, separated from Erik's own assault by the few men who remained on their feet. By Bjørn's count, there were less than forty warriors still standing with Ake, creating a ring of iron as they fought to protect their jarl. He spied Olaf and his father fighting side by side as they hacked and slashed at the unflinching circle of shields. Yngvar too was still fighting, but even as Bjørn watched a spear lunged forward from between two shields and pierced his right bicep before being ruthlessly withdrawn, releasing a fountain of blood. 'Finnir,' he said, turning quickly and instantly regretting the action as Hoelun's stitches were pulled tight. Beside him Hoelun swore and pulled his head back around, telling him to stay still. He ignored the irritated tone in her voice. 'Go and help Yngvar, and bring him here. Take Sindri with you,' he added, pointing to where the ranger was helping pull wounded warriors back from the fighting.

Nodding, Finnir ran for the battle, calling to Sindri as he passed before diving into the fray together. They emerged moments later with a struggling Yngvar between them, and Bjørn stifled a laugh as they fought to extract him from the fighting. Finally, Finnir gripped him from behind in a giant hug and dragged up the hill where he arrived swearing and bloodied as Hoelun, finished with her stitches, leaned forward to cut the gut-thread with her teeth before tying them off neatly.

'Get yourself fixed up, Yngvar,' Bjørn said when they arrived, watching as the fire left his friend's eyes and he registered the blood flowing freely from his arm. 'You'll be back at it in no time.'

He earned nothing more than a grunt for his efforts as Yngvar's eyes locked on Erik and Olaf as they cut their way through to Ake. 'I need to be there,' he grumbled. Hoelun was already slicing away at his sleeve so she could examine the wound more closely while Sindri dipped another cloth into the barrel of ale they'd found and began cleaning it roughly.

'You need to rest, Yngvar,' Bjørn said firmly, but not unkindly as he climbed to his feet and grasped his friend's good arm, squeezing reassuringly. 'We'll go,' he added, motioning for Finnir to join him. He hadn't missed the hungry expression in his eyes whenever he turned towards the fighting.

When they were just paces from the fray, Bjørn skidded to a halt, holding his hand across Finnir's chest beside him to slow him. 'Finnir,' he said urgently. 'Go to the first five houses you can find and tell them to open the doors. Get the women out and tell them to see to our wounded warriors. The men folk can help carry them up to where Hoelun is while the children spread the word. We may be able to save more than many men yet.'

Frustration flashed briefly across Finnir's face as he was again denied the fight, but he didn't argue the order. Instead, he sprinted towards the first house he saw and began knocking, crashing his sword against the wooden door in his urgency to carry out the order.

Bjørn waited long enough for the knocking to begin before turning to rejoin the fight, briefly catching sight of Uffe and his rangers as they rushed past Hoelun with barely a glance in their eagerness for the fray.

Erik could see Ake through the throng as he hid behind the wall of wood and iron that his warriors had formed around him. The mood of the battle had shifted, divulging from the organised ranks of shield on shield to the chaotic maelstrom he now found himself in. His sword arm ran red with the blood of at least five men and was made redder as he led his warriors deeper and deeper into Ake's ranks to encircle the usurper. Ake's warriors were surrounded on all sides, his defeat certain, and still he fought.

'*Good,*' Erik mused, showing his teeth as he ducked an axe blade before burying his sword in his would-be killer's eye socket. Ever since Ake had gloated over the deaths of his sons, a cold fire had taken root in Erik's gut, his entire being consumed with the need to rip Ake from Miðgarðr and send him screaming and broken to Helheim. The sight of Bjørn and Yngvar's warriors charging into Ake's flank had gone some way towards mollifying him, but until he saw Toke as well, he would seek vengeance in the blood of his enemies. Beside him, Olaf fought with the same stoic calm and economy of movement he had come to expect of him. He had little of Sigurd's or Toke's humour, or Bjørn's careless bravery and Loki-cunning, but he was a born leader. He watched with pride as Olaf raised his own shield to block a spear before twisting at the last second to draw his opponent off balance, bringing his sword down on the back of the man's head with a sickly thud. Ake's remaining warriors were thinning rapidly, but they were reaping a terrible harvest as they fought for their lives, and Erik felt the twist of it in his gut as more and more of his young warriors fell back dead or wounded. His armoured húskarlar and hirðsmen were faring better, but even they were taking losses. Snarling, he called his men to push harder as he locked his shoulder to his shield and charged against the men ahead of him, knocking one from his feet. Slowly, he forced a breach, calling on Olaf and the rest to follow his lead. Step by bloody step they pushed and sweated their way deeper and deeper into the ring surrounding Ake, ripping his men from life with ruthless efficiency.

Without warning, the pressure facing Erik suddenly disappeared as a spear shot forward over his shoulder, burying itself in the eye socket of the warrior facing him. As the man fell, Erik saw that his path to Ake was clear; there were no more guards to cut down, no ring of steel to protect him. Ake realised the danger at the same moment, his face clouded by fear when their eyes met before he remembered himself and attacked.

Erik rushed forwards to meet him, his face twisted into a cold mask of hatred as he blocked Ake's attack with ease before bringing his own sword down like a hammer. It was an ugly, chopping blow, driven by hatred and rage, and he grinned mirthlessly when he heard Ake bark in surprise and pain as blood blossomed on his forearm. Erik's blade had driven straight through the wooden planks of his shield, splintering them in an explosion of painted wood. Seizing the advantage, Erik drew back and struck again, his blade crashing against the ruined shield boss as Ake barely managed to raise it in time, his arm weak and leaking. More by luck than by design Ake shifted his feet to deliver a furious counter strike that would have buried his blade in Erik's gut. A cry of frustration escaped his lips as Erik twisted easily to avoid the blow, letting the blade slide harmlessly along his gold-ringed brynja before smashing the hilt of his sword into Ake's face, shattering his nose in an explosion of blood.

'That's for my wife,' he snarled, watching with satisfaction as blood blossomed from Ake's ruined face. 'This is my home, Ake. Mine! And you took it for what? Gold, silver, cattle? Fair fame?' Spitting rage he struck again, their swords ringing as Erik battered Ake's blade aside with contemptuous ease before bringing Freki back around in a vicious slash. Ake barely managed to pull his head back in time to avoid the blow, earning a bloody slice across his chin where he could have lost the jaw. 'You're no jarl, Ake. What kind of a man would lead so many to their deaths, would break the nose of a jarl's wife, or fail to keep even unarmed women prisoner? You're an argr nithing,' Erik snarled in disgust. 'Just die, Ake. I have no use for you.'

Battering aside another attack, Erik drew his sword back and lunged, aiming to sunder Ake's brynja and push the blade through into his heart. Focused as he was on the attack, he was unprepared for the enormous force that suddenly struck him from the left, sending him sprawling in the mud. Desperately shoving his helmet back into place, he looked up to see Canute, already on his feet, marching towards him with his Dane axe at the ready. Snapping into action, he threw his weight backwards, his movements made heavy by the iron rings as he narrowly avoided the axe that buried itself in the mud where his head had been. Charging to his feet, he managed to get his shield up in time to block Canute's next swing as he brought the axe back around, this time aiming for his ribs.

The impact tore the shield from his arm as the blade smashed through the wooden planks, trapping itself. Seizing his moment, Erik took a sharp step forward before Canute could react, tightening his grip on the blade as he moved. Canute realised his mistake too late, and awkwardly tried to smash his left fist into Erik while reaching for his sword with his right. Grunting, Erik dipped under the awkward punch before driving his sword up under Canute's brynja, feeling the blade grate against bone as he pushed until only the hilt remained.

Canute's eyes widened in surprise and shock as his organs were ruptured, his mouth filled with blood that began to trickle between the iron rings that hung from his helmet in a slow stream. Gasping for breath, he forced his head around to meet Erik's gaze, their eyes meeting briefly before the light faded forever and his body collapsed.

Erik felt as if his arm would be pulled from the socket as Canute's body crashed to the ground, pulling him with it as he struggled to keep his grip on his sword. Ake was on him before he could free the blade, screaming wordlessly through his bloody mess of a face as he swung Geri in a wide arc, his eyes wild.

Erik felt nothing. Just a thud, followed by a deep, dull ache, as if he'd fallen against *Fjord Ulf's* strakes in a storm. He didn't feel the impact of Geri breaking apart his armour, nor the burning sensation of the blade as it crashed through his ribs to describe its bloody path through his body. He felt nothing, though he heard the distorted scream as it pierced the air. It sounded as if he was under water. *'Turid is still on the boats...'* he thought dully, his thoughts slow. He tried to turn towards the sound, but the ache in his side became worse as he moved, forcing him to press a hand on the pain. He struggled to understand the warm wetness he felt, or the gloating look of satisfaction on Ake's face as he looked down on him. It was only then that he realised he was on his knees. He felt tired. So incredibly tired. He knew that if he could just close his eyes for a moment, he would be all right, that he could continue the fight. He just needed to rest.

'No, Jarl Erik,' a voice whispered with a deep, soothing firmness. *'Your time is almost at hand, but the corpse hall is not ready for you, yet. Not yet, but soon, Jarl Erik,'* the voice whispered, fading away into nothingness.

Something stirred within him, like a storm brewing suddenly on the whale road, furious and unstoppable. Fighting back his exhaustion, he forced his eyes to open, focusing on the pain in his side it as he struggled to find a final burst of energy. With a roar, he charged to his feet and threw himself at Ake, oblivious to the torrents of blood that flowed from him as he moved. Ake may as well have tried to hold back the tide itself for all the good it did him in breaking Erik's grasp, this victorious expression changing into one of utter terror when he met Erik's eyes. Snarling, Erik brought his helmeted head down on Ake's ruined face, putting everything he had behind the blow. What was left of Ake's nose disappeared in an explosion of blood and cartilage, his forehead cracking as the raven-crested helmet crashed against it. Dazed and blinded by the blood in his eyes, Ake was powerless to avoid the knife that Erik drew tiredly from his belt, his energy disappearing as quickly as it had appeared as he drove the blade up through the jarl's chin in a final act of defiance. His face twisted as the scent of voided bowels reached him and he spat contemptuously on the body as he staggered, struggling to keep his footing.

'*Soon, Jarl Erik,*' the voice whispered, flowing through him like a cool breeze before fading again. '*Soon...*'

The sight of Erik falling to the ground filled Olaf's vision, causing a wordless roar of pain to escape his lips that forced the axeman facing him to step back in surprise. The instinct to survive was overridden by his desperate need to reach his father, consuming him as he threw his shield at the axeman, distracting him long enough to whip his sword across his throat. He bit back the tears that threatened to unman him as he fell to the ground beside Erik, heedless of the battle raging around him. His heart jumped when he saw that he was alive, his hands clawing in weak desperation at the ground around him. Olaf spied Freki's hilt protruding from Canute's stomach, but he ignored the blade. He knew what his father was looking for, which sword he wanted to carry with him through the gates of Valhöll. After a few furtive moments he found it, the hilt poking out from beneath Ake's leg. 'I'm here, Father, I'm here,' he whispered, holding his father's left hand as he pushed Geri into the grasping fingers of his right. 'I'm here.'

'I'm... proud of... of you, Olaf; of all of you. No father ever... ever had better sons, not even the... the Allfather...'

'Don't talk like that,' Olaf said, swallowing his tears. 'You're going to be fine.'

Erik smiled, blood filling his mouth as he looked up at his son. 'I can see... see the valkyries... can feel their... feel their wings. It's ti... time to return to my father.'

A shout on his left briefly distracted Olaf, causing him to reach for his sword even as he watched Sigurd bowl over one of Ake's men and stomp on his throat, shattering the man's spine. Bjørn was right behind him, severing the head of a warrior aiming their spear at Sigurd's back. Neither of his brothers looked at the men they killed, their vision consumed by the sight of their father as he lay dying. They crossed the ground together, coming to kneel in the mud with Olaf as Erik breathed his last. Sven came next, unashamed of the tears cutting silent paths through the blood on his face as he stood vigil over his jarl and his sons. Erik's men were howling like banshees in their desperation to end the battle and reach their jarl, the sound filling the air as they quickly overwhelmed the last of Ake's men in their fury. Finally, unable to keep fighting, one of Ake's warriors raised a horn to his lips and blew, ending the battle as he forced his way through the scrum of stabbing warriors towards the unguarded gates. At the sight of their escape, Uffe unleashed his rangers, sending them through Erik's exhausted warriors to launch wave after biting wave of arrows into the retreating figures.

Bjørn didn't see any of it, his entire world taken up by his father as his breathing continued to slow. He felt, more than saw, Bjarni and Red Orm as they arrived at his side, watching quietly over the scene.

'Bring Toke,' he said through his tears, 'he needs to be here for this.'

They nodded silently and moved to where Toke lay under Hoelun's care.

Time seemed to slow as Bjørn listened to his father's breathing soften, whispering over and over that they were there together. He didn't notice when Turid arrived, carrying a limping and wounded Arleigh with her. It was only when his mother gasped in pain as she was lowered to the ground that he noticed her. He stared without understanding at the vicious cut to her leg.

'Spear thrust,' was all she could say as her own eyes filled with tears at the sight of Erik while Turid wept freely next to her. Toke arrived borne by Bersi and Bjarni, the two brothers carrying the injured warrior between them as if he weighed nothing while Váli and Red Orm followed silently behind with a slowly bleeding Yngvar. All around them, the people of Vágar were emerging from their houses as the news spread that the fighting was over, the sounds of battle replaced by the cries of the wounded. Some stood dumbly as they stared uncomprehendingly at the silent vigil around their jarl while others began moving amongst the fallen, separating friend from foe and administering to the living.

'O... Ol... Olaf,' Erik stuttered, struggling for breath. 'The hi... the high seat is your... yours, son. Take Freki and... and rule with honour.'

'I swear it,' Olaf said, steeling his voice. 'You have my oath, Father.'

Erik forced a smile onto his face, nodding faintly at Olaf's words. 'Listen to your bro... brother in all things, my warrior sons,' he said, throwing his weak gaze across each of them as they sat around him. He lingered briefly on

Bjørn, his expression softening before he turned his gaze on Turid. 'Goodbye, my love,' he said gently, exhaling for the final time. To Bjørn and his brothers, the breath felt heavier than the last, and he couldn't help but imagine Óðinn's winged maidens as they waited patiently to lead Erik Golden Hand to the Allfather's hall. There would be drinking aplenty that evening as Erik walked under the roof of shields, leading his victorious dead in all their glory.

They sat in silence for a long time after Erik passed, each remembering the man in their own way. It was Turid who stood first, beckoning for those who could to do the same. Bjørn groaned as his exhausted muscles were called on again, the uncountable bruises and cuts making themselves known as he climbed painfully to his feet.

'Arleigh, Hoelun,' Turid said quietly, the tears falling unhindered. 'Will you help me to prepare him for burial? We will send him off as he deserves,' she whispered, stuttering through her tears, before turning to embrace Olaf.

Bjørn watched the pair embrace silently, joined by Sigurd and Toke's lame arm as he grasped his mother's skirt. He crossed the ground to hold his own mother, grasping her tight as he pulled Hoelun to him. The sounds of battle were gone, replaced by the plaintive cries of the dying, while the survivors walked or crawled to where Erik lay, standing in weary silence around the body of their jarl.

It was impossible to miss the creeping sense of uncertainty that was spreading through the crowd and Bjørn was unsurprised by it. Erik had been an enormous figure in the lives of hundreds, and his death was a bitter price to pay for their liberation from Ake. Yngvar and Sven felt it too, and he felt a moment of immense gratitude wash through him when he they turned together to face Olaf, bowing their heads as they began speaking.

'Olaf, Jarl Eriksson,' they intoned together. 'Accept our oath of salt and blood, of steel, sweat and silver. Accept our loyalty and honour our service, as we swear to honour your leadership in all things. Let the Allfather witness our words, and should we break oath with one another, let us never see Valhöll, and instead be cursed to wander the nine realms nameless and alone,' they finished, remembering the words they had spoken to Erik, years ago in their youth. None commented on the tears trickling down their faces as the seiðr wove around them.

Like ripples on an ice-still fjord the oath spread, starting with the sons of Erik as they bent their head towards Olaf and intoned the words. As one, the men and women of Vágar joined their oaths together and pledged their loyalty to their new Jarl, the words echoing around the quieting battlefield. Once it was done, Váli led his own men forward to speak his own oath of fealty and alliance, promising to come when Olaf called, and to recognise him as his overlord.

Bjørn watched with pride as Olaf stood tall among the sea of faces and accepted their oaths, his tears carrying blood and grime from his face. It was as if he grew taller in that moment, his back straightening and his body filling out, oblivious to the wounds and bruises he had taken. As Bjørn bowed his head, his eyes were drawn to Freki's hilt where it protruded from Canute's body. The sight of the blade stirred him and he bent over to heave it free, cleaning it as best he could on Canute's breeches before offering it hilt-first to his brother.

'The high seat is yours, Jarl Olaf,' he said seriously, bowing his head.

'Thank you,' he mouthed quietly, accepting the blade. A moment of stillness came over him as he held his father's sword, his grip tightening and loosening as he held it. 'Ake is dead,' Olaf said, raising his voice as he spoke. 'The threat to our homes, our lives, is dead. Cut short at the hands of Jarl Erik Golden Hand, who even now flies with the valkyries to the Allfather's hall, his enemy banished to the wastes of Hel. Stand now and let us move forwards together!' he cried.

The people cheered as they stood, watching with admiration as Olaf seemed to grow into the role of jarl before their eyes, standing tall as he raised Freki high and added his cry to the cacophony. Vágar was safe.

# Epilogue

Erik's funeral was unlike anything the people of Vágar had seen before. Ten of Ake's men had escaped the battle, all that remained of the four ships' worth that had dared to claim Vágar as their own. Bjørn had watched tiredly as they limped into the fjord on the smallest of their ships, oar-short and unlikely to survive the journey home, wounded and bloody as they were. Uffe had claimed that not a single warrior had escaped without an arrow somewhere in their body, and Bjørn had no cause to doubt him. Ake's remaining three ships had been packed full of straw and filled with those who had died alongside Erik, ready to join their jarl on his final journey. Over fifty warriors had fallen in the final battle, their seats in Valhöll assured by the blood and fury they had brought down on their enemies. The cost of battle had been high, and Olaf had honoured the men's sacrifice by joining their funerals with Erik's. Ake's men on the other hand had been stripped and left for the ravens, carried high into the hills by thralls where they were left to rot. Even as he stood on the shore and watched his brother – his jarl, he corrected himself – walk along the wharf before him, Bjørn imagined he could hear the cries of the carrion birds as they feasted.

Erik had been laid to rest on Ake's flag ship, the mast removed, and the hull lined with straw and oil. To it, Olaf had added his father's weight in gold and silver, as well as the bodies of nine húskarlar who had died in the battle. Each of the men had been cleaned and laid out in a pattern that placed their jarl in the centre. Their families had watched with pride as, brynja-clad, they were laid carefully alongside Erik, ready to protect him in the next life. Their battle-worn shields covered their legs, while drawn swords rested on still chests, clasped tightly in cold hands. Two horses had been sacrificed, their blood flicked over the dead warriors before the corpses had been curled at the bow and stern of Erik's ship, ready to serve their master, along with two slave girls. Erik was dressed in his gold-ringed brynja, with gold and silver bands around his arms and a thick golden torc around his neck. In his hands he held Galti's hilt, the blade broken in three then laid out as if whole, its story ending with Erik's, as he had always wished. Beautifully wrought spears lay either side

452

of him, along with several knives and axes, all of them polished and shining in the summer sun. Only his shield was unrepaired, the battered and beaten planks of wood carrying the scars of its final battle with pride. Finally, the boat had been loaded with ale and meat, ensuring none would go hungry on their final voyage. No man would say the sons of Erik Golden Hand had sent him unprepared to the Allfather's hall, and the gleam of gold amidst his carefully repaired brynja caught more than one man's eyes. Only his helmet was missing, replaced by the one Olaf had worn the day of the battle. Olaf had said that his father would want something of his on the journey and none had debated the trade. Unbidden, his sons had given their own gifts. Toke had offered the axe he had captured during his first raid, while Sigurd lovingly lowered the great Dane axe he had used to cut his way through Ake's men. Bjørn had given his hnefatafl mat and game pieces, setting the board so that the shield-biting warriors sat ready alongside the jarl. He had also added the whalebone comb he had won from Erik what seemed like a lifetime ago. Olaf had smiled at the gift, commenting that their father would need more than meat and ale, or the sacrificed slave girls, to entertain himself on his final journey.

The two other ships were secured on either side of Erik's, each carrying over twenty men apiece. They lay in silent ranks with what arms and armour their families could spare. Olaf had ensured that none would meet the Allfather unarmed, and every single one lay with at least the spear and shield Erik had gifted them weeks before. Their own families had watched with pride as their young jarl looked on each and every one of them individually, adding their souls to the army Erik would lead to Valhöll. Turid had stood alongside her son as he silently watched his father's ship drift into the waiting fjord, flanked on either side by ranks of archers armed with bows and flaming arrows. Hoelun amongst them. Olaf had honoured his father's promise and granted her her freedom and had been thanked with the request to help send the jarl off.

Bjørn looked on with pride as Olaf gave the order before adding his own arrow to the arc of flaming shafts that cut across the sky to plunge into the waiting ships. The whale oil caught quickly, and before long all three ships were ablaze, the orange flames making the people of Vágar night blind as they watched. None looked away.

Arleigh stood silently beside her son, tears streaming silently down her face as she watched the ships carve their blazing path down the fjord. Torr's knife rested at Bjørn's hip and she fought again with the indecision of sharing the truth of his paternity. For a while, she had worried that her wound might claim her and she would die without him knowing, but she had survived. Now, she couldn't bring herself to shatter the security Bjørn felt as he watched the only father he had ever known disappear into the night. He had already lost one father; there was no need to take away a second. Quietly, she folded her arm through his, taking comfort from his strength and the warmth of his body while she watched Erik burn. She had once thought that seeing the death of the man who had robbed her of her life in Shorewitchshire and killed her true love would bring her joy, but she felt only sadness to see him go. She realised that, in her own way, she had truly come to love Erik, and she could feel pleasure in the way Bjørn had adopted his best qualities, and took after him in so many ways.

As the smoke rose from the body of Erik Golden Hand and his glorious dead, Arleigh contented herself with knowing that her son was on his own path now. With Olaf now sitting on the high seat, her son would rise further than Torr could ever have imagined, and she could live with that.

'*Let the dead keep their secrets,*' she decided, stealing a glance at Ake's head where it had been set to rot above the gate to Vágar, as Erik had vowed it would. It was better that way.

Wyrd.

# Glossary

**Gods and Mythology:**

**Ægir** – God and personification of the sea who, with his wife Rán, had nine daughters who personify the waves.

**Æsir** – One of the two main tribes of gods.

**Angerboda** – A giantess, mother of Hel, Fenrir Wolf and Jörmungandr.

**Asgard** – One of the Nine Worlds and home to the Æsir tribe of gods.

**Baldr** – Son of Óðinn and Frigg, God of light, joy, purity, and the summer sun.

**Bjørn Ironside** – A legendary Nordic king from legend, famous for his exploits along the English and Frankish coasts, and for reaching the Mediterranean Sea.

**Dvergr** – Dwarves. Well known for their skill as smiths and craftsmen. The dwarves Brokkr and Sindri were credited with crafting Thor's hammer, Mjölnir, amongst other things.

**Einherjar** – The immortal warrior dead of Valhöll who drink, play hnefatafl, and fight every day in preparation of Ragnarök. Those that are killed rise again in the evening ready for dinner with the Æsir where they eat the boar Sæhrímnir who is roasted daily and, whole again the next.

**Fenrir Wolf** – Fenrisúlfr. The monstrous wolf who was tricked by the Æsir and was chained up until Ragnarök. The son of Loki and Angerboda.

**Freki** – Óðinn's wolf, the "Ravenous One." The name of Erik's new sword.

**Freyja** – A member of the Vanir tribe of gods and an honorary member of the Æsir. The goddess of love, sex, beauty, fertility, gold, war, death and seiðr. Sister of Freyr, daughter of Njörd.

**Freyr** – A member of the Vanir tribe of gods and honorary member of the Æsir. The god of sexual and ecological fertility, bountiful harvests, wealth and peace. Brother to Freyja, son of Njörd.

**Frigg** – Óðinn's wife, the highest goddess of the Æsir gods.

**Fyorgyn** – The earth goddess.

**Geri** – Óðinn's wolf, the "Greedy One." The name of Erik's first sword.

**Gullinbursti** – Freyr's boar, created by Eitri and Brokkr.

**Gungnir** – Óðinn's spear, fashioned by the Sons of Ivaldi and which is said to never miss its target.

**Hel** – Goddess of Helheim, the realm of the dead. Loki's daughter.

**Hildisvíni** – Freyja's battle boar.

**Huginn** – Óðinn's raven, Thought. The name of Bjørn's sword.

**Jörmungandr** – The Miðgarðr serpent and sworn enemy of Thor, who is so large that he encircles the entire world to clasp his own tail in his mouth. A Child of Loki and Angerboda.

**Jötunheim** – Jotunheim, home of the giants.

**Kvasir** – Formed from the spit of the Æsir and Vanir gods at the end of the great war. He was the wisest human ever to live.

**Loki** – The god of cunning and trickery with the ability to change his shape and gender. Father to Hel, the Fenrir Wolf, and Jörmungandr.

**Mímir** – The Rememberer; The Wise One. Renowned for his knowledge and wisdom, he was beheaded during the Æsir-Vanir War, and his head was later carried by Óðinn on his belt, reciting secret knowledge and counselling him.

**Miðgarðr** – Midgard. Earth, the realm of men.

**Mjölnir** – Thor's hammer, crafted by the dwarves Brokkr and Sindri.

**Muninn** – Óðinn's raven, Memory. The name of Bjørn's knife.

***Naglfar*** – 'Nail ship'. Formed solely of fingernails, the *Naglfar* is the greatest ship ever made, and grows larger and larger with the passing of time. At the coming of Ragnarök, it will be large beyond imagining and carry a cursed crew comprised of the drowned dead, and the warriors of Hel, bringing them to the final battle. Captained by Hyrm, the giant, Loki will stand at the tiller and guide the ship to war.

**Njörd** – A primary member of the Vanir tribe of gods and honorary member of the Æsir. God of wealth, fertility, the sea, wind and seafaring. Father to Freyr and Freyja.

**Nornir** – The Norns. Ancient beings who rule the destinies of both gods and men and weave the threads of fate.

**Óðinn** – Odin. King of the Æsir, God of wisdom, war, death, poetry, divination, and magic. Married to Frigg and father to Thor, Baldr, Höðr, Víðarr, and Váli. He is accompanied by his two ravens – Huginn and Muninn – and two wolves – Geri and Freki. Also known as Allfather, The Wanderer, The One-Eyed, The Wise One, Wish-Granter, Spear-Shaker, Weather-Ruler, and Glad of War.

**Ragnarök** – The end of days, when Fenrir Wolf will break his chain and the dead will rise up against the Æsir and the einherjar of Valhöll.

**Rán** – Goddess and personification of the sea, wife to Ægir.

**Skídbladnir** – A massive ship crafted by the sons of Ivaldi that could be folded up like a piece of cloth and fit in a pocket. Owned by Freyr.

**Skoll and Hati** – Wolves that chase the sun and moon. They will catch their prey at Ragnarök as the skies darken and collapse.

**Sleipnir** – Óðinn's eight-legged horse.

**Svartalfheim** – Home of the dwarves, also known as Nidavellir.

**Thor** – Son of Óðinn by Fyorgyn. God of stormy weather, the sky, and fertility. Husband of Sif, a goddess of fertility.

**Tyr** – God of honour and law; a warrior's god known as the Lord of Swords. He gave his hand when the gods chained the Fenrir Wolf.

**Valhöll** – The corpse hall; The hall of the slain. Home of the einherjar, received by Óðinn in preparation of Ragnarök. Also known as the Allfather's hall, the corpse hall, and the hall of the slain.

**Valkyrie** – Female figures who choose who among the battle slain will spend their afterlife in Valhöll preparing for Ragnarök, and who will go to Fólkvangr, Freyja's afterlife.

**Váli** – Son of Óðinn and the giantess Rindr.

**Vanir** – The second tribe of gods.

**Víðarr** – An Æsir god associated with vengeance.

**Yggdrasil** – The world tree connecting the nine worlds of Norse mythology, whose roots are gnawed by Nidhogg the serpent.

**Ships and Place names:**

**Dubh-Linn** – Dublin, Ireland.

**Fótrfjord** – Jarl Ake's home.

*Fjord Elg* – one of Erik's snekkja

*Fjord Ulf* – Erik's flagship, a sixty-oared raiding drakkar.

*Fjord Uxi* – A forty-oared raiding snekkja, captained by Halfdan.

*Hrafn* – Váli's thirty-oared snekkja.

*Jörmungandr* – one of Erik's snekkja.

**Shorewitchshire** – Arleigh's home in England. A fictional location.

*Slatra* – One of Jarl Ake's snekkja.

*Sleipnir* – A forty-oared raiding snekkja, captained by Yngvar.

**Vágar** – Jarl Erik's territory, Bjørn's home. A fictional location.

## Nordic words:

**Alnir** – Old Nordic unit of measurement, roughly 50 cm in length.

**Argr** – Cowardly.

**Beserk** – Or beserkrs were Viking champions who fought in a trance-like fury with very little fear of pain or death.

**Blót** – An offering or sacrifice, usually of an animal but sometimes a human. The blood would be caught in bowls or over stones and flicked over onlookers with twigs

**Bóndi** – Farmers and craftsmen, effectively the middle class. They were allowed to bear arms, own land, and speak at things (assemblies).

**Brynja** – Chainmail.

**Draugr** – Undead creatures from Norse mythology, loosely translated as 'again walker.'

**Drengr** – A courageous or daring warrior.

**Thegn** – The most highly ranked person in a village, answerable to an Ealdorman who is the official in charge of a shire, or group of shires.

**Elg** – Old Norse for elk or moose.

**Eyrir** – An old Norse unit of weight. One eyrir is roughly twenty-eight grams. (pl. aurar)

**Faering** – A small open boat with four sets of oars.

**Fífl** – Fool; idiot.

**Fyrd** – An English militia.

**Goði** – A prominent chieftain and religious leader; a priest.

**Holmgang** – Island going. A duel used to settle disputes, traditionally undertaken on an island where it was neutral ground in a specially marked out square.

**Hirð** – Professional warriors, but not necessarily part of a household guard or band.

**Hnefatafl** – Kings Table. An early Nordic/Anglo-Saxon board game often referred to as *Viking chess*.

**Húskarl** – A professional warrior and part of a lord's household, literally a hearth guard or house warrior, similar to a bodyguard. (pl. Húskarlar).

**Jarl** – A Scandinavian Chieftain, similar to an English Earl.

**Krab** – Crab

**Longphort** – A shore fortress built by Viking raiders used to protect their ships, commonly found in Ireland.

**Nithing** – A person who is miserly or stingy, a nothing.

**Ring fort** – A circular Scandinavian fortification with four entrances with an earthen wall topped with a wooden palisade.

**Rôst** – A unit of measurement, roughly equal to a mile.

**Saga** – An epic poem about heroic deeds and men.

**Seiðr** – Magic / sorcery.

**Skjaldborg** – A shield wall.

**Skyr** – A Nordic version of yoghurt.

**Slatra** – Slaughter.

**Strand Hogg** – A land-based raid.

**Styrisman** – Helmsman on a longship.

**Svinfylking** – Swine array formation (Boar snout), used to break apart enemy shield walls.

**Thing** – An assembly, presided over by a law speaker.

**Thrall** – A slave.

**Úlfheðnar** – Wolf Skins. Wearing the skin of wolves, the úlfheðnar were devoted to the Allfather and fought as if immune to pain.

**Weregild** – Man price; blood price. A price established for a person's life which would be paid as a fine or in compensation for damages to the family when that life is taken or is otherwise injured.

**Wyrd** – Fate.

**Vikingr** – To go raiding; to be a Viking.